Trisha Telep was the romance and fantasy book buyer at Murder One, the UK's premier crime and romance bookstore. She has recently re-launched this classic bookshop online at *www.murderone. co.uk*. Originally from Vancouver, Canada, she completed the Master of Publishing program at Simon Fraser University before moving to London. She lives in Hackney with her boyfriend, filmmaker Christopher Joseph.

for Bridget ~

Enjoy it

The Mammoth Book of

Regency Romance

Edited by
Trisha Telep

RUNNING PRESS
PHILADELPHIA · LONDON

ROBINSON

Constable & Robinson Ltd
3 The Lanchesters
162 Fulham Palace Road
London W6 9ER
www.constablerobinson.com

First published in the UK by Robinson,
an imprint of Constable & Robinson, 2010

A copy of the British Library Cataloguing in Publication
Data is available from the British Library

UK ISBN 978-1-84901-015-3

1 3 5 7 9 10 8 6 4 2

First published in the United States in 2010 by Running Press Book Publishers

US Library of Congress number: 2009943385
US ISBN 978-0-76243-992-8

Running Press Book Publishers
2300 Chestnut Street
Philadelphia, PA 19103-4371

Visit us on the web!

www.runningpress.com

Printed and bound in the EU

Contents

Acknowledgments

"Desperate Measures" © by Candice Hern. First publication, original to this anthology. Printed by permission of the author.

"Upon a Midnight Clear" © by Anna Campbell. First publication, original to this anthology. Printed by permission of the author.

"The Dashing Miss Langley" © by Amanda Grange. First publication, original to this anthology. Printed by permission of the author.

"Cynders and Ashe" © by Elizabeth Boyle. First publication, original to this anthology. Printed by permission of the author.

"His Wicked Revenge" © by Vanessa Kelly. First publication, original to this anthology. Printed by permission of the author.

"Lady Invisible" © by Patricia Rice. First publication, original to this anthology. Printed by permission of the author.

"The Piano Tutor" © by Anthea Lawson. First publication, original to this anthology. Printed by permission of the author.

"Stolen" © by Emma Wildes. First publication, original to this anthology. Printed by permission of the author.

"Her Gentleman Thief" © by Robyn DeHart. First publication, original to this anthology. Printed by permission of the author.

"The Weatherlys' Ball" © by Christie Kelley. First publication, original to this anthology. Printed by permission of the author.

"The Panchamaabhuta" © by Leah Ball. First publication, original to this anthology. Printed by permission of the author.

"Angelique" © by Margo Maguire. First publication, original to this anthology. Printed by permission of the author.

"Like None Other" © by Caroline Linden. First publication, original to this anthology. Printed by permission of the author.

"The Catch of the Season" © by Shirley Kennedy. First publication, original to this anthology. Printed by permission of the author.

"French Intuition" © by Delilah Marvelle. First publication, original to this anthology. Printed by permission of the author.

"A Suitable Gentleman" © by Sara Bennett. First publication, original to this anthology. Printed by permission of the author.

"Gretna Green" © by Sharon Page. First publication, original to this anthology. Printed by permission of the author.

"Little Miss Independent" © by Julia Templeton. First publication, original to this anthology. Printed by permission of the author.

"The Devil's Bargain" © by Deborah Raleigh. First publication, original to this anthology. Printed by permission of the author.

"Kindred Souls" © by Barbara Metzger. First publication, original to this anthology. Printed by permission of the author.

"Remember" © by Michèle Ann Young. First publication, original to this anthology. Printed by permission of the author.

"Moonlight" © by Carolyn Jewel. First publication, original to this anthology. Printed by permission of the author.

"An Invitation to Scandal" © by Lorraine Heath. First publication, original to this anthology. Printed by permission of the author.

Introduction

Sweet, sexy, heartbreaking and erotic, confined by corsets (all that complicated lacing be damned!) or secreted away behind closed doors, love in Regency England was a murky business. It was hardly recognizable – laced into ballgowns, peering out coquettishly from behind ivory-handled fans, whispering inappropriately under the noses of chaperones and being seduced into compromising positions. It was an emotion dealt out cruelly by a voracious and debauched high society on the one hand, and a great hypocrisy of social graces and propriety on the other. With innocence forever in the middle, trampled, torn and abused – as usual.

There were some things love and lovers should not do. But rules were made to be broken and all it took was a little ingenuity. When denial and frustration come to a boiling point, sparks fly bright and hot. Matches are made in haste to settle the possibility of scandal, marriages are bargaining chips to elevate stations and cancel debts – where there's a will, there's a way. And mothers! Those infernal, social climbing, unrelenting mothers! The bane of every debutante during her seasons out.

Under these circumstances, sometimes love needs a little harmless dishonesty, a liberal use of ruses, dupes and tricks, to flourish. For all those secrets and lies needed to maintain the order of the day, sometimes it takes a little underhandedness to get to the heart of the matter. Under the threat of Regency villainy, sometimes that's what it takes for young lovers to come together, or older lovers to find their hearts again.

The gentlemen seem to be missing their appointments with their barbers left, right and centre, and the slightly long and unfashionable look attracts the ladies in droves. It is the carelessness, perhaps, among the almost-feminine care lavished by some of the men of the age, that appeals, I imagine, and promises other lapses in convention

– like clandestine kisses, a quick grope in the sitting room, or maybe even some hot sex?

Take a look at all the well-dressed skeletons in the Regency closet. Because for all the babies out of wedlock, the midnight elopements to Gretna Green, the young women suffering marriages to old men in penance for a moment of brief happiness on a chaise longue in an empty retiring room – this jaded society has seen and done it all. Any discretion is just one more thing to hide away, to deny, to refute or to forget. But some sensations can be harder to forget than others.

Desperate Measures

Candice Hern

She was going to commit murder. If that scoundrel Philip Hartwell did not show up soon, Lydia Bettridge was going to track him down and rip his heart out. After all, this whole scheme was his idea. If he hadn't suggested it in the first place, and if he and her brother Daniel had not gleefully concocted the plan, she would not now be waiting on pins and needles to learn whether or not it would work.

Or perhaps all that gleefulness had been at her expense. Had they been making a game of her, playing on her disappointment, poking fun at her unrequited affections?

By God, she would rip out both their hearts. With a rusty blade.

Lydia scanned the ballroom again, maintaining as casual an air as possible as she sought out Philip's bright red hair among the crowd milling about in groups, waiting for the first set to begin. She was just about to stomp her foot in frustration when she saw him. Not Philip, but . . . *him*. Dear heaven, it was Geoffrey Danforth, the secret object of her scheme, and he was at that very moment making his way across the room directly towards her.

Her belly seized up in a knot of panic. What was she to do now? And where the devil was Philip?

"Here comes Danforth, my dear," her mother said in hushed tones. "And he is smiling at you and looking exceedingly handsome in that gold waistcoat. The colour sets off his hair nicely, don't you think? I hope you will not reject him like all the others. I suspect poor Philip must be delayed. You would certainly be forgiven if you did not wait for him any longer."

Lydia had claimed a prior commitment for the opening set when asked to dance by three other perfectly suitable gentlemen, causing her mother to cluck and twitter with vexation. She was not pleased that Lydia had promised to be led out for one of the most important dances of the evening by her brother's best friend, who had no marital intentions towards Lydia or anyone else, and for whom Lydia had no more than a sisterly affection. "Such a waste," her mother had said more than once.

And here came Geoffrey Danforth, with his flashing blue eyes and a smile to make a girl weak in the knees. Oh dear.

He stood before them and sketched an elegant bow. "Mrs Bettridge. Miss Lydia. You are both looking very fine this evening." His eyes swept over Lydia, hopefully admiring her new dress, which was cut a bit more daringly in the bodice than her usual attire. It had been a part of the plan, of course, to look as dashing as possible.

His gaze turned to her mother. "The yellow plumes are quite fetching, Mrs B. All the other ladies here must be seething with envy."

Her mother giggled behind her fan and muttered something about a shameless flatterer. Geoffrey turned to Lydia and said, "I believe this is our dance."

What?

"I beg your pardon?" She could have bitten off her tongue. Philip Hartwell was obviously not coming so their plan had to be scrapped. And yet here was Geoffrey, the object of her every dream and heart's desire, asking her to dance – and she demurred. Why did she not simply take his arm and be quiet?

He grinned, an endearing lopsided grin that was somehow both boyish and rakish at the same time, and had set her heart aflutter since she was fifteen. "Hartwell is detained indefinitely and asked me to take his place." Turning his head so her mother couldn't see, he winked at her.

Dear God, did he mean what she thought he meant? Was he to take Philip's place in more than just the dance? No, surely not. Philip would not be so heartless, would he? But then, he didn't know.

Geoffrey took her hand and placed it on his arm. With a little tug – she was almost rooted to the spot, barely able to think, much less move, and so needed that bit of physical encouragement – he gently led her to the centre of the floor where sets were forming. "Don't worry, Lydia." He kept his voice low so others would not overhear. Deep and soft as butter, it was a voice that always made her want to close her eyes and allow it to melt all over her. "I know you must be disappointed, but I will do my best. In fact, not to put too fine a point on it, but I daresay I can do a better job of it than old Hartwell." He winked again, and her feet stopped working properly.

He placed his other hand firmly over hers and manoeuvred her skilfully across the floor without further incident. Surely he had noticed her falter, though he did not mention it. While they waited for the music to begin, he bent his head near hers and said, "Will you trust me to do the job properly?"

She took a deep breath to calm her nerves and decided to feign ignorance. "I have no idea what you mean." Her voice sounded surprisingly steady, and she was rather proud of herself.

He smiled and gave her a little nudge with his shoulder. "No need to be coy, my girl. Hartwell told all. Had to, of course, since I was to take his place. But, quite frankly, Lydia, I was shocked to learn that you believed such a stratagem was necessary."

"Oh dear. I suppose it does seem rather foolish." More foolish than he would ever know.

"Indeed it does. I cannot imagine you have to work so hard to make some worthless chap take notice of you."

"Worthless? You do not even know who he is."

"Then tell me. It will make this easier if I know the object of this game."

"No, I'd rather not tell who he is." She'd rather die.

"It doesn't matter. I know who he is."

Panic prickled the back of her neck. "You do not. You can't know."

"I can and I do. He is an undeserving moron, that's who he is. If he needs encouragement to notice your beauty, your charm, your wit, then he is certainly not worthy of you."

His words sent a powerful yearning rushing through her veins. Did he mean it, truly mean it, or was he simply using flattery to squirm out of taking part in this fool's errand?

"Does the fellow show an interest in some other young woman perhaps?"

"No one in particular, as far as I know."

"And he pays you no notice whatsoever?"

She shrugged. "Very little. Or, at least not in . . . in that way."

It wasn't that he didn't notice her, or that he ignored her. No, he was well acquainted with her. They had known each other for years, as he was one of Daniel's closest friends. That was, perhaps, the problem. He treated her just as Daniel did, as a sister. Or worse. She sometimes wondered if he was even aware that she was female. He never looked at her as certain other gentlemen did, with a spark of interest in his eye, or the slightest hint of desire.

Yet, whenever she saw him, for her it was *all* spark and desire. Among her brother's friends, Geoffrey was the only one who made her so thoroughly aware of his . . . maleness. She never much noticed how other men's pantaloons stretched taut across a well-muscled thigh, or the impressive set of shoulders beneath their tight-fitting coats. But she had been noticing such things about Geoffrey for several years. The sight of him had been making her warm all over since long before she understood what it meant.

"Hmm." His brow furrowed as he studied her. "And so I am to make this chap jealous?"

No sense in denying what he already knew. Maybe there was still hope for this scheme after all, even if it had been turned topsy-turvy. "That is what Philip and Daniel suggested, and Philip agreed to do it. They said that nothing piques a man's interest in a young lady like seeing another man shower his attentions on her, especially if that man is generally known for avoiding such things, for keeping himself above any potential entanglement." She tried to sound blasé but her cheeks flushed with warmth.

"Well, then, I am your man." He slapped a hand against his chest. "I have never singled out any woman, publicly or privately, so if I am seen acting the mooncalf over you, it will certainly be noticed. Ah, the dance is about to begin. Pay attention, my girl. Observe my uncanny ability to make everyone here believe I am madly in love with you."

And he did. He even made her believe it. He never took his eyes off her, except for those moments when the steps required him to link arms or hands with another man's partner. At all other times, his gaze never left her. Sometimes it was so intense, locked so ardently with hers that she almost felt as though they were alone on the dance floor.

It was all perfectly glorious. Except, of course, that it was not real. He was merely play-acting, and doing a splendid job of it.

When the second dance of the set was about to begin, Geoffrey led her out of the line. "Parched, did you say? Then by all means allow me to procure you a restorative glass of chilled champagne." Lowering his voice, he said, "Let us find the refreshment room and make our plans for the rest of the evening."

Ever the proper gentleman, Geoffrey first located her mother and told her where he was taking Lydia. She looked puzzled – it was the first set, after all, and had so far not been lively enough to have worked up much of a thirst – but nodded her approval. One small ante-room had been set aside for light refreshments and, as it was still early in the evening, it was almost empty of guests. Geoffrey led her to a table in a corner, then flagged down a footman who brought them glasses of champagne. She had not often partaken of the pale sparkly wine, and smiled when the bubbles tickled her nose, which made Geoffrey laugh. She had been too nervous to eat before the ball, so even a few sips had her feeling slightly giddy. Maybe the champagne would help her get through this odd evening, allow her to enjoy the ridiculous situation instead of walking around in alternate states of confusion and panic.

"How am I doing so far?" he asked.

"You are playing the part beautifully, Mr Danforth."

"Excellent. Has he noticed?"

"Who?"

"The man I am trying to make jealous, of course."

"Oh. I . . . I am not certain."

"I say, Lydia," he said, his brow furrowed into a frown, "you had better tell me who the chap is. How am I to make sure he sees me mooning after you? In fact, I believe this whole scheme is doomed to failure unless I know its object. So, tell me. What lucky man has stolen your heart?"

Suddenly the bubbles in her stomach had nothing to do with champagne. Who was she to name? Should she simply look him straight in the eye and tell him that *he* was the one he was supposed to make jealous? That *he* was the one whose attention she wanted so badly that she had resorted to such desperate measures?

No, she couldn't possibly confess the truth. It would be too mortifying for both of them. But what to do? She must name someone. The doors of the ante-room were open so that she could see into the ballroom. Just then, she caught sight of the infamous rake Lord Tennison leaning against a pillar and shamelessly leering at Lady Dunholme's impressive bosom.

A fraction of a second later, before her brain could tell her how absurd it was and stop her from making an even greater fool of herself, she blurted his name. "Lord Tennison."

Geoffrey's jaw dropped and he glared for a moment in wide-eyed disbelief. "Good God. You can't be serious."

In for a penny, in for a pound. She drew herself up and said, "I'm quite serious. I find him exceedingly charming. And handsome."

He stared at her as though she'd lost her mind. Which wasn't far from the truth. "But you have no idea what he is, my girl. Trust me, Lydia, he is not the man for you."

"Oh, really?"

"Really. He is a . . . a . . ."

"A rake. I know. That's what makes him so—" she smiled dreamily and gave a little shiver "—exciting."

Geoffrey narrowed his eyes. "Exciting, eh? That's what you're looking for?"

"Yes, why not?"

"I don't know. It just doesn't sound like you, Lydia."

"Perhaps, sir, you do not know me as well as you think. Besides, who wants a dull, respectable gentleman who offers little more than a lifetime of tedium and propriety? A woman wants a man who makes her feel . . ."

"Desirable?"

Heat rose in her cheeks, but she soldiered on. "Yes, desirable. Is that so wrong?"

A corner of his mouth twitched upwards. "Not a bit. Tennison certainly knows how to do that, as he's been openly desiring women for years. He is quite a bit older than you, of course, but I don't suppose that signifies."

"I like a mature man."

"I do not doubt it." The twitch became a full-blown grin. Was he mocking her? Did he guess that Lord Tennison was a ruse?

"Well, my girl, you have given me a formidable assignment. However, I shall do my best to see that Tennison not only notices you, but is overcome with jealousy. He will be falling at your feet by the end of this evening, I assure you."

Oh dear. She wondered if she was in over her head, but was not inclined to turn craven just yet.

"Here's what I will do," Geoffrey said, keeping his voice low even though there were only a few other people in the ante-room with them, and no one close enough to overhear. Did he do that deliberately? Did he employ that low, smoky tone because he knew it unnerved her? "I have been seen dancing with you. Now I will be seen *not* dancing with anyone else. I shall linger about making calf's eyes at you while you dance with other men. And I shall not dance at all until the supper dance, when I shall lead you out again. Remember, you must save that dance for me. We'll be cosy over supper and make sure Tennison sees. Does that sound like a good plan to you?"

"It sounds brilliant. I will watch for those calf's eyes."

His expression softened, his eyebrows lifted and his eyes filled with a sort of woebegone yearning. Then his shoulders sagged as he gave a heartbreaking sigh, and Lydia burst out laughing. He was the very picture of a young boy in the throes of his first infatuation. "Do not overdo it, sir, I beg you. No one would believe it of you."

He cast off the moonstruck look and was himself again. "You think not? You think no one would believe I could fall in love?"

"Oh, I believe you could fall in love." She pinned all her hopes on it, in fact. "But I daresay it would never be a simple schoolboy's passion with you."

"You are quite right, my girl." He laid his hand over hers. "I am no longer a boy. It will be a much more complex experience for me. When I fall in love it will be deeply and completely and for ever."

It was her turn to sigh. How she wished she could be the object of such a love. His love.

He rose and took Lydia's hand to help her from the chair, then kissed it. "For luck," he said and led her back to her mother.

For the next hour and more, Lydia danced with other gentlemen. Her mother encouraged her to accept the attentions of each of them, as it was her fondest hope to see Lydia engaged by the season's end. It was, after all, her second season. One more and she would be edging closer towards bona fide spinsterhood. Frankly, if she could not have Geoffrey, she would as soon be a spinster. It was not in her nature to settle for second best.

It was a heady experience to watch Geoffrey gaze at her across the room as though he could not tear his eyes from her. She could at least pretend it was real, couldn't she? Or was it worse to know what it would feel like to have him look at her with love in his eyes than never to have known it at all? Was she setting herself up for disappointment and heartbreak?

Others noticed Geoffrey's obvious attention. Her friend Daphne Hughes pulled her aside and peppered her with questions, certain that Lydia was hiding something from her. Worst of all, her mother noticed. "I cannot fathom what has come over him," she said. "It's as though he suddenly realized what a beauty you are. I won't quibble over it, though. He'd be a fine catch for you, my dear. With your glossy dark curls and his golden hair, you will make a stunning couple."

Her maternal hopes were encouraged when Geoffrey came to claim her for the supper dance – a waltz, no less. She positively beamed when he led her daughter on to the floor.

"You might want to ease up on the calf's eyes, Mr Danforth," she whispered. "My mother is getting ideas."

"Is she? Well, that only plays right into our plans, does it not? If my blatant attentions are seen to meet with Mrs Bettridge's approval, then we have Tennison exactly where we want him: very much aware that another man desires you. Look, he has just led out Mrs Wadsworth for the waltz. Let's move a bit closer to them so he won't miss the way my rapt gaze drinks in the perfection of your bosom."

The music began before she could respond, and soon she forgot all about his impertinence. His hand was warm at her waist and, as her hand rested upon his shoulder, she could feel the strength of his muscles beneath the fine velvet of his jacket. He moved with such grace and confidence that she barely had to think about where to put her feet. His lead was sure.

It might just be the nearest she would ever come to being held in his arms. She closed her eyes and relished the moment.

"Tired?" he asked. "You have danced every dance. You will no doubt welcome the respite of supper."

"Hmm," she said, meaning: *I will welcome any time I can spend with you, but especially twirling about the floor in your arms.* She opened her eyes, looked directly into his, and hoped he might somehow read her thoughts.

"You are playing your part very well, too, Lydia. I swear you look as besotted as I do. And don't look now, but Tennison is actually paying attention. Our ploy has worked. His eyes are all for you, my girl." He muttered something else under his breath but she couldn't be sure what it was.

He pressed his hand against the back of her waist and pulled her a fraction closer.

Lydia supposed she ought to glance over at Lord Tennison now and then, just to maintain the charade, but she only had eyes for one man, and she was dancing with him. The sheer bliss of the waltz ended too soon, and as it was the supper dance it was a short set. Geoffrey kept his hand lightly on her back as he led her into the supper room.

He guided her to a small table meant for two, and surreptitiously winked when Lord Tennison and Mrs Wadsworth took an adjacent table. Geoffrey placed her with her back to the other couple, then leaned down and said, "He shot an interested glance in your direction. He is most definitely intrigued. Let's see if we can keep it that way." He grabbed two glasses of champagne from a passing footman. "I shall go fill a couple of plates from the buffet. Don't you dare let another chap take my seat." He grinned and walked away towards the tables set out like groaning boards.

She realized she was starving, as she hadn't eaten since breakfast. She'd been nervous all day, but now she was surprisingly calm, despite the rather startling turn of events. How strange to think that she had come tonight hoping to make him jealous and perhaps to see her in a different light, and instead . . .

But wait a moment. That was still her ultimate objective, was it not? To make him see her as a woman, a desirable woman worthy of a man's attention. It was possible that all the play-acting had forced him to see her differently. Was that enough?

When this scheme had been hatched, it was because men were supposedly susceptible to jealousy. It had come about on a dreary, rainy day too wet to do anything out of doors. Daniel and his friend Philip Hartwell had been sprawled upon the drawing room sofas, bored to tears and itching to be out and about. With nothing else to do, they had deigned to spend time in her company – a novelty as she was five years younger than Daniel, the little sister only occasionally tolerated. They had been talking of the Erskine ball and who they might dance with or whether they should simply haunt the card room. Philip had asked Lydia about her friend Daphne Hughes and if she would be attending. She was quite sure he had a *tendre* for Daphne, though he would never admit to it. He asked Lydia whom she was hoping to dance with, and soon both he and Daniel were teasing her about several gentlemen. The gloomy day had affected her mood and she told them, rather snappily, that she did not care tuppence for any of those men, that the only man she cared about didn't know she was alive.

That confession had set them off. They begged his name but she refused to tell and soon wished she'd kept her mouth shut. Eventually, they both dropped their teasing, especially Daniel who seemed genuinely concerned that his sister's heart was in danger of being broken. The two young men commiserated over ways she might attract the unnamed gentleman, but it had all seemed horribly embarrassing and she had more or less ignored their advice.

Until, that is, they had struck upon the notion of making the man jealous. That had seemed a more logical approach, especially as they cited several romances where jealousy had turned the tide. As the Erskine ball approached, she'd become less sanguine about the plan they'd concocted, but the idea of jealousy as a means of encouragement still held a ring of truth for her. Upon consideration, Lydia decided the original plan ought not to be completely discarded just yet.

She looked up to see Lord Tennison returning to the adjacent table with a plate of food. He was tall and lean, and quite fit for a man of his age, which must be at least thirty-five. He was dark-haired and dark-eyed, his face chiselled into sharp planes and angles. His eyes were heavy-lidded and his lips were more often than not curled into a seductive leer. Lord Tennison was considered a dangerous man, with an unsavoury reputation and no honour where women were concerned. Yet, he was an infamous rake with many high-born conquests, so clearly a good number of females were drawn to him. He was still handsome, in a world-weary sort of way, but he held no appeal for Lydia. His dark, swarthy looks were the antithesis of Geoffrey's golden beauty. She had, however, named him, and so she might as well make use of him.

She caught his eye and smiled. He paused, arched an eyebrow, then returned her smile. "Miss Bettridge. You are looking remarkably pretty this evening."

His gaze flickered momentarily down to her bosom, which seemed to be generating inordinate interest tonight. She hadn't minded Geoffrey admiring her figure, or even the other gentlemen she'd danced with, but Lord Tennison's open appraisal made her decidedly uncomfortable. She was tempted to reach down and tug up the bodice, but decided that the rather daring neckline served her purpose. When Tennison's eyes once again met hers, she broadened her smile, leaned ever so slightly forwards, giving him a better view, and batted her eyelashes. Once. Twice. But no more. She hoped to appear provocative, not silly. "Thank you, My Lord. It is kind of you to say so."

He regarded her more closely, with a sort of melting warmth, and all at once she could understand how so many women had fallen under his spell. With nothing more than the look in his eye, he made her feel as though he'd touched her in a shockingly intimate manner, and while other more sophisticated women might welcome such a look, Lydia did not like it at all. To maintain her pretence, though, she dropped her gaze demurely and batted her eyelashes once more.

"Kindness had nothing to do with it," he said in a lazy drawl. "I merely spoke the truth. See here, is someone getting you a plate? Or would you allow me the honour of doing so?"

"Someone has already done so, Tennison."

She hadn't seen Geoffrey approach, but the timing could not have been more perfect. His furious expression was an encouraging sign. Lydia put on her very best smile and turned to Lord Tennison. "Thank you so much for asking, My Lord. Perhaps some other time?"

"I look forward to it," he said, glancing at Geoffrey with a gleam of mockery in his eye before returning to Mrs Wadsworth.

Geoffrey put a plate of food in front of Lydia and took his seat. His scowl was one of the sweetest things she'd ever seen. He really *was* jealous. At least, that is what she hoped. Maybe he was just angry, and feeling protective of Daniel's sister.

"Dammit, Lydia, you truly are determined to have that scoundrel woo you?"

"I have said so, have I not? And I must say, Mr Danforth, that peevish look on your face does not signal that *you* are wooing me, which, you may recall, is the plan."

He gave a resigned shrug. "Right you are. I must not forget my role."

"It must be working, don't you think? Did you see the way he looked at me?"

"Humph. How could I not? Ah, but you should see the way Eugenia Wadsworth is looking at you. Do you feel her daggers in your back?"

Lydia laughed. "Is she jealous, do you think? Of me?" It boosted her confidence to think that the beautiful, fashionable widow would see her as competition.

"Apparently," he muttered, "jealousy is the name of the game tonight."

Better and better, she thought. It was all going according to plan. The revised plan, anyway.

"Well, I really do not care about Mrs Wadsworth," she said, and fluttered her fingers in a dismissive gesture. "It is Lord Tennison who concerns me. We are to make *him* jealous, in case you have forgotten."

Geoffrey tore his gaze from the other couple and returned his attention to Lydia with a smile so beguiling it poured over her like warm honey. Thank heaven she was seated.

"I have not forgotten. Let us resume our performance. Can I tempt you with something to eat?"

She noticed, for the first time, the plate in front of her. Besides the sliced ham, lobster patty and pickled mango, there was a small pile of the tiniest strawberries. "Oh, strawberries!" She popped one in her mouth and it was like the richest of sweetmeats. She closed her eyes and savoured it. She was very much afraid she'd actually moaned with pleasure. When she opened her eyes, Geoffrey was studying her intently with an expression she could not immediately identify. Could it be . . . hunger? The air in her lungs suddenly felt thin, starving her of breath. She held another strawberry in her fingers, but could not seem to lift it to her mouth.

"I remembered about the strawberries," he said, his eyes locked with hers.

"Hmm?"

"That picnic at your aunt's home in Richmond. You almost became sick from eating too many wild strawberries. You fell back on the blanket and said there was no better way to die."

Her heart gave a little skitter in her chest. "You . . . You remembered that?"

"Of course. You looked so charmingly . . . sated."

He took her hand and lifted the berry to her mouth. When she took it, her lips touched his bare fingers, for he had removed his gloves for supper, and the brief taste of his skin overwhelmed even the strawberry. He watched intently as she ate it and then licked her lips to capture every hint of flavour left behind. She watched him watch her and, all at once, with their gazes locked, she sensed a new connection between them, something deeper and full of understanding, through eyes and lips and fingers, and the sweet scent of ripe strawberries enveloping them. It felt so right. And very real – at least for her.

Please, please let this not be entirely an act for him.

He leaned back and the moment ended. He grinned, as though nothing out of the ordinary had occurred, while she reeled as though the earth had moved.

"You might try the lobster cakes," he said. "They are devilish good."

"I'm not very hungry."

"Even for more strawberries?" He waved his fork over the remaining pile.

She shook her head. She might never eat again. But she could happily sit there and watch him dine. Or watch him do anything. Dear God, she was lost to him.

And yet he merely play-acted.

While he ate and she pushed her food around the plate, they spoke of ordinary things, of friends and family, books and plays, and a dozen other mundane topics. All the while, though, Geoffrey kept up the pretence of infatuation, touching her, smiling boldly, staring at her with those splendid blue eyes. Anyone watching would assume they were in love. He was a fine actor. She teased him about treading the boards if he somehow lost his inheritance.

"Some roles are easier than others," he said. "I confess I am enjoying this one."

Most of the guests were still dining when Lord Tennison and Mrs Wadsworth left the room. She watched the rakish nobleman with feigned interest. "What are we to do now?" she asked. "We cannot dance a third set together without causing gossip, not to mention giving my mother palpitations. How shall we proceed with our plan? Or perhaps Lord Tennison is leaving the ball? Oh dear." She infused her voice with disappointment.

Geoffrey turned slightly to watch the departing couple. "No, they are not leaving. They are going out the terrace doors."

"Oh. Do you think we should follow them?"

"A capital suggestion, my girl. Let's go ogle each other in the moonlight. Nothing could appear more romantic."

She felt many pairs of eyes on them as they left the supper room. No doubt tongues would be wagging as soon as they were out of sight. "Are you certain this is wise?" she whispered. "I fear people may get the wrong idea."

"That is the point, is it not? To make one particular person get the wrong idea?" He patted her hand where it rested on his arm. "Do not vex yourself, Lydia. Taking a bit of air after supper with your brother's best friend is no scandalous thing. Trust me, no one will care."

She hoped he was right. She would hate for a general expectation to arise, forcing him into a situation he did not want, even if she wanted it desperately.

When they reached the terrace, Lydia saw Lord Tennison in a far corner, standing very close to Mrs Wadsworth. It looked as though they might have just ended a kiss, and Lydia turned away, embarrassed. Geoffrey led her to the opposite corner. He stood with his back to the balustrade and pulled her gently to his side so that she faced the garden. It was a beautiful, clear, temperate evening. The stars were out in force and the moon almost full, the air redolent of lilac and horse chestnut. It was the perfect setting for romance, with the perfect man at her side. If only . . .

He took her hand and discreetly held it behind him so that no one looking out from the ballroom could see. Neither could Lord Tennison, if he bothered to look, so she wondered why Geoffrey did it. She wanted to believe it was for himself and not for the sake of their ruse, but she tried not to get her hopes up. Though both were gloved now, she nevertheless felt the warmth of his fingers, especially when he began sketching lazy circles on her palm.

"I think we need to up the game a bit," he said.

"What do you mean?"

"If Tennison is the man you want, you must be prepared to play at his level. He is a man of the world, as you know, with a great deal of experience."

"With women."

"Yes. A great many women."

"And you think I am no match for all those other women? That he may find my youth and inexperience tiresome?"

He reached up and stroked her cheek. "You are more than worthy of any man's attention, my girl. To be perfectly honest, I don't think *he* is worthy of *your* attention. I may not like him, but it is not my place to judge your heart's desire. If he is the one you want, then I am here to help you win him. But, because he *is* so worldly, I suspect a few dances and moonstruck gazes are not enough to incite his jealousy. Tennison is a bold choice, Lydia, and you must be bold to win him."

A frisson of anticipation skittered down her spine. "What did you have in mind?"

"Come with me," he said. Keeping hold of her hand, he guided her to the steps leading down from the terrace.

"Where are we going?"

He merely smiled and led her into the garden, where gravel pathways were lit by paper lanterns hanging from trees. "I don't understand," she said. "How can we make Lord Tennison jealous if he can't even see us?"

He'd stopped at a stone bench tucked among the shrubbery. "It's what he will see when we return," he said, and pulled her to sit down beside him. Very close beside him.

"What will he see?"

"A woman who has been thoroughly kissed."

And there, bathed in the lush scent of a nearby lilac tree and the silvery light of the brilliant moon, he kissed her. Tenderly, at first. His hand spread against the back of her head, angling his mouth over hers, while his other hand settled low on her back.

She did not care if he did this merely to provoke another man, she was in his arms and he was kissing her – it was what she had always wanted, her every dream and fantasy. And, by God, she was going to take advantage of the moment. She kissed him back for all she was worth, twining her arms around his neck and pressing her body against his.

She felt the thumping of his heart beneath his shirt and waistcoat, or perhaps it was her own heartbeat. She could no longer distinguish his heart from hers. They were as one, synchronized, merged, united.

He parted her lips with a gentle nudging from his own, and all at once the kiss became lush and full and potently carnal as his tongue began an urgent twirling dance with her own. Good God, what was he doing to her? It was like nothing she had ever experienced or could even have imagined. It was earth-shaking, soul-shattering – a kiss filled with hunger and tenderness, with promise and desire. She melted into it, allowing him to draw her tongue deeper into his mouth, and everything within her dissolved into molten liquid.

They kissed and kissed for what might have been hours or mere moments. When he finally lifted his head, he murmured her name. "Lydia, ah, sweet Lydia." He skated his lips along her jaw to the hollow beneath her ear. Unprepared for the intense sensation his lips wrought on that particular spot – she'd had no idea it was so wonderfully sensitive – she caught her breath on a gasp and shivered with almost unbearable pleasure. She arched her neck in shameless invitation as his mouth moved lower. His lips parted and the velvety tip of his tongue against her flushed neck sent ripples of pure bliss shimmering along every inch of her skin. The jumble of new sensations was so dazzling that all rational thought vanished. A moan rose from the back of her throat. She gasped his name, over and over, while kneading his back and shoulders with restless desire.

The sound of his name seemed to renew his passion, for he brought his lips back to hers and plundered her mouth again, almost savagely. She responded with equal hunger, and they kissed until her head swam in a sort of dark, sensual haze.

When they finally broke the kiss, she leaned her forehead against his, her breath ragged and her heart in turmoil. "Geoffrey? Is this real? Or are we still play-acting?"

"Does it seem like play-acting to you?"

"No. Oh, I don't know! You have my mind all in a whirl. I don't know what to think."

He lifted his head and gazed into her eyes. "Sweet Lydia, I have a confession to make."

"Oh?"

"Hartwell was not detained, and he did not ask me to replace him tonight in your little scheme."

"He didn't?"

"No, I asked him. In fact, I all but begged him to allow me to take his place. When he told me of your plans, I knew I wanted to be the one to play the lovesick fool."

"But why?"

"So I would have a good excuse to do this." And he kissed her again. "And this." He trailed his lips along her jaw and down her throat. "And this." His tongue dipped into the cleavage of her bosom while one finger slipped inside the lace at her neckline until it found her nipple, just barely covered by her stays. She uttered a moan of shocked pleasure as he teased it.

"Oh God, Lydia." His voice was raw and breathless. "We must stop."

She buried her face in the crook of his neck. "This is real, then? You are kissing me because you want to and not because of Lord Tennison?"

"I have wanted to kiss you for ages, Lydia. And the devil take Tennison. Surely you do not really want him, do you? Would you give me a chance instead?"

She threw her head back and laughed for joy. "Silly man. Of course I do not want that odious Lord Tennison. I have a confession, too, you know. What I told Daniel and Philip was true. I was indeed pining away for someone who never noticed me, and they really did help me contrive a plan to make that someone jealous. But it was not Lord Tennison, it was you."

"Me? I had assumed it was Garthwaite or Lonsdale or any of a number of eligible gentlemen – but when you named Tennison, I began to have my doubts. I knew you were up to something, and I dared to hope it might involve me."

"Wretched man! You knew all along I had lied about Lord Tennison?"

"Of course I did. You would never be attracted to such a jaded libertine. But you did give me pause in the supper room, when you flirted with him. You see, your scheme worked after all. I was seething with jealousy! Though I didn't need that ploy to make me notice you. I've been noticing you since you gave up plaits and put your hair up."

"Truly? I had no idea. I thought you entirely indifferent to me. You never hinted otherwise."

"Because I was convinced you disliked me. With all Daniel's other friends, you were fun and lively. With me, you always seemed a bit cool. But still, I found you irresistible."

"Oh no, you resisted me quite easily! If I seemed aloof, it was because I was afraid to reveal how I truly felt."

"And how is that?"

"I have loved you forever, I think."

"And I love you, Lydia. With all my heart."

"Deeply and completely?" she teased, throwing his words back at him, hoping he had meant them.

He laughed, took her face in his hands, and stroked his thumbs along the line of her jaw. "Deeply and completely. What fools we have been, eh? Each of us secretly pining after the other. We must name our first child after Hartwell for hatching the scheme that finally brought us together."

She smiled at the implication of his words, and was tilting her mouth up for another kiss when a shriek from the shrubbery interrupted them.

"Lydia! What on earth are you about?"

Dear God, it was her mother. She looked anxiously at Geoffrey, who kissed her hand and rose from the bench.

"Not to worry, Mrs Bettridge. Miss Lydia and I have come to an understanding. I trust you will forgive us for behaving improperly, but we were too excited and happy to resist a kiss or two."

"Well." Her mother frowned, but she did not fool Lydia. She was surely thrilled beyond measure. "I suppose one must forgive high spirits at such a time. You will, naturally, call upon Mr Bettridge tomorrow."

"You may tell him to expect me."

"Good. In the meantime, Lydia, come with me. You must not been seen coming out of the garden with Mr Danforth, regardless of his intentions. People will talk, you know. Come along now."

Her mother linked arms with her and walked towards the house. Lydia cast one last, longing look at Geoffrey before following her mother out of the garden and up the terrace steps.

"Well, my dear." Her mother gave her arm a fond squeeze. "What an interesting evening you have had. Aren't you glad Philip Hartwell didn't show up for that first set?"

"I have never been so glad of anything in all my life."

And she would thank him for it – for staying inside on a rainy day, for explaining the male psyche, for concocting a most excellent plan and for giving up his role in it. But mostly, for helping her to achieve her heart's desire. At long last.

Upon a Midnight Clear

Anna Campbell

North Yorkshire – December 1826

The crash of shattering wood and the terrified screams of horses sliced through the frosty night like a knife.

Sebastian Sinclair, Earl of Kinvarra, swore, brought his restive mount under control, then spurred the nervous animal around the turn in the snowy road. With cold clarity, the full moon shone on the white landscape, and starkly revealed the disaster before him.

A flashy black curricle lay on its side in a ditch, the hood up against the weather. One horse had broken free and wandered along the roadway, its harness dragging. The other plunged in the traces, struggling to escape.

Swiftly Kinvarra dismounted – knowing his mare would await his signal – and dashed to free the distressed horse. As he slid down the icy ditch, a hatless man scrambled out of the smashed curricle.

"Are you hurt?" Kinvarra asked, casting a quick eye over him.

"No, I thank you, sir." The effete blond fellow turned to the carriage. "Come, darling. Let me assist you."

A graceful black-gloved hand extended from inside and a cloaked woman emerged with more aplomb than Kinvarra would have thought possible in the circumstances. Indications were that neither traveller was injured, so he concentrated on the trapped horse. When he spoke soothingly to the animal, the terrified beast quieted to panting stillness, exhausted from its thrashing. While Kinvarra checked the horse, murmuring calm assurances throughout, the stranger helped the lady up to the roadside.

With a shrill whinny, the horse shook itself and jumped up to trot along the road towards its partner. Neither beast seemed to suffer worse than fright, a miracle considering that the curricle was beyond repair.

"Madam, are you injured?" Kinvarra asked as he climbed up the ditch. He stuck his riding crop under his arm and brushed his gloved hands together to knock the clinging snow from them. It was a hellishly cold night.

The woman kept her head down. From shock? From shyness? For the sake of propriety? Perhaps he'd stumbled on some elopement or clandestine meeting.

"Madam?" he asked again, more sharply.

"Sweeting?" The yellow-haired fop bent to peer into the shadows cast by the hood. "Are you sure you're unharmed? Speak, my dove. Your silence strikes a chill to my soul."

While Kinvarra digested the man's outlandish phrasing, the woman stiffened and drew away. "For heaven's sake, Harold, you're not giving a recitation at a musicale." With an unmistakably impatient gesture, she flung back the hood and glared straight at Kinvarra.

Even though he'd identified her the moment she spoke, he found himself staring dumbstruck into her face – a piquant, vivid, pointed face under an untidy tumble of luxuriant gold hair.

He wheeled on the pale fellow. "What the devil are you doing with my wife?"

Alicia Sinclair, Countess of Kinvarra, was bruised and angry and uncomfortable and horribly embarrassed. And not long past the choking terror she had felt when the carriage toppled.

Even so, her heart launched into the wayward dance it always performed at the merest sight of Sebastian.

She'd been married for eleven long years. She disliked her husband more than any other man in the world. But nothing prevented her gaze from clinging helplessly to every line of that narrow, intense face with its high cheekbones, long, arrogant nose and sharply angled jaw.

Damn him to Hades, he was still the most magnificent creature she'd ever beheld.

Such a pity his soul was as black as his glittering eyes.

"After all this time, I'm flattered you still recognize me, My Lord," she said silkily.

"Lord Kinvarra, this is a surprise," Harold stammered. "You must wonder what I'm doing here with the lady . . ."

Oh, Harold, act the man, even if the hero is beyond your reach. Kinvarra doesn't care enough about me to kill you, however threatening he seems now.

Although even the most indifferent husband took it ill when his wife chose a lover. Kinvarra wouldn't mistake what Alicia was doing out here. She stifled a rogue pang of guilt. Curse Kinvarra, she had absolutely nothing to feel guilty about.

"I've recalled your existence every quarter these past ten years, my love," her husband said equally smoothly, ignoring Harold's appalled interjection. The faint trace of Scottish brogue in his deep voice indicated his temper. His breath formed white clouds on the frigid air. "I'm perforce reminded when I pay your allowance, only to receive sinfully little return."

"That warms the cockles of my heart," she sniped, not backing down.

She refused to cower like a wet hen before his banked anger. He sounded reasonable, calm, controlled, but she had no trouble reading fury in the tension across his broad shoulders or in the way his powerful hands opened and closed at his sides.

"Creatures of ice have no use for a heart. Does this paltry fellow know he risks frostbite in your company?"

She steeled herself against the taunting remark. Kinvarra couldn't hurt her now. He hadn't been able to hurt her since she'd left him. Any twinge she experienced was just because she was vulnerable after the accident. That was all. It wasn't because this man could still needle her emotions.

"My Lord, I protest," Harold said, shocked, and fortunately sounding less like a frightened sheep than before. "The lady is your wife. Surely she merits your chivalry."

Harold had never seen her with her husband, and some reluctant and completely misplaced loyalty to Kinvarra meant she'd never explained why she and the earl lived apart. The fiction was that the earl and his countess were polite strangers who, by design, rarely met.

Poor Harold, he was about to discover the truth was that the earl and his countess loathed each other.

"Like hell she does," Kinvarra muttered, casting her an incendiary glance from under long dark eyelashes.

Alicia was human enough to wish the bright moonlight didn't reveal quite so much of her husband's seething rage. But the fate that proved cruel enough to fling them together, tonight of all nights, wasn't likely to heed her pleas.

"Do you intend to introduce me to your *cicisbeo*?" Kinvarra's voice remained quiet. She'd learned that was when he was at his most dangerous.

Dear God, did he intend to shoot Harold after all?

Surely not. Foul as Kinvarra had been to her, he'd never shown her a moment's violence. Her hands clenched in her skirts as fear tightened her throat. Kinvarra was a crack shot and a famous swordsman. Harold wouldn't stand a chance.

"My Lord, I protest the description," Harold bleated, sidling back to evade assault.

Was it too much to wish that her suitor would stand up to the scoundrel she'd married as a stupid chit of seventeen? Alicia drew a deep breath and reminded herself that she favoured Lord Harold Fenton precisely because he wasn't an overbearing brute like her husband, the earl. Harold was a scholar and a poet, a man of the mind. She should consider it a sign of Harold's intelligence that he was wary right now.

But somehow her insistence didn't convince her traitorous heart.

How she wished she really were the impervious creature Kinvarra called her. Then she'd be immune both to his insults and to the insidious attraction he aroused.

"My Lady?" Kinvarra asked, still in that even, frightening voice. "Who is this . . . gentleman?"

She stiffened her backbone. She was made of stronger stuff than this. Never would she let her husband guess he still had power over her. Her response was steady. "Lord Kinvarra, allow me to present Lord Harold Fenton."

Harold performed a shaky bow. "My Lord."

As he rose, a tense silence descended.

"Well, this is awkward," Kinvarra said flatly, although she saw in his taut, dark face that his anger hadn't abated one whit.

"I don't see why," Alicia snapped.

It wasn't just her husband who tried her temper. There was her lily-livered lover and the perishing cold. The temperature must have dropped ten degrees in the last five minutes. She shivered, then silently cursed that Kinvarra noticed and Harold didn't. Harold was too busy staring at her husband the way a mouse stares at an adder.

"Do you imagine I'm so sophisticated, I'll ignore discovering you in the arms of another man? My dear, you do me too much credit."

She stifled the urge to consign him to Hades. "If you'll put aside your bruised vanity for the moment, you'll see we merely require you to ride to the nearest habitation and request help. Then you and I can return to acting like complete strangers, My Lord."

He laughed and she struggled to suppress the shiver of sensual awareness that rippled down her spine at that soft, deep sound.

"Some things haven't changed, I see. You're still dishing out orders. And I'm still damned if I'll play your obedient lapdog."

"Can you see another solution?" she asked sweetly.

"Yes," he said with a snap of his straight white teeth. "I can leave you to freeze. Not that you'd probably notice."

Her pride insisted that she send him on his way with a flea in his ear. The weather – and what common sense she retained under the anger that always flared in Kinvarra's proximity – prompted her to be conciliatory.

It was late. She and Harold hadn't passed anyone on this isolated road. The grim truth was that if Kinvarra didn't help, they were stranded until morning. And while she was dressed in good thick wool, she wasn't prepared to endure a snowy night in the open. The chill of the road seeped through her fur-lined boots and she shifted, trying to revive feeling in her frozen feet.

"My Lord . . ." During the year they'd lived together, she'd called him Sebastian. During their few meetings since, she'd clung to formality as a barrier. "My Lord, there's no point in quarrelling. Basic charity compels your assistance. I would consider myself in your debt if you fetch aid as quickly as possible."

He arched one black eyebrow in a superior fashion that made her want to clout him. Not a new sensation. "Now that's something I'd like to see," he said.

"What?"

"Gratitude."

He knew he had her at a disadvantage and he wasn't likely to rise above that fact. She gritted her teeth. "It's all I can offer."

The smile that curved his lips was pure devilry. Another shiver ran through her. Like the last one, it was a shiver with no connection to the cold. "Your imagination fails you, my dear countess."

Her throat closed with nerves – and that reluctant physical awareness she couldn't ignore. He hadn't shifted, yet suddenly she felt physically threatened. Which was ridiculous. During all their years apart, he'd given no indication he wanted anything from her except her absence. One chance meeting wasn't likely to turn him into a medieval robber baron who spirited her away to his lonely tower.

Nonetheless, she had to resist stepping back. She knew from bitter experience that her only chance of handling him was to feign control. "What do you want?"

This time he did step closer, so his great height overshadowed her. Close enough for her to think that if she stretched out her hand, she'd touch that powerful chest, those wide shoulders. "I want . . ."

There was a piercing whinny and a sudden pounding of hooves on the snow. Appalled, disbelieving, Alicia turned to see Harold galloping away on one of the carriage horses.

"Harold?"

Her voice faded to nothing in the night. He didn't slow his wild careening departure. She'd been so engrossed in her battle with Kinvarra, she hadn't even noticed that Harold had caught one of the stray horses.

Kinvarra's low laugh was scornful. "Oh, my dear. Commiserations. Your swain proves a sad disappointment. I wonder if he's fleeing my temper or yours. You really have no luck in love, have you?"

She was too astonished to be upset at Harold's departure. Instead she focused on Kinvarra. Her voice was hard. "No luck in husbands, at any rate."

Kinvarra suffered Alicia's hate-filled regard and wondered what the hell he was going to do with his troublesome wife in this wilderness. The insolent baggage deserved to be left where she stood, but even he, who owed her repayment for numerous slights over the years, wouldn't do that to her.

It seemed he had no choice but to help.

Not that she'd thank him. He had no illusions that once she'd got what she wanted – a warm bed, a roof over her head and a decent meal – she'd forget any promises of gratitude.

In spite of the punishing cold, heat flooded him as he briefly let himself imagine Alicia's gratitude. She'd shed that heavy red cloak. She'd let down that mass of gold hair until it tumbled around her shoulders. Then she'd kiss him as if she didn't hate him and she'd . . .

From long habit, he stopped himself. Such fantasies had sustained him the first year of their separation, but he'd learned for sanity's sake to control them since. Now they only troubled him after his rare meetings with his wife.

This was the longest time he and Alicia had spent together in years. It should remind him why he avoided her company. Instead, it reminded him that she was the only woman who had ever challenged him, the only woman who had ever matched him in strength, the only woman he'd never been able to forget, desperately as he'd tried.

He smiled into her sulky, beautiful face. "It seems you're stuck with me."

How that must smart. The long ride to his Yorkshire manor on this cold night suddenly offered a myriad of pleasures, not least of which was a chance to knock a few chips off his wife's pride.

She didn't respond to his comment. Instead, with an unreadable expression, she stared after her absconding lover. "We're only about five miles from Harold's hunting lodge."

The wench didn't even try to lie about the assignation, blast her. "If he manages to stay on that horse, Horace should make it." Fenton showed no great skill as a bareback rider. Kinvarra recognized the wish as unworthy, but he hoped the blackguard ended up on his rump in a hedgerow.

"Harold," she said absently, drawing her cloak tight around her slender throat. "You could take me there."

This time his laughter was unconstrained. She'd always had nerve, his wife, even when she'd been little more than a girl. "Be damned if you think I'm carting you off to cuckold me in comfort, madam."

She sent him a cool look. "I'm thinking purely in terms of shelter, My Lord."

"I'm sure," he said cynically.

In spite of their lack of communication in recent years, he'd always known what she was up to. Since leaving him, she'd been remarkably chaste, which was one of the reasons he'd allowed the ridiculous separation to continue. Clearly living with him for a year had left her with no taste for bed sport.

Recent gossip had mentioned Lord Harold Fenton as a persistent suitor, but Kinvarra thought he knew her well enough to consider the second son of the Marquess of Preston poor competition. He should have listened.

Her taste had deteriorated in the last ten years. The man was a complete nonentity.

Perhaps one day she'd thank her husband for saving her from a disastrous mistake.

And the bleak and stony moor around them might suddenly sprout coconut palms.

"No, my love, your fate is sealed." He slapped his riding crop against his boot and tilted his hat more securely on his head with an arrogant gesture designed to irritate her. "Horatio travels north. I travel south. Unless you intend to mount the other carriage horse or pursue the clodpole on foot, your direction is mine."

"Does that mean you will help me?" This time, she didn't bother correcting his deliberate misremembering of her lover's name. She was lucky he didn't call the blackguard Habakkuk and skewer his kidneys with a rapier. Alicia was his. No other damned rapscallion was going to steal her away. Especially a rapscallion who didn't have the spine to stand up and fight for her.

Kinvarra strode across to his mare and snatched up the reins. "If you ask nicely."

To his surprise, Alicia laughed. "Devil take you, Kinvarra."

He swung into the saddle and urged the horse nearer to his wife. "Indubitably, my dear."

Her cavalier attitude made it easier to deal with her, but it puzzled him. Her lover's desertion hadn't cast her down. If she didn't care for the man, why choose him? Yet again, he realized how far he remained from understanding the complicated creature he'd wed with such high hopes eleven years ago.

He extended one black-gloved hand and noted her hesitation before she accepted his assistance. It was the first time he'd touched her since she'd left him and even through two layers of leather, he felt the shock of contact. She stiffened as though she too felt that sudden surge of attraction.

He'd always wanted her. That was part of the problem, God help them. He'd often asked himself if time would erode the attraction.

Just one touch of her hand and he received his unequivocal answer.

She swung on to the horse behind him and paused before she looped her arms around his waist. He'd always been cursed aware of her reactions and he couldn't help but note her reluctance to touch him.

Good God, what was wrong with the woman? She'd been ready enough to do more than just touch that milksop Harold. Surely her husband deserved some warmth after offering assistance. With damned little encouragement too, he might add.

The mare curvetted under the double weight, but Kinvarra settled her with a word. He never had trouble with horses. It was his wife he couldn't control.

"What about my belongings?" she asked, calm as you please. The lady should demonstrate proper shame at being caught with a lover. But, of course, that wasn't Alicia. She held her head high whatever destiny threw at her.

It was one of the things he loved about her.

He quashed the unwelcome insight. "There's an inn a few miles ahead. I'll get them to send someone for any baggage."

He clicked his tongue to the horse and cantered in the opposite direction to the one Harold had taken. Which was lucky for the weasel. If Kinvarra caught up with Harold now, he'd be inclined to drag out his horsewhip. What right had he to interfere with other men's wives then scuttle away to leave them stranded?

Alicia settled herself more comfortably, pressing her lovely, lush body into his back. She hadn't been as close to him in years. He was scoundrel enough to enjoy the contact, however reluctantly she granted it.

Maybe after all, he should be grateful to old Harold. He might even send the bastard a case of port and a thank you note.

Well, that might be going too far.

"Is that where we're going?" She tightened her arms. He wished it was because she wanted to touch him and not just because she sought a firmer seat. He also wished that when she said "we", his belly didn't cramp with longing for the word to be true.

Damn Alicia. She'd always held magic for him and she always would. Ten long years without her had taught him that grim lesson.

The reminder of the dance she'd led him made him respond in a clipped tone. "No, we're headed for Heseltine Hall near Whitby."

"But you can leave me at the inn, can't you?"

"It's a poor place. I couldn't abandon a woman there without protection." He tried, he really did, to keep the satisfaction from his voice, but he must have failed. He felt her tense against his back, although she couldn't pull too far away without risking a fall.

"But who's going to protect me from you?" she muttered, almost as if to herself.

"I mean you no harm." In all their difficult interactions, he'd never wished her anything but well. "You didn't come all the way from London in that spindly carriage, did you?"

"It's inappropriate to discuss the details of my arrangement with Lord Harold," she said coldly.

He laughed again. "Humour me."

She sighed. "We travelled up separately to York." Her voice softened into sincerity and he tried not to respond to the husky sweetness. "I truly didn't set out to cause a scandal. You and I parted in rancour, but I have no wish to do you or your pride damage."

"Whatever your discretion, you still meant to give yourself to that puppy," Kinvarra said, all amusement suddenly fled.

Alicia didn't answer.

The weather had worsened by the time they reached the inn. Alicia realized as they came up to the building that it was indeed the rough place Kinvarra had described. But just the promise of shelter and a chance to rest her tired, sore body was welcome. Surely Kinvarra couldn't intend to ride on to his mysterious manor tonight when snow fell thicker with every minute and their horse was blowing with exhaustion.

The earl dismounted and lifted her from the saddle. The flickering torches that lit the inn yard revealed that he looked tired and strangely, for a man who always seemed so indomitable, unhappy.

As he set her upon the ground, his hands didn't linger at her waist. She tried not to note that she'd touched Kinvarra more in the last few hours than she had in the entire preceding ten years.

"Let's get you into the warmth." He gestured for her to precede him inside as a groom rushed to take their horse.

Alicia had expected him to spend the journey haranguing her on her wantonness – or at the very least her stupidity for setting out for the wilds of Yorkshire so ill prepared for disaster. But he'd remained quiet.

How she wished he had berated her. She'd spent ten years convinced she'd been right to leave him. A moment's kindness shouldn't change that.

But when his back offered her a warm anchor and his adept hands unerringly guided their horse to safety, her resentment proved fiendishly difficult to cling to. And when she wasn't constantly sniping at him, it was harder to ignore his physical presence. He'd been a handsome boy. He was a splendid man, with his clean, male scent – horses, leather, soap, fresh air – and the lean strength of his body. The muscles under her hands were hard, even through his thick clothing.

She'd forgotten how powerfully he affected her. And the pity of it was that it would take her too long to forget again. He made every other man she'd met pale into insignificance.

It was vilely irritating.

The landlord greeted them at the door, clearly overwhelmed to have the quality staying. The tap room was crowded to the rafters with people bundled up for an uncomfortable night on chairs and benches. A few hardy souls hunched near the fire drinking and smoking. Alicia drew her hood around her face before she moved closer to the blaze. The sudden warmth penetrated her frozen extremities with painful force. Even holding tight to the radiating heat of Kinvarra's big, strong body, the ride had been frozen purgatory.

For all that she remained standing, she'd drifted into a half-doze when she became aware of Kinvarra at her side. He spoke in a low voice to save them from eavesdroppers. "My Lady, there's a difficulty."

Blinking, trying to return to alertness, she slowly turned to face him. "I'm happy to accept any accommodation. Surely you don't intend to go on tonight."

He shook his head. He'd taken off his hat and light sheened across his thick dark hair. "The weather will get worse before it gets better. And my horse needs the stable. There isn't another village for miles."

"Then of course we'll stay."

"There's only one room."

She drew away in dismay. "Surely . . . surely you could sleep in the tap room."

She felt like the world's most ungrateful creature the moment she made the suggestion. Her husband had rescued her in extremely good spirit, given the compromising circumstances. He was as tired and cold and hungry as she. It wasn't fair to consign him to a hard floor and the company of a parcel of rustics, not to mention the vermin that flourished on their persons.

His lips twisted in a wry smile. "As you can see, there's no space in the tap room. Even if there was, I won't leave you on your own with the place full of God knows what ruffians."

Aghast, she looked at him fully. She'd suspect him of some design, if she didn't know he too must recall the wretchedness of their lives together. He must be as eager as she for this unexpected meeting to end so they could both return to their separate lives. "But we can't share a room."

His eyes glinted with sardonic amusement. "I don't see why not. You're my wife. It's too late to play Miss Propriety. After all, you were about to hop into bed with Herbert."

"Harold," she said automatically, a blush rising in her cheeks.

"I hope to hell he hasn't sampled your favours already or I'll think even less of his stalwart behaviour."

"We hadn't . . . we hadn't . . ." She stopped and glared at him. "That is none of your concern, My Lord."

She didn't imagine the sudden smugness in Kinvarra's expression. Curse her for admitting that she was still to all intents faithful to him.

The cad didn't deserve it. He never had.

"Can't we hire a chaise?" she asked on a note of desperation.

Suddenly the prospect of a night at the inn wasn't so welcome. Tonight had left her too exposed. Easy to play the indifferent spouse when she met the earl in a crowded ballroom. Much more difficult when she'd just spent an hour cuddled up to him and he sounded like a reasonable man instead of the spoilt young man she recalled from their brief cohabitation.

At least he wouldn't touch her. She was safe from that.

He shook his head. "There are none. And even if there were, I'm not going to risk my neck – and yours – on a night like this. Face it, madam, you've returned to the bonds of holy wedlock for the night. I'm sure you'll survive the experience."

She wasn't so sure. Leaving him ten years ago had nearly destroyed her. All this propinquity now only reopened old wounds. But what choice did she have?

She raised her head and stared into his striking face. "Very well."

"I'll tell the landlord we'll take his last chamber." He bowed briefly and strode away with a smooth, powerful gait. He'd grown into his power over the last years. As a young man, he'd been almost sinfully beautiful with his black hair and eyes, but the man of thirty-two was formidable and in command of himself in a way his younger self had never been.

She watched him go, wanting to turn away but unable to shift her gaze. What would she make of him if they met for the first time now? Honesty compelled her to admit she would probably like him. She'd certainly notice him – no woman could ignore such a handsome man with his air of authority and competence.

She hated to say it, but she was glad Kinvarra had arrived to rescue her from that ditch. Harold would have left everything to her. They'd probably still be standing by the roadside.

Given the shambles downstairs, the bedchamber was surprisingly clean and wonderfully snug to a woman shivering with cold. A troupe of maids delivered hot water and a substantial supper, then disappeared.

Silently, Alicia removed her gloves, slid her cloak from her shoulders, folded it and placed it on top of a carved wooden chest. It seemed ridiculous to feel shy in the presence of the man she'd married eleven years ago, but she did. She tried not to look at the massive tester bed in the corner. Did he mean to share that bed with her? If he did, what would her response be? She shivered, but whether with nerves or anticipation, she couldn't have said.

Kinvarra poured himself a glass of claret and took a mouthful, then turned to watch her lower herself gingerly into an oak chair with heavy arms. He strode towards her, frowning with concern. "You told me you weren't hurt."

She shook her head, even as she relished the blessed relief of sitting on something that didn't move. "I'm bruised and stiff from cold and riding so long, but, no, I'm not hurt."

"You were lucky. The curricle is beyond repair. I know the road was icy but the going wasn't hazardous, for all that. Was Henry driving too fast?"

"Perhaps." She paused before she reluctantly admitted, "And we were quarrelling."

"You? Quarrelling with a man?" Without shifting his gaze from her face, Kinvarra dropped to his knees before her. Clearly he meant to help her remove her boots. "I find that hard to imagine."

Her lips curved upwards in a smile as she looked down into eyes alight with sardonic amusement. Nobody had ever teased her. Even Kinvarra when they'd lived together had been too intense at first, then too angry. She found she liked his playful humour.

"Shocking, isn't it?"

He extended his half-full glass and she accepted it. His focus didn't waver when she raised it to her lips. Warmth seeped into her veins. From the wine or from the unspoken intimacy of drinking from the place his lips had touched? It was almost like sharing a kiss.

Stop it, Alicia. You're letting the situation go to your head.

"What were you quarrelling about?" Kinvarra asked with an idleness that his grave attention contradicted.

Still smiling, she returned the glass. "I decided I'd been reckless to take up Lord Harold's invitation to visit his hunting lodge. I was trying to get him to take me back to York."

She prepared to suffer Kinvarra's triumphant gloating. He didn't want her. But she'd always known he didn't want her sharing her body with anyone else either.

Her husband's serious, almost searching expression didn't change. "I'm glad to hear that," he said quietly.

She tried to sit up and glare at him but the effort was beyond her. Instead she tilted her head back against the chair. She closed her eyes, partly from weariness, partly because she didn't want to read messages that couldn't possibly be true in his dark, dark stare.

"He wasn't worthy of you, you know, Alicia." Kinvarra's soft voice echoed in her heart, as did his use of her Christian name. He hadn't called her Alicia since the early days of their marriage when they'd both still hoped they might make something good from their union. "Why in God's name choose him of all men?"

Shock held her unmoving as she felt Kinvarra's bare hand slide over hers where it rested on the arm of the chair. His palm was warm and slightly calloused. Harold's hand had been softer than a woman's. She cursed herself for making the comparison.

She opened her eyes and stared into her husband's saturnine face. Into the black eyes that for once appeared sincere and kind.

And she chanced an honest answer.

"I chose him because he was everything you are not, My Lord."

Even more shocking than the touch of his hand, she watched him whiten under his tan. She hadn't realized she had the power to hurt him. It seemed she was mistaken about that too.

He drew back on his heels, removing his hand from hers. She tried not to miss that casual, comforting touch. The distance between them felt like a gaping chasm of ice.

"I . . . see." His voice was harder when he went on. "At least I'd never leave a woman alone to face down an angry husband with a snowstorm about to descend upon her."

Shamed heat stung her cheeks. She'd felt so brave and free and self-righteous when she'd arranged to go away with a lover. After ten barren years of fidelity to a man who hardly cared she was alive.

But in retrospect, her behaviour seemed shabby. Ill-advised. Bravado had kept her to her course until she'd reached York and that journey across the moors with no company but Harold and her screaming conscience. She hadn't wanted to feel guilty, but she had. And with every mile they'd covered, she'd become more convinced she'd made a horrific mistake in succumbing to Harold's blandishments.

"You wouldn't hurt me," she said with complete certainty.

"No, but Harold didn't know that."

She noted that he was upset enough to use Harold's correct name. She tried to make light of the subject but her voice emerged as brittle and too high. "Anyway, no harm was done. I'm still the impossibly virtuous Countess of Kinvarra who doesn't even lie with her husband. You can sleep easy in your bed, My Lord, knowing your wife's reputation remains unblemished."

An emotion too complex for mere anger crossed his face, but his voice remained steady. "Why now, Alicia? What changed?"

"I was lonely." Her face still prickled with heat and she knew from his expression that her shrug didn't convince. "I thought I needed to do something to mark that I was a free woman. It was, in a way, our ten year anniversary."

A muscle flickered in his cheek. "And you wanted to punish me."

Did she? Even after all this time, turbulent emotion swirled beneath their interactions. She spoke with difficulty. "It's been over ten years since I had a man in my bed. I'm twenty-eight years old. I thought . . . I thought it was time I tested the waters again."

"With that cream puff?" He released a huff of contemptuous laughter and made a slashing, contemptuous gesture with one hand. "If you're going to kick over the traces, my girl, at least choose a man with blood in his veins."

"I've had a man with blood in his veins," she said in a low voice. "I didn't like it."

That couldn't be regret in his face, could it? One thing she remembered about Kinvarra was that he never accepted he was in the wrong. But when he spoke, he confounded her expectations.

"No, that's not true. You had a selfish, impulsive boy in your bed, Alicia. Never mistake that."

Astonished, she stared at him kneeling before her. "You blamed me for everything. You said touching me was . . . was like making love to a log of wood."

This time it was his turn to flush and glance away. "I'm sorry you remembered that."

"It was rather memorable."

"No wonder you hated me."

She shrugged again, uncomfortable with the turn of the conversation. She hadn't always hated him. During most of their year together, she'd believed she loved him. And every cruel word he'd spoken had scarred her youthful heart.

His unexpected honesty now forced her to recall how she'd called him a filthy, rutting animal and how she'd barred him from her bedroom when he'd accused her of lacking womanly passion.

He'd had provocation for his cruelty. And he'd been young too. At the time, his four years seniority had seemed a lifetime. Now she realized he'd been a young man of twenty-one coping with a difficult wife, immature even for her seventeen years.

No wonder he'd been glad to see the back of her.

She swallowed the lump in her throat that felt like tears. "There's no point going over all this history. Really we're just chance-met strangers."

He sent her the half-smile that had made her seventeen-year-old heart somersault. Her mature self found the smile just as lethal. "Surely more than that." He raised his glass. "To my wife, the most beautiful woman I know."

"Stop it." She turned away, blinking back tears. This painful weight of emotion in her chest was only weariness. It wasn't the recognition that she'd sacrificed something precious all those years ago and it was too late to get it back. "We just need to endure tonight, then it will be as though this meeting never happened."

Even in her own ears, her voice sounded choked with regret. She'd thought when she accepted Harold's advances that she was over her inconvenient yen for her husband. How tragically wrong she'd been. Tonight proved she was as susceptible as ever.

She straightened her backbone against the chair in silent defiance. Kinvarra studied her with a speculative look in his black eyes and she gave a premonitory shiver. If she wasn't careful, he'd have all her secrets. And she'd have no pride left. "Are you going to drink all that wine yourself?"

He laughed softly and raised his glass in another silent toast, as if awarding her a point in a contest. "Here. Have this one."

He passed her the glass and tugged at her boot. She took a sip of the wine, hoping it would bolster her fortitude. It didn't. She supposed Kinvarra meant to attempt a seduction. Any man would with a woman in his bedchamber for the night. Although God knew why he'd be interested. If he'd wanted her any time in the past ten years, he could have sent for her. His long silence spoke volumes about his indifference.

His hands were brisk and efficient, almost impersonal, as he pulled her boots off. Automatically she stretched her legs out and wriggled her toes. A relieved sigh escaped her.

He looked up with a smile as he sat back. "Better?"

"Better," she admitted, taking some more wine. The rich flavour filled her mouth and slipped down her throat, somehow washing away a little more of her bitterness.

He laid one hand on her ankle. Even through the stocking, she felt the heat of that touch. "You always had cold feet."

She closed her eyes, refusing to obey the dictates of common sense telling her to pull back now. That she entered dangerous territory. "I still do."

"I'll warm them up."

"Mmm."

She was so tired and the cosy room sapped her will. When Kinvarra began to rub her feet, gentle warmth stole up her legs. If his touch even hinted at encroaching further, she'd pull away. But all he did was buff her feet until she wanted to purr with pleasure.

"Don't stop," she whispered even when her feet glowed with heat and he had to reach forwards to rescue the empty wine glass from her loosening hand.

As he straightened, he laughed softly and she struggled not to hear fondness in the sound.

Kinvarra wasn't fond of her. He'd never been fond of her. She'd been foisted on him by family arrangement, an English heiress to fill the coffers of his Scottish earldom. Her foul behaviour during their year together had only confirmed his suspicions that he'd married a brat.

"Let's have our supper before it gets cold. You're exhausted."

She let him take her hand and raise her to her feet. It seemed odd that so much touching was involved in sharing this room. She hadn't expected it. But she was in too much of a daze to protest as he led her to the small table and slid a filled plate before her.

She was so tired that it hardly registered that Kinvarra acted the perfect companion. When she couldn't eat much of the hearty but simple fare, he summoned the maids to clear the room. He left without her asking to grant her privacy to prepare for bed. She was too tired to do more than a quick cat wash and she had no intention of removing her clothes. When he returned from the corridor, she was already in bed.

What happened now? Trepidation tightened her belly and she clutched the sheets to her chest like a nervous virgin.

He looked across at her, his eyes enigmatic in the candlelight. Inevitably the moment reminded her of her wedding night. He'd been the perfect companion then too. Her gentle knight, the beautiful earl her parents had chosen, the kind, smiling man who made her laugh. And who had taken her body with a painful urgency that had left her hurt and bewildered and crying.

After that, no matter what he did, she turned rigid with fear when he came to her bed. After a couple of weeks, he'd stopped approaching her. After a couple of months, he'd stopped speaking to her, except to quarrel. After a year, she'd suggested they live apart and he'd agreed without demur. Probably relieved to have his troublesome wife off his hands.

She lowered her eyes and pleated the sheets with unsteady fingers. "Are you coming to bed?"

He arched one eyebrow in mocking amusement. "Why, Lady Kinvarra, is that an invitation?"

She felt her colour rise. How ridiculous to be a worldly woman of twenty-eight and still blush like a seventeen-year-old. "It's a cold night. You've had a hard ride. I trust you." Strangely, so quickly on top of her earlier uncertainty, it was true.

He released a short laugh and turned away. "More fool you."

Confused she watched him set the big carved chair beside the fire. He undressed down to breeches and a loose white shirt. "It's only a few hours until dawn. I'll do quite well here, thank you."

When he'd insisted they share a room, she'd wondered if he had some darker purpose. Some plan to take the wife who so profligately offered herself to another. To teach her who was her legal owner.

But his actions proved her wrong.

What did she expect? That he'd suddenly want her after all this time? She was a fool. She'd always been a fool where Sebastian Sinclair was concerned.

The constriction returned to her throat, the constriction that felt alarmingly like tears. She lay back and forced herself to speak. "Goodnight, then."

"Goodnight, Alicia."

He blew out the candles so only the glow of the fire remained. She listened to him settle. He tugged off his boots and drew his greatcoat over him for warmth. There was an odd intimacy in hearing the creak of the chair and his soft sigh as he extended his legs towards the blaze.

She stretched out. The bed was warm and soft and the sheets smelled fresh. She was weary to the bone but no matter how she wriggled, she couldn't find that one comfortable spot.

Recollections of the day tormented her. Harold's desertion, which should have been a considerably sharper blow than it was. If her original plans had eventuated, she'd now be lying in his arms. She should regret his weakness, his absence, but all she felt was vast relief. Her mind dwelled on Kinvarra's unexpected gallantry. The fleeting moments of affinity. The powerful memories of their life together, memories that tonight stirred poignant sadness instead of furious resentment.

Kinvarra had turned the chair towards the hearth and all she could see of him was a gold-limned black shape. He was so still, he could be asleep. But something told her he was as wide awake as she.

"My Lord?" she whispered.

"Yes, Alicia?" He responded immediately. "Can't you sleep?"

"No."

Their voices were hushed, which was absurd as there was nobody to hear. The wind rattled the windowpanes and a log cracked in the fireplace. He had been right, the weather had worsened.

"Are you cold?"

"No."

"Hungry?"

"No."

"What is it then, lass?" He sounded tender and his Scottish burr was more marked than usual. She remembered that from their year together. When his emotions were engaged, traces of his Highland childhood softened his speech.

Strangely that hint of vulnerability made her answer honestly. "Come and lie down beside me. You can't be comfortable in that chair."

He didn't shift. "No."

"Oh."

She huddled into the bed and drew the blankets about her neck as if hiding from the cruel truth. Hurt seared her. Of course he wouldn't share the bed. He hated her. How could she forget? He just played the gentleman to a lady in distress. He'd do the same for anyone. Just because Alicia was his wife didn't make her special.

When they'd first married, she'd tried to establish some rapport between them in the daylight hours, but when she'd rebuffed him in bed, he'd rebuffed her during the day. He hadn't wanted her childish adoration. He'd wanted a woman who gave him pleasure between the sheets, not a silly little girl who froze into a block of ice the instant her husband touched her.

She blinked back the tears that had hovered close so often tonight. She'd cried enough over the Earl of Kinvarra. She'd cried enough tears to fill the deep, dark waters of Loch Varra that extended down the glen from Balmuir House, his ancestral home.

"Hell, Alicia, I'm sorry. Don't cry." She opened her eyes and through the mist of tears saw he'd risen to watch her. The fire lent enough light for her to notice that he looked tormented and unsure. Nothing like the all-powerful earl.

"I'm not crying," she said in a thick voice. "I'm just tired."

His mouth lengthened at her unconvincing assertion. He reached out with one hand to clutch the back of the chair. "Go to sleep."

"I can't." She wondered why she didn't let him be instead of courting further misery like this.

"Damn it, Alicia . . ." He drew in a shuddering breath and the hand on the chair tightened so the knuckles shone white in the flickering firelight.

"I'm not . . . I'm not attempting to seduce you," she said, and suddenly wondered if she was being completely truthful. What in heaven's name was wrong with her? Surely she couldn't want to revisit the humiliations of her married life.

Kinvarra was as taut as a violin string. Tension vibrated in the air. "I know. But if I get into that bed, there's no way I'll keep my hands to myself. And I don't want to hurt you again. *I couldn't bear to hurt you again.*"

She was shocked to hear the naked pain in his voice. This wasn't the man she remembered. That man hadn't cared that his passion had frightened and bewildered his inexperienced bride.

This man sent excitement skittering through her veins and made her ache for his touch. She raised herself against the headboard and drew in a breath to calm her rioting heartbeat. Another breath.

Her voice was soft but steady as she spoke. "Then be gentle, Sebastian."

Alicia hadn't used his Christian name since the earliest days of their marriage. The shock of hearing her say "Sebastian" meant he needed a couple of seconds to register what else she'd said.

His grip on the chair became punishing.

He must be mistaken. She couldn't be offering herself. She'd never offered herself in all these many years. Even in the beginning, he'd always had to take. He'd come to hate it, so that when she'd finally suggested a separation after those miserable months together, he'd almost been relieved.

Of course, he hadn't realized then that his agreement would lead to ten excruciating years without her.

She sat up in the bed and watched him with a glow in her blue eyes that in any other woman he'd read as blatant sexual interest. She'd taken her beautiful hair down and it flowed around her shoulders, catching the firelight. She became his fantasy Alicia. He had to be dreaming.

A frown crossed her face, he guessed at his continuing silence. "Sebastian?"

"You don't know what you're asking," he said in a constricted voice, wondering why the hell he tried to talk her out of fulfilling his dearest hopes.

He'd wanted his wife for ten lonely years and now she was near enough to touch. He'd always been blackguard enough to want more from their forced intimacy tonight than mere conversation.

Then he'd remembered those disastrous encounters at Balmuir House. He couldn't bring himself to inflict himself upon her once again.

She raised her chin, a signal of bravado that had been familiar in the young Alicia. The memory made his gut clench with longing.

"You've chased one lover away. Honour compels you to offer recompense." Then in a less confident voice: "Sebastian, once you wanted me. I know you did."

He swallowed and forced his response from a tight throat. "I still do."

She'd taken her thick red cloak off when she entered the room. Now she raised trembling hands to the buttons on her mannish ensemble. An ensemble that looked anything but mannish on her lush figure.

Her travelling garb was cut like a riding habit and the white shirt was suitably modest, high at the throat. Even so, when her fumbling fingers loosened that top button, every drop of moisture dried from his mouth and his heart crashed against his ribs.

The Earl of Kinvarra was accounted a brave man. But he recognized the emotion holding him paralysed as ice-cold fear.

Tonight provided a miraculous second chance to heal the breach in his marriage. But if he hurt Alicia again, he'd never have another opportunity to bring her back to him.

He needed patience, restraint and understanding to seduce his wife into pleasure. Yet he burned like a devil in hell. What was he to do? He wanted her too much. And wanting her too much would destroy the fragile, uncertain intimacy building between them in this quiet room.

When his family had presented him with such a beautiful bride, he'd been sure they'd find joy in each other. Instead every coupling had been furtive and shameful, accomplished in darkness and ending with his wife in tears. No wonder he'd lost his taste for forcing himself upon her, although to his endless torment, his desire had never waned.

The shirt fell open another fraction, revealing a delicate line of collarbone and a shadowy hint of her breasts. She still studied him with an unwavering stare. Her hand dropped to the next button.

"Stop," he said hoarsely.

Her hand paused. "Stop?" The vulnerability that flooded her face carved a rift in his heart. "You said . . ."

He shook his head and finally released the chair. He flexed his aching hand to restore the blood flow. "And I meant it. But let's do this properly."

Her hand fell away from her shirt to lie loose in her lap. "Shouldn't I take my clothes off?"

Dear God, she was going to kill him before she was done.

He closed his eyes and prayed for control as images of Alicia's naked body crammed his mind and turned him as hard as an oak staff. When he opened them, she stared at him as if he were mad. She wasn't far wrong.

"We've got plenty of time." He stepped towards the bed, his hands opening and closing at his sides as he fought the urge to seize her and tumble her back against the mattress. "Why rush things?"

"Kinvarra . . ." she said unsteadily.

"You called me Sebastian before."

"You weren't looking at me as if you wanted to eat me before." She clutched at the sheet although she didn't pull it higher. He was close enough now to notice the wild flutter of her pulse at her throat and the way her breathing made her swelling breasts rise and fall.

"Believe me, I'd love to." He couldn't move too quickly. He had to rein himself in or the sweet promise of joy would disintegrate into dust.

Her scent washed over him, floral soap and something warm and enticing that was the essence of Alicia. He drew a deep breath, taking that delicious fragrance deep into his lungs.

Slowly, he reached to hold the hand that clutched the sheet. At the contact, she jerked and released a choked gasp.

"Don't be afraid, Alicia," he murmured. "I won't hurt you." He hoped to hell he spoke true. His hand tightened on hers even as he told himself he needed to be careful with her.

"I'm . . . I'm not afraid," she said on a thread of sound.

He laughed softly and lowered himself to sit on the bed. "Liar."

She blushed. As a girl, her blushes had charmed him. They still did, he discovered.

"I'm nervous. That's not the same as afraid."

He raised her hand to his lips and kissed it. He felt her shiver. Turning her hand over, he kissed her palm. As he heard her breath catch, desire spurred him to take more, satisfy his pounding need. With difficulty he beat the urge back.

Tonight what he wanted didn't matter. The only thing that mattered was his wife's pleasure.

She remembered him as a selfish lover. He needed to vanquish those unhappy memories and replace them with bliss. His voice deepened into sincerity. "Alicia, trust me."

He held her gaze with his. Doubt, fear and something that might have been reluctant hope swirled in her eyes. He felt tension in the hand he held. In desperate suspense, he waited for her to agree. Surely she wasn't so cruel as to deny him now.

The silence extended. And extended.

Then finally, *finally*, she nodded. "I trust you, Sebastian."

Relief flooded him, made him dizzy. Relief and gratitude. He didn't deserve her consent. Now he had it, he'd make sure she never regretted it.

"Thank you," he whispered, wondering if she knew how deeply he meant those simple words.

He leaned down to brush his lips across hers. A light kiss. A glancing touch that promised more. A salute to the woman who would be his partner in rapture tonight.

Her lips were impossibly soft. Smooth. Satiny. He lingered a second, savouring the sensation. He hadn't kissed his wife in nearly eleven years. He'd kissed her before they'd married. He'd kissed her during their first weeks together, but the spiralling misery of their days had soon made kissing seem a travesty.

Kinvarra started to pull away, even as the beast inside him surged against restraint. Then Alicia made a soft sound deep in her throat and her lips parted.

Her warm breath filled his mouth. She tasted familiar. Yet as fresh and new as a fall of snow. Hot darkness exploded inside his head and reaction ripped through him. He longed to ravish her mouth with all the passion locked in his heart. He clenched his hands in the blankets. His control already threatened to shred and he'd hardly started his seduction.

She reached out and cradled his head between her hands, holding him close. He shut his eyes and prayed for fortitude, even as she tilted her head and pressed her mouth to his.

Her kiss was clumsy, as if she hadn't kissed anyone in a long time. Shock rocketed through him. On an intellectual level, he'd known she'd never been unfaithful. But that passionate, needy, unpractised kiss assured his soul that in all the years they'd been apart, she'd belonged only to him.

Automatically his arms encircled her, curved her against his body. She moulded to him as his mouth opened over hers. Blazing heat threatened to incinerate his good intentions. Even as he kissed her deeply, ravenously, stroking her tongue with his, he struggled to remember that he couldn't yield to this fire.

His resolution faltered when her tongue moved in unmistakable response. Restraint became even shakier when she sighed into his mouth and rubbed her body against his.

His shaking hands rose to her head to hold her as he plundered her mouth, stoking her passion with every second. His heart slammed hard at her unfettered response. He'd never guessed she had such wildness in her. She was glorious. When he finally raised his head, she whimpered in protest and her eyes were dark and slumberous under heavy, drooping eyelids.

A soft, shaken laugh escaped him as he feverishly stroked his hands through the soft hair at her temples. He couldn't resist touching her – he couldn't rely on fate being generous enough to keep his wife in his arms. "I'm struggling to be gentle, my darling, but you make it almost impossible."

Her breath escaped in uneven gasps from moist, parted lips. Her face was flushed with arousal. "I'm not seventeen any more, Sebastian," she whispered. "I won't break."

Almost reverently, he cupped her jaw. "You deserve tenderness and respect."

Her smile was tremulous. "Is that what you feel for me?"

"Of course," he said immediately. Then after a pause: "And desire."

"Show me the desire."

He bit back a groan. Leashing his hunger was the most fiendish of tortures. "I promised I wouldn't hurt you."

Her gaze was steady. "You won't."

Shame bit deep, chastened his craving, although nothing could ease his need apart from having her. And he already suspected that one night, no matter how dazzling, wouldn't be enough even then. "I did once."

She touched his cheek with a tenderness that filled him with guilty awareness of how badly he'd once treated her. "We've both grown up since then, Sebastian. I trust you. Please, trust yourself."

The yearning to prove himself worthy of her confidence flooded him. He couldn't fail her now. But nor could he continue to treat her as if she were made of spun glass. It would destroy him. As he looked into her beautiful face, he realized she was right. She was no longer the frightened girl he'd first married and he was no longer the greedy, thoughtless young man who hadn't appreciated the treasure he held in his arms.

Time had changed them and now it offered the opportunity to start again, to move beyond their mistakes and create something new and invincible and shining. He wanted to insist on promises from her, but he was wise enough to know that it was too early to burden the moment with talk of the future.

His hands were gentle as he undid the next button on her shirt. By the time he slid the garment from her shoulders and let it fall to the floor, she was trembling. Her hands had dropped to her sides.

It seemed she left everything to him. Was this a test?

Her scent filled his head and his thirst for her maddened him. Even so, he held back. Carefully he undressed her. Finally she was bare to his sight and he paused in wonder. In ten years, she'd changed. Her body was a woman's, ripe, voluptuous, alluring.

He drew a shuddering breath and reminded himself of all that was at stake. His blood beat hot and hard but he managed to cling to control.

Just.

Alicia lay before him in shy wantonness. A flush lined her slanted cheekbones and the breath came fast between her lips. Almost hesitantly, Kinvarra reached out to cup one full breast. It curved into his hand as if created for his touch and the raspberry nipple pearled into tightness. When he bent to kiss that impudent peak, Alicia's surprised gasp of pleasure was his reward. He drew harder on the nipple and ran his hand down the soft plain of her belly to the curls at the juncture of her thighs.

She was already damp. This slow seduction worked its magic on his wife too. He took her other nipple between his lips and nipped gently at the crest. She shifted restlessly under his hand and he caught the scent of her arousal. She buried her fingers in his hair, urging him closer.

He needed no further encouragement. But even as he licked and bit and suckled, let his hands roam her soft skin, some trace of reason lingered. She wasn't ready yet, however her touch and her sighs of pleasure urged him to further depredations. He kept coming back to her mouth. He had ten years of kisses to make up for. Each kiss was hotter than the last.

"You're wearing too many clothes," she said in a broken voice.

"Whereas you're dressed just right," he whispered with a low laugh, tasting her breast again.

She'd been lovely as a girl, fresh and dewy and as rich with promise as a furled rose. But the woman in his arms now took his breath away.

With every minute, he felt her confidence increase. When she dragged his shirt up from his breeches, her touch on his naked back shot lightning behind his eyes.

"Sebastian, I want to see you."

He couldn't remain immune to her pleading. He rolled off the bed and tore his clothes off, flinging them into the corner in his haste. Then he paused, wondering if he should have been more circumspect. Would the sight of his rampant nakedness terrify his wife? When she was a girl, his unabashed maleness had frightened her. Could that have changed?

She slid up against the headboard, making no pretence at modesty by covering herself with the sheet. Dear Lord, she was a sight to set any man's passions afire. Her face was flushed, her lips were full and red, her body was a symphony of curves and hollows. Her thick golden hair cascaded around her shoulders, teasingly covering one breast and leaving the other bare. Kinvarra felt himself grow harder, larger, needier.

Her eyes widened as her inspection continued down past his chest and belly. Hell, what would he do if she stopped him now?

Could he stop?

Yes, something inside him insisted.

"You're magnificent," she said softly, her eyes glinting blue fire under their heavy lids.

She sent him a smile of such joy that his foolish heart performed another somersault. She'd always been able to confound him with a word. Ten years without her hadn't changed that. She stretched out one hand in invitation. To his astonishment, she wasn't shaking. All her earlier uncertainty seemed to have vanished.

"Come to me, my husband."

Alicia watched the expressions cross Kinvarra's striking face. Somewhere in the last years, she'd learned to read him. When they'd first married, she hadn't known how to pierce the shell of physical perfection to reach the man beneath. He'd seemed a godlike creature, too far above mere mortals for her to feel worthy of being his wife.

But the man who stood before her now, superb in his nakedness, was all too human.

For all his strength and beauty, he was vulnerable. How had she never seen that before?

Tonight she'd learned that he blamed himself for their marital difficulties. How odd, when finally she admitted that she'd been at least as much at fault as he in the disaster that had been their early married life. She'd been spoilt, demanding, headstrong, too quick to take umbrage, too slow to offer understanding.

Tonight she surveyed her husband's powerful body and felt a woman's desire. And a woman's ability to forgive. Sensual need raged in her blood, made her heart pump with eagerness to know this man's possession. Fear lurked too but she refused to acknowledge it.

As she watched his face, she recognized he was still unsure of her, unaware how she'd changed. He didn't know that, after a long and difficult road, she'd discovered exactly where she ought to be.

In Kinvarra's arms. For ever.

How had she imagined poor, pathetic, inadequate Harold Fenton could compare with the man she'd married?

"Sebastian, I want you," she said softly, surprised at how easily the words emerged. "Don't make me wait."

Something in her voice or her smile must have convinced him she had grown beyond the skittish girl he'd married. Determination flooded his face, hardened his jaw, set his eyes glinting in a way that, for all her arousal, made her pulse race with trepidation.

And excitement.

How had she never recognized what an exciting man she'd married? She must have been insane ten years ago.

This was no time for regrets. Not when her tall, handsome, overwhelmingly virile husband prowled towards her with such purpose. There was none of his earlier hesitation in the way he drew her into his arms and tugged her under him. There was just hunger and a masculine strength that made her feel both delicate yet stronger than steel.

When he'd kissed her, she thought she'd measured his passion. But now he was insatiable. He touched her everywhere, he kissed her as if he couldn't get enough of her mouth, he whispered praise and endearments until she was intoxicated with delight.

He touched her between her legs, stroking the sleek folds. She shuddered against him as sensation streaked through her. New, strange, astonishing pleasure. She cried out his name and jerked her hips up to meet him. She wanted him to take her, to fill the lonely reaches of her soul, to appease her hungry senses. Her arms closed hard around him, feeling the coil and release of the muscles in his back.

He rose above her and she caught the turbulent emotion in his face as he stared down at her. The moment spun into eternity then shattered when he joined his body to hers with a sure command that made her heart slam against her chest.

Her body tightened. After the years without him, the invasion felt frightening and unfamiliar. He was a large man and she'd been chaste for so long. She dragged in a shuddering breath, struggling to adjust to his size and power.

Another breath, heavy with the musky, male essence of Kinvarra. She shifted, angled her hips, felt him slide deeper, more surely. Then magically all awkwardness flowed away and, with perfect naturalness, she arched up to join him in a union as much of soul as body.

And recognized with despairing clarity she'd never stopped loving him.

Her hands clenched in the hot, bare skin of his shoulders as the inexorable truth rolled over her like a huge wave. Then she closed her eyes and gave herself up to Sebastian.

Right now he was hers. She refused to let fear of the future destroy this moment of ultimate closeness. She refused to accept fear at all. Fear had already cost her so much.

She felt his tension as he held himself still, then with hard, purposeful strokes that built her arousal to an inferno, he began to move. The dance wasn't new to her, although the deep, joyous intimacy of this moment was.

She spiralled higher and higher until she touched the sky. This was beyond anything she'd ever felt. Beyond anything she'd even imagined.

At the peak, glittering light blinded her and she cried out. Such rapture. Such glory.

Such love.

Vaguely through the swirling storm of passion, she heard Sebastian's deep groan. He shuddered and liquid heat spilled inside her. For a long moment, he held himself taut before he slumped, his body heavy with exhaustion.

The air was redolent of their lovemaking. It was as if she breathed the memory of pleasure. She tightened her hold on his back, feeling the sinews flex as he settled himself against her without withdrawing. She'd never felt so close to another person.

The fire burned low, leaving the room in darkness. Alicia stared up at the ceiling, watching the shadows gather. Nothing could dull the glow she felt or dam the satisfaction rippling through her body. She felt made anew. She felt ready to conquer the world. She felt tired and languorous and ready to sleep for a week.

So this was what a man's possession could be. She'd had no idea. No idea at all what she'd been missing.

With sudden desperation, her fingers dug into his back. Oh, dear heaven, don't let fate be so cruel as to take Sebastian away from her now that she'd discovered him again. Not now that she was finally woman enough to be his wife in every sense.

He'd undoubtedly wanted her when he'd taken her, not even the most inexperienced woman could have thought otherwise. But had Sebastian meant what just happened as a last goodbye to a bitter, unhappy past? Or was it the first step in a long, joyful journey together?

Kinvarra gasped for breath, his heartbeat drumming in his ears like a wild sea.

An ocean of satisfaction flooded his body. He'd intended to take his time, prepare Alicia, raise her to peak after peak of ecstasy before he found his own pleasure. But when he'd touched his wife's naked body and read desire in her shining eyes, he couldn't hold back.

He'd been as hungry as ever the eager young man had been, although at least this time, praise the angels, she hadn't closed away from him in misery. Instead she'd achieved her own delight in his arms. He'd felt the way she tightened, and he hadn't mistaken her broken cry as she'd arched to take him.

His big body still pressed her into the mattress. She must feel crushed, suffocated. He was a brute not to move away from her.

But how sweet it was to lie here in the aftermath, to let his hands wander her silky skin, to listen to the soft music of her breathing, to rest surrounded by Alicia.

Heaven couldn't offer an eternity of bliss purer than this moment.

What had just happened offered a profundity of experience he'd never known. He'd mourn forever if this was all the happiness allotted to him. If he was to possess her only this once.

Tonight they'd moved from hostility to a brittle trust to a conflagration of joy. But was this truce only a pause in their warfare? Or could it form the foundations of a future? He prayed for the latter, but ten years of yearning had taught him not to trust the promise of happiness.

Just like that, reality descended. He and Alicia had found shattering pleasure tonight, but he needed more. He needed her commitment beyond one tumble between the sheets, no matter how earth-shaking that tumble was.

He'd wanted this woman since he'd first seen her. He wanted to build a family with her. He wanted to grow old with her. Nothing in ten years of separation had changed that.

But he was wise enough now to know that wanting wasn't enough.

He could probably compel her to return to him. After all, the law was on his side. But for all his faults, he'd never been a bully. Could he bear to let her go if she rose from this bed and announced she would return to London alone? He might not be a bully, but the primitive savage inside him howled denial at the prospect of losing her again.

Slowly he raised himself on to his elbows. He smoothed the dishevelled blonde hair away from her face. She looked beautiful, replete, weary. In spite of his good intentions, he'd used her ruthlessly. He'd wanted to cherish her, but passion had swept them up into a whirlwind where all that mattered was the endless drive to blazing fulfilment.

Piercing tenderness overwhelmed him and he bent his head to kiss her gently on the lips. Not the hard, demanding kisses of earlier, although the ghost of desire lingered in the soft touch. "Are you all right?"

She smiled up at him and he struggled against believing that the radiant light in her eyes was love. "Better than all right." Her slender throat worked as she swallowed. "That was . . . that was astonishing."

"Yes." He fought against saying more. She was tired and defenceless. It wasn't the right time to harangue her about the future. Instead he kissed her again then rolled to the side. "It's nearly morning."

"Mmm."

When he drew her against his side, she was slack with exhaustion, a delicious bundle of warm, sated womanhood. He paused to savour the moment, praying it promised a beginning and not an ending. He'd sell his soul for the chance to hold her like this for the rest of their lives.

He held her until she slept, but for all his weariness and the throb of sexual satisfaction through his body, he couldn't settle. Eventually he rose and padded over to the window.

Very quietly so as not to wake Alicia, he parted the curtains. Immediately white light flooded the room. It was later than he'd realized. The storm had blown itself out overnight and now the pale sun rose over the horizon, painting the fresh snow with gold and making it sparkle like diamonds.

The idyll of a winter's night had given way to a new day. This morning he and his wife had hard decisions to make.

Would his glimpse of paradise prove cruelly brief? Could all the lovely harmony of these last hours crash on the rocks of past wrongs and his insatiable demands?

He didn't know how to be anything but demanding. He wanted her with him. He wanted her in his bed. He couldn't stop himself.

"How beautiful."

He'd been so lost in his troubled thoughts he hadn't heard her rise from the bed. His heart slammed to a stop as she slid her arms around his waist and pressed her warm nakedness to his back.

"I thought you were asleep," he said softly.

"I missed you."

His aching heart crashed once more as she brushed a kiss across his bare shoulder. "I've missed you for ten years," he said before he could stop himself.

"I thought you were glad to be rid of me." Her voice was muffled against his skin. "I was such a silly girl."

"You were enchanting. You still are."

Silence fell, a silence heavy with the weight of remembered pain and everything still unspoken. Because he couldn't resist touching her, he rested his hands lightly on hers. The urge stirred to seize, to grab, to compel, but he crushed it. Last night, she'd given herself to him freely. He refused to compromise that memory.

She sighed softly, her breath a warm, sensual tickle against his skin. "The snow is so clean. Even after the storm, it's perfect. It's waiting for us to make the first footprints."

He tightened his hold on her hands. So much hinged on the next moments. He struggled to find the right words, wondering if the right words even existed.

"Our future could be like that, Alicia. A new path. A new life." He paused, swallowed, and his voice was husky when he spoke what was in his heart. "Come back to me."

He felt her stiffen although she didn't move away. His gut cramped in anguish as he wondered if he'd ruined his chances. Permanently this time.

"For how long?" Her voice was quiet.

He stared at the glittering scene outside without seeing it. Instead, all his mind, all his soul focused on his wife. Again, he risked honesty, even if honesty cost him all chance of achieving his dream of a life with her.

"For ever."

This time she did draw away, and he read the inches between them as absence. "Why?"

He turned to study her. She looked unhappy and uncertain and remarkably young. Almost as young as the girl he'd married. "Because I love you."

"No . . ." She shook her head as if she didn't believe him.

Kinvarra smiled at her, even while she broke his heart. Again. "Yes."

Alicia raised her chin and stared at him as if what he said made no sense. "I was so awful to you. How can you forgive me?"

"How can you forgive *me*? Let's rise above the past, my darling. I want you with me. I've never wanted anything else. Don't let old mistakes destroy our hope of happiness." He paused and swallowed. "If you love me, come back to me."

For an unendurable moment, her expression didn't change. Sebastian heard his every heartbeat as a knell of doom. Then the tension drained from her face and her eyes turned as blue as a clear sky. Suddenly, in the depths of winter, he basked in the reviving warmth of summer sun.

She stepped towards him although she didn't touch him. "Sebastian, I love you too. We've wasted so much time. Let's not waste any more."

Shaking, he reached out to curl his hands around her upper arms and drag her against him. He could hardly believe what was happening. Yesterday he'd been lost in an endless mire of despair. Today the world offered love and hope and a future with the woman he adored. The swiftness of the change was dizzying.

"My wife," he murmured and kissed her with all the reverence he felt in saying those two words.

The vivid, passionate woman in his arms kissed him back with a fervour that sent his blood rushing through his veins in a hot torrent. A bright, unfamiliar joy flooded him as he realized that Alicia at last was his.

Then because it was cold and he wanted her and he loved her – and they'd been apart for longer than mortal man could bear – he swung her up in his arms and strode across to the rumpled bed.

The Dashing Miss Langley

Amanda Grange

It was a perfect summer morning in 1819 when Miss Annabelle Langley drove her curricle through the streets of London, weaving in and out of the brewers' carts and carriages with consummate skill. She was a striking sight, her Amazonian figure clad in a sky-blue pelisse and her fair hair topped with a high-crowned bonnet. She had no chaperone except for a tiger perched behind her. He was a splendidly clad urchin and he grinned impudently at the crusty old dowagers who looked on with a frown as the curricle whirled by.

In anyone else such behaviour would have been considered fast, but as Annabelle was twenty-seven years of age and possessed of a large fortune, she was grudgingly allowed to be eccentric.

She brought her equipage to a halt outside a house in Grosvenor Square and, handing the reins to her tiger, she approached the porticoed entrance. She lifted the knocker, but before she could let it drop, her sister-in-law opened the door.

"My dear Annabelle, I am so glad you are here," said Hetty with a look of relief.

"But you knew I was coming. Why the heartfelt welcome?" asked Annabelle in surprise.

Hetty linked arms and drew her inside, much to the disapproval of the butler, whose expression seemed to say, *Ladies opening the door for themselves? Whatever next?*

"It is Caroline," said Hetty, her silk skirts rustling as the two ladies crossed the spacious hall.

"What, do not tell me that she is not ready?" said Annabelle. "I suppose she has overslept and she is still drinking her chocolate? Or is it more serious? Is she standing in front of the mirror wondering which of Madame Renault's delightful creations she should wear?"

"It is worse than that," said Hetty with a heavy sigh as she guided Annabelle into the drawing room.

It was an elegant apartment with high ceilings and tall windows, and it was sumptuously furnished. Marble-topped console tables were set beneath gleaming mirrors, and damasked sofas were positioned between silk-upholstered chairs.

"Worse?" asked Annabelle.

"Much worse," said Hetty emphatically. "It is A Man." Her tone gave the words capital letters.

Annabelle stopped in the middle of stripping off her gloves and said, "I see. And who is this man?"

Hetty looked at her helplessly and groaned. "You will never believe it. If I did not know it to be true then I would not believe it myself. It is the Braithwaites' gardener!" she said.

Annabelle raised her eyebrows in surprise. "Unless I am very much mistaken, the Braithwaites' gardener is seventy years old!" she said.

"Oh no, it is not Old Ned. He has retired. It is his grandson who is the cause of all the trouble. Able. And a very handsome young man, it has to be said. But quite unsuitable. And, even worse, he is engaged."

"Do you not mean, *even better*, he is engaged?" enquired Annabelle, removing her pelisse and bonnet.

"I only wish I did. If Caroline would accept that he was spoken for then all would be well. But you know how headstrong she is. She is convinced that he does not love his fiancée and that he is only marrying the girl to please his grandfather, who happens to be friends with the girl's grandfather. The two men have had a very enjoyable rivalry over the last fifty years, concerning who can grow the best roses."

"And what does Able say about it all?"

"Nothing. He shifts his weight from one foot to the other when she challenges him, and goes bright red, then pulls his ear, and says, 'I don't rightly know, Miss Caroline, I reckon I love 'er.'"

"Oh dear! But surely this must deter Caroline?" said Annabelle, bubbling with laughter.

"Not a bit of it. She simply says that he does not know his own mind, and that he needs a good woman to know it for him!"

"And the good woman in question, I suppose, is Caroline?"

"Of course," said Hetty, sinking into a chair.

Annabelle looked at Hetty's woebegone face and tried to pull a sympathetic expression but she could not help herself. It was too ridiculous! She burst into outright laughter.

"Really, Belle, it is no laughing matter," said Hetty crossly.

"Oh, Hetty, I'm sorry, but of course it is! Caroline is a minx, but in six weeks' time she will have forgotten all about Able, and she will be content for him to marry his sweetheart and grow roses for the rest of his days."

"I only hope it may be so, but what am I to do with her in the meantime? She declares she won't go to Whitegates Manor with you, and if she stays here, she will make everyone uncomfortable. The Braithwaites have already asked me not to bring her with me the next time I call. She distracts Able from his work. The last time we called he sent a cabbage indoors for the flower arrangements, and then enraged the cook by sending a basket of hollyhocks into the kitchen for dinner."

"Never fear," said Annabelle soothingly, putting her hand reassuringly on Hetty's. "I will take Caroline to Whitegates with me, I promise you, and you can have some respite."

"I only wish you could," said Hetty dolorously, "but she has sworn she will not go."

"A little of the sun, instead of the wind, will work wonders I am sure," said Annabelle. Seeing Hetty's bemused look, she said, "When the wind and the sun had an argument about which of them was the stronger, they agreed to a contest to decide the matter. There happened to be a merchant walking below them and they agreed that whichever one of them could part him from his cloak would be the winner. The wind blew as hard as it could, but to no avail, the merchant only held his cloak closer. Then the sun shone down and the merchant set his cloak aside, making the sun the winner."

"And you plan to warm Caroline with sunshine?" asked Hetty dubiously.

"I do. The sunshine of flattery, coupled with an appeal to her generosity. And if all else fails, I will sweeten it with a treat."

"I only hope you may succeed. I am at my wits' end." Hetty stood up and moved towards the bell. "I will send for Withers and she will fetch her."

"There is no need for that. I will go myself. Is she in her room?"

"Yes," said Hetty.

"Then I will go up to her now."

Annabelle went out into the hall, threading her way between the marble columns and crossing the black-and-white squared floor before going up the stairs.

Twenty sets of ancestral eyes gazed down at her from Hetty's family portraits, some haughty, some placid and some disdainful, but she ignored them all as she mounted the stairs and came at last to the bedrooms.

She went to Caroline's door and knocked discreetly.

"Go away!" came a voice from inside.

"That is not a very friendly greeting," Annabelle replied, "especially as I have come all this way to see you."

"Oh, it is you, Aunt Annabelle," said Caroline, appearing at the door of her room a minute later. "Mama has sent you to speak to me, I suppose."

"No, I came of my own accord. Your mama thought it would not do any good for me to speak to you. She believes you are a hopeless case."

"And so I am," said Caroline, sinking down on to the bed with a dramatic sigh. "Hopelessly in love with Able."

"Well, he is a very handsome young man by all accounts," said Annabelle sympathetically.

Caroline looked surprised. Then a crease appeared between her brows. "And?" she asked suspiciously.

"And?" enquired Annabelle.

"Are you not going to say that Lord Deverish is handsomer, or that Able, for all his handsome face, is nothing but a gardener, and that I can do better; or that I am a foolish, obstinate, headstrong girl?"

"No. Why should I?" asked Annabelle.

"Because that is what everyone else says. They have lots of different reasons for complaining, but the moral of every story is that I must forget all about him."

"If Able is your choice, then what business is it of mine?"

Caroline looked startled.

She really is very pretty, thought Annabelle, even with that open mouth and those widened eyes. With her lustrous dark hair and her entrancing green eyes, she is positively charming.

"I cannot understand it," said Caroline, perplexed. "I was sure you would be just like Mama, and tell me it would not do. Oh!" she exclaimed suddenly, in a different tone of voice, and her face took on a sympathetic expression. "Of course, I was forgetting. You had an unhappy love affair, too! Aunt Annabelle, I am so sorry," she went on, stricken. "This must have awakened painful memories for you, and now I have added to your pain by distrusting you. But of course, with your history, I should have known that you would take my side."

Annabelle refrained from pointing out that her own unhappy love affair had been nothing like Caroline's infatuation, for she had come to know and love a man who had been suitable in every way. But she made allowances for her niece's youth, and she did no more than give an exasperated smile.

Fortunately, Caroline construed her expression as one of sympathy.

"If only Mama and Papa could see it as you do." Caroline patted the bed beside her and invited Annabelle to sit down. "But they keep telling me that I cannot marry Able because they say that, in a few weeks' time, I will forget all about him. Which is absurd, because I will never forget about Able, not for as long as I live."

"Which is exactly why you should come to Whitegates Manor with me," said Annabelle. "It will prove to your parents that you are serious about Able, and that your feelings will not change. Only imagine, when you return here and you are still as much in love as ever, they will not be able to accuse you of inconstancy, but will be forced to admit the strength of your attachment."

"So they will," said Caroline, much struck. "And then they must give their consent to the marriage."

Annabelle was just congratulating herself on her stratagems when Caroline cut short her rejoicing by reverting to a lachrymose manner. "But no, I cannot be away from Able for so long. It would be insupportable. In fact, it would kill me."

"Ah, well, we cannot have that. I see now that I must go by myself," said Annabelle, rising. "A pity, for I was hoping to teach you to drive. There is an excellent avenue at Whitegates Manor that would be perfect for the purpose; it is long and straight, and the surface is very good. But if you cannot leave Able then there is nothing more to be said."

She had gone no more than halfway to the door when Caroline asked, "Teach me to drive?"

"Yes. I thought it might amuse you. I have two new horses. Have you seen them? Perfectly matched bays. And such high steppers, with such soft mouths. They are a treat."

"And you would let me drive them?" asked Caroline, half rising from the bed in her eagerness.

"But of course. Every young woman should learn to drive."

She almost laughed as she watched the emotions playing across Caroline's face, but out of deference to her favourite niece's feelings she remained straight-faced.

"Perhaps you are right," said Caroline consideringly, as a desire to drive her aunt's dashing curricle won out over her desire to swoon over the hapless Able. "If I go with you, it will prove to Mama and Papa, once and for all, that I am really in love."

"Then make haste and finish dressing. The sooner we are away, the better."

"Do you know, Aunt Annabelle, I think it is for the best, after all. I will be with you directly."

Leaving her niece to ready herself, Annabelle went downstairs.

"Ah! She would not come. I did not expect it," said Hetty, as Annabelle entered the drawing room alone. "It was good of you to try. Girls! Everyone says that boys are difficult to handle, but boys are nothing to girls. Thank goodness I have only the one, or my head would be full of grey hairs."

"She will be down in a few minutes," said Annabelle.

Hetty looked at her in amazement. "You do not mean that you have persuaded her? How did you manage it?"

"By telling her that a few weeks' absence will prove to you that she is really in love – and by promising to teach her to drive."

"Oh, thank goodness! We are to have a few weeks' respite! And, of course, at the end of it, she will have forgotten all about Able, and be ready to think of someone more suitable instead. I cannot thank you enough. Now, sit down, my love, for you have a long drive before you. I do so wish you would hire a coachman, but I suppose it is too late now to persuade you to change your ways?"

"It is."

"Then let me offer you some refreshment before you set out. You will take a cup of tea, and some seed cake?"

"No, thank you, Hetty. I must not keep the horses waiting. As soon as Caroline is down—Ah! Here she is.'

Caroline entered the room with a sunny smile. She was dressed in a green silk pelisse, which brought out the colour in her eyes, with matching gloves, and on her head was a splendid hat, topped by a dancing plume.

"I thought I told you that that hat was too dashing for a girl of your age!" exclaimed Hetty in vexation when she saw it. "What have you done with the straw bonnet?"

"Oh, that," said Caroline nonchalantly. "I decided it did not suit me after all, and so I returned it when I went into town with Charlotte. The only other hat that fitted me was this one."

"I think it is time for us to leave," said Annabelle diplomatically.

And before Hetty could react, she swept Caroline out of the house.

"It was very wrong of you to buy that hat against your mother's express wishes," she said, as they went down the steps.

"Mama never expressed a wish either way, she simply said it was too dashing for a girl of my age, but as I was then only sixteen years old, and as I am now seventeen, of course that changes things."

"Ah," said Annabelle, smiling at Caroline's youthful logic – or should it be youthful impudence? "Of course!"

They waited for the curricle to return from the end of the street, where the tiger had been walking the horses, and then they climbed in.

"What—?" asked Annabelle in surprise, for a portmanteau and a hatbox had been crammed into the carriage. "Did your mama not send your boxes on?"

"Yes, she sent them on yesterday with my maid. But I forgot to put a few things in, and so I packed a box this morning and had the footman carry it downstairs," said Caroline airily.

"And no doubt the 'few things' you forgot are dresses of which your mama would not approve."

"There is nothing wrong with them, I do assure you. They are both of them quite adorable."

"I am sure they are. But are they respectable?"

"They are respectable enough for a vicar's daughter," replied Caroline. "But they happen to be in various colours, and Mama is so fussy about me wearing white. I cannot think why. It does not suit me, and, anyway, young ladies no longer wear exclusively white. That fashion went out when Mama was a girl."

"As long ago as that?" enquired Annabelle.

"Are you laughing at me?" asked Caroline suspiciously.

"Not at all."

They seated themselves in the carriage. Annabelle took the reins, and then they were off.

Caroline revelled in the admiring glances that were directed towards them as they set out, though she was sensible enough to realize that they were directed towards Annabelle rather than herself, and she dreamed of the day when she would be the one holding the reins. What a figure she would cut as she dashed through the streets!

"How did you learn to drive?" asked Caroline. "Did your papa teach you?"

"No," said Annabelle. "It was . . . someone else."

Her mind flew back to the day when Daniel had said to her, "It is about time you learned to handle the reins." And she remembered him putting them in her hands, then putting one arm around her so that he could show her how to hold them properly, and the way it made her feel, with his hands around hers and his breath on her cheek and . . .

"Aunt Annabelle!"

Caroline's cry brought her back to the present just in time, as a brewer's cart rolled out from a side road and she had to swerve in order to avoid it. The carriage behind her was not so lucky, and the sound of heated cries and barrels rolling on to the road followed them as they headed out to the country.

Green fields took the place of crowded streets. The air was fresh here, without the smell of fish or pies or a hundred other things, savoury and unsavoury, which perfumed the London streets. Annabelle breathed in deeply. It was good to be alive.

"I am looking forward to the party," she said.

"But I am not. It will be very boring," said Caroline with a yawn. "House parties always are."

"There might be some interesting people there," said Annabelle.

"And there might not."

"There speaks the experience of seventeen," said Annabelle, laughing.

"I know already who will be there. A retired general who will pinch my cheek and call me a clever puss. An old admiral who will talk of nothing but the sea and try to tell me all about the Battle of Flamingo—"

"I believe you mean the Battle of St Domingo."

"And a whole bunch of mamas who will look daggers at me because I am prettier than their daughters."

"But once they learn you are to marry, they will breathe a sigh of relief. They will thank heaven for Able because they will know that, for all your pretty face, you are no competition for their daughters. A girl in love has no interest in anyone else. She does not like to dance with the most eligible bachelors, she prefers to sit at the side of the room."

Caroline looked at her suspiciously, but Annabelle preserved a countenance of angelic innocence, and they carried on their way.

They stopped shortly after midday, choosing an idyllic spot in a country lane. The tiger climbed over the stile and into the neighbouring field, where he spread out a rug and began to unpack the picnic hamper. Annabelle and Caroline strolled along the lane to stretch their legs before settling themselves on the rug, beneath the spreading arms of a chestnut tree.

"How much farther is it to Whitegates?" asked Caroline.

"We have a few hours more to travel," said Annabelle.

"Can I drive for part of the way?"

"Very well. I will give you your first lesson after lunch."

They started to eat their picnic. It was a delicate affair of chicken and ham, with crusty bread and newly churned butter, and they finished their repast with peaches and grapes.

Their meal over, Caroline looked at Annabelle hopefully, and, with a laugh, Annabelle said, "Very well. I was going to suggest another stroll first, but I see that you are eager to begin. The road here is straight and flat. You may set us on our way."

Their things were soon packed and the two ladies climbed into the curricle, followed by the tiger.

With the reins in her hands, Caroline's childishness dropped away, as Annabelle had hoped it would, and she applied herself seriously to the task in hand.

"Very good," said Annabelle approvingly, as the curricle rolled smoothly along a straight, flat stretch of road. "You have light hands."

Caroline glowed under the praise.

She was reluctant to give the reins back to Annabelle when the road became more difficult, but after a moment's hesitation she did so with a good grace.

They had not gone very much further when the wind turned colder and the sky darkened. Soon it began to rain. It was nothing more than a light drizzle to begin with, but as the curricle had no hood, they were exposed to the elements.

"Urgh!" said Caroline, as the rain began to fall more heavily. "Is there nowhere we can shelter? We will soon be wet through."

A quick glance at the countryside showed that there were no barns or stables in sight.

Annabelle said, "We must just go on and hope the rain lets up. It is only a shower, no doubt, and the sun will soon be out again."

The English weather answered this optimism with its usual reply, and no sooner had Annabelle finished speaking than the sky clouded over threateningly and transformed itself from blue to grey. The horses became skittish, and when a flash of lightning sent them rearing, it took all of Annabelle's skill to hold them.

"It is no good, we cannot go on," said Annabelle, shouting to make herself heard above the thunder.

"Look ahead! There!" said Caroline, who had been looking about them. She pointed through the pouring rain, which had rendered the summer afternoon as dark as night. "I can see a light!"

Annabelle saw an orange glow shining through the blackness and, hunching her shoulders against the rain, drove the horses cautiously onwards. They did not like the weather any more than she did. They tried to turn their heads against the wind but she held them true to their course.

To make matters worse, the road was slick with mud, and the curricle slid from side to side. She saw Caroline gripping her seat tightly with her hands.

"Don't worry, I won't overset you," she said.

The glow became clearer as they moved forwards. To her relief, Annabelle saw that it was attached to an inn. The hostelry looked well cared for, with white walls showing up brightly against dark oak beams. It had a pretty thatched roof. A freshly painted sign proclaiming it to be the White Hart swung in the wind.

Annabelle guided the horses carefully into the yard. She gave a sigh of relief as she brought the curricle to a halt, for if they had been forced to go any further she was sure they would have had an accident.

The thunder rumbled overhead, making the horses dance, and a minute later the ostlers appeared and hurriedly took the horses out of the traces. Assuring Annabelle they would be well cared for, the ostlers led the horses off to the stables.

Another flash of lightning sent Annabelle and Caroline hurrying towards the door, whilst the rain jumped in the puddles all around them, splashing up against their ankles and soaking their stockings. They gained the door and went in, to find themselves in a cheerful corridor with wild flowers in jars on the deep window ledges. In front of them were two bedraggled ladies, one with a sodden hat whose plume sagged over her eyes, and the other with water streaming down her face from her high-crowned bonnet. It took Annabelle a moment to realize that the two ladies were herself and Caroline, and that she was looking in a mirror. Caroline realized it at the same time and they both laughed to see themselves in such a state.

The landlord hurried forwards to greet them. "A terrible day," he said sympathetically. "We haven't seen a storm like this in years. What can I do for you, ladies?"

"I think we had better have a room, landlord, if you please," said Annabelle. "We cannot go on today."

"Shocking this weather is," he agreed. "I said to my wife this morning, as soon as I saw the sky, 'Depend upon it, we will have rain.' 'Aye,' she said, 'and a storm, by the look of things.' But don't you worry, we have a fine room here, I'm sure you'll be very comfortable," he continued, as he led them upstairs.

Along the corridor they went, with its oak beams and its white walls, and then through an oak door and into a very pleasant chamber. The windows were latticed, but large enough to let in what little light the storm allowed, and the room was clean and spacious. A large bed was set in the centre, with a smaller one pushed to the side, and both were covered with clean counterpanes. Rustic pictures hung on the walls, and a brightly coloured rug lay on the floor. The grate was empty, but the landlord told them that there was a fire in the parlour.

"It's a private room, just right for you ladies," he said.

"Thank you, that will be most welcome," said Annabelle, looking down at her sodden clothing.

He offered to light a fire in the room as well, but Annabelle declined the offer. It was not cold and she did not want to put him to any trouble.

"I am sure the fire in the parlour will suffice," she said.

He bowed his way out of the room.

"Thank goodness I brought some extra clothes!" said Caroline, who had snatched her portmanteau and hatbox from the curricle before it was taken away. "I am longing to get out of these wet things. I would lend you one of my dresses, but I am afraid they will be too small," she added in dismay, looking at Annabelle.

"Never mind, I will go down to the parlour and dry myself by the fire," said Annabelle. She removed her gloves, bonnet and pelisse, and set them down on the window ledge, then tidied her hair as best she could.

"I will join you as soon as I have changed," said Caroline, stripping off her wet clothes.

"Would you like me to help you?"

"No, thank you, I believe I can manage, and if not, I will ring for the landlord's wife. Do not let me delay you, Aunt Annabelle, I will never forgive myself if you catch cold."

Satisfied that Caroline could not get up to any mischief in such a short space of time, in a respectable inn, Annabelle went down to the parlour.

She opened the door . . . and then hesitated, because the parlour was already occupied. A gentleman was seated by the fire. Steam was rising from his clothes, showing that he too had been caught in the downpour.

She was just about to apologise for intruding when he stood up and turned towards her, and the words died on her lips.

"Annabelle!" he said in surprise, adding more formally, "That is, Miss Langley."

"Daniel!" she said.

And indeed it was he, as handsome as ever, with his dark hair arranged à la Brutus, his brown eyes, his aquiline nose and his full mouth. His figure was hardened by exercise and his height topped her by six inches: no mean feat, as she herself was five feet eight inches tall.

Memories came rushing back: a house party the previous summer, where she had danced with him, finding him the most amusing partner she had ever had.

She remembered her delight when she had found herself alone with him in a rowing boat the following day, and how they had both laughed when a frog leaped into the boat.

And she remembered the way in which he had taught her to drive, taking her out in the country lanes, where he had shown her how to control his horses and how to guide his carriage. When he had put his arms around her in order to show her how to hold the reins, she had started to tingle. It had been the most delicious sensation, and she had turned her face up to his in surprise and delight. He had seized the moment and kissed her, and it had been quite magical.

Then other, less welcome memories returned: that he had been called away by the death of his brother and that, once the mourning period was over, he had not sought her out as she had expected him to do.

She had been forced to realize that, whilst she had been falling in love with him, he had been indulging in nothing more than a mild flirtation.

And now here he was again, standing before her.

"What a surprise. I did not expect to meet you here," he said.

"Nor I you. I am just passing through. But I must not disturb you . . ." she said, feeling suddenly awkward.

"Not at all, it is I who should vacate the parlour and leave it to you."

"There really is no need . . ." she said.

There was a silence, and then they both laughed.

"We are talking to each other like strangers!" he said. "There is no need for either of us to retreat. We can be comfortable here together, can we not? But you are wet," he said. "Will you not sit by the fire?"

She took the seat he held out for her gladly, for her damp clothes were starting to make her feel cold, then he sat down opposite her.

"You are just passing through, you say?"

"Yes. We are on our way to stay with friends."

"We?"

"My niece and I. She is upstairs at the moment, changing her dress. We were caught unawares by the rain, and as we were travelling in my curricle we were soon drenched."

"Ah, yes, your curricle. I am glad you have continued with your driving, and put your inheritance to such good use. I should have congratulated you on your good fortune, but I have not spoken to you since the lucky day."

"Thank you. It was totally unexpected. Great-aunt Matilda had always declared her intention of leaving everything to my brother, but when he married he displeased her and she changed her will and left everything to me. It was no loss to Alistair, as he already had a fortune, and it was a great piece of good luck for me. Although if I had not inherited it," she added ruefully, "I would not have bought such a dashing carriage, and I would probably have been travelling in a sedate coach and be perfectly dry now!"

He laughed. "You cut quite a figure."

She looked at him enquiringly.

"I saw you once, in town. You handled your cattle very well," he said admiringly.

She warmed at his praise. "I was taught by an expert," she replied.

"Those were good days," he said. "And what does your niece think of her dashing aunt?"

"She likes me well enough at the moment, for I have promised to teach her to drive."

"Indeed? You must think a great deal of her then."

"I do. I like her very much. She is a good girl, for all her headstrong ways, and she will make a fine woman when she is fully grown. But that is not why I made her the offer."

"No?"

"No. You see, it was the only way I could take her thoughts from an unsuitable attachment."

"Ah. That would never do. Attachments must be suitable, must they not?"

There was something in the way he said it that made her feel it was more than a general comment.

Daniel came from an old and well-respected family, whilst her family engaged in trade.

So that is why he found it so easy to forget me, she thought.

She felt downcast, but her pride came to her aid and she said, lightly, "Of course." Then, changing the painful subject, she said, "I was sorry to hear about your brother's death. He was too young to die."

"He was."

The subject had been badly chosen and the atmosphere became sombre. They fell silent until they were interrupted by the landlord.

On seeing them together, he apologised profusely for having recommended the parlour to Annabelle when his wife, unbeknownst to him, had recommended it to the gentleman. He gratefully accepted their assurance that they were already acquainted, and that they did not object to sharing.

He asked them if they would be dining.

"Yes, indeed. Both my niece and I would like a hot meal," said Annabelle.

"The ordinary is very good, but maybe you would like something else?" the innkeeper asked.

"What is the ordinary?" asked Annabelle.

"Steak pie with minted peas and tender potatoes, followed by plum tart and cream," said the landlord.

"That sounds very good. I'm sure my niece will like it, too," said Annabelle.

"Three ordinaries, then, landlord, if you please," said Daniel.

The atmosphere had warmed again and despite herself Annabelle was looking forward to further conversation with Daniel. But no sooner had the landlord left the room than Caroline entered it. She was dressed in a startling gown of green silk, which was suitable for a woman twice her age

"Goodness!" said Annabelle, gazing at the vision which was Caroline, and thinking that her niece looked as though she had raided the dressing-up box and put on one of her mama's old gowns. She did not say so, however, but gravely introduced her, saying, "May I present my niece?"

"Charmed," said Daniel, rising and bowing.

Caroline glowed, and dropped a small curtsey.

"Caroline, this is Lord Arundel," said Annabelle. "We are old . . . acquaintances."

"Really, Aunt Annabelle, you never told me you knew such fascinating people," said Caroline.

Annabelle turned her laugh into a cough, for Caroline's attempt at coquetry had all the sophistication of a newborn colt's attempts to walk. However, she thought that Caroline could do worse than to try her newly discovered feminine charms on Daniel, for he was a gentleman and she would come to no harm with him.

Caroline was invited to sit by the fire.

"Thank you," she said charmingly to Daniel, with a dimple.

She swept her gown beneath her, producing a wonderful rustling noise, but unfortunately she spoiled the effect by knocking over a stool in the process. However, Daniel picked it up without comment and Caroline seated herself by the fire. Then she began to fascinate him with her conversation.

"Tell me, Lord Arundel, have you ever met Lord Byron?" she asked.

"I have not had that honour," he said.

"They say he is a terrible man, and yet I cannot believe it. If he were truly so terrible he would not have chosen to write a poem about an innocent little child."

"Ah. You are talking of his renowned work *Childe Harold's Pilgrimage*?" he asked.

"I am," she said graciously.

Daniel's eyes twinkled, but he kindly refrained from saying that *Childe Harold's Pilgrimage* was definitely not about an innocent little child. He managed to retain a straight face, whilst Annabelle sighed in silent exasperation at her niece's ignorance.

Caroline was saved from further blunders by the arrival of dinner.

The food was good and the hot meal was welcome. Whilst they ate the plum tart, Annabelle could not help thinking of the previous summer, of eating plums on a picnic and afterwards going to a ball and dancing with Daniel, of being in his arms . . .

And then she was forced to pay attention, for they were talking of the London galleries, and her opinion was being sought. The conversation moved on to the theatres, until at last Annabelle said, "I believe we must retire."

Caroline had by this time talked herself to a standstill. She took a warm leave of Daniel before leaving the room, so that Annabelle and Daniel were alone for a minute.

"Miss Langley," he said, bowing over her hand.

He held it a fraction too long, and there was something tender in his touch, or so it seemed to Annabelle. But then she warned herself against making the mistake she had made a year ago and bid him goodnight.

"It was good to see you again," he said, as reluctantly he dropped her hand.

"And you." She smiled and walked out of the room.

"What a delightful gentleman," said Caroline, as they went upstairs.

"Yes, indeed," said Annabelle.

And she could not help thinking that, in all her life, she had never met one more delightful.

Annabelle gave a sigh of relief as the landlord's wife drew back the curtains the following morning, for the sun shone out of a clear blue sky.

She washed and dressed before Caroline was awake, glad of the landlord's wife's assistance, and then she helped Caroline to dress.

"What a coincidence, meeting Lord Arundel," said Caroline, as they went down to the parlour for breakfast. "I wonder if we will see him again this morning?"

Annabelle privately wondered the same thing, and although she would not have asked about him, she was not sorry that Caroline did so.

"The gentleman?" enquired the landlord. "Left early this morning, he did, just after dawn. Said he had urgent business to attend to."

"A pity. He was a most amusing companion," said Caroline with dignity.

Oh, yes, he was, thought Annabelle with a pang. The most amusing companion she had ever met with.

"What will you ladies have for breakfast?" asked the landlord.

"Chocolate, I think, and hot rolls," said Annabelle, rousing herself.

Caroline agreed, and they ate a hearty meal before setting out once more to Whitegates Manor.

Annabelle allowed Caroline to take the reins for a short while before reclaiming them, and was pleased to see that her niece showed promise. She told her so, and Caroline wriggled with happiness.

The rains of the previous day had taken their toll and in places the road was so deep in puddles that it was almost like a ford, so that the going was slow. They stopped for lunch at a tavern and did not reach Whitegates Manor until four o'clock in the afternoon.

They turned off the road and rattled through an impressive

pair of gates. The manor itself was an imposing residence. Large windows flanked the front door in perfect symmetry, gleaming in the summer sun. Gravel walkways surrounded it and meandered invitingly through formal gardens and over immaculate lawns.

The curricle swept around the turning circle and rattled to a halt. A couple of grooms ran forwards as Annabelle and Caroline descended, looking about them with interest.

"There you are at last! Wondered what had happened to you!" said Lord Carlton as he came down the impressive stone steps to greet them.

Lord Carlton was a jovial man of some fifty years of age. He was running to fat, but by virtue of a good tailor he managed to disguise it. His coat, a well-fitting garment of black, was complemented by cream breeches and buckskin boots. His linen was simple, and consisted of a starched shirt and a simply tied cravat.

Annabelle took his hands. "We are glad to be here."

"Storm held you up?"

"Yes, alas, it did. We had to spend the night in an inn. I hope you were not anxious on our account?"

"Guessed what had happened. Couldn't drive in that rain!" said Lord Carlton. "Wretched weather. But that's England for you! Come in, come in." He led them up the stone steps and into the house.

The hall was light and spacious. A staircase swept upwards from the far end, drawing the eye towards a magnificent chandelier that sparkled above them.

Having glanced around her, Annabelle began to unfasten the strings of her bonnet. At that moment Lady Carlton came into the hall.

"Annabelle! My dear! And Caroline!" she said, coming forwards and kissing them both on the cheek. "I have only just been informed of your arrival."

They embarked on the customary exchanges, with Lord Carlton enquiring after the horses, and Lady Carlton anxious to know that the sheets in the inn had been aired. Then Lady Carlton took Annabelle and Caroline by the arm and said, "Come, let me show you to your rooms."

Leaving her husband to see to the other guests, Lady Carlton led them up the imposing staircase, chattering all the time. She was a small, birdlike woman, quick and light in her movements, and was some ten years younger than her lord.

They reached Caroline's room first. Annabelle and Lady Carlton left her to the ministrations of her maid, who had travelled previously by coach, as had Annabelle's maid, because the curricle would not hold so many.

"This is your room. I hope you will like it," said Lady Carlton, as she led Annabelle into a beautiful bedroom.

Large windows gave into the gardens. A four-poster bed was set against the left-hand wall, whilst opposite it was an Adam fireplace.

"It is beautiful, Laura," said Annabelle.

As Annabelle removed her bonnet and stripped off her gloves, Laura moved around the room with her quick, light movements, now smoothing the red damask counterpane, now adjusting a pair of Sèvres vases that stood on the mantelpiece, one on either side of an ormolu clock.

"It is such a pleasure having you here," said Laura, at last turning to face Annabelle. "When your dear mama passed away I promised I would do all I could for you, and . . ."

She stopped, disconcerted, as Annabelle began to laugh.

"Oh, dear," said Annabelle, trying to bring her features back under control. "I should not be laughing. It is so wonderfully kind of you. But I do hope you are not going to introduce me to a string of eligible young men?"

Laura looked momentarily put out. But then she replied, with a twinkle in her eye, "Not a string of them, no. And not all of them young, either. Some of them are quite old! But you mustn't blame me for trying. Seeing you married was the greatest wish of your mother's heart. She was so happy in marriage herself, you see."

Annabelle sighed. "That is the problem. Mama married for love, and I can do no less."

"Which is why I have invited some perfectly saintly men for the summer," said Laura. "Men you are sure to fall in love with."

"I will have a difficult time if I am sure to fall in love with all of them! Although, perhaps I will leave one for Caroline."

"Ah, yes, Caroline. Hetty wrote to me. Is it serious, this fixation with the gardener, or just an infatuation?"

"An infatuation, of course, but I pray you will not tell her so. If you do, it will only take her longer to see it for herself."

"I will not breathe a word of it. I will only mention it if she mentions it first, and then I promise to treat it seriously. I remember my own youth. For me, it was a dancing master. He had the most wonderful calves! My sisters and I could not take our eyes from them! But I must not keep you talking. I had better leave you to change." She gave Annabelle an affectionate kiss and left the room.

Annabelle looked around her, taking in her new surroundings in more detail. The room was lovely, with its light furniture and pale cream walls, and the view out of the window was inviting. She might like to take a walk in the grounds before dinner, she thought. After spending most of the day in the carriage some exercise would do her good.

The door opened, and Sally, her maid, entered the room.

"They said as how you'd arrived. Worried sick I've been, thinking you must have taken a tumble," said Sally.

"Well, here I am, in one piece, having suffered nothing worse than a wetting," said Annabelle. She sat down at the dressing table. "I think I will take a turn around the gardens when you have finished with my hair."

"And changed your frock. What did you do, sleep in it?"

"Almost. I had to sleep in my chemise."

Sally threw up her hands in despair. "Why you can't get yourself a nice steady coach with a nice steady coachman I don't know. You can afford it."

"But I like my curricle."

"Break your neck in it, you will, one of these days," grumbled Sally, as she helped Annabelle out of her creased muslin and into a jonquil sarcenet.

"There, that looks better," said Sally.

"Thank you, Sally."

Slipping into her pelisse and tying her poke bonnet on top of her fair curls, Annabelle picked up her gloves and proceeded to make her way downstairs. She found a side door and decided to stroll through the gardens. The roses were just beginning to come into bloom. A few unfurled flowers dotted the banks of bushes, and buds were swelling on the stems. She breathed in, but it was too early in the year to catch their perfume.

She heard a crunching sound and looked up, prepared to greet her fellow guest with a cheery, "Good afternoon," but was rendered speechless when she saw Daniel walking towards her.

"Daniel!" she said in astonishment. "I thought you had some business to attend to."

"And I thought you were seeing friends!" he said, equally taken aback.

"So I am. The Carltons are my friends."

"So you are staying here?" he asked, a smile breaking out over his face.

"Yes. And you?"

"Yes. My business is with Lord Carlton. I am staying here, too."

She smiled warmly, feeling ridiculously pleased.

"May I accompany you?" he asked.

"Yes, I would like that."

He offered her his arm and she took it.

"Will you be staying at Whitegates long?" he asked as they strolled along the gravel path together.

"For a month, certainly," said Annabelle. "Lady Carlton is an old friend of my mother's, and has kindly invited me to stay for as long as I choose. And you?"

"Until my business is done."

"Have you known Lord and Lady Carlton long?"

"Lord Carlton I've known for many years. He and I are joint guardians of my nephew. That is why I am here, to talk over our joint responsibilities and to think about the boy's future. Lady Carlton I know less well."

"I am glad to find you here. I know very few of the other guests, and it is always nice to see a familiar face," she explained hastily.

"Ah."

They had by this time almost reached the end of the formal gardens and, as they rounded a corner, they saw a family coming towards them. The mother, a buxom matron, was clad in a voluminous cape, and was puffing along beside her three, very pretty, daughters.

"Ah! Lord Arundel! There you are!"

"Mrs Maltravers."

"We were just looking for you, were we not, my dears?" she asked her daughters.

The three girls giggled in unison.

Daniel replied politely enough, giving them a slight bow and then making the necessary introductions.

Faith, Hope and Charity, Annabelle repeated to herself with amusement as he named them. Somehow the giggling girls did not suit their idealistic names, but they seemed good-humoured enough, and she thought they would provide Caroline with some companionship of her own age.

"Now you promised to show us the water garden," said Mrs Maltravers girlishly, tapping Daniel with her fan. "And we are not about to let you disappoint us, are we, girls?"

A chorus of giggles followed her sally.

But Daniel said, "Unfortunately, I must ask you to wait a little longer. I am just escorting Miss Langley back to the house."

"Oh, pray don't worry about me," said Annabelle, feeling the danger of being too much with Daniel. "I can manage quite well from here."

Mrs Maltravers beamed at her. "Well, now, if that isn't handsome. But won't you come with us, Miss Langley?"

"Thank you, no. I must see if my maid has finished unpacking my things."

"Quite, quite," said Mrs Maltravers, not displeased to be able to secure such an eligible gentleman for the sole entertainment of her three unmarried daughters. "Well, then, let us go," she said, beaming up at Daniel.

The last thing Annabelle heard as she strolled back across the lawn to the house was the high-pitched giggling of Faith, Hope and Charity as they jostled each other to claim his arms.

She returned to her room, where she found that Sally had indeed finished unpacking her things. A glance at the clock showed that she had an hour before dinner, so she luxuriated in a scented bath before choosing which dress to wear. As she looked at each one in turn she thought how lucky she was to have inherited her fortune, for before it she had had to dress in far less fashionable style. The gown she chose was of the latest design with a stand-up ruff at the back of the neck, a lace-trimmed bodice and six inches of embroidery around the hem.

"I see you've chosen your best frock. I knew you'd want to make an impression," said Sally.

"On Lord and Lady Carlton?"

"No, miss. On the gentleman you were walking with."

"I don't suppose it will do any good to pretend not to know what you're talking about?" asked Annabelle.

"No, miss, none at all. A very fine gentleman he looked. In fact, he looked a good deal like Lord Arundel to me."

"You know very well that he was Lord Arundel."

"Well?"

"Well?"

"Sweet on him, you were, not long since."

She sighed, for she could keep nothing from Sally. "Perhaps I was, but unfortunately, he was not sweet on me."

"He gave a good impression of it," remarked Sally.

"It was a flirtation and nothing more, at least on his part. He saw me as someone to pass the time with."

"Then more fool him," said Sally. "All men are fools."

"Then it is a good thing we neither of us wish to marry, for neither of us would want to live with a fool."

Sally grunted in reply, and proceeded to help Annabelle to dress. Chemise and drawers went on first, followed by a pair of clocked stockings and light stays. Then the evening dress, with its high waist and long flowing skirt.

Annabelle adjusted the scoop neckline and straightened the lace that adorned the bodice, then slipped her feet into dainty satin slippers. She seated herself in front of the mirror so that Sally could dress her hair. She arranged it in a fashionable chignon and then teased out delicate ringlets around her face, before adding the feathered headdress.

"There," said Sally with obvious pride. "It's done."

Annabelle stood up. Sally fastened a string of pearls round her neck and then Annabelle pulled on her long white evening gloves and went to collect Caroline. Caroline, she was pleased to see, was in a demure white muslin, with satin slippers and a simple string of pearls. No doubt she had wanted to wear something more dashing, but had been dissuaded by her maid.

The two of them went downstairs, to find that the drawing room was already full of people.

"Have you met Mrs Maltravers and her three daughters?" Annabelle asked Caroline.

"Unfortunately, yes. I have never met three sillier girls," said Caroline.

However, she went over to join them and they were soon laughing together.

Laura wandered over to Annabelle, saying, "It is good to see the young people having fun. And now there is someone I would like you to meet: Lord Fossington."

Annabelle sighed.

"Now, Annabelle, you have not even met him yet. He might be everything you ever dreamed of."

"You are right, of course, dear Laura. Pray introduce me."

Laura led her across the room and made the introduction.

Lord Fossington was a tall man of military bearing, handsome in a rugged way, with a scar across one cheek.

"Miss Langley," he said. "I was hoping to have an opportunity to speak to you. I believe you know Mrs Granville, my aunt?"

They talked of their shared acquaintances, and of his time in the army, where he had served faithfully for many years.

"How do you like being at home again? Is it very dull after being in the army?" asked Annabelle.

"On the contrary. I have had enough of war. I like being in the country. The quiet suits my nerves," he said, as he led her in to dinner. "But perhaps it sounds boring to you?"

"I must confess I like the bustle of London. But in the summer, there is nothing I like better than the country."

They took their places and to her secret delight Annabelle found herself sitting opposite Daniel. He looked up as she took her place and there was unmistakable admiration in his eyes.

As the soup was brought in, she saw him open his mouth to speak to her but Mrs Maltravers, seated to her right, began to talk about the latest scandal. Mrs Maltravers denounced Princess Caroline, the Regent's wife, as a national disgrace. "Running round Europe like a lightskirt. Setting up home in Spain—"

Italy, thought Annabelle, not realizing she had mouthed it until she caught sight of Daniel's amused expression, and the two of them shared a secret smile. They continued to glance at each other and smile throughout dinner, though Annabelle did her best to keep her eyes away from him. She could feel all too clearly the attraction she had felt the year before, so that she was relieved when it was time for the ladies to withdraw.

"We must have an outing tomorrow," said Mrs Maltravers, as the ladies settled themselves in the drawing room.

"Oh, yes, Mama. A picnic!" exclaimed Hope.

"May we, Lady Carlton?" asked Faith.

"Oh, please say we may," entreated Charity.

"I see no reason why not," said Laura. "As long as the weather holds."

"It is sure to," said Caroline, caught up in the idea.

"And what do you think?" murmured a deep voice in Annabelle's ear.

She turned to see Daniel, who had just entered the room with the other gentlemen.

"I think it will probably rain!" she said mischievously.

"So you are not in favour of a picnic?"

"On the contrary, I am looking forward to it," she said, "rain or shine!"

"You have a rare gift for enjoying life," he replied with a smile.

"I shall go on horseback," declared Faith.

"And so will I," declared Hope.

"Nonsense," said Mrs Maltravers firmly. "You will travel in the carriage with me. The gentlemen will not run away, my dears, and once we are at Primrose Hill you may flirt with them to your hearts' content." She beamed at the assembled gentlemen, and then, hiding behind her fan, she whispered to Annabelle, "Never fear, my dear. You may be a bit long in the tooth, but there are plenty of gentlemen for us all."

"Perhaps you would prefer to ride?" Daniel asked Annabelle, then added, with a humorous glint in his eye, "That is, if your rheumatism permits?'

Annabelle's eyes danced. "Do you know? I think I might."

At last the party began to break up and Annabelle and Caroline retired for the night.

"Are you sure you will be able to manage tomorrow?" asked Caroline solicitously.

"My dear girl, Lord Arundel was teasing. I am not in my dotage."

"Of course not, dear aunt," said Caroline kindly. "You are only just middle-aged."

"Ah, well, it is better than being elderly!" said Annabelle. "Thank you for that, at least!"

"Not at all," said Caroline, taking her arm fondly. "You will not be elderly for another three years, for no one is ever old until they are thirty, you know."

"In that case, I am glad I have three years of youth left to me," said Annabelle, as she said goodnight to her niece.

"A good attitude," said Caroline. "You must make the most of the next few years, and not squander them. They will go all too quickly, you know."

"You are right. The ride tomorrow will give me something to remember when I am sitting alone by the fire with a blanket over my knees!"

Caroline gave her an affectionate hug and they parted on the landing.

As Annabelle walked back to her room she told herself that she must not read too much into Daniel's attention, but she could not quell a rising tide of pleasure at the thought of the outing to come.

The party assembled early the following morning, meeting in front of the house, where they mounted their horses or climbed into carriages, ready for the journey. The day was fine, but not too hot: ideal outing weather.

As Annabelle set off, Daniel fell in next to her, riding an impressive black stallion. His animal was spirited, but he controlled it with ease, and they set out at a good pace.

"Have you visited Primrose Hill before?" asked Annabelle.

"No. As I believe I told you yesterday, this is my first visit to Whitegates."

"And I should, of course, remember everything you say!" Annabelle teased him.

"That is not a very flattering remark," he replied with perfect good humour.

"Ah! I did not know you required flattery. If that is the case, then nothing is easier. Allow me to tell you, Lord Arundel, how well you ride!"

He laughed. "I will return the compliment, and say that you have a good seat and light hands."

"Please do. If flattery is to be the order of the day, I demand my full measure!"

And before she knew it, they were bantering again, as they always had done in the past, and she thought to herself, I must be careful for I am in danger of falling in love with him all over again.

The landscape was all that Annabelle had hoped it would be. Although it was not the time of year for the primroses that gave the hill its name, the area was picturesque, with a wooded area giving way to a grassy slope, and the views were magnificent. The countryside rolled away into the distance, disturbed only by dry stone walls and the silvery snake of a river, and was overtopped with a blue sky.

"Does it match your expectations?" asked Daniel. He leaned on his pommel and surveyed the area, as the carriages rolled to a halt a little way ahead of them.

"Indeed it does; in fact it surpasses them. It is a long time since I have seen anywhere quite so pretty."

He dismounted in one easy movement and then held out his arms to her.

She was about to refuse his help when she saw that the grooms were busy and, without a mounting block, she knew she would need his assistance. As she slid from her horse she felt a tingling sensation as his hands closed around her waist, and then it was gone as her feet touched the ground and his hands relinquished their hold on her. She felt the loss of it, and to cover her emotion she looked around for her niece. She saw that Caroline was fascinating a young man nearby.

Daniel, seeing where her gaze tended, offered her his arm. "If you are thinking of playing chaperone, it will be less noticeable with two," he said invitingly.

She laughed. "My niece is rather headstrong, and I would rather she did not know I am keeping watch over her. She is likely to resent it," she admitted, taking his arm. "She believes herself to be in love with a young man at home, but she is volatile, so that she could easily end up compromising some other poor young man if she takes a sudden fancy to him! I wonder whom she is with now? Do you know him?"

At that moment the young man turned round and Daniel gave an exclamation of surprise. "Why, it's my nephew, James! I wonder what he is doing here?" He added with a sigh, "He is in some scrape, no doubt, and wants me to get him out of it."

James, hearing his name, looked towards them and coloured.

"Will you excuse me?" said Daniel.

Annabelle watched him go with regret, but she was reminded that every cloud has a silver lining when she was joined by Caroline who, having lost her companion, sought out her aunt.

"You seem happy," said Annabelle.

"I am. I was just talking to James—"

"James?" asked Annabelle. "Isn't it a little early to be calling him James? You have only just met him."

Caroline gave a despairing sigh, as if to say, *Aunt Annabelle, you are so behind the times.*

"He happened to be in the neighbourhood," Caroline went on. "Hearing that his uncle was staying close by, he came to pay his respects. Ah! They have finished talking. I must not monopolize you, Aunt Annabelle. I am sure there are some old people here you would like to talk to." And so saying, she returned to her new swain.

Annabelle watched her go.

To her dismay, she saw that Daniel, having spoken to his nephew, seemed to be about to leave. He was walking towards the horses with a resolute air. Annabelle experienced the same sinking feeling she had felt the last time he had left a house party at which she had been present. But this time she quickly rallied, for she had been half expecting it ever since she arrived.

And then suddenly he stopped. He hesitated, as if he were wrestling with himself, then he turned and walked towards her with a serious look on his face.

"Annabelle," he said, taking her hands. "My fool of a nephew has managed to entangle himself with an opera dancer who is threatening all kinds of things if he doesn't marry her. He has not the age or experience to deal with her and I have, so I am on my way to London at once. I have no right to speak to you, but today's leave-taking has reminded me of another one, a year ago, when I would have asked you to marry me, had not my brother's sudden death called me away from you.

"I thought it was only a temporary separation, since I intended to seek you out and propose to you once I was free to think of myself again. But circumstances changed so radically that I could not, in all honour, speak. You see, I had to settle my brother's many debts and so I was a great deal poorer than when we had first met, whilst you had inherited a fortune and so you were a great deal richer.

"I set out to mend my fortunes, so that I would be able to offer you my hand honourably. But when I met you by chance in the inn, fate stepped in. I have no right to ask you to wait for me, but I cannot let my chance slip away again. You see, I love you, Annabelle. I have loved you for a very long time. So I ask you, though I have no right to do so, will you wait for me?"

"No," she said, shaking her head.

His face fell.

"It might take years for you to restore your fortune," she said, smiling, "by which time I will be in my dotage, if my niece is to be believed. So I rather think we should seize our youth whilst we can and marry without delay!"

He laughed and squeezed her hands. "Your niece is a very wise girl," he said. Then he pulled her into his arms and kissed her soundly. "I have been wanting to do that again for a very long time," he said.

"And I have been wanting you to," she replied.

In answer, he kissed her again.

They would have continued thus for the rest of the afternoon had they not been interrupted by a startled cry and then a gasp of horror.

Annabelle, surfacing from Daniel's embrace, saw Caroline standing there.

"Aunt! I wondered where you were! I wanted to tell you it was time to go, but I see now that I have arrived not a moment too soon to rescue you from this . . . this seducer!" She grabbed Annabelle's wrist and pulled her away from Daniel, glaring at him all the while.

"My dear girl . . ." began Annabelle.

"I assure you, my intentions are honourable!" said Daniel to Caroline. "Your aunt has very kindly consented to become my wife."

Caroline let out a cry of horror. "No! Aunt Annabelle! Say it is not true!"

"I am afraid it is," said Annabelle.

"But at your age! You will be a laughing stock!" said Caroline in horror. Then her face fell and she added tragically, "But of course, now that you have been compromised, you can do nothing else. And perhaps it is a good thing after all. You will be thirty soon and will need a companion for your twilight years." She smiled bravely. "I am very happy for you, after all."

"That is very generous of you," said Annabelle with a twinkle in her eye. "To make you feel better, I hope you will consent to be my bridesmaid."

"Oh, yes!" said Caroline, brightening at once. "I will need a new dress, new shoes . . ."

"Yes, you will need all those things, and have them, too. And then, perhaps, you will invite me to be the matron of honour at your own wedding to Able, which must surely soon follow mine."

Caroline looked at her in astonishment. "My dear Aunt, what can you be talking about? I am not going to marry Able. Whatever gave you such an idea?"

"I rather thought you were in love with him."

"How absurd! Of course not. A slight infatuation, perhaps, contracted when I was only sixteen. But I am older and a great deal wiser now. I am going to marry James!"

Cynders and Ashe

Elizabeth Boyle

One

London – 1815

"You expect my daughter to wear that gown?" Lady Fitzsimon's acid tones carried to every corner of the elegant dress shop on Bond Street.

"My Lady, it is exactly the gown you ordered," Madame Delaflote replied. Used as she was to the fits and fleeting fancies of London ladies, she took Lady Fitzsimon's protests in her stride.

Either the lady was doing this to get her bill lowered – which would never happen, for Madame Delaflote never gave up a shilling that could possibly be wrung from a client – or she was just being aristocratic merely because she could.

In that case, Madame Delaflote had naught to do but wait her out.

From behind the curtain that separated the showroom from the workroom, Miss Ella Cynders flinched with each protest as if she were being flogged. For the dress was her creation, her finest – if she was inclined to boast – but she knew that it had been a risk making it for Lady Fitzsimon's daughter.

"The Ashe Ball is tonight, Madame!" Lady Fitzsimon was saying. Ella glanced out and found the matron waving her invitation about for all to see. Invitations to the Ashe Ball were so coveted, so limited, that most who held one kept it carefully guarded. For without that printed invitation, one could not enter. Proof of this being demonstrated at the moment by her ladyship, who was keeping hers on her person, never far from sight, and, better yet, close at hand to flaunt over those who hadn't been invited. "My daughter cannot go in that!"

Ella watched the lady point at the dress her daughter was modelling as if it were made of rags – when nothing could be further from the truth. The fair green silk, embroidered with silver thread and adorned with thousands of seed pearls, was an artistic triumph. Ella and the two other assistants, Martha and Hazel, had all but worn their fingers to the bone to get the gown ready in time.

It was a fairy-tale dress destined for an unforgettable night.

"My good lady," Madame Delaflote said, "your daughter shines like the rarest jewel in that gown. Lord Ashe won't be able to take his eyes off her."

"Of course he won't – she looks naked in it," the lady declared.

Not exactly naked, Ella would have told her, but the illusion was there. As if she were a woodland nymph stepping from her hidden grove. Sleeveless and cut low in the front, the dress clung to the wearer as if it were a second skin.

"That gown is ruinous! Why, she looks—." Lady Fitzsimon's hands fluttered about as she searched for the right words.

From behind the curtain, the three assistants finished her sentence for her.

"Gorgeous," Martha whispered.

"Breathtaking," Hazel added.

"Unforgettable," Ella said.

"Common!" Lady Fitzsimon declared. "As if she's just stepped from the stage of a revue. I want Lord Ashe to fall in love with my daughter. *Marry her.* Don't you realize he must choose his bride tonight? Tonight, Madame! The gown Roseanne wears must be perfect!"

"Stupid cow," Martha muttered, her less than refined origins coming out. "That gel fair on sparkles in it."

"Aye, she does," Hazel agreed. "Like a princess."

Ella agreed, for she and Roseanne were of similar colouring and build, and she had tried the dress on herself to make sure the blush green silk – like the first verdant whisper of spring – would bring out the girl's fair features.

"If you think I am paying for this, you are sadly mistaken," Lady Fitzsimon said, sounding more like a shrewd fishwife than a baroness.

Madame Delaflote took a furtive glance at the curtain, where she knew her assistants were most likely eavesdropping. Her brows rose in two dark arches, the sort of look each of them knew was a dangerous harbinger.

If Lady Fitzsimon refused this dress, someone would pay for it.

"And whatever are those things sticking out from her back?" the lady continued.

"Wings, My Lady," Madame Delaflote told her. "You asked for a fairy costume, and those are her wings."

"They are a nuisance. However is she to dance? They'll get crushed in the crowd before the first set – and then what? She'll be in the retiring room for a good part of the night having them clipped off." Lady Fitzsimon shook her head. "No, no, no, this will never do. And I blame you, Madame Delaflote. Everyone says your gowns are the finest, but I hardly see what you were thinking to dress my daughter like a Cyprian." She turned to Roseanne. "Take it off at once, before someone sees you in it and thinks we actually ordered such a shameful piece."

Ella cringed. For the gown had been her idea, her creation. And if Lady Fitzsimon wouldn't pay for it, refused it, well, she knew very well who would be paying for it – her.

"She's not taking it?" Hazel whispered, as Roseanne slipped into the changing room and Martha hurried after her to help her out of the gown.

Meanwhile, Madame Delaflote and Lady Fitzsimon continued their heated exchange.

"My Lady, that gown is exactly what you ordered." If there was one thing that could be said about Madame Delaflote, she was a determined soul.

"I ordered a gown that would set my daughter apart – not have her appear like some Covent Garden high-flyer."

Madame Delaflote sucked in a deep breath to be so insulted, for her gowns were sought after, fawned over, ordered months in advance (as this one had been) and no one called them tawdry.

And certainly no one had ever refused one.

Yet here was Lady Fitzsimon in high dudgeon, having gathered up her daughter, by now properly dressed in a blue sprig muslin day gown, and leaving.

Ella closed her eyes and wished herself well away from this disaster. But a loud *whoomph*, and Hazel's muffled giggle brought her back to the present.

The other two had parted the curtain and there in the front of the shop lay Lady Fitzsimon on the floor.

In her rush to depart the shop, she'd run right into a footman who was delivering a missive. His notes and messages had fluttered up in the air as he had tried to catch the lady from falling, but her girth had defied even his strength and the two of them had ended up in a tangle at the doorway.

Madame rushed forwards to help the baroness, as did Roseanne, but the matron was too furious to have any assistance. She righted herself, caught her daughter by the arm and marched from the store, her nose tipped haughtily in the air.

An embarrassed silence filled the shop, but only for a moment. Madame snapped her fingers, as if that was enough to dismiss the situation, then got back to business, calling for her assistants, and greeting the waiting clients with her usual French airs.

The footman gathered up his notes, with Hazel's help – for the girl had a romantic nature and flirted shamelessly with all the handsome footmen who came and went from the shop. They all knew Hazel and she knew them.

The cheeky fellow handed over a pair of missives and winked at the girl before he turned to leave.

Madame, however, was in no mood for such behaviour and snatched the mail from Hazel's hands. She sent the girl a scathing glance that sent her scurrying to the back room.

"Take these and see to them," Madame told Ella. "We will discuss that gown later."

Ella bowed politely, took the notes and also fled to the back room.

She didn't know whether to continue her work on the gown for Lady Shore or begin the task of packing her bags. It had only been lucky happenstance that she'd gotten this job when she'd returned to London six months ago.

Luck, and her skill with a needle. Another job might not be so easily gotten.

For to be dismissed yet again and always without references – Ella shuddered at such a prospect.

"She'll not sack you," Hazel said, as if reading her friend's bleak expression. "She's made too much money from your designs."

Ella absently sorted through the notes in her hands. "That gown cost a fortune, and if Lady Fitzsimon doesn't pay for it—"

Hazel nodded in grim agreement.

It would come out of Ella's salary. Glancing over at the silk, which now lay on the work table, she sighed, for it was ever so lovely a dress and it had been meant to be worn this night and this night only.

Lady Fitzsimon was utterly mistaken on the matter. Lord Ashe would never have thought that gown common. He would have loved it.

"Gar, Ella! Whatever is that in your hand?" Hazel said, coming around the work table in a flash.

Martha had slipped into the workroom just then, a stack of sample brocades in her arms. Her mouth fell open and she nearly dropped her burden when she saw what Ella was holding. "Oh, as I live and breathe! It is."

"Is what?" Ella said, before she glanced down at the thick cream card in her hand.

> *Viscount Ashe*
> *Invites the bearer of this invitation*
> *To his masquerade ball*
> *The 11th of April*

Ella's mouth fell open. An invitation to the Ashe Ball.

Hazel began to laugh. "That old cow must have dropped it when she went off in a huff."

"She won't be able to get in without it." Ella crossed the room and caught up her cloak. She started for the back door, when Hazel caught her by the arm.

"And just what do you think you are doing?"

"Returning this to Lady Fitzsimon."

"Why would you be doing that?" Hazel held her fast.

"Because she can't get in without it," Ella told her, pulling her arm free and reaching for the door.

"Well, she don't need it now, does she?" Martha said. "Since her daughter hasn't got a gown to wear."

Something about the girl's words – nay, suggestion – stayed Ella's steps. "Whatever do you mean?"

Martha glanced over at Hazel, who nodded in agreement. "That we didn't work our fingers raw to see that gown spend the night here, being taken apart, so the mistress could not only charge you for it, but sell the makings off again to someone else, taking the profit twice over."

Hazel nodded.

"You could go, with that gown and that invitation," Martha whispered.

Ella shook her head. "I couldn't—"

"And why ever not? It isn't like you aren't quality, and it isn't like that gown doesn't fit."

"You could see *him* again, Ella," Hazel said.

"No," Ella gasped, staring down at the name on the invitation. *Viscount Ashe*.

Him.

"I can't . . . I would be discovered . . . Think of the trouble . . ."

"Think of seeing him again," Hazel said. "You know very well that you sewed that gown with him in mind. So he would think it was you."

"I did no such—" But she stopped herself. She had. Shamelessly designed and embroidered every stitch for his eyes, his favour.

"Wouldn't seeing him again be worth a bundle of trouble and then some?"

"Julian, you vowed tonight would be the last time," Lady Ashe said, over the tea table.

The Ashe residence was a flurry of activity as the servants and the added help that had been hired for the ball continued working at a furious pace to ensure that everything went off as planned.

"Yes, yes, Mother, I recall my promise," Julian, Viscount Ashe, told her.

"You will choose a bride tonight and no more of this foolishness about finding 'her'."

Julian glanced out the window at the garden beyond. Her. His mysterious lady love. The one who'd come to the first Ashe Ball five years earlier.

The Ashes had always been a romantic lot, and family tradition held that the Ashe viscount had five seasons to find his true love. Five. A bride to be plucked from a masquerade before the five years were out.

Julian had found his the very first year.

Found her and lost her.

He'd spent the last five years searching for the mysterious lady who'd come to the ball, danced with him, kissed him – Julian glanced over at his mother who was deep in discussion with the housekeeper over where to find their extra plates – the lady whose virginity he had stolen in an impetuous moment of passion.

But it wasn't just her passion that had intrigued him, it was her lively nature, her bright eyes, her sharp wit.

She'd stolen his heart that night, just as the Ashe legend said a lady would. But what the Ashe legend didn't say was what to do when the love of your life, your future viscountess, ups and disappears into thin air.

And now tonight was his last chance to find her.

It wasn't as if Julian hadn't searched for her – but all he'd come to were dead ends.

At first, he'd thought his choice was Lady Pamela Osborn. Everyone had assumed that the young lady, who the elder Lady Osborn hauled out of the ball just before the unmasking, had been her daughter. But, as it turned out, Lady Pamela had given her costume to another and used the night to elope with Lord Percy Snodgrass. Who Lady Pamela's twin had been was the real mystery, for Lady Osborn had refused to give Ashe any information about the scandal. And the newly minted Lady Percy had sent back his enquiries unopened.

He'd even taken to haunting the streets outside the Osborn townhouse in hopes of spying a maid or companion who might fit the bill, or one willing to be bribed to give a hint who his mysterious lady love might be. But not a one would give Ashe even a crumb of information about the lady in green silk who had haunted his every day for five years.

Two

The Ashe Ball – 1810

Miss Ella Cynders, companion to Lady Pamela, the daughter of the Earl of Osborn, stood at the entrance of the Ashe Ball, her knees quaking with fear and her heart hammering with excitement.

Fear, because if she were discovered impersonating Pamela, she'd be sacked without references.

Of course, if she was honest, her being sacked was a given. By the morning, there would be no way to conceal Pamela's runaway marriage and she, Ella, would be let go.

But Pamela, the soon-to-be Lady Percy Snodgrass, had promised to hire her immediately as her companion to come live with her in the country. So if Ella were to be unemployed, it wouldn't be for long.

Still, Ella couldn't help but allow a bit of excitement to nudge aside her fears. This was the legendary Ashe masquerade after all. There hadn't been one in twenty-seven years, not since the last Lord Ashe had plucked the unlikely Miss Amelia Levingston out of the crowd as his perfect bride.

Tonight would be their son Julian's first attempt to find his viscountess, and the ton was abuzz at the opportunity the ball afforded on a lucky young lady. To become Lady Ashe.

"Pamela," Lady Osborn said, "remember, if you are to catch his eye, do not be obvious, but not so shy that he doesn't notice you."

Ella nodded, but didn't say a word. Luckily, she and Pamela were of the same height and build, and with Ella's red hair powdered and done up in a crown of flowers, it was impossible to discern that it wasn't Pamela's blonde locks beneath.

And it helped that Lady Osborn was dreadfully near-sighted.

"Certainly, Lord Ashe's mother has left nothing to chance," Lady Osborn was saying as they walked deeper into the room. "There are the Damerells, and the Sadlers. And I see Lady Houghton has both her daughters here. I daresay, Lady Ashe knew what she was doing – including only the best families, so there was no chance of some undesirable *parti* catching her son's eye."

Ella flinched. Undesirable *partis* were the bane of Lady Osborn's existence. Such as the one Lady Pamela was running away with this very night.

"I am glad you had Ella rework your costume," the lady said. "She has such an eye for these things, for I daresay your costume is the finest in the room. I had my doubts when we hired her, but she has the most exquisite hand with a needle." The lady sighed. "Now, make the most of this evening. While Ashe is only a viscount, at least he has a title and lands."

This was a pointed snub about the attentions of Lord Percy, who claimed only a courtesy title and no property. Second sons held little appeal to an ambitious mother like Lady Osborn and being in love with one was nothing short of treason.

So Ella nodded and smiled, thankful the lady really spent so little time with her daughter and cared so little for her opinions and even less for her conversation. Thus, Ella wasn't required to do much more than nod obediently.

They continued to wade through the crush, and Ella felt a bit light-headed, for the crowd was dazzling in its costumes and masks – she'd never seen the likes of such a party. Certainly she'd been to other affairs as Pamela's companion, but she'd always spent her time alone on the periphery, watching Pamela being courted, while the marchioness was off getting caught up with her cronies.

"I wish I knew how Lord Ashe was disguised," Lady Osborn mused, tapping her fan against her lips and scanning the crowd, though it was unlikely she could tell a Robin Hood from a Cavalier. "But then again, I have to imagine there isn't a mother here who wouldn't give up a year's worth of pin money for that confidence."

Lord Ashe . . . Ella had heard nothing but talk of him and his ball for the last two months. Certainly everyone knew what he looked like – burnished gold hair, a square jaw and wide shoulders. Tall and elegant, he made lady after lady swoon. He would be hard to disguise, so like everyone else she couldn't help scanning the crowd trying to discover him.

But her quest to find Lord Ashe suddenly paled.

Dutifully following Lady Osborn through the crush of bodies, she spied a tall man dressed in a long, embroidered surcoat and form-fitting hose and boots coming towards them. She didn't know if it was her own love of medieval stories or the way he carried himself, but she was utterly and instantly mesmerized. From the dark mane of hair brushed back, to the straight line of his shoulders, to the way his leggings showed every muscle in his long legs – it was as if Lancelot or Richard the Lionheart had just stepped out of the Crusades or a tournament, minus the chain mail and sword. He came closer, prowling through the crowd as if it was his to command, and Ella's breath caught in her throat.

She, who had no business falling in love, fell. Fell in an instant. If that was what this was – being unable to breathe, afraid to move, afraid even to blink, lest he disappear from sight.

Oh, save me, came an errant thought. Save me, oh, knight.

And as he passed by, his gaze met hers, and something inside her flamed to life. A spark passed between the two of them.

It was as if they had always been together, were destined to be united. That they had known and loved each other until the ages had torn them apart, and now . . .

Now they had found each other once again.

Even as she continued past him, their gazes held, her head turning so she could gape after him. Then he was surrounded by the crowd and disappeared from sight and, in a flash, the connection was broken.

Ella shivered. *I cannot lose him.* It was a cry from deep within her heart, a place within her that until now had been silently slumbering. Sleeping no longer, she couldn't do anything other than stop and whirl around.

She forgot all about being Pamela, all about deceiving Lady Osborn – who had waded ahead, having spied a friend she knew would have the most current *on dits*, and had all but forgotten her daughter.

And to her shock, as she turned to determine where he had gone, he was no more than a few feet from her. For he had stopped as well. Frozen and fixed as if he couldn't take another step away from her.

Gazing at her, his eyes sparkled beneath his mask, and a smile rose on his lips. And that connection, the one that had brought them to this moment, sparked anew. It drew her closer to him, even as he closed the final bit of difference between them.

"Good evening, oh, fair, fey creature," he said, reaching out and taking her hand, bringing it up to his lips. "I have sought you for an eternity."

Then he kissed her fingertips and sent a tremor of desire racing through her. Ella willed herself not to snatch her hand back, for she'd never felt anything like it. And it seemed she wasn't alone. He looked at her anew as if the sensation had been something he had hardly expected.

"You . . . you have?" she stammered as she looked down at her fingers, which still tingled. Biting her lip, she hazarded a glance up at him.

"How could I not?" he said, bowing slightly. Then he leaned closer. "I believe they are about to start the dancing. If you are not already engaged, may I have the honour?"

She nodded wordlessly and he led her through the crowd.

Again, a thrum of desire raced through her as she walked alongside him and out on to the floor. Couples were taking their places, and soon they were surrounded, but Ella couldn't shake the sensation that they were all alone. When the music began, they moved through the steps that pulled them apart and pushed them together and then separated them yet again.

"Your costume is lovely," he said, as he returned to her. "Are you Titania?"

She blushed. "Goodness, no. I am merely one of her court." Out of the corner of her eye she spied Lady Osborn watching her, then turning her gaze on Ella's partner. Once she'd taken his measure, she turned to the lady next to her and got to work. To discover whether or not he was an eligible *parti*.

Not that any of that mattered to Ella. She'd never danced at a ball, never held a man's attention, never even been kissed. Not that she expected such a thing, but stealing a glance at the firm line of his lips, she had to imagine a kiss would be heavenly. This was her own fairy tale, one she doubted very many ladies in her position ever lived. And instead of being cautious, instead of remembering her place, she allowed herself to believe that this night was hers to discover her heart.

"I feel as if I have met you before," he confessed, as they moved around each other, their hands entwined and his gaze never leaving hers.

"I you." Ella wasn't about to play coy, or engage in all the elongated trappings of courtship. She hadn't the time. She knew if she was ever to have a night, this one was it.

This one night. Her night. *Their night.* And then it would be off to the country to Lord Percy's family estate in Shropshire. Certainly, there were no such men there – no knights like this, capable of sweeping a lady off her feet.

The dance continued and they said little, just stealing glances at each other, and revelling in the moments when his fingers entwined with hers, when his hand would come to the small of her back and guide her through the steps.

When the music ended, Ella held her breath. For she didn't want this dance, this night to ever end.

Apparently, neither did he.

"Have you seen the conservatory?" he asked.

She shook her head.

"It is rumoured to have oranges blooming right now. Would you like to see them, my lovely fey creature?" He held out his hand to her.

"Oranges?" she said. "Oh, I do love orange blossoms. The fragrance is heavenly."

"Then come along and indulge yourself."

Ella smiled and twined her fingers with his. "Do you think we should?" she asked, as he led her from the ballroom. Stealing one last glance over her shoulder, she could see Lady Osborn with her gaze fixed on the dance floor as she searched for some sign of her daughter.

"Certainly. Lord Ashe is a particular friend of mine," he confided. "He won't mind in the least."

It was exactly from this sort of scandalous adventure that she'd been hired to keep Pamela – and then again, here she was disguised as Pamela so her charge could run away with Lord Percy.

So she might as well fall into her own mire.

"I can't help thinking that we've met," he was saying.

"I feel the same, but I can't think of where or when." Ella looked at him again, searched for something familiar, wondering if he was an officer who might have served with her father. For certainly he had the confidence and bearing of a man used to being in command. But she could hardly ask who he was, for then he would ask for her name.

And she would have to lie. The one thing Ella didn't want to do to this man was tell him half-truths and fabrications. She couldn't. But the truth? That she was naught but a pauper hired by Lady Osborn because her services could be had for very little?

Would that matter to him? He was a few paces ahead of her, leading the way to the back of the house, and she glanced at his back. His pace reminded her of a lion's, the surcoat doing little to hide the muscled strength beneath it.

"Whatever are you smiling at?" he asked, as they stopped at the door to the conservatory, which had been built in the gardens behind the house.

"Your costume. I can't determine if you are Galahad, Richard or Percival."

"I would prefer a Templar," he said, taking a fighting stance and grinning wickedly at her.

She laughed. "You do realize that most of them were nothing more than expert brawlers, men trained for naught but waging war."

This took him aback. "You know of the Templars?"

"Certainly. My father was in the army, and adored military history. I have no brothers, so I grew up on a steady diet of books featuring the campaigns of Hannibal and Alexander, and ever so many histories – including the Templars. My mother feared I would be quite unmanageable from such an education."

"No, I think you are most surprising," he said, opening the door. The warmth and moisture of the air inside swarmed over them. "But I suppose I must leave the unmanageable part for further discovery."

"I am hardly unmanageable," she told him, as she stalked past into the warmth of the conservatory.

His brow arched.

"Well, I do make my mistakes from time to time. And I fear I don't always exhibit the demeanour expected of a lady." Which is why she'd been fired by Lady Gaspar *and* Lady Preswood.

He folded his arms over his chest and eyed her. "Let me see how outspoken you are." He paused. "What do you think the likelihood of the Americans joining France against us?"

"Very," she told him. Forgetting Lady Osborn's dictum that ladies never discussed politics. *Never.* "But it will be a dangerous situation."

"Yes, well, I doubt the Americans have much sense over the matter. A hot-headed rabble is all they will ever be."

"No, sir, you mistake me. I mean it will be a dangerous situation for us."

"For us?!" he sputtered. "I think your mother was right."

"No, sir, you aren't looking at it from a military vantage," she said, feeling the thrill of debate outweigh any dictum by Lady Osborn. "We will be spread too thin. If we make war in the Americas, we weaken our ability to defeat Bonaparte quickly."

"So you think we cannot defeat the French?"

"I didn't say that," she said, pacing around him. They were circling like cats, but to Ella it was exhilarating. "It is just that every military leader in history who has spread his troops over greater and greater distances thins his lines to the point where gaps are created. Dangerous gaps."

He paused for a second and eyed her, an astonished respect in his gaze. "But Napoleon is faced with the same problem. He called for Spanish recruits last month and the bloody Spaniards raced for the hills rather than be conscripted."

"And yet there are eighty thousand Frenchmen who have been conscripted, and another forty thousand in the waiting. And how many able men are in America? We are but one island." She crossed her arms over her chest and waited.

Her knight scratched his chin. "But there are the Spaniards who are joining our troops in Majorca – they will fight at our side."

"Yes, in Spain, but not in New York, or Maryland, or the Carolinas. Will they defend our hold in Canada?"

He grunted and paced in front of her.

"Bonaparte knew exactly what he was doing when he gave the Floridas to the Americans, and stirred their wrath against our Navy – as well deserved as it is."

"So you would criticize the might of the Royal Navy, you bold minx?"

She nodded emphatically. "When they anger a sleeping bear, yes. Not one of those captains thinks of the consequences of taking a single American ship, but what will they do when that country's Congress acts? When that country begins to build ships? *Fleets of ships*. They have a continent of forests. They can build frigates for the next hundred years – and man them. Can we?"

He threw up his hands and strode away a few steps. "I can't believe I am arguing this with a lady!"

"And being bested," she pointed out.

"Routed!" he declared. "Your mother was entirely correct – you are unmanageable."

Ella didn't feel the least bit insulted. "I daresay, you don't mind."

This gave him pause and then he grinned. "No, I actually don't. But if you tell anyone I've conceded—"

She shook her head and crossed her fingers over her heart. "Never! I swear."

"It shall be our secret," he told her, moving closer again. As he passed an orange tree, he reached and plucked a blossom from the branch and handed it to her. For a moment all Ella could do was gaze down at the delicate blossom cradled in her hand, for she didn't dare look up at him.

"Does your father still read you military tracts?" he asked.

She shook her head. "My parents are both gone."

He paused and gazed at her. "I am so sorry. You have sisters?"

"No, I am . . . I am all alone now."

"Not any longer," he told her, taking her hand and leading her down the long aisle.

The conservatory was glassed on three sides, running the length of the garden wall. A stove provided extra heat and lamps overhead illuminated the wild, exotic collection of plants flourishing in the artificial tropics. As they drew closer to the middle, the intoxicating scent of oranges in bloom curled around her, enticed her to come closer and inhale . . . deeply.

"It is just like our garden in Portugal," she told him, reaching out to touch the narrow leaf of a palm.

"You lived in Portugal?"

"Yes. Though not always. I was born in the West Indies. Then my father's regiment was sent to Portugal."

"I imagine you find London quite different."

She laughed. "I find London ever so cold."

They both laughed.

"Is it still a cold place?" he asked, drawing her into his arms.

"No," she said, shivering, and definitely not from London's notorious chill.

His hands, firm and warm, pulled her closer, until she was nestled right up against his chest. Her hands splayed over his surcoat, and marvelled at the hard plains beneath.

Like a Templar reborn.

"I don't even know your name," he whispered as he lowered his head, drew his lips closer to hers.

"Does it matter?" she whispered.

"No. Not really," he said, his breath warm on her lips. And then that breath became his lips, covering hers and stealing a kiss.

Ella didn't know what to expect, but this . . . this invasion . . . this breach of her defences, left her breathless. His tongue sallied over her lips, teased her to open the gates, to let him storm forth. Everything she knew about defences gave way to his very expert onslaught.

Besides, how was she not to let him in, when he was creating this breathless storm inside her?

Desire, new and exhilarating, raced through her, as his hands held her even closer, began to explore her, running down her sides, curving around her backside.

Ella was starting to burn.

His kiss deepened and, instead of being frightened – as she supposed she should be, as she ought to be – she welcomed him, drawing him closer, her arms winding around his neck.

She had to hold him like that, for her knees, her legs, her insides, had become ever so unreliable, quaking with need, with desires, leaving her shaky and unsettled . . . and eager for more.

He drew back from her, lips parted for a moment, and gazed at her, a wonder in his eyes that startled her. For even in her innocence, she knew this was different. This wasn't what he had expected.

Or had he known all along, just as they had found themselves drawn to each other in the middle of the ballroom?

"Ahem," came a polite cough from the doorway of the conservatory, breaking into their intimate moment of wonderment. "Sir?"

Her knight looked up. "Yes?"

"You are required inside," the fellow said, staring down at the floor.

"Yes, thank you, Shifton."

The man bowed and left.

"I must—" he said, waving at the door. "But only for a little bit," he added hastily.

"Yes, I understand," she said. "I think I should go to the retiring room and put myself in order."

"I will only undo it later," he told her, leaning over and kissing her brow tenderly. Ella should have realized then, it was actually a promise.

Three

Ella rushed into the empty retiring room, her cheeks completely flushed and her heart hammering. *Whatever is happening to me?*

She was falling in love. Oh, and it was perfect and delicious and wonderful. She hugged herself and spun around, only to come to a complete stop when she realized she wasn't alone.

For there in a chair in the corner sat an elderly matron.

"Oh, I didn't know—" Ella stammered, glancing towards the door and then around the room.

The lady's gaze narrowed and then she rose and crossed the room. As she got closer, Ella's eyes widened in recognition. "Mrs Garraway!"

"Ella Cynders, oh, my dear!" The lady took Ella into her arms and hugged her tight. "You wicked, wicked girl! You don't know how I have worried after you. And here you are." Mrs Garraway held her out at arm's length and examined her, smiling widely.

"How is the Colonel?" Ella asked, as she took off her mask to get a better look at her mother's dear friend. Colonel Garraway had been her father's commanding officer, and Ella and her mother had spent countless hours with Mrs Garraway, sewing and gossiping and keeping each other company in Portugal.

That is until Ella's parents had died, and Ella had been sent home to live with an aunt. But unbeknownst to the kindly Garraways, the lady had also recently died, leaving Ella without friend, family or a home. That was how she had ended up as Lady Pamela's paid companion.

"He's just the same, always in a fine fettle over something. But won't he be ever so happy to see you. We've been so worried, for when we got to London and discovered that your aunt had passed away and there wasn't a word of you, I feared the worst. But I see I was worried for naught, for here you are and looking perfectly lovely." She hugged Ella again and looked to be ready to burst out in tears. "Wherever have you been?"

"I took a position, Mrs Garraway. I work for Lady Osborn as her daughter's companion," Ella told her.

Instead of being shocked or disappointed, Mrs Garraway nodded approvingly. "That's my girl. You were never so above yourself that you couldn't find your way. That's what the Colonel kept saying. 'Got her father's nerve,' he'd say when I would get to fretting." She paused and looked Ella over again. "And they must be very fond of you to give you such a lovely costume and let you have suitors."

Bad enough that the colour in her cheeks drained away, Ella couldn't even look the lady in the eye. Oh, she was in the suds now. More so than for just taking Pamela's place at the ball.

"Ella!" Mrs Garraway said, her voice turning from welcoming to stern. "I can see it on your face. What mischief is this?"

She bit her lip and looked over at the woman who was the closest person she had left to family. And with her thoughts in a whirl, she turned to the lady and confessed all. "Mrs Garraway, I am in such a tangle. Lady Pamela begged me to take her place tonight. Lady Osborn thinks I am her daughter."

"Is the woman so daft that she can't see her own daughter?"

"She's a bit near-sighted," Ella confessed. "And has paid little heed to Lady Pamela until now. She confuses me with her daughter often, so we thought, well, Lady Pamela knew that her mother wouldn't notice the difference."

Mrs Garraway shook her head. She'd raised three daughters herself, all while following the drum, and seen them all married to good men. But she'd done so by keeping a close eye on them. And her maternal ways returned in full force. "And where is this Lady Pamela?"

Again, Ella blanched. "She's run off." And when the good lady gasped, she continued quickly, "He is a good man – Lord Percy Snodgrass, the second son of the Marquess of Lichfield. They are very much in love."

The Colonel's wife pursed her lips. "And if it is a good match, Ella Cynders, why ever are they eloping?"

"Their parents don't approve."

This didn't win any favour from Mrs Garraway. "Oh, good heavens, gel, however did you get mixed up in such a scandal? You'll be sacked. Did you think about that?"

Ella shook her head. "Oh, no, it won't be like that."

Mrs Garraway's brows rose into a pair of question marks.

"Well, yes, I will be sacked, that much is for certain," she conceded. "But Lady Pamela has promised to hire me as her companion, so I will have a job once again when they return to London."

"Oh, Ella, think on this. Does Lord Percy have an income? Estates? The capacity to keep a wife? Do his parents approve of the match?"

"Well, not exactly—" In fact, they had forbidden it. They wanted an heiress for Percy, since he was unlikely to inherit. And Lady Pamela, while a lovely creature, would come to her marriage with little, considering her father's shaky finances.

"And if his parents don't approve of the match, do you honestly think they will take you – the one who helped to make this mésalliance happen – into their employ?"

Oh, that had never occurred to her! As Pamela had laid out her plans, it seemed so simple. And now . . . "You don't think I'll be—"

"You'll be dismissed without references, gel. You've landed your-self in a great deal of trouble."

Ella's breath froze in her throat. No, it couldn't be. But, in her heart, she knew the truth. Tears welled up in her eyes. Oh, she was done for.

"Now, now, no need for all that. It isn't your fault – entirely – that this Lady Pamela is a headstrong piece, not that her ladyship is like to see it that way. Still, I can see you haven't changed a bit. You romantic thing. You likely thought Lady Pamela's marriage would be just like your parents', didn't you? But your mother fully understood the consequences that her marriage wrought."

Ella nodded. Her own parents had made a runaway marriage and been blissfully happy despite the family cutting their daughter off completely. Her grandparents had even refused to acknowledge Ella.

"They loved each other, and they never lacked for anything, and neither will Lady Pamela," Ella said, trying to sound more confident than she felt. Despite her father being an officer with no background, her aristocratic mother had been more than content to follow him. The likelihood of the pampered Lady Pamela living happily in reduced circumstances wasn't so certain. Not even with Lord Percy at her side. For he was just as spoiled. "Oh, Mrs Garraway, I am in ever so much of a coil."

"That you are, lass. That you are." Then Mrs Garraway smiled. "But it is your good luck that I've found you when I did. The Colonel is being sent back to Portugal and I am off with him. We sail in the morning, and you will come with us. I've missed you, gel. So after her ladyship sends you off with a flea in your ear and you are in complete disgrace, make haste to the docks, so you can come and keep me company in my dotage. That is, if you don't mind coming to Portugal? Better than the streets of London, I have to say."

Ella didn't know what to say. So she threw herself into the lady's arms and hugged her tight. "Oh, Mrs Garraway, whatever have I done to deserve you?"

"You might not say that in a few months when you've grown tired of me!" she laughed, a fond glow in her eyes. "Oh, now, don't gape so, gel." She glanced again at Ella's costume. "I must say, dear girl, you are going into your disgrace in an elegant fashion. You sewed that costume, didn't you?"

"You would know, you taught me every stitch," she said, finally finding her voice, and swiping at the tears that had bubbled up in her eyes.

"I might have taught you how, but you have an eye, lass. Your mother's eye for colour. And for handsome fellows, I must say. Whoever is that swain of yours?" The lady grinned and glanced at the door, for the music was striking up again.

"I don't know," Ella confessed. "But he is so handsome, and so kind. Yet, I am hardly—"

"Bah! He'd be lucky to have you," the lady said. "And if things were different . . ." The dear woman sighed and hugged her one more time. "Oh, Ella, it isn't fair, but it is the way of things."

She knew exactly what Mrs Garraway meant. *If Ella wasn't in service . . . if her parents hadn't married in disgrace . . . If she were really a lady . . .*

Mrs Garroway took Ella's mask and tied it on to her face once again. "Never you mind, gel. I was young once. And in love. Besides, that knight you've found is a handsome devil. I'd dance with him too if I was your age. Do more than dance, I daresay," she said with a laugh.

Ella blushed. "I never imagined—" Her fingers went to her lips.

"Oh, so he's gone and kissed you, has he? Good. Give you something happy to remember of this night." She shooed her towards the door. "Go with him tonight. Make your memories, gel. Then come dawn, take your lumps from her ladyship, pack your bags – if she gives you time for that – and make your way to the docks. We sail first thing."

"Mrs. Garraway . . ." Ella began, pausing at the door.

"Yes, lass?"

"However can I thank you?"

"Enjoy this night," she told her, her blue eyes asparkle with mischief. "The reckoning will come soon enough."

Enjoy this night. Mrs Garraway's encouragement filled Ella's heart with hope as she slipped out of the retiring room and paused in the hallway, wondering which way to go.

Back to the conservatory and hope her knight would come to her? Or back to the ballroom where he had been summoned?

Of course, then she risked running into Lady Osborn, who would surely be searching for "Pamela" by now. No, probably best to go to the ballroom and make some muttered excuse about not feeling well.

Then again, she realized, she couldn't confess to being too ill. Lady Osborn, in some rare pique of maternal concern, might decide to take her home.

No, that will not do, Ella decided.

But as it turned out, it wasn't for her to decide. Just before she got to the ballroom, her knight came swooping out of an alcove.

"Good heavens, I thought you'd never come down from there." He caught her in his arms again and kissed her anew. This time his lips were hungry and quick and ever so wonderful. "Whatever is it that you ladies do up there?"

"You wouldn't believe me if I told you," she said, thinking of Mrs Garraway's advice.

"Would you like a tour of the house," he offered. "I know for a fact that Lord Ashe shares your penchant for military history, and has a fine map room upstairs."

"Do you think that would be right?" she asked, looking up the stairs. The retiring room was the first room of a long hall, but one never ventured past the safety of the retiring room into parts unknown.

Then again, ladies didn't kiss strangers in conservatories either.

"Upon my honour, I know Ashe wouldn't mind in the least."

"If you don't think Lord Ashe would mind," she agreed, all too curious.

He took her hand, and then glanced around to make sure no one noticed them. They darted up the stairs like a pair of wayward children.

Down the hall they went and into the study, where there was only the glow of coals in the fireplace. It was a grand space, with a large map table in the middle – atop it were spread several charts and city plans held down with lead soldiers. The table was ingenious, designed so that roll upon roll of maps could be stored in the cubbyholes built into the base.

Bookshelves lined one wall, while a desk and chair took up another corner. A long, wide settee, with a chair opposite, sat before the fireplace.

It was the sort of place she could imagine a general plotting his spring conquests. Then her gaze flitted over to the rare light in her knight's eyes. It was the light of another sort of conquest. And when he caught hold of her and kissed her, she knew she should raise her defences, flee for the safety of the ballroom, but all she could consider was that this was her last night here.

Then it would be off to Portugal, to a life as Mrs Garraway's companion. And yes, the dear lady would do her best to marry her off to some officer or other, but Ella knew it would never again be like this.

Like this starry brush with the heavens. As if the Fates had brought them together to remind them of what could be had . . . And lost.

And so Ella caught hold of him and held fast to what chance had offered her.

It was wrong, it was foolhardy, but if she didn't . . . oh, if she didn't, she would regret it the rest of her life.

As her mother had said often enough, *If I'd had only one night with my Roger it would alone have been worth every bit of disgrace . . .*

And that kind of talk was another part of growing up in army camps, travelling with soldiers, living far from the drawing rooms and strict society of London.

Ella, at one and twenty, had a pretty good notion of what happened between men and women. Having seen enough camp followers in her days, lived around the rough talk of common men, the physical act was no mystery to her.

So when her knight kissed her, carried her over to the settee, she wasn't afraid. No, she was ever so curious. Ever so desirous – for he had awakened inside her an insatiable need.

They fell into the wide, warm depths of the settee in a tangle of limbs.

They kissed, deeply, hungrily, until it seemed to flame a fire of need neither could deny.

He kissed her neck, sending tendrils of desire dancing through her limbs. He freed one of her breasts and kissed it tenderly, taking the nipple into his mouth and sucking on it – first slowly, gently, then pulling it deeply into his mouth. At the same time, he tormented the other with his hand, bringing both nipples to taut points.

Ella arched beneath his touch, his kiss, for he was bringing her body to life. When his hand slid beneath her gown, ran up her leg, up her thigh, touched her so intimately, traced circles around the tight, throbbing nub hidden there, instead of being shocked, she gasped, for his teasing touch only made the torment so much more inescapable. She sought out his lips and kissed him, her hands ran beneath his surcoat, around his leggings.

Unlike breeches, his leggings left no means to conceal what was beneath them – a hard masculine line straining to be freed. And she ached to release him. Find her own release from this wild fire he stoked inside her. So she brazenly traced her fingers over his form, stroked him, boldly reaching inside his leggings to free him.

He moved, instinctively, atop her, poised to take her, fill her and then, suddenly, his eyes widened, as if he were awakening from a dream.

He brushed the hair back from her face, his breath coming in ragged sighs. "You've never—"

She knew what he meant. Never done this. Not trusting herself to say the words, she just shook her head.

He started to pull away. "This is madness. We shouldn't . . . But dammit, my fey little beauty, you have bewitched me."

And him her. "Then take me," she whispered, feeling the morning tide pulling her away from him. "Please, I am yours," she said, shocked by her own bold and impassioned plea.

"Then you realize what that means. If I have you now, I will have you for ever." His mouth curved into a smile.

But how could she tell him there was no for ever for them. That tomorrow she would be well and gone from London. There was no time for him to save her.

Save from the bonfire of desire crackling inside her.

"This is how it ought to be," she told him, reaching up and cradling his face. To reinforce her words, she arched her hips up to brush against him, nudge him to come closer, to fill her.

She pulled his head down and kissed him. They began again, kissing and touching and exploring and the fury of their early moments became an exquisite dance. And when he entered her, he did it slowly, allowing her to feel the pleasure of each stroke, so when he breached her barrier, it was over and done and then there was only pleasure . . . Sweet euphoric pleasure that surrounded them both, drove them both until once again they were riding that wild cadence that had ensnared them earlier but this time it brought them both to a heady release.

Ella gasped as the first wave of sensuous gratification came over her, filled as she was by him, covered by him, surrounded by him and so she caught hold of him and clung to him, as her body drowned in the sweet pleasure.

And she wasn't alone, for he made a deep groan and stroked her wildly and deeply as he too found his release.

He collapsed into her arms and they clung to each other, marvelling in the starry world they had found in each other's arms.

A little while later, he rose from the couch and pulled her up as well. Glancing behind her, he laughed a bit. "I fear I've broken more than just your wings."

She caught a glimpse of herself and saw the real problem – there was no disguising the fact that she'd been tumbled. Besides her dishevelled curls, the lost petals in her crown, the wrinkled state of her gown, there was no mistaking the starry light of wonder in her eyes.

Oh, good heavens, that is what it means to be loved, she realized, her hands coming to her cheeks. She doubted very much that this was what Mrs Garraway had meant when she'd told her to enjoy herself.

Behind her, her knight took her in his arms and pulled her against his chest, then he tipped his chin up and kissed her. After a few more kisses, he tried to straighten out her flowered crown and resettle it atop her tangled hair. He finally gave up and laughed at his own lopsided attempts, handing her back the fairy crown. As she went over to the mirror to set it to rights and make what repairs she could, she heard him say, "I never believed in the legend, until tonight."

"The legend?" Ella said, distracted by the tangle of curls before her. Oh, good heavens, she wouldn't have to wait until tomorrow to be sacked. Even near-sighted old Lady Osborn would be able to see what she'd done.

"The Ashe legend," he said over his shoulder as he pulled on his boots. "About finding a bride at the ball. I had rather thought it a bit of madness cooked up to get reluctant heirs to marry."

Ella stepped back and eyed her work – not bad, she almost looked as she had earlier, save one missing earbob. Turning to look for it, she told him, "Well, you needn't fear such a legend, because I believe it only applies to Lord Ashe."

Then there was a long silence, one that said more than a declaration of the truth.

Lord Ashe? "No!" she gasped, as she slowly raised her gaze to his. He couldn't be.

"I thought you knew," he said. "But it is no matter, the only problem is my mother."

"Your mother?" she forced past her suddenly parched throat.

"Yes. She'll be crowing for weeks. She worked over that damned invitation list of hers and vowed I would find a suitable bride tonight. She left nothing to chance as she wanted me well matched. And now I am. Perfectly so."

"And you think—" It was all Ella could manage to get out.

"That you are perfect? Yes, in every way."

Ella groaned. "Oh, this cannot be." He couldn't be Lord Ashe.

"I thought you knew," he repeated.

She shook her head. "No, I never!"

"Does it make a difference?"

However was she to answer that? Did it make a difference to her? No, he was still the most wonderful man she'd ever met. But he thought her to be a lady. One of his mother's eligible misses.

Not Ella Cynders, a mere companion. Make that a "disgraced-without-references-and-unemployed" companion.

Suddenly the blare of a trumpet pierced the solitude that had surrounded them.

"Excellent," he said. "Time for the unmasking and our announcement." He held out his hand for her.

"Announcement?"

"Of our engagement." He drew her close again and kissed her forehead. "That was the point of the ball. So I could find a bride. And I have found you. If you think I am letting you go, you are most mistaken."

"But I-I-I . . ." she stammered. "That is . . . Oh, the devil take me, this is happening too fast."

He glanced at her as he towed her from the room. "Don't you want to get married?"

"Well, yes," she said without thinking, for she was too busy trying to find a way out of this muddle. She couldn't be unmasked, couldn't have him announce his engagement to a mere hired companion.

He'd be the laughing stock of London.

She had to tell him, and tell him quickly, that she couldn't be his bride.

"I suppose you will want to tell your guardian first. Of course," Lord Ashe was saying as he drew her closer and closer to the ballroom. "That is understandable."

Tell her guardian? She didn't have a guardi . . . Ella's panic had her digging her heels into the carpet. Not that Ashe noticed her reluctance. He all but carried her along, as if her leaden steps were nothing of note.

As for Ella . . . She had to imagine that Mrs Garraway's ship wouldn't be sailing soon enough to get her out of London. Lady Osborn would have her thrown in Newgate before the sun was up, for bringing this scandal down upon them.

If I can find Mrs Garraway, maybe she can help, Ella thought desperately. *Maybe she can get me out of here before . . .*

Just then they slipped into the ballroom and Lord Ashe turned to her, beaming. "Go speak to your guardian and be ready when I call for you." He winked. "Just for a few more moments, and then you will be mine always." Before she could stop him, before she could confess the truth, he turned and strode confidently, proudly, through the crowd, towards the dais where his mother was waiting for him to announce the unmasking.

Ella drew an unsteady breath as he moved away from her. The further he went the more she felt him slipping away.

"There you are!" Lady Osborn said, coming up from behind her. "Where have you been, Pamela?" And then she looked at the young lady she assumed was her daughter.

Ella had to imagine that her hasty attempt to salvage her costume and her tumbled hair had failed given the lady's wide-eyed expression of horror.

"What have you done?" she hissed, coming closer and taking Ella by the arm, dragging her towards the door. "Who did this to you? Is it that wretched Lord Percy? Because if he thinks to press his suit in this sort of despicable manner, he is sadly mistaken. Your father and I will never allow you—" By now Lady Osborn had dragged Ella out to the foyer and had her pinned in an alcove. The lady stood so close that not only could she see every bit of evidence of Ella's rumpled condition, but one other pertinent fact.

That the girl she held wasn't her daughter.

"Ella!" she said, releasing her and stepping back.

"Lady Osborn," Ella replied, tipping her head, and fixing her gaze on the floor.

The matron glanced around and then caught Ella by the arm, rattling her like a rag doll. "Where is my daughter?"

Ella bit her lip and tried to speak. She tried to confess the truth, but the woman was hurting her, her unforgiving grasp like a pair of steel pinchers.

"Never mind, I can guess." Lady Osborn pulled her towards the door. "She's run off with that wicked boy."

Ella took a furtive glance at the ballroom, where Lord Ashe stood unmasked. She could see him scanning the room, looking for her.

The last thing she saw before Lady Osborn hauled her out the door was the startled expression on his handsome face as he caught sight of her.

But it was too late. Ella was about to pay the piper for her impetuous nature and there was naught her knight could do to reach her in time.

Four

The Ashe Ball – 1815

Ella took a deep breath when the carriage stopped before the Ashe townhouse. *I shouldn't be doing this. I shouldn't.*

But now it was far too late to back out, for too many others had put their own employment on the line for her to disavow them.

Oh, Hazel, what did I let you do? she thought, as the handsome footman – one of three – opened the door and held out his hand to her. This was all Hazel's doing – the elegant carriage driven by a well-appointed set of matching white horses, a coachman, and three footmen, all courtesy of the Marquess of Holbech, who was currently in Scotland at his hunting box and had no knowledge of his brand-new and as-yet-unmarked carriage being used in this manner.

But Hazel's flirtatious romance with one of his footmen was enough to gain its illicit use. And, as it turned out, the Marquess' old coachman had a romantic streak. He managed to rummage up some old, unremarkable livery for them to wear so they wouldn't be identified.

"Remember, madam," Hazel's swain said quietly as he handed Ella down to the kerb. "Before midnight. We must be away."

She nodded, drawing her cloak around her and pulling its hood down over her face. She ascended the stairs to the grand front door. Other guests were arriving as well and there was a bit of a queue to enter – for each guest had to present their invitation to pass inside.

As she neared the door, a familiar voice cut through the excited whispers around her. "I say, I have an invitation but it was stolen!" Lady Fitzsimon complained. "Now let us in!"

Ella glanced up to find the matron and her daughter standing before the butler, holding up the procession. Ella was glad for her mask, and did a second check to make sure her gown wasn't showing under the concealing cloak. But still, if the lady recognized her . . .

Not that this was likely to happen, for Lady Fitzsimon was in a rare mood, facing down the Ashe butler like Wellington's troops charging forth. She was going to breach this party if it took her all night.

The butler snapped his fingers at one of the footmen to continue checking invitations so the front steps didn't turn into a crush.

Ella handed over her invite and held her breath until the man waved her inside, and began checking the invitations of the others behind her. She hurried along, Lady Fitzsimon's shrill notes chasing her inside.

"I say, I was invited!" the matron complained, her voice rising sharply, almost hysterically. "I will not be denied entrance. If you would but tell Lady Ashe to come to the door, she would order you immediately to admit me and my daughter."

"Madam," the butler intoned, "Lady Ashe's rules are simple. No invitation, no entrance."

A tall, graceful lady and her equally noble husband came to a stop beside Ella. The woman glanced over her shoulder at Lady Fitzsimon and then back at Ella. "Dreadful woman. No manners."

"Yes, quite," Ella replied, imitating the same bored, elegant tones.

"Oh, heavens, I can't recall where the retiring room is," the woman said, before turning to one of the footmen. "Which way?"

He bowed slightly and then pointed up the stairs, not that Ella needed directions. She'd imagined the Ashe house over and over these past five years.

"Come along, my dear," the lady said. "I do so hate going up alone."

As they made their way up the stairs, Ella shot a glance towards the ballroom, searching for her knight errant. But in the crowd of guests, it was impossible to find him – then again, she remembered, he would be in costume.

Not that she thought he could hide his identity from her. Not even after all these years. Still, whatever was she going to say to him?

They went upstairs and, to Ella's relief, Hazel and Martha were there, helping the guests and making small repairs to various ladies' costumes. Madame Delaflote often hired them out, at a considerable profit, to provide these services.

Hazel nudged Martha when Ella arrived, and Hazel hurried over to help her take off her cloak.

The moment the cloak was removed, an awed hush came over the crowded room, as all eyes turned towards Ella. Her costume, her hair – done up in a cascade of curls that fell down to her back – the glitter of the silver embroidery, and the soft glow of a thousand seed pearls, caused a sensation.

"You made it in," Hazel whispered, as she checked Ella's back to make certain her wings were still intact.

"Yes, your friends played their part perfectly."

The girl grinned. "This is the best lark—"

"That could end with us all being sacked. Lady Fitzsimon is downstairs determined to get in."

Hazel waved her off. "Let her try. She hasn't an invitation. As for being sacked . . ." The girl shrugged and then glanced around the room. Every eye was on the two of them. Well, on Ella. Hazel went back to work, with her nose in the air, setting Ella's gown to rights. "We'll not be sacked. For when you are Lady Ashe, Madame Delaflote won't dare." She knelt down and straightened the hemline. And with that completed, Hazel curtseyed slightly and said, "All is well, your highness."

Ella's eyes widened even as a gossipy trill ran through the room.

"A princess?"

"But from where?"

"Have you seen such a gown?"

Hazel sent her a cheeky wink and then there was nothing left for Ella to do but to go and face her past.

Lord Ashe stood in the ballroom and watched the parade of masked and costumed debutantes, ladies and likely brides stroll past.

But none of them was her.

And tonight was his last chance to find her. Not that he had much hope left. For every year, as each subsequent ball came and went, and she hadn't arrived, he'd begun to wonder if she'd ever existed, his lady in green silk.

Where are you? he mused. We are running out of time.

Then a strange hushed air moved through the crowd, followed by a tremor of whispers. One after another, the guests turned towards the entrance to gaze at the latest arrival.

Ashe stilled as he spied the graceful lady making her entrance.

No, it couldn't be her. It couldn't be.

But then she turned her head and he spied something he had dared not hope to see. For on the back of her costume perched a pair of gossamer wings. *Fairy wings.*

Ashe pushed his way forwards without thinking. He ignored the insulted gasps of his guests pressing his way through the crowd, even as speculative whispers whirled around him.

"A princess, I heard."

"Russian, I believe."

"Wherever did she get that costume?"

Then before he realized it, she stood before him.

"You!" he exclaimed. "I've found you!"

She smiled at him, her blue eyes twinkling behind her mask. "No, I believe I found you."

"It doesn't matter how you've come back," he told her, catching her by the hand and drawing her into his arms. "I won't lose you again." Then, to seal his vow, his head dipped down and his lips captured hers.

The night from five years ago came back to him in rich clarity. It was her, the same sweet response, the same curves, the same soft sigh as he deepened his kiss and plundered her lips without any thought of propriety. And when he pulled back and held her at arm's length, he could only exclaim, "Devil take me, my love, I cannot believe I have found you."

"Believe again," she whispered, raising her lips to his and again, they kissed, much to the shocked gasps of the company around them.

"I have imagined this so many times," he whispered in her ear.

"You have?" She sounded surprised.

"Yes, of course," he told her. "You left me bewitched and lost that night."

"I did?" Truly, how could she be so surprised? Hadn't that night meant as much to her?

"Yes, you did," he told her with every bit of his heart, and an unabashed grin from ear to ear.

Her eyes sparkled beneath her mask. "And now?"

He grinned even more if that was possible. "I am still yours, my fey sweet love, if you will have me."

"I . . ." she stammered, much as she had years before, and he realized he had to tread carefully lest he frighten her off yet again. He hadn't another five years to wait.

The musicians struck up their instruments and Ashe smiled at her, holding her slim hand in his. "Come, you owe me this dance. One of many, I might add. I've been waiting all these years for your return."

He unmasked himself then led her out to the dance floor, to the amazed and scandalized stares of his guests. For it appeared to one and all that the Ashe legend was about to come true and the viscount had found his bride.

More than one matron with an unmarried daughter in tow and her hopes now dashed for an advantageous marriage, cursed this interloper, this princess from out of nowhere.

Ashe led her out to where the couples were lining up for the first set and, when the music began, it was as if time had not moved a tick since the ball five years earlier.

"Your hair is red," he teased as they came together.

"Are you disappointed?"

"No, enchanted. It is glorious," he whispered. He knew what it felt like, but now he could see the ginger strands and honeyed colours. He imagined what those silken tresses would look like spread out over his sheets, unbound and cascading all over her naked shoulders. "The colour matches your unmanageable temperament, as I recall."

She laughed. "You remember!"

"There is nothing I have forgotten," he told her.

They turned and moved down a long line of dancers before being reunited at the end of the floor.

"I see you found new wings," he commented. "Did you lose your other ones when you took flight last time?"

She shook her head at him. "I outgrew them. Besides, they were never mine to wear."

"So I discovered when I went looking for you."

Beneath her mask, her eyes widened. "You looked for me?"

"How could you imagine that I would not?"

Once again they made their way down the line of dancers and when they got to the end, she turned to him. "Do you know who I am?"

He grinned and shook his head. "And I'm not the only one curious to discover the truth, my fairy princess." Ashe nodded to the circle of guests around the ballroom, all gazes fixed on the two of them. "I believe you've created a sensation, Your Highness."

She leaned in a bit. "There was a mistake in the retiring room – a suggestion that I am a princess."

"Are you?"

His lady love laughed, this time heartily. "Oh, good heavens, no!"

"I am glad of that."

"Why?"

"Because I suspect there would be all manners of protocol and such to marrying a princess, and I have no patience now that I've found you again."

She shook her head and glanced shyly up into his gaze. "And it doesn't matter to you who I am?"

"No. I was destined to find my bride that night, and I did. You wouldn't have been there that night if we weren't meant to be together."

She laughed, a musical sound that brought back memories for him. "When did you become such a romantic?"

Now it was his turn to laugh. "When you ran out and left me naught a clue to be found. You could have at the very least left me a slipper."

"Or my wings?" she teased back.

"They might have helped, but I doubt the mothers of London would have appreciated me wandering about trying them on their daughters," he said, before he leaned closer to her ear, "or asking them if their little girl had a cute bit of freckle on her—"

She swatted him playfully and danced down the line away from him. Ashe watched her every step and, when they rejoined each other, she said, "I see you haven't lost a bit of your wickedness."

"Do you mind?"

"Not in the least," she replied.

They danced for a few more minutes in silence, just gazing at each other. To Ashe, she was lovelier than he remembered, from the gorgeous mane of red hair down to her slippers. She seemed less fragile than she had those many years earlier.

"Where have you been?" he asked. "And don't you dare tell me you got married."

"No, nothing like that." She tipped her head slightly. "I went away. It seemed the sensible solution at the time."

"Sensible? Not to me! And what do you mean, away? Away where?"

"Far away," she told him. "I thought it best."

"Best for who?" he said. "You stole my heart, you minx." He pulled her close, closer than was necessary for the dance, and whispered in her ear, "Let me guess, you were deserting heartbroken men from one side of the Continent to another."

She shook her head, lips twitching with mirth. "No. I haven't been doing anything like that."

"And when did you come back to London?"

"Six months ago," she confessed.

"And why didn't you come to me?"

It seemed an eternity before she answered. "I almost did," she said, a tremble to her voice. "But I didn't know—"

He stopped in the middle of the floor. "Know what?"

"I didn't know if you would forgive me. Or what that night had meant to you—"

"Did it mean anything to you?"

"More than you could know."

"Then prove it. Say you will marry me."

Then came a loud outburst that drowned out her response. For a red-faced, furious matron at the doorway to the Ashe ballroom stopped the evening cold, as she shouted at the top of her lungs, "That woman is a thief and an imposter!"

Five

Ashe stalked back and forth in front of the breakfast table where his mother sat eating her morning repast as if nothing were amiss.

"I lost her, Mother! Again!" In the chaos of the Lady Fitzsimon's shouted accusations, his lady love, his fairy queen, had managed to slip through the crowd and get out of the house.

One of the servants had seen her leaving through the garden.

Lady Ashe nodded and smiled and buttered her toast without a word.

"How will I ever find her again? I don't even know her name."

"You looked as if you knew each other quite intimately," his mother said. It wasn't so much a scold . . . But really, such a kiss! And in front of the guests. Then again, hadn't her husband kissed her in much the same manner the night they had fallen in love? But he'd had the decency to steal her off to the conservatory on some ridiculous pretence that the oranges were in bloom.

"What if Lady Fitzsimon gets to her first?" he said. "She'll have her thrown in prison."

"Lady Fitzsimon *will* most likely get to her first," Lady Ashe said.

That froze her son's steps. "Mother, that is the last thing we want to happen."

She shrugged and continued eating her breakfast.

Julian paused before the table. "How can you be so certain that Lady Fitzsimon knows where she is?"

"Because I, just like Lady Fitzsimon, know exactly where that dress came from."

She glanced up at him and he looked ready to burst. Yes, he was in love with that girl and there would be no setting her aside. He'd loved her all these years and no other lady would brighten his heart. Good. It was exactly as it should be. So she pushed aside the tablecloth and pulled from beneath the table a set of gossamer wings. "She lost these last night."

"Why didn't you tell me this before?" he exploded.

Lady Ashe smiled, wiped her lips with her napkin. "Because I wanted to finish my breakfast before we went and fetched your future wife home."

Ella emerged from the basement room that she shared with Hazel and Martha a miserable wreck. She'd been able to escape the Ashe Ball the night before – her knowledge of the house suddenly becoming rather convenient.

Once she'd found her trusty carriage and helpers, they had whisked her home and scattered into the night. When Hazel and Martha had arrived so many hours later, she had sobbed out the entire story on their sympathetic shoulders.

Now the morning had come and Ella knew the reckoning, the one she'd avoided all those years ago, was about to come to roost. But perhaps it was as Hazel averred – there had been no crime committed. Madame Delaflote had demanded that Ella pay for the gown, so technically it was hers. She had found the invitation on the floor of the shop. There was no theft whatsoever.

Not that Madame would see it that way. She'd sack Ella for bringing this scandal down upon her shop, she'd—

Ella's wayward thoughts came to an abrupt halt as she parted the curtain before going about the business of opening. She spied a crowd of ladies and onlookers outside, all queued up and waiting for the shop to open. Several of them waved at her and others pointed at the door, in hopes of enticing her to open the shop early.

Lady Fitzsimon stood front and centre with a pair of Robin Redbreasts at the ready. She hadn't wasted any time and was here to exact her reckoning. But that sight didn't frighten Ella as much as did the tall, handsome figure of Lord Ashe standing at the back of the crowd.

He was here!

Ella whirled around and hid behind the curtain. He'd found her after all.

Hazel and Martha had just come upstairs and were rubbing their sleepy eyes.

"What is it?" Martha asked.

"Is something wrong?" Hazel said, then glanced over Ella's shoulder. "Is *she* out there?" "She" being Lady Fitzsimon.

Ella nodded her head.

"Is *he* out there?" Martha asked.

She nodded again.

"Well, let him in and see what he has to say. I still wager he's here to propose. Then he'll send that old cow packing." Hazel pushed past Ella and went out into the main shop but then came to an instant standstill, much as Ella had done previously. "Oh, my stars! He's brought half of London with him."

At this point, Madame arrived, coming down the stairs from her rooms above. She glanced at the lot of them and sighed. "What is this? Standing about? The shop needs to be readied. I want—" She pushed open the curtain and discovered the mob outside.

She whirled around on her employees. "Whatever have you done?" But before any of them could answer, she took another glance at all the anxious and happy faces outside – well, except those belonging to Lady Fitzsimon and her police officers. "Oh, *la*! It matters not – I'll be rich before this day is out. Get those doors open!"

Martha bobbed a curtsey, and made her way to the door. The moment the doors sprang open the shop was filled with people and a cacophony of requests.

"I would like a gown from that green silk."

"Can you do my costume for the Setchfield masquerade?"

"I would like the same design of gown as the princess wore last night."

"I want that gel arrested for theft! She stole my gown and my invitation!"

But the loudest and most commanding request came from Lord Ashe. "I am here to fetch my bride. Bring her out immediately."

This stilled every pair of lips in the shop. Even Lady Fitzsimon's.

"Gar," Hazel whispered. "It is just like a fairy tale." Then she pushed Ella through the curtain and into Ashe's waiting arms.

And like any good fairy tale, it all ended with a kiss.

His Wicked Revenge

Vanessa Kelly

Wapping, London

It started with a woman and it would end with a woman. This woman. The one Anthony Barnett had been dreaming about for thirteen years. The one who would now be the instrument of his revenge.

Lady Paget – Marissa, to her close friends and family – studied his sombre office, taking in the dark, heavy furniture and the stacks of bound shipping ledgers. She looked everywhere but at him.

Not that he could blame her. His summons to her brother, Lord Joslin, had been carefully worded, but the threat had been clear. Marissa was to appear at Nightingale Trading by noon today or the entire Joslin family would suffer the consequences.

Anthony maintained his silence, knowing victory would be sweeter when Marissa finally came to him of her own volition. Step by reluctant step. She had already taken the first one by coming down to his dockside warehouse. The next would be when she worked up the nerve to look him directly in the eye.

The casement clock by the door ticked out the seconds as she inspected everything in the room worth inspecting. Eventually, like a disobedient child dragging her feet, she slowly lifted her gaze to meet his. Her pale eyes, the colour of a clear winter sky, fixed on him with reluctant attention. A hint of shame pooled in those cool blue depths. At the sight of it, a grim satisfaction settled in Anthony's chest. She could no longer ignore him, and had now stepped willingly into his carefully laid trap.

He finally had Marissa where he wanted her, and there wasn't a damn thing she could do about it.

"The light is poor in here, but I think you are greatly changed," she said in a flat, toneless voice. "I hardly recognize you."

He frowned. What had she expected? The last time she had seen him, he'd been a callow youth, and a weedy one at that. Years spent at sea had toughened him – hardened him in ways she couldn't imagine. She had changed as well, and in ways he had not expected.

Marissa retained the feminine power to command his complete attention, of course. But she had always chattered and sparkled like a rippling brook, full of laughter and mischief. Now she was subdued, even colourless – a muted reflection of her youthful self.

Reluctantly, he recalled the last time he had seen her, the night his life reached both a beginning and an end. Then she had been full of life and beauty – so joyously in love that his heart had well nigh burst with glory of it. The beauty remained, with her tall, slender figure and hair spun from moonlight. But the glow that had lit up his world had faded. Now her allure had become unearthly, even remote. Lovely but cold, like an Alpine lake before the spring thaw.

Anthony abandoned his post by the window that overlooked the docks and his growing shipping empire. He prowled across the room, halting in front of her, deliberately crowding her against a bookcase. This close, he could inhale her perfume – faint and scented with jasmine – and the sweetness that had always been Marissa. That, at least, had not changed. His body recognized the subtle scent, responding with a flash of heat and a sharpening of all his senses. Almost unconsciously he leaned into her, wanting more.

As she flinched and stepped back, Anthony scowled. Marissa had never trembled before anyone, not even her bastard of a father in one of his towering rages.

He waged a brief internal struggle to ignore the long and lamentably ingrained impulse to protect her. She had forfeited such a right years ago, and his current plans called for exactly the opposite of protection.

"Lady Paget, please sit down. I'm sure you're as eager to begin our discussion as I am."

She muttered something under her breath and stepped around him to the hard cherry-wood chair in front of his desk. With a spine as straight as an oak mast, she perched on the edge of the seat, looking as if she were facing a roomful of Barbary pirates.

He wasn't a pirate – he was her first lover. The man she had sworn to love for ever but instead had betrayed, breaking all the vows they had made so many years ago.

Rather than settling into his own leather chair, he leaned against the edge of his massive desk, deliberately looming over her. She edged back in her seat, trying to put distance between them. But distance between them, at least of the physical sort, wasn't part of his strategy.

Marissa took a deep breath and raised her gaze to meet his. Heat infused those eyes now, fire and ice clashing to a devastating effect. It jolted him that look, sending a heady lust roaring through his veins. He smiled, knowing he wouldn't wait much longer to bed her.

His smile seemed to discompose her. She cleared her throat.

"Mr Barnett—" she began.

"Captain Barnett," he interrupted, nodding towards the window. "Those are my ships out there in the Thames."

Frost clashed with the fire in her eyes, dousing the heat. Her lips curled in an aristocratic sneer. "Forgive me. I had no idea you had done so well. As I was about to say, I would be grateful for an explanation behind the missive you sent my brother. He was not well pleased to hear from you. It was only with great reluctance that he agreed to your demand that I come to your office, unescorted but for my maid."

"I do like to observe at least the appearance of propriety," he replied sardonically.

Obviously, Lord Joslin had not seen fit to explain to his sister why he was forced to accede to Anthony's demands. Marissa likely had no idea just how far in debt her brother really was.

With a puzzled shake of her neatly trimmed bonnet, she continued. "Since I am here, I would like an explanation. Your business is clearly with Edmund – Lord Joslin, rather. I fail to see why I must be brought into it. Whatever it is."

With that last phrase, some of the old defiance came back into her voice. Time to switch tack and keep her off-balance.

"You have a daughter, I understand," he said, stretching out his legs so his booted feet almost touched her shoes.

She froze, gloved hands clutching her large reticule in a convulsive grip. Long-lashed eyes searched his face, as if looking for the answer to a question she didn't want to ask. "Yes," she replied in a hesitant voice.

"How old is she?"

She paused. An odd expression, one almost akin to panic, flashed across her features.

Bloody hell.

You'd have thought he'd asked her to strip down to her shift, right here in his office. Not that the idea hadn't crossed his mind. He'd already calculated how long it would take him to unfasten the long line of buttons that marched up her elegant but severely tailored pelisse. That pleasant task, however, must wait for another day.

She pressed her rosy lips together, as if holding in a great secret that longed to escape. "My daughter is not yet twelve," she admitted grudgingly.

Anthony gave her a disdainful smile. "You didn't waste any time, did you? How long were you married to Paget before you whelped?"

She flared up at him, just like the Marissa he used to know. "It's not like I had any choice in the matter," she retorted. "I was engaged to be married to Sir Richard, as you recall."

"Oh, yes. I recall everything," he said. "I remember how desperate you were to break your engagement. So desperate you begged me to elope with you to Gretna Green."

She closed her eyes, fighting to regain her control. After a few moments, she opened them. Her stare was once again cool and remote.

A reluctant admiration stirred within him. Marissa would never have reined in her temper so quickly. Lady Paget was obviously made of stern stuff.

"What is your daughter's name?" he asked abruptly.

A muscle in her cheek jumped, but she gave him a fierce scowl. "Why these pointless questions, Captain? Please get to the business at hand and be done with it. I have no intention of spending the entire afternoon in Wapping."

He shrugged, crossing his arms over his chest. "My point is simple. I assume that you would do anything to protect your daughter, is that not correct?"

Marissa had always been pale, but what little colour remained in her cheeks leached away. Her perfect features froze into immobility. Except for her blazing blue eyes, she might have been carved from alabaster.

"Why . . . why would you ask me such a thing?" she stuttered. "Of course I would do anything to protect my child."

"Then we shall deal very well together," he said, not bothering to hide the triumph in his voice.

She gasped, swaying in her chair. He launched himself up from his desk and caught her by the shoulders as she began to slide off the polished seat.

"Damn it, Marissa!"

Anthony kept a firm grip on her shoulders, letting her head rest against his stomach. Guilt lanced through his gut. He clamped down hard, resisting the compulsion to sweep her out of the chair and into his embrace.

Her slender body trembled under his hands. He couldn't see her face, couldn't even tell if she had actually swooned. The rim of her bonnet not only obscured his view, it was poking him in the gut.

Carefully, he slid her across the polished seat of the chair to rest against the high ladder-back. With a quick tug, he untied her bonnet and dropped it to the floor. Her corn silk hair, coiled around her head in tight braids, gleamed in the dull November sunlight coming through the window. Like her simple pelisse, her grey kid gloves and her sturdy reticule, her glorious tresses were as neatly contained as her emotions.

Until he had made his thinly veiled threat against her daughter, that is.

He hunkered down before her, taking her hands in a gentle clasp. "Would you like a brandy? It will help to revive you."

She gave a small shake of her head. "No. Please give me my reticule."

He plucked it from the floor by her chair, where she had dropped it. "What do you need? Smelling salts?" He began to rummage around in the voluminous bag.

"My handkerchief, please," she said in a thin voice.

Pushing away the growing remorse that threatened to destroy all his exacting plans, he dug around in the overstuffed reticule until he felt a square of starched linen. "What in God's name are you carrying around in this thing?" he grumbled as he extracted the handkerchief. "You could store a frigate's cargo in here."

She ignored him, keeping her eyes closed as she blotted her fore-head, cheeks and then her full, ripe lips.

His mouth suddenly went dry. He remembered those lips very well. They could take a man to heaven. "Marissa, are you sure you don't want a brandy?" Of its own accord, his voice had fallen to a deep, husky note.

She opened her eyes. A gaze as hard as diamonds – and just as cold – stared back at him. She jerked her hands from his loose grasp. "I did not give you leave to use my name, Captain Barnett. Do not do so again."

The treacherous warmth stealing over him fled under her withering look. Anger – his daily companion – took its place. He welcomed it.

He rose to his feet, resuming his perch on the edge of the desk.

"Now, Marissa," he chided. "We're the oldest of friends. Why should you stand on ceremony? You never did before."

"I was young. I didn't know any better," she retorted.

Her temper brought the roses back to her cheeks and the heat back into her eyes. For the moment, the ice maiden stood in no danger of fainting.

"And neither did I," he said in a hard voice. "But you came to me, remember? You begged me to save you from marriage to Paget. You swore your undying love. Your eternal devotion if I eloped with you to Gretna Green."

"I was only seventeen," she protested.

"And I was but eighteen."

In the world's eyes, Anthony had been a man when he and Marissa lost their virginity to each other. But he had been so sheltered, raised by his widowed father in a small country parsonage. When he was ten, his father had died and Anthony had been dispatched to live with his distant cousin, Lord Joslin, and his family. He spent the rest of his youth on their estate in Yorkshire, deep in study, preparing to follow in his father's clerical footsteps.

Through those years, he had also fallen in love with Marissa, and she with him. Or so he had always thought. Anthony's mouth twisted into a sour smile, remembering how young and foolish he had been. In many ways, Marissa had always been more worldly than he.

"Do you want to know what happened that night?" he asked. "After Edmund discovered us together in my bed? After your father horse-whipped me and drove me from Joslin Manor?"

She blanched and, for a moment, he thought she might faint after all. But she took a deep breath and regained her composure.

"I don't know what kind of cruel game you are playing, Captain," she replied with quiet dignity. "But if reciting your tale will bring this tawdry scene to a conclusion then, yes. I do want to know."

Anthony gave her a humourless smile. "I'm sure you'll find my tale of woe edifying, Lady Paget."

He pushed up from his desk, tasting the bitterness in his mouth and throat. It was always thus whenever he recalled those months after he first arrived in London – those months spent waiting for her to come and find him. Those months of back-breaking work and near starvation, his life barely a step up from the mudlarks who scavenged along the Thames.

"After discovering us naked in each other's arms," he said, prowling around his office, "your brother ran straight to Viscount

Joslin. Your father had two grooms hold me down, then he beat me until my back was shredded raw."

Marissa made a choked sound, but held her tongue. What could she say to soften such a painful and humiliating memory?

"Did you know Edmund stood there grinning while he watched your father beat me?" he asked, curious to find out how much she knew about the scene that remained burned into his memory.

"No," she said, her eyes betraying her shock. "And Father forbade me to ever mention your name again."

He resumed his prowl around the room.

"After he beat me half to death, your father threw me out of the house without a shilling to my name. Thank God the housekeeper took pity on me and gave me some coin to make my way to London. Her brother was a clerk at Nightingale Trading. She said he would find me work if he could, or at least give me a few days' shelter while I looked for means to support myself."

"Was there no one else you could turn to?" she asked, looking miserable.

"I had no friends who could be of assistance. As for relations," he said dryly, "that would be your family. The Joslins were the only relatives I had left in the world after my father died. Not that the Viscount had wanted me. He only took me in because your mother insisted."

She gazed down at her lap. "I'm truly sorry."

Anthony paused, surprised by the heartfelt sorrow in her voice. Perhaps she did regret betraying him after all.

But he hardened his heart. Marissa had always been able to twist him around her little finger. He wouldn't let that happen again, not when he was inches away from his vengeance against her and her pig of a brother.

He resumed his pacing. "I made my way to London – some of it on foot, by the way. From Yorkshire."

She winced, but he kept ruthlessly on.

"I came to Wapping, and to the housekeeper's brother. He found work for me on the docks. It wasn't steady, but it gave me enough to rent a garret and to eat. Not often, mind you. And never enough. But I had something else to keep me alive. Something to give me hope that things would get better."

With a quick step he moved in front of her, reaching out to grasp the back of her chair, caging her in with his body. She gasped and shrank away in startled retreat.

He lowered his head until he could stare directly into those amazing eyes. Her pupils dilated, her breath coming in rapid pants. She smelled sweet, like sugar plums and mint.

"Do you remember your promise to me?" he whispered.

Her lips opened on another gasp, and he watched fascinated as the tip of her pink tongue slipped out to wet her lips. His groin took notice, as did every other part of his body.

Soon, he promised himself. He would take her – body and soul – and slake his never-ending thirst.

"I know you remember," he breathed, hovering just inches from her pretty mouth.

She ducked, sliding out from under his arms. In a flash, she was by the door to his clerk's office, her ridiculously large reticule clutched in front of her like a weapon. Which, given how heavy it was, it very well could be.

He let out a reluctant laugh. She had always been as quick as a lark spiralling over a meadow in springtime.

"Obviously, you do remember," he said. "You made a promise – a vow – that you would never abandon me. That we would never abandon each other. No matter the separation, you would find me, or I, you." He paused, waiting for a response. But her face was a blank, revealing no emotion. "I waited for you, Marissa. For months. Certain you would find me. I worked like a slave, putting away every shilling I could against that day. I thought that when you finally found me, we would leave England for America, where we could start a new life."

An acid taste rose in his mouth as he thought of the idiotic boy he had been.

"There was nothing I could do," she replied in a bleak voice. "Father made sure of that. I didn't know where to look. What to do. And then . . ." She trailed off.

"And then you married Sir Richard so you could be the pampered wife of a wealthy baronet, didn't you? Only four weeks after I was run off like a mangy cur. But I didn't hear of the wedding until six months later. Six months spent slaving on the docks, going hungry, saving every coin I earned for you – for us."

The old sense of loss rushed in on him, squeezing his chest with iron bands. Suddenly, he found he had backed her into the corner of the room.

Her back stiff and straight against the wall, Marissa tilted her head to meet his gaze. The coldness in those blue depths thrust leagues of distance between them.

"What would you have me say?" she challenged. "That I'm sorry? Of course I am. More than you'll ever know. But I can't do anything about it, nor can I erase the terrible things that happened to you."

He shrugged, feigning indifference. "No, you can't, and thank God for it. When I heard you were married and had been for months, I realized what a fool I was. That I meant nothing to you. All those expressions of undying devotion were meaningless – just smoke in the wind."

This time she did flinch, turning her head away. He waited for her to say something, but her lips remained pressed together in a thin, unforgiving line.

Anger and an odd sense of disappointment pulsed through him. What had he expected? That she would profess her undying love for him? After all these years? Disgusted with himself, he retreated behind his desk and sat.

"Don't you want to hear the rest of the story?" he asked, affecting a bored voice.

Without a word, she walked to the chair and sat down again. Her weary eyes seemed full of shadows and ghosts.

After a short struggle to repress a stirring of pity, Anthony resumed his tale. "After I learned of your marriage to Sir Richard, I had no more reason to stay in London. I signed up as a deckhand on one of Nightingale's ships. Oddly enough, I discovered I had an aptitude for the sea, and I moved up quickly. The company made me captain of a frigate by the age of twenty-six – their youngest ever. Nightingale Shipping prospered, especially during the war years. By twenty-nine, I was rich, and able to buy out Thomas Nightingale when he was ready to retire."

He turned, looking out the window at the sea of masts on the river. "Those beautiful ships are mine," he said with intense satisfaction. "And Nightingale is one of the finest trading companies in all of England."

Her soft voice held a wistful note. "You've done well, Captain. I'm happy for you."

He swung around, putting her directly in his sights. "But that's not the best part, My Lady. As you can imagine, I never forgot what your family did to me. To my regret, your father died before I could settle with him, but your brother will stand in quite nicely. After all, it was he who betrayed us to your father in the first place. Because of him, I lost everything."

She stiffened, her lovely face now wary. "What do you mean, 'settle'?"

He smiled, showing his teeth. "You didn't think I would forgive and forget, did you? I have thought of all of you constantly since I was driven from Joslin Manor. Two years ago, fate and circumstance showed me the way."

He opened a drawer and pulled out a sheaf of notes, tossing them on to the polished desktop. "Edmund never did have a head for commerce, did he? After your brother came into his inheritance, he invested very poorly, particularly in high-risk trading ventures."

"Which I'm sure you knew all about," she interjected in a hard voice.

He bowed his head in silent acknowledgment, enjoying the furious snap in her ice-maiden eyes. "Edmund's financial bumbling forced him to take out substantial private loans to cover his losses. I won't trouble you with the details. Suffice it to say that I'm now the sole holder of those notes."

He waved a negligent hand over the papers on his desk, as if it were not a great matter. As if it had not taken months of horse trading, greasing palms, and one or two carefully applied threats of business reprisals to get his hands on every last note. But it had been worth every shilling, because it gave him what he wanted most – control over Marissa.

She grew still, as understanding dawned. "How much does my brother owe you?" she asked in a hollow voice.

"Fifty thousand pounds."

She took in a huge breath, working to pull the air into her lungs. Her eyes seemed to blur, as if she couldn't focus on anything but the thoughts in her head.

Anthony drank in the moment he had worked so long and hard to achieve. Marissa *would* be his, and she was now beginning to realize it.

A full minute, measured by the casement clock, ticked by. Neither of them broke the silence.

Then she stirred, an alabaster statue coming to life. "You want your revenge against my family for what they did to you."

He hesitated, puzzled that she didn't include herself with the rest of the Joslins. Then again, why did it matter?

"Revenge is an ugly word, Marissa. I prefer to call it justice."

"As I said, I did not give you leave to call me by my first name," she snapped. "You will not do so again."

He smiled, sprawling back in his chair. Anger made her even more beautiful – driving the blood to her face. It made her flushed and ripe. Within a few days, he would be taking all she had to offer, and then some.

"You've given me leave before, Marissa. In fact, you gave me a hell of a lot more than that, as we both know."

In her frustration, she actually bit down on her plump lower lip, like an actress in a melodrama. He became hard thinking of all the ways he was going to put those lips to good use.

"I prefer not to recall the past," she said in a haughty voice.

He let out a harsh laugh. "Indeed. So would I, but that luxury has been denied me. There is, however, one thing I don't mind remembering, and you know what that is."

She glared back, refusing to respond.

"How you felt beneath me," he purred. "I remember your naked body squirming in my arms. You were slick and hot, and so very tight. All softness and silk, and begging me to take you."

Perspiration misted her face. She turned from him, pressing a gloved hand to her brow. "Anthony, please," she said in a suffocated voice.

A sharp wave of pleasure took him at the sound of his name on her lips. "Ah. That's better. You actually brought yourself to use my name."

She jumped up from her seat and slapped a hand on his desk. "Enough of this! What do you want from me?"

He rose slowly, feeling the power uncoil within him. She would be his war prize – his by right – and he would no longer be denied. "I thought it was obvious, Marissa. I want my revenge, and I want it now."

Marissa had never forgotten Anthony's eyes. How could she? A pair exactly like them gazed up at her every day. Her daughter Antonia had eyes like Russian amber – golden and full of fire.

Antonia had Anthony's eyes. Her father's eyes.

Eyes that could blaze with emotion, as Anthony's were right now. His gaze swept over her, burning so fiercely Marissa half expected it would scorch the clothing from her body.

Tamping down her frustration and fear, she answered him in the same calm voice she used with her daughter. "Perhaps I misunderstood you, Captain. I thought you were seeking justice, not revenge."

He strolled around the desk, closing the distance between them.

Ignoring the urge to flee, she held her ground. Anthony had always been tall, but now he was also brawny from his years at sea. A man, when she had only ever known the boy. And this particular man – with his dark hair, rough-hewn features and broad shoulders – was so intensely masculine that it made her tremble.

"In this case, justice and vengeance are one and the same," he answered, his voice a dark, menacing purr.

She shivered, sensing his implacable will, but was irresistibly drawn to his sensual power. That hadn't changed. As a young girl she had been madly in love with Anthony, willing to do anything to be with him – even turn her back on the family and elope with him.

If only she had.

Marissa took her seat, keeping her spine straight and her hands folded neatly in her lap. If a long and unhappy marriage had taught her anything, it was how to mask her emotions. And ever since Anthony's note arrived yesterday, Marissa had been trying to hide everything she felt – from Edmund, from Antonia, even from herself. But deep inside she could hardly breathe, swamped by waves of emotion she had repressed for years, and secrets long stashed away.

Too many secrets, ones Anthony would never forgive. Not after all he had suffered and lost.

Her insides twisted with anxiety, but she calmly met his gaze.

"Again, what do you want from me?" she asked.

He loomed over her, his face a grim, brooding mask. It hurt to look at him, for no trace of the sweet boy who had loved her remained. Her father and brother had destroyed that boy's life, just as they had destroyed hers.

"I want you," he growled.

Her heart lurched. "I . . . I don't understand."

He crossed his arms over his broad chest. "If you consent to be with me, I will extend Edmund's loans until such time he can afford to pay me back. You have my word on it."

She gaped at him. "You're saying you want to marry me?"

He laughed so harshly she cringed.

"You're such a romantic, Marissa. Why would I want to leg-shackle myself to you for the rest our lives? No. I want you in my bed – for as long as I want, and in any way I want. Do that, and the Joslins are safe."

Her stomach cramped and, for a moment, she thought she would be sick. She tried to think, but her mind was stuffed with cotton batting. "You're not making sense," she finally managed.

"It's quite simple. You live with me as my mistress, and I will not call in your brother's debts."

"But . . . but everyone will know," she stuttered. "Think of the gossip. We couldn't possibly keep such an arrangement a secret."

He snorted. "Of course not. That's the point. I will escort you to the theatre, the opera, the Royal Academy . . . whatever amuses me. You will be my companion, both in public and private. I'm rich now. Very few doors are closed to me, and with you by my side I might be able to open a few more."

"That's ridiculous," she blurted out. "The scandal will ruin me."

He shrugged, as if he didn't care.

She could barely speak past the panic and anger clutching at her throat. "I have a child. If I'm ruined, I won't be able to provide for her."

"You can't provide for her now. That's why you moved back to Edmund's house after your husband died, isn't it? You were Paget's second wife. His estate was almost entirely entailed to his oldest son, leaving only a small widow's portion to support you and your daughter."

Anthony didn't know the half of it. Her husband had drastically reduced her portion after their first year of marriage when he finally realized Antonia wasn't his child. It left Marissa poor, completely dependent on her brother's support.

She closed her eyes, trying to get past the fear, searching to find a way out. If not for Antonia, she might have agreed to Anthony's demands – if for no other reason than to atone for her family's sins against him. But she wouldn't give up on her daughter. Not for him. Not for Edmund. They could both go to hell before she would sacrifice Antonia.

She opened her eyes. "Yes, that's true," she grudgingly acknowledged. "But I must still protect her."

He remained grim and silent, his mouth pulled into a tight line. "Very well," he finally said. "I'll not make your daughter a victim of your brother's arrogance. She'll be provided for. I'll draw up the necessary contracts, giving her a generous allowance and stipulating that Edmund must always provide a home for her."

Marissa gasped. She had to clutch the seat of the chair to keep her balance. "Absolutely not! You will not separate me from my child."

"Then she can live with us," he said impatiently. "You may be certain I will provide for both of you – you have my word. But either way, Marissa, you will come to me, or see your family in ruins."

The room spun in a dizzying whirl, dark and cold. She took a deep breath, allowing the rage to clear from her mind. Somehow, she had to fight back. "Tell me, Captain, would you have forced me to be your mistress if my husband were alive?"

He frowned and slowly shook his head. "No. I may be a devious bastard, Marissa, but I wouldn't have made you betray him." His mouth twisted into a sardonic smile. "One betrayal in a lifetime is more than enough. And this is so much better. I'll have you without the annoyance of any minor scruples, and I get the added benefit of shaming your family. Your brother will be in my debt and, at the same time, he'll suffer the knowledge that his sister is in my bed. Without the benefit of clergy."

Marissa clenched her hands into fists. If she needed any proof that Anthony must be kept away from Antonia, this was it. The loving boy she had known was dead, and a cold-blooded monster had risen in his place. God only knew what he would do if he ever found out he had a daughter.

"Why must you do this?" she challenged. "You're successful now. You can have anything you want."

All traces of cold-blooded amusement disappeared from his features. His eyes glittered with an anguished fury that wrenched the breath from her body. "Your family forced this on me. They ripped me from the life I was meant to have. The one thing I truly loved and wanted, your father and brother denied me. As did you, Marissa." He flung the words at her. "But now you have the chance to atone for that by finally giving me what I deserve. If you don't, I'll see every last one of the Joslins rot in hell."

His words sliced through her like shards of broken glass, his pain so raw and immediate that it became her pain, too. She swallowed a sob and a vital part of her – the one that had never ceased loving him – reached out, yearning to heal the wounds that marked his soul.

"I never meant to hurt you, Anthony," she whispered.

He surged up from the desk with lethal, masculine grace. Big hands curled around her shoulders and he pulled her straight up from her chair.

"I think you lie," he growled.

He looked wild and dangerous as fury blasted through his shell of cynical detachment. But in those golden eyes she saw his grief and longing – saw *him*, the Anthony who her father had torn away from her, leaving her alone and incomplete.

She let her hand drift across his tanned cheek. "No, Anthony. You weren't the only one who was hurt," she murmured. "I longed to go after you . . . I was desperate to find you. But Father kept me locked away in my room, and he continually threatened to beat me. He said he'd send me to live with strangers if I didn't marry Richard." Her voice broke as his fingers dug into her arms and his gold-shot eyes searched her face. "I missed you so much, but I was still a child," she pleaded. "I didn't know what to do."

A different kind of heat, forbidden and dark, flared in his eyes. His big hands moved down her arms and slid to her waist, pulling her flush against him. She gasped at the feel of his erection pushing hard against her belly.

"But you're not a child any more, Marissa. And I've waited for this for too damn long."

She clutched at his waistcoat as he swooped to capture her mouth in a punishing kiss. Her head fell back and his tongue slipped between her lips to plunder her mouth. She whimpered, giving him everything he demanded. There was no resisting him – no resisting the passion he'd ignited. The passion unleashed for both of them after years in solitary exile.

His bold tongue tasted her, stroked deep inside to claim her with a searing hunger. Marissa had forgotten the fierce beauty of Anthony's kiss. But now everything came back in a blazing rush. The heat, the wet slide of a greedy, open-mouthed kiss, the feel of his strong hands moving over her body.

She stretched up on her toes, winding her arms around his neck. A raw need throbbed deep within as her body came alive to his touch. Her breasts grew full and heavy as she rubbed against him, her nipples pulling tight with a prickling ache.

Anthony murmured a low growl of approval as his hand drifted down to squeeze her bottom in a kneading grip. Gradually, his kiss grew softer, and his tongue slowly traced her lips before slipping back into her mouth. It was sweet and hot and reckless – just as it had always been.

As she slid into total surrender, he broke the kiss. Marissa murmured a confused protest, and his hand came up to hold her chin. She panted, struggling to shake off the confining grip, eager to taste him again. His fingers tightened on her jaw.

"Open your eyes," he ordered in a husky voice.

She did. His face was flushed under the bronzing of his complexion, and sexual hunger flickered in his rapacious gaze. But she saw something else in those golden eyes, something wary and very determined.

"What is it?" she whispered.

"I want your decision, Marissa. Of your own free will. Do you agree to be my mistress, or shall I send word to your brother that I intend to collect the fifty thousand pounds he owes me?"

For a moment she froze, stupefied, then she wrenched herself free of his grasp. Anger and shame flooded her body in equal parts. "Go to hell," she blurted out.

His lips curled back in a predatory grin. "Most likely I will, but I don't care. As long as you do what I ask. You have until tonight to make up your mind. I'll send my carriage to Joslin House to fetch you. Eight o'clock, shall we say?"

She snatched up her bonnet and reticule and stumbled to the door.

"I'll be waiting," he said.

His mocking laugh followed her from the room.

Berkeley Square, London

It had taken her thirteen years, but Marissa finally acknowledged how much she hated her brother.

Edmund lumbered across his richly appointed study, his jowly face red with ill-contained fury. He halted before her, smelling of port, snuff and outraged dignity.

"I will be ruined, I tell you," he blustered. "Forced to sell everything if that bloody bastard calls in those loans. This is your fault, Marissa. You should have been able to talk him out of it. He *was* your lover."

"Keep your voice down," she hissed. "Do you want everyone in the house to know that?"

He gave her a sizzling glare but his voice subsided to a dull roar. "Father should have killed Barnett years ago, when he had the chance."

Marissa dug her nails into her palms. "You almost did. You and Father. And for what? The only sin Anthony ever committed was to love me."

"Is that what you call it?" he sneered. "I never understood how you could let him touch you, much less rut on you like a barnyard animal. You, the finest catch in London during your first season. What a fool you were, to have debased yourself with that country bumpkin."

She itched to slap him, but refused to sink to his level. "I loved him, and he loved me, Edmund. Anthony was the only person who loved me after Mother died. God knows I never had a tender word from Father or you."

"What did you expect after you behaved like a whore? If Father hadn't acted decisively, no respectable man would have married you. As it was the damage was done, but at least it was too late for Paget to do anything about it."

He cast her a black look, then flopped into a leather club chair, which creaked ominously under his weight.

"Not that it did us any good to marry you off to Paget," he whined. "I still have to support you and your daughter. And now I stand to be ruined, all because you succumbed to your craven lusts."

Marissa thanked God there were no pistols within reach, because she likely would have added murder to her list of sins. Edmund had flung these horrid accusations at her more times than she could count. They had always made her sick with shame and regret, beating her down until she almost believed them herself.

But not any more. She was done with shame – and with her brother if he didn't own up to his own failings, and the mess he had made of the family finances.

"What do you intend to do?" she asked. "Anthony wants an answer by tonight."

His jowls actually quivered with indignation. "Not a thing. *You* created this problem, Marissa. It's up to you to save the family. If you can't persuade Barnett to forgive the loan or give me sufficient time to pay it back, then you must give him what he wants. Family honour demands it."

His callous words sent anger and shock surging through her body. "Family honour! Are you mad? I shall be ruined."

"You were ruined long ago, dear sister. It pains me that the world will now be made aware of that fact but, thanks to you, we have no other choice."

The taste in her mouth was so foul, she could have spit. Her brother would rather abandon her to a sordid fate than take responsibility for his own foolish mistakes.

She forced herself to remain calm, though her heart banged against her ribs. "Edmund, there's always a choice, good or bad. You chose all those years ago to destroy Anthony's life when he was little more than a boy. Your present situation is of your own making. I am not the person who drove the estate into debt, and I am not the person who should beg for Anthony's forgiveness. You should."

He regarded her with contempt. "Don't be ridiculous. I wouldn't soil my good name by going anywhere near the man. But since you're already damaged goods, I suggest you do whatever you can to avert this disaster. For your family's sake."

He looked over at the ormolu clock on the mantelpiece. "You'd better get ready. Barnett's carriage will be here soon enough." Edmund heaved himself up from his chair and crossed to his desk. Without giving her a second glance, he began shuffling through some papers.

A cold disgust settled in her chest. Anthony was right. Edmund had earned his destruction and, if not for Antonia, Marissa wouldn't have lifted a finger to help her brother.

"Edmund."

He looked up, irritation wrinkling his balding pate. "What now?"

"I will do as you insist, but let us be clear about my daughter. You and your wife will care for her as if she were your own. Anthony has offered to settle a handsome allowance on her, but Antonia must have a home, is that understood? She cannot come with me."

Edmund seemed genuinely shocked. "Of course not. I wouldn't let the girl anywhere near that bastard. He's already done enough damage to the family's good name, as have you. Antonia will be much better off with us."

The old shame threatened to creep back into her heart, but she beat it back. Antonia had always been loved and protected, much more than Marissa ever was.

She turned on her heel and marched from the room, slamming the door behind her with a satisfying bang. Taking a deep breath, she closed her eyes until she could fold her rage into a neat little bundle and put it aside for later. But, as the anger faded, the implications of what would happen next swept through her like a howling gale, sucking the air from her lungs.

A small, sharp voice brought her up short. "Mamma, are you ill?"

She spun around to see Antonia standing in the curve under the entrance hall staircase. Her daughter inspected her, eyes wary and bright with concern.

"Antonia, what are you doing there?" Marissa asked more sharply than she intended. "You weren't eavesdropping again, were you?"

Those golden eyes widened, the picture of offended innocence. "No, Mamma, of course not," Antonia protested. "I was just coming up from the kitchen. Cook made gingerbread today."

Her beautiful girl held up a thick piece of fragrant cake. She looked so pious that Marissa gave a reluctant laugh.

"Very well, my love. I believe you. This time. But you know very well you shouldn't be snooping about the entrance hall."

Her daughter's face split into an enchanting grin. She took a healthy bite of the gingerbread, ignoring the motherly reprimand.

Antonia's slight figure went fuzzy as Marissa blinked away the tears blurring her vision. How in God's name could she ever leave her own child behind? The pain of it just might kill her.

She silently scolded herself for the momentary weakness. What she did, she did for Antonia. To keep her safe, untainted by the mistakes of her family. It was Marissa's choice, and the only one that made sense.

"Come along, darling," she said, forcing a smile. "I must go out soon, but there's still time for us to read a story together."

Antonia slipped a warm hand into hers as they mounted the stairs. "What were you and Uncle Edmund talking about, Mamma?"

Marissa frowned, trying to look stern. "Nothing you need to know. You're far too curious, Antonia. It's not at all ladylike for you to pry into other people's affairs, especially those of your elders."

Antonia looked aggrieved. "But no one ever tells me anything."

Marissa ran a gentle hand over her daughter's glossy curls. She would have to tell the child everything, and soon enough. But not tonight.

The words caught in her throat. "You should be happy that they don't."

Russell Square, London

Marissa stood quietly before him, garbed in a grey, modestly cut evening dress – a perfect example of an aristocratic widow, so untouchable she might as well have been on the moon. But touch her Anthony would, and soon. In fact, it would be a miracle if he didn't pull her down on to the carpeted floor of his study and shred every article of expensive clothing from her body.

Even if it made him feel like the most callous brute in England.

"There's no need to stand on ceremony," he said. "Please have a seat."

She frowned and remained where she was, likely because his suggestion came out sounding like a command.

He sighed. "Marissa, I would rather you not stand there like a disobedient child waiting for a scold."

She made a small, scoffing noise but took his hand and allowed him to lead her to the sofa. Her trembling fingers betrayed her nervousness. He thought he should be deriving some satisfaction from that, but he wasn't.

Ever since she left his offices that afternoon, he had been struggling with a growing sense of remorse. He didn't like it. But her outburst had forced him to consider that Marissa probably *had* been a target of her father's retribution, just as she claimed. He was a fool for not realizing that sooner, but the wounded boy of thirteen years ago had lacked the understanding that came with being a man.

Not that Anthony was ready to forgive her – at least not yet. The possibility still existed that she was trying to manipulate him with her tale of woe. Better to wait and hear what she had to say.

And he hoped to God she said yes. He had been in a painful state of arousal all afternoon, all because of one damn little kiss that hadn't lasted much more than a minute.

"Something to drink? A sherry, perhaps," he offered. Whatever she had to say, alcohol would make it easier for both of them.

She took her seat, perching on the edge of the sofa, ready to bolt. Clearly, it would take more than one drink to settle her nerves.

"I'll have a brandy. And please make it a big one," she said in a clipped voice.

He bit back a smile and poured out two glasses of the finest French brandy his ships could smuggle into England.

After handing her the glass, he settled into a chair opposite the sofa. As much as he wanted to crowd her, something held him back. That damned remorse, he supposed, or the strained look around her eyes and the slight quiver of her pink mouth. Marissa had always been pluck to the backbone, but tonight she seemed as fragile as a butterfly emerging from its cocoon.

"Have you reached your decision?" His voice came out on a husky pitch.

"I have," she said, her air both tragic and dignified. "I will agree to your terms if you will defer my brother's debt to his satisfaction and provide appropriately for my daughter."

His heart stopped, then started again, thumping out a painful tattoo. His intellect had told him she would agree – she had no real choice – but his bone-deep sense of her had expected more resistance.

"I'm gratified by your decision," he said, struggling to keep the sound of relief from his voice. The last thing he wanted was for her to realize the power she still wielded over him.

He came to his feet and moved to sit next to her. She stiffened, but didn't shy away.

"I'm curious, though," he continued. "Why did you decide to agree?" He was more than curious. Suddenly, it seemed imperative he know the reasons why – as if his future depended upon it.

"Not for Edmund's sake, if that's what you're thinking," she said with a scowl. "You were right about him – he's not worthy of the sacrifice. I do this to provide for my daughter."

Her azure eyes briefly met his. She looked pathetically valiant, like a tragic queen in a melodrama. Or Joan of Arc consigning herself to the flames.

Frustration had him clenching his teeth as it dawned on him that he had no desire to take a martyr to his bed. Not even if that martyr was Marissa. Her noble self-sacrifice would freeze him more thoroughly than a winter storm in the North Atlantic.

"Is that the only reason?" he growled.

Her startled gaze flew to his. He didn't bother to hide his irritation. She studied his face, probing for answers to unspoken questions. Then she blushed an enchanting shade of pink and dropped her gaze.

"No," she whispered. "It's not the only reason."

He waited impatiently. "Well?" he finally prompted.

She met his eyes, and he saw a hint of her old fire. "You didn't deserve what happened to you."

"So, you're offering yourself up as a means of atonement, is that it?"

Her mouth kicked up in a wry smile. "Something like that."

He took a gulp of brandy, feeling gloomier by the minute. This was not how he had envisioned the scene playing out. He should be feeling triumphant after all those years spent developing his schemes, step by careful step. Vengeance against the Joslins – against her – had given his life purpose. And now, when he had prevailed and Marissa was finally under his thrall, what did he truly feel?

Not triumph. Not even simple satisfaction. What he felt was . . . hollow. As if he'd lost something important he could never get back.

Anthony captured her elegant chin between his fingers. "Did you mean what you said today?" he asked harshly. "That you were desperate to find me?" She tried to pull away but he tightened his grip, forcing her to meet his gaze. "I want the truth, Marissa. No more lies or secrets. Not any more."

Her pupils dilated as she drew in an unsteady breath. She seemed almost frightened.

"It's all right," he murmured, giving in to the compulsion to reassure her. "You can tell me."

Her eyes grew soft and misty. "Yes. I would have given anything to find you. My heart was broken with the thought of never seeing you again. I wasn't exaggerating when I said my father locked me in a room for a month. No matter what I did, no matter how hard I tried, I couldn't escape. And no one would help me."

Her gaze filled with anguish, an anguish that became his. He brushed her cheek, wiping away a single fallen tear.

"Then what happened?"

"When I told Father I would never marry anyone but you, he lied to me. He said you had boarded a ship to America and were never coming back. He threatened that if I didn't marry Richard, he would exile me to one of his smaller estates in the country – indefinitely."

His heart ached with guilt and he longed to take her in his arms and comfort her. All these years he had failed her, never knowing the truth but choosing to believe the worst.

She sniffed and tried to look brave. Anthony extracted a handkerchief and handed it to her.

"Father was determined I not break my engagement to Richard. I know I was weak, but I simply didn't have the strength to fight him any more," she said with an unhappy shrug. She scrubbed her cheeks with her handkerchief, finishing with a prosaic wipe of her nose. "What happens now?" she asked, looking wary.

He got up and crossed to the mantel, needing to put distance between them. "Nothing," he said. His chest ached, as if someone had punched him in the ribs.

She frowned. "I don't understand."

"You're free to go. I'll write to your brother tomorrow, setting out reasonable terms to pay back what he owes me. You have my word that no harm will come to your family."

He forced himself to look at her. She seemed dazed, frozen into immobility. He should have derived some satisfaction from that, but it only confirmed she had expected the worst of him.

"I'll ring for my carriage." He felt like the lowest kind of villain. "You may return to Berkeley Square immediately."

He crossed the room, reaching for the bell-pull. As his fingers wrapped around the cord, a slender hand touched his forearm.

"Anthony, don't," she murmured.

He pivoted. She gazed up at him, her cheeks flushed with colour and her eyes luminous with unshed tears. Never had she looked as beautiful as she did in that moment.

"Don't send me away." Her voice was throaty. "I couldn't bear it. Please . . . I don't want to lose you again."

Anthony gazed down at her, looking stunned and at a loss for words.

"Are you sure?" he finally managed in a hoarse voice.

Marissa pressed a hand over her pounding heart. Taking a deep breath, she stepped off the cliff.

"I'm not sure about anything except my feelings for you. I want to be with you, Anthony, more than you could ever know."

Shyly, she placed a hand on his chest. His heart pounded drum-like beneath her fingertips. With renewed courage, she stretched up and pressed a kiss on a jaw carved from stone.

As if her touch had unleashed a genie from a bottle, his powerful body roared to life. Arms lashed about her waist, pulling her up flat against his chest. She shuddered, relishing the feel of all that solid muscle plastered along the length of her body.

"That's all I needed to know, my sweet." He trailed a pattern of shivery little kisses across her cheek. "I'll take care of everything else."

She wriggled her arms free and took his face between her hands. For long seconds they simply gazed at each other, drinking in the wonder of the moment. His bright stare smouldered with passion and a fierce, complicated love.

That look tore through her, blasting away the heartbreak and suffering of all those lonely years, infusing her with a joy so transforming it almost frightened her.

"I love you, Anthony," she whispered. "I never stopped loving you."

His lips covered hers in a kiss so raw and needy she could have wept. This was the Anthony she had known. Loving, claiming, protecting her. She had forgotten for a while – they both had – but now they remembered. Now they had at last found their way back to each other.

She clung to his neck, opening her mouth to draw him in. Energy, hot and carnal, flowed between them. Desire licked through her body, settling deep in her womb.

Anthony reached up to gently grip the tidy braids of her hair, pulling her head back as he kissed his way down from her mouth. She pulled in a sobbing breath as his lips fastened on her neck with a teasing suck.

"Anthony," she moaned.

He gave a soft, guttural laugh, then licked the base of her throat as he gently pulled her back into an arch. Her breasts, aching in the confinement of their stays, rubbed against the silk of his waistcoat. Sensation streaked out from her nipples, gathering in the cove between her thighs. She whimpered and shamelessly rubbed herself against his erection. It was all so delicious, so overpowering, her senses swam.

"Wait," she gasped, clutching his shoulders.

He growled in frustration but eased her away from his body. "Damn it, Marissa! I've been waiting thirteen years for this. And you want to stop me?"

If she hadn't been so light-headed, she would have giggled at the aggrieved masculinity in his voice. "Anthony, my legs feel like jelly. Can we please sit down?"

A predatory grin curled the edges of his sensual mouth. "I'm yours to command, My Lady," he purred.

He swept her up – this time she did giggle – and carried her to the sofa. He set her down and began to pull her clothes off with impatient hands.

"Anthony," she squeaked as one of her buttons popped, ricocheting off the low table in front of the sofa.

"I'll buy you a new dress. I'll buy you a hundred new dresses," he said through clenched teeth. "But right now I'm getting you out of this one."

A moment later, he tossed her gown over a chair. A few moments after that, her stays and chemise followed. Leaving her stockings on, he lifted her in his arms and carefully placed her on the sofa.

"Now you," she murmured, reaching for his waistcoat. "I want to see all of you."

He pulled off his coat, ripping a seam in the process, and then divested himself of the rest of his clothing. As he turned to her, candlelight flickered along the hard vaulting of his ribs, his broad shoulders, and the dense, tightly knit muscles of his chest and abdomen. She caught her breath at the impressive size of his erection – that part she *had* somehow managed to forget – and her innermost flesh grew soft and damp.

He came down on her, pressing her into the velvet cushions of the sofa.

"Open for me, darling," he whispered, as he settled between her spread thighs.

Marissa groaned and let her head fall back. Draping her arms loosely around Anthony's shoulders, she gave herself up to all the fantasies she had ever had about him.

But the reality was so much better.

He propped himself on his elbows, studying her body through slitted eyes of gold. Marissa panted as her breasts quivered and her nipples stiffened under his gaze. She squirmed, trying to increase the contact between their bodies.

A long breath hissed out between his teeth. His dark head lowered to her breast and his tongue flicked one nipple. Once, twice, three times.

"Please," she gasped, arching up into his chest. "Anthony, I can't wait."

"God, Marissa," he groaned, "neither can I."

He clamped his calloused palms around her face, holding her still for his devouring kiss. As his tongue slid between her lips, hot and demanding, he pressed his length against her. He slipped one hand down to her bottom, tilting her hips up to meet him. Then, with a long, low thrust, he pushed inside.

She cried out, breaking free of his kiss to thrash her head against the velvet pillows. It was like nothing she remembered. He filled her, possessed her, as he had never done before. Anthony was no longer a boy, but a man, with a man's power and a man's way of loving a woman.

He flexed his hips, moving slowly at first until she heard her own voice – breathless and needy – begging for more. And he gave her everything she needed, taking her with long, powerful strokes. The end came quickly, like a rip tide, driving her to a shattering climax.

Anthony came with her, growling out her name as he thrust into her one last time. She gripped him with her arms and legs, curling around him as joy flooded her soul, obliterating years of shame and denial in an overwhelming rush of emotion.

He collapsed on to her, big, sweaty and heavy. Marissa didn't care. She wanted to lie there all night, with him inside, loving her as it was always meant to be. She was safe, home at last.

Her eyes flew open.

Home. Where Antonia was. Anthony's daughter.

Suddenly, he was crushing her. A surge of panic squeezed her chest and throat. "Anthony," she gasped. "I can't breathe."

His head came up. His eyes narrowed as he studied her, but he moved, shifting their bodies so that she came to rest between the back of the sofa and his chest. One big hand stroked down the length of her spine as he murmured soothing words and planted soft kisses on the top of her head.

Under the influence of that comforting voice and hand, her breath slowed and her reason returned. Of course she had to tell him that Antonia was his daughter. He would know it, anyway, as soon as he caught sight of her eyes. Unless Marissa intended to hide Antonia away – which would be well nigh impossible – he was bound to meet her sooner or later.

She squeezed her eyes shut, snuggling into the warmth of his body as his arms tightened around her. She *should* tell him, right now, but she couldn't force the words past the lump in her throat.

Tomorrow. She would tell him tomorrow. Or the next day, after she'd thought about the most sensible way to break the news. After all, Anthony might not want a ready-made family. Or he might be furious that she hadn't already told him. Marissa couldn't bear the thought of ruining this moment between them – not when they had just found each other after so long apart.

And she had to think about Antonia, too. What in God's name would she say to her daughter about all this?

Anthony's deep voice rumbled through his chest and into her body, startling her out of her uneasy reverie. "What troubles you, my sweet?"

She looked up. He gave her a loving smile, but his eyes were sombre and watchful. Her heart twisted at the idea that he might reject Antonia. He might reject her, too, for keeping such a dark secret.

Tomorrow, whispered the coward's voice in her head.

She stretched up to kiss him. "Nothing, my love. Everything is just perfect."

Anthony strode along Bond Street, feeling as light as a gull skimming over the whitecaps. For the first time in years, all was right with the world.

As he skirted a pair of dandies preening at their own reflections in a shop window, he patted his waistcoat to check that the small box from Phillip's jewellers remained safely stowed in his pocket. Marissa's engagement ring was a stunner – a large sapphire surrounded by diamonds. The stone matched her eyes. That made him a sentimental fool, of course, but he didn't care. He would propose to her this evening, and he wouldn't take no for an answer.

As he made his way to a hackney stand on Piccadilly, he spied a woman walking hand in hand with a young girl as they turned into Hatchard's bookshop.

Marissa. He'd recognize her graceful figure anywhere. The girl must be her daughter.

He smiled. No time like the present to meet his future step-daughter. Not that he would drop any hints, but surely Marissa couldn't object to introducing him, especially under these circum-stances. Meeting her might even be easier this way – running into them in a casual fashion. And he had to admit he was eager to meet the child. Marissa obviously adored her, and Anthony had every intention of loving her, too.

He crossed the street and followed them into Hatchard's. After a short search, he found them looking through a pile of books, their backs to him as he approached.

"Lady Paget," he said, affecting surprise. "How do—"

Marissa spun on her heel. She gasped, all the colour leaching from her complexion as she stared at him in horror. The girl turned with her, lifting a questioning gaze to his face. Her big amber eyes opened wide and her mouth gaped into a surprised little oval.

Anthony's mind whirled as he stared into a living picture of himself as a child, especially her eyes. He had never seen eyes like that anywhere but reflected in the mirror.

After he managed to pound his brain into a semblance of order, he dragged his gaze to Marissa's dead-white face. Her desperate eyes pleaded for mercy.

"How old is she?" he rasped. "She's older than you told me, isn't she?"

Marissa pressed a hand to her mouth, looking like the world had just come to an end. Maybe it had – for him, anyway.

"I'll find out, whether you tell me or not," he threatened.

"My daughter is twelve," she finally whispered.

He could barely comprehend the words, or even hear them through the roaring in his ears. Not that he needed to. Proof was in that childish gaze, darting back and forth between the two adults.

"Did you think I wouldn't find out?" he growled at Marissa.

She cast an anxious glance around the store. "Captain Barnett, please keep your voice down."

The girl tugged on her mother's arm. "Mamma, what's happening?"

Marissa dredged up a weak smile. "Just a small misunderstanding, darling. Don't worry."

Anthony gave a harsh laugh. "Is that what people call it these days?"

"I'll explain everything later," she replied, looking frantic. "But I beg you, don't make a scene."

Anger and a sickening sense of betrayal lifted him on a cresting wave. "Beg all you want, Lady Paget. But tell your brother I expect payment in full by the end of the week, or I'll see every last Joslin rotting in debtors' prison."

How could he have been such a bastard?

Anthony paced from one end of his office to the other, re-enacting the disastrous scene at Hatchard's in his head. What a brute he'd been, making threats in front of a little girl – his own daughter. No matter what Marissa had done, it could never excuse such unforgivable behaviour.

He came to a halt by the window, thoroughly disgusted with himself. A small fleet of ships – his ships – floated on the Thames. They might as well have been toy boats bobbing around in a tub for all it mattered. The only thing he could focus on was the face of a little girl, staring up at him with amber eyes.

And Marissa's eyes, too, pleading for understanding. The worst of it was that he *did* understand, now that his fury had cooled. What else could she have done when she discovered her predicament? Pregnant and alone – her lover supposedly on the other side of the ocean. She had protected her daughter – their daughter – in the only way she could.

But she hadn't trusted him with the truth, and that knowledge twisted in his gut.

A knock sounded on the door, and a clerk stuck his head into the office. "There's a young lady to see you, Captain. Says she's Lady Paget's daughter."

He jerked around. "What? Who's with her?"

"She's alone, sir."

Anthony muttered a curse and strode to the outer office.

The child sat on his clerk's high stool, her feet swinging inches above the floor. She looked like she hadn't a care in the world as she twirled her little beaded reticule around her fingers.

He glowered at her. What was she thinking? Coming all alone to Wapping – home to sailors, thieves and whores. "Good God, child! What are you doing here? Where's your mother?"

She scrambled off the stool and gave him a polite bob. "Good afternoon, Captain Barnett. I was hoping to have a word with you. Is there someplace we can be private?"

He eyed her, reluctantly impressed by her audacity. Pluck to the backbone, his daughter was, and full of brass. "Step into my office," he growled.

She sailed past him, a dignified miniature of her mother – except for the eyes. Those were all his.

"I don't have much time," she said. "Mamma thinks I'm taking a nap."

He sighed. "How did you know where to find me?"

"I heard Mamma talking about you to Uncle Edmund. Then I snuck out of the house and found a hackney."

He stifled a groan. Clearly, his daughter was both precocious and in need of supervision. He'd have to talk to Marissa about that.

It suddenly occurred to him that he didn't even know her given name. "Forgive me if I sound rude, but what's your name?"

"I'm Lady Antonia Paget. But you can call me Antonia."

His heart lurched. Marissa had named their child after him. With effort, he marshalled his wits. "Best get on with it, then. I've got to get you home before your mother discovers you missing."

She studied him, as serious as a parson in a pulpit. "You've made Mamma very unhappy. She cried. I wish you wouldn't do that."

He blinked. Were all little girls so blunt?

"I'm sure I haven't," he managed.

"You have. It's not very nice of you, especially since she loves you."

That hit him low and fast.

"Ah, I don't think that can be right," he replied. Not after today, anyway.

She impatiently tapped her foot. "Oh, no. I'm right. She told Uncle Edmund she did."

He wished his heart would stop jerking about in his chest. It made it difficult to think. "You heard her say that?"

The look she gave him clearly expressed her opinion of his intellect, and not a favourable one, at that. "Are you really my father?" she demanded.

His brain, as heavy as an overloaded frigate in a gale, struggled to keep up with her. "Why would you think that?" he hedged.

She looked thoughtful. "I'm not surprised. My other father, Sir Richard, that is, was never really fond of me."

A flare of anger cleared the fog from his brain. "Did he mistreat you?"

"Not at all. He was a perfectly adequate father, under the circumstances."

He'd lost her again. "What circumstances?"

She sighed dramatically. "The very large circumstance that I wasn't his daughter. You're not very bright, are you? I do hope I take after Mamma, in that respect."

He choked back a laugh. It wouldn't do to encourage her. "Did Sir Richard tell you he wasn't your father?"

"Of course not. But I overheard him fighting with Mamma a few months before he died. It was about me, but I didn't really understand what he meant. Of course, now it's all perfectly clear. How silly of me not to have realized before."

Anthony wondered if someone had knocked him on the head when he wasn't looking. His daughter, however, seemed completely at ease with the bizarre conversation.

"You seem to do quite a lot of eavesdropping for a little girl," he said, latching on to the one thing in this whole muddle that seemed clear.

She shrugged. "I know. Mamma says it's my greatest fault. But how else am I to know what is happening? Adults never tell children anything. Not anything interesting, that is."

He really couldn't let that one pass. "Well, stop it. It's not at all becoming in a young lady."

She crossed her hands in front of her, looking as meek as a Spanish nun. Except for the mischievous smile playing around the edges of her mouth, of course. "Yes, Papa. Whatever you say."

He shook his head, dazed by the odd creature already fastening herself like a little barnacle on to his heart. "You're rather terrifying, Antonia," he said thoughtfully. "But I suppose you already know that."

Her smile widened into a grin. "Then I do take after you – at least a little."

He laughed. "I refuse to believe you were the least bit frightened by that scene in Hatchard's."

"Not really. I was a little nervous in the hackney coming down here, though. I've never been to this part of London."

He was about to deliver a stern parental lecture on that subject when he heard a commotion in the outer office. A moment later, Marissa, looking like a wild woman, came bursting into the room.

"Antonia," she cried, clutching her daughter by the shoulders. "Thank God! You scared me half to death!"

Anthony crossed his arms over his chest and, with some effort, wiped the grin from his face. He was a wicked man, but he couldn't help taking his revenge on the two females who would no doubt lead him a merry dance for the rest of his life.

And thank God for that.

"Ah, Lady Paget, come to collect your errant child. I'm amazed you allow her to wander about town like a street urchin. You really shouldn't unleash her on the unsuspecting citizens of London without any warning. Mayhem would no doubt ensue."

Marissa pokered up, just as he had known she would. "I beg your pardon, Captain," she said in a cold voice. "She won't trouble you again. Come, Antonia."

Antonia resisted her mother's efforts to drag her from the room. "Mamma, I don't want to leave yet. Papa and I were just getting acquainted."

Marissa stumbled to a halt. Her mouth opened, but no words came out. She looked stunned, anxious and defiant, all at the same time. But mostly, she looked like the woman he loved.

He couldn't tease her any more, not even for the fun of it. Crossing the room, he took one of her trembling hands in his. "My love, I've been a brute, and I beg your forgiveness. But why didn't you tell me about Antonia last night?"

Her beautiful eyes filled with remorse. "I wanted to. But I was afraid you would hate me for the lies I told. And for not remaining true to you all those years, no matter what the consequences."

When her voice broke, Anthony pulled her into his arms. She put up a token struggle before relaxing against his chest.

"And I didn't know what to tell Antonia," she whispered. "What would she think?"

He nodded grimly. "You were ashamed of me. Of what I had become."

"Never!" she exclaimed, giving him a fierce hug. "You're the finest man I've ever known."

He let out a tight breath. "Then what were you afraid of? You should have known I would never let anyone hurt you – either of you."

She looked woeful. "I was afraid Antonia would despise me. My life was a lie, and I made hers a lie, too."

Antonia propped her hands on her hips and gave her mother a severe look. "Mamma, I worry that your mind is as disordered as Papa's. How could you think such a thing? I love you more than anything in the world."

Marissa extracted herself from Anthony's embrace and gently grasped her daughter's shoulders. Mother and child gazed into each other's eyes, seeming to communicate in some mystical, female way.

"Then you don't mind that you have a new father? Your real father?" Marissa finally asked.

Antonia looked puzzled. "Why would I? He seems nice, and you love him. Plus, he's rich. You are rich, aren't you, Papa?" she asked, suddenly looking worried. "Mamma and I wouldn't be happy if we had to live with Uncle Edmund, instead of with you."

Anthony pulled the two most important people in the world into his arms. Each fitted snugly against him, as if they'd both been there from the beginning of time.

"No man could be richer," he said.

And with the prizes he had captured, no man ever would.

Lady Invisible

Patricia Rice

Cotswolds – 1816

One

"'It is a truth universally acknowledged, that a single man in possession of a good fortune must be in want of a wife,'" quoted Mrs Higglebottom, the vicar's wife, reading from the novel on her husband's desk.

Ill at ease, Major Lucas Sumner stretched his shoulders against the confinement of his civilian attire. He had hoped Reverend Higglebottom might be available for consultation. He did not remember the vicar's wife being quite so ... enigmatic ... in her younger days. They'd both grown up here among the rolling hills of Chipping Bedton, but Lucas obviously had been away too long. He must adjust his military sense of order to village idiosyncrasies.

"My fortune is a major's pension and a small inheritance," Lucas corrected. "I am in want of a wife because I have a daughter in need of a mother."

Mrs H. – Lorena, as he'd known her – waved a careless, plump hand. "The extent of your fortune does not matter these days. The village has lost most of its available young men to war and to the city and to marriage. You can have a choice of ladies, from fifteen to fifty, I daresay. The task is to find the *right* one."

"Well, yes, that is why I thought I would consult with Edgar—"

"Edgar did not grow up here as we did," Lorena admonished. "My husband has a worthy, virtuous mind, but not necessarily one connected to the realities of life. Women are far better at matchmaking than men."

Lucas granted that possibility. He'd married in haste as a young man, and the result was currently uprooting daffodils from graves in the churchyard, if he did not mistake.

With an apology, he rose, pushed up the vicar's study window, and shouted, "Verity! Stop that at once. Where is your aunt?"

His seven-year-old hoyden waved a bunch of yellow flowers and dashed off. Lucas could only hope it was in the direction of his much-put-upon sister.

"I have a lot to account for in this life," he said, striding back to the chair. "Verity's mother died far too young, and I've neglected my daughter's upbringing. Now that the war is done and I've come home, it's time I find a mother for Verity who can teach her to be a lady and turn my bachelor household into a home."

Lorena nodded and consulted the list she'd evidently drawn up in anticipation of his visit. "Jane Bottoms is still unmarried. She's a bit long in the tooth, but a very respectable, proper sort."

Lucas tugged at his neckcloth. He remembered Jane. Thick as a brick, they used to call her. "My daughter needs someone a little more—"

Lorena cut him off, as she seemed to do regularly. "Yes, yes, of course. Verity would tie her to a tree and forget about her. How about Mary Loveless? She's a bit plump and her mother tends to dictate . . ." She caught Lucas' eye and hurriedly looked at the list again.

Impatiently, Lucas snapped the paper from her hand and scanned the names. "Harriet Briggs is still unmarried?" he exclaimed in amazement. "How is that possible? She's the Squire's daughter and had a dozen beaux before I left, but she was much too young to be interested in any of them."

Lorena crossed her plump hands on the battered desk. "She is still not interested in any of them. She has not changed since the child you remember. You need a mature, proper lady to teach your daughter manners. Harriet is totally unsuitable."

This time Lucas was the one to interrupt. "I remember her as a spirited little thing. Perhaps she was a bit of a tomboy riding to the hounds because her father never told her no, but she could argue intelligently. Verity needs a smart woman to guide her."

Lorena vehemently shook her head. "Now that her mother has passed on and all feminine influence is lost, Harriet has become quite impossible. Rumour has it that she called off two perfectly respectable arrangements while she was in London, even though her looks are nothing to brag about." She shook her head and cut herself off. "Her father has refused to give her another season."

Lucas conjured a mental image of Miss Harriet Briggs the last time he'd seen her, when she wasn't quite sixteen. He had been twenty and sporting his newly purchased officer's colours. He'd been home to say farewells to family and strutting about in hopes his new uniform would impress the ladies.

The Squire's daughter had been sitting on the doorstep of one of the village houses, showing a youngster how to feed a baby pig. She had not been impressed by his uniform but had appreciated his aid when the pig had squirmed free. They'd had a rational discourse on the care and feeding of abandoned farm animals, a conversation that he could not imagine having with any other female of his acquaintance.

Hope surged, despite Lorena's warning. His household was in dire need of the discipline a lady could bring to it.

"She must be twenty-three or twenty-four by now?" In the eight years of his absence Harriet should have grown into her lanky limbs at least. Lucas didn't think he'd care for a skinny woman, although a mother for Verity should be more important than attractiveness.

Well, perhaps not, or he'd have hired a nanny. So he needed a wife who appealed to him, as well as a mother for Verity. Doubt crept in at the seeming impossibility of that task. Perhaps he should have gone wife-hunting in London.

His sister should not have to deal with Verity while he danced through society. There *had* to be someone local, who would want to live here and raise his child among his family.

"Harriet should be a good age for looking after a child." A man of action and decision, Lucas rose from the chair. "I don't think anyone younger would be up to the challenge."

Lorena looked harassed. "No, really, Lucas. Don't be foolish. I do not wish to speak ill . . . Look, here is Elizabeth. She's an extremely attractive young lady . . ."

Having made up his mind – and worried that Verity would be digging up the dead next – Lucas was already halfway out the door when Lorena leaped up, waving the list. "And Mary Dougal! Mature, quiet, and very lovely . . ."

"I will consider them all, of course," Lucas said, making his bow, although he privately thought Elizabeth to be a simpering ninny and Mary Dougal to be a pinchpenny prude. Verity was a bright child. She needed a disciplined woman up to the challenge of taming her. And a patient one to ease them into their new domestic routines.

"I told you not to climb the trees!" he roared, after departing the vicarage. He crossed the cemetery in long strides to where his sister stared upwards in dismay. He could see the bright blue of his daughter's gown several limbs from the ground. "Come down from there at once, you little monkey."

He nearly had failure of the heart when Verity's small foot slipped and missed the branch below her. Without a second's thought, he swung up on the lowest limb, heedless of his best trousers, caught Verity by the waist, and lowered her to Maria.

"I have three of my own, Lucas," his sister called back. "I cannot do this much longer. You should hire a circus trainer."

"I am amazed you did not hire her out to a zoo before this," he said in exasperation as the child took off running before he could climb down. "Does she never speak?"

Maria shrugged and followed Verity across the church lawn at a slower pace. "She can talk if she must. Mostly, she does what she wants rather than ask, because she knows she'll be told no. I have three young boys. It's all I can do to keep up with them. I hate to burden you, Lucas, but now that you're home safe and sound, she's your responsibility."

"I agree. And someday I hope to repay you if possible. You have been a saint, and I don't know what we would have done without you." He caught up with Verity when she stopped to pet a shaggy mutt. She was no longer a toddler for Lucas to heave over his shoulder and carry off as he had the few times he'd been home when she'd been younger. He'd missed almost her entire childhood.

"Your safe return is payment enough," Maria promised. "If you never go to war again and can provide a home for Verity, that will ensure our happiness."

Lucas thought of his sister's request as he knocked at Squire Briggs' door the next afternoon. Now that Napoleon had been routed, he would not be going to war again, but that meant he had no other purpose.

Lucas' father had died before he could attend Oxford or obtain any type of training. Other than the cottage and the lot it sat on, he had no lands of his own. The only trade he knew was soldiering. It was a problem he must solve after he found a mother for Verity.

Before setting off on this visit to the Squire, he'd left his daughter with Maria, had his hair properly barbered, and had his old cutaway coat with the broad lapels brushed and pressed. And still he squirmed like a raw lad on the brink of courtship.

He had been far too young to have encountered Squire Briggs

regularly before he'd left for war, so he didn't know the man well. The unfamiliarity of civilian life threw him off balance, forcing him to recall that he had earned his major's stripes and fought battles far worse than the encounter ahead.

A maid led Lucas inside to a fusty parlour in dire need of a lady's care. He frowned over that. Even if Lady Briggs had been deceased for some years, should not Miss Briggs have directed the servants in cleaning? Or at least replaced the cat-tattered pillows?

Cat hair was everywhere. He declined the maid's offer of a seat.

Lucas liked to do his own reconnaissance and had made several enquiries before setting out on this call. From all reports, Squire Briggs was a hearty man who loved his horses and his hounds. His lands were fertile and well tended, and his tenants spoke well of him. Lack of funds or servants did not explain this lack of order.

The tenants had spoken well of the Squire's daughter, as well, but with a certain degree of caution. Lucas trusted that was out of respect, but Lorena's warning rang in his memory.

He heard the Squire roaring at a rambunctious hound somewhere deeper inside the house and smiled to himself, thinking taming a dog was very much like taming Verity. He'd nearly broken his neck falling over her this morning when she'd darted out from under a table on her hands and knees.

"Sumner!" the Squire boomed as he entered the parlour. "Good to see you home, lad! Major now, ain't ye? Made the town proud, you did. Shame your father is no longer about to brag on you." He pounded Lucas on the back and gestured towards the door. "C'mon back to m'study. We'll have a bit of brandy and celebrate your return."

Brandy was an excellent idea. Lucas thought he needed fortifying before he explained his presence. He was starting to think he should have sought out Harriet first, but he'd forgotten the protocol, if he'd ever known it. How did one woo a lady without going through her parent? He was no dab hand at courtship.

Outside, several hounds gave voice at once, and a woman shouted sharp commands.

The Squire ignored the commotion, reaching for a decanter on a dusty tray. Cat hair seemed less prevalent here, Lucas noticed. An ancient basset lay sprawled and snoring in front of the empty grate.

"You're a military man. What do you know of hounds and hunting?" the Squire enquired, handing Lucas a glass.

"A great deal, as it happens, sir. I've spent the better part of these last years on horseback, chasing enemies wilier than foxes."

Outside, the dogs howled louder, and a screech resembling a brawl between penned pigs and enraged hawks ensued. The woman's shouts escalated.

Lucas had begun to wonder if he shouldn't investigate, when Briggs threw open a sash of his double study window and shouted, "Harriet, get them damned hounds back in the pen where they belong and shoot the peacocks!"

Lucas blinked. Things had changed mightily if one shouted at young ladies these days and ordered them to perform a stable hand's duty.

In coming here, he'd had some vision of a benevolent, ladylike Harriet gliding into the room carrying a tea tray and somehow divining why he'd called. After all, Lorena had said he was an eligible catch, and the Squire's daughter was the most eligible female around. The purpose of his call should be obvious.

Perhaps he should have listened a little more closely to Lorena.

A childish shriek raised the hair on the back of his neck. Lucas dashed to the other window and threw open the second sash.

"Dash it all, Harry, I told you to get them hounds back in the barn!" the Squire was shouting in frustration while Lucas scanned the grounds for some sight of the origin of the childish scream. "We've got a guest! You need to get back in here."

A pair of peahens and a cock flapped around three baying beagles, who were racing around the base of an oak as if they'd treed a squirrel.

Surrounded by the circling hounds and birds, a slender female in honey-coloured riding habit, with the skirt scandalously rucked up to reveal her tall boots, and her jacket missing, smacked the snout of the nearest dog. Lucas couldn't hear what she was saying, but the animals crouched down and wagged their tails in anticipation of some treat.

The wildly colourful birds scattered to alight on various bits of shrubbery.

The young lady turned her uncovered head upwards to study the tree's branches, and Lucas' gut lurched. His gaze followed hers.

The child he had thought he'd left securely at his sister's house was instead perched on the lowest limb of the oak, swinging her toes and watching the dogs, probably with interest, if he knew his daughter. The earlier scream had been for effect. Verity was fearless.

"Verity Augusta, get down from there this instant!" Lucas roared, heedless of the Squire's startled reaction.

"That your young one?" Briggs asked. "What the devil is she doing in my tree?"

"As if I know what goes through her mind," Lucas muttered, pulling his head back in the window. "I'd best prise her down and take her home."

"Harry can do it." Briggs stuck his head back out the window again and roared, "Harriet, bring the girl inside to her papa."

The half-dressed lady sent her father what appeared to Lucas to be a look of exasperation, before crouching down to scratch the hounds and sending them scampering towards the kennel.

Verity, on the other hand, climbed to her feet and appeared to be considering the next highest branch.

Lucas didn't think shouting at the females had put a dent in their behaviour.

If he'd had an undisciplined soldier who disobeyed him like that . . . He'd already confined Verity to quarters without result, and he couldn't court-martial her. And he'd never resort to whipping. How did one command loyalty and obedience from a female?

As if in answer to his guest's unspoken question, the Squire poured their brandies, handed Lucas one and said, "Never understand women. Contrary lot, don't know what's good for them. Don't suppose you've come to take Harry off my hands, have you? Good girl, but damned if I can make her see sense."

Lucas took a healthy swallow of his drink. Did he need *two* contrary females on his hands? He thought not, but he was a man who required information before making a life-altering decision. Discipline could be instilled in anyone, eventually.

This wife-getting business was more difficult than he'd anticipated.

"After all these years, I can't say that I know Miss Briggs well," Lucas replied circumspectly. "It would be a pleasure to become reacquainted."

Briggs snorted again and leaned back in his chair. "I offered a handsome dowry, told everyone that she will inherit all I own someday, and she still garnered only two offers in London. And she turned those down. Take her off my hands, and you'll be the son I never had."

Studying the lady's attire, Lucas suffered an uneasy notion that *Harriet* wanted to be the son her father never had.

Two

Harriet Briggs tilted her head back to admire the small girl straddling the oak branch above her head. "The dogs didn't frighten you, did they?" she enquired with interest.

The child shook her mop of orange curls vigorously. "I like trees."

"And is there some reason you like this particular tree?"

The child didn't answer, but Harriet had a strong suspicion the reason stood in her father's study window. Tall, broad-shouldered and wearing his bottle-green swallowtail coat as if it were a military uniform, the gentleman had arrived only shortly before the child. Both had walked, so they could not live too far away.

Harriet had seen the child in church on Sundays with Maria Smith and her brood of boys. She'd been told the girl was the boys' cousin, but Harriet and Maria were a decade apart in age and never close, so she didn't know more than gossip.

As far as Harriet knew, though, Maria's only sibling was Lucas Sumner. She tried to find a resemblance to Lucas in the child's oval face, but it had been too many years since she'd seen her childhood idol. She was long past the age of believing in human deities anyway. Children developed foolish fantasies, and she was firmly grounded in reality these days.

Blifil, the lame kitten, suddenly tumbled from the boxwoods, chasing after Partridge, her tame squirrel. The squirrel dashed up her skirt and into the tree, much to the child's startlement. Harriet prayed the girl didn't fall before she got her down.

"Do you have a name?" Harriet asked, ignoring her father's bellows from the window. Really, he ought to know by now that she wouldn't shout back like a field hand.

"My name is Verity. You're Miss Harriet, aren't you?" the child asked, proving she was observant for her age.

"I am. If you climb down from there, we can have tea and biscuits. Do you like kittens?" She swept Blifil from the ground before he could follow the squirrel.

"My papa will make me go home if I climb down. He told my Aunt Maria he needs a wife to take care of me, and I want to see who he picks."

She stopped there, as if that said everything. Which it did, Harriet supposed, fighting a shiver of expectation and annoyance. Lucas had always been smart. He would seek out the wealthiest available woman in the neighbourhood before looking at the less eligible or the more beautiful. She was simply surprised he wasn't looking in London instead of Chipping Bedton.

She supposed she would have to watch the last of her childhood illusions crumble. Major Sumner had to be able to see her from the window, so she was probably missing the show already. Would he bluntly express dismay at her unseemly attire and ragged manners? Or bite back his thoughts and just tighten his lips in disapproval over a mature young lady who displayed such inappropriate behaviour? She had little entertainment any more, so perhaps she could drum some up at the Major's expense.

"I'll tell your papa you're my guest so he can't send you home," she told the child. "I'm a bit peckish and would like a sandwich with my tea, I believe. Do you think I might help you down?"

The child considered the suggestion, then finally nodded. "I climb like a monkey, my papa says." Before Harriet was prepared, Verity caught the branch she sat on and swung her feet loose.

Dropping the kitten, Harriet tried not to gasp in terror as the girl trustingly fell into her arms. Harriet had watched her creatures perform dangerous acrobatics, but she'd never endured the terror of a human child risking death in such a manner. Major Sumner had his hands full with this one.

Staggering slightly as she lowered the child's chunky body to firm land, Harriet suffered a brief glimpse of what it must be like to love and care for a precious, fragile life. It was difficult enough tending to a wounded pet. She didn't think she could tolerate seeing a child hurt.

Really, she had nothing to worry about. She need only meet Lucas, let him see how utterly unsuitable she was, and go about her merry way. Her father and the tenants and the animals needed her. She had a very full life without an annoying man providing obstacles, objecting to everything she did or wanted. It was not as if she *needed* a man for anything. And she already had one yelling impossible orders all day long. She certainly didn't require another. Taking a deep breath to settle her racing pulse, she swung Verity's hand and was smiling when she entered the study where the men waited. Her confidence faltered a little at sight of the tall, immaculately dressed gentleman nearly filling the furniture-stuffed room.

Lucas Sumner had grown from lanky lad to a huge, square-shouldered man with shadowed eyes that had seen too much suffering. Harriet's soft heart nearly plummeted to her toes. She could ignore laughing, handsome men. She could not ignore wounded ones.

"Thank you for rescuing my obstreperous daughter, Miss Briggs. I must take her home, where she belongs."

A small hand clenched Harriet's. The child very properly did not argue, but Harriet knew how it felt to be invisible. She tickled Verity's palm while nodding pretend agreement. She would give Major Sumner one more chance at a little empathy.

"I have promised Verity tea and biscuits," she said in her politest hostess tones. "Perhaps we could retire to the parlour and have a bite before you must leave?"

"No, she's not capable of sitting still," he responded dismissively. "I would not ruin your rugs with spilled tea and crumbs. It's a pleasure to make your acquaintance again, Miss Briggs. Perhaps another time?"

Ah well, such a pity that he was a blind fool like all the others, but then, attractive men often thought they owned the world. And society allowed them to continue thinking that.

Harriet supposed it was naughty of her, but she would like Verity to recognize that she was not lacking in any way. She was simply being a child, and her father was simply being . . . well, a stiff-necked man.

At her father's curt dismissal, Verity tugged her hand free and fled the room. Major Sumner uttered an impolite word and stalked after her.

Harriet blocked his path. Giving the Major a warning look, she called after the fleeing child, "If Invisible Girl will wait outside the front door, I will follow shortly. I do not break promises!"

The front door slammed. She hoped Verity was bright enough to listen. And be curious.

"I promised Verity tea and biscuits. Now I shall have to walk with her and explain they'll have to wait for another day or she will think I've lied to her." Harriet pasted a sweet smile over her irritation.

The glowering gentleman appeared prepared to bodily remove her from his path, and her smile grew more challenging.

Three

Lucas did not know what to make of the annoying Miss Briggs. She walked alongside him without a coat to cover her thin lawn blouse. Even her dishevelled lace jabot did not conceal her plump bosom. Her riding skirts and boots allowed her to take long strides that matched his, proving she was not so demure as her pursed lips and silence would lead him to believe.

She had a veritable cloud of frizzy mouse brown curls that she had made no attempt to tame or cover. She had not really grown out of her gangliness either. Her limbs were long and ungraceful, but her waist was small, and she curved in womanly places as she had not as a fifteen-year-old. He supposed, in an evening gown, she would reveal far more than this unconventional costume did. He could not quite put a reason to his shock . . . or attraction. She was as undisciplined a hoyden as Verity and not at all the polite sort of female he'd envisioned.

Perhaps he should have visited a dolly-mop or two in London before returning to the village if his idea of luscious womanhood was this defiant filly.

As they strode along the village lane, Verity scampered behind the stone fences and hedgerows, just out of sight, but following closely, as she must have earlier when she'd trailed him here. His daughter was far too clever and bold for her own good.

The silence grew awkward. Lucas sought for some means of breaking it, but he did not have much experience in conversing with unattached females. He had rather hoped for a businesslike transaction. Courting was another matter entirely – provided he wanted to court a woman who defied him before they even exchanged greetings.

"Do you prefer rural society to London?" he asked, wincing at his stilted tone.

"I believe I prefer animal society," she responded without inflection.

Perhaps he should have listened to Lorena. Miss Briggs was not a comfortable companion, at the very least. Just a little annoyed that she ignored him to keep her eye on Verity, he released some of his frustration.

"Pets cannot talk back?" he suggested with a hint of sarcasm.

She shot him a sideways glance but whether of surprise, appreciation or distaste, he could not discern.

"Animals *do* talk back, if only one listens. Rather like children, actually." Her small boots kicked up dust on the rutted dirt lane.

"Children aren't supposed to talk back. They are too young to offer intelligent observation and must be educated."

She made a rude noise that startled him. He was very much out of touch if ladies these days made uncouth sounds instead of pouting prettily.

"I have not been back in the country long," he admitted cautiously. "Perhaps I am missing the nuances of your reply."

She bestowed a laughing look on him. "What would you think if your batman snorted at your priggish assertion?"

He'd definitely been around men too long. Her laughter stirred his interest more than a little, despite her insult. "I would think he needed his pay docked," he responded tartly. "Would you take that attitude from a kitchen wench?"

"I would if she was speaking about something of which she knew more than I did," she said.

There was the spirited girl he remembered, although he'd rather forgotten that she had a tart tongue to match her intelligence. But she was wrong if she thought a child ought to be allowed to talk disrespectfully to her elders.

"Invisible Girl shouldn't climb trees," Harriet abruptly called as Verity headed for a low-hanging apple branch. "Trees make her visible."

Verity darted back into the cover of the hedge.

Now he was more than intrigued. "Invisible Girl?" he enquired.

She shrugged. "Women and children are expected to be invisible. That works for some of us. Not all."

"Expecting Verity to behave is not asking her to be invisible. There is a reason discipline and authority are required," he objected. "If my men didn't follow my command, they could put themselves or others in harm's way."

"Provided your command was correct," she argued. "You do not allow for independent thinking."

"Not while I'm the one responsible for what happens! That's the entire point of being in charge – to know what is best for those relying on my expertise and knowledge. Verity cannot simply run unchecked about town, not acknowledging anyone's authority but her own."

"She is a child! She cannot be expected to respect the authority of someone she barely knows. And who barely knows her! Have you even tried to understand your daughter, Major Sumner?"

"I shouldn't have to *understand* her, Miss Briggs," he declared. "She should simply obey the adults in her life until she's reached an age of reason."

Miss Briggs gave him a look of incredulity, emitted another rude snort, and climbed the turnstile to join Verity in the field. Together, they ran laughing in the direction of the village.

Lucas didn't think his suit was going very well. Perhaps he should consider plump, henpecked Mary after all. He marched down the lane, realizing this was the first time he'd seen Verity laugh since he'd returned home. He tugged uncomfortably at his neckcloth.

Striding down the lane after Sunday dinner, Harriet knew she'd behaved badly earlier in the week. And she'd done so deliberately, rejecting Major Sumner before he could reject her. She'd seen the disapproval in his eyes, let it raise her temper and then she'd goaded him into behaving like a military high stickler. Which he was, or at least, he had been. That did not mean he was a bad man, just one accustomed to certain behaviour.

The kind of behaviour a child could not follow. Nor Harriet, for all that mattered, but that did not mean Major Sumner was *wrong*. It just meant that he and his daughter would have a very hard time of it, if someone did not intervene.

She was probably not the right person to do so, but who else would? The other unattached ladies in town simply whispered to each other behind their hands, wearing their best bonnets in hopes that Major Sumner would notice them. As if he was likely to notice a bonnet full of roses and birds! They'd do better to wear stiff military caps to make him feel more at home.

Mary had taken him a basket of muffins. Jane had taken him a pie. The child and Major Sumner would not go hungry, at least. But Verity would be ignored and feel even more like an Invisible Girl.

Verity was the only reason Harriet was marching down the lane this fine April Sunday afternoon, carrying a basket containing an adorable black-and-white kitten that would create havoc in Major Sumner's orderly household. Perhaps he needed to be reminded – as the other ladies would not – that he was not the only person in his home.

She supposed she ought to apologise for her earlier behaviour while she was at it, but she was not so certain on that matter. She had, though, dressed carefully for church that morning. If Major Sumner had noticed, he had not given a sign. He'd been too busy trying to keep Verity behaving like a proper major general.

So Harriet was taking the liberty of calling on the child this afternoon, while still wearing her Sunday sprigged muslin. She'd even tamed her hair to stay inside her bonnet, except for a loose curl or two. She wore her gloves and kid slippers and looked as much like a lady as she possibly could, so Major Sumner would have no reason to disapprove of her disreputable untidiness and set off her temper again.

Perhaps she might show him she could be proper, if she must, but neatness had never been overly important to her. She'd kept the family housekeeper on even though Agnes was half-blind and unaware of the damages Harriet's pets caused. Harriet preferred her pets and Agnes to orderliness. If the Major wanted tidy, he should court Mary Loveless and her overbearing mother.

Nor could she compete with pretty Elizabeth or sweet-tempered Jane. Harriet was plain. Sometimes, when she did needlework, she even wore spectacles. And no man had ever called her sweet. So all Harriet could hope was that if she looked respectable enough, Major Sumner would allow her to be a friend and help with his daughter.

She had ascertained that Lucas had returned to his father's old cottage on a small lot between her father's farm and the village. His father had been the town physician until his death last spring. Harriet had often visited his home with her father's tenants. She was familiar with the two-storey cottage.

The lilac by the front door needed trimming, but it would bloom wonderfully in another month. Harriet rapped the knocker. Before anyone could answer, a childish shriek of fear and a masculine shout of panic erupted from the yard behind the house.

Setting the kitten basket on the doorstep, she lifted her Sunday skirt and raced past a few bedraggled jonquils and a struggling peony, around the corner, to the old stable.

Seeing no one in the yard, she followed the sound of angry shouts into the stable – where Verity hung upside down from the rafters with a large harness around her waist, in peril of slipping out on her head at any moment.

If it were not so terrifying a situation, it would have been funny. How had the child ended up swinging like a trapeze artist?

The rafter was tall and Verity was short. Major Sumner stretched between the ground and his daughter's hair, barely keeping her from falling but unable to grasp her sufficiently to lower her to the ground. Hence the furious shouting. Men despised helplessness.

There was no point in explaining that a little girl did not know how to grasp leathers and climb back up from whence she'd fallen, as her father was encouraging her to do. Tucking the back of her skirt into the front of her petticoat ribbons, Harriet hastened up the ladder into the loft as she often did at home.

"If you tug the strap, she will fall!" Lucas warned from below. "And you are likely to fall with her."

"I know my limitations," Harriet retorted, stripping off her gloves. "Verity's coming down. Stand under her and grab for her shoulders." She found the buckle the little imp had wrapped around the beam and carefully undid it, hanging on to the leather with all her strength. "Verity, reach for your father because I cannot hold this for long."

Verity shrieked. Lucas yelled. And the harness whipped from Harriet's hands, leaving a burned streak across her palms. Shaking, Harriet closed her eyes, too terrified to see if she'd killed them both.

Verity began weeping loudly. Probably frightened out of her mind. Lucas scolded. Not the best of reactions for either, but at least she knew they were alive. Opening her eyes again, Harriet attempted the ladder, only now realizing how very unladylike she would appear with her stockings and garters exposed.

A strong arm caught her waist and lifted her free of the ladder. "I've got you. Let go."

She did, and Lucas swung her to the ground, while keeping a tearful Verity tucked under his other arm. The man's brains were in his brawn.

She liked the feel of his brawn a little too well. Shaking now that the incident was done, she wanted to bury her face in his big shoulder and weep out her fear as Verity was doing.

Lucas had apparently removed his frock coat after church and was in only waistcoat and shirt. She could smell his shaving soap and the manly aroma of his skin. While she fought back tears, he held her a little longer than was necessary, steadying himself as well as her.

Apparently realizing that fact at the same moment as she, he released her waist, but then remained uncertain what to do with the hysterical child he'd so rudely tucked under his other arm.

"Verity, sweetheart," Harriet murmured, still shaken but unable to resist a sobbing child. "Give over." She slid her arms around the girl and lifted her away from Lucas. "Verity, you terrified us. You have no idea how much it hurts your father when he thinks you're in pain or danger. He can't cry as you do, so he has to yell and shout."

Lucas snorted rudely, as she had once done, and Harriet shot him a retaliatory look. He rubbed his hands through his already dishevelled hair, like a man who had reached his last tether.

Verity flung her skinny arms around Harriet's neck and buried her runny nose in the pretty sprigged muslin. Too rattled to care,

Harriet rocked her and patted her on the back as if Verity were a babe. Her arms ached with the weight, but Lucas had not yet learned to comfort his daughter. Someone must teach him.

Calming down enough to learn his lesson, he lifted Verity from Harriet's arms. "You scared me out of ten years' growth, child. Whatever were you doing up there?"

Verity sniffed and rubbed her nose on his waistcoat and finally wrapped her arms around her father's neck long enough to stop sobbing. Harriet thought perhaps she ought to sneak out now that the two were learning to get on, but she was interested in hearing Verity's reply.

"I wanted to be big!" she wailed. "Davy said he stretched his arms big by swinging on ropes, so I wanted to swing!"

Four

"Oh, dear." Miss Briggs snickered and turned away, as if to depart.

Holding Verity in one arm, Lucas caught his saviour's elbow with his free hand. His heart still hadn't stopped attempting to escape his chest at the sight of his daughter hanging upside down in danger of breaking her neck.

If Miss Briggs had not come along, he would have had to learn to fly. He'd never seen a more level-headed, courageous lady, and even if she was a tart-tongued hoyden, he *needed* her. Verity needed her.

"Don't go." He tried not to plead, but he could see disaster written on his future unless he kept this woman with him. "We haven't thanked you. I don't suppose it's proper to invite you in for tea." He hated being uncertain but he was too overwrought at the moment to care. He just didn't want her to go until his heart stopped pounding in his ears.

"I think it might be a good idea for Verity to go inside and wash up and lie down for a little while. Keeping up with her cousins is very tiring."

Davy was one of Verity's older cousins. Lucas caught the lady's implication. He'd left his baby girl to compete with three older male cousins. His fault. Everything was his fault. It was up to him to undo what he had wrought.

"We will be just a minute," he told her, looking for some way to persuade her to stay. "There is some pie left. We can eat it under the tree, where everyone can see we are very respectable." He started for the house, trying not to notice as Miss Briggs brushed her skirt and petticoat back where they belonged.

She had long, lovely legs.

And shapely arms that cuddled a child the way he wouldn't mind being held.

He wondered if Miss Briggs might ever rest her head against his shoulder as Verity did. That wasn't a proper or respectable thought.

"I don' wanna take a nap." Verity hiccupped on her protest.

"Just lie down and rest your eyes a little," Miss Briggs said soothingly, matching Lucas' stride with ease. "And if you're good and rest long enough, I'll have a surprise waiting for you in the kitchen."

"A surprise?" Verity lifted her damp cheeks. "For me?"

"Yes, just for you. Are you big enough to run upstairs and wash and take off your dress or do you need help?"

"I'm big enough!" Verity pushed off Lucas' shoulders and wriggled to get down. When he let her go, she raced ahead of them.

"I've never seen her hurry so to take a nap," he said wryly. "I hope you really do have a surprise for her."

"You'll hate it, but I do. She needs to feel she's important, so I brought her a kitten. Learning to take care of a pet will teach her that others rely on her, and that she's very important, indeed. But you'll have to put up with the mess."

"You're laughing at me," he said accusingly, steering her towards the tea table his mother had set up beneath the beech tree.

"Perhaps, only a little, because I'm still quaking in my shoes. She could have been killed!" Miss Briggs wailed, almost collapsing into the chair he held for her.

"Exactly my thought twenty times a day. Wait here, and I'll bring out the cups and things, after I see Verity into bed. Did you leave the kitten in front?" At her nod, he made a mental note to fetch it. He doubted Verity's ability to take care of a kitten, but his heart warmed that Miss Briggs had thought of her.

He could foresee cat hairs in his future, but Verity was more important than tidiness. Somehow, he must learn to rearrange his priorities.

His daughter had already stripped off her grubby and ruined Sunday dress and was splashing cold water as if she were a duck at play. Lucas scrubbed off some of the grime on her face and hands and watched her climb between the covers, before returning downstairs to the kitchen and setting on a kettle of tea. He supposed he should have done that first. He needed to hire a maid to think of these things, but it seemed awkward unless he had a wife first. He missed his batman.

He had imagined a sweet little woman ordering his household about, one who smiled cheerfully and arranged for delightful meals to appear on the table and pottered about keeping order, until it was time for her to come up to his bed. He could see now that his imagination was considerably rosier than actuality, rather like his youthful idea of war.

Life had a habit of not living up to his expectations. He could not even live up to his own. In the military, it had been relatively simple to follow orders, understand his men and take action. Women, on the other hand, were a mysterious universe he might never comprehend. How did he persuade one that he needed her without sounding desperate?

Remembering the kitten, he stopped at the front to pick up the basket. It smelled of lavender and sported pink ribbons and a little black nose was pushing aside a gingham cloth. He hoped it was a male cat or he'd be outnumbered.

Carrying basket and tea tray, Lucas geared up his considerable courage to approach the intrepid Miss Harriet Briggs. He needed a wife who could rescue children from barns more than he needed a lady to look pretty and make tea. He simply had to find some way of asking her

Harriet thought about running and hiding before Lucas returned. Just the fact that she was thinking of him as *Lucas* instead of Major Sumner spoke much of the familiarity of her thoughts.

She had no mirror and couldn't straighten out the frizzy mess her hair had become when the pins loosened in her climb. She shoved as much as she could inside her bonnet, then discovered she'd left her gloves in the barn. Her hands were bare, revealing her broken nails and dirt from the leather. She was an unmitigated hoyden, just as her father claimed.

Fine, then, she had nothing about which to worry. Major Sumner would not be interested in anyone as indecorous as she, so she could simply sip tea and discuss Verity's welfare.

She hurried to rescue him from tea tray and kitten as soon as he appeared. She couldn't help her heart from making an odd leap at the sight of the big strong man biting his lip while attempting to balance tray and swinging kitten basket at the same time. Even though he'd properly donned his Sunday cutaway coat and looked beyond dashing, the self-confident Major wasn't quite as intimidating or perfect in domesticity.

She had already dusted off the old table and now used the

gingham from the kitten basket to cover it before she set the tray down. "Is Verity all settled in?" she asked nervously when he hovered too close, forcing awareness of how large he was. He'd *lifted* her from the ladder, while holding Verity! Her heart did another little jig.

"I think she was frightened enough to be glad of a moment alone."

"She's a bright child, with a strong imagination. Once you learn of what she's capable, you'll enjoy her company, Major Sumner," Harriet said stiltedly. She'd been to London and had learned to make polite small talk with gentlemen about the weather and the music and the company. She'd never had to pretend restraint in the village. Until now.

"Please, call me Lucas. I am no longer in the Army and, after this episode, I would like to call you friend, if I might."

She nodded and poured the tea, aware of how ugly her hands looked. "I am Harriet, although everyone calls me Harry. I fear my name is as unladylike as I am."

"Ladylike is not a quality useful in dealing with Verity, I fear." He sat uncomfortably in the small wrought-iron chair. Even the teacup looked frail and useless in his hand.

Harriet winced at his unintended insult and sipped her tea. She was good at caring for animals but not so quick at witticism. Still, she tried. "Real ladies would not be so inclined to ruck up their dresses and climb ladders," she agreed with innocence.

He nodded. "That is precisely what I mean. Action and quick thinking is what is required around Verity. Polite manners and pretty dresses are irrelevant."

Thinking polite manners might prevent her from dumping the tea over his head for implying she wasn't a lady because she could *think*, Harriet bit back an impolite retort. "I daresay ladies are irrelevant on all counts," she agreed maliciously. "They are merely decorative, are they not? Rather like stained-glass windows. Perhaps they should be left in church."

He looked startled. Instead of replying, he apparently made a hasty reassessment of their exchange. "I did not mean to imply—"

"Oh, no need to apologise." She waved away whatever he meant to say. "I'm aware of my shortcomings. Instead of sitting prettily in my parlour, I climb in haylofts and trees. I shout at dogs. I crawl about in henhouses. I will never be considered decorative, by any means!"

"As you say, decorative is for churches. I'd much rather see a woman who isn't afraid to help a child or an animal." He said it uneasily, as if afraid he was walking into a trap.

"One who argues," she suggested, listing her many flaws. "And speaks up for herself. You do not prefer polite, pretty ladies who demurely nod their heads and make men swoon with a smile."

"Exactly," he said, apparently pleased that she understood his requirements. "I hope I am not being too forward. When I went to your father, it was because I remembered you with fondness and hoped to press my suit. But Verity . . . Verity does not make it easy for me to court in a traditional manner. You are a woman of exceptional understanding. I would like to call on you, if I might be so bold."

"You wish to call on a woman who is not a lady, one who argues and rudely rucks up her skirts and isn't remotely attractive enough to be decorative?" she asked in feigned astonishment, raising her eyebrows. "I think not, sir. You may call on me when Verity needs rescuing again, perhaps. Until then, I give you good day."

Ribbons bedraggled from being crushed by an unthinking military man, Harriet rose from her chair and, head held high, sailed from the yard with bits of straw stuck to her crumpled muslin.

Five

Dropping his best visiting coat over a chair, Lucas rubbed his aching head. After an hour of listening to Miss Elizabeth Baker and a few of her dearest friends prattle in high-pitched voices about London fashion and the best teacakes, he was ready to stick his head in a bucket to clean out his ears. He was evidently not meant for feminine company.

He stared morosely out the kitchen door at the fields separating his cottage from the Briggs' estate. He wished he understood the feminine mind. He'd thought he and Miss Briggs had reached a level where they could talk honestly. He'd hoped . . .

But she'd thought he was insulting her, when he thought he'd been showering her with fevered compliments and his genuine delight at finding a sympathetic ear. He had porridge for brains.

He'd sent round a note of apology. He'd asked the vicar to put in a word for him. He'd spoken to the Squire himself. But nothing had worked. They muttered platitudes about Miss Harriet coming around in her own time. But she was never at home when he called.

He sighed as he watched his daughter climb the back fence to gather wildflowers from the field. Verity apparently had a passion for flowers. He didn't know one from another. A woman could help Verity grow a garden. He didn't even know where to acquire seeds.

Perhaps he could ask Miss Briggs how one went about finding flower seeds. He could help Verity collect a bouquet, tie a ribbon about it and deliver it as a peace offering. Or gratitude for the kitten wrecking the furniture. Verity adored the creature.

He could practise a few compliments, although he felt a fool telling her she had eyes the colour of the sky and skin as soft as silk. She did, but he didn't know how to say that.

After spending an hour in the company of the village ladies, Lucas knew of a certainty that Miss Briggs was the only local woman who met his needs, *all* his needs. He could hire a maid to clean cat hair. He could not hire an intelligent, desirable wife, one who could keep up with Verity and not drive him mad with inanities.

He saw no reason to give up on the woman he wanted, if all that parted them was his thickheaded pride and her damnably sensitive feelings. He would not have made major had he given up and simply obeyed orders instead of thinking for himself. Which was what Miss Briggs had been telling him – although he had difficulty applying such leadership to women. He'd learn.

The day was warm and there was no sense in making his laundry more difficult by dirtying a coat while hunting flowers. With no one about to see him, he abandoned his coat and followed Verity into the field.

Verity looked up in surprise when Lucas leaned over to pick a daffodil. She laughed in delight when he handed it to her. Together, they wandered deep into the field and a wooded area, collecting a ragged assortment of blooms that might make a lady smile. Maybe.

"Do you think we should put a ribbon around these and take them to Miss Harriet?" he asked when Verity seemed to be tiring of the game.

She nodded eagerly. Lucas was about to lift her on his shoulders and carry her back to the house, when he heard an impatient shout. He might be a thickheaded oaf, but he recognized Miss Harriet's voice.

It was coming from the pasture where the Briggs' tenant farmer had just loosed his bull.

He shoved the bouquet into Verity's hands. "Take these back to the house and put them in water. I'll bring Miss Briggs to visit shortly."

He didn't have time to wait and see that she obeyed. He took off at a lope around the fence, racing in the direction of the Briggs' estate. He had a feeling Miss Harriet was much like Verity, often climbing into situations from which she could not easily be extracted.

The one he found her in caused him to stumble in horror.

The redoubtable Miss Briggs had climbed over a stile on the far side of the field, in apparent pursuit of a puppy. While she was scolding the terrified hound, a ton of beef on the hoof pawed the ground and swung its massive head back and forth behind a bush, where she could not see it. Even the puppy could sense the danger and cowered on its belly amid the grass.

Lucas would strangle the woman if he did not have failure of the heart first.

He had no weapon other than himself. Trotting alongside the fence, he sought to distract the bull from this woman in her unfashionably shortened riding skirts. He waved his arms to catch the animal's attention and, when that was not sufficient, he climbed the fence and sat atop the rail, roaring curses.

Astonished, Miss Harriet looked up at his odd behaviour, then turned to follow his gaze. Her eyes widened as she glanced behind her to the bull pawing the ground.

Lucas nearly fell off the rail when she grabbed the pup, and the bull snorted and lowered his head at her motion.

"Don't move!" he shouted at her. "He's just looking for an excuse to attack."

"I can't very well stand here for the rest of my life," she retorted, holding the wriggling pup.

"It will be a very short life if you move." Too furious and terrified to be polite, Lucas leaped off the fence and began running around the bull's rump, away from Miss Briggs.

The bull swung its head in his direction, bellowed and charged.

Running for his life, and Harriet's, Lucas raced across the corner of the enclosed field, reaching the hedge on the other side with the bull's hot breath on his neck. Grabbing a hawthorn branch that gave beneath his weight, he vaulted across the wizened limbs – into a mud puddle on the other side of the hedgerow.

"Major Sumner, Lucas!"

He heard Harriet's panicked shouts as he tried to catch his breath after having lost it. Mud puddles were softer than the ground, but not by much.

Dainty ankles exposed, she climbed the stile, her expression gratifyingly concerned. He wanted to shake her until her teeth rattled for being so careless, but the frightened tears streaking her cheeks dampened his temper. And in the end, she *had* listened to his orders and stayed still.

Thankfully, she'd used her excellent head to go against his less than clear orders and escape the field the minute it was safe to do so. Dazed, he wondered if he could appoint her to be general of his household. But that wasn't what he wanted either.

Setting the pup on the ground, she raced to help Lucas up. "I am so sorry, Lucas. You are so brave! I had no idea . . ."

She was a mess in grubby wool and tousled curls. She was an angel of concern with tears flowing down her cheeks as she offered her bare, broken-nailed fingers to help him up.

He grabbed her hand. Admired her slender form in tawny yellow. Wanted to drive his fingers through her wild curls.

And tugged the hand she offered, yanking her into the mud wallow with him.

"You could have been killed!" he shouted. "Do you never look where you are going? Does it never occur to you that *you* might be more important than a damned animal?"

She spluttered, shoved her hands against his chest, and glared down at him. "What do you care? I'm just another nuisance who won't fall in line and behave as I ought!"

He rolled her into the grass beside the mud wallow and swung over her, propping himself on his hands so he could trap her until she heard him out. "I don't need a field sergeant! Or a decorative piece of church plaster. I need a *woman*, one who understands Invisible Girls and is willing to put up with Impossible Men. I need a soft woman who cuddles children and lets me pretend I'm useful. I need a woman who looks beautiful with mud in her hair and straw on her hem. And you're the only damned one I know who fits the bill!"

She blinked, and her heavenly sky-blue eyes stared up at him in wonder. "Me? I am not beautiful. Or decorative," she reminded him.

"Decorative is useless. Decorative sits about collecting dust. Beautiful is alive and glittering with sunshine and smelling of roses. Don't make me speak poetry because I don't know any."

"I think you just did," Harriet murmured in awe, watching the passionate play of expressions across Lucas' strongly masculine face. She had not thought him capable of feeling anything. She had been wrong. He looked like a man in torment. In wonder, she daringly touched his jaw.

His head instantly descended to cover her lips with a kiss that heated her blood in ways she'd never known possible.

When he finally came up for air, his eyes glittered with triumph. "Marry me, Miss Briggs. Show me what I've missed all these years."

Left breathless, she could scarcely gather her thoughts. "I am outside more than I am in. I am not much at supervising the laundry and housekeeping," she warned, even though she wished to bite her tongue. "And if you are in the habit of dripping mud, I suspect you have a great need for both."

"I suspect between the three of us, we can use an entire village of servants," he countered. "I can command the housemaids to clean and you can command the stable boys to muck, if that is your preference."

"I like animals and children," she added, heart in her throat, fearful she would drive off the one man she'd ever wanted. "I will look after them before I look after the house."

Undeterred, he planted kisses across her face. "If you will think of me and Verity as your pets, I will come courting properly. I can buy you candy. I have a bouquet for you back at the house."

She shook her head, put a finger to her lips, and glanced sideways.

Lucas followed her gaze.

Clutching the ragged bouquet, Verity waited in the shrubbery until they noticed her. Then, holding out the flowers, she said, "Will you marry us, Miss Harriet? We love you."

Weeping, Harriet flung herself into Lucas' arms and let him reassure her that finally, *finally* she had found someone who loved and understood *her*, and not her dowry.

"We love you, Miss Harriet," Lucas repeated softly, hugging her as she had longed to be hugged. "Will you love us back?"

And she nodded fiercely, speechless for possibly the first time in her life.

The Piano Tutor

Anthea Lawson

"My Lady." The butler tapped at Diana Waverly's half-open door. "The piano tutor is here." He hesitated, a furrow marring his usually placid brow.

"Well, it *is* Wednesday." Diana laid her last black dress in the trunk she had been filling, then carefully closed the lid. "Tell Samantha it's time for her lesson. I'll be down directly."

The butler remained in the doorway, shifting his weight from foot to foot. "Forgive me, My Lady, but it . . . er, it is not the customary piano tutor. It is an altogether different gentleman."

She blinked. "But Mr Bent is Samantha's tutor. We have no other."

"I tried to tell him as much, but the gentleman insists."

Diana stood, frowning. "I'll see to him." They had few callers – the inevitable result of turning down a season's worth of invitations – and never unannounced visitors.

Tucking up a stray auburn curl, she started down the hallway towards the wide second-floor landing. Mr Bent had said nothing of this. He was quite reliable – if a bit dour to be tutoring a girl still recovering from the loss of her father.

At the top of the stairs she halted, pulled from her thoughts by the sound of music pouring from the parlour below. Someone very skilled was playing the piano.

She rested her hand on the mahogany banister and listened. Note after note tumbled through the entryway, reverberating between the high ceiling and marble floors. Sunlight streamed through the landing windows, making the dust motes swirl and glitter like gilded dancers.

Her stepdaughter Samantha joined her, her wiry twelve-year old body leaning over the railing. "I didn't know Mr Bent could actually *play* the piano."

"It's not Mr Bent." That much was clear, though who it might be and why he was in her parlour was a mystery Diana could not fathom.

She descended the stairs, the music growing fuller and more present with every step. She paused a moment at the parlour door, then – with a fortifying breath – went in. The instant she crossed the threshold, the music ceased. The magic that had been spilling into the house folded in upon itself and disappeared.

But its source remained – a broad-shouldered man with brown hair and intelligent grey eyes. He stood when he saw her and bowed with an easy grace. "My Lady."

She studied the stranger. Handsome, undeniably, with those compelling eyes and a smile that seemed genuine. He looked nothing like the stoop-shouldered and outmoded Mr Bent. For one thing, he was a good deal younger – he looked to be no more than a handful of years older than herself.

"Sir?" She hardly knew what to say. "Please explain yourself."

"Viscountess Merrowstone." The stranger's voice was rich and complex, the syllables of her title unexpectedly smooth to her ears. "Mr Nicholas Jameson, at your service. I've come to substitute for Mr Bent, who has been called away unexpectedly."

"This is most irregular. I was not informed there was to be a replacement." She faced him squarely, ready to send him on his way. That was what she intended to do, but the words came out all wrong. "You play quite well."

He tipped his head, a smile lifting the corners of his mouth. "That would be a requirement, wouldn't it?"

"One would assume so." Though his bearing made her think he would be more suited to leaping a stallion over hedgerows than giving piano lessons to a twelve-year old. "You're quite certain you're a piano tutor?"

"Let me assure you of my qualifications." He extended an envelope. "I've a letter of recommendation from Lady Pembroke. You're acquainted, I believe?"

Diana nodded. Indeed, Lucy was a good friend, possessed of a generous spirit – though she was more than a little scandalous. Henry had not approved of their friendship. Diana's gaze slipped past Mr Jameson to the portrait of her late husband, Lord Henry Waverly, Viscount Merrowstone. His stern, formal features watched impassively, a cultivated remoteness in his expression. Solid and predictable in the portrait, just as in life. Lucy had annoyed him to no end.

Swallowing a sigh, Diana turned her attention to her friend's curling script.

> *Dearest Diana – I commend Mr Nicholas Jameson to you as a piano tutor. He has provided my own Charlotte with lessons and has proven quite satisfactory. May I also point out – in case you had not noticed – that he is extremely handsome? He strikes me as a perfect diversion now that you have finally come out of mourning. I encourage you to take him on – in whatever capacities suit your needs. Pianists have such skilled hands.*

Diana felt her cheeks burn as she glanced up at the gentleman in question. No doubt it had amused Lucy to have Mr Jameson deliver such an outrageous "reference" in person.

"I see that she recommends you highly, sir," Diana said, biting her lip to avoid an embarrassed giggle. "I suppose we might consider having you." Oh dear, that hadn't sounded quite proper. She cleared her throat. "I mean *hiring* you. It wouldn't do to neglect Samantha's lessons while Mr Bent is away."

"Oh, please hire him," Samantha said, peeking out from behind the doorway. She came in and stood on tiptoe to whisper in Diana's ear. "He seems ever so much nicer than Mr Bent."

It was quite outside the regular course of things, yet there was no mistaking the eager note in Samantha's voice. No mistaking that Mr Jameson was, as Lucy had mentioned, a very handsome man.

Her stepdaughter turned to him. "I heard you playing. It was marvellous! How do you do the part with your left hand? Could you show me?"

"Of course." He gave her an encouraging smile. "It's simple once you get the trick of it. Have you played any Mozart?"

"Oh yes!"

"Then you'll be able to master it easily. That is . . ." He raised a questioning brow at Diana.

"Oh very well," she said. "It appears you will be our replacement tutor until Mr Bent returns." She ignored Samantha's muffled squeal. "Can you begin today?"

A spark leaped into his eyes. "Immediately."

Looking at him made heat creep into her cheeks. Despite herself, Lucy's advice rang in her head. As if she would consider something so scandalous as commencing an affair with the piano tutor. Really, her friend had no sense of propriety.

Samantha hurried to seat herself at the piano bench. "I'm ready!"

Diana was not sure whether she herself was ready, but events seemed to be carrying her along. She settled into the nearby wing-back and straightened the rich indigo skirts of her new dress. It was odd to wear colours again. She had grown so accustomed to the solid black of mourning that she felt vulnerable without it. A part of her wanted to retreat back into its safety – but that was not fair to Samantha. Diana could not deny the hopeful light in the girl's eyes, the flash of her rare grin as she attempted to mimic Mr Jameson's command of the keyboard.

As was customary during Samantha's lessons, Diana picked up her newest copy of the *Ladies' Monthly*, but the fashion plates held no interest for her. Her eyes kept wandering from the illustrations to steal quick glances at the new tutor – his long-fingered hands as he played a run of notes, the way his brown hair tumbled over his collar. More than once he seemed to sense her attention and she had to quickly drop her gaze back to the unseen pages.

The sound of his voice was so different from Mr Bent's dry tones, and his praise and encouragement drew another flashing smile from Samantha. Something inside Diana uncoiled a notch, a deep tension she had not realized she had been carrying.

The shape of his muscular shoulders was barely concealed by the cut of his coat as he leaned forwards to demonstrate some point. He radiated confidence and mastery. She imagined that everything he did would benefit from that focused energy.

From this angle he was in profile. His jaw was firm, his nose straight, his mouth strong, yet sensitive. She traced her own lips with a fingertip, then caught herself and hurriedly dropped her hand before he could notice.

Mr Jameson turned to face her. "Will you?" he asked.

Diana's breath faltered as their gazes held a heartbeat too long. Clearly she had missed an important turn in the lesson while daydreaming.

"Sing for us," Samantha said, a touch of impatience in her voice. "Mr Jameson has been showing me a marvellous pattern for accompanying songs, but I don't think I can sing and play at the same time."

Diana set aside her magazine. "Oh, I really couldn't. It's been so long." There didn't seem to be enough air in the room for her to breathe, let alone sing.

"Of course you can." Mr Jameson's tone was assured. "Miss

Samantha says you have a lovely singing voice." There was a challenge in his expression, as if he were curious to see what she would do.

"Please, Mama. Let's do 'The Meeting of the Waters'."

"Very well. If it's part of the lesson." She stood and took her place beside the piano, oddly reluctant to disappoint Mr Jameson. Still, it had been a very long while. What if she had lost the knack altogether? "Samantha, you and Mr Jameson must help by singing with me."

The piano tutor counted the tempo then signalled Samantha to begin. Diana took a deep breath and sang the first words. Mr Jameson's rich baritone joined her, while her stepdaughter concentrated on the keyboard.

At first her alto sounded husky to her ears, the notes unsure. Soon enough, though, her body took over and she remembered how to breathe, how to put herself into the song and carry each tone to fullness. Mr Jameson was solid beside her, his singing voice even fuller than she had imagined. When her pitch wavered, he was there, and soon their voices began to blend in a most pleasing manner. Unbidden, her eyes met his, and the appreciation there nearly made her lose the words. She forced her concentration back to the final phrases of the song.

Samantha was giggling as she played a last flourish on the piano.

"Splendid!" Mr Jameson said. "Miss Waverly, you have a deft touch on the keyboard. And Viscountess – your voice is lovely."

Diana smiled back at him. The parlour had not rung with such happy sounds for too long. It seemed that Mr Jameson would be a splendid substitute.

The clock on the mantel struck the hour, and Samantha let out a protest. "So soon? But we've just begun!"

Indeed, the time had sped.

"Thank you, Mr Jameson. Shall we expect you next week?"

"I would be delighted." He took Diana's hand and, bowing, lifted it to his lips.

The warm press of his mouth on her skin sent a shock of sensation through her. It was very forward, yet she could not bring herself to reprove him, not with the heat of his kiss disordering her senses.

Still clasping her hand, he looked into her eyes – a look full of promise that made her heart race. "Until next Wednesday."

The tea shop on Bond Street was filled with the cheerful babble of conversation. Diana had requested a table in the nook – the safest place for a chat with Lucy, whose voice had a tendency to carry.

"Tell me, darling—" Lucy arched an elegant eyebrow "—is Mr Jameson proving to be . . . satisfactory? I'd like to know if my recommendation was well advised."

Mr Jameson. Diana let out a slow breath.

She could not stop thinking of him – his grey eyes and handsome features, the confidence that accompanied his every movement. The past three Wednesdays had found her with a giddy lightness of spirit. She was attuned to each nuance of his expression, addicted to the desire that his slow smiles sent through her. At the conclusion of every session, he had kissed her hand. Last Wednesday, his lips had seemed to linger, the heat of his breath playing against her skin for a long moment. The memory of it sent a fluttery breathlessness winging through her even now.

"He . . ." Diana ran her fingertip back and forth across the rim of her cup. "He seems an excellent teacher – very patient with Samantha, and kind. She is enjoying music lessons far more than she ever has before. It's a pity he's only a *temporary* tutor. There's a certain quality about him . . ."

She took a hasty swallow of tea. Goodness, she shouldn't be prattling on. Whatever secret thoughts she had of the new piano tutor should stay exactly that – secret. Although, of anyone, Lucy would understand.

Her friend tilted her head, a speculative light in her eyes. "Why, Diana. Are you developing an *interest* in Mr Jameson? How marvellous. As I told you, I think he would prove an excellent diversion. You should commence an affair immediately."

Diana set her cup down so quickly that some tea sloshed over the edge. "Lucy, you are shocking."

Even worse than Lucy's suggestion were the images that flooded Diana's mind. Fire bloomed in her cheeks. What if Mr Jameson did not stop when he kissed her hand? What if he continued, his warm lips laying kisses up her arm, along her neck? What if he reached her mouth and covered it with his own?

Her friend gave her a shrewd look. "High time you began thinking of yourself. You're out of formal mourning now. And you've admitted that your marriage to Lord Waverly was never one of deep passion."

"A marriage does not need passion if it has respect and . . ." She searched for the proper word. "Goodwill."

Lucy waved her hand. "Goodwill is all very well, in its place. But now you have an opportunity, you should seize it! If you are careful and discreet, no one will suspect. You are free to follow your heart, or your whims – or both."

Lucy made it sound so simple.

"I must admit—" her chest tightened, excitement firing through her blood as she spoke aloud the words she had been holding inside for weeks "—I find Mr Jameson quite attractive. And his manner very pleasing."

Lucy nodded approval. "Indeed."

"What does it mean," Diana continued, "when a man's presence makes one feel so very *awake*? I can scarcely sleep for thoughts of him, and when I do, my dreams are . . ." She lowered her voice. "Oh, my dreams are most wicked."

"That is excellent news." Lucy's eyes were bright. "Perhaps you should make them come true."

Diana dropped her gaze to the tablecloth. "I doubt I'm ready to embark on such a course." It was one thing to indulge in such imaginations, quite another to act upon them. She had never considered herself bold of spirit.

"Well." Lucy dabbed her lips with her napkin. "It is your choice – but regardless, it's high time you began going out in society again. Gracious, Diana, people will scarcely remember you if you keep yourself locked away."

"In due time, Lucy." Her friend was a master at manoeuvring people when she thought she knew what was best for them. Which was most of the time. "There's Samantha to think of, and – well, I'm comfortable as I am." Though she was markedly less content since a certain piano tutor had come into her well-ordered life.

"*Comfortable*?" Lucy lifted her nose in disdain. "That's almost as bad as 'goodwill'. You need more interesting words to fill your life. *Passion*, for one. And *delight*. And best of all—" her eyes sparked with mischief "—best of all, *ravishment*."

"Lucy!" Diana clapped a hand to her mouth to stifle her giggles. "You're outrageous!"

Her friend joined her laughter, oblivious to the disapproving looks of the nearby patrons. When their mirth finally subsided, Lucy assumed the commanding tones of Lady Pembroke.

"Call me what you please," she said. "I only speak the truth. Regardless of your obvious fascination with the new piano tutor, you *will* come to the musicale I'm hosting on Tuesday. It will be a small gathering, nothing too overwhelming. I'll expect you promptly at eight."

"I—"

"Pray, do not disappoint me. If you don't arrive promptly, I'll dispatch my burliest footmen to fetch you."

"Oh very well," Diana said. There was no arguing with Lucy. "As long as there is no more talk of affairs and . . ." She could not even say the word "ravishment" aloud, though it echoed through her thoughts. "I'll come to your musicale." She made no promises, however, as to how late she would stay.

Her friend gave a nod of satisfaction, then consulted her dainty silver pocket watch, as if recalling something urgent. "Goodness, the time has flown! I'm nearly late for the modiste. Delightful to see you, Diana. Till Tuesday." She brushed a kiss across Diana's cheek, then hurried off, leaving Diana alone with her unsettled thoughts.

Their chat had left an edgy restlessness humming through her. Her carriage awaited outside, the driver ready to take her wherever she pleased. If only she knew where that might be.

Diana gathered her reticule and pelisse and left the shop. The air outside was pleasantly warm, and she turned her face up to the pale May sun. It was too lovely a day to waste in simply going back to Waverly House and going over menus with the cook.

She lingered, looking in the shop windows. A glorious fan painted with swans – she could nearly imagine herself with it at some ball, laughing and dancing. Or that bracelet set with sapphires, clasped about her wrist. It was frivolous, the gems sparkling beautifully in their settings. Still, she turned away from the window. No purchase could soothe her restiveness.

She had just resolved to return home when she caught sight of a certain broad-shouldered, brown-haired gentleman striding towards her. Sparks raced through her entire body. Mr Jameson! The loveliness of the day exploded into fiery brilliance.

He met her eyes, a smile spreading across his face as he made his way to her side. "Viscountess." He doffed his top hat. "It's a fine day. Would you care to join me for a stroll in St James' Park?"

"That would be—" ill-advised, besotted as she had become with him "—delightful."

He offered his arm and she tucked her hand through with no hesitation. She was keenly aware of the places their bodies touched, and it was difficult to resist the urge to lean too close.

They walked side by side down Bond Street to the park. The feel of his firmly muscled forearm was not disguised even through the layers of his coat and her glove, and she found it deliciously distracting. The rest of him seemed as toned and muscular as his arm. Diana shot him a sideways glance. His well-fitted breeches showed his thighs flexing taut with every step, and his stomach seemed perfectly flat beneath the blue silk of his waistcoat. Lucy's words echoed through her. *Passion. Delight.*

The green trees of St James' closed over them as they entered the long promenade. A lazy pond curved to one side, insects buzzing beside the water. The day was fine, the scene peaceful, but Diana felt unbalanced and strangely giddy.

There were so many questions she dare not ask. They scalded her tongue. She wanted to know everything about him, yet was afraid the answers would spoil the perfection of the day. Where are you from? Have you a wife? A mistress? She swallowed them unspoken.

"Do you enjoy teaching the piano?" she finally asked.

He nodded, his twilight eyes regarding her. "I'm finding a great deal of satisfaction in it. Miss Samantha is a quick study, and a fine musician. As are you, My Lady. Have you ever considered taking lessons on the piano?"

"Taking lessons myself?" She blinked up at him. "I have always simply sung, Mr Jameson. That is enough for me."

"How do you know?" His hand covered hers. "You should try something new. You might find that you like it very well." His smile held more than a little wickedness. Goodness! Was he suggesting . . .

Diana dropped her gaze, hoping her blush was hidden by the fashionable plumes in her bonnet. It seemed to be an afternoon for improper conversations.

With a sudden daring, she asked, "If I were to become your pupil, when might these tutorials occur? Before or after Samantha's lessons?"

"Not on Wednesday." His voice was warm honey, drizzling over her senses. "My instruction would require sufficient uninterrupted time. Perhaps Thursdays."

"Surely your other pupils would object to the change of schedule."

The pressure of his hand over hers increased. "It's all a matter of priority."

They were passing a weeping willow, the leaves tender and newly green, swaying lightly in the breeze. Diana took a deep breath of the soft air to steady herself.

"I would be your priority on Thursdays?"

He stopped and gave her an intent look. "You would be my priority every day."

Oh, it was the purest flirtation, she knew it, but still her heartbeat stumbled in giddy joy. "Really, Mr Jameson—"

"Call me Nicholas." He drew her off the pathway, beneath the sheltering canopy of the willow tree.

"Nicholas." She half-whispered it, a bold exhilaration tingling through her. "Then you must call me Diana."

Suddenly they were not tutor and lady any longer, but only man and woman. The air between them was alive with possibility, the spaces where bodies were, and were not. And could be.

Had she taken complete leave of her senses? She did not care. In one twist of an afternoon a gate had opened that she had thought closed for ever. A pathway back to herself. Not the young widow. Not the capable stepmother, but *her*, Diana, who had once been full of passionate dreams.

Her senses were sharpened by an almost unbearable anticipation. Everything was magnified – the light breeze, the scent of his bergamot cologne, the sound of water quietly lapping the shore. There was something excruciatingly wonderful about knowing she was about to be kissed. He leaned forwards, a smile dancing in his eyes, and she tilted her face up to him.

His mouth brushed hers, their lips meeting, parting, meeting again – like a musician sounding a note over and over, until it was perfect. She slid her hands up to his shoulders, learning the shape of his mouth against hers.

He increased the pressure of his lips. The smooth slide of his tongue against her lower lip made sparks scatter through her, and she willingly opened her mouth to him. Nicholas dipped his tongue inside. He tasted of tea and desire, and something inside her gave way, melting like late frost before the sun.

This was no debutante's kiss. It carried the full knowledge of how a man and a woman fitted together. The plunge of his tongue into her mouth, her yielding softness – all this was part of the dance, a promise of deeper intimacies. She pressed herself closer to him, yearning spiralling out from her centre.

Nicholas Jameson was a wonderful kisser.

It was more than the way he fitted his lips so perfectly over hers, or the velvety warmth of his tongue. More than the feel of his hand curving around her shoulder, the brush of his thumb over her bare collarbone. His kiss flared through her entire body. She was aware of her toes, warm and content in her buttoned boots. Her legs, cased in silk stockings with ribbon garters above her knees. The soft cotton of her chemise where it lay against her skin. The fine silk of her drawers, heated at the juncture of her legs.

And she was aware of him. Wonderfully aware of the slight roughness of his jaw as he kissed her, the warm maleness of him as they leaned into one another, the smell of spring willows and fine wool, and arousal. His. Hers.

They kissed and kissed, and then it was over. Diana opened her eyes and smiled up at him, as though she had just woken from a perfect dream.

Diana set a smile across her face and nodded at the conversation flowing past. Oh, she should never have agreed to come to Lucy's musicale. She had no heart for it. It had been too long – she did not know any of the current on dits and was relegated to standing awkwardly at the edges of the company.

Besides, how could she possibly be a witty conversationalist when all she could think of was Nicholas' hands at her waist, drawing her into that intoxicating kiss?

With his talk of "piano lessons", had he truly been suggesting that they become lovers? Her pulse sped at the thought. Her sleep had been restless, her skin too sensitive ever since that kiss. Even now the slide of her petticoats against her legs sent a shiver through her. What if Nicholas touched her there – and everywhere? How would it feel to embrace without the constraints of coat and skirts, to lie together skin to skin? Her throat went dry with longing at the thought.

"Ladies and Gentlemen!" Lucy stood at the front of the room and clapped her hands together. "Please take your seats so the musicale may commence."

Diana sidled to the end of the back row. Perhaps, once they put out the lights, she could make her escape. She did not think she could bear more awkward conversation during the intermission.

The featured performer of the evening was introduced – a young harpist who was the newest musical sensation. The room darkened, and Diana let out a breath of relief. Now she could lose herself in thoughts of Nicholas. She closed her eyes as the harpist plucked the first chord.

Someone took the seat next to her, startling her from her reverie. Cloth rustled, and then the familiar scent of bergamot cologne tickled her nose. Her eyes flew open and she turned, surprise jolting through her as she glimpsed the white gleam of Nicholas' grin. It was as if her thoughts had summoned him.

He leaned close. "Good evening, Diana." His breath was warm against her cheek.

"Nicholas – whatever are you doing here?"

His hand found hers in the dark, his clasp sure as he twined his naked fingers through her gloved ones. The intimacy of it made her gasp. Surely her heart was beating so loudly that everyone could hear.

"Come," he said.

A glissando of harp notes shivered through her. What were his plans for her? What if he had no plans?

She would never know unless she went with him into the wicked shadows. For a moment fear held her in her seat. She could not, she could not . . . Then he tugged gently at her hand and desire rose up in a wave and lifted her to her feet.

Nicholas drew her out of the darkened drawing room. The lamps in the hallway shed a beckoning light, their flames echoing the excitement flickering through her. No one was there to mark their illicit departure. He led her down the hall and up a short flight of stairs, the music growing fainter behind them. Without pause, he opened a door and ushered her through.

They were in the library. Lamplight glinted on gold-lettered spines and she breathed in the scent of books and leather. And Nicholas. He closed the door, shutting out the last lilting notes. When he turned back to her his expression was intent, his grey eyes lit with desire. For her.

Diana caught her breath, heat blossoming inside her.

Without a word, he strode forwards and took her in his arms. Her breasts pressed against his silver-embroidered waistcoat – softness against hardness, woman against man. Her breath swept between her lips, flavoured with passion. When he bent his head, she eagerly opened her mouth.

It was as delicious as she had remembered. His tongue played against hers, sweet and hot, and she felt her fears dissolve into acceptance. A low, insistent pulse began within her, as if she were an instrument responding to his touch.

She slid her hands to his shoulders, then dropped them in frustration to tug urgently at the fingertips of her gloves. She needed to feel his bare skin beneath her palms, the planes of his cheek and jaw, the softness of his dark hair tangled between her fingers.

He helped her strip the gloves off, as hungry as she. For a moment he held them dangling in his hand and gave her a penetrating look.

She stepped forwards and kissed him. By heaven, she had made her choice, and she was going to embrace it with all the long-banked fire in her soul. She tasted his laughter, and then his arms came around her and the kiss deepened.

So sweet and fierce. Embers flickered to flame, scorched to need. His palms smoothed the emerald satin of her gown and she leaned into his touch. There was no doubt he found her desirable – his body proved it, the hardness of him pressing against her centre. He bunched her skirts in his hands, drew them up, cool air caressing her legs.

Wordlessly, she stepped back and let him pull her gown off. Her chemise tangled in her arms and then it, too, was gone. She stood before him, naked but for her undergarments. It was outrageous, and wonderful.

"So beautiful," he said, his eyes alight with hunger.

He stroked his hands up her sides, then covered her breasts. She sucked in a sharp breath. Little fires quivered beneath his palms, and she could feel her nipples tauten under his touch. She arched into his hands, threw her head back, and sighed. What a picture she must make, wearing only her stockings and drawers, wanton and sensual under the hands of this darkly handsome gentleman.

But he was wearing too much clothing. Her hands went to his cravat, making quick work of the elegant knot. Next, the buttons of his waistcoat, his fine linen shirt. She tugged the fabric free of his breeches and, hands trembling, pushed his shirt open. His chest was firmly muscled; a light dusting of hair tickled her fingertips as she stroked his skin.

He made a sound of longing, then pulled her to him, his chest hot and hard against hers. It was as delicious as she had imagined. Another blazing kiss, and then he stepped back. She helped him pull off his coat and shirt, then he pushed his boots off and removed his breeches.

Diana peeked between her lashes, curious and eager, then caught her breath at the sight of him. He was erect and strong, and she felt suddenly powerful, to bring him to such a rampant state.

Henry had always insisted on taking his husbandly prerogatives with the lights off, the two of them securely between the sheets. He had never made her feel like this, had never openly admired her, or told her she was beautiful. It had been pleasant enough, their marital relations, but nothing like the fire that now seared through her.

And that fire was nothing compared to the sensation that engulfed her when Nicholas took her in his arms and dipped his hand between her legs. This tempest of want scorching her to her soul – this was new. This was *passion*.

"Ah!" she cried as his fingers stroked and played beneath her drawers. She gripped the strong sinews of his arms – she was going to fly to bits if she did not hold tightly to him.

Nicholas withdrew his hand and she moaned in protest. With a devilish smile, he stripped off her drawers, then manoeuvred her backwards until her legs bumped the settee. They tumbled down together on to the gold velvet cushions and he braced himself over her, setting his member where his fingers had been. Slowly, inexorably, he pressed forwards, opening her. Their gazes locked as their bodies fitted together, imperfectly at first. Then easier as he slid back, and forwards again.

"Yes," she breathed.

It was lovely and heated and, oh, she couldn't bear how deliberately Nicholas moved in her. She caught at his shoulders and tilted her hips up, urging him to stroke deeper, faster. His breath hitched as he quickened his pace, the pulse at the side of his neck beating urgently.

More. Yes, and *more*, until the pressure she felt coiling inside her finally released, exploded like an errant firework to spangle her senses with light and colour.

He let out a muffled shout and pulled free, spilling himself on the fine linen of his shirt. Sweat gleamed on his arms, his chest.

She let out a sigh of pleasure, her body sated, her whole being utterly, perfectly content. She brushed her fingers through his silky hair. Nicholas Jameson – masterful and tender, patient and passionate. The door to her heart swung open.

A smile illuminated his face and he brought one hand up to cup her cheek. "Now that, my Diana, was splendid indeed."

It was Wednesday.

Diana sat in the music room, waiting for the sound of the knocker to reverberate through the entry. Nicholas would be here at any moment. Anticipation fluttered all the way down to her toes.

Samantha played another run of notes, then glanced at the clock. "Perhaps Mr Jameson has forgotten," she said. "He has not developed the habit of coming to Waverly House."

"Nonsense. He's been our piano tutor for weeks now." Diana infused her voice with certainty. "He has only been delayed twenty minutes. There could be any number of reasons for it."

"Perhaps he has been crushed by a carriage, or—"

"Samantha, enough! I'm certain Mr Jameson will be here momentarily."

After the lesson, she would ask him to stay for tea. She would ask him everything, and have no fear of the answers.

He had brought music and light into Waverly House. He had coaxed her from behind her comfortable boundaries and shown her what true passion was. Every day from now on would be richer because of it. She would be richer. The memory of his touches, his words, flared through her. She had never felt so beautiful.

"It's half past the hour." Samantha sounded glum. "He's not coming."

Diana bit her lip. Where was he? Anticipation curdled into apprehension. "Practise a bit more, dear. I'll go check with the butler." Though of course he would have shown Mr Jameson straight in.

The heels of her boots clicked across the marble floor of the entryway. When she pulled the heavy front door open, the butler raised his eyebrows, but said nothing.

The street outside was quiet. No handsome grey-eyed man striding up to her door, no cabs to be seen the entire length of the block. She stood on the threshold for several minutes, the distant clamour of London washing past her, but the street remained empty.

The butler cleared his throat, and she slowly shut the door. Head high, she re-entered the parlour.

Samantha's expression lit. "Is he . . . ?"

"No. Not yet." She couldn't help but glance at the clock. The entire hour had run. Did she mean nothing to him? An ugly sob rose in her throat.

"Mama?" Samantha sent her a concerned glance.

Diana swallowed. "I suppose something important has detained him. You may go." She blinked rapidly against the sting of tears.

Samantha gave her a hug, then slipped out of the room. Diana bowed her head. Had she been such a fool to listen to Lucy? It had not felt that way at the time. But it seemed she had made a dreadful mistake.

She had practically seduced him. The piano tutor. He must be too embarrassed to face her, here with her stepdaughter, after what had been between them. He must despise her, think her a woman of exceedingly loose morals, to take such base liberties with her employee.

Yet he was far more to her than that. Her heart ached with lost possibilities.

They had, neither of them, promised more than a single hour of unbridled desire. Their banter about tutoring had hardly been talk of courtship, of love. If her actions had been spurred by deeper feelings, as she must now admit, what had she been to him? Only a willing female – one whom he evidently had no more use for.

She knew nothing about him. Nothing except that he made her feel more alive, more daring than anyone she had ever met. And now it was ended.

She could not bear the thought.

The servants at Lucy's mansion knew Diana well enough to admit her without hesitation.

"Is Lady Pembroke in?" she asked.

"She is, madam," Lucy's butler said. "She is taking the air in the garden. Shall I escort you?"

"That won't be necessary." If, as she feared, she was going to burst into tears the moment she saw her friend, she would prefer to do so unobserved.

"As you wish." The butler bowed her towards the French doors overlooking Lucy's grounds.

Diana stepped out and took a deep breath of the late-spring air. Lucy would know what to do. A woman of her experience surely knew all about broken hearts.

Rounding the yew hedge, Diana heard voices. Lucy's. And a man's, painfully familiar. Sudden fear knifing through her, she crept forwards.

"Damn it, Lucy, I have to tell her." Nicholas' voice was strained. "It's gone too far. She deserves to know the truth."

"She's not ready." Lucy sounded resolute. "Think up some excuse – tell her you were unavoidably detained. But don't tell her what you and I have been up to."

Ice swept over Diana, comprehension settling cold and dreadful against her bones. Lucy's talk of handsome piano tutors. Nicholas, here in her garden, using Lucy's given name so intimately. His presence at the musicale last night, his familiarity with Lucy's house . . .

Anger flared through her. The scoundrel! To use her so, when all along he had been Lucy's lover. What a contemptible rake, to seduce her – here of all places.

She swept out from behind the hedge. "Unavoidably detained?" She raked her gaze over Nicholas. His eyes widened and he took a step towards her.

Lucy grabbed at his arm. "Diana. We were just speaking of you—"

"Yes," she said. The word was coated in frost. "And what exactly were the two of you doing while my *employee* was supposed to be giving a piano lesson?"

Nicholas shook himself free of Lucy's grasp. "Let me explain—"

"You should have explained before the musicale." Her voice caught, snagged on memory. "But it seemed you had *other* priorities. Perhaps you had forgotten you had a music lesson to teach while you were 'unavoidably detained'. You've behaved most unprofessionally, sir." She fought to speak against the tightness in her throat. Nicholas reached for her and she pulled away. "I no longer need your services, Mr Jameson. You are *fired.*"

Hot tears blurring her vision, she turned and ran. Dimly she heard Nicholas calling after her, Lucy remonstrating, but she did not pause. She rushed back to her carriage and flung herself inside, slamming the door before the footman could even approach.

It was far worse than she had suspected. And still a part of her had wanted to stay, to listen to his pleas. She was so unbearably weak. As the wheels rattled over the cobblestones, she dropped her head into her hands and abandoned herself to grief.

"Mama?" Samantha pushed open the parlour door. "Are you ill? I had cook make you some chocolate."

She entered the room, carefully balancing a tray holding the silver chocolate pot and two cups. Diana mustered a smile for her step-daughter and hoped her eyes were not too red from weeping.

"Thank you, dear. I am not unwell, just a bit tired." Did heartsickness count as an illness? She did not think so. "Come, sit by me." She patted the settee.

Samantha set the tray down and curled up close. Diana put her arm around the girl's shoulders and gave them a squeeze – the reassurance as much for herself as for her stepdaughter.

"I have some unhappy news for you." She heaved a breath. "Mr Jameson will not be returning as your piano tutor."

"Oh." The girl's shoulders slumped. "That is too bad. He was ever so charming, and smelled much better than Mr Bent."

Diana smiled – it was the only way to keep the tears from welling up again. "That he did." She leaned over and rested her head against Samantha's. All brightness was not gone from her life, no matter how dreary the day might feel.

"My Lady." The butler bowed at the parlour door. "Forgive me for interrupting. You have a caller. Are you at home?"

She straightened. Nicholas wouldn't dare – not if he had a shred of sense. It had to be Lucy. One way or another, she would have to face her friend.

"Yes, I am receiving."

"Very good." He extended the silver salver, a vellum card centred on it. "Shall I show him in?"

"Him?" Her lips pressed tightly together, she took the card. If it was Mr Jameson . . . "The Marquess of Somerton?" She stared at the unfamiliar name. "I don't believe I know any such person. Please tell the gentleman I am not taking visitors today." Particularly uninvited ones. She could not face another stranger in her house.

"Very good." The butler departed.

"Thank you for the chocolate, Samantha." Diana gave her step-daughter another quick embrace. Really, she ought to bestir herself. There was no use sitting in the parlour when it held such memories of Nicholas.

"I'm glad it helped. Chocolate often does." The girl jumped up and gathered the cups and tray, then paused and kissed Diana's cheek before bustling out the door.

Voices filtered from the hallway, and then the butler was back.

"I am sorry, My Lady, but the Marquess insists he will see you. He vowed to toss me into the street if I stood in his way."

Diana rose, then nearly folded back down on the settee when she saw who had followed the butler in.

Nicholas. The breath squeezed from her lungs while a wild, giddy clamour started up in her blood.

"Please go," she breathed. No matter how much she wanted to remain unmoved, the expression in his familiar grey eyes nearly undid her.

He was carrying an exuberant bouquet of roses, which he handed to the butler. "See to these."

Clever man – if he had given her the flowers, she would have flung them back in his face. As soon as the butler departed, she turned on Nicholas. Piano tutor, marquess, whoever he claimed to be today. "How dare you?" Her ribs felt as though a band of silk were wrapped around them, pulled too tight. "To think, what we did under Lucy's very roof! And then you come here, bullying my servants, and—"

"Diana." He closed the distance between them and took her by the shoulders. Fool that she was, she could not move away from his touch. "I don't think my cousin begrudges the use of her library. She has done far worse in my best carriage, with never a word of apology."

"Your . . . your cousin?" She blinked up at him, her heart catching with a wild, irrational hope. "Lady Pembroke is your cousin?"

"Yes." A mischievous light sparked in his eyes. "Lucy. My meddling plague of a cousin. The one who bribed Mr Bent to take an extended holiday, then suggested I pose as a piano tutor and tempt you out of hiding." He shook his head. "But it didn't work."

"No?" She had been tempted, all too easily. Even now she felt breathless.

He smiled at her, rueful and amused all at once. "My plan was to slowly draw you out. To, as Lucy put it, 'help ease you from your widowhood'. But falling in love with you made things bloody awkward."

Falling in love? Happy tears tingled at the back of her eyes. The Marquess of Somerton? "But . . . you make an excellent piano tutor."

His hands tightened on her shoulders and he drew her forwards. "I assure you, I make a far better suitor."

She went willingly, lifting her face to his kiss. A kiss that swirled her senses, even as it anchored her fully to herself. A kiss full of passion. Delight. Life.

Stolen

Emma Wildes

One

As a partner in crime, Stephen Hammond was an abysmal failure so far.

Lady Sabrina Pearson shot the man crouched next to her a withering look. "Can't you do this faster?"

He muttered something unintelligible in response, which she had a feeling was not meant for her innocent ears, and his long fingers worked the metal picklock in the door.

Five minutes later, still no success.

"Stephen—"

"It isn't as blasted easy as it looks, Sabrina." He hissed the words and almost the minute he spoke there was a clean, smooth click that signalled success. With a graceful, mocking bow, he opened the door for her. "I wish you joy in your burglary, My Lady."

Dignifying that ironic tone was beneath her, so she swept past him into Lord Bloomfield's study, adjusting her lantern so it illuminated the space better. The room was cluttered and smelled of stale tobacco smoke, spilled claret and musty books she doubted the man had ever read.

Bloomfield was an academic buffoon, a charlatan of the worst order, and without the papers and notes, he would be exposed as such. His Lordship had stolen her father's life's work and she intended to get it back. It was her only legacy and, since Bloomfield claimed the papers had been lost during a fire at their last encampment in Egypt after her father's death, he could hardly charge her with the theft, even if he knew who had broken in and taken them.

It was really, in her opinion, a brilliant plan. It hadn't been quite so easy to convince Stephen to help her, but in the end, he'd grudgingly agreed. Now all she had to do was find where the papers were stashed.

"See if the desk has any locked drawers," she suggested, keeping her voice low. "If it does, go to work on them, please."

"Whatever Your thieving Ladyship desires," he murmured in a mocking tone, but did go over and begin to examine the desk. In the dim lamplight, his dark hair looked dishevelled, and a wavy lock fell over his brow as he frowned in concentration. Sabrina, in turn, roamed around the room, scouring the shelves for any hiding place, taking out books, even lifting a painting off the wall to see if there might be a cubbyhole behind it.

"The bottom left drawer is locked." Stephen's voice held an audible sigh. "I'll do my best, but I think this is all confirmation that I should hold to my chosen profession as a solicitor and help uphold the law rather than break it."

"It isn't theft to take what should be yours," Sabrina pointed out.

"Rationalization has its place. I suppose this is one of those occasions." He bent down and went to work on the drawer. The scrape of the picklock came clearly, the little clicks loud in the otherwise quiet, shrouded room.

If we are caught . . .

No, they wouldn't be, Sabrina assured herself, replacing a small statue of Isis on the mantel. It was a huge house, all the servants were abed, His Lordship had left for London that morning, and this was the perfect time to regain the documents.

It felt like an hour but was probably only a few minutes before Stephen said, "There it goes. I've got it open. You'd best come over here. I am not as confident of recognizing what we're looking for. Is this it?"

She crossed the room, handing him the lantern, excitement making her heart beat rapidly. In the bottom of the drawer was a leather pouch, and, sure enough, as she lifted it out with shaking hands, her father's initials were engraved on the front of it.

How many times had she watched him tuck away a bit of vellum into that pouch? How many times had he turned to her, his quick, affable smile curving his lips, his face alight as he talked of the latest discovery?

Tears blurred her eyes and she had to clear her throat as she untied the leather strings that kept it closed and saw his familiar scrawl across the papers inside. "This is it. I knew his notes were here."

Stephen touched her shoulder. It was light, just a brush of his fingers, but it was comforting. "Even if this is the most reckless thing I can remember doing since you talked me into trying to fly by jumping out of the top of one the tallest trees on your father's estate, I'm glad we came. However, in the interest of prudence, I think we shouldn't linger. An undetected escape would make me feel much better than the broken leg I suffered after the misbegotten flying attempt."

Sabrina gave a muffled laugh. "I felt awful. If you remember, I was most contrite and came over every day with sweets I wheedled from our cook while you recovered. I'm surprised you didn't emerge from that injury as fat as a piglet."

"Yes, well, let's reminisce over our childhood escapades later, shall we? I think we should just go out the window. Either way, His Lordship is going to know he's been robbed. Going back through the house carries more risk."

He was undoubtedly right. Stephen was always right. It was infuriating at times, actually. She was the impulsive one; he was the steady logical antithesis of her personality. Where she had dreams . . . Stephen had *plans*.

She followed him to the window. He unfastened and lifted it, a tall, lean form in the dim light. He looked outside and then eased over the sill to drop into the dying autumn garden below. As she sat and swung her legs over, he turned to catch her, the leather case clutched in her arms. Stephen quickly lowered her to the ground. Her hand firmly grasped in his, he practically dragged her across the lawn of the park to the edge of the wooded area where they'd left their horses. In a swift motion he lifted her into the saddle of her mare, swung on to his own horse, and they walked at first back towards the road, where they urged their mounts to a trot. It was a clear evening, but cool, a hint of chimney smoke in the air and a scattering of stars above in the velvet sky.

"There's an inn a few miles on." Stephen glanced over, his face chiselled to planes and hollows in the indistinct illumination. "Bloomfield is in London and so it isn't as if we have to avoid heated pursuit. At a guess, no one will know anything is amiss until his return. Even then he can't really raise a hue and cry over what he supposedly never had in the first place."

For a man who had been firmly opposed to her plan and had to be coerced into helping, he certainly sounded smug now that the deed was done and the mission successful. Sabrina arched a brow. "True. It's rather a perfect crime in my opinion."

"Humph. No such thing," Stephen argued, all smugness fading from his voice. "We have the advantage of his lack of desire to make a scandal over this, but on the other hand, he is going to know for certain who invaded his house to take those notes and letters, Sabrina. There still could be retaliation, as this will ruin his career. He's already proven himself to be underhanded. Let's not underestimate him."

She didn't. There was no question her father's former partner was greedy, manipulative and wily.

But she'd won, she thought in elation as they spotted the lights of the inn down the darkened road. She'd *won*.

He was a blackguard. A knave. A lustful fool.

Stephen Hammond opened the door to the small room at the top of the stairs and motioned his companion inside.

If you seduce her, you'll forever know you got what you wanted through coercion. Shouldn't it be fairly won? The annoyingly chivalrous voice in his head, one he'd heard too many time before, spoke in strident tones.

Damn that voice.

Sabrina walked in a few steps, her cheeks looking suspiciously flushed, her eyes holding an accusing look. "You told the innkeeper we were married."

So he had. Step one in his diabolical plan. Except really he hadn't had a plan at all until she'd come to his office in London a few days ago and asked him to help her on tonight's ridiculous quest, so maybe that excused him at least a little bit. He'd even argued before capitulating and agreeing to take her to Surrey on their nefarious mission. It wasn't really a surprise he'd given in, because by his recollection he'd never been able to deny her anything his whole life.

And now they were here. Alone.

"I had to," he said smoothly, "if we are going to share a room."

A single lamp was lit and shone on her pale, blonde hair. Her face, the features delicate and feminine, drew into a frown. "Good heavens, Stephen, I would be fine by myself. There's no need for you to watch over me like a mother hen. I'm two and twenty, not some schoolroom miss. This way, there's only one bed."

Exactly.

"You'll have to sleep in a chair or on the floor," she continued.

Like bloody hell I will.

"There weren't any other accommodations," he lied, committing what was the second sin of the evening but hopefully not the last.

"Oh." She looked uncertainly around the plain interior of the little room as if she could conjure another bed miraculously out of thin air. "I see. I suppose it is late and we don't have much choice. I daresay riding on at this time of night would hardly be safe."

"Ah, do I see the aberrant head of practicality rearing?" He strolled casually – or at least he hoped it looked casual, for in fact he was about as nervous as he'd ever been in his life – towards the fireplace and tugged at his cravat, discarding it over the back of a worn chair. "How remarkable. I've long maintained you were born without the inclination."

"Don't tease me," she said with a laugh. "I refuse to be baited. Please admit this evening turned out perfectly."

Perfectly? Well, not yet, but he had hopes it would. "We didn't get caught," he admitted, "but it isn't like we are free and clear either. When we are back in London, I'll feel better."

Sabrina sank gracefully down on the edge of the bed. She wore a fitted dark-blue riding habit that exactly matched her eyes, and tendrils of curling golden hair had escaped her chignon and framed her lovely face. "I owe you a great debt."

"No, you don't." It came out clipped. Whatever happened between them this evening, he didn't want to look at it that way, as if she was just grateful. He wanted her warm, willing, swept away . . .

The trouble was that he wasn't the type of man who swept women away. Yes, he had his share of experience with the other gender, but he wasn't rakish, wasn't dashing or notorious. Instead he was the third son of a baron who had to work for a living because his family fortunes were modest at best. He'd known Sabrina since childhood because he was just three years older and they had grown up as neighbours, but he really wasn't suitable for the daughter of an illustrious earl. Lord Reed had enjoyed a reputation for academic achievement and a sizeable fortune. At his death, his daughter had become an heiress and independent, not that Sabrina had ever been anything but independent since the day she could walk.

Still, he *loved* her. Surely it should count for something.

In his life, it was *everything*.

"No, it's true." She sighed. "I might have told myself I could do this without you, but I'm not sure I would have."

"Sabrina, surely you know always I'd help you. There is certainly not a chance I'd allow you to attempt tonight's folly on your own."

Her sudden smile was on the mischievous side, lighting her face. "I rather counted on that. I think if you will cast back to our conversation in your office last week, I might have slightly – just marginally, mind you – intimated that I would do this even if you didn't come along. I suppose that *could* constitute as blackmail."

"You suppose right." Stephen began to unbutton his shirt.

"Of the most innocent sort," she said defensively, her eyes following the motion of his hands, a tinge of incredulity entering her expression as if she just realized what he was doing. She stammered, "You . . . you are my best friend. Of course I'd ask you for help."

"Of course," he echoed, slipping the last shirt button free and tugging the hem of the garment from his breeches.

Her tone was faint now, her eyes wide. "Stephen! You are undressing."

"As I'm your best friend, then you won't mind if I don't sleep on the floor." He shrugged the shirt off his shoulders and sat down to take off his boots. "It occurs to me we've slept together before. What's one more night?"

Would he burn in hell for that one? Maybe.

In a choked voice, Sabrina protested, "When we were very young children. I don't think this is proper."

"Didn't we just break into a man's house and rifle his study? Please excuse me if I point out with all due logic that we are so past proper it makes me wonder at the meaning of the word." He lay down on the bed and theatrically clasped his hands behind his head. The seeming nonchalance was undoubtedly belied by the tell-tale growing bulge in his breeches. Just the thought of lying next to her all night had a predictable effect on his libido. It was the curse of being male, for there was simply no hiding sexual arousal.

Maybe she was too innocent to realize it.

Only he was mistaken there. Her gaze narrowed in on that hardening part of his anatomy and he heard her take in a sharp breath.

Two

Her palms were damp, her breath fluttering in her throat. Sabrina stared at the half-naked man on the bed and felt as if he were suddenly a stranger. Oh, the familiar features of his face were the same: the clean masculine line of nose and jaw, the cheekbones and forehead and, of course, always, always those clear grey eyes under the arch of ebony brows. Stephen had a way of looking right through you if he wished, and his moods were clearly reflected in his striking eyes.

The way he gazed at her *now* was not something she recognized and she'd known him her entire life.

She was not completely naïve. Even after her father's death, she had travelled fairly extensively: Italy, Greece, India, and several times to his beloved Egypt. Her Aunt Beatrice had been a perfect companion, proper but not stuffy, intellectually curious and equally eager to drink in the antiquities and history of each place. Instead of a London season, Sabrina had visited the catacombs, seen pyramids and ridden donkeys up steep mountain trails. Not all cultures were as proper as the English and during the course of such travels she had seen some indelicate things.

She did her best to not look at the juncture of his legs, for there did seem to be an indelicate bulge there.

"I . . ." she began to say but trailed off.

"You?" he prompted after a moment, one brow lifted quizzically. His chest was muscular and defined as he clasped his hands behind his head and lay there in a relaxed pose. At the moment, he didn't in the least resemble the staid, respectable solicitor she had visited in London just a few days ago. Nor was he the boy she remembered so well, so much a part of her life she'd simply taken him for granted.

He was a *man*.

And she was supposed to share this small room – and apparently that small bed – with him.

All night long.

"I forgot what I was going to say," Sabrina confessed. "I must admit it didn't occur to me we would have to stay overnight someplace. I suppose we might have planned better."

"Being novices at the art of burglary, I think we can be forgiven for the oversight." Stephen's gaze was intense, watchful. "But you are right, we are here now. Together."

Together.

Why had she never noticed how handsome he was? she wondered frantically. Oh, she supposed she had seen that from the gawky boy she'd known as a child had emerged a very nice-looking man, but she really hadn't ever thought about it. He'd gone to university, she'd embarked on her journeys with Aunt Beatrice while he was still at Cambridge, and they hadn't seen each other nearly so much in the past few years. She spent the holidays with his family though, as a rule, and they just seemed to naturally pick up their friendship where they'd left it, without any awkwardness at all.

Until now. This was deuced awkward because she had no idea what to do or even say.

"Stephen."

"Yes?" A faint smile curved his mouth. Unfortunately, it made him look even more attractive.

Stephen. Attractive. She was attracted to Stephen. It took a moment to assimilate.

She blurted out, "I will be ruined if anyone finds out I spent the night with you." It was a desperate stab at trying to sound calm and practical.

"My dear Sabrina, you will be ruined if anyone finds out about anything we've done – or not done yet – this evening. Let's be practical, you have jumped into possible scandal with both feet. I believe I pointed that out when you suggested this outrageous scheme back in London. You insisted we go ahead with it. For that matter, it will not do my career much good if our activities are discovered either."

She really hadn't thought of that. He had to make his own living, for the Hammond family fortunes weren't solid enough for inheritances for the younger sons.

"It was selfish of me to ask you to help me," she said, stricken.

"Not at all. Let's keep in mind I am a grown man and if I wished to refuse, it was an option all along. Maybe we are both reckless at heart or at least when we are together. Shall we continue the trend?"

"What do you mean?" she mumbled, though she had a feeling she knew *exactly* what he meant.

. . . or not done yet . . .

A blush swept upwards, the heat climbing up her neck and scalding her cheeks. She stared at him.

He looked back and didn't explain.

Really, there was no need. What was about to happen – yes, *about* to happen, for she found to her amazement she'd already made up her mind – would change her life and yet she found the decision to be easy; effortless even. Part of it was, as she had gotten older, she found her curiosity about the sexual experience had grown. However, a woman – especially the daughter of an earl – usually needed to marry to discover the answer. This was a rare opportunity. If she had thought of it, she might have propositioned Stephen herself. He was the one man who wouldn't force her into matrimony if she didn't wish it. Neither was he after the fortune her father had left her.

Why hadn't this occurred to her? If she wanted to discover for herself one of life's most basic secrets, Stephen would be *perfect.*

A certain exhilaration spiked through her, making her catch her breath.

"Do you remember when I learned to swim?" she asked, her voice sounding off-key, even to her. "I wanted to so much. You and your brothers looked like you had such great fun jumping in the river whenever you wanted while I had to sit on the bank and just watch. You coaxed me just to try it."

Stephen nodded. His eyes had gone from steel grey to stormy skies.

"I believe I said I wasn't frightened." Sabrina started to unfasten her jacket. "I lied, you know."

"I know. I knew *then* you were at least a little frightened. Don't you remember how I was right there, ready to help if you needed it?"

Sabrina was surprised she could even still breathe. Her heart pounded and she seemed to have forgotten how to unfasten buttons. "You were a good teacher."

"I'm not ten now either, I'm twenty-five." The words were said softly. "I'd like to think my instructional skills have improved."

Good heavens, she was really going to do this. Sabrina dropped her jacket on the floor, then she sat down, removed her half-boots and stockings before standing to unfasten her skirt with shaking hands. It slid off her hips, and she went to work on her blouse. In moments all she wore was a flimsy chemise.

Stephen watched her disrobe, his lashes slightly lowered. When she finished – when she stood there doing her best to not visibly tremble – he extended a hand. "Join me."

It was symbolic. *Join me.* The inference was, of course, he wished to join with her in the oldest way a woman and man could be joined.

Sabrina walked the few paces to the bed and placed her hand in his. Long strong fingers closed over hers and the matter was settled.

This moment, the one he'd fantasized over countless times, was like a dream. Maybe, Stephen thought, his breathing was too shallow to supply the right amount of air to his brain so he was hallucinating. Maybe his heart jerking in erratic bursts in his chest made him light-headed. Maybe all the blood in his body was concentrated in his growing erection and he hadn't any left circulating in his veins.

All he knew was Sabrina was more alluring than even in his very vivid, colourful imagination – a vision of soft curves, pale skin and loosened gold curls that tumbled over her slim shoulders and down her back. The girl he'd known was a shadow compared to the glory of the woman. Soft rose lips were parted just slightly, and full breasts lifted the lacy material of her shift in quick repetitive motion. Her eyes, the colour of an azure summer sky, were framed in long, lush lashes.

Once, long ago, he'd kissed her. He'd been about eleven, he remembered, both of them curious. After the brief touch of their lips, she'd declared herself unimpressed.

It was time to change her mind.

Stephen tugged her closer and caught her slender body in his arms, shifting so he could lower her to the mattress. Her slight gasp drifted in the air as he covered her, and the descent of his mouth to capture her lips stopped any other sound.

It was a hungry kiss, despite his determination to go slow and not rush things. He feasted like a starved man, tasting, savouring, the pent-up longing of the past merging with the present. The indulgence went on until his muscles felt knotted and tight, and his arousal strained against his breeches with uncomfortable urgency.

"I want you," he murmured against her lips. "I need you."

"I can tell." Sabrina's laugh was a muffled sound, sweet like a sigh. If she was afraid, it didn't show.

Her arms, he realized with triumph, were twined around his neck and her hips cradled him perfectly. "You're a virgin?"

The hint of question in his voice wasn't an insult to her honour, but he just wasn't sure if she was. She'd travelled widely, she had shown no inclination to look for a husband and, the truth was, if she didn't want one, she didn't need to get married. Her father had left her a fortune, and with it came the freedom of choice. As a young, beautiful heiress, she would be a premium on the marriage mart, but so far her interest hadn't been evident. Stephen knew full well she had an independent spirit.

He didn't want to conquer it. That quality was one of the things he loved the most about her. The light in her eyes when she contemplated a new idea, the mischievous edge to her personality, the innate sentimental loyalty that made her unique and set her apart from the young women he knew.

"Yes."

The shy, breathless admission made him relax a fraction. The jealousy he felt for the lover she'd never had evaporated. He wasn't even aware he harboured the feeling so intensely until that moment.

He nuzzled the sensitive spot under her ear. "I hoped."

"You doubted?" There was prim censure in her tone.

He laughed, blowing his breath across her fragrant skin. "Can I say I have always recognized your disdain for a guiding hand?"

"True." Sabrina touched his cheek, turned his face and looked into his eyes. "What are we doing?"

"I want to make love to you," he said in a constricted voice.

"And here Aunt Beatrice thinks you are such a good influence on me."

"When we were younger, we did her the favour of keeping her in the dark over some of our daring childhood pursuits that would have given her the vapours." He kissed her neck. "We could be just as kind over this matter."

"Good suggestion." Exploring fingers ran over the muscles of his back, sending tingles like licks of flame up his spine. Her voice husky, Sabrina said, "You are ever the voice of reason. She never has to know."

"And you ever embrace an adventure." He eased the ribbon on the bodice of her chemise free. "I will do my best to make this an exciting one for you. Can I interest you in a trip to paradise?"

"Is it really?" Her eyes widened.

Now then, he'd just issued himself a challenge, hadn't he? Stephen admired the shadow between her breasts as he parted the delicate lace of her chemise and tugged the garment downwards. Her breasts were perfect: firm, high and full enough to fill his palm. He cupped her and, with his thumb, caressed a rosy nipple. Sabrina gave a very satisfying gasp.

"You may let me know if you agree afterwards." The whisper was said against her skin as he slid his mouth downwards, tracing the graceful curve of her throat, across her collarbone, and lower, until he kissed silky mounded flesh and kneaded the opposite breast in a gentle rhythm. The small arch of her spine as he suckled the delicious taut crest told him volumes.

"Oh, Stephen." Sabrina's hands caught his arms, holding tight. "Should you do that?"

"We can do whatever we want," he murmured, lightly licking her nipple, pleased to see how tight and budded it became under his ministrations. "In a world full of rules and censure, what we do in private is only between us."

"I . . . I . . ."

Whatever she was going to say was lost as he pulled her chemise lower, over the subtle flare of her hips and length of her legs, exposing all of her to his hungry gaze as he tossed it on the floor. Outside the moon was high enough to send slivers of light through the small casement window and illuminated each curve, each seductive hollow, the shadowed apex between her slim thighs graced by dark gold curls. With a reverent touch, he skimmed his fingertips down her belly, feeling the reaction in the muscles, seeking that tantalizing juncture. "You what?" Stephen asked as he found warmth and sleek dampness.

Supine, gloriously nude, Sabrina was the very essence of his dreams, so desirable he couldn't ever imagine how fate had schemed for this night to finally happen. He was actually grateful to the nefarious Bloomfield.

Now, to make this an event she would never forget.

"You were saying?" he teased, his brows lifted, watching her face as he put just the slightest pressure on just the right spot, braced on one elbow, his hand stroking between her legs.

Sabrina made an interesting sound in her throat, and her thighs, which had been pressed together in maidenly modesty at his intimate touch, fell apart a little. "That feels . . . oh."

"Perfect," he supplied softly. "You feel perfect."

He watched her face as he began to bring her to climax, the heightening colour as it spread across her cheekbones, the droop of her lashes as she began to get lost in the building sensation, the way her lips parted to let out small delicious moans. When it happened, she cried out and trembled, her eyes flying open in surprise so he could see both her passion and stunned wonder.

When he stood up and started to unfasten his breeches, he couldn't help but give a masculine grin at the dazed look on her lovely face. It wasn't often he saw Sabrina at a loss for words, but she did appear tongue-tied, especially as he freed his erection. She stared at the hard length against his stomach. In the aftermath of her first sexual culmination, she was all lush feminine enticement as she lay there, nude and flushed, and then – though he knew it wasn't deliberate – she wet her lips.

It almost undid him, then and there.

Stephen took in a shuddering breath, found control, and said hoarsely, "Did I mention paradise was even better together? Let me show you."

She wasn't sure what the man had just done to her, but Stephen had told her the absolute truth. Just as he had promised years ago that swimming was not hard once you relaxed and trusted the buoyancy of the water, and that if she practised the pianoforte with a joy for the music, not as a chore, she would become more proficient, he was right yet again. The exquisite pleasure she had just experienced was a revelation, and though she supposed she should be frightened, or at least nervous, she just wasn't because whatever happened next, he would take care of her.

"Are you typical?" she couldn't help but ask, always inquisitive and especially so at this moment. The impressive length of him was a bit daunting, even for someone who had once faced a leopard in the midst of a tropical jungle. She had the same feeling, actually: awe for the splendour and beauty of the beast, but also an understandable trepidation for what might happen next.

"How the devil would I know," Stephen muttered. "Trust you to be analytical at a time like this. I'm happy to say that whatever the flaws of my gender might be, we do not compare ourselves to each other when in this state."

It hadn't been the most logical of questions, she conceded, but then again, logic didn't seem to apply to this evening.

"But I accept the compliment." There was a cheeky edge to his quick, boyish grin, but nothing boyish in the heavy light in his eyes. His voice dropped to a low whisper and he shifted so he was on top of her, arms braced, his mouth just teasing the juncture of neck and shoulder. "Open for me, Sabrina. I need you."

If the hot, hard press of his erect length against her hip was an indication, he told the truth. It always irked her if Stephen knew more on any subject than she did – and later she'd have to find out *how* he knew more about this particular subject – but for now the warm press of his lips on her skin was beguiling and she didn't resist when he nudged her legs apart and settled between her thighs.

The sensation of his entry made her suck in a deep breath and her hands grasped his biceps, holding tight, but Stephen merely murmured in a husky tone, "Relax, my love."

He'd never called her that before and it startled her enough that she barely noticed the sting as her innocence was lost, her gaze riveted on his face as he deeply sheathed himself.

And then suddenly they were fully joined and it was . . . indescribable.

"It doesn't really hurt," she said breathlessly. "I was under the impression there would be more pain. It's just a little uncomfortable. Do most women—"

"If you please, do not bring up other women right now," he

ordered, his face holding an intense expression belying the amused irritation in his voice. "How *you* feel is important, no one else. Can I move?"

She didn't have the slightest idea what he meant.

"Like this."

He slid backwards and she felt a pang of loss until he surged forwards again and small blissful pulses racked her body. "Yes," she whispered, "by all means move . . . oh, Stephen."

He did it again, a low sound emanating from deep in his throat. Sabrina watched in fascination as his lashes drifted downwards and the expression on his face grew taut. Her body lifted naturally into the next thrust and her hands slid upwards to rest on his shoulders.

Any discomfort eased as the rhythm increased, lost to the strange upwards spiral she'd experienced earlier and, when he reached between their moving bodies and touched her *there* again, she couldn't help a shuddering response, the pleasure was so acute. Paradise, she discovered, was a delicious, wicked pleasure in a simple bed in an obscure inn.

Above her, Stephen went very still at once, and his breath whistled outwards in an audible gasp, and he shuddered, dropping his head, his eyes closed. The moment stretched on, drifting, the little room quiet except for the hurried sound of their respiration.

It had all been . . . what was the word? she wondered, as she tested the sleek dampness of his skin over the muscles of his back, running her fingers lazily along the defined hardness. Sublime? Rapturous? Both fitted, but weren't quite right. Exquisite?

"I knew it would be like this," Stephen spoke first, his voice slightly strange.

Maybe *he* had the right word. "Like what?" Sabrina queried, noting her voice wasn't quite normal either.

He didn't answer. "Are you quite all right?" he asked instead, easing over to his side but not withdrawing, instead urging her to go with him so they stayed intimately entwined.

"Of course." She raised her brows. "Why wouldn't I be? Do you recall my father telling you about the time we were forced to outrun Barbary pirates and they were firing on our vessel and one of the bullets actually tore through my sleeve and grazed my arm? I assure you that stung far worse."

"I see." His habitual dryness returned to his tone. "Well, how does a man compete with bloodthirsty pirates and open-sea chases? Rather a daunting task, that. As an adventure, how did this rate?"

Before she could respond, he kissed her passionately, one hand smoothing suggestively over her bare hip.

And she forgot entirely about that wild trip to Gibraltar.

Three

The clatter of the busy street outside added to his distraction, but the noise was hardly the main culprit. Stephen frowned and tried to concentrate on the documents spread across his desk in an untidy fashion, then sighed and rubbed his hand across his jaw.

It was no use.

A week.

A full week since he'd returned Sabrina to her fashionable town-house, the precious notes in hand, and bid her a polite farewell. Not a lover's goodbye, but his usual casual leave-taking, for if there was anything he refused to do, it was pressure her for anything that would ruin their friendship.

But surely she understood everything had changed.

Actually, being Sabrina, she might just blithely count their night together as another escapade – albeit a scandalous one – and dismiss it as a new experience, no more. She hadn't so much as sent a note, even neglecting to invite him to tea, which her aunt usually did when they were in town.

Dear God, he might expire from frustration if he never touched her again, and—

"Whatever it is that put that grim look on your face, I am sure it can be eased by a good whiskey. It doesn't look like you are getting much done anyway. Care to join me?"

Jerked out of his abstraction by the sound of the voice from the doorway of his small office, Stephen saw his oldest brother, Kenneth, one shoulder propped against the doorway, his expression slightly amused. The weather had turned and it was drizzling outside, droplets of moisture gleaming on his dark hair.

Stephen had to admit his mood was about as cheery as the dismal skies.

Well, brooding wasn't doing him much good, and it was getting late anyway. He got to his feet. "Sounds capital, actually. Let me retrieve my coat."

They walked two streets over to a busy tavern that catered to both tradesmen and well-dressed merchants, and found a table in one of the corners. Kenneth ordered two whiskeys from the harried barmaid, and folded his hands on the scarred wooden tabletop, lifting his dark brows. "So, what has you so blue-devilled? A difficult client?"

"Who says I'm blue-devilled?" Stephen muttered.

"The clerk, for one. As I came in and asked for you, he mentioned you hadn't been yourself lately. Just the few moments I stood there waiting for you to as much as notice my arrival supports his claim."

It was true, but galling to admit it. He'd finally realized his deepest fantasy, made love to Sabrina, not just once, but for a good deal of the night, drifted to sleep with her luscious naked body in his arms . . . and now he was at a loss as to what to do next. If he declared himself, exposed his true feelings, and she declined to accept an honourable offer of marriage, their friendship would be shattered.

It was a possibility. He knew her well enough to have no illusions. Sabrina had no desire to give up her adventurous lifestyle for a staid husband who made a living poring over legal documents. She would have to want him more than her freedom, and was one night of passion and a childhood friendship enough?

He accepted the glass from the barmaid and took a searing drink that burned as it hit his throat. He suppressed the urge to cough, and confessed, "It's a woman."

Kenneth, five years his senior and recently married, the heir to the title and what modest fortune their family had left, simply nodded. "Sabrina."

Arrested with his glass at his mouth, Stephen stared.

"We've all known since . . ." Kenneth furrowed his brow. "Well, since you were both children probably."

"Known what?"

"Don't look so surprised." His brother chuckled. "It was obvious, always, even when you squabbled and got into trouble. There was a special connection between the two of you. Does it strike you how she's never been interested in pursuing the kind of highbrow marriage an heiress from a family so high up in society could contract? She's beautiful also, don't forget, so—"

"I'm not likely to forget," Stephen interrupted more curtly than he intended, recalling satin soft skin, and golden hair spilled across the bed sheets.

"No, I don't suppose you are." Fingering his glass, Kenneth said mildly, "While I don't think any male living on this green earth could claim to understand women, I am a married man, so I have some experience trying. Maybe I can help if you explain what precisely our lovely Sabrina has done lately to put you into such a dither."

"Dither?" Stephen shook his head. "Couldn't you have chosen a more masculine word? I'm not dithering, for God's sake, I'm ... conflicted, that's all."

"In what way?"

"I cannot decide if asking her to marry me would be a huge mistake or not." He took an inelegant gulp of whiskey before continuing. "I should, but she doesn't seem to think I should, or at least I've gotten no indication of that kind. It's a devil's own dilemma, to be honest, for you are right, we have a very comfortable friendship. It is inevitable that would change if she knew how I feel about her."

There was a burst of raucous laughter from a small group of patrons, punctuated by the clink of glasses. At least someone was celebrating, Stephen thought morosely.

His older brother cleared his throat. "You *should* marry her?"

Stephen gave him a level look and said nothing. Not even his brother, of whom he was very fond and trusted implicitly, would he tell about that magical night at the inn.

"I ... see." Kenneth sipped his drink, a faint frown furrowing his brow. Then he sighed. "Sabrina is unconventional, I'll give you that, a direct result of her father's fascination with travel and antiquities. She has the means to do what she wishes."

"Exactly," Stephen agreed, not encouraged by the observation – not that he didn't already know that point to be valid. "Personally, jungles, remote mountaintops and blistering deserts don't hold a lot of appeal, but she's always been adventurous. Even if she agreed to marry me, I worry if I held her here in England she'd grow restless, but I can't picture letting her continue to travel to dangerous places. Even now, when I have no influence to stop her, I worry constantly."

"Marriage is about compromise, little brother." Kenneth leaned back in his chair, his expression a hint of sardonic amusement. "Tell her you'll ride a camel and sail with her to tropical islands if she wishes, but she must also agree to stay here for part of the year and share the kind of life you enjoy."

It sounded logical, but when it came to women, Stephen had discovered, the term all too often didn't apply. Quietly, he said, "I really have nothing to offer her, Ken. No fortune and no title. As you pointed out, she could marry any time she wishes and she certainly would not have to settle for a junior solicitor who most definitely works for his modest living."

"Actually, what I pointed out was she *could* have married, but hasn't. It seems significant to me. Perhaps she is just waiting for you to ask."

Was she? Stephen wasn't sure, devil take it.

Perhaps she was wanton.

Sabrina had never thought of herself that way, but maybe it was true. In any case, all she had done since her return to London was dwell on the outrageous – and marvellous – way Stephen had touched her that fateful night after their mission to retrieve her father's notes. She blushed when she recalled the less than ladylike eagerness with which she'd responded. She'd lain against his lean body, neither one of them wearing a stitch of clothing, and he'd ravished her mouth with long, passionate kisses, while his hands—

"You are certainly distracted."

The prim sound of her aunt's voice interrupted the delicious recollection. Startled out of her reverie, Sabrina glanced guiltily over to where Beatrice sat on a brocade settee in the drawing room, busy with her embroidery. "I was . . . well, thinking of something."

Oh, that was articulate.

"I would guess so," Aunt Beatrice replied. "You had quite the oddest look on your face. I take it this subject is a pleasant one?"

Before Sabrina could mumble another nonsensical answer, a voice spoke from the doorway, "Madam, My Lady, you have a visitor."

The butler delivered the engraved card to Beatrice, who sat closer to the doorway. She peered at it – she needed spectacles but refused to admit it – and then nodded. "Please show His Lordship in, Seton, and see that a bottle of claret is brought up from the cellar, if you please."

"Very good, madam."

Lord Bloomfield. Sabrina didn't have to be told; she knew it. She'd been expecting some sort of communication from her father's colleague once he discovered the notes were missing and nothing else had been taken. While he couldn't come right out and accuse her of stealing what he claimed not to have in the first place, she didn't think for a minute he'd not try to at least wheedle them back from her. He was due to present a paper to the Royal Society in a few months and he undoubtedly needed those notes. He wasn't a scholar in his own right, and he never had been. Her father, on the other hand, had been a devoted scientist, and his scrupulous, detailed observations were like beautiful prose poems.

Had Lord Bloomfield asked for permission to use her father's research material instead of acting as if the papers were his own work, Sabrina probably would have loaned them to him. But the moment she'd read the published work that had brought Bloomfield such acclaim, she'd known it was her father's composition.

"Be polite." Beatrice said it in a brisk tone. "I know neither of us care for His Lordship, but he was a friend of your father."

"Some friend," Sabrina muttered, but she obligingly plastered a false smile on her face when Bloomfield strolled into the room.

Instantly, a quiver of alarm went through her. The Viscount was a large man, going to fat in his middle age, with a shock of thick brown hair just beginning to show grey at the temples. He was dressed for the evening in tailored formal wear, their drawing room evidently not his final destination. His immaculate cravat was tied in an intricate, fashionable knot, and above it his florid face wore what could only be described as a triumphant smirk.

"Good evening, ladies." He bent over Beatrice's hand, and then turned to Sabrina who reluctantly allowed him hers, though she longed to snatch it back immediately and give it a good wash.

"So nice of you to stop by, My Lord." Beatrice smiled graciously. "Please do sit down and have a glass of wine, won't you?"

"Perhaps one glass," he answered, choosing a chair and lowering his not inconsiderable bulk into it. "I have a full evening of social engagements but I could not keep from stopping by to offer my congratulations to Lady Sabrina."

What did he have up his sleeve? Sabrina eyed him warily and said nothing. It was Beatrice who asked, "Congratulations?"

"On her recent marriage, of course." Bloomfield watched her reaction with a gloating expression. "I must have missed the announcement in *The Times* but I understand she and her husband recently stayed at an inn near my country estate in Sussex."

Damnation.

The unladylike word seemed the appropriate reaction to the current situation. Lord Bloomfield might not be much of an archaeologist, but apparently he was a fair detective.

"You must be mistaken," Beatrice said with a small scowl. "Sabrina hasn't married."

"Ah." There was a wealth of innuendo in that small word. He dug in the pocket of his jacket, produced a slip of paper and theatrically squinted at it. "How odd. The innkeeper at the Lamb and Rooster swears a young woman answering Lady Sabrina's description stayed there a week ago with a tall, dark-haired young man, who several times in the proprietor's presence called her by the name Sabrina. The man claimed they were husband and wife, and I assumed it to be true, because, after all, they shared a room."

By now Aunt Beatrice had caught the not-so-subtle tension between them for she said in a frosty voice, "I am sure this innkeeper misheard."

"Perhaps, but he had an uncanny memory for he could describe the young woman perfectly. Golden curls, he said, and the most unusual midnight-blue eyes. She wore a dark-blue riding habit and rode a sorrel mare, and—"

"I was in Cambridgeshire last week, My Lord," Sabrina said as calmly as possible. "Visiting a friend."

"I see. And here I was delighted to think my old friend's daughter had finally decided to quit the mannish pursuits of her travels and settle into married life as a woman should." He put the piece of paper back into his pocket and shrugged, but there was nothing casual in the menacing look in his eyes. "If it wasn't you, then I'm glad. Because if you aren't wed, of course, and it *was* you, I'm afraid that would spell social ruin."

The arrival of Seton with a tray and a bottle of wine prevented any response to that overt threat. His Lordship took the opportunity to rise, decline refreshments after all, and take his leave.

The moment they were alone again, Beatrice demanded, "What was that all about?"

Though normally she drank sparingly, Sabrina reached over, filled a glass with claret, and took a bracing sip. She could lie, but then again, she wasn't good at telling falsehoods and she adored her aunt. "As I have maintained all along, he had Papa's research notes. I merely reclaimed my own property."

Beatrice digested this, her plump face registering a succession of emotions from indignation, to dismay, to resignation. "Let me guess who helped you do this. Tall? Dark-haired? That was Stephen, of course, for no matter how foolhardy it might be, that normally level-headed young man would fall in with your scheme. You could persuade him to have tea with the Devil if you wished to do so."

"Bloomfield *had* the notes," she pointed out defensively. "It isn't as if we stole anything. That odious man lied to us."

"That odious man," Beatrice said in clipped tones, "is going to smear your good name. Oh, Sabrina, what have you done, child? Did you and Stephen really spend the night together at the inn?"

A betraying blush heated her face. Despite her best effort to look bland, she could feel the crimson journey up her throat and into her cheeks. "The roads are dangerous at night and we could hardly waltz into His Lordship's home during the day, now could we?"

Her aunt looked at her and shook her head. "You have escaped disaster in your wild travels more than once, my dear, but I am afraid it has finally struck."

Four

It was late. Stephen shook himself out of a half-doze and glanced at the ormolu clock on the mantel. Past midnight wasn't an unfashionable hour precisely, but it was a strange time for someone to be knocking on his door. He snapped shut the book that had put him to sleep and rose to see who on earth was calling this time of night.

To say he was surprised to see Sabrina standing there was an understatement. She'd never once visited him in his modest lodgings before, for the obvious reason that unmarried young ladies didn't visit gentlemen. He always went to the fashionable townhouse in Mayfair where she resided with her aunt. Nonplussed, he just stood there staring at her.

At least she'd had the sense to wear a concealing cloak. When he didn't speak, she pushed the hood back. "The least you can do after I climbed out my window, bribed one of the footmen to hire a hack for me, and crept up your stairs like a character in a lurid novel, is invite me in."

That explained why she was without a chaperone, but not why she'd gone to such lengths. He had a feeling he didn't want her discussing it in the hallway, so there wasn't much choice but to step back and watch her brush past him in a swirl of velvet and a drift of light sweet perfume.

Stephen finally found his voice. "Have you lost your mind?"

"I had to see you."

She unfastened her cloak and he automatically stepped forwards to take it from her. She wore a simple day gown in a light material and her hair was caught back only with a satin ribbon. She looked young, fresh, and so damned beautiful that when she gazed at him with those entrancing dark-blue eyes he found himself irrationally unconcerned about why she'd come after all.

She was *there*.

Still, however he might feel about her presence, it was a very reckless thing for her to do. London at night was not the safest place for an unaccompanied female. "You little fool, couldn't this have waited until tomorrow? If you sent a note to my office, I would have paid a call at once if it was urgent, you know that."

"I know, but Aunt Beatrice would be there also. I wanted to talk to you alone. Besides, there is no possible way I could go to sleep." Her smile was strained. "We have a bit of a crisis, I'm afraid."

"I see. In that case, shall we go into my study where there is still a fire and I can hear this with some brandy at hand?"

"I drank two glasses of claret earlier," Sabrina said with a moue of distaste, "and you know I loathe the stuff. You might need the brandy."

"In that case," he muttered darkly, "by all means let us go into my study."

He led her down the hall and stirred the fire while she settled into one of the shabby chairs he kept meaning to replace but hadn't gotten around to doing so yet because, truthfully, it was comfortable and he was the only one who used it. Sabrina looked more feminine and alluring than ever against the backdrop of his masculine furnishings and dark panelled walls. She settled her skirts around her in a dainty way as she glanced around at the cluttered bookcases and the papers piled on his desk. When she caught sight of the watercolour above the fireplace she'd painted years ago of the very river where they'd played as children, her eyes widened. It probably wasn't a work of art in the eyes of most people – even she admitted her artistic bent did not lie with the brush – but he liked it and had kept it.

"Now then," he said to distract her attention from the painting and forestall her asking why he'd hung it in his study, "what is this 'crisis'?"

"Lord Bloomfield called on me this evening."

He wasn't too surprised. The man was a charlatan in the way he presented himself to the scientific world, but he wasn't a fool. All along they'd both known he would easily guess who had broken into his house because of what was missing. "Don't tell me he had the nerve to accuse you of rifling his desk?" Stephen propped one arm on the mantel and raised his brows in enquiry.

"No." Sabrina glanced away. Her cheeks looked suspiciously pink. "He knows we spent the night together at the inn. He came by to ostensibly congratulate me on my marriage."

Stephen digested this, the ramifications immediately evident, his feelings in flux. Having to marry him because she was forced by looming scandal was different than *wanting* to be his wife. "He's more resourceful than I gave him credit for," he said finally, trying to gauge Sabrina's expression. "I assumed he would know it was you, but hardly thought he'd bestir himself to play detective over how the deed was accomplished."

She lifted her slender shoulders, her eyes shadowed by long lashes and not quite meeting his. "He had a piece of paper with him that I assume is the innkeeper's description of us. He pulled it out of his pocket like it was a holy relic. I'd guess the man signed it, for Lord Bloomfield acted as if it was irrefutable proof."

And while Sabrina had led an unconventional life up until now, what with all her travels, her reputation had been pristine.

This was entirely his fault. The seduction at the inn, while not planned when she'd asked him to help her, was an opportunity seized.

"So he is going to make this public knowledge, I take it." His voice was remarkably calm.

"That was the threat. He mentioned that if I stayed overnight at an inn with a man who wasn't my husband, well, that would be unfortunate for my reputation."

Was this the opening he hoped would one day present itself? Stephen still wasn't sure. Sabrina wasn't obviously hinting she expected an offer. Instead, she looked at him as if she wanted him to miraculously come up with a solution for this problem.

He had one, he just wasn't sure she would like it.

On the other hand, for him, it would be a dream come true.

"He wants the notes back, obviously."

"No," she instantly responded. "That is out of the question."

"Then perhaps it would be advisable for us to marry as soon as possible." He did his best to look and sound neutral.

Sabrina's soft mouth parted. She visibly swallowed and her hands clenched in the material of her muslin skirts. "Stephen, I did not come here to coerce you into marrying me, I—"

He interrupted smoothly, "It's a legitimate offer. I'll visit your aunt tomorrow . . . no, today." A pointed glance at the clock emphasized the late hour. "After all, I did dishonour you, Sabrina, unless you've forgotten what we did that night."

I did dishonour you . . .

Is that how he referred to those hours of tender pleasure? Sabrina wasn't sure if she wanted to laugh hysterically or pick up one of his books and throw it at him – preferably a heavy tome. He was propped casually against the mantel, his expression neutral, the midnight silk of his hair distractingly rumpled around his clean-cut features, his white shirt casually unbuttoned at the neck.

He'd just proposed marriage in the most unsentimental way possible.

"No," she said succinctly.

Something flickered in his eyes. "No," he repeated. "I guess I am not surprised the idea doesn't appeal to you, but let's keep in mind it is possible you carry my child."

What she'd meant was no, she hadn't forgotten all those wicked and wonderful things they'd done together, but she didn't wish to force him to commit to a marriage he didn't want just because of her reckless inclinations.

"I've thought of that," she admitted. What was curious about it was her reaction to the idea of being pregnant with Stephen's child. It filled her with an unexpected joy that took her off guard. "We should know within the next week or two. If I'm not with child, then the point is moot."

"Is it?" he asked, looking at her with an enigmatic expression.

"Yes . . . I mean, or no . . . it isn't that," she muttered, not sure what question she was answering or even what she was saying.

Her and Stephen . . . *married*? If she was honest with herself, she'd thought about that quite a lot. Before this most recent escapade, she'd always considered him her very best friend, the boy who'd been her childhood playmate. But now that perception had certainly changed. He was very much a man and, moreover, a very attractive man.

He ran his hand through his hair. "A little clarification would be appreciated. If you don't wish to marry me, I understand. I have little to recommend such a match. No fortune, no title, and we both know you could do better."

Is that what he thought? Men were such obtuse creatures. Sabrina stared at him and took a deep breath before replying. "Can I point out how little titles and money impress me? I need neither. Don't be a complete idiot, Stephen. It's just this is my fault, for I'm the one who wanted to break into Bloomfield Hall. You needn't shoulder the problem to protect me."

A faint smile quirked his mouth. "As I recall, staying at the inn and what happened next was *my* idea. We always did manage to get into trouble together."

Sabrina shoved herself to her feet and paced across the room.

"I came here to warn you there might be a scandal unless we do something to keep Lord Bloomfield from spreading rumours, *not* to reminisce over our past misbehaviour. Do you have any ideas?"

"I believe I put one forth but it wasn't met with enthusiasm." He crossed his arms over his chest. "You could trade His Lordship the notes for his silence."

"Never." That was out of the question. Her father's life's work was not going to be claimed by a fraud.

"I thought that's what you'd say. Then marry me."

Sabrina looked at him in exasperation, but something in his expression suddenly held her arrested, locked in the moment. It reminded her of how he'd gazed at her before he kissed her that first time, how reverently his hands had drifted across her skin, the sensation of him over her, inside her, how deliciously pleasurable that night had been.

If she married him, that passion could be hers for ever. It was a tantalizing idea.

But she was a romantic at heart and she hated the thought he was offering out of duty, or even friendship. It was just so *Stephen* to take on the problem without a thought about his own happiness.

She faltered. "I . . . I know you are sincere because you specialize in rescuing maidens in trouble, but—"

He straightened away from the fireplace and took a step towards her. "Just one troublesome maiden," he interrupted, his voice soft, persuasive. "Only you, Sabrina. Always you. It has always, always been you. And just in case you wish to keep harping on how this is all your fault, I have a confession to make. There were more rooms available at the inn that night."

The intensity in his eyes made her catch her breath. "There were?"

He nodded and advanced. "I'd waited for years for a chance like that. You and me, and a convenient bed . . . how could I let it pass by? I suppose I should feel guilty for lying to you, but I don't."

Years?

Strong hands caught her waist and Sabrina found herself in his embrace, his mouth nuzzling her neck. There was no helping the small sigh of pleasure that escaped her lips, or the shiver of anticipation that rippled through her when he murmured against her skin, "Would it be possible to worry about Bloomfield in the morning? It seems to me I need to convince you my solution is a sound one. Will you stay a little longer?"

She shouldn't.

They shouldn't. But then again, when they were together long enough their actions bordered on reckless.

It wasn't too surprising she melted against him, her fingers curling into his dark hair, her breasts pressing against his chest. She gasped when he swept her up in his arms and walked out the door into a small hallway, but it was a sound of delight, not protest. His bedroom was austere, like the rest of the rooms, but it did have a nice bed, which she discovered was quite comfortable when he deposited her on the mattress and began to unfasten her clothes. Just as eagerly, she unbuttoned his shirt, the warmth of his skin under her questing fingertips causing a curl of excitement deep in her belly. Her gown, chemise, garters, stockings and slippers were carelessly tossed aside. When Sabrina fumbled trying to undo his breeches, he ended up doing it himself.

"I'm seducing you again," he murmured as he settled on top of her body in a smooth athletic movement. "And if this time doesn't do it – fair warning – I'll continue to seduce you until even someone as reckless and unconventional as you agrees to take the respectable route and become my wife."

Sabrina gave a breathless laugh, the length of him pressed against her inner thigh, hot and hard. "You *can* be infuriatingly determined when you want something."

He nibbled her lower lip. "Think of the adventures we can share. I've never seen a rainforest or ridden a camel."

It was a generous offer, for she knew he loved England and was at heart a respectable gentleman. She would wager most of the trouble he'd gotten into in his childhood was due to her instigation. Very lightly she touched his lean cheek. "I don't think my wanderlust is quite what it once was. Staying home holds a certain appeal and, for your information, riding a camel really isn't all that much fun. They are rather ill-tempered creatures."

He laughed and kissed her, and then the kiss turned molten and his hands were everywhere, caressing, exploring, evoking small tingles of pleasure. And when he joined their bodies and sank deep inside her, she experienced a bliss that wasn't just due to the physical enjoyment of the moment, but also to the poignant way he whispered her name.

That glorious summit rose, the peak promised rapture and, when she gained it and toppled over, she clung to him and quivered in unabashed erotic release, made all the more intense and satisfying when he went rigid and she felt him shudder.

"I suppose I *could* marry you to foil Lord Bloomfield's malicious revenge," she teased as they lay in damp contentment afterwards, her head pillowed comfortably on his muscular chest. "Though I do have one stipulation."

"Oh? How clever of you to strike a bargain when I am in my current weakened condition." His lazy smile made him more devastatingly handsome than ever. "Do tell."

"You must promise to continue to seduce me."

"I believe I can make that concession." His grin faded and those crystal grey eyes glimmered with a serious light. "I think you know I would give you anything within my power. I've loved you as long as I can remember. It changed, of course, as we got older, but it was always there."

"I think I have always loved you too," Sabrina said slowly, "though I admit I didn't recognize the difference between friendship and romance. You were just *you*. It's funny to think I didn't see it. After each trip, the moment I return to England, my very first order of business is to see you. Once I do, I am truly home. And when I am away, though it is all exciting and interesting, I miss you and think of you often."

"Picture me here, worrying over what kind of danger you might be in and myself a continent or ocean too far away to help you." His voice held just a hint of a ragged edge and his long fingers smoothed her hair. "It was torment."

It was galling to think she had Lord Bloomfield's devious machinations to thank for her current state of happiness, but in a convoluted way she supposed she did. "If we are going to marry," she said, snuggling even closer, relishing the feel of Stephen's arm around her, "Lord Bloomfield's petty threat is foiled, but he could still remain vengeful and isn't without influence. I suppose I could loan him the notes needed to finish the paper he has started if he agrees to credit my father as an equal partner."

"That sounds like a reasonable bargain to me." Stephen brushed a kiss across her forehead. "I am, after all, a solicitor. I could draw up a legal document for him to sign."

"You are, as always, quite handy to have around." Sabrina rose up and her smile was deliberately mischievous. "Who would think such a mild-mannered gentleman would make such a marvellous partner in crime? If it wasn't for your skill with the picklock, we would never have been able to steal back the notes."

Without warning, she was tumbled to her back so quickly she gasped.

"Would a mild-mannered gentleman do this?" Stephen demanded teasingly as his fingers did something very, very wicked between her legs. "Besides, as you've pointed out, we didn't steal anything. The notes were yours to begin with."

"But something was stolen that night," Sabrina whispered, drowning in sensation.

"What?" He went very still.

"My heart."

Softly, he kissed her. "Well, do not expect me to give it back."

Her Gentleman Thief

Robyn DeHart

Annalise Petty sat primly on the carriage seat, hands folded neatly in her lap. Outwardly, she probably appeared to be the perfect genteel lady, full of grace and peace. But inside, a battle raged. Her heart beat wildly and her stomach felt like a gnarled mess of knots. In two days she would become wife to the most boring, proper man in all of London. A man she had foolishly fancied herself in love with when he'd first begun to court her. Then he'd revealed his true self. Now she knew he was rather indifferent to her and only interested in the business deal the union brokered.

She chewed at her bottom lip. The carriage rumbled along through the dark night. Her parents had already made the journey to Kent, but Annalise and her younger sister, Penny, had stayed behind for one last fitting of the wedding gown. The dress, in layers of cream-coloured gossamer silk, was the finest garment Annalise had ever owned. Her betrothed had purchased her an entire wardrobe of appropriate clothing, which would be delivered to his estate sometime next week. The wedding gown, though, sat neatly in a trunk on the back of the rig.

Hildy, their maid, rested quietly across from them, pretending not to nap, though her level breathing and spontaneous snores betrayed her. Penny sat quietly, her expression blank. Sweet and beautiful Penny. Annalise sighed. This should have been her trip, her wedding gown in the back.

As if her sister had read her mind, Penny placed a gloved hand over Annalise's. "You should be excited," Penny said. "Your grin belies your worry." She smiled warmly. "Relax."

Annalise thought to argue, then nodded. "You know me far too well, sister. I cannot help but think that all of this should be for you. This is your season, your introduction to society."

"And you never had either." She put a hand against her chest. "I am so very happy for you. Your union with Lord Benning has no bearing on my finding a good match. Besides, you are older, you should marry first."

Yes, but Cousin Millicent hadn't offered to sponsor a season for Annalise, and, though her father was an earl, they had no money to provide either a dowry or a proper coming-out. So Annalise had neither, which was fine with her. She had resigned herself to never marrying. But when the opportunity had come along for Penny, well, the entire family had moved in with their distant cousin in the hope of a quick marriage. This had not been what any of them had planned.

At three and twenty, Annalise knew she should consider herself lucky to have found a man willing to marry her. She certainly wasn't unattractive, but she was fleshier than most society beauties. Still, she hadn't been properly introduced at Almack's. She'd only gone to London at Penny's request to act as a chaperone of sorts. And as she'd sat in the corner at that first ball, she'd seen the tall, handsome Griffin Hartwell, Viscount Benning moving in their direction. She'd even reached over and squeezed Penny's hand in excitement for her younger sister. Then when the rich baritone voice had asked her to dance and the masculine hand had extended not to Penny, but instead to Annalise, it had been scandalous. She'd wanted to decline, had known it would have been the more appropriate thing to do, but as she'd looked up into his handsome face, all her girlish fantasies had come to life and she'd found herself nodding and extending her own hand.

That one dance had led to three more that evening and had tongues wagging all over London. He'd played proper court to her after that scandalous evening, never once seeking time alone with her and only speaking about her, rarely to her. Her parents had eagerly accepted his offer of marriage and in one afternoon Annalise had gone from the unassuming sister to betrothed to a viscount. It wasn't that she didn't want to marry – she did – but she was foolish enough to long for a marriage with love and warmth. All her life she'd been dutiful and obedient, but her parents had not once asked her how she felt about this union. Nor had Griffin, beyond the polite proposal staged perfectly in front of her entire family. An impossible situation for her to say, "No thank you."

She supposed matters could be worse. Griffin could be old or cruel, and he was neither. Instead he was only a few years her senior and polite and so dashing she had nearly choked on her lemonade the first time he asked her to dance. Then had come the proposal and she'd wondered at her great fortune. It hadn't taken long for her to see the truth. A man so handsome and dashing – a man so rich – he couldn't possibly want *her*. He'd only asked for her hand because he wanted some property her father owned. Her lack of dowry hadn't been an issue, so they'd brokered a deal and she was the price. She exhaled loudly, but thankfully did not disturb Hildy.

Suddenly the carriage jerked to a stop. Outside she heard muttering, men's voices. Perhaps they'd lost a wheel or taken a wrong turn. She peeled the curtain away from the window, but in the dark of the night, she could see nothing but outlines of the trees lining the road.

Hildy stirred. "Why are we not moving? Have we arrived?"

"I don't believe so," Annalise said, still trying to make something out of the dark shadows. She placed a hand on Penny's knee to offer comfort.

Then the door flew open. "Out, ladies," a male voice said curtly.

"Out?" Hildy said, clearly outraged. "It's dark. If there is a problem with the carriage, we shall sit here until you fix it."

A masked man stepped in front of the opened carriage door. Annalise noted that most of Penny's form remained hidden in the shadows, so she sat forwards, trying to hide Penny. Her heart slammed against her ribcage.

Good heavens, they were being robbed!

Without thought, Annalise tossed her cloak over her sister. "Stay still," she whispered.

He showed them a small pistol. "I said out."

"Do not leave this carriage," she warned her sister in a whisper. Annalise made haste to climb down the carriage steps. Hildy promptly fainted at the sight of the gun. *An excellent chaperone, that one.* The lanterns hanging off the carriage afforded her enough light to take in her surroundings. Annalise noted their driver and footman were both blindfolded and tied to a tree.

"Sir, we don't have many valuables with us, but what we do have is yours," Annalise said. "If you would simply let us be on our way." She fought the urge to glance behind her to the carriage. She knew Penny would obey Annalise's instructions and stay hidden.

"Indeed." The masked man came to stand in front of her. If she hadn't known any better, she would have sworn recognition flickered in his eyes. The carriage door remained open and Annalise knew the robber could see Hildy's large body slumped over inside. Eventually the woman would awaken, but for now her silence kept Penny safe and unseen. "You ladies are out quite late this evening."

Annalise bravely looked up to meet the highwayman's gaze and found herself arrested by the most stunningly beautiful green eyes.

And were it not for the black silk domino mask obscuring part of his face, she might have forgotten who he was and what was happening. The lantern light flickered off his features and she could clearly see a strong jaw, sculpted lips, a hint of a day's growth of whiskers. It was quite evident that he was devilishly handsome.

The highwayman leaned against the carriage, crossing his feet at the ankles. The pistol dangled from his hand, almost as if he held nothing more than a handkerchief. There was a casual air about him, as if this situation were a perfectly normal occurrence for a Monday evening.

His sensual lips curved into a smile. "And where are you going at this hour?"

"My wedding," she said.

But as the words left her mouth a realization surged through her. After this incident, there would be no wedding. No one here could attest to the fact that this man, this thief, had not ravished her. Hildy had not roused and the other two servants were blindfolded and tied up. There was no one save Penny to vouch for her and, if she were to speak up, she too would be ruined. Simply being stopped by this highwayman was enough to sully her reputation and her virtue. And who was to say he wouldn't ravish her still? But Penny could be saved. She needed only to get Penny to safety.

Before she could further think on the matter, she reached out and placed a hand on the highwayman's chest. "Take me with you," she said.

If she didn't know better, she would have thought he looked affronted. "I beg your pardon," he said.

"Please, I won't be a burden, you can simply take me and drop me off in London," Annalise said. Her heart pounded so rapidly, so loudly, her very ears seemed to vibrate.

One eyebrow rose above his mask. "What of your wedding?"

What to say? There was no reason to tell this man that her fiancé was no more interested in her than he was her meagre collection of coloured ribbons. He might even know Griffin – though that seemed unlikely considering this man's profession. She did not believe Griffin consorted with such fellows. Though if she didn't know better she would have sworn this man was a gentleman too. The way he spoke, the way he moved – there was something utterly genteel about him. But that was foolish. Gentlemen were not thieves. She shook her head. "My parents arranged the marriage. To a dreadful man, boring, priggish and only interested in the land my father offered him."

The highwayman's lips tilted in a slight smile. His head quirked. "So not a love match, then?"

"No, most certainly not," she said. Though she had once thought – hoped – it might be. She'd been a fool. A mistake she would not make again.

"And you want me to help you run away?" he asked.

She heard stirring in the carriage behind her. She stepped forwards, closer to the highwayman, and nodded. "Yes, please. Help me run away."

He stepped closer, so that he stood but a breath away from her. His gloved fingers ran down her cheek. "Are you not afraid of me?"

She steeled herself, straightened her shoulders to stand taller. This was precisely why she'd had to hide Penny – to protect her sister's reputation, but more so to protect her actual virtue. Penny was not a woman most men could resist, with her lithe figure and pale blonde hair. She was a classic beauty, unlike Annalise who was rather easy to ignore. It seemed unlikely Annalise would get ravished. "No." She reached into her reticule and pulled out the jewellery she had been given to wear on her wedding day: a lovely pearl and diamond set necklace with matching drop earrings. "I'll pay you." She cupped the jewellery in her hand and held it out to him.

"I am a highwayman in case that has escaped your attention. I would take that regardless," he said with a grin as he pocketed the jewels. He didn't wait for her to answer, instead he leaned over, picked her up and tossed her over his shoulder as if she weighed no more than a child. "You will regret this."

She thought he was probably right, but for some reason she felt no fear, only excitement and expectation. Penny would be safe. Eventually Hildy would awaken and she'd untie their driver and ensure Annalise's sister got home safely. She'd always wanted an adventure. Well, now she'd all but stumbled head first into one. Perhaps her wedding day would not be so dull after all.

Griffin Hartwell breathed in the heady lemony scent of his bride's hair as she sat nestled against him on his mount. The mask he wore itched and pricked at his skin, but he didn't dare remove it. Not now. Instead he was forced to ponder his situation in physical discomfort.

He'd lost a damned wager and because of that he'd ended up out here on this road playing the thief. He was only meant to steal a single piece of jewellery, a piece that would have been mailed back to the rightful owner as soon as he'd returned to London. But as his rotten luck would have it, he'd stopped the carriage carrying his own betrothed and she'd begged him – no, not him, the highwayman he was pretending to be – to save her from a marriage to a bore. That was what she'd called him. Perhaps it hadn't been poor luck at all, but a boon considering she would have made the same request of an actual thief. No, he could at least ensure she remained safe.

The irony was not lost on Griffin, but he was too addled to enjoy it at the moment. He shouldn't have complied with her wish to take her along, but as he saw it, he didn't have much choice. Her reputation would have already been in shambles simply by being alone in the woods with a highwayman, and since her silly maid had succumbed to a fit of the vapours, and he'd conveniently tied up the driver and footman, they'd been hopelessly alone. He and his betrothed.

He'd ruined his own would-be bride. He nearly chuckled.

Of course he'd still marry her, convince her parents that he believed her tale of not being ravished. That would work only, though, if she fought for herself. And evidently she had no real desire to marry him. She found him to be a bore. And priggish. And that was an irony even more profound than the first. He'd only pretended to be righteous and proper to prevent further scandal. When he'd first asked her to dance he'd not known she hadn't been properly introduced to society and was only acting as a chaperone to her younger sister. But shock waves had rocked through the ton as they'd danced not once, but four times that night.

She'd been utterly enchanting: charming and witty and easy to converse with. Her laughter had come easily and had been authentic. She'd been sincere, not at all like the pretty, but empty shell that was most marriageable women he'd encountered. Annalise had been different and he'd been intoxicated by her.

It would seem he'd done such a convincing job that he was at the very height of propriety. Annalise was not interested in him in the least. Though he would have sworn that hadn't always been the case.

Her full bottom pressed against his inner thigh stirring his desire. It would have been impossible for her to ride side-saddle, as was customary for ladies, so he'd snuggled her against him, her position mirroring his own. Annalise Petty was a desirable woman. It was why he'd sought her out at the Draper Ball. Why he'd first noticed her in that shop on Bond Street the day before when she'd turned her righteous anger on Lady Henwick and given the matron more than one afternoon's worth of gossip. The woman had had it coming. She'd been ruthless towards Annalise's younger sister. Still Annalise's behaviour was shocking. She'd intrigued him, so different when compared to all the rest of London's marriageable misses. So when he'd seen her the following evening at the ball, he'd been unable to resist crossing the ballroom to ask her to dance. Because of the ensuing scandal, he'd pursued her and had eventually asked her parents for her hand, but that initial attraction had not yet faded for him.

She was lovely, with her large brown eyes and wide mouth, her honey-coloured locks and rounded figure. Griffin loved her fuller curves. Though her modest dresses didn't give too much away, he knew she had lush hips and shapely legs to match her bountiful breasts. Where some girls had to dampen their petticoats to pronounce their assets, Annalise's figure demanded attention. And he'd imagined every inch of her, and precisely what he would do to her on their wedding night. She would be worth the wait, worth the sacrifice he'd made in not enjoying her company these past few weeks.

If Annalise didn't marry him, his mother would select a bride for him. She'd given him a deadline and he knew, as wonderful as his mother could be, a bride of her choice would not match his own desires. She'd select someone pretty and sweet and demure, and he'd be in for a lifetime of boredom. Much the same as what Annalise clearly expected from him.

Clearly he had only one option. The highwayman who had just abducted Annalise would have to convince her to marry her bore of a fiancé. He wouldn't take her to London at all. In fact their current location was rather perfect. There was a small cottage on the edge of his property that would give them safe shelter for the night. The cottage was empty this time of year, generally used as a hunting cottage in pheasant season. It was the perfect place for them to hide and rest until morning light when he could send her on her way to Kent. On her way to their wedding.

He had to convince her she was making a mistake running away. And he'd have to do all of that while keeping his identity hidden.

Half an hour later they pulled up to the cottage. It was dark, though Griffin knew it would be well stocked with candles and blankets.

"Where are we?" she asked.

"Looks to be an abandoned cottage," he said. He jumped down from the horse, then helped her to the ground. "We'll stay here for the night. It's far too late to ride all the way back to London."

"Is this your hiding place? Where you keep all your stolen goods?" she asked, her voice an odd mixture of intrigue and horror.

He led her to the front door, then made a show of breaking the lock to make it appear as if he didn't already know there was a key concealed within the hanging fern. "I have no such hiding place," he murmured.

"Well, I would think as a thief you would need some place such as that," she said. "Unless you are not successful in your wicked endeavours."

He quickly found two candles and lit them. A soft glow permeated the darkness and illuminated the lovely Annalise. He met her gaze. "I can assure you that when given the opportunity I can be appropriately wicked." He'd imagined this very scenario, only on their wedding night, with her wearing a filmy robe, her golden hair cascading down her back, her feet bare.

Now though she stood before him fully clothed. Her travel gown was basic and brown, with matching boots. While her dress remained intact, her hair was windblown from the ride, the remaining pins still holding her curls but several tresses had escaped and now framed her face. He noted that she wore no cloak or outer garment. "You do not wear a cloak in this chill weather?"

She chewed at her lip and shrugged. "I must have left it in the carriage."

He eyed her. He knew Annalise to be fiery and bold, but never impractical.

"Are you going to take that mask off?" she asked.

His heart thundered. Had she recognized him? He didn't think so, but it was a possibility. The sound of his voice or perhaps his eyes? Any of that could clue her into his true identity. They hadn't spent much time together, but she had certainly seen him, stood close to him, had heard him speak. He eyed her, searching her face for signs of recognition, but her blank expression gave him nothing.

"Unless you tell me your name, it is not as if I can lead authorities to you," she reasoned.

So no, she did not recognize him. "No, I'm perfectly comfortable just as I am."

She shrugged. "Very well." She turned around slowly, surveying the cottage. They stood in the seating room, which consisted of three wooden chairs and a worn sofa. She rubbed her arms, obviously chilled.

He made quick work of getting a fire going in the hearth. The flames crackled to life and warmth began to spread through the small cottage.

She swallowed visibly. "And we are to sleep here? Together?"

Her eyes widened as she lowered herself to the worn green and brown sofa, as if the weight of the situation had just crashed down upon her. To her mind, she was alone in an abandoned cottage with a dangerous highwayman. Highwaymen had dreadful reputations as thieves who preyed upon carriages of the wealthy, stealing jewels and money and virtues as they prowled the countryside. Yet she hadn't seemed afraid of the situation as she'd climbed down from the carriage, nor when she'd asked him to take her with him. And even now, although she seemed hesitant, perhaps cautious, he saw no actual fear lining her lovely face. Perhaps she feigned bravery.

But she *should* be afraid.

She was to be his wife. He certainly couldn't allow her to ride through the countryside befriending miscreants and thieves. What if he hadn't been the one to pull over her carriage? What if a true blackguard had taken her with him? Perhaps she needed to see the full weight of the situation, feel the repercussions of her reckless behaviour.

He took a step towards her. One finger at a time, he pulled his gloves off. "Yes, this is where we will sleep for the night." He trailed a hand down her cheek. "I suspect we'll find an appropriate bed in one of the rooms down that hall."

Her eyes followed his nod to the darkened hallway.

"Rethinking your request to come along with me?" he asked.

She inhaled sharply and took a steadying breath. "I am merely coming to terms with my reputation."

"You weren't too worried about your reputation back on the road when you begged me to rescue you."

Defiantly she crossed her arms over her chest. It did little to hide the curves of her breasts, but instead drew closer attention to their fullness. "Perhaps I was a measure too hasty in my request. But it is far too late now. My reputation is already in tatters." She pushed out her chin. "I assume you intend to ravish me, then?"

He felt his lips twitch with humour. He turned away from her to hide his expression. He should be angry with her – hell, he *was* angry – but she made it damned difficult to stay that way. "I would not have to ravish you," he said. "If I want you, I will have you." He turned back to face her and met her gaze. Momentarily, it felt as if he was looking at her, Annalise, his fiancée and she was looking at him in return, seeing Griffin beneath the mask.

The masked man sat in a wooden chair and stretched out his long legs in front of him. His tan breeches moulded against his well-formed legs, his Hessian boots shone in the candlelight. He certainly did not dress like a highwayman.

She crossed her feet at the ankles and folded her hands in her lap. Her mama had always told her she was impetuous and head-strong, but she'd never done anything this foolhardy. But here she was, holed up in an abandoned cottage with a masked thief. Her family would wonder what Griffin would say when he discovered his would-be wife had been abducted. Hopefully Penny and Hildy had made it safely to Kent.

If I want you, I will have you. His words rang in her head. *If.* Leave it to her to be so uninspiring to the opposite sex that even a ruthless highwayman could resist her charms. The fact that a thief didn't want to ravish her should make her feel better about her current situation, instead she felt defeated. No wonder Griffin was indifferent to her.

"Tell me about this fiancé of yours," he said.

"He's a gentleman," she began, not quite certain what else to add. She'd spoken so poorly of him earlier in the evening. But there was part of her, the part that was uneasy with her current situation, who wished he were here now. Not that he'd ever been particularly protec-tive, in fact he'd mostly ignored her. But that first evening when they'd met, when he'd not been able to keep his eyes off her, when they'd danced again and again, he'd seemed, perhaps not protective, but most definitely interested. And she supposed he was an athletic sort and he might be able to fight this highwayman for her honour.

"A gentleman," he repeated, clearly amused. A smile played at the corners of his mouth, which drew her eye to his lips. They were perfectly crafted, she couldn't help but notice, sensual, almost pretty. The kinds of lips she'd heard other ladies talk about, the sort that would know how to kiss a woman to make her insides quiver.

She didn't remember ever noticing Griffin's mouth. Of course he didn't speak to her very often. And, of course, he'd never so much as kissed her cheek. Annalise refolded her hands in her lap. "He's kind and gentle."

An eyebrow quirked over the domino mask. "You said he was boorish," he reminded her.

She had said that. And she'd meant it. There was nothing romantic or exciting about her betrothed. He was a typical English gentleman, more interested in land and politics and drink than his intended. Being in the same room with Griffin was a constant reminder of how forgettable she was as a woman.

So much like the family she'd grown up in. Her father was always far more concerned with their coffers, and what the neighbours were doing. Her mother spent every last minute doting on Penny, the prettier daughter. Annalise had been ignored. Which had suited her perfectly since it allowed her plenty of uninterrupted reading time.

That was until Griffin had started to pay attention to her, then it was as if her parents had noticed her for the first time. He'd been the only man to show an interest in her and, initially, when they'd danced at the ball, she'd thought he wanted *her* – Annalise, the woman. But as time progressed and he more or less simply courted her parents, she'd realized he'd been attracted to nothing more than the land she provided.

"I did say that," she said. Truth was, she didn't have much to say about her future husband. She didn't know him. She knew his name and she knew what his hand felt like in hers, the other resting on her lower back. She knew how she'd felt that first moment in his arms, the furious agitation in her stomach and the hope that had bloomed in her heart. And she knew the resulting disappointment when he'd come to call and spent the time discussing horses with her father.

"And you meant it," he said.

"I did." She crossed her arms over her chest defiantly. What did it matter what she said here tonight? She did not know this man; he did not know her. And tomorrow everything in her life would be different. "He is awfully boring and polite. And terribly respectable."

He feigned shock, his mouth fell open. "However do you bear it? Respectability is indeed a terrible thing."

"I am quite serious," she said, feeling the frown crease her brows.

"Of that, I have no doubt." He sat quietly for several moments before he folded his hands across his abdomen. "So what shall you do now that you've left this dreadful man at the altar?"

Annalise allowed his words to sink in. No, it would never appear that way to Griffin, nor her family. They would see her as tarnished goods because of her fate at the hands of this highwayman. But she knew the truth. As did this man. She had walked away from Griffin. Jilted him. Indifference or not, he hadn't deserved that, but what of Penny's reputation? Annalise couldn't have allowed her sister to be ruined alongside her.

"I never said he was dreadful," Annalise said quietly.

"But a respectable boor," he corrected.

She sighed. "I shouldn't have said those things."

He was quiet for several moments before he said anything else. "So tell me, is leaving this fiancé of yours the only way in which you can acquire excitement? That is what you're after, is it not? Some manner of adventure?"

She hadn't left with this man to seek adventure, she'd done so to protect her sister. But she couldn't tell him that, so she played along. "I am most disappointed as to how my life is turning out. It seems the only way," she said. And it wasn't as if any of that was a lie. She *was* disappointed.

"What of marrying this boring bloke, as planned, then finding your adventure elsewhere?" His head tilted as if he were truly curious about the matter. Or had that been an invitation . . . to dally with him? Certainly not. He'd said himself, if he wanted her, she would be his. Evidently he did not want her. And she was grateful for that. No woman wished to be ravished, regardless of how dashing the highwayman might be.

"It is practised quite heavily in society, as you must know. Perhaps a virtuous woman such as yourself has not heard of such a thing. But I can assure you it is most common." Was that resentment she heard lining his voice?

"I would never do such a thing," she said. "Infidelity is unthinkable. I do realize men find it palatable, but I could never participate." She sat straighter. "And, of course, I have heard of liaisons outside of the marriage bed. Griffin might be boring, but he is a kind man and I would never be so disrespectful of him."

He was quiet for a moment as if he were trying to make something of her admission.

Her eyes travelled the length of his legs and again she was struck by the shine of his Hessians. Simple thieves did not dress in such a refined manner. "It doesn't appear as though infidelity is the only way to seek out adventure." She inclined her head in his direction.

"To what are you referring, madam?" he asked.

"This." She motioned her hand in his direction. "Your mask, your thievery. Kidnapping an innocent lady."

He held up a finger. "At her request," he added. "I did not don the mask for adventure."

"Perhaps not, but you are no ordinary highwayman, are you?" she asked.

"I suppose you've met other thieves then, to compare me to? And I am somehow lacking in an area?" he asked.

She smiled in spite of herself. "No, I have met no others. But you are well born, I can see that much. In the way you handled the ride. The manner in which you speak, sit, hold yourself, your fine clothes." She paused, then met his eyes. "The fact that you have not handled me inappropriately. You are a gentleman."

A slow smile slid into place and he was so utterly handsome, so devastatingly dashing, she sucked in her breath. She would have sworn her heart paused for an entire minute before it beat again. As if the blood pumping through her veins stilled as she inhaled, stopped simply for his smile. "A well-born man," she continued in an attempt to hide her reaction to him, "who becomes bored with society can traipse about the countryside playing at thievery. A well-born lady has only gossip and shopping to entertain her."

He shrugged. "Perhaps. But looks can certainly be deceiving."

"Indeed. Regardless of who you are, you must acknowledge that women do not have the same opportunities men do when it comes to life choices, especially well-bred ladies. I may marry a man of my family's choosing or I am doomed to spinsterhood, relying on the generosity of my family members."

"Forgive me if I offer you no sympathy." He leaned forwards, bracing his elbows on his knees. He shoved his shirtsleeves up, revealing well-muscled forearms. "Men do not always have choice in their marriage partners either."

"More often than women do," she argued, knowing it was childish to do so.

"Marriage to the right person could be an adventure. Have you considered that?" he asked.

"Of course." And initially she had thought Griffin to be that very person. He'd been so charming, so funny, and then turned so cold. "Marriage for love," she said quietly.

"So you do not love him?" he said. His words came out slowly.

"He does not love me," she said vehemently, perhaps revealing too much of her disappointment. She paused before adding, "It was not a love match, but rather a business transaction between him and my father."

"He has told you he does not love you?"

She frowned. "No, of course not. He would not be that cruel."

"Then how do you know?" he asked.

"Because a woman can tell these things. In the way that he looks at me." Or rather the way he never looked at her. "And the way that he speaks to me." She didn't owe this highwayman an explanation. "A woman knows when a man loves her." She had thought she'd felt it with Griffin, felt the gentle bloom of love in his touch, his words. Then as suddenly as their relationship had begun his polite indifference had replaced his wooing.

"Women do not know everything." He stood and paced the length of the small room. He stood in front of the tiny window, but made no move to push aside the faded curtain. He simply stood there staring at nothing.

"What does a highwayman know of love?" she tossed out.

He chuckled, but it did not seem to be a particularly humour-filled laugh. "Perhaps I know nothing about love." He turned and slowly lowered himself on to the sofa next to her. Far too close. She could feel warmth emanating off his legs.

She swallowed hard and fisted material from her skirt, twisting it. Trying her best to ignore her fear, she raised her chin up a notch. This close to him she could smell his scent, woody and musky, complete masculinity. There was something oddly familiar about it.

"You are quite lovely," he murmured.

"There is no need to taunt me. That is cruel," she said.

"Taunt you?" He leaned forwards, twirled one of her stray curls around his finger. "I thought I was paying you a compliment."

"I am not a beauty, everyone knows that," she said defiantly.

"That is a foolish thing to say." He ran a hand down her cheek. His fingers were warm as they trailed down her face. "I might not know love," he said, bitterness seeped into his tone. "But I do know beauty and you are beautiful."

Again he touched her. Shivers scattered over her flesh, but nothing touched her the way his words did. As much as she didn't want to, she believed him. He thought her beautiful. Perhaps that said more about her than it did him, that a thief would find her appealing. But she didn't care. In this moment she felt beautiful. And it nearly erased all of her nerves about being trapped in this cottage with a potentially dangerous man.

"Your complexion is exquisite, your skin so soft. And your hair – I want to pull those pins from it and run my hands through your golden locks."

In that moment she wanted him to. Not to simply threaten it, but to do it, to pull those pins out and pull her to him, kiss her senseless. It was wrong, she knew that, still there was something so compelling about this masked man.

"You have lovely brown eyes," he continued. "But more than all of those, you have a luscious mouth, lips so full and tender, I want very much to kiss them." He was so very close now, she could smell the faint hint of liquor on his breath as well as cold.

Without a thought to the consequences, Annalise closed her eyes and leaned forwards ever so slightly. He chuckled lightly, then his lips brushed against hers. The first touch of his mouth warmed her entire body. He settled closer to her, placed one hand on her back as he pulled her to him. His other hand cupped her cheek.

His lips moved against hers, softly, slowly, seductively. Annalise opened her mouth to him. He deepened the kiss, sliding his tongue across her teeth, then into her mouth. Desire pooled through her body, blood tingled through her veins.

Oh my.

His fingers kneaded her back. And she still sat, ankles crossed, hands fisting her skirts. She wanted to touch him too, but did not know where to put her hands. This entire situation was wrong, she knew that, but what did it matter now? She was a ruined woman. Fated to life as a single woman, much like her Aunt Triny. Should she not simply enjoy this moment of desire for what it was?

He kissed her for several moments and she enjoyed every brush of his lips, every sweep of his tongue. Good heavens, what was he doing to her?

With both hands he pulled her towards him so her torso lay partially across his body. His warm, firm chest pressed against her and still he kissed her. She had heard other girls mention such embraces, usually found in the arms of blackguards who preyed on the virtue of innocent females. But none of that mattered any longer. She felt a pang of regret as an image of Griffin's face formed in her mind. She'd imagined kissing him in such a fashion, passion overcoming them both. But he did not want her, not truly, she reminded herself.

His hand came up and cupped her breast, the touch so intimate, so unfamiliar, yet so utterly devilish, that she made no move to stop him. He kneaded her sensitive flesh and deepened the kiss. Tentatively she kissed him back, running her tongue against his.

"Annalise," he whispered.

Her eyes flew open, and she leaned back. "I never told you my name."

Without another thought, Annalise reached over and tugged on the black mask. The black silk fabric tore away from his face. She came to her feet and her eyes widened in shock. "Griffin!" she exclaimed.

He gave her a mocking bow. "Sorry to disappoint you."

Several conflicting emotions flitted across her face. She stood stock-still, her hands fisted at her sides, and continued to gape at him. "But how? Why?" Her brow creased in a heavy frown.

"How did I come to be a highwayman?" he asked. He walked away from her then, casually making his way to one of the tiny windows.

He stared outside and said nothing for several moments, then he slowly turned to face her. "It was a wager. A foolish wager with an idiot friend." He shook his head. "I was only meant to steal one piece of jewellery and then be on my way. Harmless enough."

"Harmless," she repeated.

He'd seen Annalise's wrath and he fully expected to be on the receiving end any moment, but after several moments of silence he began to wonder. Still she stood, but she no longer faced him, instead she looked in the opposite direction.

"Annalise," he said, gripping her elbow.

She turned to face him, her expression flamed with indignation. "You deceived me, played me for a fool." She shook her head. "I said things I never would have—" She choked on the rest of the sentence.

Was she looking to him for an apology? Yes, he'd deceived her, but she'd walked out on him. Chosen a thief over a fiancé who . . . who what? Who was mad with lust for her? These were not the romantic words of love that a lady longed to hear. Still, she didn't seem to be longing for such words from him so what did it matter if he had tender feelings for her or not?

"There is nothing harmless about this night," she said quietly. She pulled away from him and faced the sofa.

So she regretted that too, his touch, his kisses. It was a kick in his gut because he knew that had she not ripped his mask off, she would have allowed him to continue, to push their passion further. But with Griffin, it was all regret.

He watched Annalise now as she lay on the sofa. Then he made his way to the front door. He wouldn't leave, not now, but he needed some air. And the cold night breeze. Already his blood heated for her, desire surging through his body.

"I need some air," he said as he headed out the front door.

He shouldn't have touched her. He'd known that all along about Annalise, that once he started he wouldn't be able to stop. Wouldn't want to. Despite her good breeding, she was a fiery woman, one with passion and pluck. She would never be the perfect wife who sat in the corner and nodded and smiled. No, not his Annalise. She would argue and fuss.

He knew that for a lot of men that would bring nothing but aggravation. And he'd be a fool not to admit that her feisty behaviour would bring its share of frustration. But he wouldn't want her any other way.

With other women he'd always been bored. They all looked the same and they sounded the same. But Annalise had her sumptuous curves, her wide, easy smile, and her eyes shone with intelligence. Her father had even warned Griffin that the girl was too well read for her own good. "Those books put too many opinions in her head," he'd said. Her parents had even tried to convince Griffin that Annalise's younger sister, Penny, was a better choice for him. But prim and proper Penny did nothing for him.

Hell, he'd known he had to be careful with her. It was why he'd kept his distance. They were explosive together. And he didn't want to give his mother any reason for sabotaging this union so she could marry him off to a girl of her choosing. But he'd kept his distance so much so that he'd convinced his would-be bride that he was indifferent to her.

He had betrayed her, that he could not deny. But she had abandoned him. Begged a stranger to kidnap her so she could escape their marriage. He'd be a liar if he said that didn't anger him. Other men might be perfectly satisfied with marrying a woman who did not want to become their wife. But Griffin was not that man. He wanted Annalise, but only if she wanted him too.

Oh, she'd desired him. In those heated moments when he'd still worn his mask. Did that mean the fire in her burned so hot merely because of the adventure? Was it the danger of the unknown and the idea that a common thief had his hands and mouth on her body? He wanted to believe that somehow she'd known it was him, and that was why she'd been so wanton. But he was no fool and he was not given to silly boyish fantasies.

He knew what he had to do. He'd give her the choice. If she chose to walk away perhaps her reputation would not be too damaged.

"What do you mean, you're leaving?" Annalise asked the following morning. Her voice was shrill, she knew that, but it panicked her to think he'd leave her, not simply alone here in this cottage, but that he would walk away completely. He'd lied to her and betrayed her, she reminded herself. But hadn't she left him first? Begged a strange man – a man, to her mind, who was a common thief – to take her away from him?

"I have an appointment in Kent," he said calmly.

She opened her mouth to speak, then said nothing. He still intended to marry her? Or was he planning to merely make an appearance to show good faith to her parents? Preserve his own name while he watched hers sullied? "Penny and Hildy will have told everyone what happened to me," she said quietly. "No one will blame you for deserting me."

"I'm not deserting you. I've called a carriage and it will take you wherever you choose to go," he said.

"And what of the wedding?"

He inclined his head, then looked at her. "I'm planning on being in the church as we planned. If you so choose, you can meet me there and we will be married."

"And if I do not?"

He shrugged. "Then I suppose I will be jilted and you will be free to do as you desire. Escape the propriety and boredom and chase that adventure you're so desperate to find."

She flinched, but took a step towards him regardless. "That's it?" she asked, not knowing what she wanted him to say, but knowing she wanted more. Much more. *Fight for me*, her heart whispered. *Want me, Griffin, love me.*

"That's it," he said softly. He turned to go, then paused. "If you decide to go to London, you might want to leave fairly soon, the weather is getting colder and it might snow later. You wouldn't want to get stuck on the road." His eyes searched her face. He closed the door behind him, and he was gone.

She stood alone in the cottage. He'd never told her why he wanted to marry her, or if he even did. She knew he was honourable, despite his foolish wager that landed him the highwayman stunt. He would marry her because he said he would. Even though her reputation would now be in tatters. It would affect his name. He knew that. It mattered not that her virtue remained intact or that he was the only man who'd ever touched her. Society wouldn't care about those details. All they would know was that she had been kidnapped by a highwayman two days before her wedding.

She realized now that what she'd wanted him to do was declare his love. Beg her to marry him because he couldn't face another day without her. But men did not speak of such things, at least not to her. Why would she want to hear those things from him of all people? Certainly she did not love him. He was boring and inattentive . . . and passionate and utterly charming. She'd seen glimpses of those very characteristics that first night, then they'd all but disappeared.

The previous night though, as they'd played captor and captive, everything had been different. They'd talked, conversed, almost as friends would. They'd teased and flirted. He'd treated her as if he was courting her, wooing her. But that would mean he had tender feelings for her, which she knew could not be else he would have fought for her. But fought for what? A woman who'd declared she did not want him? Could not love him?

Annalise stared out into the woods surrounding the cottage. She strained her ears, trying desperately to hear the sound of hooves, willing him to return. But of course he would not. Which left the decision to her. What if she took that carriage and went to London? Showed up on the doorstep of her aunt and worked with her at her orphanage? She might have some satisfaction in her life from working with those who were less fortunate than her. She certainly adored her aunt and they always had a wonderful time together.

But what of love? What about being a wife and a mother? What of the passion she'd tasted for the very first time the night before? Perhaps Griffin did not love her now, but that did not mean he never would. Did it? He had asked her to be his wife and, even though she'd been horribly hurtful about his person, he had not walked away from her. He'd left for the church fully intending to marry her.

Or perhaps he intended to walk away from her once she met him at the altar? No, he could never be so cruel. Griffin, ah, handsome Griffin, who certainly had more adventure and passion in him than she'd ever realized.

Not to mention the way he'd touched her. The sensations he'd caused. She closed her eyes and, despite the chill from the morning air, warmth surged through her as she remembered his mouth on hers, his hand on her skin.

Her heart raced and thunder shook in her belly. Oh dear. Could it be? Did she love her very own husband-to-be?

Griffin ignored Annalise's family who collectively had nearly paced a hole in the narthex floor. Every time her mother looked at him, she burst into tears. Her father had tried, on more than one occasion, to tell Griffin that no one expected Annalise to show her face at the wedding. Though her sister Penny looked appropriately worried, not one other member of her family was concerned about Annalise's safety. To them, she was carelessly kidnapped by a villain. All they seemed to care about was Griffin's feelings regarding her virtue.

They were mad, the lot of them.

He caught sight of Annalise's sister again, standing quietly in the corner. Penny. What had Annalise said before he'd left? That Penny and Hildy would have told everyone what had happened to them. That meant Penny must have been in the carriage.

Griffin made his way over to the tall blonde. "Penny," he said tersely. She swallowed, but stepped over to him.

"Were you in that carriage?" he whispered.

She nodded. Her clear blue eyes welled with tears. "Yes, I was. Annalise covered me with her cloak and bid me stay inside, hidden."

"To protect you," he said.

"My reputation, My Lord, she was trying to protect my marriage prospects," Penny said.

"So no one else knows you were in that carriage."

"No, My Lord, my parents forbade it."

He nodded and walked away from her. He'd thought Annalise had been so desperate to rid herself of him, she'd thrown herself at a common thief, but she'd merely been protecting her sister. Sacrificing her own reputation to salvage that of her beloved sibling. Perhaps that meant there was hope for them, for their future. If she decided to marry him. But damned if he wouldn't have fought harder for her had he known the truth.

The wedding was a mere thirty minutes away and Griffin did his best to keep his own nerves from being rattled. Still he'd seen no sign of Annalise.

"Where is she?" his mother whispered from behind him.

"She'll be here," he said, willing it to be true. He would give her another hour and if she didn't come, he'd go after her. Tell her how he felt, that he loved her and that he could wait until she learned to love him too. Though he tried not to be hurt and disappointed, he kept longing for the sound of a carriage rolling over the hillside.

And as if his heart had created that sound for him, he heard wheels crunching against rocks and hooves beating against the road. Annalise's family continued to argue and speculate and do everything they could to be as insensitive and annoying as possible. Griffin stepped outside of the church, allowing the heavy door to slam behind him. He cared not if he was rude. All he cared about was whether or not she'd returned to him, and decided to marry him after all.

The carriage rounded the curve at the top of the hill and came in full view. It was definitely one of his, the Benning crest emblazoned on the door.

His heart thundered. He felt very much the eager schoolboy as he wiped his palms against his breeches.

Finally the carriage came to a rolling stop. He stepped forwards. The door opened. One delicate ankle stepped on to the step, then another as Annalise emerged from the carriage.

She'd come. Griffin fought the urge to run to her, to throw his arms around her and kiss her senseless.

"You came," he said quietly as she walked towards him.

"I did."

"Why didn't you tell me that Penny was in the carriage with you?" he asked.

"It didn't matter."

"The hell it didn't. It means everything. It means that you weren't choosing a dangerous thief over a life with me. You were protecting your sister." He paused. "Does this mean you'll marry me?"

"I have a question first," she said. She swallowed visibly and her lovely brown eyes looked up at his. "Why do you want to marry me, Griffin? I know my parents offered you Penny. Why would you choose me instead?"

He searched her face, looking for meaning behind her question.

She chewed at her lip. Her expression was so heartbreakingly vulnerable he fought the urge to pull her to him.

"I wanted to marry you because I love you," he said.

Her mouth opened in a silent gasp. She gave him a shy smile. "You do?"

"Yes, Annalise, from the moment I first saw you in that dress shop on Bond Street. You so effectively put Lady Henwick in her place, I'd never seen anything like it. You intrigued me, amused me, your boldness, your fearlessness. I sought you out the following evening."

"The Draper Ball," she said.

"Yes. You looked perfect in your lavender gown."

She frowned. "I didn't know you remembered that."

"I remember everything about you."

"Then why? Why all that time during our engagement did you ignore me? Why did you spend so much time chatting up my parents while not so much as passing me a glance?" she asked.

He smiled. "Because I knew that if I spent too much time with you, I would not be able to keep my hands off you."

"Truly?"

He pulled her to him, close to him, and inhaled the sweet scent of her hair. "Truly."

"I love you, Griffin," she said.

He squeezed her tighter. "Even though I'm boorish?"

She smacked his arm. "Yes, despite that, I still love you."

The Weatherlys' Ball

Christie Kelley

One

Tessa stared out across the ballroom, nervous apprehension running through her body. The Weatherlys' ball looked no different than it had five years ago when she had raced from it in scandal. Only then, she had thought her lover would be a gentleman and correct the situation before marching off to war. How wrong she'd been.

"Are you all right?" Grace asked, squeezing Tessa's hand in support.

"I am well." She smiled over at her cousin. After the disaster that ruined her reputation, Grace had remained her only friend. Once Tessa had married Lord Townson and gone into seclusion in the country, Grace had been her only contact in town. Even Tessa's parents had disowned her.

"I am glad you decided to come to town this season. Your mourning time is finished, now you can enjoy yourself again."

"And find a new husband," Tessa said with a touch of hardness to her voice. She knew marriage was the only option for her but dreaded the idea. After four years with Townson, she'd hoped for some freedom. But the bastard had left her with barely a pittance. Not even enough to support herself, much less Louisa.

Her daughter had been her only source of happiness since her marriage. Townson, of course, had been displeased that in four years she had only managed to give him a daughter. He'd assumed marrying a woman forty years younger than himself would help to produce an heir where his first two wives had failed. Tessa blinked and shook her head to rid herself of the dreadful memories of her marriage. Reminiscing about the past five years only saddened her.

She glanced over at Grace and wondered why her cousin seemed to be nervously assessing the ballroom. "Who are you looking for?"

"No one in particular," Grace replied quickly. "I am just trying to see who is here."

Tessa looked around the room and noticed a few faces familiar from her second season. But after almost an hour in the ballroom, not one person had come to speak with her. How was it that one mistake could mark a woman for life, while men could make multiple errors and no one chided them?

Money.

Men had the money and women did not. Nor did most women have a way to accumulate any. So, unless they were born an heiress, they had to count on their looks. And at five and twenty, the bloom was nearly off the rose for her. She had nothing to offer a husband except her intelligence and wit – neither a commodity most men looked for in a wife.

"Harry has finally returned from the gaming room," Grace said. "Would you mind if I went to speak with him?"

"Of course not. Go to your husband."

"Thank you, cousin. I shall return promptly." Grace walked away, her blue silk swishing about her ankles.

Tessa sipped her wine and wondered how much longer Grace and Harry would want to remain at the ball. They had only accepted the invitation in order to get Tessa back out on the marriage market. Obviously, marriage would be a slow process.

"Lady Townson, how lovely to see you again. How are you?"

Tessa blinked and noticed the man beside her. "I am very well, Mr Harrington. And you?"

Harrington smiled in such a manner she thought he meant to devour her. "I am very well now. Would you care to dance?"

She bit her lip for a moment. Harrington had been a rake when she'd been out before, was he still the same? Without Grace, Tessa had no one from whom to seek guidance. Her gaze slipped to the dancers twirling across the floor in a parade of coloured silk. A pang of sadness flitted through her. It had been so long since she danced at a ball. "I would love to dance with you, Mr Harrington."

"Excellent." He held out his arm for her to take.

As they walked towards the dance floor, she studied him. Nearing thirty now, the past few years had been more than kind to him. His blond hair was still thick, with a touch of curl to it. His blue eyes sparkled like sapphires when he smiled, which he was doing right now. With his chiselled jaw, he was every woman's fantasy . . . except hers.

Even now, she continued to dream of a man with black hair and light-green eyes. Perhaps it was true that people never forget their first love. Or maybe he was the only man she had been meant to love.

"I do believe a waltz is next. Are you still willing to dance with me?"

The last time she'd been out the waltz was a scandalous dance that only a few hostesses would allow at their balls. Grace had told her that it had become more acceptable, but still Tessa hesitated. She'd spent the past two months relearning all the dances she'd forgotten since her marriage and the waltz was one of them. "Yes, Mr Harrington."

His smile turned almost devious. "I see your tendency towards scandalous activities hasn't changed over time."

She stiffened.

"Don't be upset with me," he whispered near her ear. "I always liked that about you. In fact, I was hoping to speak with you about a proposition that might suit us both."

"Oh?"

Harrington laughed softly. "Don't sound so prudish, Lady Townson. Being a widow gives you much more opportunity for pleasure than marriage to an old lord did. I can show you what it's like to be with a real man. A strong virile man."

Tessa blinked back the tears that blinded her. "I believe I have changed my mind about the dance, Mr Harrington. Good evening."

She turned and left before he could say another disgusting word. How dare he just assume she would be interested in a lascivious affair because she was now a widow! Looking about the room, she tried to find Grace or Harry, to no avail. Where could they have gone? She backed herself up against a pillar and snatched a glass of wine from a passing footman. After a quick sip, she stared across the room.

"Still running away from men, I see."

Tessa turned to face the one woman who had never caused her anything but grief. "Good evening, Georgiana. Lovely to see you again."

"Am I to assume you are here to find your next victim . . . I mean, husband?"

"Yes, it was so enjoyable five years ago to win the love of the man you had hoped to marry. Shall we do it again this year?" Tessa plastered a smug grin on her face.

"Oh, but you didn't really win that competition, did you?"

Before she could think of a witty reply, Georgiana turned and walked away towards the refreshment table. That woman had been a thorn in Tessa's side all during her two seasons out. Georgiana had made it her mission to stop Garrett courting her, but Garrett and

Tessa had seen right through Georgiana's tricks. Tessa sighed and returned her attention to the ball.

A flash of black caught her eye. She watched the man as he walked towards the refreshment table. She was only able to see his black hair, but her heart pounded against her chest.

For a quick moment she thought it was he. But that was inconceivable. He'd been dead for almost five years. Perhaps it was his older brother, Laurence, a man she had no desire to speak with again. Laurence had not even found it necessary to inform her about Garrett's death in person. Instead, he'd sent her a note.

Her eyes refocused on the dark-haired man at the table. Something about his mannerisms reminded her of the only man she'd ever loved. The only man who had broken her heart so completely. Not a day passed that she didn't wonder how different her life might have been if he hadn't gone off to the war.

But this gentleman was surely different. His black hair was longer, almost reaching to the collar of his emerald coat. And he had a slight limp as he walked past the table. Still, the way he cocked his head as someone made a comment seemed vaguely familiar.

Tessa looked down at her wine and noticed how badly her hands trembled. This had to stop. Garrett had been dead for five long years and nothing could bring him back. And yet, even as she scolded herself, her gaze returned to the man at the refreshment table. She smiled slightly, knowing he was about to turn around and then she would see for certain that he was not the man she'd loved.

The black-haired man turned towards her.

It couldn't be him. Garrett was dead!

Tessa's wine glass fell through her cold fingers.

Two

Everyone's gaze, including Garrett's, turned as the sound of breaking glass rent the air. A flash of red hair could be seen before the woman raced from the ballroom and out a terrace door. His heart stopped for a moment. It couldn't be her. After what had happened, she would never attempt to go about in society again.

"It truly amazes me that anyone would invite Lady Townson to a ball," whispered a female voice behind him.

"Poor Mrs Billings felt she had no choice but to bring her into her home after the old lord died. After all, she is her cousin," another woman commented.

"She should have stayed in the country."

Fury washed over him at both the comments, and at the idea that Tessa was at the ball. Had she seen him and dropped her glass? He almost laughed at the thought. The cold-hearted woman had probably only been flirting with another man when she let the glass slip. She was likely just trying to attract more attention to herself.

But watching her scamper off to the gardens had sent his anger even higher. It was high time he confronted her about what she'd done to him. With her living in the country, he'd never felt a need. But now that she had returned, he would deal with her. He strode towards the terrace, attempting to ignore the pain in his hip and the looks of pity from the people around him.

The cool April air was like a slap in the face after the stifling conditions inside the ballroom. The fresh scent of the evening air refreshed him. He moved along a row of rose bushes, the gravel crunching under his feet as he listened for any sound. The chilly temperatures had kept most of the amorous couples inside. A few torches lit the path as he ambled towards the brick wall to the back of the garden. He paused for a moment to listen to the rhythmic shuffle of pacing on the gravel path ahead of him.

He found her with her hand over her mouth, muttering, pacing, her eyes frantic.

"How can he be alive?" she whispered.

He didn't move for a moment but just stared at her, remembering exactly how she had looked five years ago. So beautiful it took his breath away.

With her red hair and blue eyes, a heart-shaped face and curves exactly where a man wanted them, she had been one of the most popular girls out during her seasons. She had favoured him with her smiles and her dances. And he had craved her attention. Now she had matured and sorrow marked her face. Could she have loved her older husband so much that she still missed him a year after his death?

"What are you doing here, Tessa?"

She glanced up with a gasp and shook her head. Tears trailed down her cheeks and her blue eyes looked like wet sapphires. "What am *I* doing here?"

"That was my question."

She rose from her seat and stared at him. "You are supposed to be dead."

Dead? "If you think you can attempt to fool me with your duplicitous words, you are mistaken."

"Fool you!" She walked over and slapped him across the face.

Damn. He rubbed his cheek as the pain lessened. "Try that again and you will find yourself over my knee."

She laughed caustically. "Over the knee of a dead man. I doubt you will be able to manage it."

"Why do you insist that I am a dead man?" he asked.

"Why don't you ask your brother? I'm sure he can tell you why he wrote me a letter stating that you had died. Or maybe you can explain why I received *your* letter. The one I was only supposed to receive after your death."

"And what about my other letter?" he demanded.

Her brows furrowed deeply. "There was no other letter. The only note I received from you was the one that just about killed me."

Before he could even begin to understand, she picked up her skirts and ran from him. Not unlike how she'd run from him five years ago. And as much as he would have liked to chase after her, his damned hip prevented him from anything more than a slow walk. By the time he reached the ballroom, he knew she had departed.

Not that he could blame her. Now, he would have to wait until tomorrow to call on her and ask for an explanation. But he had no way of justifying his brother's actions, if he was to take her remarks as truth. No way of discovering why Laurence would have sent her such a note. Could Tessa have been so secluded from society gossip that she didn't know Laurence had died over a year ago? Or that Garrett had inherited the title?

He walked back out to the terrace and sat on a stone bench, remembering a night like this five years ago. Making love to her out in the garden had been one of the more foolish things he had done in his life. And yet, the most memorable. She had been driving him insane with desire for a month before she finally let him kiss her. But one kiss hadn't been enough for either of them.

Why she'd agreed to marry Townson had never made any sense to him. Garrett had written her a letter the very next morning offering to marry her via proxy once he arrived with his unit in Belgium. But she had never replied. Instead, he'd received a letter from Laurence stating that she had married Townson. Laurence had implied she married him for the title and money.

Garrett went a little mad after receiving his brother's letter. Placing himself in dangerous situations, perhaps hoping God would take him. Obviously, God hadn't wanted him any more than Tessa had.

Still, he owed her an explanation, just as she owed him one.

Three

"Why didn't you tell me?" Tessa demanded of Grace the next morning. "You knew he was alive and you never told me. How could you do that?"

Grace stared down at her hands. "By the time I discovered he was alive, it was too late, Tessa. You had already married Townson. There was nothing you could have done."

Tessa strode across the small parlour of Grace's home. Dodging Louisa, who lay on the floor petting the cat, Tessa stalked past the wingback chair where Grace sat, then stopped.

"Why didn't you tell me after Townson died?"

"I didn't want him to hurt you again," she replied quickly. "I was only trying to protect you. The only reason I agreed to go to that ball last night was because I'd heard he would not be there."

Tessa looked up at the white ceiling. "Grace, you know I would have discovered the truth sometime. You should have told me so I didn't embarrass myself in front of all those people . . . again."

"I'm sorry, Tessa. I honestly never meant to hurt you."

"I know." She walked the length of the room again, this time stopping by the fireplace. "Has he married, then?" she whispered.

Grace shook her head. "No. His brother died a little over a year ago and now that he is Viscount Haverhill, everyone is expecting him to start courting an eligible lady."

Tessa swallowed back the bitter taste that filled her mouth. The idea of Garrett marrying someone made her clutch her stomach. Now she would have to spend the whole season watching him court some young woman.

"He said he wrote me a letter that I never received." Tessa resumed her pacing. "I wonder why I never learned of it."

"Do you think he was lying?"

Tessa frowned and shook her head. "He seemed quite sincere."

"Your parents might have intercepted it," Grace said, looking up at Tessa as she passed the chair again. "You know they didn't approve of him. They felt his prospects were limited at best."

"He was an officer in the military. The second son of a viscount. There is nothing wrong with that."

"True. But they had higher expectations for you than a military man."

Tessa shook her head in disbelief. Could her parents have been so deceitful? In her heart, she knew they could. All they had wanted for her was a wealthy peer who would marry her and take her out of their home.

A knock scraped the door and Grace's butler peered into the room. "Lady Townson, you have a caller."

Tessa frowned. "Who is it?"

"Lord Haverhill, ma'am. Shall I inform him that you are not at home?"

"No, show him to the receiving salon. I shall be there presently," Tessa replied, as nervous energy filled her.

As the door shut, Tessa looked back at Grace. "What am I to do now?"

Grace smiled sympathetically. "Talk to him and find out where your letters crossed."

Tessa nodded. With a breath for strength, she walked to the receiving parlour. And there he was. He rose to his full height upon her entry. Could she really have forgotten what a handsome man he was?

His black hair was longer than he used to wear it, but still just as striking. His green eyes were the lightest she had ever seen, almost the colour of a peridot. His square face, straight nose and brilliant smile made him hard to resist. And resist him was exactly what she should have done five years ago. Today, those intense eyes burned her as she walked slowly into the room.

"Lady Townson," he said with a quick bow.

"Lord Haverhill." She took a seat as far from him as possible.

"I believe we should talk about what happened last night." The stiffness in his voice carried through to his body. He crossed his arms over his chest as he waited for her to speak.

Tessa's heart pounded. "I am not sure there is any more to discuss."

"You told me you received a letter from my brother stating I had died. I find it difficult to believe my brother would have done such a thing. He knew how I felt about you at the time."

She blinked in surprise. "You don't believe me?"

"I said, 'I find it difficult to believe'. Not impossible."

His cold tone sent a shiver through her. "I still have the letter," she whispered. She had kept all of Garrett's letters. She had reread them every night after Townson left her bed.

He closed his eyes and blew out a long sigh. "Might I see it?"

Tessa hated the tension this discussion brought. The two of them used to be able to talk about everything. Now, he could barely stand being in the same room as her. "It is in my bedchamber. I will ask a footman to retrieve it for me." She rose and walked to the door. After speaking to the footman, she returned.

"You never received another letter from me after the one from my brother?" he asked quietly.

"No. What was in it?"

"Nothing of importance," he muttered then swore under his breath. He rose with the assistance of his cane and walked to the fireplace. "Are you lying to me, Tessa?"

She watched him limp to the fireplace and her heart went out to him. He had been a brilliant horseman before the war and now he looked as if he could never ride again. She wondered if the wound pained him.

"Tessa, are you lying to me?"

"Of course not," she snapped. "What purpose would I have in lying to you?"

He turned at her outburst. "Excuse me?"

"Your letter broke my heart, Garrett."

His smile turned nasty. "I'm certain you were so heartbroken that you let your parents marry you off to old Townson. Of course, he was a much better catch, being a viscount."

"Get out of this house," she said, pointing towards the door.

"Not until I see this *supposed* letter you received." He walked towards her, leaning heavily on his cane.

Each step brought him closer, until she could smell the aroma of his sandalwood soap. She shouldn't feel this attraction to him. This desire to run her hand down his cheek, just to feel the rough stubble there.

"Why did you marry him?"

"I thought you were dead," she whispered. "I didn't care who I married after I had lost you."

He closed his eyes. "I see."

"I don't think you do." She should tell him the real reason for her marriage, but that news would only cause him more pain.

"Did your parents force the marriage?" He opened his eyes again and stared at her.

Tessa nodded. "They felt it was the best for me. My reputation was in ruins. I had no prospects for a decent marriage."

"Excuse me, ma'am," a footman paused at the threshold. "Here are the letters you asked me to fetch for you." He handed them to her before disappearing.

Tessa stared down at the bundle of letters tied together with a blue ribbon. She pulled out the top letter that she had read hundreds of times. In it, he had expressed his love for her and his sorrow at losing her so soon. Slowly, she held out the worn paper to him.

"This is your letter." She then sorted through the other letters until she found the one from his brother. "And this is your brother's note."

He opened the first note and stared down at it. For a long moment he said nothing, and then he handed the papers back to her. "I am dreadfully sorry, Tessa. That note was not supposed to go to you unless I died. I can only assume that Laurence decided he wanted you out of my life and this was the best way to do it. Unfortunately, we will never know for certain."

He retrieved his cane and walked towards the door.

He was leaving? She couldn't let him go just yet. There was more they had to discuss, wasn't there?

"How were you injured?" she asked.

"I was shot in the hip." He continued to shuffle to the door. His limp was much more pronounced than it had been yesterday.

She bit down on her lip and tried not to cry. He could have lost his leg to an injury like that or, worse, died from an infection. Had things worked out between them, she could have been the one to help him recover, or rub his hip when it pained him. Now he was walking out the door, and if she didn't try to stop him, she might not see him again.

"Would you like to stay for some tea?"

He stopped and slowly turned to face her. "Tessa, I believe it would be best for both of us to continue with our lives as usual. What happened is in the past. Nothing can change it. Good day." Then he was gone.

She couldn't move as he walked out of her life again. Dropping to a chair, she stared at the low fire glowing in the fireplace. While she still had feelings for him, perhaps he felt nothing for her? Perhaps he was right – they should continue as if they had never found each other again.

A burning flame of anger lit her. Standing up, she walked across the room to the window. Pulling back the heavy velvet curtain, she watched as he clambered up to his coach. Something was keeping him from letting her back into his life. And she did not believe it was her marriage or the deception of his brother, or her parents.

She was determined to find the true cause of his reluctance.

Four

As his coach eased away from Tessa's home, Garrett stared up at the window where she stood watching him. This was for the best, he told himself. The last thing she needed was to be burdened with a cripple.

He leaned his head back against the squabs. Dammit! Why did she have to come back to town? She should have stayed in the country and found a homely squire to marry and give her babies. She shouldn't have returned where he would see her every time he attended a ball. Just being in the same room with her had been torture. It had taken all of his resolve and military training to walk away from her.

When she had asked him to stay for tea, he'd wanted to say yes. Wanted to spend more time in her company. Wanted to kiss her until she moaned with pleasure. Not that he understood why she would want to spend a second longer in his company than needed. He had discovered quickly that his injury frightened many of the young ladies away. They wanted a whole man, not someone who could not even dance with them.

The best course of action was to stay away from her. After he'd been wounded, he decided he would never subject a woman to marrying half a man. His younger brother Robert, or one of Robert's sons, could inherit the title and estates when the time came. For now, he would continue on, rebuilding the fortune that Laurence had lost over the years. And he would not think about Tessa.

Garrett almost laughed at the thought.

He had thought about Tessa almost every day for the past five years. Seeing her had only relit the flame of his desire. Knowing that tonight he would most likely run into her again, only made him want her more.

Somehow, he would fight his feelings for her.

Garrett scanned the audience, determined to find her. The opera would be starting soon and he knew if he didn't see her before it started he would never be able to watch the performance. Remembering her favourite colour was sapphire, he examined every woman dressed in any shade of blue. As the orchestra started, he moved to violet gowns, another of her favourites. Again, he didn't find her.

Finally, as the curtain started to rise, he found her sitting in the back of a box with her cousin Grace Billings. Tessa looked pale and uncomfortable as she shifted in her seat. Perhaps she had noticed his gaze, but her eyes remained focused on the stage.

Now that he knew she was there, he could ignore her and watch the opera.

And yet, not five minutes later, he found himself staring at her again. This obsession was maddening.

"So, who exactly are you staring at?"

Garrett turned to his friend, David Harris, sitting next to him. If it weren't for David, Garrett would be dead. It was David who had pulled him to safety after he was shot in the hip. "No one," he replied with a scowl.

"Indeed?"

Garrett moved his gaze back to the stage and attempted to watch the performance. Nonetheless, his eyes slid to the side, where he could just make out Tessa.

"He's doing it again," David said to his wife Anne, who was sitting in front of them with her younger sister.

Both women glanced back at him with a smile.

"Leave him alone," Anne said with a compassionate smile to Garrett.

He shook his head and forced himself to concentrate on the opera. During the intermission, he walked the corridors to loosen the tightness in his hip. Sitting for long periods always caused him pain.

"Good evening, Lord Haverhill."

Garrett halted his hobbling stride and looked over at Tessa. She sipped her lemonade with a smile. A damned seductive smile. "Good evening, Lady Townson. I hope you are enjoying the performance tonight."

"Not particularly," she replied with a little shrug.

Seeing her up close was far worse than from across the expanse of the opera house. Her jonquil dress was cut low enough to display her full, rounded breasts to perfection. Damn his unruly desire. Just standing this close to her was enough to make him hard. He had to get his mind off her.

"So where would you prefer to be, then?" he asked.

Her smile deepened until two small dimples appeared in her cheeks. "At home. In bed."

Not the words he needed to hear when his imagination had already placed her in a bed with him on top of her. "Oh?" was his only insipid response.

"Do you plan to attend the dinner party at the Byingtons'?"

"Yes," he muttered, before realizing he should have said no and avoided her.

"Excellent," she said with a smile. "I shall see you there."

Her cousin approached them slowly. "There you are, Tessa. It is time to go back to our seats."

Garrett almost laughed as Tessa rolled her eyes. Something about her look made him wish he could rescue her. But he didn't have that option now. Nor would he ever.

Five

Garrett watched Tessa as she assessed the salon with a hint of a smile on her face. His heart raced just seeing her standing on the edge of the crowd in her yellow gown. How he wished he could ask to escort her into the dining room. But he couldn't. Keeping his distance was the only option. The woman was young and vibrant and didn't need a cripple for a husband.

"Why don't you stop staring at her and ask her to take a turn around the room with you?"

Garrett glared over at David. "She is the last woman I would ask."

"Of course," David replied with a light chuckle. "That explains why you couldn't keep your eyes off her during the opera."

"She means nothing to me," he lied. "I have been over her since I discovered her deception years ago."

"Deception? Or forced marriage?"

"It matters not either way." She could have refused her parents' wishes. This wasn't the Middle Ages where a woman was forced to marry a man against her will.

"Then why are you still staring at her?" David asked and then walked away.

Why was he staring at her? Because he knew she would never disobey her parents. And as she told him, she thought he was dead. As he watched her, her lips moved upwards until she smiled fully . . . at him. She strolled over.

"Good evening, Lord Haverhill."

"Good evening, Lady Townson," he replied stiffly. "Are you enjoying the dinner party?"

She sipped her sherry and glanced over at him. "Oh, I think you know where my preferences lie tonight."

At home. In bed. How could he have forgotten? "Still, it must be enjoyable to be back in town?"

Her face drew into a frown. "For most people it would be."

"But not you?"

"The majority of society would prefer I go back to the country."

A thought he'd had only yesterday. "There is no reason you should not be here."

"Indeed? Do you want me here?" she whispered.

He closed his eyes for a moment but that only brought thoughts of her lying naked in his arms. He blinked quickly and focused on the question. "What I want is of no importance."

"Still, I would be very interested in knowing what you want," she said in a seductive tone.

Thankfully, Lady Byington announced that dinner would be served in the dining room. Saving him from venturing a reply to her flirtatious words.

"Garrett," she whispered. "Will you escort me? I am quite certain no one else will."

He couldn't ignore the pleading tone, no matter how much he knew he should. "Yes."

"Thank you," she said, then slowly licked that luscious lower lip.

As seductive as she looked, he remembered it was only a nervous reaction that caused her to do that. She had done it many times when he courted her. Unfortunately, he still reacted in the same manner, as he felt himself stiffen.

She looped her arm with his and a shock of awareness raced up his arm. He had to find a way to distance himself from her. He could not become involved again.

Walking into the dining room, he quickly found her seat . . . right next to his. Could she have planned this? Did she specifically ask Lady Byington to seat her next to him?

"Well, this is convenient," she said with a smile. "I am seated with you."

"A little too convenient," he muttered.

"At least sitting here, I know someone will converse with me. Had I been seated next to another man, I might have been ignored."

Bloody hell, he thought. Who could ever ignore Tessa? He would have no choice but to include her in any conversations. It would take every ounce of control he had to survive this dinner.

Tessa sat next to Garrett with a secret smile. Very few people knew Lady Byington was her godmother. When Tessa asked her to seat Garrett next to her, Lady Byington thought it was a splendid plan. If only Tessa knew what to do now that she was next to him.

While she had found flirting with Garrett easy years ago, now he was a different man. Harder. Far more in control of himself. She wondered if her efforts would be in vain. But remembering his reaction to her comment about wanting to be home and in bed, she believed she might have a chance.

She placed her hand on Garrett's forearm and leaned in close. "Lord Haverhill, do tell me what you have been doing with yourself since your return from Belgium."

He tightened his muscles under her hand and grimaced. "I have spent the past year attempting to sort through the mess my brother left me with the estate."

"And before that?"

"Recovering."

Tessa removed her hand and picked up her wine glass. It would not be easy to break through the wall he had around him. She brushed her leg against his, savouring his hard muscles. "Tell me about the estate."

He clenched his fist around his own glass before drinking a long draught. "I believe I told you about it several years ago. Nothing else has changed."

"Very well," she whispered. After wiping her mouth with her napkin, she placed it back in her lap. Slowly, under the cover of the tablecloth, she skimmed her hand up his thigh.

Suddenly, a hard hand caught hers and abruptly stopped her caress. Garrett leaned in close to her and whispered, "Stop now or I shall make you look like a fool in front of everyone. Do you understand?"

Embarrassment heated her cheeks as she nodded. She understood perfectly. Garrett wanted no part of her flirtations. Once again, she had made an error in judgment.

Six

For a week, Tessa tried to ignore the feelings she had for Garrett. She had only seen him once since that dreadful miscalculation at the Byingtons' dinner party. But he would be at the Seatons' ball tonight. She inhaled deeply and entered the ballroom.

Tessa scanned the room for Garrett. Where was he? Grace had said he would be here, but as she searched the room, she could not find him. She casually strolled to the gaming room. And there he sat, playing faro with his friend Mr Harris. For a moment, she could only watch him. But her yearning to be close to him brought her nearer.

"Are you winning?" she asked softly.

Both men stood and bowed towards her. Mr Harris looked over at her with a slight frown. "Good evening, Lady Townson."

She nodded at him. "Mr Harris."

Garrett finally glanced at her. "I am winning a small amount."

"Ahh," she said, wishing she could have come up with a witty retort and not one that sounded completely simple-minded. "Perhaps I will see you later."

"Perhaps," he muttered.

Mr Harris smirked at Garrett's mumbled reply.

Feeling rather dejected, she returned to the ballroom and the scornful looks from the ladies. There were days when she wondered if it would have been better to stay in the country. She might have found a nice man to marry there. But after seeing Garrett again, he was the only man she wanted.

After standing alone for a few moments outside the gaming room, Garrett finally approached with a wary look on his face. "Did you wish to speak with me?" he asked.

She did, but she had no idea what to say to him. "I've missed you," she whispered.

He tightened his jaw but said nothing.

"Did you enjoy the play two nights ago?" she asked, hoping for some reply.

"Yes," he admitted.

"I'm glad," she said softly.

"Why?"

Why? "Why wouldn't I be?" She pulled out her fan and swept it near her face a few times. "It is stifling in here."

"I suppose we could take a turn in the garden."

Her fan stilled in front of her face. Did he just offer to take her to the garden? *Alone?* While she knew she should rebuff his advance, she heard herself answer, "Yes, I would like that."

He held out his arm, and she linked hers with his. They walked slowly, allowing him to keep up without limping too much.

"Are you ever going to tell me how you were shot?" she asked as they reached the terrace door.

"There was nothing terribly fascinating about it." They walked towards a bench. "Napoleon's forces were bearing down on us. My unit was trying to defend our position. I took a shot in my hip and fell off my horse. Dreadfully embarrassing to fall off your horse in front of your men."

"But you had been shot!"

"True," he said with a slight smile. "But I should have been able to hold on to my horse. I resigned my commission after that and returned home once the surgeon had patched me up."

Tessa shook her head with disbelief as she sat on the bench. Were all men worried about embarrassing themselves? Her own brother had never seemed to care.

She looked up at him and patted the place next to her. "Please sit down so your hip doesn't bother you."

He looked away, but even in the dimly lit garden, she noticed the colour stain his cheeks. She would have to remember that any talk of his wound apparently shamed him.

"Very well," he said, reluctantly taking the seat.

The scent of his sandalwood soap filled the air around her, overpowering the scent of spring flowers. His shoulder brushed against hers and tingles of desire crept through her body. She pressed her hand to her belly.

"Are you all right?" he asked.

"Yes." She smiled over at him. "I was just remembering the time we were at the Halsteads' country party."

He frowned for a moment before nodding his head. "I remember."

"We played that game of chess and talked for almost two hours." Tessa sighed, remembering what a wonderful night they had shared. That was the evening she realized she loved him. Hearing his excited tone as he spoke of leaving for the war had softened her heart. She understood his need to defend his country from the dreadful Napoleon.

"And you told me how you wished you'd been born a man so you could fight beside me."

She laughed lightly. "Well, I was only twenty and my brother had just gone off to the war."

"How is Mitchell?"

"I don't know," she whispered, staring down at the tips of her shoes peeking out from her skirts. "He hasn't written me or even called on me since . . ."

His large gloved hand covered hers. "I am so sorry, Tessa. If I had known what would happen, I never would have made love with you that night."

"It was worth it," she mumbled. She had wanted him so desperately back then.

"How can you say that? It cost you your reputation. Even now, after paying your penance by marrying that old bastard, you are still being cast out."

She turned her head and stared into his light green eyes. "I was in love with you, Garrett. I wanted you to make love with me. I wanted to . . ."

"To?"

She turned her gaze away from his prying eyes. "To marry you," she whispered.

"Oh, Tessa," he said with a sigh.

She looked over at him as his head slowly inclined towards hers. Her lips parted instinctively as his lips brushed against hers. He deepened the kiss, shattering her senses, and his tongue swept across hers. She shifted and pulled him closer.

He drew away slightly. "I missed you, too," he whispered before kissing her again. Only this kiss was more heated than the previous one.

She moaned. Desire flooded her body for the first time in five years. Heat seared her as his hand cupped her breast, his thumb rubbing her nipple. She wanted desperately to be closer to him, to feel his naked body against hers and erase the memories of her late husband's pathetic attempts.

Kissing him brought back images of their one and only night together. She could still remember the sensation of his mouth on her breast. The fullness of him deep inside her.

Oh, God, how she wanted that again.

"My, my, one would think you would have learned your lesson five years ago," a sharp feminine voice sounded.

Tessa pushed away and looked up to see Georgiana Chambers staring down at them both. Heat crossed Tessa's cheeks. The woman continued to glare at them.

"Haverhill, I do hope once we marry your penchant for chasing this little slut will stop." She turned and strode away, leaving Tessa gape mouthed.

Marry! He planned to marry Georgiana Chambers! The same woman who had ruined Tessa's reputation by spreading her poisonous venom about finding them in the garden? She took one look at Garrett's guilty face and raced from the garden . . . just like five years ago.

Seven

Guilt slammed into Garrett as he watched Tessa run from him. God, he was a fool to let her go. But he didn't stop her. He knew this was for the best, so why did he feel so damned dreadful about it?

Because he loved her.

He'd loved her since the first time he saw her. She deserved better. She'd suffered enough with Townson; she didn't need another burden.

Slowly, he stood and walked back towards the house. His heart ached with every step he took. The love he'd felt for her had never died. Even if he still didn't completely understand why she'd married Townson, it didn't matter. He loved her.

As he reached the small terrace a voice stopped him. "Did you accomplish what you'd hoped?"

When he'd seen Georgiana enter the ballroom earlier, he knew he had found his way to stop Tessa's flirtations. He didn't have the strength to resist her. She was and always had been his weakness. Georgiana had reluctantly agreed to help him.

He turned to her and nodded slowly. "I suppose I did."

"Well, that is a shame," Georgiana replied and started to walk towards the door.

"What do you mean?"

She stopped and stared at him. "I was married for two years before my husband died. I would have given anything if he had looked at me the way you look at her."

"It's for the best."

She shook her head and blew out a breath. "You are the only one who considers your slight limp to be a defect. Why would you discard a woman who loves you and doesn't care about it? She's not after your money or your title. She only wants to love you, and be loved by you."

Garrett stood there unable to say another word as she walked away. He leaned his head back and looked up at the stars. This was supposed to be the right thing to do. Having Georgiana find them again had been his plan. A plan that suddenly seemed very foolish indeed.

He had to talk with Tessa.

Tonight.

He walked back into the ballroom. After speaking with a few

people, he discovered that she'd left. Not that that would stop him. He collected his things and departed for her cousin's home. He impatiently tapped his cane against the coach floor as they drove the few blocks. Walking up the short flight of steps, he then pounded on the door, determined to rouse everyone in the house if needed.

"My Lord, do you realize the time?" the butler asked as he opened the door.

"Yes, I do. I will speak with Lady Townson now."

"Sir, she is not at home."

Garrett pushed his way past the butler but stopped after seeing the two hulking footmen.

"What is going on down there, Gates?"

Garrett looked up to see Tessa's cousin and her husband staring down at him. "Mr Billings, please excuse the interruption. I must speak with Lady Townson immediately."

"Lady Townson has no desire to speak with you," Mrs Billings stated.

"I am sorry, My Lord," Mr Billings said, "but my wife is correct. Lady Townson will not speak with you tonight. You may try to call on her tomorrow."

"If she doesn't come down, I will find her," Garrett warned. Hearing another door open, he waited for her to look down the stairwell at him, too. Instead, he saw a small figure with long, curly red hair. She couldn't have been more than four years old.

"Who are you?" she said from the top step.

He knew the Billingses had no children. This little girl had to be Tessa's.

Oh, dear God, was she his child, too?

He reached for the newel post for support. She couldn't be his daughter. Tessa would have told him.

Except Tessa had thought he was dead.

It all made sense now. She was the reason Tessa had married Townson. Guilt slithered through his mind. If he hadn't made love to her that night and gotten her with child, she never would have married Townson. It was all his fault that she married that old bastard.

"Go back to bed, Louisa," Mrs Billings shouted.

"What is all the commotion?" Tessa asked as she exited another bedroom. "Louisa, what are you doing out of bed?"

The little girl ran to Tessa and confirmed Garrett's suspicions by burying her head in her mother's nightdress.

"Tessa, I need to speak with you now. If you don't come down, I'll be forced to come up." Garrett crossed his arms over his chest and waited.

"I will be down after I get Louisa back to bed," she replied. "Wait in the parlour."

"As you wish." Garrett followed the butler into the parlour. He poured himself a snifter of brandy. He drank it down before finally hearing Tessa's light footsteps approaching.

She stopped on the threshold and stared at him. The redness in her eyes told him how badly he'd hurt her. He never wanted to hurt her again. She wore a white wrapper that only accentuated the pale colour of her cheeks.

"Tessa, please come in and sit down."

"Just tell me why you are here so I can go back to my room."

Obviously, she wasn't about to make this easy on him. "Tessa, please."

"Very well." She walked into the room and dropped into the wing-back chair closest to the doorway. Crossing her arms over her chest, she asked, "Why are you here at this hour?"

"I came to apologise."

"For what? Kissing me? Making me think that maybe you felt something for me again?" she choked out.

"For all that and more." He finally sat down in a chair near her.

"Go on."

"Mrs Chambers came out into the garden because I asked her to," he mumbled. Saying this aloud made it sound even worse than when he'd thought up the foolish plan.

"What?"

Hearing the cold tone in her voice made him wonder if she would ever forgive him. "I thought it would be best if you realized that I wasn't going to marry you."

"Of course not, you plan to marry Mrs Chambers."

"No, I have no intention of marrying her. She only said that so you would think it possible," he admitted. "Because I told her to."

Tessa blinked rapidly as if attempting to hold back the tears. "How could you be so cruel? All you had to do was tell me you didn't want me and I would have left you alone."

"I *do* want you, Tessa," he muttered. "I've wanted you since the first time I met you."

She shot to her feet and stared down at him. "Then why would you do such a hurtful thing?"

"Because . . . because I am a cripple."

Eight

Tessa stared at him, unable to conceive of what he'd just admitted. How could he think that his insignificant limp could be a burden? Her heart swelled with so many emotions that tears slipped down her cheeks. She fell to her knees and placed her head on his legs.

"You foolish man," she whispered. "I don't care if you have a limp."

"I can't even ride a goddamned horse."

"Then we shall take carriages," she offered.

"I can't dance with you," he said softly. "You have no idea how badly I want to dance with you. I want to see your face light up with pleasure as you dance across the floor."

"Then we shall stand in the background, holding hands and watching the others dance. None of those things matter, Garrett. I love you," she sobbed. "I never stopped loving you even when I thought you were dead."

"I love you, too."

"I have to tell you something else," she whispered.

"Is it about your daughter?"

Tessa nodded. She knew it would hurt him to learn the truth, but they needed to start fresh with no secrets between them. "I married Townson because I was with child. Your child. That is the only reason I married him. I thought you were dead and I was unmarried—"

He lifted her up and let her rest on his lap. Caressing her head, he said, "Shh, Tessa. After seeing her I figured everything out."

"No, Garrett." She shook her head and more tears fell. "She's not your daughter."

He stilled in her hair. "She's not?"

"No. A week after I married Townson, I miscarried." Tears burned her cheeks. "I had lost you and then I lost our baby too."

"Oh, God," he whispered against her head.

"The only positive thing I had to look forward to in that marriage was having your child and knowing that a little piece of you had survived. And then I lost that, too." She wept.

He pulled her against his chest as tears flooded her. "So we both went through our own hell." He shifted her slightly on his lap. "I thought you hadn't loved me."

"I never stopped loving you, Garrett. Not in five years. Not a single day passed that I didn't think of you at least once." She wiped away a tear. "When I saw you at the Weatherlys' ball, I thought I must be going mad. No one had told me you were alive. I thought you were a ghost."

"Have you talked to your parents about the letter I sent you?"

"No."

"Why not?"

"I haven't spoken to them since my wedding day. They told me I had embarrassed them completely, and I was never to be seen in their presence again." She bit her lip until she tasted the metallic flavour of blood.

"It doesn't matter," he said firmly. "We both did what we thought was necessary at the time. And, despite that, we found each other again."

She pulled away and looked at him. "I guess that means we are meant to be."

He drew her closer and kissed her softly. "I believe it does."

Nine

Tessa smiled down at the infant on her lap. How was it that he seemed to get cuter every day? The love she had for her son was almost a perfect match for the love she felt for the man sitting next to her.

"Is it me or did Will just smile at you?" Garrett asked with a grin.

"He's far too young for a real smile yet. Perhaps in a few weeks."

Louisa raced into the room and plopped herself on Garrett's lap. "Papa, you promised to teach me to ride this morning!"

"So I did," he replied with a slight wince at Louisa's weight. "But first I need to speak with your mother in private."

Louisa's bow-shaped mouth formed a pout.

"Go ask your nurse to dress you in your new riding habit," Tessa said to appease her daughter.

Louisa's pout quickly turned into a smile. "I almost forgot about my new habit!" She ran from the room with a giggle.

"Ah, there is nothing like a new dress to make a woman do as you wish," Garrett said with a chuckle.

"Indeed?"

He leaned in closer and kissed her cheek. "Not all women can be so easily swayed. But maybe this will help." He took her hand and placed a long box across her palm. "Happy anniversary, darling."

Tessa blinked back tears as she stared at the box. The past year had been the happiest of her life. A new husband who loved her completely. A new father for Louisa – one who loved the little girl as if she were his own. And now little Will.

"Do I have to open it for you?" Garrett asked.

She shook her head and carefully opened the box. Inside, on a bed of black velvet, was a sapphire pendant. "It's too much," she whispered.

"It matches your eyes. And you can wear it for the Weatherlys' ball. I don't believe you will have to run from it ever again."

"Not now." She moved closer to her husband and kissed him softly.

The Panchamaabhuta

Leah Ball

Wells, England – 1817

Francis studied the massive ruby ring that winked on her finger. The Panchamaabhuta had always been her good luck charm. The Indian ring was named for the golden geometrical figures that flanked the square-cut ruby on either side. The symbols represented the forces of nature in the Hindi religion: earth, water, fire, air and ether. According to Hindu beliefs, the five elements combined together to form a powerful force that flowed through all living things. Francis believed in the power of the ruby to protect her from harm. It had been her husband's gift to her, and now it was the only possession of value that she had left.

Francis darted an anxious glance around her. The dining room of the Horse and Hounds was filled with rough-looking men who had crowded in with her to take refuge from the storm. She cupped a hand over her ring, screening it from view. Her survival depended on delivering it to Bath tomorrow.

Her skin prickled. The man leaning beside her at the counter of the tap seemed to be looking at her hand. He had a bold, well-proportioned face with a strong chin. A tight silk vest clung to his massive chest. His fair hair was clipped short and he was a full head taller than the other men in the room. If she was not mistaken, he had been eyeing the Panchamaabhuta. Francis gave him a reproving look, and their eyes met and held. A spark flashed between them. Francis felt a tingling sensation travel down to her belly. She found it difficult to look away from the curious, light green eyes that gleamed in his dark face. His buckskins were still slightly damp, and he carried an earthy scent of animal skin and sandalwood. Francis realized that her hands were trembling. Under the influence of his brazen stare, her skin prickled first hot, then cold. She crossed her arms over her chest, trying to will the disturbing sensations away.

"Well, then." The innkeeper appeared at her elbow. "You look as if you took a right beating in the storm."

Francis shrugged, scattering droplets of water across the counter. The traveller beside her chuckled, and she supposed she looked a fright. Her soaked hair clung to her forehead and little rivulets of water were trickling down her neck.

The innkeeper waved to a table in the corner of the room that was being cleared. "Can I get you a proper seat? Nothing like a meat pie and a hot tureen of soup to warm you!"

Francis' stomach churned at his words. She looked longingly at her fellow traveller, who was attacking a plate of country ham. His jade eyes glinted with enjoyment as he chewed and swallowed. Francis swallowed too. Her last hot meal had been two days ago. She felt a little faint at the sight of those translucent slices of ham, slathered with mustard.

"Just hot coffee with cream, please." Skipping meals had become a habit with her. Francis had lost at least a stone since her husband's death. She had stopped eating out of grief, and then it had become a necessity. The angles of her wrists now jutted out from her slender hands. Her bosom, which once had been very fine, now seemed to be the only plump part of her. Robert had loved her bosom. It warmed Francis to recall his sigh of contentment when he buried his face between her breasts. She absently ran her fingers over her soft flesh, remembering.

A chuckle sounded in her ears. Francis looked up, startled. Her neighbour's stare, like a pinprick, had invaded her reverie. The tanned rogue winked, ogling her bosom. She flushed and moved her hand away from her breast, realizing he must have thought her unconscious gesture was a sexual invitation. She looked around the throng of gentlemen, uncomfortably aware that she was the only woman present in the public room. Her stagecoach had broken a wheel in a muddy rut and Francis and her fellow passengers had walked an hour through the rain to take refuge in the Horse and Hounds. The coach would not leave until early in the morning. The price of the inn's modest room would eat up most of what was left of her meagre resources.

Francis slumped against the counter, feeling a heaviness settle in her limbs. Her breathing turned shallow, and her vision blurred. The voices of the men at the tap dimmed in her ears and she curled into the shell of her own thoughts, blotting out her surroundings. This journey to Bath was just one stop along an endless journey that moved her body from one place to another, while her mind remained rooted in Brussels. Robert had fallen on the battlefield of Waterloo two years before, bayoneted by a French soldier. Francis dwelled in Brussels still, repeating her husband's parting words in her mind until they had become a daily prayer. The bitter loss at Waterloo had left her with an eerie feeling of detachment towards the scenes that played themselves out around her. Perhaps that was why she had been unable to hold on to any kind of steady employment. She had hired herself out as a governess for the children of one of the colonels in her husband's regiment, but he had let her go after less than six months. Try as she might, Francis could not like the Burroughs' pampered girls, who threw tantrums every time she tried to enforce some discipline on them. She had watched their squalling with a cold feeling as if she saw them through a pane of glass. It was as if she were merely marking time, waiting to follow Robert to the other side.

Something brushed her leg, sending a jolt through her. Francis gave a little gasp and jerked her head up. The tanned stranger flashed her a wicked grin, and she realized he had momentarily pressed his muscular thigh against her leg. She glared at him, but then found it difficult to withdraw her gaze. Those brilliant green eyes ensnared her. There was fire in their translucent depths and she stood, as if hypnotized. A surge of energy crackled between them and Francis swayed on her feet, clutching the counter for support. The spell broken, she turned her eyes to his plate of ham, now half empty and furrowed with mustard.

The gentle pressure of fingers on her hand made her jump. He held a fork out to her. "The name's Jared White." He nodded at his plate. "I have more than enough food here for two. Go on, help yourself."

Francis looked from the pink slices of ham, drowning in grease, back to Mr White. The gnawing pain in her stomach almost tempted her to accept his offer. But she mistrusted the rakish gleam in his eyes. Perhaps offering to share his meal was a ploy so he could take advantage of her.

"No, thank you."

Mr White frowned, but the innkeeper reappeared, saving Francis from further embarrassment. The innkeeper was a stout man with a balding pate who looked to be respectable, in spite of the shabby state of his hostelry. "Your room is ready, Mrs Taylor. If you'd like to go up and get dry, I'll bring the coffee up to you."

Francis smiled with real gratitude. The kindly man seemed to understand how vulnerable she felt in this public room, surrounded by strangers.

She turned to follow the innkeeper, but Mr White touched her arm. "You are sure you won't join me? At least take your coffee here."

"No, thank you." Francis' arm was not entirely steady when she pulled it away.

"Then I wish you pleasant dreams." Something about the sly way Mr White murmured those words put Francis to the blush. She could feel his intent gaze on her as she jostled her way out of the crowded room.

The innkeeper wheezed as he led Francis up the stairs towards a small room at the end of the hall. Inside was a timbered chamber with a low roof that looked as if it had not been dusted for a long time. Cobwebs encrusted the mirror and windows. Two narrow iron beds, a washstand and a wicker chair were the only furniture. The window fronted a wood-planked balcony that seemed to extend along the backside of the inn. Francis gave a little moan of delight at the sight of the crackling fire in the grate. She ran to the hearth and stretched out her hands.

"I've given you as many blankets as I could spare."

Francis hardly heard the innkeeper, for she had closed her eyes to soak in the blessed warmth. He must have gone, for a few moments later, she heard a knock at the door, and the portly man handed her a tot of hot coffee.

"I am indebted to you," Francis said, curling her fingers around the hot metal cup.

He gave her a harried look. "I have to be getting back. A new group's just come in. I don't know where I will lodge them all!" Throwing up his hands, he rushed from the room.

Francis drank the coffee down in a few scalding gulps. She stripped off her dripping wet clothes and draped them over the mantelpiece to dry. She grimaced at her reflection in the mirror. Her bright blue eyes looked unnaturally large in her pointed face, and the golden curls of her braid were tangled into a bird's nest. Her firm mouth drooped with fatigue. Wrapping herself in a woollen blanket, Francis sank into the wicker chair that stood next to the fire. For the first time in almost a day, she felt her shoulders begin to relax. Perhaps she would be all right after all.

She looked down at the Panchamaabhuta gleaming in the light of the flames. The refraction of the light created a star-shaped pattern in the ruby's crimson depths. It was a man's ring, and it looked enormous on Francis' slender finger. Her husband's good-luck charm had seen her home from Brussels. It was the only thing of value that Robert had left her, and now perhaps it would give her a new start. Francis took up her reticule and dug around inside it. Shivering, she extracted the announcement she had cut out of *The Times*. "Seeking the Pancha-Maabjoota. Will buy it at any price." A description of the star ruby from Madagascar and its gold setting followed. Francis examined the gem on her finger. Robert had called his ring by that name, and a jeweller had assured her that it was a genuine star ruby. Even its golden setting matched the description in the paper. Francis frowned at the announcement. Who knew how many Indian rubies were to be found in England? But the gentleman in the advertisement, one Mr Davis, had said the ring had once belonged to his family and had been lost at Oxford. Francis thought Robert had said he had won it in college at a game of faro. Her intuition told her that her good-luck charm was the one. According to Hindu superstitions, the Panchamaabhuta could be counted on to protect its wearer from harm. Francis was determined to believe that her talisman had drawn Mr Davis to her when she had exhausted every other avenue of support.

When the fire had dimmed to a dull glow, Francis climbed, shivering, into bed. But she was too cold to sleep. She lay in the darkness, wondering what she would do if the announcement in *The Times* turned out to be a prank. One trouble after another had followed since Robert's death. Without him, Francis felt as if the bottom had dropped out of the centre of her life, leaving it as dark and oppressive as her unlit room. In the adventurous years she had spent following the drum, accompanying a ragtag army of men through Spain and France, Francis hadn't minded lodging in flea-infested quarters and living on scraps. But then she had had Robert at her side. Without him, the dark English winter pressed in on her until she longed for her own release.

"Please come for me," she whispered into the darkness, running her fingers along the square-cut ruby.

Francis dreamed she was trying to cross a frozen lake. She strained to move her legs, but they had frozen into blocks of ice. Her body was getting colder and colder. Soon the falling blizzard would cover her entirely. "Help!" she shouted, but the words came out in a pathetic whisper.

There was a slight sound, and she felt warm breath on her face. Suddenly, she could move her limbs. She reached up and felt the silken texture of fine hair beneath her fingers. The teasing currents of his breath tickled her face. "Kiss me," she whispered.

He didn't move. She looked up, surprised, but the fire had almost died out, making it difficult for her to see Robert's face. "I need you," she said, her voice throaty with longing.

He bent towards her, and she could hear his breathing quicken. When their lips met, she let out a moan of surprise. His mouth was warm, his lips surprisingly soft. She opened her mouth to him. The kiss was tender. The velvet tip of his tongue brushed hers. He traced her lips, and then plunged his tongue into her mouth. The intensity of his heated kisses sent a jolt straight to her core. Francis gasped and reached for him, pulling him down on top of her. He sucked her tongue into his mouth, devouring her. She panted beneath him, lost in sensation. His heavy body pressed her down into the mattress, his weight solid and arousing. Francis massaged his firm buttocks, and he groaned. When he thrust against her, she felt a hard ridge press into her stomach. His mouth tasted deliciously of brandy. Arching up, Francis bit into his neck. He tasted of curry and sandalwood. Francis shivered, confused. His smell reminded her of something. She tried to speak, but his mouth closed over her nipple, sucking her through the thin muslin of her nightgown. Francis cried out in pleasure, sinking her nails into his back. "Oh, yes, please!" she cried, thrashing underneath this delicious assault.

A door slammed, somewhere down the hall, bringing Francis fully awake. She stiffened, realizing with the suddenness of a lightning bolt that the man in her bed was not her husband. "Who? What . . . what are you doing?" she cried.

The man jumped up from the bed and darted to the window. She heard a rasping sound, and realized that the intruder was escaping.

"Stop!" Francis jumped out of bed, her mind reeling. The window closed with a rattle, and then she heard a slamming sound farther off. She dived for the candle and ran to light it in the dying embers of the fire. The flickering taper revealed the bare fingers of her right hand. The Panchamaabhuta was gone.

Francis wailed, a low, keening note that seemed to rise up from the depths of her being. The deep, guttural lament went on and on. Iron bands squeezed her lungs. It wasn't just her hope that had gone; the ring was all she had left of Robert. The finality of her loss struck Francis with full force. "No, no, no, no!" She pounded her fists against the mantelpiece. "Oh, God, Robert, Robert." She crumpled over, racked with sobs. After some time, the blackness receded. Her stomach growled, forcing her back to the present. If she didn't get the Panchamaabhuta back, she would starve.

She lifted her head, thinking. What did she know about the man who had stolen her jewel? He had the same smell of buckskin and spices as the stranger from the public room. Mr White had been eyeing her ring, hadn't he? Francis remembered his teasing look when he had wished her pleasant dreams. Suddenly the words took on a sinister meaning.

Francis ground her teeth. Whoever he was, the thief had leaned over her bed because he was trying to steal her ruby. She was the one who had, inadvertently, offered him another prize. She remembered the intruder's searing touch, and shivered. It had felt so right, being held in his arms, but he had only been taking advantage of her. She touched her swollen lips, remembering the hungry way Mr White had stared at her mouth when they stood together at the tap. He had pressed his thigh against her leg beneath the counter. It must have been him. The blackguard had misused her and robbed her into the bargain.

Francis' gaze flew to the window. He had escaped that way, and then she had heard a muffled thud. Her chamber was located in the back corner of the inn, and there was nothing but wood beams to her right. The sound had seemed to come from the chamber to her other side. Perhaps the thief had deliberately taken a room next to hers. There was only one way to find out.

Stumbling in her haste, Francis pulled a thick woollen shawl over her nightgown and slipped on her kid half-boots. She strode to the window and pushed it upwards with a grating sound. Stealthily, she lowered herself on to the balcony on the other side. A board creaked beneath her feet. The wooden planks of the balcony seemed to connect all the rooms along the back of the inn. Moving on tiptoe, Francis crept slowly towards the next room. The window of the chamber was bare of curtains. She stood back, in the shadow of the wall, where she thought she could look through the pane of glass without being seen.

Standing up on tiptoe, Francis craned her neck. The room was glowing with candlelight and a crackling fire. A tall man with clipped blond hair stood barefoot on the rug. Francis drew her breath in on a hiss. There was no mistaking his powerful build – Mr White had dwarfed the other men in the public room. She flattened herself against the wall, hardly daring to breathe. She was suddenly aware of how exposed she was, alone on the dark balcony with only a pane of glass separating her from a man who could very well be a dangerous criminal. He stood with his back turned. At first, she thought he was hugging himself. Then he lifted his arms, and pulled the white linen shirt over his head. The broad expanse of his bare back, rippling with muscles, was revealed. Francis bit her lip. Mr White was very well made. His golden-toned body tapered from powerful shoulders to a trim waist, and his tight buckskins were moulded to his firm buttocks. He bent forwards, tugging at his waistband, and Francis realized that he was unfastening his trousers. Embarrassed, she was about to retreat, when she saw a glint of red on his right hand. Was it the Panchamaabhuta?

Francis squinted, but his hands were on his trousers, making it difficult to see. Mr White was inching his buckskins down, revealing a tempting expanse of smooth golden skin. Francis held her breath when the round globes of his buttocks came into view. She felt a tingling sensation in her belly, and she pressed her cheek against the glass, trying to cool her heated face. Mr White had powerful thighs, furred over lightly with golden brown hair. His long, muscular legs revealed his prowess in sporting pursuits. When he turned towards her, she saw his pendulous sex swinging between his legs, cushioned in a nest of dark curls. Francis swallowed convulsively. Heavens, but he was a beautiful man. She felt little prickles along her skin as she looked at the broad expanse of his naked chest. He scratched his mat of golden-brown hair luxuriously, and Francis' teeth clicked together. She had seen the glint of red on his right hand. She couldn't mistake the golden setting of the ring. It was the Panchamaabhuta. Francis gave a fierce snort, and the sound seemed to catch his ears. Mr White looked up towards the window.

Francis ducked down, huddling in the shadows. She waited in fear for some time, scolding herself for her carelessness. A vault of darkness and silence enclosed her. When the tumult of her beating heart slowed, she straightened up and looked through the window again. Mr White had walked over to his bed. The light in the room dimmed, as if the candles had been blown out, one after the other.

Francis chewed her lip, twisting the ends of her shawl in her hands. Her fingers clenched around a tassel, and she tugged at it so hard that it broke off. The gloating look on Mr White's face had incited her beyond bearing. Robert had left her the ring as his parting gift. She would rather die than let his precious keepsake end in the hands of a cutpurse.

Francis waited, crouching in the shadows, until she thought she heard the sound of snoring. Her joints were stiff when she stood upright again. Moving out of the shadows, she peered into the darkened room. The fire was still blazing in the grate, and she saw Mr White lying, with his eyes closed, in his bed. She trembled at the thought of what she would have to do. She was going to break into the room of a strange gentleman, risking her reputation, even her safety, to steal back her jewel. But Mr White had left her no choice. Francis dug her nails into her palms. She wasn't going to let the Panchamaabhuta go without a fight.

She tugged at the window, which gave with a rasping sound. Did none of the windows have locks in this forsaken inn? Holding her breath, Francis pushed the window up and hoisted herself through it. It was a struggle, but years of arduous travel had put a fair amount of strength in her wiry arms. She lowered herself to the floor. She had done it. She was actually inside.

The crackling fire shed a dim light around the room. She darted an anxious glance at the man on the bed, wondering if all her noise had woken him. All she heard was the steady sound of snoring. Chuckling to herself, she crept towards him, imagining his look of chagrin when he woke and discovered his booty was gone. He lay under a white coverlet, and she looked him over with cautious interest. In sleep, he looked more like a boy than a man. The strong planes of his face had relaxed. His tousled blond hair gave him an innocent look. Mr White stirred, muttering to himself. Francis knew she had to act now, and quickly.

Perching on the edge of the bed, she tugged down his coverlet to reveal his right hand. She was trembling when she reached out for the ring. He stirred, moving his hand out of reach. With a deep breath, Francis seized it in hers. His fingers were warm and the hair on the back of his hands felt rough against her palm. A flutter ran through her at the contact. Francis pulled at the ruby, and then sucked in her breath. The Panchamaabhuta seemed to be glued to Mr White's index finger. She would have to use all her strength to take it off. Little goosebumps stood out on Francis' arms. The smallest touch or sound might waken him. She darted a glance at Mr White's face, but his expression was as peaceful as before. Francis curled her nails around the square-cut ruby, trying to advance it towards the tip of his finger. Suddenly, Mr White turned his head. His catlike eyes, awake and fiery, stared into hers.

"So you've come back for more." Throwing off his bedclothes, he dived for her.

Francis scampered away with a frightened squeak. Moving with a speed born of sheer terror, she raced to the window.

He reached it at the same time. Blocking her escape, he seized her wrist in a firm clasp. "We have a score to settle, you and I." He loomed over her, and Francis stared at his hairy chest. He was standing before her, naked as God made him.

Francis' heart seemed to be jumping out of her bosom, but she was still able to think. Bringing her foot up, she came down with all her weight, crushing his bare toes beneath her boot. He let go of her with an agonized grunt. She leaped to the window, and pushed up on the pane of glass. As she started to hoist herself up, strong arms seized her from behind. She kicked at him, trying to free herself, but an irresistible force pulled her down to the floor. Francis writhed, kicking and panting, as they rolled across the floor. She landed on top and scratched viciously at his face. He cursed and slapped her. Francis hardly felt the stinging pain on her cheek. Her heart was pounding, and a surge of fierce triumph shot through her. After two years of slow, burning rage at Robert's death, now she had a human target to wreak her vengeance on. It wasn't some nameless French soldier who had taken Robert from her. It was Mr White, who had violated her bond with her husband by stealing the ring.

"You bloody thieving bastard!" She hammered blows at his face. "How dare you? You miserable, mercenary wretch!" This time, her nail nicked the corner of his eye, drawing blood.

Cursing, he seized her wrists together in one hand, gripping her so hard that she cried out in pain. She wriggled, but he held her arms fast and pinned her writhing body against his chest with his other hand.

"Let me go!"

His grip tightened on her. Francis panted against his naked chest, feeling a hard button press into her cheek. Turning her head, she bit viciously into his nipple.

He gasped, and then seized her in an iron grip. A punishing hand pushed her head down, burying her face in his warm, muscular shoulder. Francis couldn't move. She realized with a sinking feeling that she was in his power. She went limp against him, as the truth sank in. He wasn't a French soldier; he was a common thief in a roadside inn. Even if she got the Panchamaabhuta back, Robert was lost for ever. Exhausted, she collapsed on to Mr White. Immediately, the painful pressure eased. He tilted her chin up, so that his luminous eyes bored into hers.

"You fight like a Bengal tiger," he said. To her surprise, there was a chuckle in his voice.

"Give me my ruby," Francis said.

"If you want it, you'll have to give me something in return." He gave her a hot look.

Francis was suddenly aware that although she was wearing a shawl over her nightgown, she had nothing on underneath. She could feel the heat of his limbs coiled beneath hers.

"What do you want?" she asked.

He flicked his hand at her, showing off the ruby. "I'm not asking for much. Just one kiss, willingly given." His smouldering gaze raked her, and Francis realized that the position he held her in, sprawled on top of him, had been deliberate. He had let her take the superior position, giving him access to the most vulnerable parts of her.

"Why should I trust you?"

His lips stretched in a devilish grin. "I wouldn't, if I were you." He moved so she could feel his breath against her cheek, ruffling her hair. The gentle caress made her shiver.

He must have felt it, for he chuckled again. The low, purring sound, so close to her ear, only added to her giddy sense of danger.

"You're actually enjoying this." She glared at him.

In answer, he pushed down her hips, shifting her until she felt his erection press between her thighs. Trembling with a mixture of arousal and fear, Francis sat motionless astride him. His hungry jade eyes bored into hers with hypnotizing effect. Some part of her began to give in to his silent invitation, and then she forced herself to look away. She struggled to lift herself off his body, but he only let her move so far away before he pulled her astride him again. Their rocking motion, as she wriggled back and forth against his erection was highly arousing. Francis felt a betraying moisture dampen her nightgown, even as she struggled to get away. This time, when he thrust her down on top of him, he nipped at her ear, and then sucked her ear lobe into his mouth. It sent a tingle straight to her belly. Panting, Francis scratched his naked chest. He gave a deep moan. Then his mouth was on hers, fierce and hot. He plunged his tongue inside, sending currents of giddying sensation through her belly. Giving in to the pleasure, Francis surrendered to the hard pressure of his embrace. His heady taste, a mixture of man and brandy, made her senses swim.

He grunted, a low, guttural noise, then tangled his tongue with hers. Unwilling to relinquish all of her power, Francis pulled back and then stabbed her tongue between his lips, ravishing him as he had ravished her. She plundered his mouth until he twisted and panted beneath her. Enjoying her new sense of power, Francis scratched the buds of his nipples with her fingernails. He shuddered and she could feel the urgency of his arousal. He pushed her off him, panting, and then took her by surprise by flipping her on to her back. Before she knew what was happening, he had removed her shawl and then he ripped her nightgown, exposing her round, firm breasts to the cold. She gasped, and her nipples puckered in the slap of frigid air. He knelt over her, and she felt his hot breath on her sensitive skin.

"Say yes." His voice was harsh against her ear.

Francis nodded, and he just barely touched her nipple with the tip of his tongue. She whimpered, but he hovered over her, teasing.

"I want to hear the words."

The flickering movement of his warm breath against her skin made her wild. "Yes," she whispered.

He lifted her up into him so that his knee was pressed into her groin. Francis gave a choked cry and dug her nails into his shoulders. Supporting her in his arms, he buried his face in her bosom. She moaned as he caressed her soft flesh with the fan of his cropped hair. Then, with a hungry look, he took one of her nipples into his mouth.

Francis cried out. He suckled her, his tongue circling the tight bud. She whimpered and moaned, waves of intense pleasure engulfing her. His tongue was warm and its teasing pressure sent shock waves to her core. Quivering, Francis tossed her head from side to side, giving in to the white-hot sensations building in her groin. The fire exploded and she bucked against him, screaming.

"Oh, God, yes, please. Oh, God," she moaned. Her sex contracted against his knee, swamping her in blinding volleys of sensation. Then she collapsed, panting, against him.

"The name's Jared," he murmured in her ear, "but you can call me anything you like."

Francis blinked at him, as if she were waking from a long sleep. Her entire body felt intensely alive. She saw Jared in sharp focus now: the beads of sweat on his upper lip, his leaf-coloured pupils, rimmed by darker green, the tawny hair of his clipped sideburns that framed his face. The intent look in his eyes was almost too much for her to bear. She rested her head against his chest, and the muffled sound of his heartbeat tugged at her senses. Absently, she put her hand on her bosom, and felt her heart contract beneath her palm. Something powerful had taken possession of her. Francis opened her mouth to ask him why he had stolen the Panchamaabhuta, but the words came out in a sob.

"Shhh." He stroked her hair, and, at his gentle touch, Francis buried her face in his chest. Sobs racked her as if a dam of pent-up grief had broken open. She wept and wept, feeling a leaden weight in her chest pressing her down, overwhelming her. Little by little, as she cried herself out, the heavy feeling began to fade. For the first time in two years, the black time in Brussels had receded. Francis hiccoughed and coughed, then raised her head, suddenly aware of how much time had passed.

"That's better." He had been rocking her gently against his shoulder, his voice a soothing murmur. Francis felt delicious warmth spread through her at his gentle touch. He lifted her in his arms and carried her, a limp armful, to his bed. She collapsed like a rag doll, looking up at him, wide-eyed. Suddenly she felt painfully exposed. Her stolen encounter had borne in on her that her bitter loss in Brussels hadn't happened at all as she had imagined. She had thought that Robert's death had taken everything from her. Instead, she had discovered a passionate, living force inside that she had never known until now. Francis straightened up, feeling strangely light and yet filled with wanting. And what she wanted, most of all now, was the stranger who stood naked before her.

For the first time, Francis smiled at him. His answering grin was brilliant even in the semi-darkness. He strode towards her and pulled her nightgown, which had pooled at her waist, down over her feet and threw it on to the floor. Then he took a step backwards. She watched him stand there motionless, his hands on his hips, studying her. His pupils were so dilated that his irises looked black. Francis lay trembling on the bed, waiting for him to come to her. But he stayed still.

She felt a surge of anxiety. She had never felt such raw desire for a man before. The carnal need to taste his hot mouth, to feel him deep inside her, was overwhelming. What if he didn't feel the same way? "Jared." She held out her hand.

He didn't move. Francis frowned and sat up against the pillows, covering herself with her crossed arms.

"No, don't," he said in a husky voice. "Let me look at you." His heated gaze assuaged a little of her uncertainty. He took a branch of candles to the fire, lit them, and then placed the light on the table next to the bed. He moved to stand at the foot of the bed. "Let me look at you," he repeated, his voice harsh with command.

As if under a spell, Francis let her arms fall to her side, and then she relaxed against the coverlet, exposing her naked body to him.

He made a low, rumbling noise in his throat. "Put your arms behind your head."

She did as he commanded, aware that she was thrusting her breasts forwards for his hungry gaze.

Jared licked his lips. The question of whether he wanted her was more than answered by the angle of his rigid sex, jutting out from his body. "For ten years I've been away from England, keeping company with women different from my kind. You are more beautiful than I could have imagined."

His heated examination of her sent little shivers travelling up and down her spine. She knew that her arms and legs were too thin, but somehow he found her beautiful. The realization sent a fluttering sensation into her core. "Come."

He didn't move. "This is too good to be true," he murmured, a rapt look in his eyes. He seemed to devour every bit of her white skin and long, wheat-coloured hair. Francis felt a stirring of pride at his evident admiration of her slender body. His eyes lingered on her flat belly, and the pink tips of her nipples, which jutted in response to the cold air. His possessive gaze was only feeding the flames of her impatience. He licked his lips again, and she realized he was examining the golden patch of curls above her sex. Inspired with a naughty idea, Francis spread her legs apart. He made a low, guttural noise in his throat. Encouraged, Francis raised a hand to her breast and traced lazy circles around her nipple. He sucked in his breath. She let her other hand drift down between her legs. Fixing him with a wanton look, she traced her folds with one fingertip.

Jared surged forwards, as if he could no longer contain himself. Climbing on to the bed, he lowered himself on top of her and entered her in one thrust. They both cried out when he sank into her. Francis thrashed beneath him, meeting his every thrust with fierce energy. He possessed her. But the more she surrendered to the sweet invasion, the more pleasure she felt. The warmth of his mouth, the fullness inside her, took her to a state entirely out of herself. His fingers, teasing her at the place of their joining, sent waves of heat through her. He stiffened, increasing his movements, and she felt the tingling sensation of a violent climax approaching. She arched up, lifting her hips to take him deeper inside her, and then she shattered against him with a breathless sob. He bit into her shoulder, muffling the hoarse sound of his own release.

He collapsed on top of her. Francis held on to him for dear life, hugging him so close that she could hardly breathe. Her nails dug into his back, as she felt his heavy weight squeeze the air out of her lungs. She couldn't bear to let go of him, of the radiant sense of pleasure and release Jared had given her. He claimed her mouth in a fierce kiss, and then rolled off on to his side. He pulled her into his chest, and Francis rested her cheek against the soft mat of curls on his chest. It felt strangely, terrifyingly right, lying in his arms. His fingers tangled in her hair, and she sighed at his soothing touch. Soon she fell into a deep sleep.

Francis was aware of an elbow digging into her side. She winced, and tried to push it away. A loud snore resonated in her ears. Her eyes blinked open to find the early morning light streaming through the bare window. Jared was tangled in the coverlet, asleep, his back to her. She looked in admiration at the taut muscles of his back. Feeling rather shy, she traced her fingers along his smooth, golden skin. It was warm and silky to the touch. She felt a stir of desire at the sight of his naked body, lying so temptingly close to her. She was free of shame about the unexpected night she had spent with Jared. Making love to him had been entirely different to her decorous couplings with her husband. She had discovered some hidden part of herself, passionate and alive, which made her see everything in a different light. Francis had discovered that she had invested all that had been good of herself in Robert, and believed that it had died with him. Now, she seemed to have taken some of it back. Looking at her lover's sleeping form, she spied the dull red glow of the Panchamaabhuta on his finger.

Francis wriggled out of bed and stood up, careful not to make any noise. Jared's long, muscular limbs were intertwined with the white coverlet, and, in her fancy, he resembled a sculpture of Apollo. His arm was crossed over his chest, elevating the ruby into a ray of morning light. Francis knew her only chance to steal it back was while Jared was defenceless in sleep. His body was limp, his chest rising and falling with the sounds of his hearty snores. She bent over him. "Jared?" she murmured in his ear, testing him.

He didn't move. His breathing was deep and regular.

Holding her breath, Francis took his hand in hers. This time the ring gave when she tugged it. Her heart was pounding in her chest when she slid the Panchamaabhuta off his finger. Slipping it on, she snatched up her woollen shawl and then struggled into her boots. The window groaned when she eased it open, and Jared stirred. Francis waited, her heart in her mouth, but he didn't move. The sonorous sound of his snoring began again. Francis clambered through the window and hurried across the balcony to her room. She dressed in frantic haste and then ran down the stairs. Collaring the innkeeper Francis paid for her room, looking over her shoulder all the while. Her fellow travellers from the stagecoach had already gathered on the front step.

Francis ran out to them. She found the burly farmer with the woollen vest who had sat next to her in the coach the day before. He was shifting from foot to foot, balancing two great baskets of apples on his meaty hips. "How long until the coach comes?" Francis asked.

"It's just on for seven. It should be any minute now," he said, creasing his round face into a friendly smile.

"If it ever comes at all. Look over there," said the slender curate, pulling a long face.

The driver was riding towards them on one of the horses from the carriage.

"That's not a good sign," the farmer murmured.

The coachman pulled his horse up in front of them and said, "Look here, now. I've just spoken to the carter, and the wheel is split more badly then he thought. It's going to have to be replaced, and that won't be until tomorrow."

An angry babble broke out from the assembled travellers. Francis shot a nervous glance around her. At any moment now, Jared might wake up. What was she going to do?

She confronted the coachman. "You can't just leave us stranded here!"

He looked down his nose at her. "You'll have to hire a convenience yourself, or spend another night at the inn. The coach isn't going anywhere today."

Francis wrung her hands. "What can I do?"

The curate looked as if he had tasted something sour. "There won't be anything in this forsaken spot. I suppose we'll have to walk into Wells proper and see if we can hire a gig or cart or whatever they have on hand." He pulled out his watch fob and shook his head. "The rector was expecting me yesterday. He'll be right put out if I don't show my face this morning."

Francis thought the rector's feelings were nothing to how put out Jared would be when he woke to discover the Panchamaabhuta was gone. The other gentlemen talked over their plans. A few of the travellers elected to stay another night at the Horse and Hounds. But the curate, Mr Pickering, and the farmer, who introduced himself simply as Samuel, decided to walk to Wells in search of a convenience. Francis ran after them, fairly twitching with anxiety. Her fear of what Jared would do if he caught her gave her a burst of strength she hadn't known she had. She ploughed down the winding country path, striding through the long grasses until she was in the lead of the two other gentlemen.

But by the time they reached Wells, her legs felt like rubber. Panting, she collapsed on to a bench at the Stag Hostelry and ordered a cup of coffee while the two men went to look for a carriage.

Mr Pickering appeared in the doorway just after she had gulped down her hot brew.

"Did you find anything?"

He gave her a disgusted look. "Nothing for a lady to ride in, I'm afraid. The smithy offered a gig that looked to be on its last legs, and in the end we settled for a wagon." Francis went to the doorway, and he waved his hand at a sturdy-looking four-wheeled vehicle. There was no top to the wagon, and only two seats in front.

"You'd better wait for the stagecoach," Samuel said, lifting up his baskets of apples and heaving them into the back of the cart.

Francis swallowed and shot an apprehensive glance down the road she had come. "I must get to Bath without delay. If you don't mind taking me with you, I will ride in the back."

"Nonsense," Samuel said. "It's a mucky farm wagon."

Francis peered inside. "I see nothing but straw at the bottom," she said.

Samuel shook his head and made for the back of the carriage, but Francis took his arm. "Please," she said rather breathlessly. "I hardly have any money, and I have to get out of town right away. I don't mind." Ignoring Mr Pickering's outraged hiss, Francis clambered up the wooden side of the wagon. The skirt of her dress snagged on the iron fastenings of the carriage and the gentlemen averted their eyes as she tugged it free. Years of travel in all kinds of conditions had inured Francis to superficial proprieties. She squatted down Indian style next to the basket of apples. "I'll keep an eye on your fruit baskets. Likely, if the road is as rough as it was back there, the apples might fall out and get bruised."

The farmer gave her a shrewd look. "Help yourself to a few, if you like. Happen you didn't have time for breakfast this morning."

Mr Pickering pinched his lips together, but apparently he was too much the gentleman to voice his thoughts about Francis' hoydenish behaviour. He climbed into the wagon next to Samuel, who took up the reigns and whipped the phlegmatic horses forwards.

Francis seized one of the rosy apples from the basket and sank her teeth into it. The sweet juice exploded against her tongue. It had now been three days since she had had a solid meal, and her stomach was burning with acid from the cup of coffee she had drunk. She ate every bit of the apple, including the core. Then she leaned her swimming head against the baskets. The gruelling run to Wells, on top of her exertions of the past two days, had left her in a stupor. She closed her eyes, trying to ease the stabbing pain in her head, and then she knew nothing more.

"Miss?" Francis awoke to the sound of an anxious voice. "Miss, can you hear me?" She cracked her eyes open to find a man in livery standing over her. She blinked at him, aware of the sounds of hooves and men's voices. She was lying sprawled in the straw at the bottom of the wagon. She struggled upright, but there was no sign of Samuel or Mr Pickering. The wagon was standing in the stable yard of what looked to be a large inn.

"Where am I?" she asked the liveried man who seemed to be a groom.

"In Bath. Your friends tried to wake you. Eh, you did give them a fright. One of them went to see a rector or somelike, but the other went for a doctor."

"Doctor?" Francis repeated, dazed.

"Samuel asked me to keep watch. Pale as a ghost, you were. I thought for a minute you weren't going to wake up. But that blond fellow who felt your pulse said you was all right."

"Blond fellow?" Francis struggled upright, and winced. There was a cramp in her leg, and her head was throbbing. She ran her hand across her eyes, and then froze. She had missed the cold pressure of the Panchamaabhuta. "My ring!" Francis looked wildly down at her hand. "The ruby! It's gone."

"Well, I'll be jiggered." The groom let out a low whistle. "That gent who felt your pulse must have been cutting a sham."

"He was blond, you said?" Francis whipped around to face the groom. "Was he very tanned?"

"That's right. Looked like a traveller from foreign parts. Dressed like a nob, with buckskins and all."

Francis drew her breath in a hiss. "Where did he go?"

The groom gestured at the inn. "He went in there. Said he was getting himself a bite."

Francis didn't hear the rest. She was running to the doorway of the inn, and then she burst into the dining room, her heart hammering in her chest.

Jared sat at a table by the window, sipping at a mug of ale. He was freshly shaven and he looked disgustingly handsome in a grey silk waistcoat and white linen shirt. A smug smile played over his lips as he leafed through *The Times*.

Francis clenched her jaw. "I'll serve him trick or tie for this." She charged towards his table. "So!"

At the fierce sound of her voice, Jared's head jerked up. But if he was shocked to see her, he gave no sign. He waved at the bench across from him. "Dinner should be here any moment."

Francis stamped her foot. "I don't give a fig about dinner. I want the ring."

His eyes narrowed, but he didn't answer.

"My ring was just stolen and, by a strange coincidence, I find you here!" Francis shot an accusing glance at Jared's right hand, and then froze. The Panchamaabhuta was not on his finger. She looked at his other hand, puzzled, but there was nothing there. Was it possible that she had been mistaken, and some other man had taken her jewel? She looked around the room, but Jared was the only tanned man present. This was not surprising, considering that it was the dead of winter in England. It must be the very reason the groom had remembered Jared so well. The thought made Francis look him up and down suspiciously.

Jared stood up from the bench and moved close to her so that their bodies were almost touching. His masculine scent, mixed with smells of exotic spices, set her pulse racing. He brushed his hip against hers, sending a crackling current between them. "I, too, lost something valuable this morning. When I woke up, I discovered she was gone." There was a sincere note of regret in his baritone voice.

Francis bit her lip. Jared had actually missed her. And the intent look he was giving her now told her that he wanted her still. When he slipped an arm around her waist, she forgot about the ruby. His hypnotic jade eyes and the gentle touch of his hand cupping her cheek made her sway a little on her feet. She reached out to steady herself, resting her palm against his chest.

"You didn't even leave me your name," he murmured in her ear. The low purr of his voice and the heat from his body were stirring Francis into a state of heightened arousal. The pressure of her hand against his chest increased, and she stiffened. There was a small, hard lump beneath her palm. Francis' breath caught, and she darted a glance at her hand. The lump beneath it felt suspiciously like a ring in the inner pocket of Jared's silk waistcoat.

"Come, have dinner with me."

"Very well." Francis forced her lips into a smile. She would play his little game, matching guile with guile. Jared didn't know yet that she had discovered his treachery. She settled herself on the bench across from him. "I won't say no to a hot meal."

"I took the liberty of ordering you some ham. I got the impression last night that you had a taste for it." There was a devilish glint in Jared's eyes.

A portly server bustled over with a plate of hot rolls. Jared thanked the ruddy gentleman and held the basket out to her. "May I tempt you with a roll, Angelica?"

"What?" Francis had already closed her hands over a warm roll, but she stopped with it halfway to her mouth, giving him a startled look.

"No, that is not exactly right. I think Theodora suits you better." He waved the butter plate at her.

She snatched the plate from him. "My name is Francis," she said crossly, slathering the roll with butter and practically stuffing it into her mouth. It had been almost a week since she had eaten freshly baked bread, and it was more delicious than she could have imagined. Jared chuckled, but Francis didn't mind, lost only to the blissful sensation of the hot, buttered roll melting against her tongue.

"Mmmmm," she moaned, dispatching it in a matter of a few bites. Some of the butter had dripped on to her hand, and she swiped at it with her tongue, forgetting her surroundings.

Jared made a strangled noise in his throat. Francis looked up to see an expression of pure lust in his eyes. So his seduction of her had not been feigned, after all. She was struck suddenly with an idea for getting the Panchamaabhuta back. Watching Jared, she slowly, deliberately, dabbed her tongue against the base of her wrist, as if there were still butter there.

Jared stiffened against the bench, and she noticed his face had flushed, the red sheen visible even beneath his tan. Francis straightened up, flexing her shoulders in a catlike gesture, and he shifted restlessly in his seat. She smiled to herself. She had found Jared's weakness, and she would use it to her advantage.

"I'm glad to see you're all right." Samuel appeared at her elbow, startling her.

Francis rose to her feet, feeling embarrassed by all the trouble she had caused the kindly man. "I'm so sorry. The stable man told me you had gone in search of a doctor. I should have sent word to you right away."

Samuel beamed. "Doesn't look as if you're in need of one now."

Jared was studying Samuel from under furrowed brows. "Will you join us, Mr . . . er . . ." There was a sharp note in Jared's voice that startled Francis. She gave him a sideways look. He had moved to stand between her and the other man. Francis could almost have sworn he was jealous.

"Samuel." The two men stared at each other, as if they were taking each other's measure. "Thank you, but I'd best be getting along." Samuel tipped his hat to Francis and turned away.

"Thank you for everything. What do I owe you for the ride?" she asked.

He chuckled. "It wasn't nothing."

"Please, I insist."

But the kindly farmer had already reached the door. Francis sank reluctantly back on to the bench.

"A friend of yours?" Jared sat down across from her, and this time she was sure she had not mistaken the harsh timbre of his voice.

"We met on the stagecoach," she said.

The furrow on Jared's brow had grown more apparent. "You shouldn't be so trusting of strangers." He took a swig of ale.

Francis gave him an ironic look. "How true."

Jared choked on his drink. His dancing eyes met hers, and suddenly the two of them were shaking with laughter. Francis collapsed against the bench, wiping her streaming cheeks. The last thing she should be doing was laughing with the rogue who had stolen the Panchamaabhuta, but somehow she couldn't help it.

His white teeth flashed in a devastating grin. "When I stayed in Calcutta, an old woman told me a story about the hazards of meeting strangers on the road."

"Indeed?" Francis said, crossing her arms. So Jared had been living in India.

He leaned his broad shoulders back against the bench. "The story is that the beautiful Kamalakshi journeyed to Shimla, where she was to marry a wealthy merchant. But she was waylaid by a road bandit who plundered her dowry jewels."

Francis stiffened. There was a mischievous gleam in Jared's eyes that told her there was more to his story than a simple diversion.

"Harmendra stole the ruby comb Kamalakshi wore in her hair. It was a priceless heirloom, each of the rubies as large as a cashew fruit. Kamalakshi couldn't bear to part with the comb, and she resolved to steal it back." Jared pressed his knee against Francis' beneath the table and gave her a sly look. "But Kamalakshi's schemes led her into Harmendra's bed.

The story reminded Francis all too much of her encounter with Jared. She realized that her palms were sweating. "What happened then?" There was a husky note in her voice.

"Three times the ornament was stolen back and forth between the lovers. Kamalakshi's nights of passion with Harmendra led her to break her betrothal vows. She pledged herself to Harmendra instead, and gave him the ruby comb as her bridal gift." Jared entrapped Francis' hand. He lifted it to his lips, pressing an ardent kiss into her palm.

Francis gave a panting breath. The ruddy tinge was back in Jared's face, and the pupils of his green eyes had darkened to the colour of coal. The morning light cast a golden glow over his chiselled face, and the sensuous movement of his lips on her fingers was reducing her to a quivering bundle of nerves. Was Jared making her an offer? The exotic syllables of the Indian names had spilled effortlessly from his tongue. India was his country, Francis was sure of it. Would Jared take her back with him as his consort, to share his life of banditry and adventure? Her heart threatened to beat out of her chest. Francis realized she would almost be willing to abandon her principles to be with him.

The server dropped a plate nearby, and the harsh clatter shattered her daydream. Francis shook her head. The truth was that Jared was nothing but a tavern thief, trading on his good looks and charm to prey on unsuspecting female travellers. Perhaps even his tales of India were a hoax, invented to cast an air of exoticism around him that women would find appealing. She pulled her hand away. "I'm afraid I'm not in a position to give the Panchamaabhuta to anyone. It was a gift from my husband."

Jared sat up. His face was suffused with crimson. "You're married?"

His outraged expression surprised the truth from Francis. "I was. Robert died at Waterloo, along with most of his friends."

Jared sank bank on to his seat. "He was a military man?" His face was still red, his voice not entirely steady.

Francis found it impossible to meet Jared's eyes. She might have shared his bed, but talking about Robert made her feel achingly vulnerable. "He was a rifleman with the 95th."

"The Light Division?"

She nodded, relaxing a little.

"I never heard of a Robert Taylor in the 95th."

"Not Taylor, Spencer."

Jared jerked his hand, almost upsetting his mug of ale. He gave her a perplexed look. "You gave your name as Taylor at the Horse and Hounds inn. Why?"

Francis was uncomfortably aware of Jared's curious eyes boring into her. She opened her lips to tell him it was none of his concern, but blurted out something else instead. "That was my family name. Robert's parents live nearby. I don't want them to know I am here."

"Why not?"

Francis looked down at her hands. "The Spencers threw us off after we married. My father was a small-time lawyer in London, with no connections." Francis' hands clenched. She had never been good enough for Robert's parents and, as a result, he had been forced to choose between her and his family. It had been a devil's bargain. Francis had never reproached Robert for his love of gaming in the years that followed, for she understood it was driven by his need to recapture the inheritance he had lost. In the end, Robert's debts of honour had swallowed up what was left of his military pay, leaving her with nothing but the ruby.

The server provided a welcome interruption by arriving with a tray of food. Francis busied herself with a piece of mutton pie, and the heavy food exercised a calming effect on her. By the time she had made short work of the pie, the rigid tension of her body had relaxed.

"Have some ham," Jared said, heaping her plate with thick slices of the roast pink flesh.

Francis sighed, inhaling the savoury aroma of the pork, and then she attacked her plate. Halfway through her second piece of meat, she looked up to see Jared frowning at her.

"When's the last time you had a decent meal?"

Francis shrugged. There was an angry look on Jared's face that warned her not to answer his question.

He crossed his arms. "Spencer seems to have done a poor job of providing for you."

Francis fired up. "Don't you dare criticize Robert! He left me the Panchamaabhuta."

"What about his arrears of pay?"

Francis toyed with a slice of ham, her appetite suddenly deserting her. "He had a run of bad luck before he died. He would have come round again if it hadn't been for Brussels." Francis closed her eyes and leaned back against the bench, trying to block out the picture of the French troops cutting her husband to ribbons on the battlefield. It was an image she had pieced together in her mind from the stories of the survivors. Her breathing went shallow as she battled the disturbing vision, forcing herself to come back to the present.

Jared's breath against her cheek startled her. "You look unwell." He chafed her wrists. "Your pulse is rapid. Let me take you upstairs, so you can rest."

Francis opened her mouth to protest that she was fine, when it occurred to her that Jared was offering her the perfect opportunity. "If you think that's best." She gave Jared what she hoped was a sickly smile.

When he went to see the innkeeper, she thought through the details of her scheme and ate every remaining morsel of ham. When Jared returned to the dining room, Francis was ready. He led the way up the stairs to a chamber on the second floor, and she leaned heavily on his arm.

When the innkeeper unlocked the door for them, Jared startled her by taking her up in his arms. The innkeeper stumped away, clicking his tongue in disapproval.

Francis wriggled in his arms, trying to get down. "For heaven's sake, what will he think of us?"

He winked at her. "Nothing to concern yourself with, Mrs White." Giving her a teasing smile, he slung Francis on to the narrow bed. Then he strode to the door and closed it. "Can I get you a glass of wine?"

"No, thank you."

Jared leaned over her to unfasten the top clasps at the back of her gown, and then he loosened her hair. "Now you should be more comfortable." He straightened up. "I'll go now, and let you sleep a while."

Francis stiffened. Jared's plan must be to escape with the ruby while she was feeling weak, unable to summon any help. She caught his hand. "Oh, no, please stay with me."

He gave her a quizzical look. "You need to rest."

She mustered the most pitiful expression she could. "I'm scared." She gave a little shiver, and blinked at him. "Please stay."

Jared sank back down on to the bed. "Shhh," he murmured, wrapping his arms around her.

Francis sighed and nestled against his firm chest, flooded with a delicious sense of well-being. Scoundrel that he was, Jared's gentle touch had an immediate soothing effect on her. Cuddling closer, Francis felt her cheek brush against a lump in the pocket of his vest. It was time to put her plan into action. She tugged at his shoulders, pulling herself up so her face was level with his. Jared's sleepy eyes flickered. Encouraged, she brushed the tip of her finger across his lower lip. "Kiss me," she said.

He barely touched his mouth to hers, the movement so tender that Francis melted against him.

"I want you." Her words came out in a husky whisper.

Suddenly, they were tangled together on the bed, his hot kisses depriving her of breath. Francis gave in to the wild pleasure of tasting him, letting her senses swim. Jared drew away and gave her a long, serious look. Francis stiffened, remembering her purpose. Whatever it was that Jared seemed to want to say, it could wait.

"Come, darling," she murmured, drawing closer and toying with his cravat.

Jared's breath came in a hot burst against her cheek. She felt for the buttons of his waistcoat and the top button gave, and then the next. Francis slipped her hand inside, moving her palms in a slow circle against Jared's chest. He moaned. His nipples were highly sensitive, she had learned. When she continued the sensuous massage of his chest, Jared arched his back. Fighting the impulse to plunder him in a different way, Francis claimed his attention with a kiss. At the same time, her fingers probed the inner pocket of his waistcoat. She moved her lips to his neck, and Jared closed his eyes. Quick as a flash, she curled her fingers around the Panchamaabhuta. Retracting it from his inner pocket, she sealed his mouth with a last, hot kiss, and slipped the ring into her décolletage. Then she levelled an assessing glance at him. Jared's eyes were still closed, his lashes fluttering against his cheek. A pang of longing shot through her at the sight of his golden beauty. His firm chin, full sensuous lips and dark tan were in stark relief to his tousled blond hair, giving him the look of a dark angel. Francis stared at him for a moment, as if she were memorizing him. Then she refastened the buttons of his waistcoat and pulled away.

Jared blinked his eyes open.

"Good heavens, I left my wrap downstairs," Francis said, wringing her hands.

"What?" There was a glassy expression in Jared's wide green eyes as if she had pulled him from a pleasant dream.

"The woollen wrap, with red flowers on it."

Jared's brow was furrowed. "You don't have it now?"

"No. When I was feeling dizzy before, I must have left it on the bench. Do please go down and get it for me." Francis took his hand and pressed it to her cheek.

"Later." Jared lunged forwards, claiming her mouth in a deep, possessive kiss.

She pulled away from him, breaking the kiss. "Someone might steal it. First my ring, and then my wrap. I couldn't bear it."

Her words seemed to have pricked Jared's guilty conscience, for he let go of her and rose to his feet. "Very well. But I'll expect a reward for it when I get back." His roguish grin flashed at her, then he slipped out of the room. The door closed shut behind him.

Francis waited for a moment, her heart pounding, and then she cracked the door open and looked out cautiously. The hall was empty. Gathering her courage, she darted to the stairs. She took the stairs two at a time on her way down. It would take Jared time to find the shawl she had hidden beneath the bench in the dining room, but there was always the possibility that he would catch her on the stairs. The thought made her pulse race. Francis breathed a sigh of relief when she reached the foot of the stairs and saw no one at the bottom save a maid carrying a stack of linens. Jared must still be in the dining room. The server had revealed there was a back entrance out of the inn, and Francis scurried towards the back passage of the hostelry. She gave a silent cry of thanks when she reached the wooden door at the end of the hall. It pushed open and she darted through it.

She took one wild look around her to get her bearings, and then she plunged into the street. It wasn't until she reached an intersection that she paused to catch her breath. Francis knew Bath fairly well; for it was there that she had met Robert. She had a fair idea of where she was and, looking up, she used the distant clerestory of the Bath Abbey Church as her guide. Anxious to put as much distance between herself and Jared as possible, she plunged down the cobblestone street in the direction of the abbey. The office of Mr Davis was located on York Street, not far from the ancient cloister. Every footfall and call behind Francis seemed to be Jared running after her in hot pursuit, and she pounded down the web of narrow cobbled paths as if her life depended on it.

A small building on York Street had Mr Davis' name on the door in gold lettering. Francis burst through the door, panting. A severe-looking man with greying hair rose from his desk, giving her a startled look. Francis knew she must look a sight with her hair half undone and a gap in the back of her dress where Jared had unfastened it. She took a gasping breath. "I read the advertisement in *The Times*. I am here to sell the Panchamaabhuta."

The gentleman gave a curt nod. "Then you have come to the right place."

"Thank heavens for that. Are you Mr Davis?"

"Yes. And you are?"

"Mrs Spencer."

A slow smile spread over Mr Davis' face. "Where is the ring?"

Francis looked down at her hand, but there was nothing there. She remembered that the ring was still in her décolletage.

Mr Davis was looking at her expectantly.

Francis shifted from one foot to the other. "It is hidden on my person. Please avert your eyes while I retrieve it."

Mr Davis raised his eyebrows but obligingly turned his back.

Her cheeks burning, Francis extracted the ruby from her undergarments. Then she straightened her dress. "Here it is." Mr Davis had turned round to face her, and she held the Panchamaabhuta out to him. "Is it the ring you were looking for?"

Mr Davis lifted the star ruby up to the light. He examined it for a long time as Francis watched, her heart in her throat. At length, he handed it back to her. "I believe this is the one. The inscription and the gem are just as my client described. But he will have to judge for himself."

"Your client?" Francis gave Mr Davis a bewildered look.

"I am a solicitor, Mrs Spencer. My client commissioned me to find the ring for him."

"Who is this gentleman?"

Before Mr Davis could answer her question, the door of his office opened, and Jared burst into the room.

Francis gave a frightened squeak. Jared's hair was dishevelled, and he was panting. There was a wild look in his eyes. When he caught sight of her, he gave a little cry of triumph. "There you are. What the devil happened to you?"

Francis backed away from him, trembling.

Jared strode forwards. "Why did you run away? I've been looking for you everywhere." He sounded furious.

Francis darted an appealing look at Mr Davis, but he stood passively watching her and Jared, a bemused expression on his face.

Francis gathered her courage and turned to look Jared squarely in the face. "I couldn't let you keep my ring. I came to Bath to sell it to Mr Davis."

Jared's eyebrows shot up. A snort of incredulity escaped him. Then he hunched over, his shoulders shaking. As Francis watched, perplexed, Jared collapsed in a paroxysm of laughter. His mirth went on for some time.

Mr Davis cleared his throat. "I was about to send you word that your ring had been found, but it seems you already learned that for yourself."

Jared chuckled. "Thank you, Davis. It seems your work is done."

The familiar tone of Jared's voice registered. Francis looked from him to Mr Davis as it dawned on her that the two men were acquainted with each other. Her teeth clicked together, the pieces of the puzzle forming together in her mind. Jared was Mr Davis' client. Her perilous quest to Bath had been all for nothing. It was Jared who had put the announcement in *The Times* in the first place and, all this while, he had been making a May-game of her.

Francis gave a little sob, and rushed to the door.

"Francis!"

Heedless of Jared's cry, Francis plunged into the street, narrowly missing a collision with a hackney. The driver shouted insults at her, but she ran on. It wasn't until she almost barrelled into a tall gentleman in the square that she realized Jared had overtaken her.

He grasped her shoulder. "Francis, please."

"All right!" Francis pulled the ruby ring off her finger and held it out to him. "Go ahead, take it. Just promise you will leave me alone!"

But Jared didn't take the ring. All traces of his former mirth were gone. He stood staring at her, his eyes dark with emotion. "It's not the Panchamaabhuta I want. It's you."

Francis stiffened. "I don't believe you."

Jared shuffled from one foot to the other. "You make it deuced difficult on a fellow. Every time I try to declare myself, you run away." He looked down at the ground. His confidence seemed to have deserted him. Francis examined his averted face, suffused with red, and realized with a chill that Jared was in earnest.

"You want to marry me?" Her voice squeaked in surprise.

Jared scuffed his shoe on the cobbles. "I've made a right mull of this. I don't blame you for telling me to go hang." He darted a quick glance at her, and a shudder ran through Francis. Jared's heart was in his eyes.

"I thought you only wanted the ruby."

"That was true at first." Jared frowned. "It's a family heirloom. It drove a wedge between my father and me, when I foolishly let go of it, years ago. Father's sick now, and I promised him that I would go back to England and try to get the Panchamaabhuta back."

Francis crossed her arms. "What do you mean, get it back? Robert didn't steal it from anyone."

"I know that." Jared grinned. "We roomed together at Oxford. I lost the ring to Robbie in a game of faro. Then I went back to Calcutta to join in my father's business, and we lost touch." His grin faded. "I looked Robbie up as soon as I got back here, and learned he had been killed. I tried to see you, but your friends gave out that you had disappeared." Francis nodded. After her dismissal by Colonel Burroughs, she had been too proud to seem to be begging from her old friends, and had moved from one cheap lodging to another, trying to find employment. Jared pressed her hand. "I am so very sorry for your loss."

"Not so sorry that you didn't try to take advantage of me," Francis flared up. "You snuck into my room, and stole the ring from me when I was sleeping!"

Jared shrugged. "I couldn't get a word out of you at the tap. And there was something furtive about the way you kept looking around, and covering up the ring. You gave your name out as Taylor. I thought you had stolen the ring from Robert, or his widow."

Francis glared at him. "You only suspected me of stealing the Panchamaabhuta because that's what you would have done yourself. I haven't forgotten your story about the road bandit!"

Jared gave her a mischievous smile. "Harmendra is my great-uncle, and he was a bandit, as I told you. Kamalakshi scandalized the family by taking on an Indian name when she married him. In return, Harmendra got into a more honourable line of work. In time, my father went out to join him in the business, and then I followed." Jared's eyes glittered with amusement. "I hate to disappoint you, but I'm merely a spice importer for a medium-sized British-Indian enterprise. I have to travel a great deal, and the climate where I live is oppressive and unhealthy to say the least." A wistful look came over his face. "Most British women wilt over there, after a few years, and have to go back home. They can't take the heat and the strangeness of India."

Francis tilted up her chin. "I'm not afraid of a little heat. I climbed the Pyrenees on horseback when we marched on France. And I don't mind living abroad either. What I don't like is deceit."

"Indeed?" Jared raised his eyebrows, and Francis flushed, remembering how deceitful she had been herself when she stole the ruby back from him earlier. She bit her lip. "I wouldn't have had to trick you if you hadn't stolen my ruby again. Why did you do it?"

Jared fiddled with his cravat. "Because it was the only way I could keep you at my side. I seemed to be incapable of making an impression on you, but the ring drew you to me like a magnet!"

Francis couldn't help giggling at this. "You must have realized at least that I was attracted to you. Why didn't you just tell me what you were about?"

Jared groaned. "Because I lost my head every time I was with you. Instead of getting out the words, I made love to you, and then you disappeared." His intent green gaze captured hers. "It cut me to the quick when I woke up this morning and found you had gone. You went off with that farmer, and left me flat." Jared frowned. "Then I remembered Kamalakshi's story. When I came of age, she gave me one of the rubies from her comb, telling me that the Panchamaabhuta would lead me to my heart's desire. It's a kind of myth in our family." Jared shrugged. "I thought it was all a load of moonshine until last night."

"Now what do you think?" Francis asked, aware that her mouth was suddenly dry.

Jared drew closer. "I think the Panchamaabhuta brought me a daring, adventurous woman to share my life in India. I want you, Francis."

Francis nodded, speechless with emotion. Jared crushed her against his chest. He kissed her for a long, breathless moment, and then let go. A catcall had sounded behind them.

Francis was suddenly blushingly aware that they were standing in a crowded square. She pulled away from Jared.

His grip only tightened on her. "Promise me you won't run away again."

"I promise," Francis removed the ring and slipped it on to Jared's finger. The square ruby looked perfectly at home there on his firm hand, bronzed by the heat of India.

He grinned. "Father will be pleased."

"I'm looking forward to meeting Aunt Kamalakshi."

He groaned. "She'll be insufferable now. Before I left Calcutta, she told me that when I found the Panchamaabhuta, I'd find my bride."

"The ring called you to me, answering my heart's desire," Francis said.

Jared gave her an impish smile. "Well, thank heavens for that."

Angelique

Margo Maguire

One

Berkshire – July 1819

The honourable Miss Angelique Drummond was so furious she could have spit. But ladies did not spit, either in public or in private, no matter how despicable their fathers might be. Even their deceased fathers.

"I do not understand the rush, Angelique," said Minerva Drummond, querying her after their maid had fallen asleep. "My brother is not yet cold in his grave and here we are, flying off to Berksh—"

"'Tis two weeks since Father passed away, Aunt Minerva. And after what he's done . . ."

Angelique tamped down the grief that threatened to overwhelm her, and allowed her anger to surface. She refused to grieve for her irresponsible, unfaithful sire who'd written his will so that she would be forced to beg for funds from the one man to whom she had not spoken in two years and refused to speak to now.

Her father, Viscount Derington, had lived his life frivolously, squandering his wealth so that he was in possession of very little beyond his entailment at his death. The meagre annuity he'd left his only child would be just enough to keep her and Minerva from the streets, but it was an unforgivable insult that he had not put her in charge of it.

He'd left the funds under the control of the Duke of Heyworth! Angelique ground her teeth in frustration at the thought of dealing with her former fiancé.

"I do not understand why you are so upset."

Angelique looked squarely at her aunt and tried to be patient.

Minerva was her father's elder sister, but never the sharpest needle in the basket. Angelique knew she was still grieving the loss of her younger brother.

"You remember two years ago," Angelique said, "when I – well, when Father and I – accepted Heyworth's marriage offer?"

Minerva's brows came together. "You seemed pleased at first. It seemed such a perfect match, and yet you left London before your nuptials. You upset your father . . ."

Yes, she had.

But his upset was naught compared to her own. Angelique had been enthralled by Heyworth. She'd fancied herself in love with him – the handsomest, most charming gentleman who'd ever requested a dance. He'd courted her diligently, as though she were the most desirable young lady in town. He'd sent her flowers and even a pretty locket on a golden chain. He'd declared his love and admiration, and then proposed.

And yet, two nights before her wedding, she'd learned the unthinkable. All through the weeks of their courtship, while Heyworth had been professing his love for her, he'd been visiting his mistress with some regularity.

Even now, Angelique's blood boiled at the thought of his disingenuous attentions. What a rake. What a rogue. What an absolute scoundrel!

She would never wed such a man – a mirror image of her philandering father – and yet it was he who now managed the trust, the annuity that was Angelique's livelihood. She would not be able to maintain Primrose Cottage – her house in Berkshire – without asking the Duke for funds. It was unthinkable, absolutely untenable, and Angelique intended to challenge her father's will in court. She did not care how long it took, she would wrest control from the odious Duke and live on her own terms.

"Yes, I refused. But Father has seen to it that I must go to Heyworth and beg for my livelihood." As though *that* might cause her to soften towards the man. If anything, it hardened her heart even more.

"My brother and Heyworth's father had strong ties. And he is a duke, besides. You could not have done better—"

"Than to marry a lying womanizer? No, thank you, Aunt."

"But most men . . ." Minerva blushed, hesitant to finish her thought aloud. But Angelique understood clearly. "Well, I understand that 'tis not unusual for a man . . . to . . . uh . . ."

"Which is why I will never wed. I have no intention of tying myself to some . . . some . . . *stud* who wants a wife merely for the purpose of breeding."

"Angelique!"

"'Tis naught but the truth, Aunt Minerva."

And when Angelique had learned of the lightskirt who was a regular fixture in Heyworth's bed, she knew she could not bear knowing that his affections lay elsewhere. That she would not be the woman who owned his heart. Her very own mother had lived through the pain of that, and it had caused her demise at far too young an age. Angelique was not about to suffer the same fate.

She would write to Heyworth and request her funds, but there was no reason to have any closer contact than that.

Brice Colton, Duke of Heyworth, knew there was going to be hell to pay.

And he relished the thought of it.

He rubbed his hands together like an old miser, although he was anything but miserly. As Duke of Heyworth, he'd always made a point to use his vast wealth in many charitable ways, but he was not so inclined to be charitable where Angelique was concerned. He intended to make her beg. For her money, of course.

The thought of Angelique begging for his attentions had not abated since the day of their aborted wedding. He'd been incensed at first, at the very idea of Lord Derington's daughter jilting him. He'd learned about Rathby's lies far too late to rectify the situation, and hadn't been able to find Angelique, either. Later, he learned that she'd fled to Italy – against her father's wishes – on the very day they were supposed to have wed.

She was gorgeous, and any man in his right mind would want her. But it was her fine spirit that had attracted him to begin with. Angel was no missish flower who swooned – or worse, wept – at the slightest hint of social irregularity. She had gumption. She had fire.

She had opinions, by God.

Which made her exactly the kind of wife Heyworth wanted. Though her abrupt departure on the eve of their wedding day caused him no scarcity of embarrassment, he could only admire her courage and determination.

Heyworth had yet to see how determined she would prove to be against the seduction he had started planning the moment he understood the ramifications of her father's will. With Viscount Derington dead, Angelique had no income. The Viscount had no son and no nephews to inherit, so his estate had passed to a distant cousin. There was nothing for Angelique but Primrose Cottage, bequeathed to her by her maternal grandmother, but she was going to need funds in order to maintain it. She could not live there without his largesse.

Heyworth expected her to arrive at any moment. Her father's heir would have taken possession of the house in town, as well as the estate in Shropshire – as decrepit as it was. And Angel could not flee to Italy, not this time. She had no choice but to come to her grandmother's house.

And deal with him.

Perhaps she would believe him this time. Trust him.

Heyworth looked around at the fine appointments in the drawing room. Primrose Cottage was far more than what its name implied. There were five or six bedchambers, and two parlours besides the drawing room in which he sat, as well as several small sitting rooms interspersed with the bedrooms. The kitchen was large and only a tad outdated. Best of all was a very fine portico that overlooked the back gardens, with a large sofa that would be the perfect place to commence his seduction.

He heard the squeaks and clatter of a carriage and waited for it to come to a halt in front of the house. Soon, there were voices and carriage doors slamming. The angel of his dreams was finally here.

"Thank heavens there is a meal already prepared," Angelique said as she entered the foyer. The delicious aroma of a roasted *something* was in the air and it made her stomach growl. "I am famished."

Footmen began to unload the carriage and, with all the commotion, Angelique hardly took note of the butler when he said, "Miss—"

"We'll take supper in the breakfast room, Thornberry. I do not wish to put you and Mrs Thornberry to any additional trouble. 'Tis bad enough that we arrived on such short notice." She removed her gloves while heading towards the small dining chamber, with her aunt right behind her, and stopped suddenly when the last man she wanted to see stepped into her path. Minerva bumped into her, pushing her into his chest.

"Heyworth," she whispered as he caught her elbows. She could not have been more shocked. She was not ready to face him.

"At your service, Miss Drummond."

Angelique tried to step back and compose herself, but failed miserably. Not only was Minerva right on her heels, Angelique had never anticipated seeing the Duke at Primrose Cottage.

He did not release her arms right away, and a powerful frisson of awareness raced up her skin. "I took the liberty of visiting your lovely cottage . . . to assess your financial needs personally."

"I'll just leave you two to . . . uh . . ." Minerva bustled away towards the breakfast room, leaving Angelique to face Heyworth alone. She withdrew her arms from his grasp, and accidentally dropped one of her gloves. They both bent to retrieve it, and inadvertently bumped heads.

One of his big hands darted out to take hold of her once again, catching her to help her keep her balance. This time, he did not release her when she started to move away. He pulled her close and bent his head, his lips barely an inch away from hers. "You are even more beautiful than I remembered."

Angelique clenched her teeth, wishing his voice had lost its power to turn her knees to pudding. He smelled like shaving soap and leather, and his dark-green eyes were undeniably striking. Her breasts touched his chest, causing her breath to catch in her throat. What a husband he would have made . . .

If he hadn't been keeping a lover while professing his love for *her*.

This time, Angelique did pull away. "I sent you a letter requesting quarterly funds, Duke. There was no need for you to travel so far on my behalf."

"Ah, but there was great need."

"I do not see why. You are not my guardian."

"But I would make a very poor trustee indeed if I did not come and see the conditions of the estate in person."

"As I said, it was not necessary. I did send you a letter which – very accurately – spelled out my needs."

If she could have taken back her last two words, she would have, for Heyworth – from the way his gaze focused upon her mouth – was quite obviously reading more into them than she'd intended. He swallowed heavily, drawing attention to his masculine throat and the chiselled line of his jaw. It was entirely unfair of him to possess such a manly chin with a hint of a cleft.

"M-my *requirements* are not extravagant," Angelique said in an attempt to turn his attention to the matter at hand. "The house is in good repair, so my father's annuity will suffice."

"How could you possibly know the condition of the house? You have not been home in, what? Two years?"

Twenty-three months, Angelique thought as her face heated. She had not planned on having to confront him at any time this decade, especially not at such close quarters. And alone.

"My father wrote." But she did not wish to think of those letters or the sharp pang of grief that had settled just below her breastbone. She was angry with him, angry with Heyworth.

"I expect he asked you to return to London."

"No. As a matter of fact, he did not." She'd explained her position quite clearly, so Derington knew better.

"I understand he visited you in Florence."

"Yes. Once."

"But you did not reconcile."

She was not about to dwell upon that awkward visit. Derington had been anything but a model father, and his desire that she wed into the wealthy, prestigious Colton family was pointless. Angelique wanted naught to do with a suitor who kept a mistress while he paid court to her.

"If you don't mind, it has been a long journey. I am tired and famished and would like to retire as soon as possible."

"Of course." He gave a slight bow and allowed her to pass.

Clearly, it had not dawned on Angelique that he would be spending the night under her roof. Heyworth had no intention of giving her an opportunity to toss him out – which she had every right to do. There was an inn only three or four miles from Primrose Cottage. He probably could have acquired a room there, in spite of the crowds that had come to Maidstone for the horse race.

But that would defeat his purpose.

His nerves tingled with awareness of the woman who could still make him burn, just at the sight of her. Even in her unrelenting black muslin gown, she was magnificent, her doe's eyes flashing fire at him as she spoke, her loose blonde curls shimmering in the candlelight. She'd given no overt indication of losing her composure, but Heyworth had noted the racing pulse in her delicate neck.

How he'd craved a taste of those plump lips.

He turned abruptly and went in search of his valet. The man was never far away, and Heyworth quickly located him. "I'm going out for a long ride while Miss Drummond and her aunt get settled in. Make yourself scarce as well, Grayson. I do not want the lady to realize we're billeted here just yet."

It was underhanded, he knew. But so had been the reason she'd fled two years ago, too. The unscrupulous Lord Rathby had spent a full year trying to injure Heyworth in retaliation for an incident at the races, and the bastard had succeeded beyond his wildest expectations. Rathby had to have known that Angelique would be horrified by his deceitful "revelations" and cry off their wedding.

It had been the most humiliating day of his life, learning *from the newspapers*, for God's sake, that his fiancée had fled to Italy rather than stay and marry him. Heyworth's anger had known no bounds. He'd searched for Rathby only to discover that the blackguard had gone to ground after doing his damage.

After his initial fury passed, Heyworth had quickly realized that Rathby was not the priority. He had to go after Angelique – he had no doubt he could convince her of his innocence. And Rathby's despicable treachery.

He made arrangements to follow Angelique to Italy, but on the morning he was to depart, his mother had fallen ill. There'd been no question of leaving London then, and the dowager duchess had lingered near death for a month before succumbing to a series of strokes that finally caused her demise.

And when the mourning period was over, it seemed that one thing after another prevented Heyworth from going after Angelique. He finally put his foot down and decided that everything else, no matter how crucial, could wait.

He'd gone to speak to Angelique's father only a week before his death, informing the man of his intention to track down his daughter and bring her home to England. And then marry her. He hadn't anticipated that she'd have to come home for Derington's funeral.

Angelique had fallen asleep within moments of going to bed. And yet now she lay awake, her encounter with Heyworth plaguing her dreams. She thought about all she'd lost two years before. If Heyworth had not been so deceitful, Angelique would have married him happily, for she'd desired him as she'd wanted no other.

And it seemed that had not changed in the least.

The fact that she could not control her attraction for Heyworth, in spite of all that had happened, was beyond annoying. Fortunately, he was gone now, so she would be able to put him out of her thoughts as she'd finally managed to do in Italy. Until the next time she needed money, that is. Every farthing she required to live on would have to come from the Duke and, judging by their earlier interchange, she would no doubt have to go through the same rubbish she'd had to endure earlier.

She was twenty-four years old and, as Aunt Minerva was so fond of reminding her, well on her way to being quite solidly on the shelf. And now she was beholden to a man whose very presence made her heart quake in her chest.

It would have been so easy to lean into the comfort of his body. But Angelique again recalled the conversation she'd had with Lord Rathby only two days before she was to marry Heyworth. She was grateful that at least Rathby had been honest with her, unlike her fiancé and her own father. Neither of them must have thought she'd mind having a husband who kept a mistress in Chelsea.

Well, she did mind, and she was not about to go through the same misery her mother had. Luckily, she'd learned of Heyworth's duplicity before she'd made any vows to him.

In need of a glass of milk to soothe her nerves, Angelique got out of bed and pulled a light wrapper over her chemise. Her nerves might be in a tizzy, but the house was quiet, and comfortably warm. Angelique crept down the stairs and headed in the direction of the kitchen, only to stop cold when she smelled smoke coming from the portico.

A fire would be disastrous. Angelique ran quickly towards the smell, afraid that Thornberry might have left one of his cheroots burning.

"You!" She stopped short when she saw Heyworth stretched out on one of the padded chaises.

He moved like an agile predator, coming to his feet without the slightest effort, and moving – stalking – towards her. He'd discarded his coat and collar, and had rolled his shirtsleeves to his elbows. In the pale lamplight, Angelique could easily appreciate the dusting of dark hair on his forearms, and his powerful hands. He tossed away the cheroot and her mouth went dry with feminine awareness.

Angelique felt next to naked. Her chemise was nearly transparent, and her dressing gown hardly better. As he came towards her, she felt her bare toes curl on the cool floor.

"I knew your hair would be even more lovely when you let it down." He touched her shoulder, but only to pick up a lock of her hair, which he rubbed between two of his fingers.

"I thought you'd left . . . gone to the inn."

He shook his head slightly. "I'm not going to let you go so easily this time."

Every nerve ending in Angelique's body was fully alert and clamouring for his touch. And then she remembered why she'd gotten off so easily two years before.

"I was very sorry to learn of your mother's death, Heyworth. It couldn't have been long after . . . after we . . . after I . . ."

"Thank you," he said, stepping even closer. "I was in no position to come after you in Italy then. But, rest assured, had circumstances been different, I would have."

His eyelashes were long and black, the perfect frame for his persuasive eyes. Angelique swallowed when he slid his hand along her jaw and cupped the side of her face. She tried to back away.

But her feet would not move. His touch felt like balm on a raw wound, far too compelling to disregard. He lowered his head and touched his lips to hers, brushing lightly against her mouth as he'd done during the earliest days of their courtship.

Angelique had tried to forget the shuddering pleasure of those light kisses, but her dreams had often reminded her of his sensual power. Far too often.

She wanted him now, wanted his arms around her, his brawny chest against her breasts, his loins against her own. She shuddered, and he suddenly deepened their kiss.

A small cry came from the back of her throat when he drew her close, changing the angle of his head for deeper penetration. His tongue touched hers, and Angelique's knees went weak, though she felt protected by the heat of his body, and his powerful embrace. His arousal was thick and heavy against her pelvis and, when he moved, a sensation of pure pleasure skittered up her spine.

Her wrapper slid off her shoulders, and Angelique yearned for more. *No, less.* Much less clothing between them. She wanted to feel Heyworth's bare skin against hers, their legs twining together. She'd dreamed of it often enough.

He lowered one strap of her chemise, and Angelique cried out with amazement when he cupped her bare breast.

"Aye, 'tis soft and full as I always imagined it. You are so perfect, my sweet."

Angelique let out a low sigh when he bent down and touched the swollen peak with his tongue. He held her securely, but she felt as though she were floating in a sea of sensation, of need. She wanted it all – it seemed as though she'd always wanted to lie with him, to finally share her physical passions with the man she loved.

"Rathby lied, Angel," he whispered, his voice harsh. He feathered kisses up to her neck. "He's a scoundrel who doesn't deserve half the credence you've given him."

Angelique pulled away suddenly, as though a pitcher of frigid seawater had been dumped upon her head. *What was she doing?* Allowing her heart to be broken yet again? By the same man who'd nearly destroyed her two years before?

Disgusted by the whimper she heard coming from her own throat, she covered her breast with her chemise and whirled away, then made haste to the staircase. It took only seconds to scamper upstairs, where she quickly entered her bedchamber, closing the door tightly behind her. If she'd had a key, she would have locked it.

Whether it was to prevent Heyworth from entering, or to keep herself from making the same foolish mistakes with him again, she was not sure.

Two

Heyworth was up early, but he didn't enter the breakfast room until Angelique and her aunt had gone in and begun their meal. He wanted to give Angelique no possible avenue for avoidance. Of him.

"Good morning, ladies," he said, drinking in the sight of her.

"Your Grace," said the elder Miss Drummond, "I had no idea you were still here. Why, I . . ."

"There is a horse race tomorrow down at Maidstone. Which means, of course, there are no rooms to be had within twenty miles." He took a seat across from Angelique, who would not look at him. Still, he took satisfaction in the blush that rose on her cheeks, for she was obviously recalling the intensely sensuous interlude they'd shared the night before.

"I hadn't heard," said Minerva. She turned to Angelique. "Did you know of it?"

"No, Aunt."

"Well, it has naught to do with us," the older woman remarked.

Heyworth did not take his eyes from Angelique as he stirred his tea and half listened to her aunt discourse on the subject of escaping to the country only to find the crowds of London encroaching on their little corner of Berkshire. He'd never spent a morning with Angelique before, their courtship always taking the conventional course: afternoon rides in the park, balls and soirées in the evenings.

In the time before their aborted wedding day, Heyworth had imagined vividly the mornings they would soon spend together in bed – making love before the servants brought their breakfast, feeding each other tender morsels between heated kisses, then making love again before they arose to face the day.

She wanted him. Heyworth had no doubt whatsoever of that. If only he'd kept his silence last night, she would never have recalled the reason for her precipitous abandonment of their nuptials. He'd have driven her as mad with desire as she made him, and they'd have consummated their bond. Then Angelique would have had no choice but to make use of the special licence Heyworth had had the foresight to procure before coming to Berkshire.

But, dash it, he wanted Angelique to trust him. It had been far too easy for Rathby to convince her of Heyworth's alleged misstep. He did not understand how she had so easily believed Rathby's lies rather than his honest declaration of love.

For he did love her. He'd buried himself in his work – and his grief – and tried to forget her two years before, but it had been impossible. He was determined not to err this time. For he knew how much he had to lose.

Angelique was never happier to have an interruption than when Squire Stillwater arrived. She had slept badly the night before, and felt exhausted – from the funeral, the travel, the late night nearly succumbing to Heyworth's seductions.

She rose quickly from her seat when Thornberry announced him, intending to go into the drawing room to receive their old family friend. Her grandmother and Mrs Stillwater had been close in years past, and she had always been more than kind to Angelique.

"Bring him in, Thornberry," said Heyworth, stopping Angelique in her tracks. "Set another place and let him join us here."

She scowled at Heyworth, looking squarely at him for the first time since he'd entered the breakfast room. She had not trusted herself to do so before.

And with good reason. He was outfitted as any gentleman might be, in a green waistcoat that perfectly matched his eyes, a black cutaway frock coat, and dun-coloured trews. And yet he filled them out as no other gentleman could do. His raw masculinity was beyond tempting, but Angelique wanted nothing to do with a man who could lie so convincingly to her.

Her father had made a far too frequent practice of it with her mother. Women, drink and cards . . . Viscount Derington had done it all, and lied to Suzette through his teeth about his women and his gaming losses. His behaviour and the pain it caused her mother had taught her well. Angelique had no intention of losing her heart to a scoundrel like her father. When Rathby had told her the truth about

Heyworth, she'd picked up her skirts and fled as quickly as possible to Florence, where she had friends.

"Good morning, good morning!" said Squire Stillwater as he entered the breakfast room.

He was barely as tall as Angelique, had the ruddiest complexion and brightest smile of anyone she'd ever known. The sight of him there, in Primrose Cottage, brought back memories of earlier days, and Angelique felt a deep twinge of grief for the loss of her father. She hadn't shed a tear for him, and yet now she was on the verge.

She took a sip of tea to clear the sudden burning in her throat.

"Oh dear," said the Squire. "I fear I have interrupted your breakfast."

"Not at all," said Heyworth, as though he owned Primrose Cottage. Angelique was temporarily glad of his proprietary manner, for it changed the cheerless direction of her thoughts. "Please join us."

"Alas, but no. I cannot. We heard word of the Miss Drummonds' arrival, and Mrs Stillwater bade me to ride over first thing . . . well, nearly first thing—" he chuckled "—to invite you to sup with us this evening at Tapton Manor. We had no idea Your Grace was here as well. You've come down for the race?"

"Aye," Heyworth replied. Angelique looked at him sharply. Hadn't he come to Berkshire . . . well, for *her*?

"The festivities are in full swing. Perhaps you'll go into town and enjoy the fair – a real medieval exhibition with . . . Oh, I beg your pardon, my dear." Stillwater seemed to take note of Angelique's mourning attire all at once. He and his wife had travelled to London for the funeral, of course, but they were not compelled in any way to observe a mourning period for Viscount Derington. "Please accept my sincere apologies . . . I should never have mentioned—"

"Thank you, Squire. Though we cannot attend any of the activities in town, my aunt and I would be pleased to join you this evening. 'Twill be an intimate gathering?"

"Oh yes, of course. Our granddaughter, Caroline, and her husband have come down, and we'll have a few neighbours as well." He turned towards Heyworth. "And of course, Your Grace, if you would care to join us."

Heyworth gave a slight bow of acquiescence. "I would be honoured to escort Miss Drummond and her aunt."

"Esc—?" Angelique closed her mouth tightly and bit her tongue. She needed no escort, especially not an arrogant nobleman who quite obviously believed that women ought to worship at the sight of him. As *she* had done last night, much to her chagrin.

She knew better now.

It was truly unfortunate that Angelique was unable to come into town and enjoy the lively fair with its jesters and jugglers, its roving musicians and craftsmen's booths. Heyworth remembered that she enjoyed such entertainments. They'd attended plays in Drury Lane and concerts in Vauxhall Gardens. They'd played cricket in the park in May of that fateful spring when Heyworth had courted her, and ridden together along the pretty bridle paths near Primrose Cottage.

But with her father so recently in his grave, she could not indulge in such frivolity. Heyworth knew it was not going to be easy for her, not that she'd been close to her sire in recent years. Derington had been an inept father, and an even worse husband, if the rumours were to be believed. He'd run through his own inheritance and, as far as Heyworth could ascertain, the Viscount had left only a small annuity to support Angelique and her aunt.

There'd been no dowry two years before, when Heyworth had offered for her, but that had been no obstacle to his intentions. She might have been destitute for all he cared. He had wanted Angelique and Angelique alone.

That had not changed. If anything, he wanted her more today than he had two years before.

It was a particularly warm day even here in the country, and Heyworth was glad to have escaped the heat and stench of London. He felt confident of his mission in Berkshire, convincing Angelique of his sincere intentions and winning her as his wife. There was nothing that mattered more to him.

A large number of London's fashionable set had arrived for tomorrow's race, and Heyworth knew he wouldn't have been able to hire a room even if he wanted one. He stabled his horse and took in the sights of Maidstone while he walked through the crowded lanes. He had one purpose in mind, but was interrupted by a sour greeting from his one-time nemesis. Rathby.

Heyworth had forgotten Rathby owned a country estate nearby. The bastard had been on friendly terms with Derington and his family, which was the reason he'd had the opportunity to tell his lies to Angelique. And why she had believed him.

"Heyworth, what are you doing here?" There was no mistaking the hostility in Rathby's voice.

"I've come down for the race, of course," Heyworth replied as smoothly as he could. He had no intention of mentioning Angelique's presence at Primrose Cottage, although it was only a matter of time before Rathby discovered it for himself. "Have you bribed anyone this time round, Rathby?"

The other man coloured deeply. "You have your nerve, Heyworth. Naught was ever proved."

"No, but you forget – I saw you with my own eyes. Paying off a jockey. My guess is that you're far more careful not to be seen these days."

The Earl sputtered, and Heyworth brushed past him before the man could refute the charge, his mind whirling with possibilities. Rathby's presence could very well work to Heyworth's advantage, if he played him just right.

Solidifying a plan in his mind, the Duke entered a little shop of novelties. Several other shoppers were looking at the wares displayed on the shelves while the proprietor looked on. Heyworth browsed the offerings, bent on finding just the right gift for Angelique.

He spied it almost immediately.

"Would you mind," he said to the shop owner, pointing to a lovely music box on a high shelf.

"Of course, My Lord," said the man, who moved a ladder into place and climbed up to retrieve the box that featured a pair of dancing dolls on its top – a blonde lady, and the gentleman as dark as Heyworth. "They dance while it plays a right pretty tune, sir."

He handed it to Heyworth, who gave the key on the bottom several twists. When he set it on the counter, the dancers moved around a clever little track on top while the box played a tinkling version of the Mozart waltz that had been his first dance with Angelique.

"How much?"

Heyworth paid the man and watched him wrap it, then he went back to the stable for his horse. He had a short visit to make at Squire Stillwater's manor before returning to Primrose Cottage. And a favour to ask.

"Tell my aunt I've gone to the lake to read," Angelique called to her maid as she stuffed a book into a small satchel alongside a spare shift, a thin blanket and a towel. Fortunately, Minerva was napping. She would be horrified to know Angelique's true intentions.

Well, it was nearly as hot in Berkshire as it was in London, and Angelique had become accustomed to swimming on sultry days while in Italy. So even if Minerva wouldn't approve, Angelique had no qualms about taking a short dip in the private lake nearby. She hoped the cool water would help clear her head.

She wanted to dispel all memories of Heyworth's touch. She would never marry the man, and such intimacies were absolutely unacceptable. She couldn't succumb to him again. The bond between them was merely physical attraction. There was no substance to his intentions – no honesty beyond the pleasure of the moment. Angelique refused to become the same kind of wretched victim her mother had been, waiting for the man she loved to favour her with his presence. Always wondering if her husband's assertion of love was sincere and true, or yet another falsehood from an inveterate womanizer.

The lake was small, and its location a secluded little glade, the perfect haven in which to spend a warm, sunny afternoon with her dismal thoughts. It was quite different from the lake near her little villa in Florence. There was hardly any beach at all, with an unkempt lawn and trees growing right up to the water's edge.

It was where her father had taught her to swim when she was a child, when he had found it amusing to pretend to be a father.

It was peaceful and quiet at the lake, but Angelique found it painful to think of her father, of the weeks he'd been ill before she'd come home. She hadn't believed his first letter, and it wasn't until the third that she'd realized he was in earnest. He was dying.

She'd been so damnably stubborn.

The sun shone brightly through the trees, and bees buzzed about the clover in the grass. Derington had once been a devoted father. In those days, he hadn't gone running off every night to chase skirts and lose his money at the gaming tables. Angelique didn't know what had caused him to change, but the change had not endeared him to her. She had barely acknowledged him as her father.

She forced aside her upsetting memories and put her satchel down beneath a tree. She pressed the blanket to her breast and smothered her sorrow, refusing to shed the tears that threatened. There was no point. She could not imagine that he'd have wanted her to weep, anyway.

Swallowing the thickness in her throat, Angelique spread out the blanket she'd brought. She sat down and removed her shoes and stockings, then took a quick look around to be sure she was truly alone before unbuttoning her bodice.

In a few short moments, she was completely undressed, but for the thin cotton chemise she wore under all her dull, black clothes.

She stepped into the water and found it refreshingly cool. After she waded out deeper, she lay back and floated, gazing up at the clear blue sky while she tried once again to empty her mind of all its troubling thoughts.

But her melancholy would not abate. Nor would her questions. Angelique could not understand why her father had thought it acceptable to make Heyworth trustee of her funds. When her father had come to Florence to chastise her for leaving England, Angelique had made it perfectly clear that she would never wed the Duke. Obviously, Derington thought they were well matched, in spite of Heyworth's philandering ways. Her father must have believed that renewed contact with the Duke to work out the disbursement of the annuity would result in a new engagement.

It would not.

A bleak sob escaped Angelique and she came to her feet. Her father did not deserve her tears, yet her eyes filled and she found herself weeping over his loss. Whatever had occurred between her mother and father, Derington had been her papa. He'd taken her on pony rides and bought her sweets. He'd carried her on his shoulders and pushed her in the swing behind the cottage.

The guilt for leaving him alone during the last months of his life had been niggling at the edges of her awareness, but now it overtook her. She stumbled out of the water, feeling anything but refreshed. When she reached her blanket, she fell to her knees, then lay down and pressed her face into the soft cloth and cried as though her heart was broken.

At first, when Heyworth had come upon Angelique wading out of the lake, he'd thought himself the most fortunate of men. Her chemise was nearly transparent, allowing him a view of her perfection. Her every move was a seduction, her high, full breasts swaying as she left the cover of the water, her long graceful legs stepping from the lake. He felt a deeply visceral reaction at the sight of her.

And then he realized she was weeping.

Her indifferent exterior had been just that – an exterior. It was clear, in spite of her anger with Derington, she felt the loss of her father deeply.

Heyworth felt like a cad for ogling her while she was in such obvious distress. Without considering how she would react, he went to her, knelt beside her and put his hand on her back, gently caressing her shoulder. She turned to him suddenly and clung to his shirt, allowing him to hold her as she wept against his chest.

"H-he made me s-so angry," she sobbed.

"Aye, I know, love."

"He was unfaithful t-to my m-mother."

Heyworth knew that, too. But he kept his silence.

"And h-he made *you* tr-trustee."

"Hush, my darling. We'll work that out."

She looked up at him with the most beautiful teary eyes he'd ever seen. "H-how? You have complete—"

"No. Whatever you need – 'tis yours to use as you see fit."

She blinked and a tear rolled down her cheek. "R-really?"

His heart twisted in his chest at the sight of her red-rimmed eyes and the tears that fell from them. "Of course. I never meant to keep you from your inheritance, Angel." He pressed a kiss to her forehead, content to merely cradle the woman he loved in his arms.

Three

Angelique slept like the dead for an hour or so, after walking back to the house with Heyworth. He had not attempted to kiss her or touch her in any way after she pulled herself together, and she . . .

She could hardly credit that she'd been disappointed. She didn't want him to touch her. And yet . . .

Heyworth's caresses were unlike anything Angelique had ever known. He was strong yet gentle, insistent but patient. She yearned for his embrace, but did not want to encourage his attentions. He'd told her she would have control over the annuity, when her father had given *him* jurisdiction over it.

It was all too much. She did not want to grieve for a father who'd hurt her mother so deeply, and who had seen nothing wrong with tying her to a fiancé who was unfaithful. And yet that fiancé was being so kind to her now.

Heyworth handed Minerva into the enclosed carriage, and when Angelique looked round, she saw that there was no horse saddled and ready for him. "You are not riding?"

He gave a shake of his head, and a lock of his dark hair fell across his forehead. She longed to touch it, to thread her fingers through the thick mass of it.

"It will be far cooler outside the carriage," she said. She did not want to spend the next half-hour in such close quarters with him.

"You aren't afraid of having me near, are you, Angel?"

"Of course not." It was a lie. Even with Minerva present, Angelique could not dispel her ridiculous longing for him.

"Very good. Shall we?"

He helped her into the carriage and off they went. Angelique tried to keep her attention on the passing scenery outside her window, but she felt his gaze on her and, whenever the carriage went over a rough patch, his knees bumped into hers, sending shivers of longing through her.

"Will you attend the race tomorrow, Your Grace?" Minerva asked.

"I doubt it," he replied, and Angelique looked up at him, puzzled by the contradiction. "I have other plans."

"Oh? Will you be returning to London?"

He looked right into Angelique's eyes. "I don't think so. Not just yet."

"There's no reason for you to stay any longer, Your Grace," Angelique said, in spite of the conflicting emotions churning within her. "Once you release the funds my aunt and I will need to live on—"

"That was done before I came down to Berkshire."

The world shifted suddenly. "*What?*"

"I had my solicitor transfer control of your funds yesterday morning. A letter was sent, but it seems you left London before it could be delivered to you."

"But then why—"

"Angelique, do not badger His Grace," said Minerva. "'Tis perfectly clear that he came all this way to tell you personally."

That could not be true. He'd sent her a letter. Angelique bit her lip in consternation. If he hadn't come for the horse race, or to talk to her about the annuity, then he must have come specifically because of their broken engagement.

Had he changed? According to Lord Rathby, a certain Mrs Dumont was a frequent recipient of Heyworth's attentions. At least it had been a Mrs Dumont two years ago. Did she dare hope that he'd changed his ways? That he was ready to become a responsible, faithful spouse?

She took in the strong line of his jaw and his intense green eyes and wished it were so. She feared she still loved him, and knew that marriage between them could be wonderful.

Or a complete disaster.

When they arrived at Tapton Manor, Angelique was quite surprised to encounter Lord Rathby. Yet his presence made perfect sense, for he had an estate nearby where her father had often gone shooting. Of course he was on friendly terms with the Stillwaters, but Angelique had not seen or spoken to him in the two years since the fateful conversation that had resulted in her abrupt departure from England.

She felt awkward facing him now, but the same was not true of Heyworth. Obviously, the Duke was unaware of Rathby's part in her abrupt departure and the cancellation of their wedding, or he would not have been quite so cordial with the Earl.

And yet his cordiality had a strange edge to it, something Angelique could not quite define.

Heyworth took her elbow, as he drew her into the house. Angelique allowed herself to enjoy his innocent touch, nearly as comforting as the caresses he'd given her at the lake. She had never felt more attracted to him than she did at that moment.

When she was in Italy, it had been far easier to deny everything she'd felt for him. It was nearly impossible now.

She'd wanted him during their engagement, had lived for their stolen kisses and the promise of pleasures she could not even imagine after they were wed. Angelique tried to curb her longing for his touch, but feared she still loved him. She feared she did not have the strength or the will to reject him again. If he took her into his arms, or kissed her . . .

She would quite possibly melt.

Mrs Stillwater embraced her lightly. "You look pale, my girl. Come inside and sit down."

"I'm quite all right, Mrs Stillwater," Angelique said. "'Tis very good of you to invite us."

Lord Rathby came and bent over her hand. "My sincere condolences, Miss Drummond, and my apologies as well, for my absence at your father's funeral. I was in York and did not hear of his passing until it was too late."

"'Tis quite all right, Lord Rathby. You were a good friend to my father."

"Aye," he said quietly and, when he slipped away to the far side of the room, Angelique suddenly wondered why he had bothered to seek her out two years before, to tell her about Heyworth's perfidy. He'd been so earnest . . . and yet now, he was not quite so bold in his demeanour. His gaze darted towards Heyworth, as though worried that the Duke would suddenly divine who had tattled on him two years earlier.

Angelique made a study of him as the conversation flowed around her. It wasn't as though Rathby himself had been vying for her hand, for he had not been one of her suitors during that season. What difference would her marriage to Heyworth have made to him?

Would he have had some reason to lie to her?

A leaden feeling of dread centred in the pit of her stomach. She'd never had any reason to doubt Heyworth before Lord Rathby's tale of loose women. Rathby might have held a grudge or had some other reason for wanting to damage Heyworth. And yet Angelique had jumped to the conclusion that her betrothed was just as unprincipled as her father. She'd been afraid to trust him, afraid to trust that he was different.

Her mind reeled with possibilities.

"Do you plan to stay at Maidstone for very long, Your Grace?" Mrs Stillwater asked the Duke.

"No. Only until tomorrow."

"Then back to London, is it?" the Squire asked.

"For a short while, then I plan on travelling."

"How lovely. Where will you go?"

"To Greece. My agents are en route now, securing lodgings and a cruising yacht for my use."

A little wave of panic came over Angelique. He could not go. She needed to speak to him, to ask him some pointed questions, something she should have stayed and done two years before. She'd been a rash and headstrong fool.

"Such a romantic trip," said Mrs Stillwater. "I would have enjoyed travelling at one time, but now I'm quite comfortable in our old house, and glad to have our grandchildren nearby."

"How do you find Maidstone, Ange—Miss Drummond?" asked her childhood friend, Caroline. "It has been some time since you were here last, has it not?"

Angelique nodded, swallowing her agitation and turning her attention to Caroline – now Mrs Gedding, a vicar's wife. Caroline was only a year older than Angelique, and yet she and her vicar husband already had two children. Angelique felt yet another troubling emotion, a pang of longing for what she'd foregone when she'd left England. Left Heyworth.

She needed to speak to him alone, to ask him . . . Dear heavens, there was so much to ask, starting with his forgiveness. "Primrose Cottage is just how I remembered it," she said, looking for an opportunity to take him aside, but finding none. "'Tis a lovely respite from the close confines of London."

Caroline glanced at her father. "There is quite the crush in town, isn't there, Papa?"

"Aye, but we will not be part of it, thank heavens." He turned to Heyworth. "Your Grace, will you escort the elder Miss Drummond in to supper?"

"Of course," Heyworth said, taking Minerva's arm. They all retired to the dining room, where Angelique was directed to a seat beside the Duke.

She'd had no good reason to doubt him two years before. He was far too kind to her now, and his civility towards Rathby rankled.

The Duke hardly looked at her, though his eyes flashed with intelligence and awareness. He seemed tense, his powerful body poised for action, while Lord Rathby remained nearly silent all through the meal. When it was over, Squire Stillwater invited the men to retire to the veranda to smoke, and Angelique resigned herself to waiting until they returned to Primrose Cottage for the private moment she intended to have with him.

It would be now or never. Heyworth was counting on the Squire to make sure that he and Rathby were left alone for a few minutes. And Mrs Stillwater was to bring Angelique into the small sitting room adjacent to the veranda. From there, she would be able to hear the men's conversation.

Heyworth sensed that Rathby was about to bolt. The Earl had done all that etiquette required after discovering that the Duke would also be dining at the Stillwaters' and now he could leave. He wouldn't want to spend any more time than necessary with the man who had not only witnessed his attempt to rig a horse race, but seen to it that he was censured by the jockey club and banned from the races for a full two seasons.

Heyworth hoped Mrs Stillwater had had time to bring in Angelique. He stood in front of the door, blocking Rathby's path of escape, and blew out a plume of cheroot smoke. "Have you got a favourite tomorrow, Rathby?"

Rathby hesitated, eyeing Heyworth with a measure of extremely justified mistrust. It was mutual. "I certainly wouldn't tell *you*. I don't want you betting against me."

"You don't *ever* want to bet against *me*, Rathby."

The man's complexion darkened. "Oh? My bet that Miss Drummond would believe my tales of your duplicity destroyed you, did it not?"

"Nearly, Rathby. You lied to Miss Drummond, but I am about to rectify that matter."

The door burst open and Angelique came through, her expression one of heated astonishment. She looked at Rathby with complete disgust. "You . . . you lied to me?"

Rathby tossed his cheroot to the ground and started to walk past, but Angelique grabbed his sleeve. "Tell me the truth now. When you came to me and told me about Heyworth's mistress . . ."

"Aye. You heard me admit it." He cast a hateful glance at Heyworth, looking more like a petulant schoolboy than a peer of the realm. "'Twas a lie. All of it. I wanted my revenge, and I got it, by God."

He made an abrupt turn and walked round the outside of the house, leaving Angelique and Heyworth alone. Angelique was speechless. Heyworth approached her and took her gently into his arms.

"I was such a fool," she finally said against his chest.

"No." He slid his hands down her back, pulling her closer. "He was your father's friend. You couldn't know—"

"I should have known." She felt tears fill her eyes for the second time that day. "I should have trusted you. You were always honest with me, but I was afraid – afraid to trust my own judgment."

"'Tis all right, Angel. Rathby's lies are in the past."

A well of despair opened up inside her. "B-but you're leaving for Greece—"

"Not without you, love." He stepped back and, keeping her at arm's length, looked into her eyes. "Marry me now. Tonight. It seems impossible, but I love you more than I did two years ago. I don't want to go another day without you as my wife."

Angelique sniffled. "I have no dowry. And I'm in mourning."

"You had no dowry two years ago, either. It didn't matter."

Angelique was shocked. He'd wanted her – a disreputable viscount's daughter – even without a dowry? "But the banns—"

He pulled a folded sheet of vellum from inside his coat and showed it to her. Angelique read the special licence quickly, then looked up at him, gazing deeply into his eyes.

"I love you quite desperately, you know," she whispered.

"I know. That's why you had to flee England."

She raised her brow in question.

He caressed the side of her face. "Because I had the power to hurt you quite dreadfully. I promise I never will, my darling."

"Oh, Brice, I love you. These past two years without you have been abominable."

He tipped his head down and touched his lips to hers in a light kiss that held the promise of so much more. If only they could leave the party and return alone to Primrose Cottage.

"We're together again. 'Tis all that matters, Angel."

Angelique slid her arms round his neck and kissed him deeply. He growled and pulled her against his body, claiming her as his own, finally.

"Shall we go and see if Squire Stillwater's son-in-law will perform the service?" he asked when they finally broke apart.

"Oh yes, my love," Angelique whispered. "'Tis all I've ever wanted.

Like None Other

Caroline Linden

One

Number 12, George Street was a lovely home. It was new, built only in the last ten years, and contained all the modern conveniences, with well-fitted windows and floors that only squeaked a little and chimneys with impeccable draw. It was part of a row of terraced houses, with a neat little garden out back and smart marble steps with a blue-painted iron railing in front. Emmaline Bowen loved her little home, even though it wasn't nearly as grand as the country manor where she'd once lived as Lady Bowen. Unlike Bowen Lodge, this house was all hers. She liked being able to paint the walls any colour she liked, from the bright yellow of her small dining room to the vivid turquoise of her bedroom walls. It was a joy to open her eyes in the morning and see that blue, brighter than a robin's egg. She often lay still for a moment, thinking that heaven must be such a colour. She said as much to her maid one morning, when the girl brought her morning tea.

"Heaven, milady?" Jane blinked suspiciously.

Emma waved one hand, leaning back against her pillows and sipping the hot tea. "Just look at the sky! Can't you see what I mean?"

Jane peered out the window. "I see clouds. Great, rolling grey ones. The blue won't last today."

"You're old before your time," Emma told her, putting down the tea and rising from the bed. "If there are clouds on the horizon, I'd better get out and enjoy the sun while it lasts."

"Won't be long, from the looks of it," muttered Jane.

Emma ignored her, going to the wardrobe and opening the doors. She took out her favourite dress, the yellow-striped morning gown with pale-green ribbons. "I'll finish my breakfast in the garden," she said. Jane merely nodded, with one more jaundiced glance out the window, and left. Emma shook her head as she unbuttoned her nightgown; poor Jane, to be so dour at such a young age. She must not have had a chance to learn one of life's hard truths – that sometimes the only way to keep from raging in bitterness was to smile and laugh, even if you must force yourself to do it.

By the time she went downstairs, armoured against any greyness of the day with her bright yellow dress, Jane had put together a tray with breakfast. Carrying her own small tea tray, Emma led the way into the garden, where the sun was blindingly bright. Only if she shaded her eyes and squinted at the horizon could she see the line of grey lurking in the distance. Like the sun, she ignored those dark clouds. She set down her tray on a small table in the dazzling light.

"You'll want a parasol, ma'am," said Jane. "And a shawl."

"I shall want neither," replied Emma firmly. "I mean to enjoy the sun this morning. But since you dread the coming rain, please go open the windows to air the house before the deluge comes."

Jane peered at the sky. "Before dinner," she said grimly. "Thunderstorms, with lightning and flooding."

"Go on," said Emma, trying not to laugh. The maid cast her an aggrieved look before heading back inside. Emma settled into her seat and picked up her tea. She raised her face to the sun. Just a few minutes couldn't freckle her complexion too badly, and she would regret missing the chance if Jane's predictions of thunderstorms came true.

As she sat in peaceful solitude, her ears caught the clink of china and the rustle of a newspaper from over the fence. Her neighbour must also be enjoying his breakfast outdoors. A moment later a deep voice called, "Is that you, Lady Bowen?"

"Yes, Captain Quentin," she called back. "Good morning."

"Indeed it is, although my man assures me it will rain later."

She smiled. "My maid predicted the same thing. Perhaps they are comparing notes before we wake."

The sound of his chuckle drifted across the high fence. "Ah, but Godfrey looks forward to the rain. It will wash the steps so he does not have to sweep them."

"He must mention it to Jane, who does not."

"He will be sure to tell her about the hurricane we encountered in the Caribbean Sea."

"Perhaps he had better not speak to her, then," Emma replied at once. "She will be certain it is a hurricane approaching, and wish to board up the windows."

The Captain laughed. Emma felt the rich, deep sound right

through her body. Captain Quentin had a very nice laugh. It went well with his voice. It was a lovely coincidence her neighbour liked spending as much time in his garden as she did in hers. He had done so many things she had never dreamed of: sailed around the Horn of Africa, been to India, seen the fantastical creatures who lived far out at sea, weathered storms and pirates and all manner of adventure. When he asked – very politely – about her own life, Emma had to laugh, a little embarrassed. She'd had no adventures. She had married sensibly, not very happily, and never travelled more than fifty miles from Sussex. They often talked over the wall that divided their properties. The Captain would tell her about his adventures, and she would sit and listen, letting herself drift out of her quiet little life and imagine seeing what he had seen.

And if the sound of his voice sometimes seemed to weave a spell over her, and made her think he was taking her with him to these fantastic places . . . She didn't let herself think too much about that. He was being polite and friendly, sharing his tales, and she was being an idiot, wondering what it would be like to swim in the tropical ocean. To feel the warm water – as warm as any bath, he said, and as clear and blue as the sky – sluicing over her skin. To lie on the sand and stare at the stars on a moonless night. To feel the wind on her face as they sailed into the unknown.

But that's what she thought of, and what made her smile, safely hidden on her side of the brick wall. The Captain would never know.

"When did you encounter a hurricane?" she asked, as much to hear him talk as to know the story. "Are they really as terrible as the stories say?"

"They are worse, and yet magnificent. The ocean itself seems to turn on you, as if it would swallow you up, tear you to pieces and fling you to the corners of the world. A man discovers his true feelings about life and death when faced by a hurricane, since he is balanced perfectly between the two, and only the storm can decide which will be his lot . . ."

Emma settled back into her chair and closed her eyes.

Two

Number 14, George Street was a grim little house, with narrow stairs and low ceilings and all sorts of things meant to be conveniences, which were never very convenient. After a neat, efficient ship's interior, Phineas Quentin could hardly believe the carelessness that obviously had gone into building this row of terraced houses in the growing city of London, for all that it was almost new. He had bought it upon his retirement from the Navy five months ago, thinking he would soon get used to being settled ashore, and instead found himself missing the ocean more than ever. He missed the wide-open sky above him, and the rolling expanse of ocean below him. He missed the camaraderie of officers aboard ship, and the regimented routine of life on a frigate. Now he found himself living mostly alone, in a dark little house, crowded right up close to its neighbours, penned in from the sun and wind like an invalid.

In fact, one thing alone had kept him from selling the house. Number 14 was directly beside Number 12, and Number 12 happened to house the loveliest woman Phineas had ever laid eyes on. Two days after he'd moved in, when crates and boxes still filled the house and he couldn't even find the strop for his razor, she'd knocked on the door, bearing a large jar of gooseberry preserves and smiling in welcome. Phineas had opened the door in his shirtsleeves, unshaven and impatient, and been rendered speechless by the sight of her. From the top of her golden brown curls to the tips of her slippers, Lady Bowen was dazzling in the morning sun, and simply perfect in Phin's eyes. No matter how many times he cracked his head on the too-short doorway at the end of the hall or stubbed his toe on the narrow tread where the stairs turned, he wouldn't have sold the house for any amount of money.

With the calculation of an admiral, he had set out to learn all he could about his beautiful neighbour. Lady Bowen was the widow of a baronet, a much older man who died of a weak heart. She was too genteel to say anything against her stepson, but her maid was not, and Phin's man Godfrey had gotten every last scrap of gossip about the new baronet. Tight with money and critical of his stepmother, Sir William Bowen had not wanted her to leave Sussex. The maid was of the opinion that the Baronet had thought to keep her under his thumb as an unpaid housekeeper and hold on to her widow's jointure. Phin was heartily glad the man was an ogre, for it kept Lady Bowen in London, right next door to him. He liked her humour. He admired her optimistic spirit. He loved the sound of her voice and the way her hair would escape her bonnet and curl madly around her temples when she worked in the garden and he wanted to get her into his bed like he had never wanted anything else in his life.

He had known that last bit since the moment she stood on his front steps and smiled up at him with those velvet brown eyes, but he had waited these last five months to be sure he liked the rest of her. He needed to choose the right approach. If she were one sort of lady, it might be only an affair. If she were another sort, he might do well to run the other way immediately, no matter how badly he wanted to have her. But everything about Lady Bowen indicated she was another sort of lady entirely, and somewhat to Phin's surprise, he was rather pleased when he realized it. She wasn't the sort a man trifled with, or the sort who squeezed a man by the ballocks for fun; she was the sort a man fell in love with and married.

That was all well and good by Phineas, except that he didn't know how to court a woman. He had flirted with many and had had a few agreeable affairs, but never had he approached a woman with such serious intent. It was daunting. Every time they talked in the garden, divided by a brick wall that came to his head, he wished he could see her face to know if she really were as interested as she sounded, or if she listened out of politeness. Even as he fell a little bit more every time he spoke to Lady Bowen, he felt less and less sure of what she thought of him.

Did she really want to know about hurricanes, he wondered now, or was it just an extension of that dreadful polite conversation about the weather? He tried his best to make his accounts of life at sea interesting, and left out all the bad parts. But he was describing a storm that had killed five members of his crew and broken his mizzenmast, and left them run aground on a sandbar for a week before they could coax their wounded ship into port. Twice he found himself straying into unpleasant details, and had to stop abruptly. The last thing he wanted to do was to shock and alarm her. If only he could see her face . . .

Then and there, Phineas decided it was time to stop talking over a garden wall. He would have to call on Lady Bowen and discover her true feelings, and what – if any – chance he had.

Three

Emma never enjoyed her mother's visits.

Mrs Hayton arrived late that morning, just as Emma finished cleaning the parlour. She was hot and dusty when her mother appeared in the parlour door, looking as cool and dignified as ever.

"Dusting, Emma dear?" she asked with a trace of disdain.

"Yes, Mother. Someone must dust, and Jane is busy upstairs airing the beds."

"You need more servants."

"I have all the servants I need." Emma pulled off her cap and grimaced as dust settled on her dress.

"No," her mother corrected her, "you have all the servants you can afford. There is a vast difference."

She shrugged. "Not in this case." She set aside her cap and dusting cloth, and made herself smile. "How are you, Mother? You're looking very well."

"I do not have to dust my own parlour. It is far easier to look well when you haven't got—" She tsked in dismay. "Emma, you have cobwebs in your hair."

"They don't hurt." She brushed one hand over her head. "Will you take some tea?"

"Yes," murmured her mother, a jaundiced eye still fixed on Emma's dusty, cobwebbed hair. "Please."

The real reason for her mother's appearance became clear as they sat and sipped their tea in the newly cleaned parlour. "I saw Lord Norton the other day," she remarked. "He asked me to give you his regards."

"Thank you," murmured Emma, steeling herself. She had heard this introduction too many times in the last two years not to know what was coming next.

"His wife died over a year ago," Mrs Hayton went on relentlessly. "I shouldn't think he'll wait much longer to wed again, what with a pair of daughters in his nursery."

"I wish him very happy." Emma, too, could be relentless, in ignoring her mother's hints.

"Darling, you must know he would be a fine match for you." Mother abandoned subtlety. "He is a viscount – not an old title, 'tis true, nor the wealthiest, but a good step up from a baronet."

"I don't need to marry a viscount. I don't want to marry Lord Norton." Mrs Hayton drew breath to respond, and Emma tried to forestall her. "I am happy as I am."

"Happy?" Her mother looked her up and down. "Dusting your own parlour and wearing last year's fashions?"

Independent, thought Emma. Free. "Yes. I shall wear this dress until it falls apart, and I adore dusting."

Her mother wrinkled her nose. "Nobody adores dusting, and that dress is horrid."

"Nevertheless, I like it. And I wouldn't marry Lord Norton if he were to show up and prostrate himself before me." Which he wouldn't, because Viscount Norton thought himself a great deal better than any of Emma's family. Her mother was scheming above herself again, unflagging in her quest for better connections at any cost.

Thankfully, Jane interrupted whatever her mother might have said next. The maid tapped at the door and came in. "You've a caller, ma'am," she said. "A gentleman."

Emma blinked in surprise. Gentlemen never came to call on her. Across from her, Mother's head came up and her eyes sharpened, like a hound scenting a fox. "Indeed," Emma said quickly. "Who is it?"

Jane hurried over to hand her the card.

"Oh!" She gave a little relieved laugh as she read it. "Captain Quentin! Jane, you gave me such a start, when it's only my neighbour."

"But I never seen him in uniform," said Jane mulishly. "He looks much finer than a neighbour ought . . ."

Mrs Hayton turned to look at Emma, eyebrows arched in enquiry. "I did not know you had a new neighbour."

"Oh, yes. He bought Number 14 a few months ago." Emma kept her expression placid. "A retired naval officer."

"Is he . . .?" Mama paused, eying Emma expectantly. "Amiable?"

"Perfectly, the few times I've spoken to him." She got to her feet. "I wonder why he's come to call. Mama, would you mind—?"

"Oh yes, I really must be going." Mrs Hayton rose with a smile. "Will you walk me out, dear?"

Emma took a deep breath. "Of course."

They met Captain Quentin in the hall. Jane was right; he did look finer than a neighbour ought. Finer than she had expected him to look, Emma realized. He wore his uniform, which made him look very tall and impressive in her narrow hall. Although, to be honest, she had only met him a handful of times outside of their garden chats. Even though she felt fairly well acquainted with him, she had almost never seen him so clearly or so close, with his dark hair brushed neatly back, his shoulders broad in his dark-blue coat, his legs long and powerful in his white breeches. He looked overwhelmingly male, and Emma had to consciously divert her mind from that fact.

She introduced her mother to him, and then Mother left, acting suspiciously uninterested in the Captain. Emma said a quick prayer that was so, and ushered her guest into the parlour. Jane had hastily whisked away the tea tray, and Emma asked her to bring a fresh one. She didn't know if the Captain would like tea, but she didn't have much spirits in the house. Not that she knew he drank spirits, either. She had some port; perhaps she should offer that? But it wasn't even noon yet . . .

She gathered her scattered thoughts. "How nice of you to call, Captain," she said as they sat down.

"I ought to have done so much sooner." He sat in the chair by the window, where the sun fell full and warm on him, and smiled at her. Emma felt the room tilt around her. He had blue eyes, the same blue as her heavenly bedroom walls. Her neighbour was a handsome, impressive figure of a man, much more so than she had realized. For a moment she stared, transfixed.

"Is something wrong?" he asked.

She jerked her gaze away from his and smiled. "Not at all! It just seems odd to speak to you face to face. We have talked so much over the fence, and so rarely called on each other."

"The failing is mine," he said with a rueful laugh, "and one I mean to correct."

Still cringing from being caught staring, Emma barely heard him. "Of course," she said, then blushed in realization as speculative surprise lit his face. And his eyes. "I m-mean," she stammered, "that would be lovely. Of course we should feel free to call on each other more, as neighbours."

"Yes." He regarded her thoughtfully. "As neighbours."

She took a deep breath. "And as more, I hope. I do so enjoy our conversations in the garden."

"I do, Lady Bowen." Again he smiled at her. Fine lines crinkled around his eyes. "Very much so."

Well. Her heart skipped a beat. Why had he called on her today? She found herself smiling back. How silly she would feel if he had merely come to tell her Jane dumped the dishwater too near his steps.

But before she could hear why he had come, the door opened. "Dear me, I seem to have forgotten my gloves," announced Mother. Her eyes darted between the two of them. "Please forgive me."

"Not at all, Mrs Hayton." Captain Quentin was on his feet already.

"I was some distance down the street when I realized I didn't have them." She smiled prettily at the Captain. "I am so sorry to disturb your visit."

"Of course not," said the Captain.

"Where did you leave them?" Emma asked, trying not to glare at her mother. She should have expected this. "I didn't see them after you left."

"Well, let me see . . ." Mother turned her head from side to side, her eyes large and limpid. "I don't see them – oh dear, they are my favourites, I shall be so distressed to lose them . . ."

"Nonsense," said Captain Quentin gallantly. "They are sure to be here somewhere. Let us look for them."

Emma, who knew very well her mother hadn't gone anywhere other than the chair where the Captain now sat, set to work, checking the table and looking behind the chair. Under Mother's direction, the captain looked under all the furniture and behind all the cushions. When Mrs Hayton exclaimed happily that she had found the gloves, Emma was sure Mother had slipped them out of her reticule. Then she thanked the Captain profusely, and before long she was sitting around the tea tray with them. Just as Emma knew she had intended, when she came back on such a flimsy pretence.

She didn't waste any time getting around to her purpose, either. "How nice of you to pay a neighbourly call, Captain," she said, smiling at him with an almost adoring air. "I'd no idea my daughter had a new neighbour."

"Not so new," he said, returning her smile. "I've lived in George Street since early spring."

"Oh, dear!" Mother glanced at Emma with wide eyes. "And you are just now becoming acquainted?"

Emma opened her mouth to reply, but the Captain didn't notice and spoke first. "We have spoken often, Mrs Hayton. I hold Lady Bowen in very high regard."

Emma closed her mouth. Her mother slowly turned her head to look Emma squarely in the face, her expression slightly victorious.

"Mother, the Captain will hardly wish to sit and chatter all day with two women," Emma said in warning. "I am sure he is a very busy man." Her mother was at it again, and if the Captain hadn't been present, Emma would have asked her mother to leave at once.

"Of course, dear, of course." Mother patted her hand. "But he came to call; that must indicate some desire to converse, surely?"

Emma flushed. Too late the Captain seemed to recognize the presence of a trap; his expression grew more closed and cautious. Mrs Hayton turned to him and smiled again. "Are you enjoying this fine weather, Captain?"

The grey clouds that had alarmed Jane were just visible through the window, although sun still streamed in. Emma glanced at the Captain just in time to meet his eyes, glimmering with wry humour.

"Very much so," he murmured.

"Until the rain comes," said Emma.

"Thunderstorms," added the Captain.

"Fierce ones, I understand."

"Really, Emma, you needn't sound so gleeful," exclaimed her mother, and Emma almost choked on a laugh. The Captain coughed.

"I had come to issue an invitation," he said. "My sister and her husband have secured a box for a performance of Shakespeare next week. I wondered if you would care to accompany us, Lady Bowen?"

"Well, that is a lovely invitation," said Mrs Hayton before Emma could speak. "But I do worry that Shakespeare is too clamorous for a lady. This Mr Kean has wrought such a change on the public, with his dramatic, violent portrayals of all those tragic heroes."

Emma gaped at her, then jerked her eyes back to her cup of tea. *Oh no. Please, dear heavens, no . . .*

The Captain's eyebrows rose slightly. "Indeed."

"I find nothing to be so enjoyable as a dinner party among friends," Mother went on. "There one can enjoy the society of the company and not be distracted by an unruly crowd in the pit."

"Er . . . yes," murmured the captain, staring at her in fascination.

Emma was almost quivering with fury. "I quite enjoy the theatre as well."

Her mother laughed, her tinkling light laugh that had enthralled so many men. "Nonsense, dear! You had dinner parties all the time in Sussex; she is the perfect hostess, Captain. Emma dear, it's certainly time you began going about again, but discreetly. You've been out of society so long."

The Captain's smile was a bit stiff. "Of course," he said. "A dinner party."

"Mother," whispered Emma between gritted teeth. "*Please.*"

"Just a small one would be perfectly acceptable," Mother said, ignoring Emma. "Don't you agree, sir?"

The Captain blinked. "Yes," he said cautiously.

She beamed at him. "I am certain Emma would be delighted to attend."

Emma wished she had locked the door when her mother had left. Now she had no choice but to raise apologetic eyes to the Captain, who looked almost desperate. He cleared his throat. "Would you honour us with your company, Lady Bowen? On this upcoming Saturday evening?"

She would try to explain to him tomorrow, across the garden wall.

For now she just wanted to help him escape, so she could tear into her mother. "You are too kind, sir," she murmured. "Thank you."

He turned to her mother. "And you, Mrs Hayton?"

Mother cast one twinkling glance at Emma as she laughed. "Thank you, but I must decline. I am engaged at the Powells' that evening."

Emma was sure she didn't imagine his shoulders easing in relief. "Well." He shuffled his feet then rose. "I should leave you to your conversation. Mrs Hayton, it was a pleasure to make your acquaintance. Lady Bowen." He bowed as Emma and her mother made their farewells, then left.

Four

"How dare you!" Emma whispered furiously the moment the door closed behind him. "Mother, that was unpardonably rude!"

Mother waved one hand. "Unpardonable, pish. He fancies you, my dear; who are his people? Where is he from? What are his connections?"

"He is my neighbour," she snapped. "He is a gentleman, and that is all I know about him. I shall have to apologise tomorrow – how could you do that?"

"Emma, my dear, you are such an innocent." Mother was unmoved. "Sir Arthur left you a pittance. You shall have to marry again, and it might as well be to a man of means and station."

"You mean someone unlike me," she retorted. "Because *I* have modest means and modest station."

"And you don't want to sink lower, either!" Mother rounded on her suddenly. "You don't know what it's like to be watched with pity and scorn," she said in withering tones. "Wearing your clothes until they are practically rags because you can't afford a new gown or gloves. Dusting your own parlour so you look like a servant – and then receiving a caller in that state! I want more for you, dearest, and you should, too."

Emma met her mother's fierce gaze. Mother's father had been a baron, but a destitute one. Mother had told her many times how the family went hungry after her father lost at the races or the card tables. There had been no money for fine clothes or servants, and that poverty had shaped Emma's mother into a woman of endless ambition. With her beauty she had caught one husband, Emma's father, who was a prosperous mill owner, and then a second. Mr Hayton had been an MP, and a decent man, although thoroughly under his wife's thumb. Even now, twice widowed and with a healthy annuity, Mother was constantly thinking how she could improve her situation, by any means necessary.

Emma had learned early on that her mother would happily use her to do it. Mother had contrived to have her compromised by a wealthy viscount, even though he was three decades older than Emma, and then tried to persuade her to seduce Mr Fitzwilliam, who had no title but owned one of the largest estates in north-eastern Sussex. In desperation Emma had wed Sir Arthur, who was kind and genial and managed to keep her mother from overrunning their lives.

"Mother, I am content as I am. I do not need a new husband so that I might wear new gowns and keep my own carriage and dine on fine china. Sir Arthur left me enough to be comfortable, as I am," she said, raising her voice to forestall her mother's impatient protest. "Now you have gone and manipulated Captain Quentin just for fun, and he was too polite to say nay! He is my neighbour, and a kind man, and you have humiliated me."

Mrs Hayton cupped Emma's cheek in her hand. "You are so like your father," she murmured. "Satisfied with so little."

Emma clenched her jaw. Her father had been an affectionate papa. "Is that what you were to him?" she whispered. "What I was to him?"

Mother released her. "The Captain is a handsome man," she said, picking up her reticule. "He is young to be retired; he must have made his fortune in the wars. I shall see what I can learn about him. Do not do anything until I speak to you again."

"My feelings, whatever they may be, wouldn't be affected in the slightest by anything you say."

On her way to the door, Mother glanced back at her. "You would ignore a man of fortune, right on your doorstep, just to spite me?" She shook her head. "Emma dear, sometimes I wonder how you can be my child."

"I do, too," she replied quietly as her mother closed the door.

Phineas walked slowly down the steps of Lady Bowen's house. That had not gone as expected. Mrs Hayton was a beautiful woman, but Phin thought he'd be careful not to be drawn into conversation with her again. She'd manoeuvred him right into throwing a dinner party when he suspected Lady Bowen would have rather accepted his invitation to the theatre. And now he would have to go tell his sister Sarah they weren't going to the theatre after all, but that she must help him plan a dinner at his house. He'd never done such a thing. Sarah would have such a laugh at his expense over this. Whom could he even invite? Sarah and her husband, of course; perhaps he could get his old mate Hakeham to come, and Morris and Campbell were genial fellows . . .

No, too many gentlemen. Phin felt a flutter of panic. Just Hakeham, then, and . . . and . . . he could ask his mother, he supposed, or ask Sarah to invite another lady. Instead of going on to his club, as he had planned to do, Phin jogged up the steps of his own home and let himself in. "Godfrey!"

"Yes, sir?" Godfrey stepped promptly from the dining room.

"Plan a dinner party," Phin told him, flexing his fingers and cracking his knuckles as he thought. "For Saturday next."

"Yes, sir. Shall I send notes around to the usual guests?"

He meant Hakeham, Morris, Campbell and some other men who had been with them in the Navy, Phin's usual companions. Phin squared his shoulders. "No. There will be ladies present." Godfrey's eyes flickered in the direction of Number 12, and he went a shade paler. "Yes, that lady," Phin told him. "Clean the house from top to bottom. Send to Lady Stanley if you need any plate or advice or . . . anything. And, for God's sake, get Smithy sobered up to cook a decent meal."

"Truly, sir? A dinner party?"

Phin nodded. Lady Bowen had looked lovelier than ever today, her chestnut hair a little mussed and her pink gown that looked soft and worn. She was a beauty, but not a hard, polished one. Phin preferred a woman who looked natural and comfortable rather than a woman who looked arranged and artful, as if she would crumble the first time a man embraced her. He had spent far too much time already thinking about embracing Lady Bowen, but Phin wanted to court her properly. If he had to throw a damn dinner party to do that, so be it. As his man hurried off to carry out his orders, Phin took a deep breath. It was like the preparation to set sail, making sure the supplies were ordered and the men instructed on their duties. But he was in charge of setting the course.

Five

Emma tried at once to rectify the situation. The next morning, she was up early, and rushed into the garden, hoping he would be there. As soon as he came out, she called over the wall to him. "Good morning, Captain."

"Good morning, Lady Bowen." He sounded as cordial as ever.

Emma said a quick prayer he wasn't holding Mother's actions against her. "I must speak about yesterday, when you called—"

"Yes, I enjoyed it very much. It was a pleasure to make your mother's acquaintance."

He was a good liar, she thought. It had been a nightmare from her point of view. She forced herself to go on. "I must apologise for her behaviour, though. To suggest you throw a dinner party—"

"But no, my dear," he protested, and Emma paused. "My dear Lady Bowen. I am delighted you agreed to join our party – it will be a small gathering, just my sister and her husband, my mother and an old friend of mine from my Navy days."

Emma pushed aside the little flicker of interest in the way he'd called her 'my dear' before adding her name. She tried not to recall her mother's blunt assessment of the Captain's regard for her. She said the only thing she could say. "I'm sure it will be lovely. I wouldn't miss it for the world."

The dinner was almost a success.

Phin had prevailed upon his mother to act as hostess, since his sister couldn't stop smirking when she looked at him. Mama had raised her eyebrows when he asked, and he knew Sarah had already told her why he was throwing together a party on such short notice. But Mama merely smiled and said it was good to see him taking an interest in society at last, and agreed.

Godfrey polished the dining room to a sparkle, and laid the table with Sarah's second-best china and silver. He impressed upon Smithy, the cook, that his employment hung on this dinner. Phin was relieved by the succulent smells that filled the house as Saturday evening approached. Godfrey brushed and pressed his best coat, and Phin dressed with care. He hadn't been this nervous even when the admiral had come aboard his ship.

Then Sarah and her husband arrived, Sarah still delighted by the image of Phin infatuated with his neighbour, and Gregory flashing Phin a glance of wry sympathy. Hakeham arrived, as good-natured and discreet as ever, and then his mother. Mama cast a critical eye over the arrangements, and then gave a satisfied nod. Phin kissed her cheek. "Thank you," he murmured.

"You know you have only to ask, Phineas. I cannot wait to meet the lady who has inspired you."

He'd told his mother all about Lady Bowen. Phin pulled out his pocket watch again and checked the time. "Perhaps I shall go escort her," he said. "Would that be acceptable?"

Mama smiled. Sarah tried to hide her laughter in a cough. "Go fetch her, Phineas."

Emma tried not to attribute too much to the evening. She wore her best dress, a glazed cotton with embroidered hem, and her favourite shawl. Her mother had called the day before, clearly ready to tell all she had learned about the Captain, and for once Emma refused to see her. She pleaded a headache and locked her bedroom door. She didn't want Mother to pollute her impression of the Captain or his guests. She didn't want to have her head stuffed with Mother's talk of advantageous matches and how to seduce the Captain, if he were good enough for Mother's requirements. She still felt a burn of humiliation over the way Mother had acted, and resolved to be as polite and restrained as possible, to prove she wasn't like that.

But as she went down the stairs, her heart ignored all her sense and sped up.

Then she opened the door, and jumped back in surprise. The Captain himself stood on her doorstep, hand raised as if to knock. He looked as surprised as she.

Emma pressed one hand to her bosom and gave a shaky laugh. "I beg your pardon."

"No, no!" He looked abashed. "I merely thought to escort you."

Emma could see his front steps from the corner of her eye. "It is only twenty feet or so . . ." He looked to his steps and gave her a rueful smile, looking up at her from under his brows like a boy. Her silly heart bumped again. "But it is so kind of you," she finished a bit shyly. "Thank you."

He extended his arm and they walked down her steps, covered the short distance between the houses, and then up his. A servant was waiting to open the door, standing stiffly at attention. Emma had seen him chatting with Jane over the railings. He took her shawl, then the Captain led her to the drawing room, where he introduced his other guests. Lieutenant Hakeham, a charming, merry fellow, had sailed with Captain Quentin. Viscount Stanley was married to the Captain's sister, Lady Stanley, who greeted Emma with warm enthusiasm. It was Mrs Quentin, the Captain's mother, who gave Emma the most pause. She was tall and regal, and seemed to size Emma up with one glance. But her greeting was polite enough, and then Lady Stanley took over the conversation, chattering gaily.

"How wonderful you could join us tonight," Lady Stanley said, drawing Emma apart. "I understand you are a gardener; my brother has often mentioned how lovely your garden is."

"Oh," said Emma, glancing at the Captain. He was talking with his mother, but watching her. Good heavens, he looked attractive in his evening clothes. His dark hair gleamed with lighter streaks in the candlelight, but his eyes were as blue as she remembered. Emma had to drag her eyes away. "Indeed."

"Oh, indeed!" Lady Stanley exclaimed. "I vow, he has described a veritable Garden of Eden! You must share your secrets."

"Oh," said Emma again. "It's really not so grand; it is only a small city garden, after all."

Lady Stanley laughed. "To Phin, any patch of trimmed grass looks grand, after all his years at sea. Tell me, do you have roses? Our gardener does not like them, but I so long for some pink ones."

Emma smiled, glad for a safe subject. She could still feel the Captain's gaze on her back, like the heat of a fire. It warmed her even as she talked, with relief, of roses and gardens until they went in to dine.

Six

It wasn't until dessert was served that everything went wrong.

Emma had excused herself to the necessary, and then took some time trying to pin up her hair again. The dinner had been marvellous, expertly prepared and served by the Captain's man with astonishing speed and economy of movement; when the Captain mentioned Godfrey had been with him in the Navy, Emma understood why. All her fears about being out of place had evaporated in the easy atmosphere as the conversation flowed like wine – rich and mellow. The Quentins were an affectionate family, and it made Emma's heart swell to see how the Captain was so easy and relaxed with his sister and his mother. It was exactly the sort of familial scene that had been so lacking in her own life, with her mother constantly worried about how such familiarity would appear.

In fact, the conversation at dinner had been so animated and lively, half her hair seemed to have slipped its pins as she laughed. As she twisted curls back into place, she caught a glimpse of her expression in the mirror. Her colour was high, her eyes bright, and her lips seemed stuck in a slight smile. Even with her hair verging on untidy, she looked rather nice, much to her relief.

It was only for female pride that she wanted to look nice, of course. She was not putting stock in what her mother said, nor taking her mother's advice to pursue the Captain. She was just enjoying his company, and he was even more interesting without a wall between them. As he related some story, with frequent asides from Lieutenant Hakeham, about fishing in the Caribbean, Emma found herself drifting away as she always did when he spoke, and his rich tenor voice carried her imagination away to some faraway place. Only when she caught Lady Stanley watching her curiously did she recall where she was.

Her hair repaired, her heart light, she walked back to the dining room. As she reached the door, Godfrey slipped out, a laden tray in his hands. When he saw her, he bowed crisply, despite his tray, and left the door unlatched. "Thank you," Emma murmured, moving aside to let him pass. She reached out to let herself back into the dining room.

"It's her connection to Mrs Hayton that concerns me." Mrs Quentin's voice, though not raised or angry, carried through the partly closed door. Emma froze. "Phineas, her mother is quite beyond the pale. Her ambition is no secret to anyone – indeed, she does not try to hide it. I warrant she took one look at you and rated you a fine catch in terms of wealth, station and advantage." Emma closed her eyes as each word struck home. "You mustn't let yourself be taken in."

The Captain's reply was too low to hear, but Emma didn't even try. It was bad enough that her mother's scheming was widely known, and now presented to the Captain. He would have heard of it sooner or later, most likely. The Bowens had come to despise Mother because of her ceaseless manoeuvring for every little scrap of status. Her stepson William had refused to allow Mother at Bowen Lodge after his father died, not even for the funeral. He'd said he couldn't bear to watch her try to catch a third husband over the cold meats, and Emma couldn't argue against it. Her mother was shameless.

Quietly she turned and walked away. She should just leave. Emma didn't want to know what the Captain himself might think of her now; her mother's behaviour the other day could only have confirmed Mrs Quentin's words. Perhaps if she stayed out of her garden for the next few weeks, the Captain would believe she hadn't been scheming to marry him. Except . . . Oh, how she would miss him.

But the door opened before she had gone more than a few steps. "Lady Bowen," said the Captain behind her. "Wait. Please, wait!"

"I must go," she said in a rush, barely glancing back. "A sudden headache . . . I don't wish to spoil everyone's evening . . ."

"Wait," he said again, firmly. He was already beside her, and took her arm. "I must have a word before you go."

"Your guests," she tried to protest.

"They can wait." He pushed open the door to a small room. When he closed the door behind them, there was only cool, bright moonlight to see by, but she had no trouble making out his frown.

"You heard what my mother said." He wasn't asking.

Emma avoided his gaze. "You mustn't think I am offended. She is, in general, correct; you saw for yourself how my mother can twist things to suit her."

The Captain turned away and put his hands through his hair. "Damn."

"But I wouldn't want you to think I came tonight because my mother wished it," Emma forged on.

He wheeled around. "Why did you come?"

"Be-because . . . I . . ." she stammered. "Because I wanted to."

Relief swept over his face, and his shoulders sagged. "Why?" he asked quietly.

Her lips parted. "Because of our friendship," she whispered. "Oh, I really must go."

"No!" He lunged for the door at the same moment she did. His hand closed over hers on the doorknob. Emma froze. He was so close, his hand so large and strong over hers. She could smell his soap, and the wine on his breath. "One more question," he murmured, his cheek right next to hers. "Just for friendship?"

Emma breathed deeply. She couldn't think, not when he was so close. He must feel how he affected her, not at all like a friend. She didn't say anything.

With careful hands he turned her to face him. "I should go," she whispered again, without making any effort to leave. He just looked down at her with those blue, blue eyes. As he raised his hand, his knuckles brushed the outside of her breast. Emma sucked in her breath; her whole body flinched. The Captain paused, his eyes searching hers, and then he slowly brushed his knuckles deliberately over the same spot. This time Emma gasped. Her heart pounded against her ribs, and her knees felt weak. Still watching her, Captain Quentin lowered his head and kissed her.

It was a kiss like no other. His mouth was hot and sweet, flavoured with burgundy and passion. It took Emma off guard, and for a moment she leaned into him, opening to him and letting him deepen the kiss. For a moment everything else fell away, and she was carried away again by the spell he seemed to weave over her so effortlessly. This was no fantasy or flight of fancy; this was his arm around her, his mouth on hers, and her body straining into his.

But, as always, the spell broke. He lifted his head and Emma crashed back to earth. She was kissing him while his family sat a few rooms away, thinking she was laying a trap for him with her mother's help. She had only ever spoken politely and properly with the Captain, and had no idea what his real intentions towards her were. And she hadn't kissed a man since Sir Arthur died four years ago. For all she knew, those years had made her awkward and susceptible, too easily swayed by the most magnificent kiss she'd ever experienced.

She backed up a step, pressing her hands to her burning cheeks. "I'm sorry," she whispered. He said nothing, just looked at her with a slightly dazed expression. "Please make my excuses."

"Don't go," he said, as she pulled open the door. Emma just shook her head and fled.

Phin let her go. He wasn't sure he could walk. His body had reacted with joyous alacrity when she opened her lips under his, and now he was so aroused, it hurt. He also wasn't sure what to do. Perhaps his thoughts would clear when he could think of something other than the feel of her in his arms. That moment seemed a long time off.

He'd thought things were going rather well at dinner. Lady Bowen – Emma – appeared to enjoy herself, joining in the conversation and laughing when Sarah teased him about something. Phin had to work at keeping his eyes away from her. She was beauty itself in a dark-green gown that shimmered in the light, her dark hair piled in loose curls that made his fingers itch to unpin them. And when she excused herself from the table, Sarah had immediately turned to him.

"Oh, Phin, she likes you," his sister hissed in delight. "Are you planning to propose?"

"Sarah," murmured Gregory.

Sarah waved him off. "Are you, Phin? She seems very sweet and not at all proud."

Phin had thought exactly the same thing, and been opening his mouth to say "yes" when his mother raised her hand in protest, and condemned Mrs Hayton. "You don't want to get taken in," she added gently.

But Phin had seen a shadow at the door. "Bite your tongue, Mama," he had growled, and then run after Emma.

He hadn't planned to kiss her. He had planned to be proper and polite all night. But the moment intervened, and left him more certain than ever that he wanted Emma as his wife.

"Sir?" Godfrey tapped at the door. Phin started out of his thoughts. "Do you need anything?"

Just her, he thought bleakly. "No."

"Shall I bring the port to the table?"

Phin adjusted his trousers and sighed. "Yes." Bring the damn port so he could bundle his guests out the door, and he could puzzle out what to do next about the luscious Emma Bowen.

Seven

Emma rushed out of the Captain's house and ran up her own front steps. She banged on her door until Jane answered, and then rushed up the stairs to her room. She ignored her maid running up the stairs behind her, squawking in concern. Emma threw open her bedroom door and slammed it behind her, turning the key in the lock with shaking hands.

"Madam! Lady Bowen!" Jane thumped on the door, her voice sharp with fear. "Are ye ill? Should I send for a doctor?"

"No!" She pressed her hands to her face; the blush was still hot on her skin. "I'm fine, Jane. Never mind. You can go on to bed."

Jane knocked again. "You'll need help with your gown."

"Not now I don't! Leave me be," Emma said sharply. There was a surprised hush, then Jane left, her footsteps almost drowning out the sound of her muttered indignation.

Emma paused and slowly raised her hand. She laid her palm against the wall, her heavenly blue wall. The plaster was cool and solid beneath her hand. His house would be the opposite of hers, the plans mirror images. If he had taken the best bedroom for his own, as she had done, it would lie directly on the other side of this wall. She took a deep, shaky breath, thinking of him undressing just feet away, separated only by a foot of plaster and brick.

And he wanted her.

She thought of his voice, smooth and strong, sliding over her like a caress. She thought of his hand, so large and strong, taking hers. She thought of his lips, brushing sensuously over hers.

He *wanted* her.

She touched the neckline of her gown; her fingers drifted along the puckered fabric. Gently she touched the swell of her breast and shivered. It had been a long time since anyone had touched her breast. Sir Arthur had thought it unseemly, even in the marriage bed. She didn't think the Captain would hesitate to touch every inch of her, in bed. The heat in his gaze, when his hand had accidentally brushed her breast, was impossible to forget – and then he had deliberately done it again, watching her as he did so. Emma knew her body had betrayed her, even if her face had not, and that he was aware of her reaction. He wouldn't have kissed her if he hadn't been sure. She stroked her breast again, imagining it was his hand that touched her, and a sharp tingle raced through her.

She wanted him.

The blue walls around her might have been the reflection of his eyes, surrounding her, watching her. Alone in her room, she admitted to herself that she had been half in love with the Captain for some time now – the Captain, with his easy laugh and deep voice and the way he could describe a hurricane and make it sound as exciting and as sensual as it was dangerous and frightening. She had known anxiety and fear, but never with any exhilaration, and never with such high stakes as the Captain had experienced, with his very life caught between the storm's tempest and his own skill as a mariner. Emma didn't want to experience a hurricane on a ship in the middle of an ocean, but maybe, just once, she should risk a tempest of some sort. She had been quiet and sensible her whole life, trying so hard not to be like her brash, calculating mother. She had married a quiet, sensible man, and they had lived a quiet, sensible life together. There had been no excitement, only a calm contentment, with Sir Arthur. Emma didn't once think it would be that way with Captain Quentin – with Phineas.

She went to her window, overlooking the garden where they had talked so frequently, and sat for a long time, thinking. When the clock chimed midnight, she pushed open the casement. It squeaked as it swung open, and she braced her hands on the frame, then leaned out to take a deep breath. She could smell the roses from her garden, and the jasmine from his. It was a sweet, wild scent, hinting of exotic lands and adventures. The jasmine had been there when he bought the house, but Emma thought it suited him. She closed her eyes and breathed deeply, feeling something a bit wild and sweet stir within her.

Then she gave a huff of laughter. After the way she had run out on him, Captain Quentin probably thought her mad, or else repulsed by his declaration. "Blast," Emma said, shaking her head. "What a fool I am."

"Lady Bowen?"

Emma started violently, banging her elbow on the window frame as she leaped backwards. Her heart nearly stopped. "Captain!" she exclaimed. "I . . . Forgive my language . . . I didn't mean . . . I didn't realize you were there . . ." Her voice petered out, which perhaps should have happened sooner. Silently, Emma grimaced and bounced her fist off her forehead. Now he would think her mad *and* a slattern.

"I have heard far worse language, and I beg *your* forgiveness," came his sombre reply. "I should have spoken as soon as I heard your window open." He paused. "I confess, I was hoping to talk to you."

Something about the way his voice dropped as he made that confession sent a shudder through her. He had been hoping to talk to her. Perhaps this way was best, when she couldn't see him and he couldn't see her. Emma wet her lips. "I am sorry for the way I left this evening."

"I am sorry you were driven to it," he answered instantly. "Please accept my deepest, humblest apology for what happened—"

"No," she said softly. "I liked it." There was a long moment of silence. The night breeze stirred the jasmine, and Emma filled her lungs with sweet wildness. "I was . . . startled."

"I know," he murmured. "I should not have . . ."

"Should I have been startled?" she asked when he stopped. "I have looked forward to our every conversation, and wished you were in your garden even more often. I have dreamed of the things you describe to me, and I can hear your voice in those dreams. I have kept those things to myself, not wishing to ruin our friendship, never dreaming you meant more. Have I been blind?"

"No. You have been everything a lady should be."

"But now I wish to discover what a woman should be," she whispered.

For a moment all was silent. "I am going into my garden," he said. "And unlocking the gate in the wall."

Emma's heart skipped a beat. She had forgotten about that gate; it was small and narrow, and she had planted roses in front of it last year, never thinking she would use it. The thorns would probably rip her dress to shreds . . . but changing would mean waiting for Jane to come help her. Besides . . . She smoothed her trembling hands over her skirt. It was only a dress, sensible and modest. Without stopping to think about anything else, she crossed the room, unlocked her door and hurried down the stairs.

Eight

Straining his ears, Phin heard the faint sound of her door opening. Good God, she was going to meet him. Without pausing even to put his coat back on, he rushed out of his room and bounded down the stairs. Godfrey met him in the hall, looking alert.

"Something wrong, Captain?"

"No, nothing," said Phin as he pushed past him. "I'm going to get some air."

"At midnight, sir?" said Godfrey in surprise.

"Yes. You can go to bed." Phin paused, thinking. "In fact, go now. Take a glass of port. Take the bottle. And whatever you do, don't set foot in the garden." Leaving his astonished man, he strode through the house to the rear door, unlatched it and stepped out into the night.

He knew Emma spent hours in her garden, weeding and pruning and even talking to her plants. Phin would sit quietly and listen, picturing her at work, her arms stretched overhead . . . or on her knees . . . or bending over to pick the flowers . . . Phin had peered over the wall a few times, and seen the bower she cultivated. His garden was nothing compared to hers. There had been a linden tree and some climbing vine growing there when he moved in and, since Phin had no talent with plants, that was all that grew there now. As he pulled aside the overgrown vines to get to the tiny connecting door, he realized the vine was flowering, with masses of small white flowers that gave off a faint sweet scent. When he dragged the door open, a shower of flowers rained down on him. He was still brushing them from his shoulders and hair when she appeared in the doorway.

For a moment she just stood there, watching him. Phin could only stare back. She still wore her evening dress, the dark-green fabric black in the night. Moonlight gilded her shoulders and hair with a silvery light. "Emma," he whispered.

She stepped forwards, into the shadows, through the door. "Good evening."

Great God. She was here, in the moonlit garden, with him, just as he had fantasized about. Now what should he do? Probably not seize her and carry her inside to his bed, which was where his fantasies usually led. "Thank you," he said lamely. "For coming out."

Her smile began in her eyes, then her lips curved and a faint dimple appeared in her cheek. "Is that all you wished to tell me?"

"To tell you?" he repeated. "No, there is a great deal more I want to tell you . . . But first . . ." He stepped closer. Her head fell back as she looked up at him, and a lock of her hair slipped free and fell across her shoulder. Phin reached out and wound it around his finger. Her eyes half closed and her lips parted on a soundless sigh of want. He shuddered, sliding his hand around the back of her neck, digging his fingers into her glorious curls, and lowering his head to hers.

The kiss began gently. His lips brushed hers, and Emma shivered. He must have thought she was cold, for his arms went around her, enveloping her in the warm, male scent of him. Through the thin linen of his shirtsleeves she could feel his muscles flex and bunch as he pulled her closer, and Emma moaned softly. She slid her hands up the front of his waistcoat, anchoring herself to him as his mouth slanted over hers, more demanding, coaxing, seductive. This was a tempest she could lose herself in, most willingly . . .

"Captain," she whispered as his kisses drifted over her temple.

"Call me Phin." His breath stirred her hair, and she shivered again.

"Phin." He smiled when she said his name, a masculine, hungry smile. His hands slid down her back, curving her spine until her body pressed against his. Emma tried not to gasp aloud as her breasts flattened against him. Against her belly she could feel his erection, growing harder by the minute, and this time she had to bite her lip to keep from moaning. He wanted her as much as she wanted him.

"Phin," she said again, trying to keep hold of her fraying thoughts. "I should tell you . . . What your mother said . . ."

"I don't want to talk about my mother or your mother." He was kissing the side of her neck now. Emma tilted her head, shamelessly begging for more.

"But my mother *is* ambitious, even grasping. She . . . oh my . . . She coerced you into having a dinner party . . ."

"Emma," he said, his voice low and ragged, "if she'd suggested I host a circus in my parlour for you, I would have done it. If she said I could call on you only if my connections were good enough, I would have lined up every relation and friend I have, just to ensure I could see you."

"But you can see me any time," she protested.

"That's not what I want, with a wall between us." He kissed her brow, smoothing her hair back. "I want to see you like this."

"Phin." She slid her hands around his neck, making him look at her. "You didn't need to appease my mother to see me."

He paused. "No?"

Emma blushed. "I didn't spend so much time in my garden before you arrived."

He blinked, smiled and then threw back his head and laughed. "And I've been plotting a careful campaign to seduce you."

"You have been, all this time," she said. "With just the sound of your voice."

"Really." Interest sparked in his face. "Just my voice?"

"Yes," Emma admitted. "And your tales of adventure and danger in foreign lands. I would imagine I was there with you."

Phin laughed. "Well! That is good to know. For I have a tale of adventure to tell you, my darling Emma, and, while there will be no danger or foreign lands, I plan to seduce you most thoroughly, and with more than my voice."

She smiled up at him as he gathered her into his arms once more. "I've been waiting months for that adventure."

"It will be like none other," he promised. He kissed her again, bearing her back into the jasmine, and a shower of tiny blossoms covered them both.

The Catch of the Season

Shirley Kennedy

In the drawing room of her family's spacious London townhouse, Miss Julia Winslow waited while her mother, Lady Harleigh, read the note Julia had just received from Lord Melton. When Lady Harleigh finished, her face lit. She gasped with delight. "I cannot believe this! Do you think he's going to *propose*?"

"It is possible," Julia replied cautiously.

Squeals of excitement issued from Julia's aunt and cousins who had all gathered for tea. "Lord Melton is the catch of the season," declared Aunt Elizabeth, who appeared to be in the same state of elation as her sister.

"An earl!" cried giddy cousin Lydia. "You will be a countess! It's almost too good to be true. Read it to us."

Julia took the note from her mother and read aloud, "'Dear Miss Winslow, if it's convenient, I would like to call upon you this afternoon at 4 p.m. on a matter of some importance. Melton.'" She regarded the assembled ladies. "So what do you think?"

"What else except a marriage proposal could be a matter of 'some importance'?" Julia's mother dropped into a rosewood armchair and began to fan herself with her inlaid ivory fan. "Oh, this is all too much. Lord Melton himself. I may need my smelling salts."

"Calm yourself, Mama," answered Julia. "Perhaps he simply wants to ask me to the theatre or to see the Elgin Marbles or some such thing."

"No," Lady Harleigh firmly replied, "he's going to propose, I feel it in my bones. What fantastic luck! Lord Melton is not only perfect in every way, he's going to be our new neighbour. Did you know that, Julia?"

"So he told me," Julia said. Her mother was referring to Lord Melton's recent purchase of Hatfield Manor, the vast country estate next to her family's own Bretton Court, not far from London.

"Imagine," Lady Harleigh continued., "we shall be connected to one of the most prestigious families in all England! True aristocrats, the lot of them."

"Except for his ne'er-do-well younger brother," contributed Aunt Elizabeth. "He's quite the rake, from what I understand, what with his drinking and gambling. But that was a while ago. Now, apparently, they keep him under wraps."

Lady Harleigh ignored her sister's comment and grew starry-eyed. "I can see it all now – the conjoining of two great estates. Hatfield Manor and Bretton Court will become as one, eventually to be inherited, of course, by Julia and Lord Melton's eldest son, and then—"

"Mama, please! Let's not get ahead of ourselves." Despite her mother's overly vivid imagination, Julia rejoiced to see her smiling again. Only a year ago, Julia's beloved brother, Douglas, had been killed at the Battle of Waterloo, plunging her mother into a period of near-inconsolable grief for the loss of her only son. Lady Harleigh had seemed to age overnight, her once pretty face grown thin and gaunt. But now what a difference! The prospect of a brilliant marriage for her youngest daughter had put roses in her cheeks again and revived her bubbling enthusiasm.

From the gilt-wood settee where she'd been sitting quietly, Julia's tiny, sharp-eyed grandmother spoke up. "What's all the fuss about? Who is this Lord Melton?"

"Where have you been, Mother?" Aunt Elizabeth asked. "We're talking about Charles Carstairs, Lord Melton. An earl! Not only handsome and charming, he recently came into his inheritance, which is considerable, I assure you. Vast estates . . . a huge fortune. If you ask me, he isn't just the catch of the season, he's the catch of any season you can name."

A chorus of feminine voices agreed.

"Lord Melton dresses impeccably . . ."

"He's so handsome . . ."

"His manners are perfection . . ."

"He's just so . . . so . . . *correct* in every way . . ."

"Humph!" Granny cast her daughters and granddaughters a sceptical gaze. "Handsome and correct? That says nothing about the man himself. Where's he been? Why have I never heard of him?"

"He's been on an extended grand tour of Europe," Aunt Elizabeth replied, "and spent considerable time in Paris, I understand."

"Sewing a few wild oats, I suppose." Granny's shrewd eyes shifted to Julia. "I'm surprised you've finally made a choice, missy. Here you are, twenty-two years old, well into your fourth season—"

"Third," Julia interjected.

"Third then. You're beautiful enough to have had your pick, yet you've shown your strength of character by not settling for the first conceited fop who came along."

"I totally disagree." Lady Harleigh cast a long-suffering glance at her daughter. "Your grandmother calls it 'strength of character'. I call it just plain pernickety. Remember Viscount Lansdale? You didn't like him because you said he had a silly laugh. I also recall Lieutenant Dashmont who looked so resplendent in his gold-braided uniform. He—"

"Was balding and wore too much cologne," Julia interceded with a wry smile. That wasn't the real reason, but who in this room except Granny would understand?

Lady Harleigh continued, "At any rate, Julia's betrothal to Lord Melton will be the coup of the season. I feel sorry for all those mothers with marriageable daughters who spent considerable time trying to trap him."

Julia held up a protesting hand. "Wait. He hasn't proposed yet, and even if he does—"

"Just think of the wedding!" With shining eyes, Julia's mother clasped her hands together. "We shall spare no expense. I shall invite the Duke and Duchess of Sherford, and – yes, why not? – I shall invite the Prince Regent himself. Julia's wedding will be the biggest, the grandest—"

"Mama, please," Julia began, then changed her mind and said no more, knowing her protests would fall on deaf ears.

Later, after the others had left, Julia sank down on the settee across from her eighty-five-year-old grandmother. Granny always looked so sweet, Julia thought, with her lace cap perched atop her snow-white head and her lavender paisley shawl draped around her frail shoulders. But she wasn't sweet at all. In fact, one of the ongoing vexations of Mama's life was having a mother like Granny who said whatever she pleased and consistently ignored society's rules of proper behaviour. Julia loved her just as she was, though, and valued her judgment. "What do you think, Granny? Is he going to propose?"

Granny peered at her over the top of her spectacles. "Do you want him to?"

"I certainly ought to. You heard what everyone said, didn't you? How could I not want to marry Lord Melton when he's so perfect in every way?"

Granny levelled one of her shrewd, assessing gazes which in the past had always made Julia admit the stark truth and nothing but. "I'll ask you again, missy. Do you want Lord Melton to propose? In other words, have you fallen madly in love with him or will you marry him simply because everyone expects you to?"

"That's a very good question," Julia replied, stalling for time. "I am *not* dying to get married, but you know how I hate coming down to London for these seasons Mama insists upon. I intensely dislike putting myself on display so some man will find me attractive enough to marry – with, of course, an eye on my dowry. It makes me feel like a slab of meat on show at the butcher shop."

"So you would marry simply to avoid another season?"

"Isn't it high time? Mama has managed to marry off all her daughters except me. I cannot stay single all my life. She would die of disappointment if I did." Julia sighed and continued, "Of course, if the choice were mine, I would be home at Bretton Court this very minute, out riding my horse or painting my landscapes, and *not* worried in the least about finding a husband." Her eyes shifted to several small oil paintings that hung in a group next to the marble fireplace. Each depicted a scene from the ruins of Swindon Abbey, which lay between Bretton Court and Hatfield Manor. She had spent many an hour there, not only painting but musing about those long gone days when Swindon Abbey had teemed with life, virtually a small city of its own. With a note of wistfulness, she added, "I could spend the rest of my life painting scenes from those ancient ruins."

"Your paintings are excellent," Granny replied. "You're a gifted artist, Julia. But however much I hate to say it, an outstanding talent such as yours doesn't mean a thing for a woman in your position."

Julia nodded in reluctant agreement. "I could be the greatest artist in the world, but all that's expected of me is that I make a brilliant marriage and then start popping out babies, as soon and as often as possible."

"Unfortunately you're right. Of course, you would have made things easier on yourself had you fallen in love with any one of your many suitors."

"Well, I didn't," Julia replied. "But perhaps I will with Lord Melton. Even if I don't, I shall probably marry him anyway. After all, he's the best of the lot, and if I haven't fallen in love by now, I doubtless never will."

"How well do you know him?" Granny asked.

"Actually not that well. I met him at Lady Gardner's ball. We've danced several times at Almack's. We've been to Covent Garden, and he took me to hear Catalanai at the King's Theatre." A thoughtful smile curved Julia's mouth. "At least he's been the perfect gentleman. He's never even kissed me."

"Have you wanted him to?"

"I . . . don't know."

Granny emitted one of her disdainful sniffs. "Then I suggest you kiss the man, preferably before you accept his proposal, and see how you feel."

Julia grinned. "You mean sparks should fly? My knees should grow weak?"

"Just kiss the man before you agree to marry him."

"All right, I shall." Not that it much mattered. Mama, Papa, everyone expected her to say yes, and so she probably would. If she didn't, she would break her mother's heart. Not only that, everyone would think she had lost her mind if she turned down the catch of the season.

"Oh, Miss Julia, you look so exquisitely beautiful!" declared Yvette, Julia's lady's maid. "Look in the mirror. See for yourself."

Julia viewed herself in her full-length mirror. For Lord Melton's visit she had chosen her new afternoon gown, a soft-blue cotton batiste with short puffed sleeves. Lace frills and bands of light blue satin decorated the bodice, sleeves and skirt. Not bad, she thought, pointing a toe to admire a slipper made from the same fabric as the gown. And Yvette had done her usual fine job on her thick auburn hair, binding it up in a topknot held by a matching blue satin band.

Yvette stood behind and fussed with her gown. "I love dressing you. That full bosom! That tiny waist! Lord Melton is sure to propose."

"Thank you," Julia answered, silently amused. She wouldn't bother to ask how her lady's maid knew about Lord Melton. The servants knew everything.

At precisely four o'clock, the butler knocked. "Lord Melton has arrived, Miss Julia. I have put him in the drawing room."

"Thank you, Gettys. Inform him I shall be down directly."

So the big moment was at hand. Julia picked up her white lace fan and started down the staircase, making a conscious effort to put herself in the proper mood. The catch of the season would soon be hers! She was going to be the next Lady Melton! Married to the perfect man, admired and envied by all!

Strange, how her heart wasn't pounding with excitement. It soon would be, though, she was sure of it.

When Julia entered the drawing room, she found Charles Carstairs, Lord Melton, standing before the marble fireplace. Always attired in the latest fashion, today he appeared even more elegant than usual in a meticulously tailored serge spencer jacket over a waistcoat and drill trousers. A chitterling frill ran down the front of his shirt, which had to be of the finest linen, Julia was sure. As for his perfectly tied cravat, she could not imagine a spot of gravy landing on its snow-white surface. It simply wouldn't dare.

His handsome face lit when he saw her. "Ah, Miss Winslow!" he said with a bow.

"Lord Melton." She dipped a curtsey, further noting how absolutely gorgeous he looked. Tall and broad-shouldered. Thick head of wavy blond hair worn fashionably short with one careless curl falling over his noble forehead. Finely chiselled nose. Wide-set blue eyes with long, thick lashes . . .

Perfect in every way.

Rich and titled, besides.

For a short while they sat on the opposing settees and chatted. The weather . . . her parents' health . . . his parents' health . . . the Prince Regent's latest escapade. All the while, Julia grew more restless. Would he never get to the point?

"I suppose you are wondering why I am here," he said at last.

Finally. "I confess, Lord Melton, I am curious. 'A matter of importance', you said?"

Totally at ease, he smiled across at her, revealing his dazzlingly perfect white teeth. "Indeed it is a matter of importance to me, and of course my mother who is most anxious – how can I put this delicately? – to see the end of what she terms my profligate ways. To put it plainly, my mother feels it is time I married. That's why I'm here."

With one swift move, Melton arose from the settee and settled himself beside her. Taking her hand, he gazed deep into her eyes. "These past weeks I have developed a great fondness for you, Miss Winslow. You're everything my mother could ever ask for. Daughter of a viscount. Fine family. Charming and beautiful besides."

Something in Julia rebelled at his words. "But what about *you*, Lord Melton?" she tartly enquired. "How do *you* feel?"

"Of course I feel the same," he smoothly replied. "Indeed, I think I've fallen quite in love with you and want you to do me the honour of becoming my wife."

So there it was – the proposal, her mother's dream come true. Why wasn't her heart pounding with excitement? Why, instead, had she bristled when he talked about his mother? But surely she was being much too sensitive. *Lord Melton has proposed!* She tried to drum this exciting, incredibly wonderful news into her head. A "yes" formed on her lips. She remembered Granny's words. *Just kiss the man before you agree to marry him.*

Not a bad idea. What could it hurt? With her hand still in his, she looked deep into Melton's eyes and declared, "Do you realize we have never kissed?"

For the fleetest of moments Melton appeared taken aback but quickly recovered. "I do not believe we have."

Never had she asked a man to kiss her before. In the past, such a request had hardly been necessary, but now, without a qualm, she asked, "Then shall we remedy that lamentable situation right now?"

"But of course," Melton replied, remaining his usual imperturbable self. He placed his hands on Julia's shoulders, drew her close, and brought his lips to hers. She placed her hands on each side of his elegant spencer jacket, pressed back with her lips and gave herself over to the enjoyment of the kiss. At last she was in the arms of the man she was going to marry! The man whose bed she soon would share!

She waited for hot excitement to strike. It did not. Instead, kissing Lord Melton was like . . .

Like . . .

Kissing a piece of paper.

Dry. Emotionless. Boring.

Indeed, she had hoped to be set aflame by his kiss – *wanted* to be set aflame – but Melton's arid lips on hers did not stir her in the slightest. And aside from a slight quickness of his breath, he didn't appear to be set aflame either, for he soon drew away and calmly enquired, "So may I have your answer?"

Again the word "yes" formed on her lips, but try as she might, she could not force herself to say it. So what would be wrong with a slight delay? Give herself some time, then say yes. "If you don't mind, Lord Melton, I need a bit of time to consider your most kind and agreeable proposal before giving you my answer."

He smiled. "But of course I don't mind. As a matter of fact, tomorrow I'm leaving for my hunting lodge in Scotland. I shall be gone two weeks. You can give me your answer upon my return."

Relief swept through her. He didn't appear in the least perturbed, as she feared he might.

On his way out of the drawing room, Lord Melton caught sight of Julia's paintings hung by the fireplace. "Those look like the ruins of Swindon Abbey," he remarked, stopping to take a closer look.

"They are indeed, sir."

"Actually I own them now that I've bought Hatfield Manor. The ruins are part of my estate." Melton bent for a closer look, examining her favourite: a full moon hanging low over the jagged walls of the ruined church. "You painted this?"

"Yes." She readied herself for a nice compliment.

"Very nice." He laughed indulgently. "You ladies must have your little hobbies."

Hobby? Words of protest rushed to her lips. *My painting is more than just a little hobby, my good sir! I take my art quite seriously and have been told it's very, very good.*

But of course she said no such thing and instead forced a smile and declared, "Why, thank you, Lord Melton, how kind of you to say."

When he bid her goodbye, Lord Melton bent low over her hand. "Good day, Miss Winslow. I shall return in two weeks, quite anxious, of course, to hear your reply."

He peered at her with knowing eyes that said he wasn't anxious at all. How could she turn him down when droves of London belles and their mothers pursued him? He was, after all, the catch of the season and had no doubt whatsoever what her answer would be.

"You said what?" Poor Lady Harleigh collapsed in a chair and stared up at Julia with horrified eyes.

"You heard me correctly," Julia replied. "Lord Melton proposed. I told him I would like time to consider his proposal before giving him my reply."

"Consider *what?*" Lady Harleigh enquired in complete bewilderment. "What is there to think about? What more could you possibly—?"

"I know, Mama, I know!" Julia knelt beside her mother's chair and took her hand. "Please try to understand. I am aware how wonderful he is, but somehow I just couldn't bring myself . . . It's hard to explain, but I need a little time. What I would like to do is go home. After all, there's no point in continuing the season, since everyone says I've already caught the best there is."

Lady Harleigh eyed her with suspicion. "Why? What would you do at Bretton Court that you cannot do here?"

"I want to see Papa. Also, I need time to think, and what better place than the ruins of Swindon Abbey? You know I love it there."

Her mother gazed at her sceptically. "What you find so fascinating about crumbling walls and messy piles of rock, I have no idea."

"I just want to go home."

"Very well." Lady Harleigh sighed in resignation. "If sitting amidst the ruins of Swindon Abbey will bring you to your senses and make you see how fantastically fortunate you are that Lord Melton has proposed, then I am all for it."

"Never fear, Mama. All will soon be as you wish. I simply need to clear my mind."

Despite the gruelling all-day coach ride home, Julia gathered up her sketch pad and charcoal as soon as she arrived and walked the short distance from Bretton Court to the neighbouring ruins of Swindon Abbey. The sun was just setting as she arrived, providing the jagged stone walls of what remained of the nave with a breathtaking background of blues streaked with pinkish gold. How good to be home again, back to these beautiful ruins she loved! She searched for a subject to sketch. As always, she had so many to choose from: the jagged silhouette of the inner cloister, the beautifully arched arcades that once led to the monks' living quarters but now led to nowhere. She chose one of the arcades and had almost completed her sketch when she heard the canter of a horse and looked up from her sketch pad.

She could not look down again.

A man on horseback was approaching, one of the most common sights imaginable, yet the graceful, easy manner in which he sat in the saddle held her spellbound. When he drew close, she saw he was casually dressed in breeches, an open-necked white shirt and plain Hessian boots. Closer still, she could see he was somewhere in his early thirties, wore his dark, wavy hair on the long side, and was regarding her with compelling brown eyes framed by a strong-featured face bronzed by the sun.

He rode to where she sat on one of the many large, broken stones scattered about. Reining his horse to a stop, he looked down at her and casually remarked, "You must be Miss Winslow."

"How did you know?" Fascinated, she watched as he swung from his horse, performing an infinitely graceful dismount, which revealed a lean and sinewy body, muscular legs and broad shoulders.

"How did I know?" Touches of humour gathered around his mouth and the corners of his eyes. "My brother has been singing your praises. He has described in great detail your full red lips, your adorable nose and—" his eyes fell to her full bosom where they lingered an extra moment "—other parts of your exceedingly well-constructed anatomy. From what I understand, you are soon to be my new sister-in-law."

"Ah!" she exclaimed, suddenly enlightened. "You must be Lord Melton's—"

"Ne'er-do-well younger brother, Robert," he interrupted with a wry smile. While he tied his horse to a nearby branch he went on, "Every family has one. Haven't you heard?"

Words failed her. "Why, I . . ."

"Don't worry about it." His shrewd eyes regarded her curiously. "Just tell me why you're going to marry Charles, will you? He's not too bright, you know, and thoroughly self-absorbed. I doubt he could actually love you since he's too much in love with himself."

For a long moment, she stared at him in astonishment, her mind not able to comprehend his outrageous words. When they finally sank in, she realized he was only trying to bait her and burst into laughter. "I take it you're not overly fond of your brother."

"He's my brother and I love him," Robert replied. "I wouldn't want to marry him, though." He rolled his eyes upwards. "My God, what a bore." He settled himself on the stone slab beside her, stretching his long legs in front of him. "When's the wedding?"

He'd had her completely baffled, but now her confidence returned. She turned to face him, tipped her head and examined him curiously. "Are you jealous of your brother? I do believe you are."

"Jealous?" He grew serious. "There was a time when actually I was. How could I not be? First sons get it all. Second sons?" His chuckle held a dry, cynical sound. "In my earlier days, I spent some time in London, leading a dissolute life feeling sorry for myself. After a rather unfortunate incident, I finally realized nobody owed me anything. It was up to me to make something of myself. That's when I took hold of my life and I've not been sorry since. So let old Charles keep his vast estates, his hunting lodge in Scotland, his fine coach and six matched greys, I'm doing what I want to do and wouldn't trade places for the world."

"Just what do you do?" she asked.

He shrugged dismissively. "I've been talking too much. What do *you* do?"

"What do I do? Only what every well-brought-up young lady does. I embroider. Study French. Play the pianoforte. And also I—"

"Draw," he said, eyeing the sketch pad she'd laid beside her. "May I see?"

"If you like." She handed him the sketch pad. "It's not finished yet."

The sun had just set, leaving just enough light for him to examine her nearly finished sketch. He examined it carefully, holding it up to catch the last of the light. "This is good," he said simply, "very good."

There was something about the way he spoke . . . It was as if he wasn't mouthing the usual empty platitudes but instead had judged her work as an expert who knew what he was talking about. "Why, thank you," she replied. Ordinarily she didn't care to discuss her artwork. Too many times she'd heard it referred to as her "little hobby", but now, for some inexplicable reason, she found herself wanting to confide in this veritable stranger. "I come here often to sketch, and often render an oil painting from the sketch. I find these ruins so beautiful I can't stay away and could paint them forever."

"Yes, they're beautiful, and haunting, too." With heartfelt intensity Robert added, "Henry the Eighth was a despot of major proportions. Between him and his pal, Thomas Cromwell, they managed to destroy virtually every monastery in England. How monstrous. How incredibly greedy. How . . ." He caught himself and smiled. "But I shall save my outrage for another day. I would like to see your paintings."

"Why do I have the feeling either you're an artist yourself, or at least you know what you're talking about when it comes to painting?"

"How very perceptive," he said admiringly. "I would like to think I'm a good judge of art. I'm an architect." With a wry smile, he continued, "That means I'm the family disgrace, of course. We all know a true gentleman does *not* work for a living. When my father learned I actually get paid for doing what I do, he was horrified. I truly believe he would have preferred I continue my dissolute ways in London where I could behave like a true aristocrat – gamble my money away and drink myself into oblivion."

She asked, "Do you like doing what you do?"

"Recently I've had some success in London, designing in the

neo-classical style, namely Palladian. Occasionally, when I get my fill of fluted Greek columns and fanciful curves, I turn to the old monastery ruins. My interest started just by chance when I was summoned by a gentleman whose estate included the site of a monastic ruin. He wanted it restored, so I happily obliged." He paused and gazed around, taking in the ruins of Swindon Abbey. "It's my fondest wish to restore these ruins, too."

"But that would be wonderful!" she exclaimed. "I often sit here and imagine what Swindon Abbey must have been like three hundred years ago before the King ordered it destroyed."

"It was like a small city here." Robert nodded towards the jagged walls of the church. "The nave with its flying buttresses could be easily restored. Did you know there's a beautifully tiled floor beneath all that rubbish? I could almost sell my soul to uncover it. Then there's the kitchen, brew house, bakehouse and kiln house. A lot of agricultural buildings, too, and of course the fields they tilled and the small gardens the monks kept for their vegetables, as well as—" The sudden bleating of a goat interrupted. They both laughed at the small herd of goats nearby. "Things haven't changed much in three hundred years. The local farmers still graze their animals here."

She had been so immersed in their conversation she hadn't noticed the sun had long since disappeared. Suddenly she realized it was almost dark and declared, "Uh-oh! I must be getting home or they'll start to worry."

"We can't have that." Robert rose to his feet and extended his hand. "It's been a pleasure meeting my sister-in-law-to-be."

She took his hand. Her pulse quickened when she felt its roughness against her own smooth palm. So different from the soft, pudgy hands of those London dandies who would not be caught dead doing an honest day's work. He helped her to her feet. They stood face to face, Julia growing increasingly aware that Robert Carstairs was a dangerously attractive man with a commanding presence which positively exuded masculinity. She gulped. Her mouth felt dry. She had a near overwhelming urge to flee before she made a fool of herself. "I was pleased to make your acquaintance," she said, making an effort to sound as prim and disinterested as possible. What was the matter with her? Why hadn't she told him she had not yet said yes to his brother? Could it be she was afraid to?

They remained facing each other, so close she could almost feel the heat from his body. "Remember, I would like to see your paintings," he said.

"Of course, Mr Carstairs. You must come to dinner—"

His hearty laugh interrupted her. "I'm the ne'er-do-well younger son, remember? Not received in polite society. I don't care to impose myself on your family. Bring your paintings here. I'll meet you tomorrow."

The very thought of seeing him again caused her heart to flip-flop. But no! What utter folly when she was about to become betrothed to his brother. "I . . . think not." She knew she would sound like a prude, but she had to say it. "It wouldn't be proper."

He laughed again, lightly clasped her shoulders, and bent towards her. "Proper or not, you *will* be here, same time tomorrow."

His nearness made her acutely aware of her breathing. She had to get away, if for no other reason than to gulp some air. "I most certainly will not, sir. Goodnight." She spun on her heel and left him standing.

"My brother's a lucky man," he called after her.

She stopped, turned, and opened her mouth to tell Robert Carstairs he was mistaken, she had *not* said yes and therefore was not yet betrothed to his brother. But the words stuck in her throat. She was definitely going to marry Lord Melton, so why allow this much too aggressive man to think otherwise?

Without speaking, she turned back and continued on, telling herself how foolish she would have been had she agreed to see Robert Carstairs again. Thank goodness she had sense enough to see that any further contact with him would lead to nothing but trouble.

That evening, Julia's two older sisters and their husbands came to dine. In the past months, these dinners had been sombre affairs, the family still mourning the loss of the son and heir. But tonight the table rocked with jokes and laughter. Julia knew why. Her mother was happy again, indeed, downright giddy with joy that her youngest daughter would soon make the perfect marriage. All evening she was bursting with elaborate wedding plans, her infectious good spirits spreading to all of them, especially Julia's father. Viscount Harleigh had also been devastated by the loss of his son, yet over the past months his main concern had been for his grieving wife. Now, as he sat at the head of the table, his kindly eyes brightened whenever he looked at her. He loved her dearly, as she did him. His delight in her newfound happiness was plain to see.

Throughout the evening, Julia stayed unusually quiet. Ordinarily she would have been actively engaged in catching up on family gossip with her sisters. Not tonight. Try as she might, she could not get Melton's younger brother off her mind. She kept thinking about those dark eyes that seemed so shrewdly assessing . . . the graceful way he dismounted from his horse . . . the feel of his hand when he pulled her to her feet . . . Wait! What on earth was the matter with her? More than once she commanded herself to stop thinking about him, but her advice never worked. Instead, she started to wonder why he couldn't come to dinner as she'd asked him to. Before she knew it, during a lull in the conversation, she declared, "I met Lord Melton's younger brother today."

From the foot of the table, her mother enquired, "Isn't he the one who isn't received?"

"Indeed!" Betsy, Julia's oldest sister, who always knew all the gossip, nodded emphatically. "The Not-So-Honourable Robert Carstairs is the disgrace of the family, or he was, anyway."

"Oh, dear," said Lady Harleigh. "What shall we do after Julia and Lord Melton are married? Must we receive him?"

"Most certainly not," her husband replied from the head of the table. "I heard he was involved in a cheating scandal at one of the London clubs. Boodles, I believe." He shook his head in disapproval. "Absolutely disgraceful. Unforgivable."

A cheater? "Are you sure, Papa?" Julia asked with rising dismay.

"As it turned out, it was all a mistake," declared Betsy, sure of her facts as always. "Mr Carstairs was proven innocent of all the charges against him. Nevertheless, his reputation was ruined anyway, and he was never seen at any of the gentlemen's clubs or any social events again." She closed her eyes and thought a moment. "Ah yes, now I remember. He receives an adequate income from his grandmother's estate, but from what I heard, he went into some sort of trade and is now actually working for a living. Can you imagine?"

Lady Harleigh looked relieved. "Then I won't feel obligated to issue him any invitations."

Julia breathed an inward sigh of relief. Thank goodness Robert Carstairs had seen fit to decline her dinner invitation. His appearance would have caused a flurry of consternation if he hadn't. Even so, her mother's firm words caused a clutch of dismay at her heart. Why that should be, she didn't know. She had much more important matters to attend to than Lord Melton's unpopular younger brother.

Contrary to her resolve of the night before, by the next day Julia found herself going about in what could best be called a daze. She could not stop thinking about Robert Carstairs to the point she could think of nothing else. During the morning she told herself she absolutely was not going to meet him at the ruins as he requested. By noon she was considering the possibility she might see him just one more time. What harm would it do? Then she would never see him again.

By mid-afternoon, not only had her resolve completely crumbled, she was trying to decide which of her paintings she should take to Swindon Abbey. Frames were out of the question, but many of her paintings had never seen the light of day and were rolled up and put away. She chose five of what she considered her best and rolled them together, after which she bathed and called upon a rather perplexed Yvette to help with her gown and hair.

"You are dressing for dinner rather early this evening," commented Yvette, helping her into a simple gown of light-green calico.

"I suppose I am." Julia hated having to sound so vague, but with a houseful of sharp-eyed relatives, plus servants who always knew everything, carrying out any sort of deception was never easy.

But she managed. During a quiet moment in the late afternoon, carrying her roll of paintings, she slipped from the house. What would one more meeting hurt? She would see Robert Carstairs one more time and that was positively all.

When she reached the ruins, she discovered Robert sitting on the same stone slab where they'd sat before, his long legs stretched comfortably before him. He rose to greet her, not seeming at all surprised she had come. "Ah, you brought the paintings." He took the roll of paintings from her hand. "Let's have a look."

One by one, he laid them on the flat part of the slab and examined each carefully. "Beautiful," he said of her special favourite which featured swirling clouds over the ancient stone monks' quarters. "The depth makes me feel as if I'm there." Another painting featured the still-intact south-west tower of the church, its dark stones etched against a brilliant sunset. After he scrutinized it carefully, he remarked, "Excellent! What harmonious colours! Your remarkable talent oozes from every brush stroke."

By the time he finished, she was positively glowing from his praise. "You're very kind," she said.

"You're a gifted artist. I'm surprised no one has recognized your work."

She smiled dryly. "I shall only be recognized for my 'work' when I manage to find a husband."

"Ah yes, we mustn't forget old Charles." He shrugged with disinterest. "But let's not think of him right now."

"I'd rather not."

After he re-rolled the last of her paintings, they sat on the slab and continued to chat. She did her best to fully engage in whatever inconsequential topic they were discussing, but she found herself so aware of his presence she soon realized there were, in essence, two conversations going on. One had to do with the obvious – their spoken words; the other, so much more subtle, had to do with the intense waves of attraction that coursed back and forth between them. She could tell from the admiration gleaming in his eyes he found her desirable. In turn, his very nearness so made her senses spin it was all she could do to nod politely and respond in a normal voice.

At last, in the midst of his description of some ancient abbey, he stopped abruptly. Drawing in a sharp breath, he clasped her upper arms and declared, "Enough of this farce. You know I'm deucedly attracted to you, don't you? So much so I—" He bent forwards as if to kiss her.

Finally. She pursed her lips, eagerly awaiting the crush of his mouth upon hers, but instead he abruptly dropped his hands and pulled away. Muttering a "Damn it," he stood and walked a few steps from the slab. For a long moment he remained with his back to her, staring at the pink and gold streaked remnants of the sunset. Finally he turned to face her. "We can't do this," he said, his voice thick with intensity. A touch of irony in his words, he continued, "You must forgive me, Miss Winslow. I fear your charm and beauty are so compelling I was carried away and momentarily forgot you belong to Charles."

"I do not belong to Charles or anyone else," she sharply declared, keenly disappointed he hadn't kissed her.

"Are you not betrothed to my brother?"

"I haven't said yes yet."

He raised an eyebrow in surprise. "You haven't?"

"I told him I would like to think about it."

He thought a moment. "But surely you will."

"Whether I will or whether I won't is none of your concern, Mr Carstairs. Suffice to say that at this moment I am most definitely not betrothed to Lord Melton or anyone else." She pointed to where he had been sitting. "Now will you please come back and finish what you started?" She was astonished at herself. *Never* in all her twenty-two years had she spoken so boldly to a man, but she so badly wanted him to kiss her that at that moment she didn't care.

Her answer seemed to satisfy him, for he swiftly returned to her side, seized her in his arms and crushed his lips to hers. She kissed him eagerly in return, wrapping her arms around his neck, pulling him closer still. She found the touch of his lips such a delicious sensation that when they finally broke apart, both gasping for air, she immediately wanted more. Their lips met again. They continued on in a series of slow, shivery kisses that put her in such a world of dreamy intimacy she forgot time, place and every admonition her mother ever gave her.

Her heart lurched with excitement when he leaned her back on the slab and she felt his hand slide up her side. As it slid ever higher, a delicious current of wanting ran through her. His hand had just cupped her breast when—

"Bleaaah!"

Startled, they abruptly pulled apart and looked to see where the sound had come from.

"It's one of the goats," said Robert. They both broke into laughter at the sight of the bearded animal only a few feet away, at that moment engaged in munching on a shrub.

Sanity returned to her befuddled brain. She sat up and smoothed her hair. "What were we thinking of?" she asked, fully aware she would surely have continued had the goat not intruded.

He inhaled deeply. "You're right. What were we thinking of?"

She saw that darkness had fallen. "I must be getting home. My family will be wondering where I am."

"Of course."

Thoughts of her family quickly returned her the rest of the way to stark, cold reality. What if the goat hadn't come along? Would she and Robert have stopped? What if she had actually made all-the-way love with Robert Carstairs? Good grief, was she about to? The man had got her so hot with desire, so aching for his touch she doubted she could have mustered the strength to say no. In fact, she'd been so carried away she suspected the word no would not have even crossed her mind.

"We had best not see each other again," she said.

"Nonsense. I'll meet you here tomorrow. Make it two o'clock. Bring your horse. We'll go riding."

The more she thought about it, the more she convinced herself she must never again be alone with Robert Carstairs, not if she valued her reputation and, in fact, her entire future. "You don't understand."

"I understand perfectly." He bowed slightly, his eyes full of mischief. "I value your friendship, Miss Winslow, as I hope you do mine. From now on we shall meet as friends."

"Nothing more?" she asked, highly sceptical.

"Nothing more. I give you my word."

Deep in her heart she didn't believe him, but she could not bear the thought of not seeing him again. "Tomorrow. We'll go riding – just for a little while, and just as friends."

For Julia, the days that followed were the happiest of her life. She and Robert went riding every day, following the beautiful trails that led through the thick bordering woods or along the nearby river. Occasionally they passed Hatfield Manor's gamekeeper's lodge where Robert said he was staying.

"You don't stay with Charles in the mansion?" she had asked.

"I told you Charles bores me to distraction," Robert had replied with a grin. "I prefer to be alone and, besides, my stay is only temporary. I shall be leaving for London soon on business." He'd feigned a lecherous expression and enquired, "Would you care to visit me in the gamekeeper's lodge? You're welcome any time, you know. We would be entirely alone."

She'd laughed as he intended, but the very thought of being alone in a secluded place with Robert Carstairs gave her a secret shiver of delight.

Robert always brought along the makings of a picnic in his saddlebag. Every day they would stop at some beautiful spot along the way to eat and just talk. "Thanks to Charles' cook we've got bread, cheese, fruit and chicken," he told her the first time they stopped. "And—" he held up a sterling silver hip flask "—a bit of brandy to keep us warm in case a storm should strike."

They talked of many things: her art, the buildings he'd designed, the ancient monasteries he'd visited and what he would do to restore them. True to his word, he made no further advances. On the surface she was grateful, yet secretly she yearned for his touch – more each day if that were possible – to the point where she thought she would scream if he mentioned one more time what good "friends" they were.

But she was well aware the idyllic days she was spending with Robert must soon end. So far she had managed to keep their trysts a secret, but how long could that last? And what did it matter? The two weeks Lord Melton was spending at his hunting lodge were nearly at an end. Soon he would return, ready to hear her answer.

Late one afternoon when Julia arrived home from a delightful afternoon with Robert, her grandmother summoned her to the drawing room. "Sit down, Julia." Spying the sketch pad in her granddaughter's hands, she lifted a sceptical eyebrow. "So you've been out sketching the ruins again?"

Julia immediately caught her meaning. Every time she'd left the mansion to meet with Robert, she'd made a show of bringing along her sketch pad. She hadn't used it once. "I've been meaning to talk to you," she began, but her grandmother raised a hand.

"A rumour has reached my ears that you've been out roaming the countryside with Robert Carstairs. Is that right?"

Julia nodded. She could never lie to her grandmother. "How did you know?"

"How could I not know? Did you think such a juicy bit of gossip would escape the servants' notice? Not that I care what you do, but your mother is sure to find out. Soon, I suspect, and you must be prepared. Are you in love with him?"

Julia was not given to excess, but her grandmother's abrupt question caused her to burst out, "I adore him, Granny! Robert Carstairs is everything I ever wanted in a man. He's a talented artist, as well as an architect. He has a love of the old monastic ruins, just as I do. Sometimes we talk about them for hours. We talk about all sorts of things. He's never boring, he's—"

"Slow down, missy," Granny said with a smile. "My, my, he must be a remarkable man indeed. Have you kissed him?"

Julia felt a slow blush creep over her cheeks. "Yes, I kissed him, and it was . . . it was . . ."

"You needn't go on. I get the point. What about Lord Melton?"

In the wake of her grandmother's penetrating question, Julia's euphoria quickly slipped away. "How can I marry Lord Melton when I have fallen madly in love with his brother?" She shook her head in dismay. "But if I don't marry him, I'll break Mother's heart."

"You must make a decision, and soon."

"But I'm not sure what to do."

"It's simple. Either you follow your head or you follow your heart. Has Robert Carstairs proposed?"

"No, but I think he loves me."

Granny shook her head in sympathy. "You poor girl, such a dilemma."

"I'm meeting Robert tomorrow. Lord Melton returns the day after." Julia gave her grandmother a rueful smile. "By then I'll make my decision. If it kills me, I won't be one of those wishy-washy women who can't make up their minds."

That night Julia lay awake staring into the darkness. Talking to Granny was one thing, but what, in reality, was she going to say to Robert? After all, he had not proposed, nor had he declared his love for her. In fact, since that never-to-be-forgotten kiss that the goat interrupted, he had behaved like a perfect gentleman, truly being nothing more than a friend. Perhaps that was how he thought of her – as just a friend. But if that were true, what were those messages of attraction and passion she had seen deep in his eyes when they talked? Had she been mistaken?

Perhaps she should cancel tomorrow's meeting with him, wait for Charles' return and simply say yes like everyone expected her to do. But no! She had to talk to Robert – find out how he felt about her and damn the consequences, even if she might very well end up making a complete fool of herself.

The next day, Julia saddled her horse and met Robert at the ruins of Swindon Abbey as usual. Immediately she felt tongue-tied. How was she supposed to find out how Robert felt about her? She couldn't just ask. That would be much too "unladylike", as Mama would say and, besides, she would be leaving herself wide open for rejection. What if, God forbid, all he wanted was her friendship? She was still searching for an answer when their ride took them deep into the woods past the gamekeeper's lodge. An idea glimmered. Perhaps in the more intimate privacy of the lodge, she could find her answer. She reined in her horse. "I do believe I would like to see the inside of the lodge," she said. "You've invited me often enough."

"What's this?" Robert remarked with feigned surprise. "Aren't you afraid you'll be ravished the moment you step through the door?"

She tilted her chin. "I'll take my chances."

When she entered the main hall of the gamekeeper's lodge, she was struck by how comfortable it was with its oak-beamed ceilings, huge stone fireplace, animal heads mounted on the walls and informal furnishings made of pine.

She settled on a sofa facing the fireplace. "I can see why you like it here. Where are the servants?"

He sat next to her and chuckled. "One or two come in from time to time to tidy the place up. Otherwise, I fend for myself. I prefer it that way, rather than staying in that huge monstrosity up the hill." A rueful expression crossed his face. "Forgive me. As the future mistress of Hatfield Manor, you might be offended by my last remark."

"I really don't care what you call it," she replied in a deliberately haughty tone. "What makes you so sure I'm going to marry Lord Melton?"

"Aren't you supposed to have your answer ready when he returns tomorrow?"

He had asked the question casually, yet Julia detected an alert gleam in his eye. "My family expects me to marry him in the worst way, as you can well imagine."

"Oh, I can imagine all right." Robert tensed. His relaxed attitude of amusement disappeared. His eyes drilled intently into hers. "And you? How do you feel?"

At long last, the moment of truth had arrived. *Follow your head or follow your heart,* Granny had said. Well, she knew for certain her heart had won. "I don't love Charles, and I'm not going to marry him."

She started to lean back on the sofa and wait for his reply, but before she could, he roughly seized her shoulders and demanded, "Tell me exactly *why* you are not going to marry my brother."

"Because . . . because . . ." Seeing the expectant gleam in his eye, she threw her last bit of caution to the winds. She laid a gentle palm on his cheek and continued, "It's because of you."

Robert drew in a ragged breath and pulled her close. "Are you sure?" he whispered in her ear.

The touch of his hands, locked tight against her spine, sent her senses spinning. "Will you just stop talking and kiss me?"

"Gladly." First he kissed the tip of her nose, then her eyes. Finally he kissed her long and hard on her mouth. It was a kiss for her yearning soul to melt in, a kiss she returned with reckless abandon. When they finally broke apart, he sat back and regarded her with such a soft warmth in his eyes she knew beyond all doubt he loved her. "I had always assumed you would marry Charles, so naturally—"

"I don't need to be a countess," she interrupted. "Nor do I need half a dozen estates, or however many your brother owns. I just want to be with you . . . unless . . ." She cocked her head and regarded him quizzically. "Unless, of course, you want us to be just friends."

With a deep sigh that combined both relief and delight, he replied, "Just friends? Surely you jest. You know you've stolen my heart. I fell in love with you the first moment I saw you, sitting amidst the ruins with your sketch pad. To hell with friendship. It's been all I could do to keep my hands off you."

"My darling, from now on you won't have to."

Robert pulled her into his arms again and began a series of kisses that left her weak with desire. When finally he murmured, "We need a bed."

She nodded in agreement, feeling a giddy sense of pleasure when he scooped her in his arms and carried her off to his bedchamber.

Afterwards, when she lay naked in Robert's arms, bursting with joy and completely satiated, she said, "I must be getting home soon. Will you come with me? It's time you met my family."

"Not yet." Robert raised up on an elbow and looked down at her. "I prefer you finish your business with Charles first. When that's done, we'll make our plans."

Never had she felt so blissfully happy, so fully alive! She could hardly wait to see Lord Melton again and give him her positive, irrefutable no.

When Julia returned to Bretton Court, she felt as if she were floating on a cloud. Robert loved her! She wanted to dance across the marble floor of the vast entry hall, just thinking about the blissful years that lay ahead. Together, she and Robert would work on restoring ancient ruins. They would raise a number of beautiful children. They would make love every night.

"Is that you, Julia?"

Her father's voice. When she saw him she stopped short. Only once before, the night they learned Douglas had died at the Battle of Waterloo, had she seen his usually cheerful face so pale and drawn. "Papa, what is the matter?"

"It's your mother. She suddenly collapsed this afternoon. The doctor says it's her heart."

In an instant her joy turned to anguish. "Will she be all right?"

"We don't know yet. The doctor is still with her. I know you'll want to see her, but first—" he laid a gentle hand on her arm "—you need to know that the cause of your mother's collapse was you."

Julia gasped and cried, "How could that be, Papa? You know I would never—"

"This afternoon a rumour reached her ears that you had been seen with Lord Melton's younger brother, Robert Carstairs. You have been seen in his company more than once, and apparently quite enjoying yourself." Papa looked her square in the eye. "You know how happy your mother has been, believing you were soon to become betrothed to Lord Melton. But now . . ." Papa's voice broke. "Is it true, Julia? Are you involved with Robert Carstairs? If you are, I fear your mother may not survive another heartbreak."

"Oh my God, I couldn't bear it if—" Julia pressed her hand over her face, fighting back tears. "I wouldn't hurt Mama for anything in the world."

"I know you wouldn't, daughter, but if you're involved with this scoundrel, you will kill your mother as surely as if you had stabbed her in the heart."

Never had her father spoken to her like that before. With a sinking anguish, she swallowed the sob that rose in her throat and asked, "Where is she? I must go see her."

Papa's jaw tightened. "I won't have her hurt."

"I won't hurt her, Papa, I promise."

"It's me, Mama." Julia bent over her mother's bed, despairing over the sight of her mother lying there, so pale and wan.

Lady Harleigh grabbed her hand and clasped it tight with more strength than Julia would have thought possible. "Is it true?" she asked in a laboured whisper. "Have you been seeing Lord Melton's brother?"

"Yes, Mama, I have, but . . ." At first the words she was about to say stuck in her throat, but she knew she had to say them. "Mr Carstairs and I are only friends. Don't worry, I still plan to marry Lord Melton."

The next morning, crumpled pieces of notepaper covered Julia's writing desk, some of them tear-stained, all the result of her painful attempts to write a farewell note to Robert. She had not yet finished when her grandmother came hobbling in on her cane. Granny seated herself on a chair beside the desk, her lined old face frowning with concern. "You look terrible, missy."

Julia gulped and replied, "I feel terrible."

"Have you heard the doctor says your mother is better this morning?"

"I know. I'm very glad."

Granny peered at her carefully. "You don't look glad."

"That's because . . ." Before she could prevent it, a tear slid down her cheek. "Oh, Granny, I'm so glad Mama's better, but . . ." She choked. Another tear followed the first.

Granny offered her lace-edged handkerchief. "I see the problem. You've lost Robert, whom you love, and you're going to marry Lord Melton whom you don't love."

Julia took the handkerchief, wiped her eyes and blew her nose. "You know everything, don't you?"

"Just about."

"Then you know my heart is broken and there's nothing I can do about it." Bitterness tinged her voice as she continued, "I shall be Countess Melton – oh what a thrill! I shall be one of the exalted leaders of the ton, everyone bowing and scraping. I shall flit from one country estate to another and . . . Oh, Granny, I'm so miserable I don't know what to do!"

Granny frowned. "Why on earth did you tell your mother you would marry Lord Melton?"

"Because she would have died if I hadn't."

"That's rubbish!"

Caught off guard by her grandmother's vehement reply, Julia sat stunned for a moment. "How can you say such a thing when Mama was at death's door, and all because of me?"

"Maybe she was and maybe she wasn't. Either way, she and your father have no right to force you into doing something you don't want to do."

Julia slowly shook her head from side to side. "I don't care what you say. What's done is done. I gave my word I would marry Lord Melton and so I shall."

Granny peered at her with her shrewd old eyes. "I cannot see you married to that foppish dolt."

"Well, you had best get used to the idea."

"I won't. And furthermore . . ." A strange expression crossed Granny's face, almost as if she'd had some sort of revelation. "I predict you are *not* going to marry him. Something's going to happen that will make you change your mind."

"Would you mind telling me what?"

"I don't know yet."

Julia laughed wryly. "This time you're wrong, Granny. I have lost Robert for ever and must make the best of it. Nothing on this earth could make me change my mind."

Notified of Lady Harleigh's illness, Lord Melton sent his best wishes for a fast recovery, adding he would await "that fervently anticipated moment when she would be well enough to receive guests again". He didn't have long to wait. After making a remarkably swift recovery, Julia's mother not only abandoned her bed, she began planning a dinner party for some of her finest, most prestigious friends, including, of course, Lord Melton. She even invited the Prince Regent himself. Though Prinny refused, citing an important engagement elsewhere, her elation knew no bounds when the Duke and Duchess of Sherford accepted. "A Knight of the Garter will be at our table!" she elatedly declared.

An invitation was sent to Lord Melton "and guest", as was the proper etiquette. Naturally Mama expected him to come alone, but when Melton returned his RSVP stating he planned to bring a guest, she grew alarmed. "Is it a woman? Do you suppose he has found someone else?"

"Nonsense, my dear," her husband reassured her, "no one could replace our daughter. The dinner party will give Julia the perfect opportunity to give Lord Melton her answer. You have nothing to fear."

Over the next few days, Julia wondered who Melton's guest could be. In her heart she fervently hoped he had indeed found someone else and had lost all interest in her. Or . . . could he possibly be bringing his brother? She had not heard from Robert since she sent him her farewell note. Not that she expected a reply – or *deserved* a reply. But despite her decision to marry Charles, thoughts of Robert filled her mind nearly every waking moment. How could she live without him? How could she ever be happy again? She wondered, too, how Robert felt. Had she broken his heart? Was he as devastated as she? Why hadn't she heard from him?

On the night of the dinner party, Julia, dressed in a daringly low-cut gown of white bombazine, performed her hostess duties as if by rote. Standing in the entry hall beside her parents, she was greeting guests when she saw Lord Melton pull up the drive to the front portico in his curricle. Robert Carstairs sat by his side.

Her pulse pounding, she watched Robert alight with infinite grace from the curricle. Never had she seen him so splendidly attired, looking every bit as dashing as his brother in a double-breasted wool frock coat with claw-hammer tails, long trousers, waistcoat, Hessian boots with a tassel, kid gloves and scrupulously tied cravat.

As the two approached, Lady Harleigh hissed behind her fan, "It's that ruffian of a brother! What shall we do?"

Her husband whispered back quickly, "We shall receive him graciously, my dear. We have no other choice."

Lord Melton approached and bent low over Julia's hand. "I am delighted to see you again, Miss Winslow. I trust you will save some private time for me later on this evening?"

"Indeed I shall, Lord Melton." Her spirits sank to a depth even lower than they already were. How could they not be low when she was only hours away from making a commitment that would last a lifetime, seal her wretched fate for ever?

Melton moved on as Robert approached and bowed. "Miss Winslow," he murmured. If he was heartbroken and devastated, it certainly didn't show. In fact, a faint light twinkled in the depths of his brown eyes, almost as if he knew something of interest she didn't yet know.

"Mister Carstairs," she murmured back. She wanted to say more, but other guests arrived and Robert moved on. She didn't get a chance to see him again until they sat down to dinner and she found both brothers seated across from her. Although she tried to avoid it, Robert occasionally caught her gaze. What *was* that faint light still gleaming in his eyes? Again, she had the feeling he possessed knowledge of something she as yet didn't know. But what? she asked herself miserably. Their affair was over. Done. She would never make love with Robert Carstairs again.

During the soup course, Lord Melton began expounding on the subject of Hatfield Manor, his newly purchased estate. As the whole table listened, one of the guests remarked, "I understand your estate includes the ruins of an old monastery."

Melton smiled, eager to answer. "Indeed, you are referring to Swindon Abbey."

"I hear it's one of the most beautiful of all the monastic ruins. Do you plan to restore it?"

Melton's laugh boomed around the table. "Actually I have just completed my plans. As you know, a good abbey ruin is a fine feature for a gentleman's park. In a manner of speaking I shall restore it, although—" he stole a quick glance at his brother "—not as some would like."

"What do you plan?"

"I will convert the south-west tower of the church into a shooting box. Perfect for hunting. Of course, those arcades will have to come down first thing. Otherwise, they'll block my view."

Robert spoke up. "Tell us your plans for a quarry, Charles." He was addressing his brother, yet his gaze was fixed on Julia, as if he was waiting to see how she would react.

"Ah, yes, the quarry," Melton enthusiastically replied. "Did you know there's good money to be made from the ruins of these old monasteries? I plan to sell the stones for paving roads and the like."

Julia nearly choked on her spoonful of turtle soup. When she was able to speak, she asked in a shocked voice, "Everything, Lord Melton? The church, the cloister, the storehouses . . . oh, surely not the monks' quarters!"

Melton nodded equitably. "Actually the old monks' quarters are the perfect size for the brewery I intend to install. As for the rest, except for my hunting tower, I intend to demolish Swindon Abbey down to the last stone." With a chuckle he added, "In other words, I shall finish what Henry the Eighth started, eh?" Amidst sporadic laughter, he sat back with a pleased smile on his face.

Swindon Abbey demolished? Throughout the rest of the meal, Julia remained in a state of shock, hardly knowing what she ate, if she ate anything at all. When she accidentally caught Robert's eye, she observed what appeared to be a faintly perceptible knowing smile on his face. Not only that, but his eyes held a question, as if he were asking, *Now what will you do? Do you still plan to marry my brother, the greedy fool?*

She thought long and hard. By the time the ladies adjourned to the drawing room, with the gentlemen remaining behind for their brandy and cigars, she had made up her mind and knew exactly what she was going to do.

Later in the evening Julia led Lord Melton into the library. After firmly shutting the door, she turned to face him and said without preamble, "I am grateful for your offer, but I cannot marry you."

Lord Melton's perennially smug mouth dropped open. His eyes bulged like some recently caught fish. "Am I hearing you correctly?"

"Indeed you are, sir. I would be doing you a disservice if I married you because I don't love you and never could. Furthermore, I could never love a man who would destroy the beautiful ruins of an ancient monastery."

Truly taken aback, he replied, "The ruins of Swindon Abbey are but an eyesore! I don't understand."

Why bother explaining? With his shallow mind he would never understand. All she could do now was soften the blow. "You are a remarkable man in many ways, Lord Melton. Handsome, charming, indeed, the catch of the season. I can name any one of a number of young ladies who would sell their souls to capture you."

Her flattery caused Melton to give her a self-satisfied nod of agreement. To her relief, although he had obviously been taken by surprise, he seemed less than devastated. In fact, she had the distinct impression he would have shown more feeling had he lost his favourite cook.

After the barest of pleasantries Melton departed, leaving her standing in the library feeling as if a tremendous load had just been lifted from her shoulders. But she didn't feel that light-hearted. She still had her mother to worry about – and Robert . . .

"May I come in?" Robert's voice. He was standing in the doorway.

"Please do, Mr Carstairs."

"Charles just told me." He closed the door behind him and strode to where she stood. "By God, I was right!" he exclaimed.

"Right about what?"

"I knew you could never marry a man so crass, so insensitive that he would desecrate the ruins of Swindon Abbey."

How well he knew her! "I could have forgiven him anything but that." Nervously she bit her lip. "I can only hope my mother will understand."

"She just might not be as upset as you might think," he said in a voice so positive she wondered if there was something else he wasn't telling her. But before she could ask, he took her in his arms, gave her one long, passionate kiss and declared, "I want to marry you. I cannot give you everything my brother could, but I have a good income, and as a matter of fact—"

"Say no more." She touched a finger to his lips. "Of course I'll marry you. I would marry you if you hadn't a farthing to your name."

As he kissed her again, she reflected that now only one dark cloud hung over her otherwise brilliantly shining horizon. She wondered if her mother would understand and could only pray the shock wouldn't kill her.

Lady Harleigh was chatting with the portly Duke of Sherford when Julia and Robert entered the drawing room. When the Duke saw Robert his eyes lit. "Ah, Carstairs! I haven't had a chance to congratulate you yet."

Lady Harleigh frowned in puzzlement. "*Congratulate*, Your Grace?"

"You haven't heard?" the Duke continued in his booming voice. "Robert Carstairs has been personally appointed by the Prince Regent to design the development of Marylebone Park. Quite an undertaking for a young architect, eh, Carstairs? You've certainly kept it quiet enough. From what I've heard, it's going to be a 'garden city' with villas, terraced houses, crescents and even a canal and lakes. Good going, man!" He gave Robert a hearty clap on the back. "Prinny himself told me he's a great admirer of your work."

Lady Harleigh stood frozen in astonishment. When finally she gathered her wits about her, she addressed Robert. "Why that's . . . that's . . . I never dreamed! I thought—"

"That he was Lord Melton's ne'er-do-well brother, Mama? Well, obviously not." Julia threw a why-didn't-you-tell-me glance at Robert, followed by a long sigh of contentment. She addressed her mother again. "By the way, whenever you and Papa can squeeze in a spare moment, Mr Carstairs and I have something to tell you."

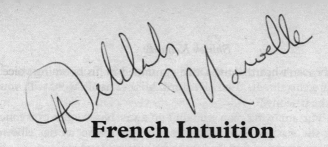

French Intuition

Delilah Marvelle

London, England – June 1828, evening
The Pickworth Ball

He hadn't come. Even though he said he would.

Of course, Lady Gwendolyn Elizabeth Redford knew all too well why her husband hadn't arrived. Instead of being a mature and rational man, he'd finally opted to believe the outrageous rumours that she was involved with Lord Westbrook. And whilst, yes, Westbrook had once ardently vied for her hand in marriage, the man had never meant anything to her. Not then, and most certainly not now. No man could ever be as handsome, or as witty, or as charming, or as . . . *annoying* as her Camden.

Somehow, this mutual agreement of theirs to spend a little time apart had led to a lot of time apart. Followed by complete chaos brought on by the ton, who held nothing sacred if it created some amusing entertainment.

Perspiration trickled its way down the length of Gwendolyn's exposed neck beneath her pinned curls. And she hadn't even been dancing. It was all due to the stagnant heat of a ballroom that harboured an unsightly amount of people. A result of too many invitations sent.

Far worse than all the heat and the people, their fading scents of oiled perfumes mingling with rancid sweat, was having to assist her younger brother's new-found aspiration to wed. Edwin's dreamy enthusiasm towards a love match achingly reminded her of herself when she was his age. But it took far more than dreamy enthusiasm to make a loving marriage thrive. She should know.

Lord Westbrook's stocky frame reappeared at her side again. For the fifth time that night.

She stiffened, but otherwise remained in place, knowing he was going to follow her no matter where she went.

Westbrook swept aside the curling, dark hair from his forehead and cleared his throat. "Lady Redford. Might I have a word with you out on the balcony?"

Gad. The annoying man wouldn't go away. No wonder everyone thought she was involved with him. He was forever at her elbow, insisting on attention that was anything but respectable.

She sighed, wishing there were no rules in society about being courteous. "I am not interested in sharing words, My Lord. And most certainly not on a balcony where our conversation may be construed as something it is not."

He scooted closer, his gloved hand curving around her corseted waist. "You cannot keep eluding me."

Gwendolyn sucked in a breath and stepped outside of his grasp, eyeing the crowds around them, including her brother who lingered only a few feet away. Of course, her brother was far too occupied with his own life to notice she was being shoved into the devil's own cupboard.

She set her chin, trying to remain calm. If she overreacted, it would bring attention. And that she most certainly did not need. "There is a very good reason as to why I am eluding you, My Lord, but I am far too civil to express that reason. Now I am demanding you cease this. You have already created more gossip than I know what to do with."

Westbrook reclaimed the distance she had set between them and leaned towards her. His dark eyes boldly traced her breasts and whispered, "I will only cease once I get what I want. Do you need me to tell you what I want? Or has your husband never properly educated you on the matter?"

She buried her right hand within the folds of her gown, fisting the silk material in an effort to keep herself from outright smacking him. She stepped away again and glared at him. "I will see to it my husband calls on you tomorrow afternoon so that you may discuss this with him in greater detail. Will that better suit you?"

"There is no need, madam. When it comes to you, Redford and I already share an understanding." Westbrook smirked, adjusted his evening coat and stared her down with haughty, dark eyes. Offering her a nod, he turned and strode over towards her brother, interrupting his conversation with a few curt words.

Gwendolyn narrowed her gaze, wishing it were legal to publicly castrate men. With each passing day, she was beginning to believe it was far better being miserable *with* Camden than being miserable *without* him. Their separation was supposed to bring them a form of uniting, healing peace – not this . . . *war*.

She wandered closer to her brother and waved a frantic hand towards him from behind Westbrook's back. She urgently mouthed, "*We must leave. Now.*"

Edwin flicked a nod in response to her silent plea, and discreetly held up an apologetic gloved hand, asking for patience. He then continued his in-depth discussion with Lord Westbrook.

It reminded her of something Camden would do. Tell her to wait a moment and then two hours would pass.

She hissed out a breath. Didn't Edwin realize that by engaging Westbrook, he was only going to further complicate her life? She flicked open her fan and waved it frantically back and forth before her heated face.

A superficial laugh – one she'd never heard in all her five and twenty years — escaped Edwin in response to something Westbrook said.

Gwendolyn blinked, freezing the tip of her fan below her nose. She lowered her chin slightly and continued to observe her brother's unusual antics. Edwin's chestnut hair fell farther out of place with each exaggerated, eager nod.

Oh, no. If she didn't know any better, she'd say Edwin was trying to impress Westbrook in an effort to gain an introduction to the man's ever-so-popular younger sister. Dear Lord, this did not bode well for her. At all. She did not want or need Westbrook for an in-law.

Someone leaned towards her, bringing the refreshing scent of citrus into the frowsty air. "Gwendolyn," her mother chimed. "You look incredibly annoyed."

"I am incredibly annoyed." Gwendolyn snapped her fan shut and released it, letting it dangle again from her wrist. She spun towards her mother. "Where have you been?"

Despite the heat that was causing everyone's rouge to fade, Lady Stanton's own remained flawless. Like the rest of her. Even with those greying tresses, her pretty, oval face held a fresh youthfulness from which no amount of grey could detract. Now why couldn't Westbrook obsess over someone like her mother who had been widowed these past six years? The woman needed attention far more than she did.

Gwendolyn leaned towards her mother. "Edwin is entertaining Westbrook. I demand you do something. He is your son and there-fore *your* responsibility. Not mine."

Lady Stanton's green eyes flicked over towards Edwin and Lord Westbrook, then back to her. She shook her head and ushered Gwendolyn away from the two, her emerald satin and lace gown brushing against her own.

Once they were a few steps away, her mother flicked open her own silk fan, hiding her lips from those around them, and whispered, "You do realize Westbrook is waiting for you and Redford to divorce, yes?"

Gwendolyn rolled her eyes. "As if I would ever—"

"What is more," her mother added in an even more hushed tone, now appearing concerned, "Redford may be planning on it."

Gwendolyn stared at her, her breath hitching. "Whatever do you mean? Camden and I aren't—"

"Apparently, upon hearing all the gossip, Redford went to Westbrook and demanded proof of your involvement with him, lest he call the man out for slander. Two days later, Westbrook provided him with proof."

Gwendolyn choked. "What proof? I never—"

Her mother grabbed her arm and shielded both of their faces with her fan. "Westbrook bribed one of your servants and acquired one of your silk stockings, then delivered it to Redford. Therein providing proof."

Gwendolyn gasped, her eyes widening in disbelief. She grabbed both of her mother's gloved hands and squeezed them in a frantic effort to balance herself and her thoughts. "How do you know all of this?"

Lady Stanton fluttered her fan for a moment and eyed her sheepishly. "With Redford moving out, I was worried about you living alone. So I . . . paid your butler and housekeeper additional funds to watch over you a bit more carefully."

Gwendolyn felt her throat tightening as she glanced back towards Lord Westbrook who was still enthusiastically conversing with her brother. "Keep me from slitting his throat from ear to ear," she rasped. "Why is he doing this to me? I never once—"

"Calm yourself," Lady Stanton hissed, snapping her fan shut. "And more importantly, keep your voice to a whisper. Now, let us fetch you a glass of wine and take you home. In the morning, we will try to settle this misunderstanding as best we can."

Gwendolyn drew in a steady breath, trying to calm herself. She let the breath out, nodding. "I believe I will require more than one glass of wine. I will require four or five. Maybe even six."

"Whatever amount will keep you calm. Now come along." Lady Stanton tucked her hand into the crook of Gwendolyn's arm and whisked her away in the opposite direction.

"*Mother!*" Edwin called out after them. He scrambled around Lord Westbrook and held up a gloved hand above the heads of other passing couples. "You cannot whisk her away as of yet. I need her."

"Ignore him," Gwendolyn hissed, rushing them forwards. "He only ever acknowledges me when an opportunity for a female introduction arises and, frankly, I feel like an underpaid chaperone."

"You needn't worry about him," her mother insisted. "I will put an end to his preening. That boy has been far too preoccupied with his own life to notice anyone else's."

"It must be contagious."

Together, they bumped their way through the crush of people and didn't slow their pace until they were on the other side of the ballroom.

Gwendolyn heaved out a sigh and glanced at her mother. "I don't understand why you keep encouraging his need for matrimony. Edwin is only twenty."

Her mother patted Gwendolyn's forearm. "You cannot fault him, dear. He's always been a romantic. You know that."

Lady Stanton suddenly yanked them both to a halt, turning them in the direction of an older gent. "My Lord!" her mother exclaimed. "Oh, thank heavens. Such divine timing I have never known."

Lady Stanton scurried them both over to a grey-haired gent whose ivory waistcoat couldn't hide an oversized belly that protruded from his dark evening coat.

Gwendolyn's heart momentarily skipped at the realization of who he was. Camden's uncle. Lord Truesdale. Why, she hadn't even heard his name announced.

"My dear Lady Stanton." Lord Truesdale took her mother's free hand and bowed ardently over it. "I demand we find a less crowded room. My carriage or yours?" He waggled his thick, grey brows and grinned crookedly, still holding on to Lady Stanton's gloved hand.

Her mother released a girlish laugh and coyly withdrew her hand not only from him, but also from Gwendolyn's own arm. "Do tame yourself," she shrilled. "We are family."

Lord Truesdale continued to blatantly grin at her, not in the least bit fazed. "Must you remind me?"

The two openly laughed.

It was like listening to debutantes prattle. Only far worse. When the opportunity of silence presented itself, Gwendolyn decided to interject. "Forgive me, My Lord, but is Camden coming? Do you even know?" There was no sense in pretending she had come for anything *but* Camden.

Lord Truesdale turned his stout body towards her, those brown eyes instantly cooling. "The boy has never been one for confrontations. You know that." He stiffly grasped Gwendolyn's hand, kissed the top of her gloved knuckles and paused, staring her down. "Camden is beside himself. As am I."

She choked, her grasp on his hand tightening. "*I* am beside myself. It is a farce, My Lord. A lie. All of it. My mother can attest."

Lord Truesdale tugged her in closer with the jerk of her hand, forcing her to stare straight into his stern, round face. "It had better be a lie. Now cease all of this nonsense, move back in with the boy and see to your duty by siring an heir. My nephew has waited long enough, has he not?"

Gwendolyn swallowed back the biting sensation of tears burning her eyes and yanked her shaky hand out of his. She had miscarried far too many times – seven, to be exact — for there to be any humour in his words. "Did your nephew not explain my situation? Or do you find yourself thoroughly amusing?"

Her mother touched her arm, silently pleading she refrain from saying anything more.

Lord Truesdale blinked, then set his hands behind his back and abruptly turned towards her mother. "Whatever the situation may be, I intend to embark upon an intervention by putting an end to these blasphemous rumours." He scanned his surroundings. "And I hope all of London is listening. Because I am a man of my word."

Gwendolyn's heart skipped at the unexpected gesture. After all, the man had never been enthusiastic about her and Camden's marriage, being the dedicated bachelor that he was. The man much preferred courtesans over a respectable woman. "You intend on assisting? Why? You never approved of our marriage."

He glared at her. "Camden has been contemplating everything but suicide. What else would you have me do?"

Oh, poor Camden. She couldn't imagine what he must be thinking or feeling. They had promised to be faithful during their time apart and now this . . .

From behind them, someone cleared their throat. "Pardon the interruption," Edwin drawled. "But I require the company of my sister for an introduction."

Gwendolyn refrained from groaning, but opted to heave out an exasperated sigh instead. She supposed if she couldn't be a good wife, she might as well be a good sister. She reluctantly curtseyed to Lord Truesdale. "Please inform Camden I am still devoted to him and him alone. Despite everything."

Lord Truesdale leaned in. "I will call on you tomorrow afternoon. I have an idea as to what should be done."

Though she dreaded his idea of "what should be done", she supposed any assistance in this matter would be helpful. "You will find me at home, My Lord," she insisted, more than ready not only to face Camden, but to reclaim him and in turn become the wife he deserved.

A firm hand grabbed Gwendolyn's upper arm from behind and yanked her off to the side. She stumbled, glaring at her brother. "Edwin, what are you—"

Her brother stalked past her and moved towards Camden's uncle. "Tell that nephew of yours I have a pair of fists waiting for him at Jackson's," he snapped, not at all bothering to lower his voice. "What breed of man abandons his own wife?"

Gwendolyn's eyes widened as she smacked her brother's shoulder with her fan. "Whatever are you doing?" she hissed, glancing around at those who were beginning to stare. "He didn't abandon me. It was a mutual separation."

Edwin spun towards her and glared down at her with blazing green eyes. "I am merely overseeing your honour. Someone has to. Now come along. There are a few marvellous women I've yet to meet." He grabbed her arm and tugged her rudely in the opposite direction.

She rolled her eyes and scrambled to keep up with him. "Marvellous? So far, every woman you've insisted on meeting has been about as entertaining as a brick."

He glanced back at her and continued to lead her through the crowds. "I'll have you know that bricks make good, solid foundations upon which to build."

It was pointless trying to stick a fork into his brain about anything. She sighed and allowed him to drag her left and right, and then right and left, for the rest of the evening for the sake of his happiness. Of course, she made a point to avoid Westbrook at every turn. After all, she didn't want to be rude and spray the man's blood everywhere when she attacked him.

Two days later, night, as the clock strikes ten
The Truesdale house

Camden Richard Dearborn, the fourth Marquis of Redford, had never once in the course of his thirty years overindulged in enough cognac, port or brandy to render himself senseless and useless.

Until tonight.

Of course, drowning the last of his rational mind was the only way he could gull himself into facing his own wife – who already appeared to be an hour late. Damn her. As always, time meant nothing to her. And apparently, neither did he.

Camden shifted against the sofa cushion and tried to focus on tightening his bare fingers against the glass of port. It was a miracle he hadn't spilled the damn thing. Or dropped it.

He glanced across the length of the candlelit parlour towards the entryway and staggered on to heavy-booted feet. He brought more port to his lips and though he swallowed, he could no longer taste the tangy sweetness coating his tongue.

The very thought of his own Gwendolyn touching another man made him want to smash his glass against his own head. Never did he think she of all people would do such a thing.

It was obvious he stood apart in his way of thinking that all a man truly needed out of life was a faithful wife, four children and a dog. For what every man in London *really* wanted these days was multiple lovers and other people's wives. Including his own! And whatever children were born were simply the results of overspent passions, not love and family planning. As for the dog? The poor dog was left to wander the streets alone. Completely forgotten. Man's best friend no more.

With each droning minute that passed in silence, Camden couldn't help but feel increasingly pathetic about waiting around for a wife who apparently was not coming. That alone bespoke of guilt. She couldn't even face him.

Regardless, he was not leaving until she arrived. He wanted a damn explanation as to how her silk stocking had gotten into Westbrook's hands. And if that explanation wasn't good enough, by God, he was getting a divorce and moving to France.

"*Uncle!*" Camden leaned forwards impatiently, swaying for a brief moment against his own movement, and glanced towards the entryway his uncle had disappeared into. "Is my wife coming or not? Where the bloody hell is she?"

After a few moments of silence, there was an echoing of boots. His uncle reappeared with . . . what appeared to be two black strips of cloth in his hands. The old man strode towards him. "She just arrived. Apparently, she couldn't decide on which gown to wear."

That most certainly was Gwendolyn. He was of the mind that a woman should only be allowed one gown. That way, there'd be no more indecision.

His uncle paused before him.

Camden watched as his uncle casually draped one of the black velvet sashes over the chair, then snapped the other strip of black velvet taut between his hands. "Lean forwards."

Camden pulled his shaven chin against his silk cravat. "Whatever do you mean 'lean forwards'? What the blazes do you intend to do with that? Put that away!"

His uncle's bushy brows went up as he extended the black velvet blindfold. "Do you or do you not wish to save your marriage?"

Camden choked. "I . . . My marriage? What is all this?"

"Lean forwards, damn you. I will not ask again."

Camden huffed out a breath, knowing that when it came to his uncle, one did not ask questions. One simply hoped for the best. To accommodate the height difference between them, he leaned forwards, as told. But for some reason, the room swayed.

Camden caught hold of his uncle's shoulder with his free hand and steadied himself as port splashed outside the glass he held in his other hand.

Lord Truesdale glared up at him. "Why would you ply yourself before her coming? The idea is to save your marriage. Not destroy the last of it."

Regaining his balance, Camden shifted towards his uncle. "I am not in the least bit pleased with my wife and am merely trying to ensure I am sedated enough to entertain her."

"She may just entertain you." His uncle smirked and placed the thick, double-folded soft velvet against the bridge of Camden's nose, covering his eyes.

Darkness flooded Camden's vision as his uncle secured the blindfold firmly against the back of his head. The glass was suddenly yanked from his grasp and, before he realized what was happening, both of his hands were yanked hard behind his back and tightly bound together.

"What—?" Camden struggled against the ties that bound him. "What is this? *Untie me!*" he boomed, unable to free his wrists from the tight binding.

Shuffles and movements floated around him in the fuzzy darkness. "Have at it," his uncle announced to someone, his booted feet disappearing out into the corridor. "I intend to go for my walk. Expect me in two hours."

The rustling of skirts filled the room.

"Gwendolyn?" Camden demanded.

"Yes, Camden?" Her voice was soft and flirtatious. "What is it?"

He froze. It had been months since her voice had been that soft or that flirtatious. "What . . . You'd best untie me. Do it. Now."

"Why would I do that? You are supposed to remain bound for the rest of the evening."

He choked. "The devil, you say. I am demanding you untie me. Before I acquire a divorce on the grounds of this alone!"

"Oh hush, already. Where is your sense of adventure? You always take everything too seriously." A pair of firm, small hands grabbed hold of his forearm and waist and guided him forcefully forwards in a direction that was anything but straight.

He scrambled forwards, trying to keep his body upright, though with his hands tied behind his back, it was difficult to balance. He stumbled and winced. "I should probably point out, madam, that I've had *far too many cognacs*. And port. Lots of port."

"So I've noticed." She eased their pace, and tucked her petite, curvaceous body against him, tightening her hold on his waist, to assist in his movements.

Camden swayed and awkwardly adjusted himself against her. Soft, abundant hair grazed his skin as she slowly led him forwards. He unwittingly leaned into her, willing himself to submit to whatever was happening to him.

The rustling of her skirts, which brushed up against his trouser-clad legs, was all that met his ears. Seeing that they weren't climbing any stairs – fortunately for him – his guess was that she was opting for the closest private room there was.

His uncle's library.

She brought them to a halt and slid out of his reach. There was a creaking of double doors opening.

A warm, soft hand grabbed his and carefully guided him through. Her other hand took hold of his arm, encouraging him to remain where he was, before releasing him again.

The doors thudded closed, and a click told him that they were not only locked, but he was now officially at her mercy.

And then . . . there was nothing. Absolutely nothing.

Camden stood in blinding darkness and silence, sensing Gwendolyn was still nearby. "What are you doing?" he demanded. "Do you find yourself amusing?"

Her skirts rustled against the movement of her legs. And without a word, gentle, yet firm, warm hands smoothed their way under his coat and against his waist in a seductive manner that made him suck in a breath.

She placed her warmth close against the front of his body, forcing him to feel every soft inch of her. Her skirts pushed against the length of his trousers. The stiffness of her corset and her full breasts beneath pressed against the front of his buttoned waistcoat.

She continued to tenderly hold him and did not attempt anything more. His pulse drummed. It was as equally wrenching as it was awkward, knowing how long it had been since she had so willingly touched him.

God save him, all he wanted to do was . . .

Camden lowered his shaven chin into a soft mass of soap-scented curls that touched his lips. "Gwendolyn. Please."

Gwendolyn readjusted in his arms and laid her head on the expanse of his chest, sighing ever so wistfully. As if it was the only place she was ever meant to be.

Camden swallowed. The way that sigh escaped her lips, and the way her hands and fingers dug possessively into the back of his waist, achingly reminded him of the way their marriage used to be. Perfect. Romantic. All the things he and Gwendolyn had lost with each and every miscarriage.

Damn her. Damn her for not using their separation to heal her body and her soul as they had agreed on. "I want an explanation as to what is going on between you and Westbrook. And I will have that explanation *after* you bloody remove this blindfold and untie my hands. Is that understood?"

Her head lifted from his chest. Pulling her arms from around his waist, she scrambled outside of his grasp. "You will get an explanation after we play a little game."

He blinked against his blindfold and huffed out a breath, trying to focus. "I would sooner demand a divorce than entertain any of this."

A hush met his ears.

Camden raised his chin slowly. Then lowered it. He tried to see her through the blindfold. "Are you there?" he ventured. "Or did I cause you to faint and somehow missed the thud?"

When she didn't answer, he attempted to move his hands against the velvet binding. He staggered during the attempt. "Your humour knows no bounds. This is all very symbolic, I assure you."

He suddenly froze, sensing Gwendolyn was not only standing before him, but was actually leaning *in* towards him. He swallowed, as the heat of her body seemed to pulse against his own, bidding him to forget everything and give in to the temptation of touching her intimately.

She obviously wanted them to be intimate. But . . . why?

"'Tis obvious your wife never appreciated you as much as she should have," she whispered, her hushed voice sounding so incredibly close it startled him. "Which is why she humbly asks to pleasure you in a manner you deserve. Will you let her?"

His breath hitched in his throat in response. Hell, he couldn't have heard her right. This was all the result of one too many cognacs, a blindfold and no access to cigars.

Camden stumbled back and away, but the floor beneath him – which he could barely feel, let alone see – swayed. He sucked in a harsh breath and squeezed his eyes shut, steadying himself and his thoughts. He shouldn't have drunk so much. He never drank and was now downright delusional. And by tomorrow, he'd be heaving for it.

Camden opened his eyes again and blinked against the darkness of the blindfold. "I . . . No. I cannot do any of this. Not until you tell me of your relationship with Westbrook."

"I will not offer you an explanation, Camden, unless you agree to play a game with me. You used to love playing games in the bedchamber. Or have you already forgotten what it is you love?"

Damn. In some ways, yes, of course, he wanted this. He was tired of using his right hand all these months. But to submit himself to her without explanation?

He was usually a rational man. Usually. Hell, even whilst rumours about Gwendolyn's involvement with Westbrook had choked him to a fury he never thought possible, he allowed reason to rein him in and decided to visit Westbrook's townhouse for an explanation. Instead of shattering the man's skull against the floor like a piece of china, as he should have, he coolly demanded proof of the man's involvement with his own wife. And the proof came, two days later, in the form of Gwendolyn's silk stocking, which he recognized all too well. The one stitched with lilies and softly scented with her favourite French perfume. The one he had burned, lest he hang himself with it.

"I want an explanation," he snapped.

"And you will get it by the end of the night. The question of more notable importance is . . . do you trust me, Camden?"

He swallowed. Hard. He wanted to trust her. He wanted to trust her with his entire bleeding heart, but . . . "I don't know if I do."

"Then you will receive no explanation and can take yourself straight to the door. I am certain London would find you quite entertaining stumbling about the streets as you are."

"Gwendolyn, for God's sake—"

"Do you know the name of the game we are about to play?"

"Yes. It's called Let Us Torture the Husband."

She snorted. "No. It is called French Intuition. According to your uncle, courtesans play it with their patrons."

He rumbled out a laugh. "You really shouldn't listen to my uncle. He flogs the bishop a bit too much."

She sighed. "Do you think I would have agreed to any of this if I did not think it would benefit us? You and I both know how much our intimacy has suffered due to our inability to have children. I wish to set all of that aside. I wish to save our marriage."

He shifted from boot to boot, struggling to understand her and what it was she wanted. "Why?"

"Because I love you and hope that you still love me." There was an aching softness in her voice. "Now please. Ask me how the game is played. Show me how much our marriage means to you."

He shifted his jaw. "How is it played?"

"You will remain blindfolded and your hands will remain tied. Nothing will be allowed to exist for you except for pleasure. Everything else, all doubts, all questions, all fear, must fall away. By allowing everything to fall away, only that which is important will remain. What one *feels*."

"A philosophical game tainted with eroticism. How very . . . *French*, indeed."

"So you will play?"

He snorted. "In my uncle's own house? Good God, woman. Never. The idea is anything but arousing."

"Your uncle has removed himself from the house and the servants have been asked to retire. We have two hours. Now if you promise to keep your blindfold in place, I will go against the rules and allow your hands to be untied. So you can touch me."

He seethed out a breath at the thought of touching her. Christ, it had been so long. So bloody long, he couldn't even remember what she felt like. Pathetic, was what he was. Pathetic. "I . . . very well. Do it. Before I change my mind."

"You promise to keep your blindfold in place?"

"Yes, yes. I promise."

She rounded him, bare fingers working against the velvet bindings. Within moments, his hands were free.

"Undress." Her voice was flirtatious but controlled and authoritative. "Remove your coat, cravat, collar, waistcoat and shirt. In exactly that order." She paused, then added a quick, "Please."

He was deranged, to be sure. To engage her like this without even knowing whether she and Westbrook . . .

Then again, that was the point of the game, wasn't it? Exhaling a ragged breath, he slowly slid his evening coat from his shoulders. Already he felt himself growing hard at the thought of having her. With the darkness that continued to press against his eyes preventing him from seeing her body or her face, he envisioned his beautiful Gwendolyn in a state of undress, and savagely hoped this was not the last time he ever touched her.

Gwendolyn drew in a shaky breath as Camden slipped his dark evening coat from his broad shoulders and pulled it down the length of his muscled arms, hidden beneath his white cotton shirt. The coat slid away from his upper body with a soft rustle and crumpled to the wooden floor of the candlelit study.

His arousal pressed against the buttoned flap of his wool trousers. Her fingers dug into the sides of her skirts and her gaze drifted back up to his blindfolded face. The fact that he was willing to play meant he wanted to save their marriage as much as she did. Which is all that mattered.

Camden's hands reached up and his bare fingers smoothly and effortlessly undid his white silk cravat, his arms shifting to accommodate the movements. His full lips parted slightly as he slid the cravat from around his neck, exposing the smooth skin of his strong neck. He gently flung the cravat over his shoulder and let it disappear somewhere behind him.

Gwendolyn bit down on to her lower lip with the top row of her teeth. Although Camden wore a velvet strip over his eyes that prevented him from seeing her – or at least she assumed he couldn't see her – the way he casually stood there, his body positioned towards her, made her feel as if he were very comfortable with what he was about to do. Unlike before. He was allowing everything to fall away in order to give himself over to her.

He lifted his shaven chin, causing a few strands of his blond hair to fall away from his forehead and, one by one, undid the silver buttons on his ivory waistcoat. He stripped it from his body and tossed it aside, standing only in his shirt and trousers. "What are you wearing? Describe it to me." There was a raw huskiness to his voice that made her stomach squeeze.

It was a huskiness she only had the privilege of ever hearing during their lovemaking. It was something she hadn't heard for months, due to her fear of miscarrying another child. But what was that fear compared to losing the only man she would ever love?

It was obvious that if she wanted to save this marriage, she needed to show him that she was still the wife he once knew and loved. The wife capable of overseeing his passion and his pleasure in the most unexpected of ways.

"A rose-coloured muslin gown," she offered in a soft, soft tone. "It tapers off my shoulders."

She shakily pushed away a misplaced curl from the side of her face. She hadn't realized how nervous she was about being intimate with him again. Especially under such unconventional circumstances. They were in his uncle's library, for heaven's sake. But that was exactly the point of this game. To let everything, including one's surroundings, disappear.

"Rose-coloured muslin tapering off your shoulders," he murmured as he undid the three small buttons at his throat. The open slit of the shirt fell open to his mid-chest, displaying those defined muscles beneath.

It was more than obvious where her husband had been spending all of his time these past three months. At Jackson's. Boxing. How many poor men had he hit far too hard because of her?

He yanked his shirt out of his trousers and drew it up and over his head. Muscles rippled in cascading unison as his shirt floated off to the side and ruffled his blond hair.

Gwendolyn would have fainted if she hadn't locked her knees into one another. For physically, Camden was still every bit of the man she remembered. And missed.

He quietly stood there, at his full height of almost six feet, his broad, smooth shoulders set and his arms lean and defined from all the boxing and fencing he'd engaged in since he was twenty. Soft golden blond hairs trailed from his chest down to a narrow path that made its way towards the only thing that remained covered.

He shifted his jaw, but otherwise continued to stand, motionless. As if waiting for her to approach.

She moved closer to him and set the slippered toes of her shoes against the tips of his large leather boots. She allowed her skirts to cover both their feet. Her gaze drifted up the length of his naked chest, which rose and fell in slow, even breaths, until she rested upon the view of his full lips. The clean and simple scent of soap mingling with cognac drifted towards her, causing her already heightened senses to flutter. He always preferred the simple scent of soap. Even on her. Which is why she didn't wear any perfume tonight. In his honour.

The clock in the room chimed, startling her for a moment. It chimed a total of eleven times before clicking back into silence.

Camden's large hands grabbed hold of her shoulders, causing her heart to nearly leap out of her throat in astonishment. He reached down and around her with his bare muscled arms. His large hands grabbed each round cheek of her bottom, hidden beneath her skirts, then yanked her body up hard, against his towering, broad body. He held her firmly in place against his erection, his jaw tight. Stating his intentions quite openly.

He slid his hands from her bottom and up along the back of her gown. His fingers gently grazed the hidden hooks on her back, which held the material of her gown in place.

Her mind blanked and nothing mattered in that moment. Nothing but his touch. She stared up at him in complete awe, her chest falling and rising a bit too quickly.

Without a single word, he released the hooks, the muscles in his taut arms shifting around her. One by one, he released them, until he had opened the entire back of her muslin gown, exposing her corset and the chemise beneath it. His jaw tightened and his lips pressed together as he slipped his large hands beneath the parted material. He swept it down from her shoulders and arms, letting it fall to her waist.

His hot hands skimmed the length of her arms, causing her to catch her breath as goosebumps frilled her skin. He slid his hands up towards her neck and dug his long fingers into the nape of her neck. He tilted her head up towards him and bent his blond head, lowering his lips on to hers.

A warm softness grazed her lower and upper lips.

Gwendolyn closed her eyes in utter bliss and slid her hands up the tight, smooth length of his muscled back. She pressed her body against his warmth. And revelled in it. She hadn't realized how much she missed the bliss of his touch until that moment.

His wet tongue slid into her mouth and touched hers. He pressed his lips harder against her and moved his tongue more urgently into her mouth, silently demanding she make love to him.

Before she could fully enjoy his kiss, he withdrew his tongue from her mouth and outlined her lips softly with the tip. Circling, tasting. Circling, tasting. He drew her upper lip slowly, playfully between his teeth, nipped it then licked. Nipped it again then licked.

Passionately kissing him, her hands left the expanse of his back to slide down between their bodies, past the folds of her muslin gown gathered at her waist. She blindly unbuttoned the wool flap of his trousers and shoved the material past his muscled thighs, wanting to touch every part of him.

Their mouths momentarily broke away from each other as she grasped hold of the hard length of him with one hand. She slid her hand against his hard smoothness, staring up at him, wanting and needing his reaction.

His lips parted in a groan, he threw his head back and held her firmly against him. His chest heaved unevenly as his body tensed. He groaned again, levelling his head. He blindly grabbed hold of her wrists, bumping his knuckles against her corseted stomach.

He yanked her hands away from his body, then grabbed hold of her waist, and dragged them both on to the floor. She gasped as the cool wooden floor pressed against the exposed, heated skin of her back.

He rolled carefully, but quickly, off to the side, threw off his shoes and all the other clothes on his body. Until he was left gloriously naked with nothing on but a velvet blindfold. He felt his way back to her and climbed atop her legs, still covered by her mass of skirts. It was the only material left separating them.

He gathered up her skirts in one hand, pushing them up and away from her legs and thighs, causing the bulk of material to cascade across the floor on both sides of her. His hands slid up the length of her stockings, past the tied garters that held them in place, and pushed her legs apart. Cool air pressed against the wetness between her legs as Camden lowered his head.

His hot wet tongue met her core. She gasped and closed her eyes as a powerful sensation of pleasure rippled through her body. His tongue pressed harder against her, and she gasped in complete disbelief that she was already so shatteringly close to divine intervention.

But then his lips disappeared, as did the warmth of his hands, as he yanked her skirts back down.

Her eyes popped open. Her breaths came in short desperate takes. She blinked.

He wound his arms around her, his body hard, yet so warm and welcoming. "I cannot deny it," he whispered hoarsely. "Despite everything, I have missed you."

Her heart skipped. "You have?"

His hand affectionately skimmed the side of her face, down the curve of her throat.

He slipped over the length of her and dragged her skirts back up her thighs, causing her to melt. He slowly skimmed his forefinger from the inside middle of her exposed thigh up to the very spot she wanted and needed him to touch most. Her heated skin tingled in response as she further dissolved into a world of pleasure she had forgotten, and to which she desperately wanted to escape again.

He slid his finger deep into her, pushing her once again towards climax. She fisted the material of her gown and her mind momentarily emptied. It was amazing. *He* was amazing. He'd always been. She'd simply . . . forgotten.

He climbed over her, placing both hands on each side of her head and rubbed his hardness against her.

His mouth found hers without hesitation, as if he knew exactly where her lips were, and he kissed her deeply, his tongue pushing hard against hers.

She moaned into his mouth as he lifted himself on to one arm and used his other hand to guide himself into her. She gasped as his hips drew back and he drove deep into her, hissing out a breath.

Gwendolyn cried out in bliss and dug her nails into the flesh of his taut skin, trying to feel and breathe her way through the moment. Trying to feel and breathe through every sensation imaginable as it enveloped her body.

He drove deep into her again. She could barely breathe as those building, wondrous sensations scorched her body. She moved against every thrust, wanting and needing more. She could feel the sensation within her core building. Growing. It had been too long.

"Gwendolyn." His voice simmered with fierce passion as he licked her entire mouth, leaving it cool and wet. He slammed repeatedly into her, grinding her harder to the floor.

A remarkable haze took over the rest of her body and mind. Her name entwined upon his lips and the escalating pressure of his hard length moving against her threw Gwendolyn into that spiralling, whirling paradise she'd missed.

She savagely held on to his naked waist and cried out as endless ripples roared throughout the entire length of her body that both tightened and released her core.

He was relentless in his savage need. "Gwendolyn," he rasped, then threw back his head and let out a guttural moan of pleasure that reverberated throughout her entire body and soul.

That flushed face, partly hidden by the black blindfold, and his heaving, muscled chest boasted of the pleasure he had taken. And she couldn't help but love it.

He settled silently beside her.

She swallowed, noticing that several candles had flickered out and that shadows were beginning to creep towards where they lay on the floor. Surely now he knew how she felt. How she had always felt.

He raked his ruffled blond hair with a hand, shifting against the floor. "I want to know," he blurted. "For God's sake, I have a right to know."

Her eyes widened. So much for him knowing how she felt. After a few harried tries, she stumbled up and on to her slippered feet, fumbling with the upper section of her gown in an effort to shove her bare arms back into the hanging sleeves. "Is that all you have to say to me?"

"Blast you, Gwendolyn!" He snapped both of his hands up and frantically tugged at the blindfold. "Why do you refuse to answer? Because of guilt?"

"No. Because if I do, I will be acknowledging that you never trusted me to begin with. And if there is no trust between us, what else is left of this marriage? Nothing. Absolutely nothing." Feeling as though her legs wouldn't hold her up for much longer, she sank to the floor before him.

When Camden ripped the blindfold away from his face and flung it aside, his eyes were instantly flooded with warm candlelight and the earthy colours of his uncle's study. It somehow snapped his fuzzy, hazed brain and body back into focus.

He blinked at Gwendolyn, who sat near him on the floor. His heart momentarily stopped beating as he wordlessly stared at the beautiful face he had missed so much.

She continued to gaze straight at him, with those blue-green eyes, and lowered her chin ever so slightly. As if not in the least bit pleased with him.

Several golden-chestnut curls, which had fallen from their pinned places atop her head, lay scattered around her bare, slim shoulders. Shoulders that were not properly covered by the lopsided sleeves of her rose-coloured evening gown.

The room wavered and tipped to the side as he leaned over and snatched hold of his shirt, which lay beside him. Her words about his lack of trust bit into him. For she was right. But that still did not explain why Westbrook had her stocking.

"Camden." Her strained voice brought him back to reality. "Why are you allowing doubts to destroy the last of us?"

He never had doubts before. Not until they had agreed to a mutual separation. All of these months without her had been consuming the last of his soul.

"If you feel an explanation is too much to ask, I will bid you a goodnight." He stumbled to his feet, veered over to his clothes scattered across the wooden floor and frantically snatched them up one by one. Cravat. Waistcoat. Collar. Trousers. Coat. Boots.

"Camden," she insisted hoarsely. "It splinters me no end that you would think the worst of me. Based on a silk stocking. Do you know how ridiculous you are being?"

He kept his back to her, his chest heaving. "And rumours, madam. Rumours of him calling upon you at unconventional hours. All that aside, are you informing me that the silk stocking I received was not yours?"

"It is mine. But Lord Westbrook did not acquire it by stripping it from my body, that I assure you. He bribed one of my servants for it in an effort to make you think the worst of me. I will gladly present that servant to you, whom I have since dismissed, if my word is not enough. Westbrook sought to bed me during our separation, but I never allowed it. Not a touch. Not a kiss. And, because of that, he sought to destroy me, and in turn, us. Though I have been suffering, I have been faithful to you, Camden. The question is, who do you believe? Lord Westbrook? Or me, your wife of four years?"

Camden turned towards her, feeling nauseous. And he knew it had nothing to do with all the spirits still warming his blood. He stared her down and whispered hoarsely, "Swear it. Swear it upon whatever love we ever shared. Swear he never touched you."

"I swear it upon the love I hope we *still* share. I would never hurt you in so cruel a manner, and I had hoped you would never hurt me by thinking that I could." She pleadingly met his gaze from where she knelt on the floor, her muslin gown spread out about her in a puddle of rose-coloured cloth. The backside of her dress, which he had unhooked sometime during the height of his fantasy, was still wide open, exposing a pale-blue corset, the chemise beneath it and a few glimpses of pale, smooth skin.

Having known his Gwendolyn for four years of marriage – and a year of courtship before that – he could tell by her eyes, her demeanour and her voice that she was in fact telling him the truth.

He choked, feeling as if the burden he'd been carrying with him all these months fell away. "Gwendolyn," he rasped, his knees feeling weak. "Forgive me. After you repeatedly denied me of your bed all these months, I have been nothing short of—"

"No, Camden. I ask that you forgive me. You are right. I was distant for too many months, never allowing you to touch me out of an irrational fear of losing another child. But it never meant I loved you any less. I simply never realized our inability to have children was destroying who I was – destroying us."

He swallowed. "I will not have you blaming yourself. I wasn't as understanding as I could have been. I expected too much of you."

"We both expected too much of each other." She raised her skirts so as not to stumble, and pushed herself up off the floor.

"I . . . should dress," he murmured, throwing his clothes on to a chair in a daze. He snatched up his trousers, shoved in his left leg, then his right, and yanked them up to his waist in a single swoop.

His hands shook as he attempted to button the front flap of his trousers. He focused on staring at the wooden floor beneath him, doing his best not to look at Gwendolyn, afraid this was all an illusion brought on by severe inebriation.

Camden yanked his shirt over his head, pulling it into place, and stuffed the ends into his trousers. He pulled on his waistcoat and his coat, and then shoved his feet into his shoes, not caring that his stockings were missing. He looped his cravat around his neck, barely aware of what he was doing.

"Camden, the only good to have come of our separation is that it made me realize I cannot lead a life without you. Please tell me you cannot lead a life without me and that our inability to have children will not keep you from loving me." Her tear-streaked blue-green eyes met his, causing his chest to tighten.

Her words, at this moment, held everything he had ever wanted from them. But, as always, he couldn't put his cursed emotions into words for fear they wouldn't match what was truly in his heart.

The clock chimed once, announcing it was half past eleven. Then there was nothing but the annoying sound of his heart beating against his ears. The mingling of laughter and voices drifted towards them from a distance.

Gwendolyn glanced over at the clock. "I suppose you have nothing to say," she whispered. She turned and made her way slowly to the locked doors.

He stiffened. No. No, no, no. She couldn't leave. Not now. Not ever again. He would find the right words to say. He would. And that was his vow to her and to himself from this night forth.

Camden sprinted towards her. He slid to a rapid halt before her – or what should have been a halt. The soles of his shoes skidded across the remaining length of the wooden floor until his backside slammed against the double doors with a loud thud.

He winced and stilled his large frame against the door, trying to appear cool, calm and collected despite the fact that he was anything but. He crossed his arms over his unevenly buttoned waistcoat, cleared his throat and eyed her. "I know I've always been a man of few words, which has always been my greatest sin against you. But I . . . I love you. I don't need children to make me happy. I need you to make me happy. I didn't want to admit even to myself that we were incapable of having children. So I can only imagine what you must be enduring."

Tears glistened in her eyes and her full lips trembled. "Come home with me," she whispered. "Where you belong. We will find the words we both lack. I know we will." She sniffed and then rolled her eyes, as if trying to draw attention away from her own sadness. She yanked her sleeves back up her shoulders and turned, exposing the open back of the gown to him. "Would you mind securing all the hooks back into place?"

God help him, what he really wanted to do was rip off the damn dress and take her again. Without a blindfold this time. So he could see everything and show her exactly what she made him feel every time he looked at her. Show her how she put his body and his mind into a state of constant weakness. Even after all these years.

She looked back at him from over her right shoulder, expectantly. She held the back of her gown together with one hand, pulling long strands of her loose hair out of the way with the other.

He stepped towards her and pushed all of her feathery soft curls to the side, so he could see better. His fingers and palms brushed against the sides of her muslin gown as he slid his hands up to her corseted waist. He managed to find the first hook at the very bottom, just above the curve of her backside. He hooked the material together one by one, up the entire back of her gown, revelling in the moment. He was her husband again. It was all he'd ever wanted and needed. That he knew.

As he reached the top part of her gown, just beneath her neck, his bare fingers brushing against the warmth of her soft skin, she whispered, "We must learn to find new ways to love each other. Seeing it will only be us."

He wrapped his arms around her waist, pulling her backside against him and leaned towards her ear, nuzzling against the warmth of her throat. "We will find endless ways. That I know."

She caught his hands and squeezed them.

His arms tightened. "By the by, I plan on gutting Westbrook tomorrow morning at eight."

She stilled. "You . . . don't actually mean that, do you? Mind you, yes, he deserves it. But I would rather not see you hang. That would be rather pointless, wouldn't it?"

That it would. "Then what do you propose I do? I am not letting that bastard walk away from this."

She nestled back against him, placing her head in the curve of his throat. "I propose we avenge ourselves by living happily ever after and making him look quite the fool."

He smirked. "I prefer to gut him and move to France."

She shifted towards him and grinned. "Are you being serious?"

He chuckled and shook his head. "I wish I were. I suppose making him look quite the fool will have to do." He paused, then added, "For now." He eyed the clock in the study and then drawled, "Do you think we have enough time to play French Intuition again? Before my uncle returns?"

She turned fully in his arms, her hands sliding up his shoulders and grinned. "I believe we do. Only this time, *I* intend to wear the blindfold."

He quirked a brow. "How about we put it around your mouth instead? To keep things quiet."

Her eyes widened as she smacked him. "Camden!"

He laughed. "It was just a thought."

"Yes. And how very few of those you have."

He smirked. "Why do I suddenly feel married again?"

She grinned. "It's good to see you, too."

"I think we ought to go home. So we don't have to rush. What do you think?"

"Even better." She held out her hand.

"Oh. But before we go—" Camden jogged over and snatched up the pieces of black velvet. He shoved them into his evening coat pocket, sheepishly cleared his throat and strode back over. "For later."

A Suitable Gentleman

Sara Bennett

A sharp breeze tossed the simple cambric skirts of the petite lady walking along George Street, threatening to display much more than her dainty ankles. Her apparel, while not of the first water of fashion, displayed a certain elegance. Dark hair curled becomingly about a pale heart-shaped face, and big blue eyes were shadowed with tiredness.

"Plain and simple" were Lady March's watchwords when it came to visiting the dressmaker with her eldest niece. "Clarinda is too old now for frills and furbelows. And of what use are they to her anyway, when her place is by my side?"

Of course Lady March would never have allowed her niece to go about Bath looking like a destitute orphan, although strictly speaking that was what she was. But her aunt had always been kind to her; Clarinda could not fault that. Lady March had taken Clarinda and Lucy into her home when they were in dire circumstances, and since then they had wanted for nothing.

Nothing material, that is.

Clarinda's face, so clearly fashioned for love and laughter, appeared drawn and serious as she considered the situation that awaited her at home, where Lady March had taken another one of her turns. If she were truly ill, Clarinda would be genuinely concerned, but her aunt treated illness as a diversion; since her husband died she had sought out ever more bizarre symptoms to while away her boredom. Now Lady March had run out of her tonic – Clarinda doubted it was more than sugar syrup – and had sent her niece out as a matter of urgency to purchase another bottle.

Buried deep in her thoughts, Clarinda did not see the top hat. Blown from a gentleman's head, it came bowling across the roadway, narrowly missing the wheels of a passing barouche, and rolled up on to the pavement. It wasn't until the hat struck her on the shin, hard enough for her to cry out in surprise, that she realized she was under attack.

The bottle of tonic wobbled in her hand and she only just prevented it from smashing on the hard paving. Another gust threatened to carry the hat away from where it was nestled at her feet, and, without thinking, she reached down to secure it. Automatically she smoothed the soft beaver fur with her gloved finger. This hat was well made – a wealthy man's accessory – and he would be missing it.

She looked about her for its owner, and spotted him at once.

Tall and dark, he was standing across the road, directly outside the Good King hostelry. The coat he wore was fashionable without being ostentatious, his neckcloth was elegantly tied and his boots were shiny. The smart equipage behind him looked as if it had just arrived, and baggage was being disengaged by bustling servants.

All that movement going on about him, thought Clarinda. How strange then that he seemed so still. So alone. As if his concerns were such that they set him apart.

Clarinda realized she was staring, but then so was he. The next moment the gentleman was striding across the road towards her. Her breath caught in consternation as she remembered she should be returning post-haste with her aunt's tonic, and yet her feet did not want to move.

As he drew closer, Clarinda could see that he was handsome indeed. A faint smile was curling the edges of his firm lips and crinkling the skin about his dark eyes. "Good morning," he said, his voice deep and with a laughing note to it. "You appear to have rescued my hat from this violent weather."

Clarinda held out the object in question, returning his smile. "Bath is famous for its weather, sir."

"Infamous, perhaps," he replied with a teasing note. "If I was not standing on dry land I would believe I was at sea, with squalls such as these." Another gust of wind blew cold splatters of rain against them and he gave a chuckle of amazed laughter. "It gets worse. And I see you do not carry an umbrella, eh . . . madam?"

They had not been introduced but that didn't seem to matter. "Miss Howitt. Clarinda Howitt. I normally carry an umbrella, sir, but this morning I was in a rush and forgot it."

As if to underline the fact, the feather on her bonnet suddenly gave way beneath the weight of water and sagged over her eyes. She laughed, and then wondered at herself. Clarinda rarely laughed in the street, and yet the gentleman's dark eyes were smiling back at her, seeming to encourage her.

"Allow me, Miss Howitt," he said. He unfurled his umbrella, then held it over her.

"Thank you, sir. You are newly arrived, I think?" she said, a little breathlessly because he was now so close to her.

For some reason the laughter in his eyes faded, their intensity hinting at something serious. Clarinda wondered what it was that had brought him to Bath, for certainly it did not appear to be pleasure.

"I am indeed newly arrived," he said. "In England, as well as Bath. I have been abroad in the army for a number of years but now I am home again, and I hope to remain in Bath for some time to . . . eh . . . take the waters. Do I have the phrase correct, Miss Howitt?"

The laughter was back and she responded.

"Perfectly correct, sir. The waters are supposed to be very benefi-cial. My aunt takes them daily, when she is well enough to make the journey to the Pump Room, that is."

"Your aunt is an invalid?"

"My aunt is as fit as a fiddle, but she has taken up illness as a hobby."

He lifted his eyebrows at her dry note.

"Forgive me," Clarinda said, and lowered her eyes. "That was unkind of me. I have had very little sleep. In fact my aunt is the reason I am out now – she required a bottle of her tonic from the apothecary."

There was a pause, and she wondered what he must think of her, complaining about her relative to a complete stranger. And yet something about him seemed to invite her confidences, as if he would understand. When he spoke again there was no censor in his voice, only the same warm friendliness as before.

"I have been remiss, Miss Howitt. Let me introduce myself. James Quentin at your service."

She allowed her gloved fingers to be swallowed by his much larger hand and felt his grip tighten. The hard warmth of his fingers was pleasing, reassuring, although she had no idea why.

"Are you in Bath visiting friends or relatives, Mr Quentin?"

"Alas, I am all alone," he said, but he didn't appear to be sorry about it, with his smiling eyes fixed on hers. "Although now I have made your acquaintance I am not quite alone, am I?"

Clarinda felt a tingle of excitement. James Quentin was hand-some, clearly with means, and a bachelor. Perfect. Lucy would bowl him over with her pretty vivaciousness, marry him and be set for life. It seemed that it was providence that brought his hat sailing towards her upon this windy Bath day.

"If I visit the Pump Room, Miss Howitt, will I encounter you and your aunt?"

Clarinda's smile was sparkling with delight. She imagined Lucy in her best muslin, pretty as a picture. How could any man, how could this man, resist her?

"I do hope so, Mr Quentin."

"Then I will haunt the place every day until you appear," he promised her, the laughter dancing in his eyes.

She realized with a sense of shock that she was still holding his hand, or he hers. The rain had eased. He refurled his umbrella and placed his hat upon his head.

"Mr Quentin!"

A small dapper man was hailing him from outside the hostelry. Mr Quentin turned and nodded, before bowing to Clarinda.

"I fear I am wanted. Good day, Miss Howitt."

She returned his bow with a curtsey and a smiling upward glance. "Good day, Mr Quentin."

"You must take my umbrella, just in case," he added, as she went to turn away. "I will not need it this morning."

Clarinda hesitated, but the umbrella would give her a reason to contact him again. She nodded her thanks, her head full of possibilities. She knew her aunt would be beside herself at the delay but even that did not worry her as much as usual. She had the urge to stand and stare after this tall, handsome figure – an urge so strong it was difficult to resist, but resist it she did. Mr Quentin was not for her. He might have been charming and polite, with an air of mystery, but once he saw Lucy he would forget Clarinda entirely.

Men always did.

Clarinda told herself that her sister's happiness was enough for her, that she didn't really mind sacrificing herself to ensure Lucy's future. Lucy would escape Lady March's household but Clarinda must remain, a hostage to her hypochondriac aunt's tyranny.

"Even my husband has not heard of some of the things with which Lady March is afflicted," Etta had informed Clarinda, a sparkle in her dark eyes, "and he is a doctor. It certainly keeps him on his toes."

"Oh, Etta, you make light of it, but how does he find the patience? She has run through three other doctors, you know."

"It is not so bad. He says he enjoys the challenge. And the tonic he prescribed has helped, has it not?"

"Yes, it has. My aunt declares it a miracle. I do not think she has had a single bout of *brain fever* since she began taking it."

Etta had laughed, but there had been a great deal of sympathy in her eyes. "Poor Clarinda, I wish there was some way I could rescue you from this situation. Sometimes I fear it must be like being in gaol!"

Gaols, Clarinda agreed, did not necessarily have barred windows and locked doors. Restraints could just as easily consist of tears and vapours and demands for attention. And Clarinda's sentence was a lengthy one, for she had long ago come to the conclusion that despite Lady March's protestations, she would outlive them all.

A rattle of raindrops fell on the pavement around her, bringing her back from her anxieties to the present. It was always raining in Bath. One grew accustomed to it. She unfurled James Quentin's umbrella. Normally Clarinda would never have forgotten hers, but Lady March had made such a fuss when she discovered her tonic was nearly gone that Clarinda had left the house at a run, and set off for the apothecary as fast as she could manage, Lady March's threats of dire consequences to her health echoing in her ears.

"I cannot possibly manage without it," she'd gasped, clutching her shawl across her ample bosom. "I feel palpitations coming on. Do hurry! Oh, my head is beginning to pound."

With such threats hanging over her, Clarinda had set out on her mission without a thought for the weather. Now she retraced her steps more slowly.

Milsom Street was not directly on her way home, but she turned down it anyway. It contained most of Bath's more interesting shops and Clarinda found herself dawdling past their windows, casting a wistful eye over the new fashions. Not for herself, of course. She'd long ago accepted such fripperies were not for her. No, she told herself, she was thinking of Lucy.

At nine and twenty, Clarinda had heard herself described as an old maid. Oddly, until now she'd thought herself accepting of the stark truth that she would never have a home and family and husband of her own, but suddenly a sense of rebellion arose in her. She imagined herself in the latest evening gown, dancing lightly in the arms of . . . of . . .

Clarinda sighed. This was the fault of the handsome and charming James Quentin. Well, there was no point in wishing herself in love with him, or him with her.

Clarinda turned her back on Milsom Street, and hurried towards home. But no matter how she tried to flatten her spirits there was an anticipation bubbling away inside her, like a child with a promised treat. She found herself quite oblivious to the raindrops and the biting wind.

A week later James Quentin stood before the looking glass, straightening his sleeves with sharp tugs and smoothing the creaseless cut of his waistcoat. He felt like a hunter pursuing his quarry, but he had learned over the years that he must be a patient hunter, if he were to succeed.

He must watch and learn and listen; he must blend into life in Bath until he was all but invisible.

This morning he was going to the Pump Room, with the added frisson of possibly seeing Miss Howitt there. He felt a lightening of his spirits as he remembered her face, blue eyes shyly peeping at him beneath the wreckage of her bonnet, and the sweet curl of her lips. She was his ideal woman, petite and pretty and intelligent. If only he wasn't here in Bath with an ulterior motive, he might consider getting to know her better. He had been alone too long and Miss Howitt was extremely tempting.

"What are these Bath waters like?" he demanded of his manservant, Dunn.

"Very nasty, I believe, sir."

"But beneficial?"

"So the inhabitants of Bath would have us believe, sir."

James would have made a visit to the Pump Room a week earlier – indeed he'd planned to do so the day after meeting Miss Howitt outside his hostelry – but he'd been forced to travel out of Bath on urgent business. His late brother had left his affairs in a damnable mess. If he'd known how bad things were he would have come home earlier rather than spending his time with the occupying forces in France, after Waterloo. But he admitted he'd been reluctant to step into his elder brother's shoes – it had never been his ambition to do so – but then he had never expected his brother to die so young in a foolish attempt at a fence that was too high.

James gave his coat another tug. "Very well, I am as ready as I will ever be. Do I take the carriage?"

His manservant allowed himself a small smile. "I believe the established modes of travel in Bath are chair or perambulation."

"And which do you suggest in the circumstances?"

"I think you should walk, My Lord."

James raised a dark brow at his manservant. "I think I prefer 'sir' just for now. I do not feel like a lord."

"Very well, sir."

James went to the door, but paused with his hand on the latch. "Do you think we will find her in Bath? Is she here somewhere?"

"Yes, sir, I am certain of it."

James nodded, his mouth losing its good humour, his eyes bleak.

"Then if she is here I will find her. I fear I cannot rest, Dunn, until I do."

Clarinda tried not to fidget. Lady March was leaning heavily on her arm, as if her legs could barely hold her up, and yet when Clarinda suggested they return home the elderly lady had given her a glare that could have curdled cream.

"I am certain the waters will do me good."

"Oh yes, Clarinda, we must stay!" Lucy piped up. "I see Isabella over there."

"Quiet, miss," Lady March said, sharply for one in such a weakened state, "no one asked you."

Lucy bit her lip, but her sparkling eyes were unrepentant. She was a girl with spirit, and it would take more than her aunt's crotchets to depress her. She fluttered through life expecting only the best to happen. Clarinda was older and wiser, but it was her dearest wish to see that, for Lucy, all her dreams came true.

Now, with a smile to her sister and her scowling aunt, Lucy hurried across the room to her bosom bow. Clarinda watched her go, aware that most of the gentlemen in the Pump Room were doing the same. Lucy was wearing one of her newer gowns, a pretty muslin with a flounced skirt, her hair was simply dressed, but the sheer simplicity of the young woman's attire only made one more aware of her beauty.

We were right to come to Bath, Clarinda told herself. Despite what she herself had to endure in payment for their food and lodging, Lucy was far better off here than she would have been, destitute, at home in the country. Here she had a chance to shine.

After their parents had died – victims of a fire that had also rendered their home a blackened ruin – they had been alone and in debt. So when their father's elder sister, Lady March, heard of the death of her profligate brother and his wife, and wrote offering them a home, Clarinda had jumped at the chance. She had not realized then that taking up that offer would mean a lifetime sentence for herself as unofficial nurse to Lady March's imaginary illnesses, but even if she had . . . Well, there was no other option if Lucy was to take her rightful place in the world.

"Lucy is looking very fine."

With a smile Clarinda turned to find her friend Etta, the doctor's wife, at her side. "She is, isn't she?"

"And you are no slouch in that department yourself, my dear," Etta added, her dark eyes searching Clarinda's face with sharpened curiosity. "What has happened to give you that sparkle?"

"Nothing. I am the same as always." And yet Clarinda felt herself blushing, as if Etta knew she had spent the past week dreaming of James Quentin's warm smile and longing for him to make a reappearance. She'd even gone so far as to send a note to the Good King, when she returned his umbrella, but their servant informed her on his return that Mr Quentin had gone out of Bath on business for a week. The disappointment she felt had been ridiculously excessive, but the week was up and this morning she was hoping to see him in the Pump Room.

"Well, I think you are looking very well, Clarinda."

Etta was a woman her own age, but sometimes her manner seemed to belong to someone much older. Although Etta said little of her past, Clarinda suspected that her life had not been easy before she married her beloved Dr Moorcroft.

"I know several gentlemen who would be pleased to offer for you, if you were to give them the slightest encouragement," Etta went on, and then laughed at Clarinda's shocked expression. "Did you truly not realize that? But then you are always thinking of Lucy's future and not your own. Clarinda, Lucy would not want you to martyr yourself for her sake."

"I want her to have the life she deserves. You make me sound like one of those saints with arrows stuck in them and a pious expression. I assure you I am not a martyr, and my life is very comfortable with Aunt March. She cannot help having a taste for the more bizarre forms of illness."

Etta gave her a look that meant she didn't believe a word of it.

But Clarinda's attention was elsewhere. In the entrance to the Pump Room stood a familiar handsome figure. Mr Quentin! She gave a little gasp.

For a moment she was quite dizzy with the confusing rush of emotions sweeping through her: relief and agitation; excitement and impatience; happiness and melancholy. There was no time to examine and understand each of them.

"Good Gad!" Lady March lifted her quizzing glass and ogled the crowd waiting to enter the room. "Who is that intriguingly handsome gentleman, Clarinda?"

Clarinda was not at all surprised that her aunt had noticed him. "I believe he is called James Quentin—" she began, and his name on her lips made them tingle.

"Quentin, Quentin? Never heard of him," Lady March replied loudly. "I am most impressed with his wheeled chair. I wonder whether I can have one made?"

Clarinda, bewildered, looked again at the group by the entrance and understood that her aunt wasn't referring to James Quentin after all. She was more interested in a large figure in a chair with wheels, a man with a sun-browned face and a shock of grey hair who was glowering at the occupants of the Pump Room from beneath his thick, black eyebrows.

"I must speak with him," said Lady March, and made a beeline towards the man in the chair, her steps strong and sure, with no signs of her previous tottering weakness.

"Oh dear," Clarinda murmured, turning to Etta. To her surprise her friend's face was quite drained of colour. "Are you feeling faint?" she said, reaching to support her. "Etta, what is it?"

But Etta shook her head. "I must go," she murmured, and with that she turned and hurried through the crowded room.

Clarinda stared after her, bewildered. If she had not known better, she would have thought Etta was running away from something. Or someone.

Alone now, Clarinda hesitated. She could join any number of groups in the room, where there were acquaintances who would welcome her and chat politely about the weather and her aunt's health. But suddenly everyone but James Quentin seemed boring and insipid. She turned towards him, and felt a sharp stab of disappointment to see that Mrs Russo – with her five unmarried daughters – had already captured him.

She wavered. It was not in her nature to be forward, to push in, but suddenly she found herself moving towards Mr Quentin with a new determination, and with each step her determination grew.

James was wondering how on earth he could escape the middle-aged woman in her hideous turban and her packet of simpering daughters. At one point he was on the verge of breaking free but she caught hold of his arm and held on to him with strong fingers.

"Mr Quentin?"

The voice was sweet and melodious. He turned, joy in his heart, and saw that it was indeed Miss Clarinda Howitt, rescuer of gentlemen's hats. She was smiling up at him, a sparkle in her serious blue eyes.

"Miss Howitt," he said, with every evidence of a long acquaintance, "how marvellous to see you again. You must tell me how your aunt is. Let us go and find some tea, and then we can chat. Do excuse me, Mrs Russo. Eh, Miss Russo and . . . eh, all the rest of your family."

He tugged. The fingers on his arm resisted a moment and then he was reluctantly released.

"Thank you, thank you, Miss Howitt," he said fervently, as they moved away. "I thank you from the bottom of my heart. I feared I was to be Mrs Russo's prisoner for life."

Clarinda bit her lip, trying not to laugh. "Mrs Russo is one of our long time residents, Mr Quentin."

"Is that what happens to someone who lives here too long?" he demanded, wide-eyed, but with a teasing smile.

This time she did laugh.

"She said I had a smell of London about me, which sounded most unpleasant."

Miss Howitt gave him a shy smile. She had the sweetest mouth and he wished she would smile more often. If she were his, he would make it his goal to see her smile each and every day.

"I think she meant to imply you had a certain style, sir, that can only be found in London."

He nodded soberly. "Thank you for explaining that to me, Miss Howitt. I thought she might be insulting me, but I hardly liked to fight a duel with a woman of her age. Indeed with a woman of any age."

"No, duels are frowned upon in Bath society. Although I believe Mrs Russo is quite an expert with a crossbow."

Her blue eyes were sparkling delightfully and a frisson ran through him and centred itself on his heart. It was a sensation he had not experienced in a very long time and he could not ignore it, no matter how urgent his current mission.

"Miss Howitt . . . " he began rashly.

But she was already speaking.

"Mr Quentin." She took a breath, as if her words were somehow momentous. Did she feel it too? This sense of the meeting of two beings who were destined to meet? He leaned closer and breathed in her scent, drowning in visions of Clarinda lying in his arms quite naked. And then he heard what she was saying.

"I want you to meet my sister, Lucy. She is standing over there, by the vase of flowers. Do you see her? The girl with dark hair?"

Confused, he glanced in the direction she indicated. There were a number of girls gathered in a group, girls who looked as if they were just out of the schoolroom. One of them did seem to have dark hair.

She was watching him with anticipation, and because he didn't want to disappoint her, he said, "Delightful."

He was rewarded with a beaming smile, her eyes shining up at him. "Yes, she is delightful. I think, although of course I am biased, she is the loveliest girl in Bath."

"Indeed your sister is very pretty, Miss Howitt."

"Come and I will introduce you, Mr Quentin." She began to make her way towards the group of schoolgirls. He stood a moment, watching her go, absorbed in the graceful perfection of her figure and the elegance of her bearing. Why did no one else in the room realize what a treasure she was? When she glanced back, surprised he was not following, he had to hurry after her.

The introductions were made, although James hardly heard them, but he must have said all the right things for no one gave him a peculiar look. Lucy was indeed an engaging girl, and smiled and chatted about Bath and then laughed when he lamented the weather. And all the time Clarinda beamed upon him like a fairy godmother who had just granted him his dearest wish.

When an older woman in a striped silk gown joined them, she was introduced as Lady March, Clarinda's aunt. She examined him coldly through her quizzing glass as though seeking fault.

"How do you do, Lady March?" he said politely.

"Particularly ill, sir. My niece misled me as to your identity."

"Aunt, I'm sorry, I thought you were speaking of Mr Quentin when you—"

"As I recall I said, 'Who is that handsome gentleman?' and you told me it was Mr Quentin. In fact it was Mr Collingwood I was referring to."

"Aunt, please . . . " Clarinda's eyes met his and darted away. She flushed scarlet.

"Mr Quentin is handsome enough," her aunt went on, as if he wasn't there, "but he is rather too healthy looking for my liking. Mr Collingwood has some very interesting ailments – he quite puts the rest of us invalids in the shade."

"You are an invalid, Lady March?" James said with an air of surprise, trying not to enjoy the fact that Clarinda thought him the handsomest man in the room. "You disguise your suffering well, I must say."

She gave him a stoic smile that did not reach her steely eyes. "There is no point in complaining, Mr Quentin. Now, come along, Clarinda. You too, Lucy. I have discovered there is a shop where it is possible to purchase wheeled chairs. We have no time to waste. I really must have one. Mr Collingwood says his sister pushes him everywhere in it," she added with satisfaction.

For a moment there was anguish on Clarinda's face, so heart wrenching that James took a step closer, but the next moment her face assumed a resigned expression.

"Yes, Aunt. Goodbye, Mr Quentin. Will we see you at the ball in the New Assembly Rooms on Thursday night?"

"Oh yes," piped Lucy, "you must put your name down in the book, sir. No one is allowed to attend unless their name is down in the book."

"Then I shall do so post-haste," he assured her, with a quizzical smile. "Where is this book?"

Aunt March was hurrying them away, showing amazing resilience for an invalid.

"Ask Mrs Russo!" Clarinda called back to him, and for a moment her smile was back, though less brilliant than before.

James watched them go. The old woman, Lady March, seemed to have Clarinda in her clutches and would not easily let her go. Well, he would see about that. At Waterloo he had helped defeat Napoleon; Lady March didn't stand a chance.

"And who, pray, is this Mr Quentin?" Lady March demanded, when they were safely back in Sydney Place.

Clarinda turned from the soft patter of rain on the window, where she had been staring dreamily into the afternoon shadows. "He is lately arrived in Bath," she said, but when Lady March continued to glare at her impatiently, she added, "He is a gentleman, and his manners are good. He is putting up at the Good King and planning to stay for some time. He—"

"He is wealthy." Lady March liked to get to the point.

"It would seem so," Clarinda replied cautiously. She glanced at her sister, who was reading upon the chaise longue. "What did you think of Mr Quentin, Lucy?"

Lucy set down her book and yawned sleepily. "Lord, I don't know, Clarinda. He's amusing enough but he's quite old, isn't he? Not like Monsieur Henri," she added dreamily.

"You can't prefer the hero in that book to Mr Quentin," Clarinda declared with uncharacteristic crossness. "Really, Lucy, he's charming and sophisticated and perfect in every way."

Lucy's pretty face took on a mulish look. "If you think that, Clarinda, then you must be falling in love with him yourself."

There was a silence. Clarinda felt too shocked to reply, not so much at Lucy's temper but at the idea that she should be falling in love with a man when her future was already set.

"I am most disappointed about my wheeled chair," Lady March announced in a loud voice. "Sold out indeed. I cannot believe there are so many people in Bath requiring them at this present time. I am sure no one needs one as urgently as I do. Perhaps I could send up to London for one. What do you think, Clarinda?"

"I think you should wait and see if you can find one closer to Bath, Aunt," said Clarinda, knowing who would be pushing her aunt around in the wheeled chair.

"Humph!"

"Perhaps Mr Collingwood could help you find one," Lucy added, with a bland look on her face and a naughty twinkle in her eye. "Do you know where he is staying, Aunt?"

"He has a disease of the lower limbs that makes them swell up enormously," Lady March said with relish. "He has invited me to tea, to examine them."

"Poor man." Lucy could not help but feel sorry for him.

"I wonder how he contracted it?" Lady March gazed into the fire.

Clarinda and Lucy exchanged a speaking glance, and Lucy gave a shudder. "I'm sorry I was cross," Lucy whispered. "I did not mean to snap at you."

"I know you did not."

"You only want what is best for me," Lucy went on in a dull voice.

Clarinda looked at her sister in surprise. "But you must want to marry and have a fine house and fine clothes and . . . and . . . Surely every young woman wants to live grandly?"

"I suppose so," Lucy agreed, but she didn't sound very certain. "But I want to fall in love first, Clarinda. I would hate to marry a man simply because he was wealthy or had a title. I do not crave to wear pretty dresses or ride in a fine carriage as much as that."

"You are very young," Clarinda began, as if this was an excuse.

"You speak as though your own life were over," Lucy retorted.

"We owe Aunt March a great deal," Clarinda said, as if this were an answer, glancing at the older woman now dozing in her chair.

"You have spent ten years caring for her," Lucy said, suddenly seeming far older than Clarinda knew her to be, "and it is time I took my turn."

Clarinda opened her mouth, closed it again. Suddenly everything seemed to be turning topsy-turvy. Slyly, the image of herself and James Quentin crept into her head. How could she dare to believe such a thing was possible? That she should be granted the chance of such happiness?

If she were to allow herself to begin to believe only to have her dreams snatched away from her, it would be too cruel. Clarinda knew she would rather lock them away now, before they could gain purchase, than be shattered by the dashing of her hopes.

"We shall see," she said firmly.

Lucy sighed. "That means you intend to have your own way," she murmured. "But this time, Clarinda, you will see. I intend to have mine."

"The Pump Room went well, My Lord?"

Dunn's curious gaze took in his master, as if trying to decide what there was about him that was different.

"Well enough, and please do not call me by that title."

Dunn took his coat. "I am sorry, sir, but you are Lord Hollingbury."

"I know I am, Dunn, I just . . . Oh dash it, I suppose you're right. I'll have to get used to it one day."

"Did you learn anything to your advantage, My Lord?"

"To my . . . ?" James repeated, momentarily dazed. "Oh, you mean . . . No, Dunn, I didn't."

James poured himself a brandy. He felt the need of it. The water in the Pump Room had been as nasty as he feared, and he told himself the brandy was to wash the taste out of his mouth. In truth it was to settle his nerves, which were rattled far more than he liked to admit.

Mrs Russo had clutched hold of him again after Clarinda left, and she had been most forthcoming. She had informed him, with false sympathy, that Lady March's two nieces were only with her because she had kindly offered them a home after they were destitute. "Poor as church mice," she added, with a sly look. "Good looking, I grant you. The younger one may make a good marriage. Miss Clarinda is obliged to remain with her aunt, but she has expressed a wish that her sister may have an independent life. So unselfish of her, don't you think? What did you think of the youngest Miss Howitt, sir? She is generally thought to be quite a beauty."

James frowned. Now he recalled the moment when Clarinda

introduced her sister and there had been something watchful in her gaze as she beamed at him. He almost groaned aloud. Clarinda thought he would fall for Lucy and she was happy with that. She did not want him for herself. Acknowledging it made him damned angry.

Now James shook his head, trying to clear his thoughts of Clarinda. He had come to Bath with one object in mind and here he was being diverted. It would not do at all.

"How can I find her?" he muttered. "Does she even want to be found?"

Dunn looked concerned. "If she is in Bath, then we must discover her, sir, whether she likes it or not. It is not such a large town and there is a great deal of gossip."

"But she has hidden herself away. Will she understand how much I want to find her and restore her to her proper station in life?" His face darkened. "My brother had a great deal to answer for, Dunn."

"It was unfortunate you were away in the army when it happened, My Lord."

"But now I have a chance to amend matters."

If only Clarinda would stop distracting him.

No, he told himself, he would put her from his mind.

But he found he couldn't. She came to him in his dreams. Clarinda Howitt was perfection, well perhaps not entirely, she did want him to marry her sister after all. But he knew he wanted her by his side when he began his new life as Lord Hollingbury.

Which was why he found himself in front of her house two mornings later, waiting for his card to be taken upstairs, and permission given for him to meet Clarinda face to face.

Clarinda felt her hands shaking as she smoothed her skirts and pinched her cheeks. She looked wan, with great dark shadows under her eyes. Her aunt had taken a turn in the night, claiming her limbs were swelling like the hot air balloon they had seen flying overhead in the summer. Clarinda knew it was all nonsense, that she had taken the idea from Mr Collingwood, whom she'd visited during the day. But when Lady March decided she was ill there was nothing to be done but ride the wave to its conclusion.

Dr Moorcroft had come and was upstairs with Lady March, listening patiently to her symptoms. At first, when there was a tap on her door, Clarinda had thought it was the doctor wishing to speak to her, but instead it was the maid with a card from James Quentin.

Her James Quentin.

No, no, that was not right. He was not hers. He could never, ever be hers. Her life, her future, was fixed. Lucy could never handle Lady March, no matter what she said. No matter how much she wished it could be so. Whatever he wanted she must send him away and as soon as possible. To let him linger was only to cause herself more pain and suffering.

With a new iron resolve, Clarinda descended to the vestibule.

He was gazing at a gloomy hunting painting that belonged to Lord March, but turned at the sound of her steps on the stairs. His smile faded a little at the chill tone of her voice.

"Mr Quentin, how do you do?"

"Miss Howitt. I am interrupting. I am sorry to intrude upon you without an invitation. I felt the need to see you."

He made it sound as if seeing her was somehow imperative, but she dared not imagine that was true.

Without answering, she showed him into the parlour and they were seated. "I cannot stay long," she said. "My aunt is ill and the doctor is with her."

"I'm sorry to hear it. Although your aunt did not seem to be an invalid when I met her at the Pump Room, and the first time we met you mentioned her penchant for imagining herself ill." His look was quizzical.

"That is neither here nor there," Clarinda said quietly. "I owe my aunt a debt. Without her Lucy and I would have been . . . well, I don't know what would have happened to us." Suddenly she looked at him, her eyes widening. "Oh." A thought had occurred to her. He'd come to offer for Lucy! After one meeting he was hopelessly in love with her sister and wished to ask for her hand. Her emotions sank even lower but she tried to smile. "Lucy is out shopping with her friends. I am sure she will be sorry she missed you."

His smile was gone. He was frowning almost furiously. "I didn't come here to see Lucy, I came here to see you. I thought I made that perfectly clear, Clarinda?"

Puzzled, not daring to believe, she gazed into his eyes.

"Clarinda, let me make myself very clear. I have no interest in your sister whatsoever. It is you I am interested in."

"I don't understand," she began, hoping for and yet dreading his answer.

"Mrs Russo informed me of your circumstances," he said dryly. "An unpaid servant to your aunt. I have come to offer you a way out, Clarinda."

"A way out?" she croaked, praying she was wrong, and yet hoping . . .

Lady March's voice drifted down from upstairs. "Clarinda!"

Clarinda stood up, shaking.

Footsteps on the stairs and a white-faced maid poked her head around the door of the parlour. "Miss Clarinda, the doctor says can you come?"

Clarinda hesitated, torn between hearing what James Quentin had come to say and her duty to her aunt. "I must go."

"Clarinda, please, I know I have put my question very badly. I should have said how much I admire you, how I dream of you, how ever since we met in the rain I have longed for your company."

Her heart was thudding so hard she could barely hear herself think. "I must go," she croaked, and with a gasp she fled the parlour.

In her brief absence Lady March's bedchamber had turned into a bedlam. Servants were running back and forth with smelling salts and lavender-soaked cloths. Lady March was wailing on her bed, clutching her head and saying her brain was boiling.

The doctor was standing, watching her, a frown on his face. Clarinda, approaching the bed, caught sight of her aunt's reading matter on the bedside table – *Strange and Unusual Diseases.*

Her aunt opened one eye and, seeing that Clarinda was distracted, redoubled her wailing.

"Aunt, please, you are frightening us."

Dr Moorcroft appeared at her shoulder. "She was perfectly all right until she heard you had a visitor downstairs," he said. "A Mr Quentin?" His eyes searched her flushed face. "Your aunt seems to have taken it into her head that he is here to take you away from her."

"Well, she is wrong," Clarinda replied bleakly. "I know where my duty lies."

His glance stayed on hers a moment more and then he squared his shoulders. "Right," he said grimly. "How odd. I have just come from Mr Collingwood, who also possesses this book. Can there be a connection, do you think?"

"My aunt has recently made the acquaintance of Mr Collingwood," Clarinda said cautiously.

Her aunt opened one eye, then closed it again quickly when she realized she was being observed. "Is Mr Collingwood as unwell as I?" she demanded in a surprisingly strong voice for one so ill. "I'm certain he cannot be."

Dr Moorcroft considered her. "It may be necessary to quarantine you and Mr Collingwood, Lady March. To ensure this ... this disease does not spread throughout Bath."

Lady March looked quite thrilled at the prospect. By the time arrangements were made, and the doctor was leaving, she was sitting up drinking tea.

"She is lonely and bored," Clarinda explained, knowing it was no excuse.

"All the more reason to find her a friend of similar mind," the doctor said, with a twinkle in his eye. He paused at the head of the stairs, waiting until the servants had passed by and they were alone. "Has she reason to fear Mr Quentin, Clarinda?"

Clarinda looked away. "No. I cannot put my own happiness before that of my aunt, or Lucy."

The doctor sighed, but said nothing.

It was not until he reached home that he allowed his anger to show. "It really is ridiculous," he said, as he and Etta sat together in their handkerchief of a garden. "Clarinda obviously loves this fellow but is refusing to allow herself to accept him because of her wretched aunt."

Etta, who wasn't her usual smiling self, said softly, "And what is this fellow's name, my love?"

"Quentin," he told her, proud he'd remembered.

A moment later Etta was in tears.

"My darling, whatever is the matter? Etta, please tell me?"

Slowly, painfully, Etta allowed him to draw out the truth. Afterwards she was drained and he put her to bed and sat with her as she fell into a deep sleep. When she woke, he was still holding her hand. He bent over her, smiling, and kissed her lips.

"I love you," he said. "I don't care about the past. We have the future to look forward to, and I am forever grateful for it."

Etta gazed at him with shining eyes.

"What are you going to do?" he asked, worriedly. "Whatever it is, you know I will stand by your decision."

Etta sighed, and, after a moment, she told him.

The Assembly Rooms were lit by lamp and candlelight, the musicians busy playing their instruments as the dancers moved gracefully or gossiped in little groups by the walls. Clarinda, feeling like a shell of her former self, was only here because Lucy had insisted, and her aunt was visiting Mr Collingwood and his sister. They seemed to have so much in common that there was little else her aunt would speak of. Clarinda was bewildered by the change in her.

"You should be pleased," Lucy said with a grin. "I am. Let her marry old Collingwood. They could be wheeled up the aisle in their chairs together, can you imagine it?"

"Lucy," Clarinda murmured reprovingly.

Her thoughts were melancholy tonight. Mr James Quentin had asked her to marry him, or at least that was what he'd intended to do, and she had cut him rudely short and rushed away. How could he forgive her for that? He must think he had embarrassed her, or she didn't return his feelings. How could he understand the conflicting demands that had been tearing her in two?

Of course he would never approach her again. She wouldn't be the least surprised if he had left Bath altogether.

"Here is Etta," Lucy whispered. "I will leave you. I see Isabella over by the potted palm."

Her sister hurried away, eager to join her friends. Clarinda smiled as Etta approached. "I did not know if you would come," she said.

Etta looked as pale as she had at the Pump Rooms, and there was something anxious about her, a sense of expectation.

"I have heard from my husband about your aunt's new hobby," she said, with a ghost of her old twinkle.

"Yes, my aunt and Mr Collingwood are very close."

Etta glanced beyond her and stiffened. She bit her lip. "Oh dear," she said in a wobbly voice.

The next moment she had hurried past Clarinda and grasped the hands of James Quentin who had been approaching, resplendent in formal evening wear. "James," Etta said, as if the name meant everything to her.

Shocked, speechless, Clarinda stared. She tried to understand what this meant but nothing occurred. There was a sick sense of despair in the pit of her stomach, and something else – a feeling of furious jealousy.

She turned away, not knowing where she was going, not caring. She was almost at the door when Etta slipped her hand through Clarinda's arm and turned her around. Her friend's eyes were shining, her cheeks flushed. She looked like a woman in love, Clarinda decided bleakly.

She was so busy being miserable she didn't at first take in the words Etta was saying to her.

"He is my brother! I . . . I was foolish enough to run off with someone totally unsuitable while James was away in the army. Our elder brother, Lord Hollingbury, disowned me, even when I begged to be allowed to come home."

"Your . . . your brother?" Clarinda whispered.

"James came to Bath to find me."

Clarinda looked up and found her eyes held and captured by those of James Quentin, and suddenly she realized how like Etta's they were – both so dark and warm and dear.

"I had sworn I would find her and make all well again," he said softly. "I had people searching and discovered she had married and was hiding in Bath, so I came to fetch her home."

Etta laughed. "Only this is my home now."

"But . . . " Clarinda looked from one to the other. "You do not mean Dr Moorcroft is the unsuitable man you . . . ?"

"Oh no. I met him later, and fell in love. I have been very fortunate."

As if her words had conjured him up, her doctor joined their little group. For a moment the emotion ran high, before Etta and her husband departed to the supper room.

"I made a bit of a hash of it, didn't I?" James broke the silence between them. They had stepped into an ante-room, hidden from the crowd by draped curtains. He smiled, his eyes seeming to caress her and warm her.

"No," she said, her voice trembling with passion, "it was my fault. I thought there was no hope and I couldn't let myself believe. I couldn't bear it. So I sent you away." She lifted her head and gazed into his face. "Did you really come to Bath to find Etta?"

"Yes. But I found you, Clarinda. My darling, will you marry me? Will you be my Lady Hollingbury?"

Clarinda allowed her whirling thoughts to settle. There was her aunt, but she seemed to have found a new life. There was Lucy, but Lucy had a mind of her own it seemed and wasn't going to fall in with Clarinda's idea of her future. And that left Clarinda.

"Yes," she said, and a wave of such happiness washed over her.

He took her into his arms. "I will never complain about Bath weather again," he whispered against her lips, "because that is what brought us together."

And then he kissed her.

Gretna Green

Sharon Page

He had caught gangs of murderers in the stews off Whitechapel High Street. Arrested opium dealers in seedy brothels near the Wapping docks. But in all the years he had worked for Bow Street as a Runner, Trevelyan Foxton had never been required to investigate in a more foreign and intimidating place.

He watched the shop from across the street, drawing smoke from his cheroot. Each time the door opened, the silver bell tinkled delicately, and he caught the faint scents of rose and lavender. Ladies flowed in and out continuously. Ladies of every age and every description – slender, giggling girls, with shining eyes, and their mamas, the formidable matrons of the ton. And from within, all he could hear was incessant feminine chatter.

Trevelyan glanced up at the name above the shop, proudly displayed on a large sign, painted in burgundy and ivory, glimmering with gilt.

No longer was she plain Sally Thomas. She was now Estelle Desjardins. He'd caught a glimpse of her when the door opened. She wore severe black and had pins stuck in her mouth. She had been pointing at a thin, sallow girl who looked miserable in an ivory dress. And, at the same time, she was lecturing the mother, a bosomy, grey-haired woman he recognized as the Duchess of St Ives.

Now that was the Sally he remembered.

She'd been the toughest, hardest and fiercest of their gang. All of the lads – the pickpockets, the mudlarks, the thieves – had been afraid of her. Except for him. He knew the one thing that frightened Sally. When he wanted her to shut her mouth, all he had to do was kiss her. Or show her he cared about her.

That had been a long time ago. Back in the days when he never would have dreamed he'd end up on the good side of the law as a Bow Street Runner. Back then he never would have pictured Sally in anything but a ragged dress, with her fists doubled and her point of a chin stuck out. Never would he have pictured her looking down her nose at grand ladies.

Trevelyan tossed away his cheroot and ground it into the cobblestones of the street.

Sally had done well for herself.

It was a shame he was going to have to destroy her.

Estelle froze. All thoughts of what exact shade of ivory the daughter of the Duke of St Ives should wear vanished from her head. It no longer mattered that the fashion was now for long sleeves. Or that it could be possible to make Lady Amelia's bosom appear more ample, with strategic pleating and a lot of padding.

He stood in the doorway, the proverbial bull in the china shop. At once her lavender sachets were overwhelmed by the rich, refined, masculine scent of him, of smoke, shaving soap, and sandalwood. His straight shoulders filled the doorway from side to side. His gaze – sharp, intelligent – glinted with an amusement that made her quake, and fastened immediately on her.

She had wondered if he would ever come and find her. It would be so easy for Trevelyan to get his revenge, which he surely must want.

All he had to do was tell every lady in her shop exactly where she had come from and who she really was.

A pin jabbed into her tongue. Estelle spat them into her hand. The attention of every woman in her salon riveted on him. He had to duck for the doorway, and he took off his beaver hat to clear it, revealing his striking coal-black hair and the one streak of white that began at his temple and followed the sweep of his unfashionably long hair to his shoulder.

"Madame Desjardins," he said, with a perfunctory bow. He straightened, then ensured he closed the door behind him, a sardonic smile on his mouth. "Is it intended to mean 'Star of the Gardens'? I like that very much."

Her stomach almost dropped away. What did he want? "May I help you, Mr Foxton?"

The buzz began at once.

"Goodness, Mr Foxton is a Bow Street *Runner*," whispered Lady Amelia to her bosom-bow, Lady Caroline.

Lady Caroline put her gloved hand to her mouth and her eyes glittered with delight. "What is he doing *here*? Do you think there's been a crime committed?"

"You mean other than these prices?" muttered Lady Caroline's mother.

"Have you heard?" one young lady whispered. "It is said that Mr Foxton is the heir to the Earl of Doncaster."

Estelle froze. She took care to know the gossip of the ton. How could she not have known this?

"That cannot be true. I heard that he grew up in the East End stews," declared the voluptuous Countess of Bournemouth. "And that he has a very sordid past." She said it breathily, as though "sordid" was a commendable thing.

"I think he is trying to look down Lady Armitage's bodice!"

That would not surprise Estelle. Trevelyan had always been a rogue. And he appeared to enjoy making her clients shocked and uncomfortable. "Madame Desjardins," he began, in a voice that had deepened and roughened and grown even more magnetic in ten years, "I hate to trouble you, but I would like a private word."

The ladies gasped. For, of course, it meant he must walk through her shop, past the curtained rooms in which women stood in various states of undress. "Miss Sims," she instructed her best seamstress, "advise the ladies to keep their curtains closed, if you please. Mr Foxton, you may come to my office. I assume a respectable representative of Bow Street will keep his eyes averted."

Oh, she was not prepared to have him in her private office. At once he went to her desk and tried the drawers. "The key, please, Sal."

That name. She had not heard it for ten years. It was *not* her name any more. "If you want my help, do not call me that, Lyan." She carried her keys in a pocket sewn into her dress, skilfully designed so as not to ruin the line of the smooth-flowing skirt.

This was her sanctuary – this office, this shop. "Do you wish to see my book of accounts? You are free to review it, if you are interested in what a satin ball gown costs these days. If it's the measurements of my clients that interest you, I will not help you there. That information rests only in my head."

He pulled out her ledger, planted his trouser-clad derrière on the edge of her desk, and flipped open the book. "I am here about Lady Maryanne Bryght."

A shudder of apprehension slid down her spine. "Lady Maryanne? I do believe she *was* a client of mine. But why—?"

Her book of accounts landed, closed, on her desk. His green eyes had narrowed, and he looked so expressionless, she shivered. The Lyan she remembered had never looked so cold.

"You're lying to me, Sal. That's why I never came to see you before. I knew all you'd give me was a pack of lies."

"Perhaps you should question me first, before assuming that's all I will do." She tipped up her chin and spoke with the bravado she'd cultivated on the streets.

"At first, I suspected Lady Maryanne never came to see you. I assumed she used your appointment in order to leave the house so early in the morning. I believed she'd headed for Gretna Green instead."

In the stews, she had stared down any number of men – from randy young toffs to vicious pimps looking to drag her into their seedy flash-houses. But she was quaking now. "Then you should be able to find her."

"Angel, that appointment was five days ago. She should have returned a happily married woman by now. I followed her tracks along the Great North Road as far as the border, and then she disappears. No one in Gretna remembers her. If she was wed over the anvil, no one will admit to performing the ceremony. She's vanished into thin air."

Estelle swallowed hard. That made no sense. She had investigated Lady Maryanne's handsome young scholar. That was what she did. She smoothed the course of true love for young ladies about to be forced into loveless marriages. She had made her choice years ago – security over love. But that did not mean she could bear to see innocent women made into prisoners in their marriages. This gave her the chance to see others have what she couldn't.

Her investigation had revealed the gentleman Maryanne adored to be exactly what he claimed – a studious, respectable, noble young man, the youngest son of a now-impoverished viscount. "Do you know who she ran away with?" she asked, trying to look shocked.

This was a nightmare. There was no one in London – in all England – who knew her like Lyan did. If anyone could see through lies, it would be he.

"Yes. Don't you?"

She imagined he hoped she would incriminate herself. But there was nothing more she could tell him. She had watched Lady Maryanne climb into a hackney, and had loaned the eighteen-year-old girl a purse filled with money to finance the journey (since, like most girls, Maryanne had no access to money on her own).

She had sent Maryanne on her escape to true love.

She had hoped Maryanne had crossed the border into Scotland, where a young couple needed no one's consent but their own to marry. As soon as they had crossed the border, lovers could marry anywhere, but Gretna Green was close and, since the couple usually wanted to be joined in haste, that was where they would stop. Vows were spoken over the anvil at the blacksmiths' shops, officiated by the blacksmith priests.

Maryanne must now be safely wed. And blurting out the truth of what she had done would not accomplish anything. It would not give Trevelyan any more information than he already had. It would destroy her. And she was not the only person she had to worry about.

"Lady Maryanne came here that morning. We had another fitting. Dresses for her wedding trousseau – for her upcoming nuptials with her guardian, Lord Cavendish." She managed not to shudder at the name. "I do not know any more than that, Lyan."

"You do, love. Everything about you screams to me that you're keeping secrets. You always looked your most defiant when you were telling me a tale. Now, how about we strike up a bargain? You tell me everything, and I won't go back out and have a nice chat about our childhood with the Duchess of St Ives."

"Don't. Don't ruin me, Lyan. It may please you to see me lose everything, but I would not be the only one to suffer. You see, I have a daughter."

She could not have stunned him more if she'd hit him with a plank. She could see that from the way all six feet of him lurched back on his heels. And she knew what he must think.

"No, she is not *your* child. But I will be damned if I will end up like my mother – poor and in some stinking, wretched flash-house. My daughter is almost nine years of age." She lied there. It had been ten years since she had last seen Trevelyan. Since she had panicked and gathered up half the money she knew he hid in his grotty room, and run away with it. "You know what her life would be like if I have to go back there." Her voice was shaking, no matter how much she tried to calm it.

"Who is her father, Sal?"

"That is none of your business."

"As I remember, the last time I saw you, you had agreed to marry me. We had our little ceremony in that warehouse. And we consummated our marriage on the floor of it."

She winced. He had lowered his voice, and his words were a smooth-as-honey murmur beside her ear. "I'd say that does make it my business."

Then, before she could stop him, before she could *react*, he spun her around, put his hands on her upper arms, and slanted his mouth over hers.

At first she froze in shock. And horror.

She stayed as rigid as her metal mannequins – or she tried. He was so much bigger than she remembered.

Then the tension – the *fear* – began to evaporate. Something else pounded in its place. *Desire*. Hot, maddening, inconvenient, disastrous desire.

He tasted of smoke, of liquor and coffee, of heat and man and sin. Every decadent thing about men she could imagine was imprinted on her lips by Lyan's mouth. He tipped her off her feet, so she had to wrap her arms around his broad back. She melted, like wax beneath a candle's flame.

Oh. Oh. Ooooh. She'd kissed him before. Made love to him before, which had been the most dazzling, wet, hot, wonderful and heartbreaking night of her life. She should be impervious to his skill – much more skill than he had ten years ago. His lips teased hers. His mouth forced hers wide and she loved it. And she moaned, breathlessly, as his tongue slid in and played and reminded her of what she'd dreamed of him doing for so many years . . .

A whole decade. And the one kiss she'd had since then had been forced upon her. A harsh, vicious assault she'd escaped when her attacker had been struck with a frying pan. After that, she'd never wanted to be touched again. Until now . . .

She had to stop . . .

But to her shock, she couldn't make herself pull away. Lyan broke the kiss, set her back on her feet and stared at her. With green eyes that gleamed as brilliant as lanterns.

"W-why did you do that?"

A sardonic grin twisted his handsome mouth. "I just wanted to see if it had been worth thinking about you for all these years."

His very answer terrified her. There was no hatred in his voice. Only regret. "And was it?" she asked coolly.

"Let's just say I can have my secrets too." But his gaze ravaged her mouth. And her lips were still so sensitive, just the heat in his vivid emerald eyes made her tremble.

"I promise you, Sal," he growled, "I will get to the truth. I will find out if you were involved with Lady Maryanne's disappearance. And I'll find out if you are keeping my daughter from me."

★   ★   ★

Lyan followed the tall, icily correct butler down the gloomy halls of Cavendish House – he felt he was trailing a walking cadaver. As he neared his client's study, he planned what he would say. What he would reveal.

He hadn't expected Sally to give him any information. But he'd observed her shock when he'd said Maryanne was missing, and it had told him more than words. Sal had known he would question her about a marriage – she'd never anticipated a disappearance.

And he hadn't anticipated kissing her. His mouth had been on hers before he'd realized what he was doing. Her kiss had burned a path through his hardened heart like a flame along a fuse. He couldn't think of anything but getting her back into his arms, keeping her there for ever, kissing and kissing and kissing her, until she was panting and needy and begging him to make love to her.

Never, on a job, did he lose control. Never had he let his sexual desire take charge. He couldn't afford to do it now.

Yet knowing that, he was still mentally undressing Sally as he sauntered down the corridor of the Marquis of Cavendish's home. He could picture her slender body naked, completely bared to him, and draped sensuously across her desk. For his pleasure, he arranged her on her front – on her small round breasts and smooth tummy – with her naked rump saucily lifted to tempt him.

Hell.

Even with their past hanging between them, with her betrayal sitting in his gut like a knife blade, he had to admire her. He'd always known she was tough, but now he appreciated she was also intelligent and clever. A better life agreed with her. She had changed from a stick-thin seventeen-year-old with dirty hair to a tall, striking beauty. Her severe hairstyle had made him hunger to tear out her pins and watch the whisky-coloured mass fall down her back. He'd never guessed her hair was that rich amber hue. As for her dress, it was a plain sheath that clung to her slender figure. It's simplicity made him speculate how she would look without it.

If he hadn't known her from the past, he would have been enjoying himself. A canny, beautiful woman – she was the type of adversary who made his work interesting.

When he looked at her, he felt . . . not anger, but sorrow and regret. When he'd walked through her feminine shop, he'd been stunned by one astonishing realization – the tumultuous ending of their relationship had been for the best. Where would they have been if she hadn't taken half their money, run out on him and built up her business?

Where would he have been if he hadn't gone after her, gotten himself stabbed by a footpad in his distraction, and discovered he had to get out of the stews before that world ate him alive?

The butler rapped upon a dark study door. "Mr Foxton has arrived to report, My Lord."

A raspy voice barked at him to enter, and Lyan found himself once again in the dark, cavelike study of Horace Beckworth, Lord Cavendish.

The Marquis tossed back a glass of brandy and stomped forwards. His jowls shook as he bellowed, "Bloody hell, Foxton, you haven't found her yet. I don't know what you hoped to accomplish by coming to see me without my ward, but if your goal was to infuriate me, you have succeeded. There are other Runners in London. And other, successful private investigators."

Lyan disliked Cavendish. "You are free to hire one of them, My Lord. But this case has become personally interesting to me. Whether I'm working for you or not, I will find out what happened to Lady Maryanne."

Cavendish grimaced. "Fine then. Have you learned anything?"

In curt tones, he gave Cavendish a report on what he'd learned at Gretna. "As yet, there is no evidence she has married," he concluded.

"So then it is possible her seducer never meant to marry her – only ruin her!"

"That is a possibility. That's why I came to you tonight. To find out if there could be someone who would seek revenge on you through your ward."

"Revenge? For what?" The eyes narrowed in the fleshy face. "I will remind you I am a gentleman of honour. If I have made enemies, they would meet me over pistols. On that you are wasting your time."

Yes, he thought he was. There had been a fleeting look of guilt in Sal's shrewd blue eyes, along with a quiver of apprehension, which told him she knew who had accompanied Lady Maryanne on her escape.

"But you could find no sign of her in Scotland?" Cavendish barked.

"None," Lyan said, and he watched his client's face.

The Marquis fell back into his large, leather chair. "Do you think it is possible she never made it to Gretna Green because she is dead?"

"It is a possibility, yes," Lyan said. Not one he would have wanted to leap to, if the girl had been under his care. However, he had a young sister. It would be his worst nightmare to lose her. But there was something different in Cavendish's expression. Not horror, nor despair. It was a look Lyan knew from his days on the streets. Anticipation.

Cavendish pulled out a linen handkerchief to mop his brow. "I have to know, Foxton," he croaked. "I have to know what has happened to her."

The back of Lyan's neck prickled. Cavendish had been the best friend of Lady Maryanne's father and was the trustee of the girl's fortune. Her father had made millions in speculative ventures and had settled a large portion of his money – that part of his estate not entailed – on his daughter.

Lady Maryanne was a wealthy woman. Lyan had gone to Somerset House and reviewed the will left by Lady Maryanne's late father. If she died, Cavendish got the fortune. Of course, when she married Cavendish, he got control of her money. But if she married someone else, Cavendish lost his chance of any of it.

"Find her. Or find evidence that she is lost to me. I want it within the week or I'm done with you. And don't think I'll just fire you. I have no patience with men who fail me. I make them pay."

"I would advise you, Cavendish, not to threaten me," Lyan growled. But he thought of Lady Maryanne. She was a sweet, gentle young lady, very much like his younger sister Laura. She deserved a better life than being locked up in this mausoleum with an old roué who hungered for her money. And he prayed she was still alive.

After his interview with Cavendish, he needed to clear the foul stench of greed and arrogance from his senses. Lyan went home. Walking up the steps to his house normally gave him a feeling of pleasure. It pleased him to know this was where Laura would remember growing up. She had spent seven years in the slums, but those memories were fading. And he wanted to keep it that way. She deserved to think of this as her world.

He gazed up at the elegant Georgian façade with its rows of mullioned windows glinting in the sun, its neat blue door, the freshly painted wrought-iron fencing, and its promise of security and position. He'd acquired it with the rewards he'd earned as a Runner. Once he became the Earl of Doncaster, he would give up this house and take Laura to the earldom's London house, an enormous mansion on Park Lane. Laura was seventeen. Now that he'd been discovered as the long-lost heir to the Doncaster title, he could give her the come-out she deserved.

Earl of Doncaster. He'd never believed his mother's tale – that she'd been wed at sixteen to an earl's younger son, abandoned by him, and finally widowed when he'd died of consumption. Trevelyan had known nothing but guilt when the solicitor found him and told him her story had been the truth.

His mother had married again when he was nine. To a Whitechapel butcher. And when that man died three years later, they were all out on the street again, but this time his mother had Laura, a fragile little child of two.

Lyan jogged up the steps, opened his glossy blue door, and stepped into his spacious, marble-tiled foyer. He handed off his greatcoat and gloves to a footman, and shook his head at the vagaries of fate.

Even then he had vowed he would keep Laura safe, no matter what. It was a man's duty to take care of the women who relied upon him. He'd always sworn he would never leave a wife, the way his father had deserted his mother. Ironically, he had been the one abandoned—

"Lyan!"

He looked up as Laura leaped to the bottom of the stairs, sailing down a half-flight, her muslin skirts flying up. "It was all the talk at Gunter's today," she cried. "That you were investigating at Madame Desjardins' dress shop. Heavens, what were you looking for there?" She flashed a coy smile. "Some of the ladies are speculating you were hunting for a potential bride – by going where you could view the debutantes in their underclothes."

He groaned, then embraced her and planted a kiss to the top of her midnight-black curls. "You know I wasn't doing that."

He had a bride. He had made a vow to Sally Thomas. It still stood, in his mind, legal or not. And whether either of them wanted it or not.

"Good." Laura nodded. She was no longer frail and sickly, but healthy and strong. "I have an appointment there tomorrow for a ball gown. I should hate to think the door was barred to me because my brother was trying to see ladies in their corsets."

In the course of his work he had often questioned madams and prostitutes. He'd seen more ladies in corsets – and out of them – than he could count. But no woman had ever haunted him like Sal. "You are going to Madame Desjardins' shop?"

"Mrs Fennings says I must, now that you are to be an earl. But I hate all the dull fittings. I'd much rather stay at home and read a book."

Mrs Fennings, widow of an earl's brother and a haughty martinet, had been employed to oversee his sister's come-out. The woman could bring a man to his knees with her glare. He'd often wondered about trying to convince her to partner him in the pursuit of criminals.

Laura assessed him quizzically. "Has Madame Desjardins committed some kind of crime?"

Did breaking his heart a long time ago count as a crime? He sighed. "I don't yet know." Laura knew a little about Lady Maryanne's disappearance. Since she was a similar age to the missing girl, he'd wanted to know her thoughts, had hoped they would give him insight into Lady Maryanne. "It is the last place Lady Maryanne is thought to have gone."

"But she wasn't in Gretna Green?"

"No. And you sound surprised."

"It's just—"

He put her arm around her. "Tell me, Laura." He didn't need to say more. She understood his fears for Lady Maryanne's safety.

"I heard that Madame Desjardins helps young women who want to elope."

"Helps them?" He narrowed his eyes. "How?"

"I don't know. These are just rumours I've heard from other girls. I think she loans them money. Most have no access to their own money, of course. And I also heard that she investigates the gentleman these ladies want to marry. To ensure they are not just fortune-hunters, gamesters or rakes. She stopped one young woman from marrying a man who was just pretending to be a Scottish earl's son. He was actually a draper's lad."

"Thank you, angel." He gave his sister a hug. Then frowned. "You aren't planning to use any services of Madame Desjardins beyond her dressmaking skills, are you?"

"Do you mean do I want to elope?" Laura's laugh was silvery and sweet. "Of course not. I simply want a dress. Anyway, no man would ever dare run away with the sister of the famously ruthless Mr Foxton."

Lyan scratched his jaw. He was afraid her answer had come too quick and with too much light-hearted laughter. "Laura—"

"Mrs Fennings is going to introduce me to other earls, Lyan. I have no intention of running off with anyone."

Tonight he had two reasons to visit Madame Desjardins. He would question her again about Lady Maryanne. And warn her what would happen if she tried to help his sister do something foolish, like eloping.

There was no way in Hades he would let the woman betray him twice.

* * *

"Are you certain this is what you wish to do? You do realize how much you will give up by marrying this man against your brother's wishes?" In a soft voice, Estelle listed what those risks could be. Estrangement from family. Loss of any hope of a dowry or marriage settlement. The discovery that love was not enough to conquer everything, after all. "There is nothing like poverty to sour a marriage. It may turn your charming suitor into a bitter, brutal husband."

Estelle watched the young woman solemnly nod. The girl had a hood pulled down to cover her dark curls and shroud her face. She had insisted all candles be extinguished. Only the light from the coals in the grate illuminated her. "I know. I've thought of those things. But my . . . my brother has received news he will inherit a title. I know he thinks he wants the best for me, but I don't want to make my choice amongst viscounts and earls. I know which man I want to marry. But my beloved is a Bow Street Runner and I know the match will be refused."

"Give me his name. Before I can help I have to ensure he is not a rogue, a criminal or a rake."

The girl shook her head. "It's not necessary. I know everything about him. He's worked with my brother for years. He's a hero! He has rescued kidnapped children and stopped criminal gangs."

"His name?"

"I can't. You could go to my brother."

"My dear, I would never betray you. But if you wish for my help, you must tell me."

But the young woman rose to her feet. "No. I will do this alone then." She spun on her heel and ran for the door of the shop, shoving a stool across the path between the worktables.

Estelle jumped up. Her scissors fell from her lap to clatter on the floor. Her patterns were whirling in the air, blown off the tables as the girl had raced by. She rushed after the girl, leaped over the stool, but as she reached the front of the salon, her door snapped shut and the bell tinkled madly. She snatched open the door, ran out into the street.

The girl had disappeared.

On a sigh, Estelle went back into her shop, back to the workroom. Moonlight slanted in through the narrow windows. Her dress patterns lay all over the floor, battered and bent. She'd torn one, as she'd run over it. If she did not finish them, she would not have the St Ives' wedding gown completed. Or the two gowns required by the twins of the Earl of Roydon, who were going to have their come-out ball.

To disappoint clients was to embrace the end of her business. It would mean her fall back into poverty again, and this time she would drag her daughter down with her.

She couldn't.

But there could be only one young lady in England whose brother had just learned he was heir to a peer, and who herself might know enough about the Bow Street Runners to fall in love with one.

Lyan had a sister. Her name was Laura.

Estelle had never once betrayed the confidence of any girl who had come to her seeking help. And the young ladies, to her surprise, had kept her secret. Her role in their marriages was shared by word of mouth, and just to those girls in the same predicament.

She had helped girls who had a real reason to flee. Girls for whom a marriage that would ostracize them from their families was a lesser evil than staying at home.

Did Laura have reason to flee her brother? And why did she believe her brother would never let her marry for love? Or was he afraid Laura could be blinded by love and end up betrayed?

Estelle paced in her workroom. Was it just because Lyan wanted his sister to move up in the world that he would refuse the match? Some Bow Street Runners were known to be motivated more by rewards than justice, and some were considered to be as unsavoury as the men they hunted. That was the very reason Lyan had fascinated all of London. He had always appeared to be moral and just.

It would break his heart if Laura ran away into a terrible marriage.

Could she betray him again, break his heart again, by keeping Laura's secret?

A soft creak sounded overhead. Directly over the rear of the workroom, where Estelle was gathering up her patterns. She cocked her head to listen. Was Rose out of bed? Had the slammed door awakened her?

She put down the stack of fragile paper, picked up her scissors, and crept upstairs. The door to Rose's room was ajar, just as she had left it—

A hand clamped over her mouth and dragged her into her bedroom. Her shoulders were pulled back hard against something unmovable. Estelle knew what it had to be: a male chest. Panic rose like a wave and she struggled against the arm that clamped around her torso like an iron bracket.

"Easy, my love. I won't hurt you."

Those words. He'd said those. Cavendish. When he'd tried to assault her here, in her own bedroom, while Rose slept innocently in the next room. He'd held a blade to her throat to make her stop fighting and had warned her not to make a sound. In a sneering, evil voice, he'd warned her she would not want to wake her daughter . . .

All those years she'd spent in the stews had not been for nothing. She'd known he didn't intend to leave witnesses afterwards, whether she obeyed him or not. So she had fought for her life. Rose came to help, hit him over the head with a frying pan. At eight years of age, just like Estelle, Rose had seen what men could do.

And now she kicked and struggled just as furiously. She had her scissors in her hand—

A strong hand pulled them out of her grip. "I wouldn't like those stabbed into my privates, thank you."

Lyan. He turned her to face him. "You wretch!" she spat. "You terrified me. You could have woken up Rose. She went through this before and it almost frightened her to death. I—"

"What do you mean, 'she went through this before'?"

When she didn't answer, he kissed her. Just like that. His mouth devoured hers. All her fear and rage tumbled around inside. But even as furious with him as she was, she became hot. Scorching hot. So much so, she feared her simple work dress would melt to her skin.

"Tell me, or I won't stop there." Then he grimaced at his words, and he brushed his hand over her cheek. "No, no threats. Threatening you with kisses won't work any more, will it? Because you've known worse. Tell me what happened, Sal. I'll kill anyone who hurt you or your daughter."

Through the heat rising inside her, a heat that fogged her mind like steam upon glass, she remembered the painful truth. She had abandoned him in a panic ten years before. Why should he care about her now? She had put her security above all else, and the simple fact he still gave a damn made her throat constrict. "Well, then," she managed to say, "that is exactly the reason why I can't tell you."

His hands traced the simple neckline of her dress. Her breasts leaped up, under her shift, as his fingertips skimmed over them. Then, shock of all shocks, he cupped them.

"I want all your secrets, Sally. Every last one." He breathed the words against her ear. The fire he'd ignited inside her consumed another piece of the wall around her soul. Just this, his hands on her breasts, his mouth nuzzling her neck, could leave her utterly defenceless.

No. She would be like her mother then. Vulnerable. What was a woman in the throes of passion but a woman waiting to be destroyed?

"You know who Lady Maryanne ran away with. This afternoon, I interviewed families of young ladies who have been your customers. Four of them ran away to Gretna Green with men."

"And those marriages are all successes," she said tartly. She tried to pull away, but he held her too tight.

His tongue ran up and down her throat. Her mind was becoming as mushy as porridge. "S—stop," she whispered.

"I will if you give me a name. A man's name." His grip changed and he stopped kissing her. He faced her, his eyes glittering with determination. "I fear Cavendish arranged for Maryanne to disappear. He found out about her plans to elope, and he had her killed so he would not lose control of her money. By the will, he gets it all if she dies without a husband or children."

Estelle gulped. "Oh yes, he could do that, Lyan. He is more than capable. He is a fiend." She knew she had to give him the name. For Maryanne's safety. "Her beloved was the owner of a small bookshop on Charing Cross Road. Mr Samuel Peabody."

His dark brow shot up. "He sounds like a little, fat, middle-aged merchant. Why would you help the girl elope with a man like that?"

"I did not help her. She simply gave me a name. As for the others—"

"You're lying, angel. I could prove you helped her – if I found the hackney driver who came to the rear of your shop and who saw you escort a young woman who matched Lady Maryanne's description into the cab. A man who saw the young lady clutch your hands before she left and thank you for everything you had done."

Her heart sank.

"You helped her run off with some scoundrel," he ground out. "Some man who might have killed—"

"No! I promised to help her. And that meant ensuring she was marrying the right man." There, she had admitted her guilt. And she knew why she'd done so. Deep down, she still trusted Lyan. She would always believe in the goodness of this man's heart. Carving her way into respectability and security, she had encountered some of the "gentlemen" of the ton. The ones who pressed their attentions on any women they believed beneath them. Who were willing to rape because they believed themselves to be untouchable. She had soon learned that birth meant nothing. Lyan Foxton had grown up in the stews, but she had learned how special, noble and wonderful he was.

Yet there were also good gentlemen. Peabody was one of them.

"He is the third son of the Viscount Marlborough, and he has a love of books. He is tall, thin, but very handsome. And I realized, when I went to his shop and spoke with him, that he truly loved Maryanne."

He frowned. "How could you know that for certain?"

"I . . . A woman can tell." She did not want him to know how she knew. That she'd compared how Peabody looked when she spoke of Maryanne to the way Lyan used to look at her.

"Thank you," Lyan said. "I pray I'm not too late."

"What are you going to do?" She knew she had to be quiet, but her voice rose in fear. "I went out this afternoon. Peabody's shop is still closed up. And I spoke to his employee and his neighbours. He hasn't come back."

"I think if Cavendish arranged for his ward's death, it would be known by now that she was killed. He'd want it done fast. It would be easy enough to make it look like a highwayman attacked her on the way to Scotland. I think the fact that she hasn't turned up dead means she is still alive. I think he wants her back to marry her himself, which gives him both the lady and control of her fortune. Hell, I *have* to believe that."

Stark pain showed on Lyan's face. How harsh and sharply cut his features were, now that he'd matured from a youth to a man.

"Why would he hire you, if he was the one to arrange for her to disappear?" she asked.

"To make it look like he's innocent. Or because she escaped his trap. He might genuinely have no idea where she is. I'm going to trace the route to Gretna again, now that I know who her suitor is. I hope they are hiding somewhere along the way and I can find them."

"I would like to come with you." She had to know Maryanne was safe. And she could help Lyan. For a start, she knew what Peabody looked like.

"On one condition," he growled. "I want you to promise you won't help my sister, Laura, if she asks you to help her elope."

She swallowed hard. Nothing had escaped him in the past. That hadn't changed. "Of course not. But why do you think she would run away rather than ask your permission?"

His brow rose sharply. "Because sometimes women do damned illogical things."

"All right. I agree. But I have conditions for *you*."

"Indeed?"

"No more kissing. No more touches. That's behind us, Lyan. There can never be anything between us again."

★　★　★

"Why did you do it, love? Why did you run out on me before I came back for you? I thought – apparently like a blind fool – that you intended to be my wife."

Estelle jerked her gaze from the carriage window, where she had kept it fixed for several hours. Lyan sat across from her, and he had looked out the opposite window ever since they had entered the carriage together. Each time she'd stolen a surreptitious glance, she'd discovered he was not looking at her.

Which was for the best. To feel anything else, any sort of girlish pang, was a stupid and irresponsible thing. She had long stowed away the desires and foolish fantasies that always began with the words "what if". From the moment she'd made her choice to run away, then discovered she was carrying Rose, Rose had been what she'd lived for.

Her future had been mapped out. Decided. It was not to be changed. But what she *could* do was help shape the futures of others.

She did owe him some sort of explanation, but although she'd had ten years to think about it, she had never come up with an account that satisfied her. "I did it so I could have what I have now."

"What do you have now?" he asked, and she wondered if Lucifer sounded like this – like smooth-flowing brandy and chocolate when it bubbled in a cup – when he promised dreams in return for souls.

She cleared her throat. As though just a little more time would clear away the heat wrapping tentative fingers around her heart, the yearning blossoming between her thighs. "My business. Enough money upon which I can survive. My daughter. I suppose what I have is success and security."

"But you have no husband. No one to protect you."

"I protect myself." She managed a smile. "You, of all people, must remember I am capable of that."

"Aye," he answered with a breathtaking grin of his own, one that carved dimples deep enough to make her knees quiver. "I still bear a few scars to prove it."

She had forgotten what this was like. For ten years, she had worked every minute of the day. Her needle would flash through cloth late into the night, while she would be desperately blinking to keep her eyes open. Hour upon hour. Day upon day. She had carved out a formidable reputation amongst the ton for her gowns. But she had not had a friend. And from behind a mound of fabric and patterns, she had watched Rose grow into a beautiful, quick-witted girl.

"I've never forgotten our wedding night," he said softly. "For ten years, I've considered myself married to you."

That startled her. "But you have the reputation of a rake."

He groaned. Though they'd lit lamps within the carriage, which made looking out the windows quite useless, shadows still lurked in the corners. He leaned back, letting the gloom hide his face. "There were times the need got a bit too much, I'll admit that. But I never fell in love, Sally. Never once."

"Oh heavens, Lyan. I wish you had." For then she could have forgiven herself. "How much longer until we reach the border?"

"We'll have to stop for the night. We'll find an inn along the road, and leave in the morn, as early as possible."

"An inn." She took a deep breath. "Separate rooms, of course."

"Of course? We made marriage vows. We had a wedding night." He leaned forwards. The teasing note in his voice did not reach his eyes, which glittered in the lamplight like cold glass.

"Ten years ago," she said. "And our vows were not spoken in a church or before a vicar."

"The passing time makes no difference. And the intention of marriage vows, love, is for husband and wife to make a promise to each other. Does it matter if it is not in a house of God?"

Estelle trembled. He had always been able to do this to her. Bring out emotions – or desires – she did not want to face. "*Legally* it does. I am not your wife, Lyan. I will never be. I do not consider our marriage to be valid. I ran away from you. Isn't that reason enough for you to think it invalid too? Don't you want to admit our vows meant nothing? For that means you would be free."

"Ah, Sal, but that's the irony. I'll never be free of you."

The Rose and Crown was the third inn at which they'd stopped. It looked more prosperous than the other two, with many coaches rumbling in and out of the yard. Coachmen drank ale around the water troughs, singing to the tune of a jauntily played fiddle.

Estelle had been commanded to stay in the carriage. But she ignored Lyan, hopped down, and hurried inside after him. He was leaning on a counter, in deep discussion with the innkeeper, a thickset bald man with a large stomach and enormous arms.

Lyan turned at the sound of her footstep. "Ah, my wife." He did the introductions. One key dangled from his hand.

"I said two rooms," she muttered.

"And there is one available. You can sleep in the stable if you'd like, but I'd prefer a bed." Then his voice dropped even lower. "They were here two days ago. Peabody and Lady Maryanne. She wore a heavy veil, but the man matched the description of her suitor. He took a room for them as husband and wife, and she was seen fiddling with a wedding ring."

Estelle felt such relief; it was like taking a long breath of air after loosening a corset. It surged in so quickly it left her light-headed. She wanted to believe she had rescued Maryanne. She wanted to believe she had carved out another happy ending in a world sadly lacking in them. But relief, like a breath, ended. "They could have been posing as married but had not yet—"

"After heading to Gretna six days ago? I suspect they would have raced up there, stopping only when necessary. They could have reached it in two days. No, I think they were wed and were returning to London."

"But why didn't they get there?" Estelle whispered. Her body ached from the tension of sitting in a carriage and trying not to look at the man who had sat opposite.

"That's the mystery," he agreed. "But dinner first, and a night here. You look as though you are ready to fall to the floor. And you, my love, can have the bed."

It was unsettling to have him lying on the floor. Rather like having a sleeping tiger in the bedroom. Moonlight slanted in through a space between the threadbare drapes. Estelle hadn't slept. She lay on her back, staring up at the silvery light that flickered over the dark ceiling. She wore a thick, unflattering flannel nightgown, buttoned to her throat.

"You aren't sleeping."

Lyan's matter-of-fact statement had her jerking up the worn sheets. He was on his knees beside her bed, elbows resting on her mattress. Watching her. He had stripped to his trousers. The last time she'd seen him, he had been a lad of seventeen. Strong and well built, but nothing like . . . like this.

"I'm intrigued," he continued. "Why do you help young women run away? Is it because it worked so well for you?"

She flushed. "No. It's because I want them to find the one thing I turned my back on. Love."

In the stark bluish light, he looked haggard. Haunted. "Before I caught you in your house, I took a peek at your daughter."

Indignant, she sat up, fisting her hands at her sides. "You had no right—"

"She was sleeping – didn't see me. I know she's mine, Sal. I wanted to see if you would finally tell me. But you won't, will you? You'd have let me go to my death without knowing I have a child." He shoved back his hair. It was loose and fell in coal-black waves around his shoulders. "Why, Sal?"

She hugged herself. This was a mistake. She should never have put herself in a position where she was alone with him. She'd believed she trusted him. But she'd never seen any man look as wounded, as tortured as Lyan did now.

"I . . . I have finally given her some happiness."

"You don't want her to blame you for the choices you made. When did you know you were pregnant? Before or after you ran away?"

"After," she whispered.

"You could have found me. I would have married you then. If there had been the three of us, Sal, you wouldn't have had to work your fingers to the bone as a seamstress. You would have known I would always be there for you."

"I didn't know that then," she cried. "All I knew was what I'd seen of my mother and men. I vowed I would never be dependent on anyone."

"You cost me ten years, Sal. Ten years I could have had with my child."

"I suppose you hate me." It was too late to run now. "What are you going to do to me, Lyan, after we find Lady Maryanne? Do you plan to hand me over to Cavendish? That would give you what you must want – revenge."

He jerked back. Anger flared in his green eyes. "Jesus, Sally. I suspect Cavendish might have plotted to murder the girl."

She was moving away from him, trying to scuttle across the bed. But he grasped her wrist and pulled her back with such force, she squeaked in pain, and fell across the mattress.

"I would never betray you. Understand that." He cursed and let go of her. "And if Cavendish conspired to kill his ward, I intend to see him pay."

"He is too powerful, Lyan." Her bitterness rang out in the room. "Men like him are never punished. He'll be free." Icy panic rushed to her heart. "Did you tell him I helped Maryanne?"

"I didn't. But he suspected you of helping her. He knew she had appointments with you." His eyes narrowed. "Cavendish seems to think you would have helped Maryanne to spite him."

Spite him. She would like to see him rot in Newgate for what he had done. For the way he had left Rose with fears and nightmares.

"What are you afraid of, Sal? Cavendish?"

Yes, she was terrified. But she couldn't let him see it. That was how she had always survived. By never allowing anyone to see her fear.

"Maryanne is likely a married woman by now," Lyan said. "She will have her fortune, and she can buy herself a lot of protection with money. How will you protect yourself, Sally?"

"I . . . I will do it somehow." For Rose. She would protect Rose. In every way and at any cost. But she was afraid. Cavendish was capable of anything. And if she were to make a mistake, if he were to kill her, Rose would be vulnerable. And she had no doubt that Cavendish, the evil blackguard, would take delight in hurting Rose too.

"There is a solution, love. Marry me." He smiled, and had never looked more devastating, more tempting. "Again. As your husband, I can keep you safe. Cavendish, for all his threats, his bluster and his arrogance, would never try to hurt you if he knew I'd rip him apart over it."

"You are going to be an *earl*. You can't rip men apart."

He lifted his brow in a way that warned he could do anything. "Oh? You just told me peers are above the law."

Her heart thudded in fear. "Not for killing other peers." He couldn't throw his life away over her. It was bad enough that he had waited for her. He couldn't give her any more. She couldn't live with that.

"It was Cavendish, wasn't it?" Low and dangerous, his voice made her shiver. "He was the man who attacked you. Who made you afraid." He had never spoken like this. Never so terrifyingly.

"Yes." She had to give him the truth. And she feared he knew anyway – that she had shown something in her eyes. "But you cannot do anything rash. Or foolish."

"I don't do foolish things, love. I wouldn't have survived so long if I did."

"You just proved that isn't true, Lyan." She managed a wry smile. "You just asked me to marry you."

"Not foolish, Sally. But I'd like to postpone the moment when you tell me 'no'." He rolled her on to her back, and crawled over her, his tawny gold body supported above hers on his powerful arms. Her breath caught. He grasped the neckline of her nightgown and pulled hard. Three buttons popped free and clattered to the floor. Her gown gaped to reveal her bosom.

Lyan captured her mouth, all the while stroking her breasts, making her feel like molten gold. She had once seen a jeweller turn the metal to liquid, had seen it splash, scalding hot, into a mould. That was how she wanted to feel – like something strong and solid which could turn to fluid with all this heat, which could be changed, reshaped, transformed into something new.

How could he kiss her like this when he knew she would turn him down?

"I . . . I want you," she whispered. "But marriage . . . I can't . . . I have to say—"

"Shh."

He began to lift up her sensible flannel nightdress. She couldn't stop him. She couldn't walk away from him now. One night. She would allow herself that. One glorious night to remember for ever.

He bent to her nipples, teasing and suckling them. Giving her pleasure she hadn't known for ten years. His hands slid down and he stroked her most private place.

Yes. Oh *yes*. But she didn't dare say that word. That dangerous word.

Then Lyan slid inside her, burying his erection deep, and his mouth never stopped lusciously tormenting and pleasuring hers, not for a moment.

She kissed him as they moved together, frantic, wild, just like when they had been young, blessedly young, and in love. She had always wanted to believe it would be easier to face the world if they were together.

She licked his neck. Devoured his mouth. Nibbled his ear. Bit his shoulder. Because if she didn't keep touching him and tasting him, she would start to think of what she'd lost. And she'd burst into tears that might never stop . . .

His lips pulled back, and she almost tumbled into the depths of his wild, hot green eyes. "Stop thinking, Sally. Just love me. For right now, this is love. Savour it."

Then he covered her mouth with his as though afraid she might argue. But she couldn't any more. And she came, she climaxed, she surrendered to a pleasure she couldn't begin to control. She burst into a thousand shimmering pieces. She flowed like liquid gold. She soared.

And he cried out hoarsely in a climax. His shout of pleasure sent her heart spinning up to heaven.

As she fell back to earth, to their hot, disordered bed, Estelle was aware of Lyan's arms around her. He had moved off her, but his embrace held her captive.

"I want to ensure," he said sleepily, "you don't run away again."

You could marry him and make love with him and sleep like this every night. Rose could have the one thing you never had and never will have – a father.

Estelle sat up. Lyan was not doing a very good job as gaoler. His long, large body was still snuggled beside her. But his arm was slack with sleep and rested on her hip.

She needed to think. And needed air. The room smelled of sex and pleasure and was so hot it made her dizzy. As soundlessly as she could, Estelle put on her cloak. While Lyan breathed steadily, she slipped out of the room, then hurried down the stairs and ran outside to the yard.

She wasn't going to run away. No, this time she had to refuse Lyan to his face. She felt as though she were a gown that was stitched up all wrong. All the pieces were where they should be, but she could never be right until she was taken apart and made up all over again. Yet she didn't have the courage to pick her stitches away.

A carriage stood in the yard. There was a light within, illuminating a girl's face.

It was the face of the young woman who had come to her last night. It was Lyan's sister's face. He'd told her the girl's name. Laura. There was one reason for Laura Foxton to be in a carriage at a coaching inn on the road to Scotland.

The girl was alone in the carriage, and she drew back as Estelle wrenched open the door. "What are you doing? Eloping?"

"I—" Laura tipped up her chin. "Yes."

"What of your brother? I'm sure it will break his heart if he finds out you've run away."

The dark-haired girl glared mulishly. "I'll go back and see him. I'm not running away for ever. You have no right to tell me what to do. Or tell me what my brother feels. He left me a note before he left last night. In it he told me who you are. The woman who broke his heart!"

Estelle fought the guilt she knew Laura had wanted to provoke. "Well, he doesn't need another broken heart then, does he? He is here, in this inn. Why not tell him what you want? Why not marry with his blessing?"

"He won't give me his blessing. I am in *love*. And I won't turn back now."

Estelle clasped the girl's hand. "If you are happy, then I wish you a lifetime of happiness. Tell your brother, wait for his blessing before you marry. Understand that it is not too late to turn back. It never is."

She left Laura then, hurrying back across the muddy yard. It was so easy to give advice she would never take. Lyan was offering her the chance to turn back. And she had said no.

Her heart grew heavier with each hurried step back to the bedroom. Lyan still slept. He lay on his stomach and the sheets had fallen down to expose his bare back. Estelle dropped her cloak and sat down beside him. Her nightdress was half open, slipping off her shoulders. What should she do – slip back into bed and betray him by letting Laura escape to Gretna? Or wake him up and betray a young girl who yearned to find love?

She touched his shoulder. Shook him gently.

Click.

Behind her, the door's latch had opened and she spun around. *Laura?*

She expected to see the girl in the doorway, but instead she breathed in the choking scent of a smouldering cheroot. Her gaze locked on the dark eyes of a strange man.

But she had locked the door. After she'd come in, she'd locked the door by instinct.

The black-haired man winked at her. He wore a grey greatcoat and gleaming black boots, the cheroot was clamped in his teeth, and his large body filled the doorway. Blocking her escape. An amused smirk twisted his lips.

Then she saw it. The almost extinct firelight glimmered along the muzzle of a pistol held in his hand.

"Who are you?" she demanded, fighting to hide fear.

"I take it you are Mrs Desjardins," the man said and his glittering eyes mocked her. "I see Lyan has been mixing business with pleasure. Well, I have some business to conclude myself. In the name of Lord Cavendish. Which means, unfortunately, I will have to get rid of you first."

He swung up the pistol to point at her chest.

Estelle stared at the muzzle, frozen, her heart pounding in wild terror. She expected to hear the roar of the shot and be blown off her feet. Instead, she saw a look of pleasure leap to the man's eyes. He was enjoying her torment.

She drew on all the bravado she'd clung to when she'd been growing up in the stews. "I will pay you more," she said, confident and cool. "I will pay you far more to leave us alive."

His finger paused on the trigger. "I doubt that. And I can't leave Lyan alive – he'd hunt me to the ends of the earth. But you . . ." His gaze moved suggestively over her.

"I have a lot of money," she purred. "I can give you ten thousand pounds." She couldn't. *Couldn't.* But she prayed he would be intrigued enough to keep his attention on her, to give her more time—

And then Lyan launched off the edge of the bed. His body ploughed into the man, his hand slamming on to the pistol. The weapon exploded with smoke and a flash and the stench of burned powder.

For a frozen second, Estelle expected to see Lyon – or herself – collapse. Then she saw the feathers drifting in the air. The only victim of the shot was the bed.

The man swung the pistol up again, and smashed the muzzle into the side of Lyan's head. Lyan recoiled and blood flowed down his face from a gash in his temple. Estelle's heart gave a leap of terror. For her entire life, she had feared being under a man's power. She'd feared being helpless.

Dear heaven, she was not going to let Lyan be killed.

She didn't have scissors in her hand this time, but the fireplace poker was in reach. While the attacker had his attention fixed on Lyan, Estelle lunged forwards, wrapped her hands around the iron handle, and struck . . .!

"Blast!" The man jumped back, avoiding her blow. But it gave Lyan enough time to grab him, snapping back the wrist that held the gun. She heard a sickening *crack*, then the thud of the fallen pistol. The man's wrist dangled limply for a second before Lyan threw him to the floor as though he weighed no more than the feather pillows.

He pressed his foot down across the blackguard's throat.

He had come so close to losing her again, losing her for ever. And he'd known, as Nick Swan levelled the pistol at Estelle's heart, he couldn't live without her. He had barely survived for ten years without her, let alone a lifetime. If she died, he knew his heart would die, too.

Lyan increased the pressure of his foot on Nick's neck. He knew full well he wouldn't have the Judas beneath his boot if it weren't for Sal . . . for Estelle. And, though her chest rose and fell with quick, deep breaths, she was already yanking a cord from the bed curtains to tie Nick's hands. She definitely hadn't left behind the woman she had once been. She was still a survivor. His heart was filled with admiration for her.

"Who is he?" she whispered.

"My former partner and Bow Street Runner, Nicholas Swan." He rapped the butt of the pistol against Nick's temple. "I take it Cavendish paid you to pursue me."

Estelle took a sharp breath. She went as white as chalk. Swan emitted a grating chuckle of pure triumph. "He paid me well, but I had another reason to come here, Foxton – the lovely lass waiting in my carriage for my return. I'm sure she's panting for me—"

"Laura," Estelle broke in. She glared at Nick. "*You* are the man she believed was a hero?"

"What?" Lyan began to wonder if he'd been the one thrown to the floorboards. It appeared he'd missed a few things. "Would one of you tell me what is going on?"

"Your sister came to me last night," Estelle admitted, "and told me she wished to elope – with a Bow Street Runner – because she believed you would refuse the match. I now see why."

"And you didn't tell me about this?" He felt a sharp pain through his chest, which just had to be the large crack slicing through his heart at that moment. "Didn't you trust me to do what was best for Laura? This is why I didn't want my sister anywhere near Nick Swan! He's a corrupt blackguard."

"And what are you going to do, Foxton?" Nick grunted from beneath his foot. "Have your sister destroyed by scandal? Let me go, and I'll wed the chit and save her reputation."

"Lyan! What in heaven's name are you doing to Nick?"

Lyan stared into the shocked and horrified eyes of his sister standing in the doorway.

Estelle, bless her, drew Laura into the room. She told Laura everything – Lady Maryanne's elopement, their suspicions about Cavendish, Nick's attack. Estelle soothed his sister through each step of the story. At the very end she whispered, "And you must know which man you can trust – the one you should keep in your life. Your brother."

Lyan dragged a bound Swan to his feet. "Was it also your job to go after Lady Maryanne Bryght?" Nick's eyes shifted and his mouth hardened, revealing the truth. "Did you find her? Hurt her?"

At Nick's silence, he gripped him by the throat. "Tell me where you found her. And what you did to her and Peabody, or I'll kill you now. Give me the truth and things might go better for you."

Nick gave a vicious laugh. "Good luck finding them. I caught them two days ago, but by then they were wed."

"And Cavendish had sent you to kill them if they were," Estelle accused.

Nick gave a sly grin. "He wanted the lovely and rich bride for himself. I was to get rid of the husband. But the little witch outfoxed me. I had cut up the gent and was ready to finish him when Lady Maryanne pulled a pistol on me. They managed to escape but I had to return to London because Laura was waiting to elope with me." He smirked to Lyan. "Even if I failed Cavendish, I assumed you would pay a lot of money to get her back and make me go away. Enough for me to live comfortably in Italy."

Laura turned a heart-wrenching shade of white.

"Where did you find them?" Lyan demanded, but Nick shook his head. Fortunately Lyan knew his former partner well. He was a coward at heart. It took another half-hour of threats – and a little pain – but Nick finally revealed the small village inn where he had discovered them.

The innkeeper had stormed upstairs at the sound of the shot, and now Estelle took charge, sending him to fetch the nearest magistrate. Lyan looked to her. "Once Nick's taken away, I've got to see if I can find Lady Maryanne."

She nodded. "I will take care of Laura."

What a shame that, at the end of this, he thought ruefully, she wanted him to walk away from her for ever.

The magistrate and several muscular village men arrived to place Nick Swan under arrest. Swan had been shackled in irons and taken to gaol. Lyan, the other magistrate, and several of those men raced off to search for Lady Maryanne and Peabody, planning to start their hunt in the village where Swan had caught the pair. Estelle stayed with Laura, who sobbed and sobbed at her lost love.

But as dawn began to blush on the horizon, Laura wiped at her eyes. "You had tea brought in, didn't you?"

"Yes." Estelle poured the girl a cup. She suspected Laura was, at her core, as strong and noble as Lyan. As the girl sipped hot tea, Estelle stroked back her hair.

"I'm crying at my stupidity," Laura said. "And at how close I came to losing my brother." Wide green eyes gazed up. "You were correct. I see how important Lyan is to me. I don't want to lose him, in any way. When I marry, I want it to bring happiness to our family. Not discord. And—" She ducked her head. "He was right."

"Your brother is a very wise and wonderful man."

The door burst open then and Lyan strode in. He grinned when he saw his sister drinking tea, still tear-stained, but also smiling. "My God, Estelle," he murmured, "you are a shining star."

Estelle grasped Laura's cup. Her heart felt full to bursting as Laura flung herself into Lyan's embrace. Over Laura's disordered curls, Lyan gave her the good news.

"We found Lady Maryanne and Peabody quickly. They had taken refuge in a nearby barn. Peabody has lost a lot of blood, but the village doctor believes he will survive. They have many years of married life ahead of them."

Estelle could have kissed him. But Laura deserved to have all her brother's hugs. Then to her surprise, Laura looked up into Lyan's face. "Are you going to marry Madame Desjardins? You could keep travelling to Gretna Green and marry her over the anvil. That's the place where everything – all love – is possible, Lyan. You both deserve to be happy."

Estelle caught her breath. What if Lyan thought she'd put Laura up to it?

But Lyan shook his head. "I have no intention of going to Gretna Green."

A fortnight had passed, and Estelle had accepted the truth. Lyan believed she would not marry him again. He would not come to ask her one more time. Really, it was madness to even hope.

How many times would any man put up with being turned down?

At least Lady Maryanne – now Mrs Peabody – was free of Cavendish. He had been faced with ruin, for he'd needed Maryanne's money for his gaming debts. His body had been found in the Thames. Whether he'd jumped or had fallen in drunk, no one knew.

The bell tinkled above her shop door. It was just closing time. She peered out from behind the workroom curtain to tell the customer to come back tomorrow.

Lyan stood in the doorway, just as he had done two weeks ago. But this time, his arms overflowed with an enormous bouquet of red roses. There were so many flowers that the red velvety blossoms almost hid his handsome face. "For Sally of the Gardens," he said softly, setting the lovely bundle on one of the chairs.

"Lyan—" But her voice died as he dropped to one knee, and a shy smile touched his lips. He held up something sparkling. It caught the candlelight and flashed light around the room. "I didn't want to whisk you away to Gretna Green, Sally. That's the place for *forbidden* love. I wanted to marry you here, properly. If you wish, we can marry at St George's as soon as I get a licence." He raked back his dark hair. "I love you, Sally. I've loved you for my lifetime. When I realized I could have lost you in that inn . . . You have to say yes, Sally. Because I'm going to stay here, down on one knee until you do. And with me filling your doorway, no one can get into the shop."

She almost laughed. The very first time he had asked her, ten years ago, she had said yes. She'd agreed then, because she had thought she could never love anyone more than she loved Lyan.

She had been wrong. She loved him even more *now*.

At her silence, his face dropped. "Angel, it can't be 'no' again, can it?"

"There are more reasons why I can't marry you than I can count. For one, you will soon become an earl. Earls do not marry simple seamstresses—"

"You are anything but a simple seamstress."

"I am a shopkeeper, Lyan. Earls do not marry shopkeepers. Unless the earls are very, very poor and the shopkeepers are very rich."

His lips twitched. "I was – am – a Bow Street Runner. My upbringing was no different than yours, and I have a profession, as you have."

"I ran away the first time because I was afraid of being trapped." There. She wanted to give him the truth. And if he still wanted her then . . . "When we were young and you asked me to marry you, I wanted you more than life itself – that was why I said yes. But then I became afraid. My mother had been treated so badly by men, I wasn't sure—"

"You thought that I could hurt you."

"I had no idea that men could be good and noble, Lyan. All I knew was my mother and the men in the stews. She had believed those men would be good to her, but she was so very wrong. I was afraid of losing control of my life. I thought what I wanted most was to be in charge of my own destiny. But when we were attacked in the inn, I realized that love and family are far more important than fighting to always be in control."

She threw up her hands. "It doesn't matter what I want. Society would never accept me as a countess. You wanted to clear Laura's way to a better life, not throw more obstacles in her path. I would be an insurmountable obstacle."

"Laura has found the man she wants to marry."

"Goodness. Already? Who?"

"The young Viscount Norbury. Once she no longer had Swan in pursuit of her, blinding her to other men, she saw Norbury's good qualities. But I told Laura she can't encourage him until you complete an investigation of him, Sal."

Her nervous laughter bubbled up.

He clasped her hand, and just the contact sent a sizzle to her toes. "I was afraid you wouldn't want to marry me because I was a Bow Street Runner," he said, his eyes serious. "The ton isn't going to be eager to accept me as an earl. But if I'm going to face whispers and sneers, I need you at my side, Sally, to give me strength. I've always needed you at my side."

She took a deep breath and tried to speak. But tears got in the way.

"I want a home with you, Sally. I want to have more children with you. Many brothers and sisters for Rose. But, more than anything, I want you, and that will never change. I don't care what the ton says about us. If I have you, I can look any peer in the eye and tell him I'm the luckiest man in England. For I'd have the two most precious things in the world. Love. And you."

Her tears broke free. They ran down her cheeks. Lyan looked nervous and got to his feet, jerking a linen handkerchief from his pocket.

She took it, and tried to wipe delicately. Then gave up and rubbed her cheeks. She couldn't remember when she last cried. But no longer did she have to hide what she felt, no longer did she have to bear everything alone. "Yes. *Yes*, I will marry you."

He grinned. "No more secrecy, no more running. No more need for Gretna Green." And he wrapped his arms around her like he would never let her go.

Little Miss Independent

Julia Templeton

One

London, England

"There was a day not so very long ago that women were pining for Lord Drayton. Who would want him now?" Elizabeth Montgomery said, her voice hinting at amusement.

Adelaide Bruce, better known as Addy to her friends, resisted the urge to toss her punch in Elizabeth's face. A newly formed acquaintance, Elizabeth didn't realize the man she spoke of so flippantly and with such cruelty was Roan, Addy's brother's best friend, who had been severely injured in battle six months ago.

"He is ghastly, I tell you."

Squaring her shoulders, Addy did her best to control her growing anger. "Miss Elizabeth, the man you speak of is a war hero . . . and a close family friend."

Elizabeth looked down her long nose at Addy, her dark eyes narrowing. "Oh dear, I did not mean to strike a nerve, my pet. I am merely repeating what others have been saying since the Captain's recent return."

"You would do well not to listen to idle gossip, Miss Elizabeth. At the very least, Lord Drayton deserves your respect."

The other woman pressed her lips together and sniffed. "I do respect the Captain, especially for his service to our country. However, there is no denying his appearance is rather . . . frightening." Elizabeth gave a little shudder for good measure. "And to think a year ago he had been engaged to one of London's most desirable debutantes. Everyone knows Sara Duggart's sudden departure to America was no coincidence. A sick great-aunt, my eye." Elizabeth cleared her throat and leaned closer to Addy. "I have heard she is newly engaged to a wealthy Virginian. What he lacks for in height, I understand he makes up for in looks."

Elizabeth's voice faded as Addy watched Roan – or Drayton, as most friends called him – enter the ballroom. Tall and broad-shouldered, Roan's long hair curled at the collar of his Navy jacket. Even as a boy he had commanded attention with his nearly black locks and intense silver eyes. In profile he looked just as he always had — handsome, powerful, masculine — but when he turned, she saw the scar that had changed his life seemingly overnight. It was raised, a mottled red and purple, running from directly beneath his right eye, down the lower lid, over his cheek and down his neck, disappearing beneath the intricately tied cravat at his throat. She had heard the burn had ravaged his entire right arm and hand, to the point he'd nearly had to have the limb amputated.

She could feel the others turn away from his stare, doing anything so as not to make eye contact. Shame on them! What was wrong with them to treat him so? His striking beauty had always made her breathless, and now she felt the familiar stirring in her breast as those piercing eyes scanned the room.

Her brother Jack came up behind Roan and whispered something in his ear. The stern expression immediately fled Roan's features and the wolfish smile she remembered well from her youth appeared, making her heart miss a beat.

Jack motioned her over and Adelaide felt a flutter of excitement ripple through her as she made her way through the throng of guests towards her brother and Roan.

It had been five long years since the last time she'd seen him. She'd been a girl then, just shy of her thirteenth year, and he a young man of three and twenty. How proud he had been to receive his commission to captain his own vessel in Her Majesty's Royal Navy. Word of his bravery had quickly made the rounds of balls and soirées and, when he came home on leave for a short break last year, he had asked Sara to become his wife.

Everyone had been envious of the fair-haired, statuesque merchant's daughter who had enchanted the rakishly handsome, wealthy lord and renowned Navy captain.

That is until word of his hideous appearance reached English shores. It was said Miss Duggart had immediately broken the engagement by way of a hastily written letter, which had left Roan shattered.

With anticipation tripping along her spine, Addy stopped in front of her brother and Roan.

Jack smiled. "Addy, how good of you to join us."

Roan abruptly turned and Addy swallowed past the lump in her throat as she made a small curtsey. "Lord Drayton, what a pleasure it is to see you again. It has been far too long."

His intense silver eyes held her hostage, and she shifted on her feet as he stared at her without blinking.

"Addy." He said her name as though he could not quite believe it was her. "You have grown up in my absence."

She'd always loved his voice. The rich timbre of his voice had not changed at all, and it made the fine hairs on the back of her neck stand on end.

"I certainly hope I have changed. It has been five years, after all," she said, pressing her lips together. To her surprise, his gaze shifted to her mouth, pausing until her brother cleared his throat.

Roan's gaze abruptly ripped back to hers. "You have grown into a beautiful young woman, Addy."

His words thrilled her beyond comprehension. "You have not changed at all," she said, and nearly tripped on her words when she heard a gasp from nearby.

Heat rushed up her neck as she realized what it must sound like to others. To her, he had *not* changed. She did not see the scar that covered his cheek, jaw and neck . . . but rather, the face she had adored for a lifetime.

"I wish that were true," he said warmly, and she shifted on her feet, wishing she could recant the words. She opened her mouth to explain herself, when Jack glanced beyond her shoulder and grinned.

"Ah, there you are, Seeton."

Addy straightened her spine. Stephan Browning, Lord Seeton – her current suitor – bowed at the waist while lifting her gloved hand to his lips and kissing the air above her fingers.

"Miss Adelaide, I am so sorry I am late." He squeezed her hand. "May I have the next dance?"

Stephan's golden locks were swept off his forehead, and he wore a perfectly tailored, dark-grey suit that fitted his tall frame nicely. His blue eyes crinkled at the corners as his gaze shifted slowly from her to Roan. He forced a smile and quickly averted his eyes.

She bit back her disappointment in him.

"Well, will you dance with me, Miss Addy?" Stephan asked.

"Yes, of course. I look forward to it."

Stephan nodded, and departed as quickly as he'd appeared, saying something about greeting his uncle.

"Lord Seeton is Addy's beau," Jack said with a wink.

Roan's dark brows lifted in surprise. "You have a beau, Addy."

The way he said her name made her blood run warm.

"He is not exactly a beau, as much as a friend."

"Do not listen to her. She is being far too coy. Seeton is one of many suitors, I might add. Our little Addy is quite the toast of the ton this season. She had her coming out in June and the house has not been silent since."

Addy could feel her blush deepen. "You exaggerate, Jack."

"I wish I did," Jack said glumly. "Addy, you have cast a spell on the young men of our fair city."

"I can certainly understand why," Roan said, and the compliment delighted her.

"Thank you, My Lord," she said, biting her bottom lip. "I am so very glad you approve. I have always looked to Jack as a father, and you as—"

"An uncle," Jack said with a slight smirk to his lips.

There was something in Roan's eyes that made her pause. Could it be that he was finally seeing her for the young woman she was? How long had she hoped for such a day?

The music stopped and, as a new song began, she gave another curtsey. "It is wonderful to see you again, Roan. We have sorely missed you. I do so hope you will not be a stranger while you are in London."

"Roan is returning to Oak Hill tomorrow," Jack said, taking a sip of punch.

"You are leaving so soon?" she asked, trying to hide her disappointment but failing miserably.

Roan cleared his throat. "I was considering leaving."

"Jack, you must talk him into staying with us for a while."

"I have already invited him to stay, but Roan seems quite determined to leave us."

"Perhaps I shall stay for a little white longer then," Roan said abruptly.

Her heart nearly leaped from her chest, and she could not keep the grin from her lips. "I am so very glad. That is wonderful news!"

Roan could not believe the beauty standing before him was Addy Bruce. His best friend's little sister had always been a mischievous, independent girl, who wore her hair in two braids on either side of her oval face, and had a hankering for getting into trouble. She always did exactly as she liked, never one for going with the crowd. Jack had often said that she was more like a little brother than a sister. He called her "Little Miss Independent". The title suited her.

He couldn't say that any longer. There was nothing masculine – or childlike, for that matter – about the woman standing before him. The plaits were gone and Addy's auburn hair was worn in a simple chignon that complemented her fragile features. Her green eyes were extraordinary, framed by thick dark lashes, and held a wisdom that belied her eighteen years. Her body had filled out in all the right places, with full breasts, a tiny waist and slightly curved hips. And, dear God, her legs were long.

Even more astonishing than her transformation from tomboy to beautiful young debutante was the shock that she did not react to his wound like everyone else had. She had not so much as blinked or stared at the hated scar. There had been warmth and excitement in her gaze, and he felt completely overwhelmed by such a welcome.

As the musicians began playing a waltz, she glanced away. "I must meet Lord Seeton on the dance floor," she said with a soft smile before excusing herself.

With his heart pumping like mad, he watched her walk off, staring at her slender back and the gentle sway of her hips as she made her way to the dance floor and the arms of her suitor.

"It's hard to believe she's our Addy, isn't it?" Jack said, a hint of surprise in his words.

"Indeed," Roan replied, pulling his gaze away with force, still trying to grasp the reality that the lovely creature now dancing with Lord Seeton was Adelaide Bruce. Addy, who as a child used to drive him crazy with her impulsive nature. His stomach clenched as he watched her move with such grace, her smile radiant as she stared up at her partner and laughed at something he said. The two were a striking young couple, and to Roan's surprise, he was jealous.

"How long has he been calling on Addy?" Roan asked before he could stop himself.

"Nearly two months now, I'd say. I do believe he will be asking for her hand very, very soon."

"*Hideous.*"

Roan heard a woman say the devastating word from nearby. When he turned to glance at her, the small group of women were watching him, but quickly looked away.

He clenched his fists, wincing at the pain that shot through his right hand as the skin pulled tight. It had taken a long time to adjust to his reflection, and he had become accustomed to expecting negative reactions from those he met – especially the opposite sex – but it certainly didn't help matters when people were so cruel.

His life had taken an abrupt turn extremely quickly. His new life was in such contrast to the one he had led before the accident. Never had he been without feminine companionship, and now, his fiancée had left him and past mistresses would not return his correspondence. In a moment of weakness he had visited a brothel, and though the women smiled at him and batted their eyelashes, he could see their relief when he picked another. His paid companion had been amiable enough, but the experience had been less than gratifying and he had refrained from visiting another brothel since.

But, like any man, he wanted a wife and children. He had sowed his wild oats, and after long years at sea serving his country, he wanted to settle down and make a life for a family, preferably at Oak Hill, his country estate in Essex. Right next door to what was now Jack's estate.

Memories flooded him of his younger years when he'd stayed with his grandparents at Oak Hill. How excited he'd been when Jack and his baby sister had come to live with their aunt and uncle. From the time Addy had started to walk she'd been precocious, but always a happy child who looked upon her brother with open adoration.

Roan cleared his throat. "So will you give your consent if he asks for Addy's hand?"

"I believe so. I mean, he is from a good family, and only very recently came upon the title from a departed uncle who had no children of his own."

"What do you know of him . . . aside from his peerage?"

"Well, he attended Oxford, and then spent the next four years touring Europe. He has an excellent reputation, and is not known to gamble or drink to excess. In all, I feel he is a good match for my sister."

A newly titled lord who was young, rich, handsome, and with a sterling reputation – who could possibly compete with that? Especially a wounded war captain whose better days were far behind him.

The last strains of the waltz floated towards the high ceiling, and Seeton rested his hand on the small of Addy's back. She looked up at her beau with flushed cheeks and a radiant smile, and Roan grit his teeth, trying hard to understand his tumultuous emotions.

"How about a brandy, old boy?"

"Of course." He had never been a big drinker, but he felt inclined to imbibe now.

He followed Jack towards the door and was annoyed as he tracked Addy's progress across the room. She was the consummate hostess: laughing, chatting, and Seeton beamed with pride.

The younger man finally detached himself from her and made his way across the room. Addy's gaze fastened on Roan. She flashed that angelic smile, exposing deep dimples he had long forgotten about.

Scandalous thoughts raced through his mind as his gaze shifted to the sapphire necklace that curved to a point above the soft swell of her breasts. An image of what she might look like naked came to him, and he shook his head, horrified at where his thoughts had wandered.

Addy was his best friend's little sister.

He should burn in hell.

He was enshrouded in the scent of jasmine as she came to a stop before him, her smile as bright as her eyes. "Dance with me, Roan," she said, her hand reaching out to him. She had reached for his right hand – his wounded hand – and he nearly jerked away.

His hesitation must have been obvious, but she pressed her full lips together. "I am so sorry. Did I hurt—"

"No," he said abruptly. "You did not hurt me, Addy."

How could he tell her he had not been touched in so long, that it felt odd to feel a woman's hand on him, especially the wounded part of him?

He could see the familiar hurt in her eyes, and he extended his good arm to her. "I would be delighted to dance with you."

Her disappointment dissipated as she slid her hand around his elbow, holding tight, her breast brushing against his biceps. He swallowed hard and tried to keep his thoughts as holy as possible.

The dance was a waltz, and she smiled as he pulled her into his embrace. Her gaze was steady as she observed him. He watched her closely, looking for the disgust to show in her eyes. But it never came.

"You look happy," he said.

"I *am* happy."

"Lord Seeton is a good match for you." He managed to say the words without sounding like a complete liar.

"We are not engaged," she said, irritation lacing her voice. "I wish that everyone would not speak to us as though we were."

"I didn't mean—"

"I know you didn't," she said. Was it his imagination or had she stepped even closer?

"I only just returned from school three months ago and already my brother is anxious to be rid of me."

Her words gave him hope. "You do not wish to marry?"

"Of course I do . . . one day. But I am still young. I have plenty of time to worry about marriage. I want to have fun, enjoy what little freedom I do have."

Her words pleased him more than they should have.

"Perhaps while you're staying with us, you could speak to Jack. Convince him that it is wise for me to wait to marry. Will you do that for me, Roan?"

"But what if Lord Seeton grows tired of waiting?"

Her green eyes stared deep into his, and he felt a lump form in his throat. His gaze slid to her tiny, tipped-up nose, to the full lips that were slightly open. Her tongue slipped out, sweeping across her lower lip and he swallowed a groan. "Stephan is extremely patient."

He didn't like the sound of that, and he wondered exactly what kind of "patience" she was referring to. He remembered being a man in his early twenties. He hadn't been too keen on patience.

"I like your hair," she said, completely changing the subject.

"Thank you." He hadn't cut it since his accident, using it as a shield to hide as much of his face as he could.

"You remind me of a pirate."

His lips quirked and he couldn't help but laugh at the whimsical smile she flashed. She'd always had an incredible imagination.

Her hand moved slightly and she touched a lock of his hair. "I wish I didn't have gloves on," she whispered.

His breath caught in his throat.

Did she not realize what she was doing to him? How her words affected him on every possible level? Her touch was like water to a thirsty man. It was all he could do not to turn his face towards that hand, to kiss her palm.

Her smile slowly faded as her eyes searched his. She lifted her face to his, her lips coming extremely close, and the music ended.

She blinked up at him, and then abruptly stepped away, but he had seen the look in her eyes, and recognized it for what it was . . . desire.

Two

Staying with Jack and his sister had been a horrible idea. And now that Addy's beau had made an appearance, it was all Roan could do not to pack up his things and leave.

And yet every time he made a move to do so, he could not help but think of Addy's expression upon seeing him. The warmth in that smile and those beautiful green eyes. Eyes that, at the moment, were focused on Stephan as they played cards. The younger man set his winning hand over her hand, and her beautiful grin diminished.

Idiot. Didn't he know he should always let the young woman win?

Apparently not, as he scooped up the handful of sweets – his "winnings" – and set them to the right of his brandy. The eighth brandy since dinner, not that Roan was counting.

What had Jack said just last night – that the boy had a stellar reputation? Not that Jack would know. He had been paying very little attention to the two all evening. If this was how he usually played chaperone, then chances were Stephan and Addy would be headed down the aisle sooner rather than later.

Seeton belched under his breath, and Roan grimaced. He had little tolerance for people who drank in excess. Having lived with a father who couldn't hold his liquor, he knew the ugly sides of inebriation. She deserved better.

"Lord Drayton, will you join us?" Addy asked in a sweet voice.

Jack, who was deeply engrossed in his book, glanced up at Roan, the sides of his mouth lifting slightly.

"Come, Roan," Addy urged. "We are only playing for sweets."

She did have a point. "Very well, if you insist."

Seeton sat up straighter and shuffled the cards while Roan made his way to the small table. He sat to Addy's right, which meant his bad side was facing Stephan, who looked exceedingly uncomfortable as he slid the cards to Addy.

Looking pleased that he'd joined them, she shuffled the cards one final time and began dealing them each a hand. Seeton finished off his brandy and motioned for a footman to refill the glass. Addy, looking serious all of a sudden, set the remaining cards in the middle of the table.

Lord Seeton lifted his brandy to his lips and took a long drink. When he set it down, he glanced at Roan. "Lord Drayton, I have heard you lost your ship in battle. What a shame."

"Yes, it was a shame."

"Taken by surprise?"

"Actually, I was taken in by a traitor, a man I respected." Little had Roan realized that the man, his first in command, was reporting back to the French. The frigate came out of nowhere, a thief in the night, taking him and his men by surprise.

Roan had looked into the eyes of his first in command before he'd slid his blade deep inside his black heart. Seconds later, he'd felt the cannon blast when an overzealous lieutenant had mistaken a wave of his arm for a signal to fire.

"Must have been quite a blow," Stephan murmured, adjusting the cards in his hand.

"Stephan," Addy said, looking aghast.

Seeton did his best to appear confused as to why she would be angry with him, but failed miserably. "I did not mean to offend you, Drayton. I merely meant that it had to be a horrific thing to live through. Is that how you were injured?"

Beneath the table Addy reached for Roan's hand, squeezing it in silent support. It was the slightest of touches, ending as quickly as it started, but a gesture that touched him to the core. He cleared his throat. "Yes, as a matter of fact, I was injured in that blast. I am lucky to have survived the attack on my ship. Many of my men were not as fortunate."

Seeton nodded as though he was interested, but Roan knew better.

The first game went relatively fast, with Addy winning. Stephan's growing irritation was extremely obvious, and determination etched his brow as he lifted his cards for the next round.

Though Addy had slid her hand away from Roan's, her stockinged toes brushed over his boot. He sucked in a breath. First she touched his hand and now his foot. Did she seek to comfort him, or was there another reason behind the gesture?

Stephan set his cards down triumphantly, his eyes bright, his smile wide. His cheeks were flushed, and Roan wondered if the alcohol wasn't to blame. That, or the excitement of competition. Either way, it was a sad display.

Roan set his cards over Stephan's and the smile faded from the other man's lips.

Releasing a heavy sigh, Seeton pushed the winnings towards Roan and finished off his brandy. Roan handed the sweets to Addy, who positively beamed with delight.

Stephan pulled a kerchief from his waistcoat pocket and mopped at the perspiration at his brow. "It's bloody hot in here. Adelaide, perhaps you would like to join me for a stroll about the gardens?"

"Not alone," Jack said from his position near the door, and Roan smiled inwardly, glad to see that his friend wasn't completely lax in his chaperoning duties.

"Do not pull yourself away from your novel," Addy said with a smile, already standing. "Roan will accompany us."

Roan buttoned his jacket and followed the young couple out the door. "We shall return shortly."

Jack nodded, looking relieved he did not have to leave the comfort of his chair and his novel.

It was an amazing night, the moon full and bright, stars as far as the eye could see . . . and yet it paled in comparison to Addy. In the span of a few days he had come to realize that his feelings for his best friend's sister had changed from doting big brother to something altogether different. Any man would be fortunate to have such a bride, and Roan felt himself disliking Seeton for the sole reason that he was well on his way to having what he himself would never have.

"Look at the moon," Addy said, lifting her face to the sky.

Roan thought of the nights on his ship, and how enormous the sky was. During those times, he had imagined what his friends were up to in London, and knew that he would never change places with any of them, for there had been nowhere else he'd wanted to be.

He still had times when he missed the ship, the ocean and the camaraderie he'd shared with his men.

Addy's laughter rang out, bringing him back to the present. Roan slowed his pace, watching the handsome young couple ahead of him, feeling far older than his twenty-eight years. His gaze lingered on Addy's slender form, at the way the pale-green silk fell on her curves and accentuated her long legs.

Addy glanced over her shoulder and then stopped as she waited for Roan to catch up. She slid her hands up and down her arms. "I forgot my shawl," she said with a shiver for good measure. "Lord Seeton, would you mind retrieving it for me? I believe I left it in the dining room, hanging over the chair."

Stephan glanced at Roan, pressed his lips together, and gave a curt nod. "Of course. I'll be right back."

"Thank you," she said, her tone sweet.

When he disappeared down the pathway, Roan turned to her with a smile. "I could have gone for it."

"I wanted him to go."

His pulse skittered. "Why?"

"Because all night I have wanted to do this," she said, pulling him towards the high hedge, and wrapping her arms around his neck.

His mouth opened at the same time her lips covered his, and all thoughts evaporated as her sweet tongue swept into his mouth.

Her breasts were pressed flush against his chest. He couldn't remember moving, and yet he had one hand flattened against the small of her back, the other at the nape of her neck. He deepened the kiss, and she moaned low in her throat.

A door opened and footsteps headed their way. He took a step back, his heart a roar in his ears. Sweet Jesus, what had just happened?

"I've wanted to do that since I was eight years old," she said under her breath, making the blood in his veins boil. Every fragile detail of her perfection was outlined in the moon's golden glow, and he had the insane urge to pull her back into his arms and kiss her until she couldn't stand.

The heavy footfalls on the pathway behind him brought him out of his musings.

"Ah, here we are," Seeton said, and Addy's gaze shifted to beyond Roan's right shoulder.

"Thank you," she said, as he slid the shawl over her shoulders.

"You're welcome, my dear," Seeton said.

Roan gritted his teeth.

"Yes, that is much better," Addy said with a husky quality to her voice. "I already feel warmer."

Her eyes sparkled with mischief, reminding him of the girl she had once been and the seductive young woman she had become.

"I want to be alone with you," Stephan whispered against Addy's neck, the smell of brandy on his breath overpowering. His lips had brushed her ear and she took a quick step back. Just moments before she had thrown all caution to the wind and kissed Roan – and it had been wonderful.

She hadn't even needed to coax him. No, his tongue had danced with her own, his lips firm, yet gentle, his hands running over her body. His fingers had slid into the hair at the nape of her neck, and she had been lost.

So lost in the moment she had not even heard Stephan return. It had been Roan who had stepped away, but he had been shaken. In fact, he was still shaken. She could see his hands trembling and she hid a smile.

He wanted her . . . just as she wanted him.

Already she could see the panic in his eyes. All she could hope was that he did not run away. That would ruin everything.

And her life would never be the same.

"Adelaide, did you hear me?" Seeton asked, sounding disturbed.

"Why do you wish to be alone?" she asked, even though she knew exactly what he had in mind. All the girls at Saint Francis' School of Young Ladies talked about men's secret desires. Sister Mary Catherine said to never trust any man, for they were truly wicked creatures.

Addy didn't know about that. She trusted her brother, of course, and always felt protected when she was with him. Protected, the same way she felt with Roan. Aside from her brother, his was the opinion that meant the most.

"I wish a moment alone with you," Stephan said under his breath, and Addy's stomach tightened. Had Roan heard his request?

The way he straightened his shoulders said he just might have.

Slowing her pace, she was relieved when Roan quickly caught up to them. Stephan didn't even try to hide his agitation as Roan joined them and they made their way to the end of the path, towards the veranda that led back into the house. She covered her mouth with her hand and forced a yawn. "It is getting late, Lord Seeton. Thank you for coming over this evening. I quite enjoyed our card game."

"You are angry with me for not letting you win?" he asked, looking concerned that might very well be the case. "I would have given you the sweets, you know that, right?"

She frowned. "I am not angry. Why would you think such a thing?"

"The night is young and you wish me to leave."

"It is nearly eleven, My Lord, and I did not sleep all that well last night." This was not entirely a lie. She had tossed and turned until early morning when she fell into a fitful slumber.

"I did not realize you were keeping track of the time."

"You know that is not what I mean, Stephan."

His eyes softened at the use of his Christian name. He glanced over his shoulder at Roan, who had once again fallen behind, and she wondered if he was paying attention to the conversation.

"Let me at least bid goodnight to your brother," Stephan said. She knew he wanted her to ask him to stay.

"Certainly."

Jack looked up when they walked into the room, and she glanced over at Roan. He appeared pale, and had a difficult time making eye contact with her brother.

Did he feel guilty for kissing her? she wondered. What would Jack say if he knew the truth? He had been the only parent she'd had these past few years since Aunt Mildred passed away. He was not comfortable in the role, she could tell that much, especially since he seemed so keen to marry her off to Stephan.

Would he approve of Roan courting her, or would he be angry with them both?

She honestly didn't know the answer. She felt Roan's gaze on her and smiled, recalling the feel of his lips against hers, the stroke of his tongue as they kissed so passionately.

Heaven.

Stephan slid his hand over hers, his fingers tight. "May I call on you tomorrow?"

She forced a smile. "I must visit an old friend."

"When will you return? Perhaps I can come by."

"I do not know how long I will be. I hate to cut my visit short, considering it has been such a long time since last I saw her. Perhaps you could come by later in the week?"

"Of course. How inconsiderate of me." Stephan glanced to something past her shoulder. "Thank you for your hospitality, Jack."

Jack closed the book. "Thank you for coming. We shall see you next time."

Stephan gave a curt nod in Roan's direction. "Lord Drayton."

Roan nodded. "Lord Seeton."

She felt Stephan's hand on her back as they walked from the room and, when he closed the door and they were alone, Stephan turned to her, taking both her hands within his.

"I care for you very deeply, Adelaide," he said, his eyes intense as he stared at her. "I hope you feel as strongly about me."

She breathed through her mouth in order not to take the full brunt of his stale breath. To her shock, he leaned in and kissed her.

Unlike the kiss she'd shared with Roan, this kiss lacked fire and intensity. Worse still, Stephan pressed a little too hard, his teeth biting into her top lip.

She took a step back, but it was too late. Roan had opened the door. He looked stunned to find them there.

Three

Sweat poured down Roan's face. Jack had always been a worthwhile fencing opponent, but Roan had not remembered him being so fluid with his rapier. Or perhaps his injuries had finally caught up to him, giving his friend the upper hand.

The skin pulled tight on his burned arm with each strike of Jack's sword. Several times Jack had hesitated, and Roan had seen the indecision in his friend's eyes. He was afraid of hurting him. The knowledge was sobering, to say the least.

"What happened during that walk last night? You left so abruptly afterwards," Jack said, coming back with a half-hearted blow that made Roan want to roll his eyes. "Did Seeton say something to offend you? He is young, and quite often does not think before he speaks."

That much was obvious.

Roan was having a difficult time thinking of anything other than Addy. He ran through every memory of their younger days, of the time since he had seen her again. From the first moment he had realized little Adelaide had grown into a stunning woman, to that heart-pounding kiss in the garden. The kiss had been so intensely gratifying that he'd been unable to sleep last night. Instead, he'd spent the hours tossing and turning, the slight pressure of the blankets against his heated loins too much to bear. Finally, he had fallen into a fitful slumber that ended with a nightmare of Addy marrying Stephan.

A nightmare that would soon be a reality.

Especially if they were kissing behind closed doors. And mere minutes after she'd kissed Roan in the gardens. If only he'd stayed put and remained in the parlour with Jack, he wouldn't have seen it.

That kiss had been as effective as a punch to the gut.

Jealousy ate at his insides, which was ridiculous. Seeton was obviously the chosen one. Jack seemed content with his choice.

And why not? Lord Seeton was everything a young woman would desire in a mate.

"You don't like him, do you, Roan?"

Good God, could his friend read minds now?

Roan cleared his throat. "I think he is a typical young English lord."

"Meaning what, exactly?"

"Meaning he's confident, self-assured, if not a bit selfish."

Jack's lips quirked.

"What?"

"Do you not recall how we were, Roan? We were all those things and more at the age of two and twenty. I am nearly thirty and the thought of marriage is only now starting to look appealing." He brushed a hand through his hair. "I think the two suit, don't you?"

"If you mean Seeton and Addy, I would say no, I do not think they suit at all."

Jack lowered his sword. "Why ever not?"

"For one she is much too young to marry. She only just had her coming out. Are you really so anxious to be rid of her?"

His friend blinked as though he'd slapped him. "Of course not. Addy has spent the past few years at boarding school, so it has been refreshing to have her back home again. You know how it is with women though – if they do not marry soon after their introduction into society, then they're put on the shelf."

"She's just turned eighteen, Jack."

"She likes him."

"Perhaps . . . as a friend. Did you not notice how anxious she was to be free of him last night?"

"She was tired. It was a long day."

Roan counted to ten . . . *twice*. "I am certain you have her best interest at heart. Far be it from me to tell you who the best man for Addy would be."

"Perhaps you wish to be in the running."

He felt his cheeks turn a little warm. "She is . . . your sister."

"Yes, I know," Jack said with a wolfish grin. "I was only trying to get a rise out of you. Can you imagine you as my brother-in-law?" His eyes went wide, as though he were horrified at the thought. He lifted his rapier. "Come, enough of this marriage talk. On guard."

Frustrated, Roan parried, and lunged away from the blade. He came back with a vengeance, his frustration of the last few days making him more aggressive than he would normally have been with his friend.

He had Jack up against the wall a second later, the blade inches from his throat.

He heard a gasp from behind him.

Both he and Jack turned to find Addy standing in the doorway. She was beautiful, dressed in a cream and blue print day dress with a low neckline that nicely displayed her full round breasts. Once again his thoughts went the way of the gutter.

Slowly he lowered the blade, and took a step away from Jack, whose brows were furrowed as he looked from Roan to Addy.

Addy's gaze slid from Roan's, down his neck, over his chest, and lower to the planes of his abdomen.

If her brother weren't there, that look would get her more than she bargained for.

* * *

Addy's thighs tightened as she stared at Roan. He had a powerful body; olive skin over muscle and sinew, which shifted with each movement. The high bones of his hips cut deep, as though pointing an arrow downwards. Realizing where she was staring, her eyes darted back to his face. His hair was tied back, allowing her to see the entire length of the burn that started beneath his right eye, covered the better part of his cheek, his neck and his arm. The last two fingers on his hand looked almost melded together.

She could only imagine the pain he had endured. Did his wounds still hurt? she wondered. Or was it the internal wounds that pained him more?

"Good morning, Addy. What are you up to today?" Jack asked, taking a seat and wiping his face with his shirt, which he had flung over a chair.

"I don't know. What are the two of you doing?"

Jack frowned. "Well, I was considering going into London. Perhaps take a ride through the park."

"Can I come?"

Roan set his blade aside and quickly donned his shirt. He didn't make eye contact with her and she wondered what it was he was thinking. Had she shocked him with her kiss last night? Did he think her unseemly? Especially after catching her kissing Lord Seeton right after? Something in his expression said he was not entirely pleased with her. She desperately wanted to set things to rights.

"I don't see why not. Perhaps Seeton would like to join us?"

Roan's jaw clenched tight.

"He is busy today," she blurted, wondering why her brother was so keen to have Stephan join them. "What do you say we all meet in the parlour at eleven o'clock sharp?"

"Very well," Roan said, walking past her towards the door. How she yearned to reach out and touch him, to tell him exactly how she felt about him.

She watched Roan's retreating back from the corner of her eye, liking the way the loose shirt hung on his wide shoulders. He looked like he had just come from a tryst, she realized, and her heart quickened, imagining him leaving her chamber after a night of passionate lovemaking.

Jack cleared his throat abruptly after Roan disappeared and Addy gave him her full attention.

"What are you playing at, Addy?"

Her stomach clenched into a tight knot. "What do you mean?"

"Roan is my friend."

"He is my friend, too."

Sliding his shirt on, Jack released a deep breath. "He is too old for you."

"Father was fifteen years older than mother. There is only a ten-year age difference between me and Roan."

"Oh dear God, you *are* serious."

"Yes, I am."

"Bloody hell," he said, running a hand down his face. "I cannot believe this."

She straightened her spine and lifted her chin a good inch. "I do not understand what is so difficult to comprehend. Roan is a good man. An exceptional man. And need I remind you that he is your *best* friend?"

"In this we agree, but he is . . . Roan." He stared at her, yet she had the feeling he didn't see her. "Has he touched you?"

The clock on the mantel seemed exceedingly loud all of the sudden. "We kissed."

"Kissed?" He stood slowly and, shaking his head, walked past her. "I'll kill him."

Roan was intensely uncomfortable. Since his accident he rarely ventured out into society, and today was the first time he had walked the streets of London.

He felt the stares of the people they passed by, noticed the way many dropped their gaze when he made eye contact. He saw his own reflection in the mirror every morning, so he knew how startling his appearance was. He didn't blame others for their morbid curiosity or astonished stares, but he did resent the way people he had considered friends before the accident now wanted nothing to do with him.

And now his best friend was angry with him. He had felt it from the moment Addy walked into the parlour. The way Jack had watched them both, his eyes shifting between them.

When they had met in the parlour, Jack had said very little, and even still, in London, he remained uncommonly quiet. However, Addy was not. She had been chattering throughout the entire ride, and seemed excited to be in the city. When she hesitated by a shop window where a beautiful scarlet gown was displayed, it had been all Roan could do not to walk in and buy it for her. Jack would hardly approve though.

The very thought that his friend found him unworthy to court

Addy was gut-wrenching. He could offer just as much, if not more, than Lord Seeton. The young man had much to learn, and he was still so immature, where Roan had seen a good deal of the world, and understood the importance of surrounding oneself with people who were true friends

"Oh, I have heard of this place," Addy said, stopping in front of an art studio. "I want a shadow portrait of all of us together. It will take but a few minutes."

"I think it will take more than a few minutes, sister. Do you remember the portrait Aunt Mildred forced us to sit for just before you left for school?"

"But this is a silhouette. It takes very little time. Lady Kelly was telling me all about it at her ball. There is nowhere else we need to be, right?"

Jack glanced at Roan. He nodded, and Jack shrugged.

An older woman met them at the doorway.

"We would like a shade of the three of us," Addy said, a wide smile on her face.

"How long will it take?" Jack asked, already looking impatient.

"Actually, it takes very little time for a shadow painting, sir. The sitting takes mere minutes, and the picture itself will be ready in an hour's time."

"Very well," Jack agreed.

"Please, come in." The woman motioned for them to follow her into a small parlour. She arranged three chairs in a row, placing Jack in the first, Addy in the middle, and then Roan in the last.

Next she closed the draperies and lit several large candles, placing the waxy pillars in front of a large screen.

The lady repositioned the lighting several times, and then took a seat on the opposite side of the screen. "Now please try to be as still as possible."

Roan was left with no choice but to stare straight ahead at Addy's beautiful auburn curls, the long swan-like neck, the slender shoulders. Gold hoop earrings hung from her ears. He wanted to buy her anything she desired . . . like the dress in the shopfront window. If she belonged to him, he would never stop spoiling her.

An image of her kissing Seeton came to him again, and he wished it far away.

"You on the left, quit fidgeting," the woman said, and Addy laughed under her breath, which made Jack and Roan laugh, too.

He was glad they were there, glad that for a few minutes the tension had been lessened and that they were once again relaxed. Friends whom he trusted and loved more than life.

The entire ride home, Addy stared at the shadow portrait and smiled.

"We cut quite dashing figures, do we not, Roan?" Jack said, surprising him.

Roan looked at his friend, glad he was finally talking to him. "Lucky for them, they captured my good side," he said cheerfully, and Jack grinned.

But Addy frowned at him. "Not everyone sees your scars, Roan. When I look at you, I see . . . you. The same Roan I have always known. The Roan who will always live here," she said, placing a hand over her heart. "You are perfect just as you are. Do not let anyone ever make you feel differently."

He stared at her, shocked by her declaration and sincerity.

Jack's gaze shifted between them.

"Thank you, Addy," Roan said, and she pressed her lips together before looking down at the picture again.

Four

"A package for you, my lady. Where shall I put it?"

Addy, who had been sitting in the parlour drinking tea and watching the clock move excruciatingly slowly, looked at the large white box with its pink bow in both excitement and trepidation.

Setting her cup aside, she motioned to the spot beside her. "Right here, Nelly."

Was this a gift from Seeton? Aside from flowers on their first meeting, he had not been prone to gift-giving, but then again, he seemed to have grown more affectionate since Roan arrived.

Addy slipped the ribbon from the box, and removed the lid. Her breath caught in her throat. It was the scarlet gown she had seen in the shopfront window yesterday.

"How lovely," Nelly said, and Addy nodded in agreement, her throat tight with emotion. It could only be from one of two people.

"Here is the card," Nelly said.

With trembling hands, she opened the envelope and pulled the card out. "To Addy . . . just for being you. Your friend always, Roan."

Nelly sighed. "How very kind of Lord Drayton. What a lovely man he is."

"Indeed, he is," Addy replied, her heart nearly pounding out of her chest.

"He's always looked upon you as a little sister, hasn't he?"

"Yes, yes, he has." But she didn't want to be looked upon as his little sister any longer, but as someone who was far more important and dear to his heart.

"Have Lord Drayton and my brother returned from their ride yet?"

"No, not yet."

"Good. Come, Nelly. I need your help."

Roan and Jack arrived back at the manor and were surprised to find Seeton standing on the veranda, smoking. Seeing them, the younger man dropped the cheroot and crushed it beneath his heel.

"Have you been waiting long?" Jack asked.

"No, I only just arrived."

"Is Addy not here?"

"Actually, I've come to speak with you, My Lord."

Roan's stomach clenched.

"Do come in," Jack said, motioning for him to follow him into the house.

Roan promptly excused himself. He walked in long strides to his chamber, shut the door and closed his eyes.

Damn it!

At this moment, Stephan was asking for Addy's hand and, knowing Jack, he would heartily agree to the match.

The wheels were set in motion and there was nothing Roan could do to change their course. After all, he was but a family friend. Stephan had been courting Addy for weeks while Roan had been convalescing at his home in Essex. He had no business to be as furious as he was . . . or so intensely jealous.

The younger man did not deserve her. Stephan had no idea how to make a woman like Addy happy.

Dearest Addy, with her love of the outdoors, her free spirit and outspoken nature.

And those lips – good Lord, those lips – lifting in that coy way, promising things she had no right to.

He removed his jacket and waistcoat, and tossed both items over the back of the chair. Reaching behind his head, he lifted his shirt, but stopped short upon hearing a knock at the door.

No doubt it was Jack, come to tell him the good news. Or perhaps he'd realized that Roan was worthy of Addy. He ran his hands through his hair and, with a steadying breath, opened the door.

Addy stood before him, dressed in the gown he had bought for her. The scarlet gown fitted her like a glove, the shade doing incredible justice to the colours of her eyes and hair.

"Beautiful," he said on a whisper, his gaze wandering down the length of her and back up again.

She was absolutely breathtaking, the kind of woman any man would be proud to call his wife.

"Thank you so much, Roan. I cannot believe your kindness," she said, stepping into the room and shutting the door.

"It fits you beautifully."

"Indeed, it's perfect." Her eyes shifted from his to his chest, reminding him that his shirt was open. He lifted his right hand and touched the scar at his neck. His skin was rough, puckered, a mixture of pink and purple – a gruesome sight for one so fair.

"Do not hide from me, Roan. Never from me," she said, her hand covering his at his neck. Her fingers slid between his, and then she did the most extraordinary thing – she kissed his neck and the thick scar there.

"Addy," he said her name on a groan.

She didn't stop. She kissed his scarred cheek, his jaw, his throat, his shoulder, made a pathway of kisses all the way to the burn on his hand, and then she kissed each of his fingers. "You are the most beautiful man I have ever known, and will ever know, Roan. Don't hide from the world. Don't hide from me. You are not changed. If anything, you are a better man for the things you have suffered through, for now you have a greater understanding of what real trials are."

Her words eliminated the last of his will power.

"Addy, we shouldn't be alone."

Her lips curved. "Why is that, Roan?"

"You know why," he replied, his voice husky.

She lifted her face to his, their breath mingling.

He should put her at arm's length. He knew that. Everything within him told him to do so and, yet, he could not bring himself to deny her, not when she had bewitched him body and soul.

He reached for her with his injured hand, his thumb brushing over her soft lips. She didn't pull away, did not flinch in the least. Instead, she smiled; her eyes warm and full of desire. A desire he understood all too well.

She turned her head the slightest bit, pressed her soft lips into his scarred palm . . . and he was lost.

He pulled her into his arms, held her close, felt the tears burn the backs of his eyes as he inhaled deeply of her scent, felt her arms come around him, holding him tight, embracing him. Comforting him.

"Adelaide!" The call came from downstairs.

"It's Jack," she whispered, a mixture of frustration and irritation in her voice.

"You had better see what he wants before he comes looking for you."

"You are right," she said, kissing him softly. "Thank you again for the gown. You didn't have to."

He smiled. "Yes, I did."

Addy entered her brother's study and was stunned to see Stephan standing there. Dressed in a tailored dove-grey suit, he looked the epitome of the English lord. His golden hair was swept off his forehead, the ends curling at his collar.

How very different he was from Roan in every way. His shoulders were not wide like Roan's, nor were his features quite so fine.

"Lord Seeton, what a surprise."

"Adelaide, you look absolutely stunning," Stephan said, taking her hand in his and kissing it.

If Jack recognized the dress from the shop window, he wasn't letting on. He folded his hands behind him. "Stephan would like a word with you . . . alone."

Her stomach dropped to her toes. Oh dear, this was not good. "Oh?" she said, forcing a smile she did not feel.

"I shall give you two a moment alone together. I'll be right outside."

Her eyes widened, but Jack did not see her distress. Instead, he slipped out the door.

Stephan squared his shoulders and released a breath, treating her to a whiff of brandy. Good gracious, it was barely four in the afternoon and he smelled like he'd been drinking all day.

"Dearest, Adelaide, we have only known each other for a short time, but I feel as though it has been forever, and I feel we are well suited. Indeed, we are so very similar."

Similar. In what way? They didn't seem to like any of the same things.

"I asked your brother for his permission to marry you and he has agreed."

She pressed her lips together, and couldn't form a reply to save her life. The awkward silence continued as she struggled for something to say.

"Well, do you have an answer?"

Swallowing past the lump in her throat, she replied, "I just did not expect a proposal so soon."

His eyes widened. "Are you refusing me?"

"No, I just . . . am surprised, that is all."

"Take the evening to decide then, my dear," Seeton said, the smile returning in force. "I am sure you will have a clear head come morning."

A clear head? She could not be thinking more clearly.

The door opened abruptly and Roan stood there. He looked just as he had when she'd left him five minutes before – save that his shirt had been tucked into his breeches. But his hair was even more unruly, as though he had been running his fingers through it time and again.

"Lord Drayton?" Seeton said, his brows furrowing as he glanced from Roan to Jack, who appeared at Roan's shoulder.

"I am afraid Addy can't marry you," Roan said matter-of-factly.

Seeton frowned and puffed out his chest. "Why is that?"

"Because I love her, and I want her to marry me."

Addy's heart soared to the heavens.

"Do not be ridiculous," Stephan said, lifting his chin a good two inches.

Jack glanced at Stephan, his eyes narrowing. "Why is Lord Drayton asking for my sister's hand ridiculous?"

"He is . . . scarred. What woman would want—"

"I would," Addy said, rushing into Roan's arms. "Yes, I'll marry you."

She saw the surprise in Roan's eyes, the intense relief. A relief she felt herself.

Stephan's face turned bright red. "I cannot believe what I am hearing. Good God, Adelaide, you would have this . . . this monster for a husband over me?"

"Indeed, I would," she replied.

"The two of you deserve each other." Stephan whisked his hat off the desk and rushed out of the room.

"I'll give you two a moment alone," Jack said, clapping Roan on the back. "I can think of no one else I would rather lose her to than you."

"Thank you, Jack," Roan said, smiling as he turned to Addy. "My beautiful Little Miss Independent."

Addy grinned, and cupped Roan's face. "I love you, Roan. I always have, and I always will."

The Devil's Bargain

Deborah Raleigh

One

London – June 1814

Contrary to many of the fine homes currently being built in Mayfair, the townhouse near St James' was a plain three-storeyed structure made of red bricks, with a columned portico that was hidden from the road by a walled garden.

At a glance, it could be easily dismissed as an old-fashioned, increasingly shabby structure, but upon closer inspection there was an undoubted charm in the weathered stones and an air of solid respectability.

And once inside . . . well, those fortunate enough to receive an invitation to Countess Spaulding's home were astonished by the recent renovations that had transformed the dark, cramped rooms into airy spaces with marble columns, ivory walls and coved ceilings that were vibrantly painted with Roman gods.

On this night, the crimson drawing room was filled with elegant guests who were busily arguing the merits and faults of the Treaty of Paris. There were those who thought that the House of Bourbon should be returned to rule France, while others feared another revolution that would tear apart the Continent.

Amelia, the Countess Spaulding, allowed a faint smile to curve her lips as the arguments became heated and a young Prussian waved his hands in violent protest. As a hostess, she invited only those guests who were capable of stirring her intellectual interest: artists, philosophers, inventors and a smattering of politicians.

She had no patience for most of society and their frivolous gatherings, which were no more than an opportunity for the vain idiots to preen and primp for one another – no doubt because those idiots had made her life a misery during her years as an unwelcome wall-flower. Even now she shuddered at the memory of being tolerated solely because her father was related to the Duke of Devonshire and her mother's father had made a fortune in the West Indies.

She thrust aside the tormenting memories as she hovered near the door of the drawing room and sipped her champagne. No one could mistake her for a wallflower tonight.

Now a married woman, Amelia was no longer a victim of her mother's unfortunate lack of style. Her dark-red hair was smoothed into an elegant knot at her nape, rather than teased into frizzy curls around her face, emphasizing her bright green eyes and the tender curve of her mouth rather than her rounded cheeks and too short neck. She had also shed the white, frilly muslin gowns that had made her appear overly pale and as round as a dumpling.

Instead she was attired in a silk gown of rich green that was cut to celebrate her lush curves, and perfectly matched the magnificent emeralds that dangled from her ears.

More importantly, having endured the humiliation of being caught in Lady Granville's conservatory half-naked, in the arms of the Earl of Spaulding, not to mention their hasty marriage by special licence despite her discovery that he was nothing more than a brazen fortune-hunter, she had developed a hard-earned maturity. She was a sword forged in fire, she wryly acknowledged, and nothing was allowed to penetrate her aloof composure.

She was now a confident woman in command of her life, not the timid child she had left behind a year ago.

Draining the last of the expensive champagne, Amelia watched as a slender gentleman in a purple satin coat and white knee breeches minced across the Persian carpet to stand at her side.

Mr Sylvester Petersen could claim ten years more than Amelia's four and twenty, with handsome features and blond curls that had taken hours to tousle to his satisfaction. It was not his male charms, or his decidedly dreary poems, however, that allowed him a place among Amelia's select circle of friends. No, it was his biting wit and his ability to imitate the fashionable elite that made him an amusing companion.

"A charming evening as always, Lady Spaulding," her companion drawled, a glint of sly humour in his blue eyes. "How ever did you manage to lure Czar Alexander to your elegant gathering?"

Amelia shrugged. "I was introduced to Alexander Pavlovich when I attended his sister, the Duchess of Oldenburg, at the Pulteney

Hotel. He was kind enough to suggest that I include him during my next salon."

Sylvester waved a delicate lace fan, his lips curling into a cruel smile.

"The Prince Regent will be furious, of course," he drawled. "It is said the Russians have flatly refused to attend several of the shockingly expensive entertainments he has planned to celebrate his grand victory over the Frenchies."

"Considering that our rotund Prince's only contribution to the war was marching his regiment up and down the streets of Brighton, it is hardly surprising that the Czar is unimpressed."

Sylvester leaned forwards, a hint of a leer on his face as his gaze lowered to her full bosom.

"And, of course, Alexander Pavlovich does not desire to bed the Prince."

Amelia stiffened in distaste. Over the past month she had noticed an unwelcome familiarity from Sylvester. Indeed, there had been several gentlemen who had made unwanted advances, perhaps assuming her husband's continued absence from London meant she was in need of male companionship. She would have to put a swift end to such nonsense.

"Behave yourself, Sylvester."

"My dear, I could hardly miss Alexander Pavlovich's languishing glances and awkward attempts to lure you from the crowd," Sylvester drawled. "He desires to make you his mistress."

"I have no interest in the Czar."

"Do not be so hasty, my dear. Czar Alexander is handsome enough, and taking him as your lover would only heighten your position among London society." The lace fan fluttered. "You would be infamous."

"Sylvester," Amelia said softly.

"Yes?"

"If you ever again suggest that I barter my body to acquire the approval of society you may consider yourself an unwelcome guest in my home."

"Forgive me, my lady." The blue gaze slowly returned to her face. "You are quite correct to reprimand me. It is all too common among ladies of the ton to take lovers. Your mysterious refusal to discuss your current paramour only makes you more intriguing."

Sensing the man was in need of a more crushing set-down, Amelia was abruptly distracted by the sound of raised voices echoing from the foyer below.

"What the devil?"

"It sounds as if an uninvited intruder is attempting to force his way past your rather terrifying butler. How very ill-bred," Sylvester twittered, his brows lifting as Amelia turned to leave the drawing room. "My dear, where are you going?"

"To put an end to this foolishness."

"But, he might be dangerous. God knows the streets are no longer safe for decent folk."

"Do not be absurd." Amelia waved a hand towards the milling guests who had yet to notice the disturbance. "See to the guests. I do not wish them to be bothered."

"But of course, my dear."

Slipping into the hallway, Amelia hurried down the corridor to the marble staircase, startled to see her uniformed butler standing on the formal landing, his arms lifted as if he were holding back an intruder.

Not that she could see anything beyond his hulking form. She had specifically chosen several large male servants to ensure her safety. Her butler in particular had once been a famed boxer who was capable of felling the most determined opponent.

"Is there a problem, Boris?"

"This here gentleman claims to be your husband," the man growled, then he abruptly bent double, as if he had taken a brutal blow to the stomach.

Amelia stumbled, her back slamming into the wall of the corridor as the tall, raven-haired gentleman shoved aside her cursing butler and prowled forwards.

Her heart beat painfully against her chest as she studied the man who she had once been convinced she loved with all her soul.

He was not conventionally handsome. His features were strong rather than refined, and his skin bronzed from the hours he spent on his estate. He had a broad, intelligent forehead and a noble nose. His mouth was carved with a sensuous fullness and his eyes a stunning gold that could shimmer with humour or smoulder with passion. And, as always, his raven hair was in need of a cut, making her fingers ache to run through the satin length.

A shiver raced through her body, stealing away her arrogant belief that she was immune to the man who had crushed her youthful dreams.

"Good evening, Amelia."

Her mouth went dry as her gaze lowered to his large, muscular body attired in a fawn jacket and buff breeches, his cravat tied in a simple knot. The Earl of Spaulding had no need of lace and frip-peries to attract female attention. He possessed an innate male arrogance that was annoyingly captivating.

"Justin," she breathed.

His lips curled in a humourless smile, his hooded gaze sliding down her stiff form with an unnerving intensity.

"I suppose I should take comfort in the fact that my wife is capable of recognizing me, even if my staff does not," he drawled.

There was a movement behind him and Amelia hastily lifted her hand to halt her butler from attacking. "That will be all, Boris," she commanded.

The servant scowled, obviously smarting from being bested by a nob. "Are you certain?"

Justin paused to glance over his shoulder. "Lady Spaulding gave you an order."

"I will handle this," she snapped, bristling at his interference. She had become accustomed to being the lady of the manor, and she had no intention of handing over her authority to anyone. Especially not her treacherous husband. "Please return to your duties, Boris."

Boris shot the wryly amused nobleman a venomous glare before offering her a deep bow. "Yes, my lady."

Waiting until the servant had made his way back to the foyer, Amelia returned her attention to her unwanted companion, her stomach clenching with a bittersweet awareness as he moved to stand close enough for her to feel the heat from his large body and catch the tempting scent of sandalwood.

Her hands clenched at her side. Damn him. She hated him, so how could he still stir her most primitive desires?

"What are you doing here?" she rasped.

"The last I knew this was the Spaulding townhouse, a home that has belonged to my family for the past century, is it not?"

Her chin tilted at his mocking tone. "If you would have possessed the courtesy to inform me of your intention to travel to London I would have taken rooms in a hotel and ensured that you would have your privacy."

Without warning Justin shifted to place his hands flat on the wall on either side of her shoulders, effectively trapping her. "You mean that you would have cowardly fled as you did on our wedding day?" he demanded, his head slowly lowering. "That is precisely why I did not inform you of my impending arrival."

She flinched, the memory of that day seared into her mind.

The brief, impersonal marriage ceremony before the Bishop. The long, silent carriage ride to the small inn where they were meant to spend their wedding night before travelling on to Rosemount, Justin's estate in Hampshire. And then her impulsive flight back to London when she noticed the mail coach waiting in the stable yard.

She could still feel the sick dread in the pit of her stomach as she had arrived at this townhouse and the hours she had paced through the shabby, dark rooms, expecting Justin to arrive at any moment.

But he hadn't arrived.

Not that evening. Or the following evening. Or the one after that.

Eventually she had accepted that her husband was content to have her in London while he settled at his beloved Rosemount. And why not? He had only taken her as his wife to salvage his heavily mortgaged estates. He was no doubt deeply relieved not to be burdened with his awkward, inconvenient wife.

But no more relieved than she had been, she sternly assured herself. Why would she desire him to chase after her, pretending that she was anything more than a means to replenish his family coffers?

Burying her pain and disillusionment deep inside her, Amelia had concentrated on building a new life for herself. First, she had overseen the renovations to the townhouse, ignoring any guilt at the vast changes she was making without regards to whether or not Justin would approve. The feckless Spauldings had allowed the place to fall into ruin. It was her money that had restored it to a habitable home. Why should she not choose what pleased her?

Next, she had set about renovating herself. Without the oppressive yoke of her mother's overbearing presence, Amelia had slowly emerged from her cocoon. She bought a new wardrobe and hired a French maid who was an artist with her hair. She slowly and carefully began opening her home to a select collection of friends, deliberately ignoring those in society who had treated her with such disdain over the years.

She had been ironically aware that her hasty marriage to an earl, combined with her presence in London while her newly wed husband remained in Hampshire, had made her the source of avid interest among the ton. And the very fact that she refused to accept the piles of invitations that arrived with the post each morning only increased the fevered desire by London hostesses to secure her as a guest.

Absurd dolts.

Briefly lost in her thoughts, Amelia was jolted back to the present as she felt the brush of Justin's warm lips over her mouth.

Shocking pleasure exploded through her body, reminding her of those dazzling days before she had discovered the truth of this man. Amelia had never comprehended passion until she had first felt the brush of Justin's slender fingers and the heat of his hard body as he had swept her across the dance floor. From that moment he had only to be near for her body to shiver with aching need.

She had blamed that shivering awareness for why she had been so easily deceived. If she hadn't been so blinded by his sweet seduction, she might have been wise enough to realize his seeming affection was no more than a cruel ploy.

Ridiculously, she had assumed discovering the truth of her husband's treachery would destroy her vulnerability to his raw masculinity. Now she realized she had been a naïve fool.

She hastily turned her head to the side, shuddering as his lips skimmed over her cheek and down the curve of her throat.

"Halt that," she husked, infuriated by the pleasure searing through her.

"Halt what?" He pulled back to study her flushed features. "Greeting you as any husband would after being parted from his wife for the past year?"

"We may possess a marriage licence, but that does not make me your wife," she snapped.

"No, I have yet to claim you as my true bride, but that is about to change." The golden eyes smouldered with a wicked amusement. "Tonight."

Her heart came to a precise halt. "Justin—"

"Do you know what today is?" he asked, overriding her protest.

"No."

"Yes you do, my love." His hand shifted to cup her cheek, his thumb tracing her lower lip. "It is the anniversary of our wedding."

She had known, of course. The thought had plagued her the entire day. Not that she was about to admit as much to her aggravating husband.

Thankfully the sound of approaching footsteps had Justin stepping away from her, his handsome face tightening with anger as Sylvester appeared on the landing.

"Is everything well, my dear?" Sylvester asked, his avid gaze taking careful note of Amelia's obvious discomfort.

"Leave us," Justin barked.

"Really, sir. There is no need to behave as a savage—"

Sylvester's words were cut short as Justin moved with astonishing speed to grasp the smaller man's elaborate cravat. "I said, leave us."

Sylvester paled at the threat, intelligent enough to realize that Justin could crush him without effort. "Yes. Of course." He held up his hands and backed away. "So sorry to have intruded."

Once again alone with her husband, Amelia slammed her hands on to her hips and glared at him with a rising fury. "Have you taken leave of your senses?" she hissed. "You cannot force your way into my home and embarrass me before my friends."

A feral smile curved his lips as he abruptly turned and, without warning, swept her off her feet. "Never underestimate what I can or cannot do, my love," he growled, heading for the stairs.

"No." She slammed her fist against his chest. "Put me down at once. Damn you, Justin."

Climbing the marble steps to the upper floor, Justin glanced down at her with a lift of his dark brows. "Such language from the lips of a lady."

Amelia trembled, telling herself it was pure outrage that made her pulse race and her breath so oddly elusive. "But I am not a lady, at least not as far as you are concerned, am I?" she gritted.

"I presume that has some deep, philosophical meaning?"

"So far as you are concerned I am no more than a means to an end. You were in desperate need of wealth and I was a convenient means of acquiring a ready fortune."

"Convenient?" His humourless laugh echoed through the silence as he made his way unerringly down the hall to the master bedchamber. "Not even you can be that naïve, Amelia. You have haunted and tortured me for the past year."

"Liar." She blinked back her ridiculous tears. She had sworn a year ago that this man would never hurt her again. "You have ignored me since you were given the rights to my dowry. I do not doubt you forgot you even possessed a wife."

A dangerous emotion darkened the golden eyes. "I was not the one to turn my back on our marriage."

Amelia nervously licked her dry lips, barely aware of Justin reaching down to shove open the door to her private rooms.

"You made no effort to halt me from leaving," she accused.

His mouth tightened, as if she had struck a nerve. "I was stupid enough to hope that with time and distance your wounds would heal and we could begin again."

"You thought I would forget you seduced and tricked me into marriage?"

"Do not pretend you were without your own selfish motives."

She sucked in a sharp breath. "What is that supposed to mean?"

"I was not alone in desiring what our marriage offered," he drawled. "You were frantic to be independent of your mother."

Heat flooded her cheeks. She should have known he would have been perceptive enough to realize it would take more than the humiliation of being caught in a compromising position to force her into marriage once she discovered he was no more than a fortune-hunter.

In truth, she had been determined to call an end to the hasty wedding once her supposed friends had arrived at her home to reveal that the gossips were busy whispering that Lord Spaulding had been quite cunning in acquiring the funds he so desperately needed. She would rather have withdrawn from society in shame than wed a man she hated.

But, at the last moment, the thought of being forever trapped with her mother had halted her impetuous need to be rid of Justin. Mrs Uhlmeyer was not an evil woman. But as the daughter of a wealthy merchant who had managed to capture a husband who could move along the fringes of the ton, she had been obsessively consumed with her desire to see Amelia married to an aristocrat. She would have made her daughter's life a misery if she were to decline a proposal from the Earl of Spaulding.

"Fine," she gritted. "We both have what we needed from our unholy union. So why are you here?"

"Because I do not yet have everything I want from this marriage."

She frowned, a strange chill inching down her spine. "You have my money, I have nothing else to offer."

"You could not be more mistaken."

His smug expression made her wish she had the small pistol she carried in her reticule. Her frustration would be considerably eased by lodging a bullet in his arse.

"What do you want from me?"

"It is quite simple, Amelia," he murmured. "I want a son."

Two

Taking advantage of Amelia's momentary shock, Justin carried her over the threshold and headed directly towards the canopied bed in the centre of the vast room.

Laying her on the mattress, he briefly savoured the sight of his wife's lustrous skin, which possessed the sheen of the finest pearl in the candlelight. Bloody hell, she was a tempting minx with her fiery curls tumbled about her delicate face and her green eyes filled with fury. Even when his wife had been a shy wallflower attired in the hideous gowns her mother had insisted upon, Justin had been acutely aware of her hidden beauty. It had caused more than one sleepless night. Now . . .

Now her beauty had ripened, becoming even more breathtaking with the air of confidence she had acquired since he last caught sight of her.

He swallowed a groan as desire slammed into him with the force of a kicking mule.

Damn it. When he had made the decision to travel to London it had been with the full intention of taking his place as Amelia's husband. In her life. And in her bed.

But he had not intended to fall on her like a ravaging beast the moment he entered the house.

Sucking in a deep, steadying breath, he forced himself to turn his attention to the connecting rooms that had once belonged to his parents. He was prepared for the lavender satin wall panels and delicate rosewood furnishings that had replaced the dark, decidedly ugly furniture preferred by his ancestors. He had, after all, been aware of every alteration made to the townhouse. A rueful smile found his lips. He might have been willing to give Amelia the time and distance needed to heal her wounds, but he hadn't been prepared to leave her unprotected. Which was precisely why he had ensured that several members of her staff happened to be his own loyal servants.

"Lovely," he murmured in genuine appreciation. "I knew that I could leave the renovations of this house in your capable hands. You have always possessed exquisite taste when not being ridden roughshod by your mother. I am anxious for you to turn your talents to Rosemount." He turned back to watch Amelia scramble to sit upright, her eyes dark with an awareness she was clearly determined to deny. "Unlike my relatives I find little to be admired in shabby medieval furnishings and dour portraits of long-dead Spauldings. I wish you to make the manor house a home." He paused, giving her a smile of anticipation. "*Our* home."

"I did not refurbish the townhouse to please you."

"And yet I am pleased." His smile widened as his gaze lowered to the enticing curve of her breasts. "Very pleased."

Her chin tilted, but Justin did not miss her tiny shiver. "I want you to leave."

He reached to thread his fingers through her satin curls, which shimmered like flames against the pure ivory of her skin, his arousal pressing painfully against his breeches.

"Not until I have what I have come for," he said, huskily.

"Are you batty?"

His lips twisted. "There are many gentlemen who would consider me mad to have waited so long to take what is rightfully mine."

"Rightfully yours? I am not your property."

"No, you are my wife." Barely aware he was moving, Justin settled next to her on the mattress, his fingers fisting in her hair as he was besieged by a surge of sheer male possession. He had waited for months to claim this woman as his own. He would wait no longer. "And soon to be the mother of my children."

He heard her breath catch. "So, that's the devil's bargain, is it? Never."

"Come, Amelia. You knew that we could not continue to live estranged."

"Why not? There are any number of couples who choose to live separate lives."

Justin bit back his instinctive words. He had known when he travelled to London that Amelia still harboured her bitter resentment. And that she was not yet prepared to accept what he had to say. He would have to tread with care.

"Only after they have produced the necessary heirs," he said. "Surely you do not believe I would have gone to such effort to salvage my estates without the hope that we will one day pass them to our children?"

"And because it is what *you* want my own desires are meaningless?"

"On the contrary. Your . . ." He bent forwards to graze a soft kiss over her mouth. "Desires are of utmost importance. That much I can assure you."

For a dazzling moment her lips softened in ready pleasure and Justin swallowed a low groan. Christ. If she only knew how many nights he had lain awake, plagued by his craving to have her in his arms, or lying beneath him as he sheathed himself deep in her body. He vividly recalled the honeyed sweetness of her lips and her gratifying moans of encouragement as he had discovered how best to please her. Then his memories were shattered as her hands lifted to his chest, pushing him away with a small cry.

"How dare you?"

Justin struggled to leash his desire, pulling back to regard her with a brooding frown.

"I have not forgotten how readily you responded to my kisses, to my touch," he said, his voice thick. "You desired me. You still desire me."

"No."

"Yes." His fingers tightened in her hair, his body clenched with frustrated hunger. "My God, I have missed you, Amelia. Do you know on how many occasions I started towards London only to return to Rosemount? Or how often I stood at the window and imagined you rushing up the drive and into my arms?"

An indefinable emotion flared through her green eyes. "No doubt there were plenty of women to comfort you?"

"Jealous, my love?"

"Certainly not," she muttered. "You are welcome to take as many lovers as you wish."

His eyes narrowed in warning. "I fear I cannot return the generous offer. If I were to discover another man in your bed I would kill him."

"You have no right."

"You are my wife." He made no effort to hide the stark possession in his tone. "I have no intention of sharing what belongs to me."

She gave a wild shake of her head. "I must have been out of my wits to ever have believed that I—"

They both stiffened as she abruptly cut off her words, their gazes clashing with the violent emotions that had never been resolved between them.

"What?" he demanded softly. "That you loved me?"

With a muttered curse, she yanked away from his grasp and slid off the bed. She wrapped her arms around her waist and nervously paced the floor. "Do not say that."

"There is no shame in offering me your heart," he said, resisting the urge to hoist her back on to the bed. "I have sworn to protect it with my life."

She glared at him with smouldering resentment. "You have brought me nothing but shame from the moment you decided I was a gullible enough fool to believe a man such as you could ever truly care for me."

"A man such as me?"

She waved an impatient hand. "Handsome. Elegant. Toasted by all of society. While I was a pathetic wallflower with nothing to recommend me but my grandfather's wealth."

His brows snapped together, his temper flaring. Amelia could brand him as any sort of scoundrel, but he would not listen to her demean herself.

"That is not true. I was fascinated by you from the moment we were introduced," he gritted. "I had never met a female who I could truly converse with on important subjects rather than having to spend the evening exchanging shallow flirtations."

"And if I had not possessed a large dowry?"

He flinched at the blunt question. "What would you have me say, Amelia?"

"What you should have said from the first." She moved with jerky steps to the window that overlooked the small rose garden below, her profile tense with the anguish that Justin knew could be laid at his feet. "That you never gave a damn about me and without my dowry you would never have taken me as your wife."

He clenched his hands, hating the knowledge he might very well have destroyed any hope of happiness with his wife.

But what else could he have done?

After several generations of reckless, devil-may-care Spauldings, the once impressive family fortune had been drained dry and the estates had slipped into ruin. By the time Justin had shouldered his inheritance, the lands had been deeply in debt and his tenants mired in shocking poverty. He could not allow them to continue to suffer.

Or at least that was what he had told himself.

It was not until he had been forced to watch the joy fade from Amelia's eyes to be replaced with a bitter resignation that he realized that some sacrifices were too great. And that he should have carved out his own heart before wounding this beautiful, excessively fragile woman.

"I have always cared for you," he said.

She absently straightened a Sèvres plate on the carved mantel, the tremble of her hand revealing she was not nearly so composed as she would have him believe.

"No, if you had then you would have been honest with me about your need for an heiress."

"Even a gentleman in my position has his pride." His smile was self-derisive. "I intended to reveal the ruin of my family fortunes in time."

"But only after you compromised me and ensured I would have no choice but to wed you or be publicly shunned."

Justin rose to his feet, his expression hardening. He had been blindly stupid for too long. Perhaps not astonishing. Mere hours after his hasty wedding, his wife had abandoned him in a painfully public fashion, and his steward had sent him a frantic note revealing that the roof of the long gallery at Rosemount had collapsed, injuring several servants and threatening to destroy what remained of his ancient home.

He had done his best to concentrate on what he could mend rather than brooding on those troubles that seemed beyond his skill.

Over the past weeks, however, he had devoted a significant amount of time to recalling the exact details of that fateful night and coming to a startling conclusion.

"I did not force you to accompany me to Lady Granville's conservatory that evening," he pointed out in soft tones. "Nor did I force you to respond to my kisses."

Her cheeks flared with colour. "So it was my own fault that I was deceived and manipulated?"

Crossing the Persian carpet, Justin grasped her hands. "We are neither to blame for what occurred in that conservatory."

"You expect me to believe that it was random fate that offered you the perfect opportunity to coerce me into marriage?"

"Not fate." He squarely met her accusing gaze. "Your mother."

Three

"You . . ." Jerking her hands out of Justin's grip, Amelia glared into his handsome face. "Bastard."

His lips twisted. "You can hurl any number of insults at me, but I most certainly am not a bastard."

With a toss of her head, she headed towards the door, more out of fear of being alone with Justin than his wild accusations. She could not think clearly when he was near. Not when her heart was pounding and her stomach fluttering with an unwelcome awareness.

How could she still ache for the damnable man when he had so ruthlessly destroyed her?

"I will not stay here and listen to you insult my mother."

She had nearly reached the door when Justin's fingers closed around her upper arm and he turned her about to meet his burning gaze.

"We can have this conversation in the midst of your friends, if that is what you prefer," he drawled, "but make no mistake we will be finishing this discussion."

"I am no longer the innocent fool you wed, My Lord," she said coldly. "You cannot lay your sins at the feet of another and assume I will blithely forgive you."

"I accept my numerous sins, but I will not be accused of seducing you in that conservatory and ensuring we would be discovered."

Amelia bit her bottom lip, the agonizing memory of that night seared into her mind.

The dazzling pleasure of strolling about the crowded ballroom on Justin's arm, knowing she was the envy of every female in London. Preening beneath his bold glances of frustrated desire, and shivering when he had bent his head to whisper in her ear. And then he had urged her from the ballroom, leading her through the maze of hallways until at last they were alone in the perfumed shadows of the conservatory.

She shivered, still able to feel the branding heat of his kisses and the intimate exploration of his hands. She had been so eager for him that she had not even considered the dangers of allowing him to peel away her God-awful dress. Her only thought was the shocking pleasure of his lips closing around the tip of her breast as he had suckled her with obvious skill.

It was not until the door to the conservatory had been thrust open and the sound of shocked voices had shattered the illusion of privacy that she had realized just how stupid she had been.

"Are you telling me that my mother urged you to lure me from the ballroom and remove my gown?" she gritted.

"No." His hooded gaze swept over her pale face. "But, I have never disguised the fact that I desired you from the moment I first held you in my arms and we waltzed across the floor of Almack's. By the evening of Lady Granville's ball I was nearly mad with my need to assuage my hunger for you." As if to prove his point, Justin wrapped his arms around her and hauled her roughly against his aroused body. "And in all honesty, if we had not been interrupted, I am not entirely certain I could have halted my urge to take your innocence regardless of the discomforts of our surroundings, or the obvious danger of discovery."

Her mouth went dry at the potent feel of his erection pressed against her hip, his warm scent teasing at her senses. A melting heat flowed like lava through her veins, pooling in her lower stomach.

"Then how can you possibly blame my mother?" she rasped.

As if sensing her grudging reaction to his touch, Justin skimmed his hands down her back, his eyes darkening to molten gold. "If nothing else, your mother has always been a clever woman capable of taking advantage of any situation."

She could not argue the truth of his words. Her mother possessed a calculating mind and a ruthless lack of sentimentality when it came to using her daughter to achieve her own social ambitions.

"My mother wanted me wed, not get involved in a scandal that might very well have ruined me," she protested.

"Correction, my love, she wanted you to capture a title. The greater the title the better."

"Why you . . ."

He easily caught the hand she lifted to slap his face, pulling it to his mouth so he could press his lips to her palm.

"Steady, Amelia," he murmured.

"Are you implying that my mother assumed that the only means for me to acquire a husband was by trapping him with public humiliation?" she hissed.

"Calm down and listen to me."

"Have you not insulted me enough for one evening?"

"I am well aware you had received any number of proposals before we were introduced."

She curled her lip in disdain. "Worthless fortune-hunters."

He ignored her insult. "And that you refused them all."

"I had a ridiculous hope that I might actually discover a gentleman who could care for more than my dowry. Stupid, of course."

He grimaced, as if her jab had struck a nerve, but his expression remained grimly determined. "It is my belief that your mother learned that my estates were heavily mortgaged and suspected that once you learned the truth of my need for . . ."

"My money?" she sweetly supplied, startled by a small pang of regret as his cheekbones darkened with a humiliated flush.

"For a loan," he corrected in a raw tone. "Your mother no doubt feared that you would turn away my impending offer of marriage as well."

"As I most certainly would have."

"Consider, Amelia." He peered deep into her eyes, as if willing her to believe his words. "Your mother was quite anxious for you to acquire a title and it was unlikely that there would be a nobleman greater than an earl to court you. Would she have meekly allowed such an opportunity to slip away without making an effort to push you into marriage?"

Amelia frowned, suddenly recalling that it had been her mother who had first entered the conservatory and promptly screamed to ensure that everyone at the ball was aware of Amelia's humiliation. She also recalled that her mother had not been nearly so shocked as she should have been when Amelia revealed Justin was a common fortune-hunter. Indeed, her mother had pressed even harder for a swift wedding.

At the time, Amelia had assumed that her mother was motivated by her horror at having an unwed daughter who was tarnished goods. Now, she realized that it might very well have been an obsessive desire to have her daughter wed to an earl.

"This is all conjecture," she muttered. "You have no proof."

"No, I have no proof," he readily agreed, "but I have spent many long nights recalling our brief courtship and the events leading up to our fateful tryst in the conservatory."

"Even if what you claim is true, it changes nothing."

"You are mistaken, Amelia, it changes everything." With a smooth movement, he swept her in his arms and headed back to the bed. "You can no longer accuse me of deliberately causing our scandal. It was never my intent to force you into marriage."

Amelia felt a dangerous crack in the ice she had built around her heart. What if he spoke the truth? What if he had never led her into the conservatory to compromise her? What if he had been as overwhelmed as she by the heady passion that even now swirled through her body? What if . . .

She shook her head. Damn him.

"Did you ever intend to tell me the truth?" she demanded as he lowered her on to the mattress and stretched out beside her, his fingers tangling in her hair.

"What truth?" he asked, a savage hunger tightening his features. "That you fascinated me from the moment we met? That I treasure our time spent together? That I desired you beyond all reason and that the thought of you carrying my child filled me with a need I could barely control?"

His child? Amelia quivered at the compelling thought of Justin's baby growing inside her.

"The truth that you wed me for my dowry," she forced herself to say, as much to remind herself of this man's treachery as to continue the argument.

His head lowered, his eyes blazing with sensual intent. "I wed you for many reasons, some of which I am still attempting to comprehend."

"Justin . . ."

Her protest was ignored as he crushed her lips in a kiss that demanded her response.

For a heartbeat Amelia stood poised on a precipice. She understood the significance of this moment. She could turn Justin away and continue with their cold, distant relationship. Or she could give in to her desires and risk opening herself to yet another betrayal.

Perhaps sensing her fear, Justin lifted his head to reveal an expression of undisguised vulnerability. "Amelia, please," he pleaded, his hand trembling as he brushed his fingers over her cheek. "I have hungered for you for so long."

His hunger could not be any greater than hers, Amelia acknowledged. But trust was a fragile thing.

"Have you . . ." She bit her lip in embarrassment.

"What? Ask me, my love," he urged. "I swear I will tell you nothing but the truth."

"Have there been other women?" she demanded bluntly.

"No, Amelia." A dark, possessive expression settled on his beautiful face. "You are my wife. I want no other."

The remaining ice that encased her heart shattered at the soft words and, with a small moan, she lifted her arms to wrap them around his neck. She did not know what tomorrow might bring, but for this night she could not deny the desire that had plagued her for so long.

"Yes," she sighed.

As if the soft word was what he had been waiting for, Justin wrapped his arms about her and buried his head in the curve of her neck.

"Amelia, if you do not want me to make love to you then you must tell me now," he muttered. "Very soon I will be unable to halt."

Her arms tightened about his neck. "I want you, Justin."

The words had barely tumbled from her lips before he was pressing restless kisses over her face, his fingers tugging at the buttons that lined the back of her dress.

"Thank God," he rasped, then with a muttered curse he roughly tore the fabric.

"Justin?"

"You have no notion of how desperately I desire you," he growled, pulling off the ripped gown and managing to tug down her corset and thin shift with exhilarating haste. Pulling back, he swept a smouldering gaze over her body that was now naked except for her silk stockings and slippers. "God, you are so beautiful."

Amelia blushed, but oddly she felt beautiful beneath the burning intensity of his gaze. Justin had always been capable of making her far more assured in his company than she had ever been before. It was the reason she had been so drawn to him from the moment they had met.

Well . . . one of the reasons, she ruefully acknowledged, staring at the dark, beautiful face that had made her heart halt the moment she caught sight of him.

Shuddering with an excitement she could no longer deny, she moaned as his hands impatiently traced her curves, his mouth trailing a path of fiery kisses down the line of her throat. She forgot about the guests who no doubt were questioning her strange disappearance and her servants who must be shocked by the sudden appearance of Lord Spaulding.

In this moment nothing mattered but the feel of Justin as he gently cupped her breast and nuzzled her tightly furled nipple with shocking intimacy.

"Dear Lord," she muttered, stirring restlessly beneath his caresses. She needed something. Something only Justin could offer.

As if sensing her impatience, he abruptly pushed himself upright, jerking off his attire with unsteady hands. Amelia watched in awed silence as he revealed his hard, muscular body. She had never seen a naked man before and she was astonished to discover the pleasure she found in the width of his chest lightly sprinkled with raven hair, the slender line of his waist and the powerful thrust of his legs.

Then her breath tangled in her throat as she caught sight of the proud thrust of his arousal. She had assumed she would be frightened in this moment, but oddly she felt nothing but anticipation as he slowly moved to cover her with his warm body, her hands tentatively stroking down the curve of his back.

"I am not certain what to do," she murmured.

"Just touch me, my love." His breath brushed her cheek as he nuzzled a path of kisses to the hollow beneath her ear. "God almighty, the feel of your hands . . ."

Emboldened by his fierce reaction, Amelia skimmed her hands lower, groaning at the sensation of his rippling muscles that clenched beneath her fingers. He muttered a curse as she cupped his hips.

"It has been too long," he rasped, abruptly grasping her hands and pinning them above her head.

Her lips parted to protest at having her tentative exploration brought to an end, but, before she could speak, Justin was covering her mouth in a kiss of searing need. Amelia squeezed her eyes shut, realizing the restraint she had always felt in his touch was gone.

There was no uncertainty as he caressed her body with experienced ease, or as his lips brushed down her collarbone and latched on to the aching tip of her breast. Or as his leg thrust between her thighs to rub at her sensitive cleft.

Amelia gasped as she struggled to breathe, assaulted by a flood of astonishing sensations.

"What are you doing to me?" she breathed.

A low chuckle was wrenched from his throat, his lips nuzzling the curve of her breast.

"What I have been longing to do from the moment we first met."

"Surely not the *first* moment," she said, only partially teasing.

He pulled back to regard her with a burning gaze. "Regardless of what you may believe, Amelia, I have never lied about my feelings for you. Never."

Her heart faltered at the harsh sincerity in his voice. "Make love to me, Justin," she whispered, her fingers softly stroking the bronzed beauty of his countenance. "Make me your wife."

He remained silent a long moment, his gaze searching her face for any hint of uncertainty before a slow smile curved his lips. "As you wish, Lady Spaulding." He outlined her lips with the tip of his tongue. "My only desire is to please you."

Without giving her time for second thoughts, Justin kissed her with an aching sweetness. She arched beneath him, pulling her hands free of his grip to shove her fingers in the satin strands of his raven hair. He moaned, moving his lips over her cheek, nipping gently at the line of her jaw and then down the curve of her neck. He lingered at the base of her throat to kiss the frantic pulse that beat there, his tongue teasing the spot before he was trailing ever lower.

Amelia forgot how to breathe. During the past year she had convinced herself that her memories of Justin's kisses must be a part of her fevered imagination. After all, she had encountered any number of handsome gentlemen over the past year and none of them had stirred so much as a flutter.

Now she realized that his touch was even more exciting, even more achingly sensuous than she remembered. Dear heavens, she wanted to drown in the pleasure of his touch.

Scattering kisses over the curve of her breasts he gave each aching nipple a lick of his tongue before nibbling a path down to her stomach. Amelia arched her back, shocked by the urgent need that pulsed deep inside her.

"You taste of honey," Justin murmured as he licked her belly button and then down the tense muscles of her thigh. "So sweet."

"Good God." Her hands clutched at his hair. "Justin . . ."

"Yes, my love?" he demanded, tugging her legs wider so he could slip between them.

"What are you doing?"

His chuckle brushed her skin as he lazily explored the length of her leg and the arch of her foot. "I have waited a year to claim my bride. I intend to savour you from head to toe."

She choked back a moan as he tormented her toes before slowly making his way back up her leg. How could she survive such a delectable assault?

She was suddenly aware of a damp heat between her legs that seemed directly connected to Justin's exquisite caresses and she squirmed in pleasure as he trailed his lips up the inside of her thigh.

Not even her dreams had prepared her for such astonishing sensations.

"Justin, please," she pleaded, raising herself on to her elbows as he tugged her legs even further apart.

"Oh, I intend to please you," he said, holding her gaze as he slid one slender finger through her damp heat. "I intend to hear you scream in pleasure."

"What are you . . ." she began, only to have her words stolen as he shifted upwards and she felt his tongue part her tender flesh. "Oh Lord."

Her elbows collapsed and she tumbled back on to the bed, her eyes squeezing shut at the intense pleasure.

His tongue was relentless as it teased and stroked her need to the very edge of bliss. There was something . . .

Something that beckoned just out of reach.

"Please . . . please . . ."

"Yes, my love." With a lingering kiss upon her thigh, he slowly moved over her, his eyes smouldering with a hunger that echoed within her. "Forgive me."

She frowned. "For what?"

In response, he settled more firmly between her spread legs and tilted his hips forwards. Amelia gasped as she felt him sliding into her body, stretching her with his steady thrust.

"Oh," she breathed, her hands grasping the cover beneath her.

"You must relax, Amelia." Justin kissed the tip of her nose. "Trust me."

For a tense moment, their gazes clashed, Amelia's heart missing a painful beat. Trust. Such a simple word. And yet such a very complicated emotion.

Then, lifting her hands, she framed his face and pulled him down to meet her soft kiss.

She was not yet prepared to make promises, but her heart was no longer filled with bitterness.

"Make me your wife," she whispered against his lips.

"My wife," he repeated, the words filled with a husky reverence that brought tears to her eyes. "My beautiful wife."

He kissed her with a stark passion, his hands moving to cup her breasts, his thumbs teasing her sensitive nipples.

Slowly, Amelia began to relax, a soft moan tumbling from her lips. Justin's thrusts fanned the flames of her desire from the embers.

Barely aware of it, she discovered her hips lifting in harmony with his rhythm as the pleasure coiled in the pit of her stomach.

Murmuring encouragement, she ran her hands restlessly up and down the curve of his back. Yes. Oh, yes. Her legs instinctively wrapped around his hips as he plunged deeper and deeper. This was what her body had ached for since that night in the conservatory.

"Christ . . . Amelia . . . I cannot . . ."

She dug her fingers into his hips, urging him to a quicker pace. "Please do not halt," she pleaded.

His hands slipped beneath her hips, angling upwards, as he pushed ever deeper within. Amelia arched her back as her muscles clenched with a breathless anticipation. Then, her keening cry echoed through the room as she shattered in shocking delight.

"Justin," she whispered, holding him tight as he shouted her name and poured into her welcoming body.

Four

Struggling to catch his breath, Justin rolled to the side, pulling his wife into his arms and pressing his lips to the top of her tousled hair.

His wife.

A surge of male satisfaction settled in his heart as he recalled the manner with which she had responded to his touch, and her startled cry as she had reached fulfilment.

Now she was well and truly his wife.

As she was meant to be.

Not that he was foolish enough to believe their troubles were at an end. After all, he had never questioned Amelia's desire for him. She had been far too innocent to hide her ready awareness when he was near. And while making love to her had been an earth-shattering experience, it did not mean that she was prepared to accept him into her life.

As if to prove his point, Amelia abruptly stirred in his arms, pressing her hands against his chest as she attempted to wriggle from his grasp.

"Dear God . . ." she muttered.

His arms tightened around her, a scowl marring his brow as he met her panicked gaze. Bloody hell, did she regret having given her innocence to him?

No. What they had just shared was . . . extraordinary. Magical. He would not allow her to dismiss their lovemaking.

Or him.

"Where do you think you are going?" he demanded.

"I have guests awaiting me."

"They can keep themselves entertained. We have not finished our conversation."

She turned her head away, her tone petulant. "I thought you came to London to get me with child, not to converse."

"Amelia, you know why I am here." He cupped her face in his hand and gently forced her to meet his searching gaze. "I want us to live as man and wife. Together for now and all eternity."

"Eternity?" She licked her lips, her expression heartbreakingly fragile. "So very long?"

"Do you want me to beg, my love?" he asked softly.

Her beautiful eyes softened in a desolate yearning that pierced Justin with an unbearable pain. Then, with another burst of panic, she battled her way out of his arms and off the bed.

"Please, can we discuss this tomorrow?" she asked in a ragged voice, her hands trembling as she tugged on the linen shift he had so recently removed from her exquisite body. "I must return downstairs and . . ."

"No, Amelia." Indifferent to his lack of clothing, Justin surged off the mattress and grasped her shoulders in a tight grip. "I allowed you to flee from me once before. I cannot bear to watch you walk away again."

"Justin . . ."

"I know that I hurt you and perhaps I do not deserve your forgiveness," he said, interrupting her protest, his heart clenching at the beauty of her fiery curls tumbled about her pale face and her eyes shimmering like the finest emeralds. Christ, he had missed her. "But if you will give me the opportunity, I swear I will prove to you that I am worthy of your heart."

She suddenly stilled, regarding him with an undisguised wariness. "Why?"

"What do you mean, why?"

"You have my dowry and we are both aware you have only to kiss me to have a place in my bed." Her tone was flat, the very lack of emotion revealing just how important his answer was to her. "Why must you have my heart as well?"

His lips twisted. "I should think that obvious."

"Humour me."

Justin steeled his courage. This was the moment.

It had taken him months to accept the truth. Oh, he had known from the moment that he had been introduced to Amelia that she was special. She did not brazenly toss herself at his feet nor had she bored him with mindless chatter and shrill giggles. In fact, he had been enchanted by her clever comprehension of the bills being debated before the House of Lords and the inherent dangers of Spain's political instability.

And, of course, he had not been fooled for a moment by her hideous gowns and frizzed hair. His discerning eye had easily recognized the lush beauty that set his body on fire.

Still, it was not until he was alone at Rosemount that he accepted that his feelings for Amelia ran far deeper than he had ever realized.

After all, he had what he wanted. With Amelia's vast dowry his estates were swiftly being restored and even Rosemount had been rescued from ruin, although he had done no more than ensure the foundation was sound and a new roof and windows were installed. He was being toasted as a saviour by his tenants and, while he expected to feel guilt and perhaps even a measure of remorse, he was not prepared for the raw, aching need to have his wife at his side.

His estates were suddenly a burden that had cost him the only thing that truly mattered in his life.

Amelia.

"It is only fair that I have your heart when you have stolen mine," he whispered.

The emerald eyes flared with an unexpected fury at his soft words. "No."

Justin frowned. This was not precisely what he had expected when he had dreamed of telling his wife that he loved her. "Amelia?"

"If you wish to discuss our future together I am willing to listen without false promises," she muttered, her voice thick with suppressed tears. "As you said, it is only to be expected you would wish an heir."

"I do not give a damn about an heir," he growled.

"But you said . . ."

"I knew that you would have me thrown out if I told you I was here because I loved you and I could not bear to spend another day without you," he admitted without apology. He had many things to regret, but not his determination to earn his wife's heart. "I had to have some excuse to be in London."

She trembled, regarding him with wounded eyes. "You love me."

"I believe that is what I just said," he attempted to tease.

"No." She shook her head. "It is impossible."

"Surely I am allowed to know my own feelings?"

"If you loved me . . ."

"Sssh." He bent his head to press a soft, aching kiss to her lips before pulling back with an expression of apology. "I am painfully aware I should have told you the truth of my financial troubles the moment we were introduced, Amelia, and if I could return in time I would do whatever necessary to avoid hurting you."

"Allow me to finish, Justin," she commanded.

His lips twitched with rueful amusement. The awkward wallflower was well and truly gone. And in her place was a woman who was in her full glory. His heart swelled with pride.

"If you loved me you would never have left me alone for the past year."

His brows lifted at her rather unfair accusation. "There are those who would argue that you were the one to leave me, my sweet."

She turned her head to reveal the tense line of her profile. "Because I was hurt. And . . ."

"And?"

"Scared."

Justin flinched, feeling as if she had just shoved a dagger in his gut. In truth, he wished she had. That would certainly have been less painful.

"Scared of me?"

"Of having my heart broken again."

"Never." He buried his face in her satin curls, breathing deep of her sweet scent. "I swear, Amelia."

A silence filled the room, and Justin battled back his agonizing need to plead for her to accept him as her husband. On this occasion she would not be pressured or coerced or seduced into her decision. Instead he simply held her, savouring just how perfect she felt pressed against him.

"Why did you stay away?" she at last demanded.

"As I said, I hoped that time would heal your wounds, but primarily because I feared that I had truly destroyed any feelings you might have possessed for me," he admitted with stark honesty. "How could I force myself into your company if you hated me?"

She pulled back to meet his burning gaze. "So why did you come here tonight?"

He hesitated, knowing that he had to speak the truth, yet wise enough to realize Amelia was bound to be angered by his confession.

"In part because you remained a virgin."

Her eyes widened with a horrified shock. "How did you . . ." She bit off her words as a blush rose to her cheeks. "Of course. My servants were spying upon me."

Justin grimaced. "Do not blame them."

"Oh, I don't," she said, her tone revealing precisely whom she did hold to blame. "Why were you so interested in my virginity, or need I bother asking?"

He gently framed her face in his hands, his thumb brushing the edge of her full lips. Against his will, his body began to stir with an urgent passion that was by no means sated. Hell, he doubted there would ever come a day when he was not consumed with desire for his wife.

He brushed his lips over her furrowed brow. "I knew that if you no longer cared for me you would have found someone else to love."

She trembled, her eyes darkening with an unconscious invitation. "You said that was part of the reason," she reminded him, her voice thickening.

His lips skimmed down the length of her nose, then nuzzled the edge of her mouth. "Yes."

She trembled, her body instinctively arching to press against him. "And the other part?"

He lifted his head to regard her with a sombre sincerity. "Quite simply, I could not stay away," he breathed. "My life, my home, my heart . . . they are all empty without you. I love you."

Tilting back her head, she studied him with a piercing intensity. As if hoping to see into his very soul.

And perhaps she was, he ruefully acknowledged. He had destroyed her trust once before. She would not easily offer it again.

Justin clenched his teeth, suddenly realizing what a man on trial must feel like just moments before his sentence is pronounced. Was he to be offered mercy or sent to the gallows?

Amelia's lips parted, but before she could speak there was a tap on the door.

"Lady Spaulding?" a maid's timid voice whispered through the door. "Your guests are concerned. Is everything all right?"

Justin frowned, but before he could order the servant to leave them in peace, Amelia had placed her hand over his mouth, her emerald eyes glowing with a happiness that nearly sent him to his knees in relief.

"Thank you, Mary, you may inform my guests that for the first time in my life, everything is absolutely perfect."

Kindred Souls

Barbara Metzger

One

"'He's dead,'" she read.

Aunt Mary grabbed for the letter that dropped from Millie's hand. "Dead? Who's dead? When did he die?"

Aunt Mary held the page closer to her eyes, as if that would help her read the solicitor's letter. It would not. Miss Marisol Cole was born of an age when women's brains were considered too small to shelter facts or figures. What she lacked in education, however, Aunt Mary made up for in eccentricity. She turned to peer at her pets, three small sleeping canines of undetermined parentage and one ill-tempered tabby guarding the window seat: Finn, Quinn, Min and Grimalkin.

"The animals are not upset, so it cannot be anyone important."

"It's Papa," Millie said through a throat that was suddenly dry and scratchy.

"You see? No one important. The dogs always know. The cat must know too, but she never tells."

Millie took the letter back. "My father. Your brother."

"Who wrote both of us off after The Incident, the cold-hearted churl. What was that, five whole years ago? And we have not heard one word since. I am certain he did not mention either of us in his will, so no, he is not worth a single tear."

Millie dabbed at the one that trickled down her cheek. "He was my father. I always hoped, that is—"

"Jedediah Cole never forgot or forgave an insult in his life. He crossed both of us out of the family Bible, didn't he?"

With a big puddle of ink, Millie thought. She'd been told this by the solicitor who'd arranged their departure from the Baron's estate. All because of the scandal.

When a schoolboy was said to 'blot his copybook', it meant his penmanship was messy, his essay or test or practice page irredeemably ruined. Ah, but when society considered that a young miss had 'blotted her copybook', her whole life was irredeemably ruined. No matter the truth, gossip labelled her loose, immoral, tainted beyond repair, unfit for polite company or prospective suitors. Especially if the man involved was not standing by with a special licence that could magically erase many a black mark. There'd been no such rescue for the motherless Miss Mildred Cole, who'd been young and in love.

Helped by that selfsame *involved* man – no gentleman, he – the scandal spread like a fistful of mud thrown against a whitewashed wall. It cost her father his good name and, worse for Jed Cole, his money. It cost Millie's brother Ned his membership at his London clubs, and her younger sister a come-out season. Neither of them forgave her either. Her letters went unanswered; the small gifts she sent went unacknowledged.

Millie and Aunt Mary (who played a part in The Incident, as well) were banished to a tiny cottage in a village outside Bristol, with a piteously small, begrudgingly given, allowance and no communication with their family or former friends. Of course they'd made new acquaintances, a place for themselves in the small community. A community where the bachelors were all farmers and tradesmen, uninterested in a dowerless bride or a penniless spinster, no matter their pedigrees.

"Five years," Aunt Mary mused, lifting the nearest dog on to her lap. "We have done enough mourning for our own lives. Why should we mourn for his?"

The dog scratched its ear.

"You see? We shouldn't bother."

Millie took up the letter again. "It seems we need not put on black anyway. Papa died six months ago, of influenza."

"And no one thought to tell us?" Aunt Mary snorted.

"Papa made them all swear not to. But now that I have reached my twenty-fifth birthday, the solicitor wishes to speak about—"

"Money!" Aunt Mary's eyes lit up. "Perhaps the old curmudgeon left you something after all." She clapped her hands, which set two of the dogs to shrill barking. "Yes, the darlings think so, too. I am sorry I spoke so unkindly of dear Jed."

"What if the solicitor wants to tell us we're being evicted? Or that our pittance ends with Papa's death?"

"That dastard!"

Papa or the solicitor? Millie wondered. "I'll write back immediately to find out."

"What would we do? Where could we go? How could we feed the dogs?"

"I suppose we could throw ourselves on my brother's mercy."

"Your brother is as clutch-fisted and cold-hearted as your father ever was. And spineless, else he would have stood by us despite your father's commands. Now that Edwin has succeeded to the barony, he'll be more insufferable. And that priggish female he married is no better."

Millie had to agree. Ned's wife Nicole had been mortally offended by The Incident. Then mortally disappointed when her dreams of becoming a grand hostess in London had disappeared in that same dark cloud of Millie's scandalous fall from grace. Besides, she was all too happy to see Millie and Aunt Mary ostracized far away across Britain, leaving her sole mistress of the baron's London residence as well as the family seat at Knollwood, in Kent. She would not want the black sheep wandering back to the fold. "We cannot know anything until I hear more from the solicitor."

"I think we should go speak to him."

The dog in her lap yelped, which Aunt Mary took to mean they should start packing. Millie thought it meant the dog got squeezed too hard.

"To London?" Aunt Mary might have suggested they consult the man in the moon.

"No, we haven't the proper clothes, and I doubt we'd be received, not after That Man guaranteed our reputations were destroyed. But your father was never one for clever City lawyers, or their fees. He always had a man of affairs near the Knolls."

Millie checked the letterhead on the thick sheet. "You are right, although I do not recognize the name."

"I'd wager he's fat and finicky and smells of snuff, but it's better to know what he wants, isn't it, rather than sit and worry while waiting for a reply?"

"But what if Ned and Nicole do not admit us to the Knolls? That would be mortifying." And they might not have funds to return to Bristol.

"They wouldn't dare, because we'd put up at the inn in the village and tell everyone they were too miserly to house their own kin. You know how much public opinion means to them at home."

Home. Millie felt a pang of longing she'd thought suppressed years ago. She'd been happy in Kent, while her loving mother lived, at any rate. She could ramble across the fields, visit with the neighbours, knowing everyone within miles. She'd played with the miller's daughters and the viscount's sons. So what if her hems dragged through the dirt or her red hair was snarled with leaves. She was her mother's cherished child then. Returning to Knollwood could never restore that love, that freedom, or that carefree innocence. Why, she'd thought she'd grow up to live happily ever after. Millie looked around the tiny room they called a parlour, where no one came for afternoon calls and where the tea set had chips and the tea was reused until it had no colour. The curtains were clean but faded, the furniture all cast-offs from the previous owner. Their gowns were home-made, and of second-rate material at that. They had one old manservant to carry wood and tend the chickens and the old horse they kept for the old carriage, and a woman who came once a week to mop and do the laundry. They'd learned to cook and clean and grow vegetables. How much worse off could they be if the solicitor had ill tidings? Or if Ned tossed them out?

"I suppose we might as well go. I have some coins put by, enough for the coach fare, I hope."

"Nonsense. The dogs cannot travel in a public coach. Henry will drive us."

Henry, the coach and the mare were equally ancient. Who knew which would collapse first on the way to Kent?

"No, we can use my savings to hire a carriage. And the egg money for rooms along the way." That might be less costly. They could bring a hamper of food with them rather than paying for mediocre meals at exorbitant prices on the road. They'd have to carry their own provisions if the dogs were to come – and sleep in the carriage if the nights were warm enough.

Millie knew better than to suggest her aunt's pets stay behind. "But not the cat. I still have scars from the last time we tried to give her a bath."

"I daresay Grimalkin wouldn't travel well. If Henry stays back, he can feed her and keep an eye on the cottage, although everyone in miles knows there's nothing to steal here. But what if we don't return? If we are invited to stay at Knollwood?"

If Ned and his wife did invite them, Millie thought, it could only be because they needed free servants in the nursery or the scullery. Either way, Millie had no intention of returning to this decrepit, draughty cottage, or to the meanest cat in creation. If worse came to worse, Millie still had her pearls, her gold locket and a pair of diamond eardrops to sell. She'd been saving them for an emergency. The end of their financial support, such as it was, counted as just such a crisis. "We can send Henry funds to take Grim home with him."

The cat rolled over and swatted at the threadbare curtains, leaving a jagged tear behind. Aunt Mary nodded. "I suppose that means she doesn't like it here, either."

So they were going. Back to the past with hopes for a better future.

That night Millie wept, not for the father who'd always been distant and disapproving, certainly not for leaving the place where she'd lived the past five years. No, she cried for the memories of what once was.

Two

"*It is I, Whitbread. Ted.*"

The white-haired butler stared at the unkempt brute at the entrance of Driscoll Hall, ready to slam the carved oak door or call for the footmen. And a blunderbuss. Then he looked past the bushy hair and the darkened skin. "Master Theodore? Is that truly you?"

The tall bearded man in rough leather – coat, boots, and breeches – stepped closer and smiled, showing even white teeth against the tan. "Truly, Whitbread. I am home at last."

"Oh, Master Theodore, how glad I am to see you after all these years. And looking so, ah, hearty. But I forget myself. I should be calling you Lord Driscoll, should I not?"

"Not yet, my friend. I still have to prove myself alive to anyone outside the family before I can officially announce my return. Then I have to prove myself innocent of countless spurious charges. I have much to do before I can present myself as Viscount Driscoll or take my seat in Parliament."

Whitbread led the way into the library, where generations of Driscolls had gone over accounts, entertained their cronies and escaped the day's worries in a glass of spirits. "I trust hiring a valet and seeing a tailor is among the first priorities."

Ted smiled again, this time with pleasure at the old retainer's unspoken affection, as well as the fine cognac Whitbread was pouring out. He pushed his long dark hair away from his eyes and smoothed out his untrimmed beard as best he could. "My first priority must be staying alive, hence the frontiersman disguise." Which was no disguise at all, simply the way he had looked and dressed for the past several years in the Canadian provinces. "I shall repair my appearance and my wardrobe in time, but not until I restore my good name and bring to justice those who tried to destroy it, and me."

Now the butler shook his head and frowned. "To think that anyone would try to murder you, much less label you a traitor and a deserter, My Lord. Not that anyone in the family would harbour suspicion for an instant. Not knowing what a fine young man you are, how loyal and honest and—"

Ted cleared his throat and gestured for the butler to join him in a welcome home libation.

The butler nodded his appreciation and filled another glass. "Kind and modest, too. Why, we were so thrilled to know you were alive, we wished to shout it from the rooftops. Except that might have put you in greater jeopardy, we feared, from reading your letters."

Ted sipped his liquor, savouring the rich, smooth taste. "It would have. The only way I escaped the firing squad was by changing my name to Winsted and my appearance to a fur trapper's, then disappearing into the Canadian backcountry. Staying dead, in effect. My father knew the truth. I wrote to him as soon as I was able."

"He kept your letter by his bedside, His Lordship did. And he passed away content to know you survived."

Ted raised his glass. "To the Viscount. The seventh Lord Driscoll."

Whitbread raised his glass too. "His Lordship informed me and the family solicitor of a secret way to correspond with you in case of necessity. Lord Jared knew, also, of course."

Ted drank and made another toast. "To the Viscount. The eighth."

"And to the ninth, My Lord."

"I should not be in the tally." Ted fell silent, thinking of his older brother, the eldest son who had succeeded their father for so brief a time. Jared and Ted had been best of friends, playmates and partners in every mischief two lively boys could find. Jared grew to a more sober lad, as befitted his position. It was he who had to study agriculture and investments, everything connected to the Driscoll holdings. Not Theodore, the devil-may-care second son, up to every rig and row. How Jared must be laughing now. Ted felt like crying.

"I wish I could have seen him again. Both of them. The mail was so deucedly slow."

"Across the ocean, in times of war, with you travelling the entirety of North America, it seemed? I found it amazing that you received our letters at all."

Sometimes it took years, sometimes Ted knew letters had gone missing. "I treasured the ones I did get. Except for all the bad news."

"Sad times for Driscoll Hall, My Lord. But at least you have finally returned to take up the title and responsibilities."

"If he wasn't already dead I would curse Jared to hell for not taking care of his duties before shuffling off. Begetting little Driscolls is the primary job of the heir, not the spare. I never wanted to step into my father's shoes, much less Jared's. He should have had a son by now. Or two, by all that's holy."

Whitbread sighed. "Before the old Viscount died, Lord Jared promised to find a wife when he turned thirty. I'm certain His Lordship never expected to meet his maker before meeting the perfect female. Not at such an early age."

Jared had been eight and twenty, the age Ted was now. A damnably, painfully, young time for his brother to die, Ted thought, feeling the familiar ache of loss and the sense of years rushing by. He'd seen many a young man die, though, a lot younger. Some in battle, some from disease, some from the harsh life in the northern territories. Ted could not let himself dwell on those tragic losses either. The present had to be for the living, not the dead. "Influenza, your letter said."

"Yes, the epidemic took many in the vicinity. The apothecary, the vicar's two infants and the entire Gorham family. Baron Cole, too."

"I will not mourn Cole's passing. If not for that self-righteous jackass I'd never have gone to Canada to make my fortune in the first place." Ted tried to shake off the gloom of past misfortunes. "But enough of dwelling on losses or rueing what cannot be changed. Tell me of Noel. My baby brother is well?"

"Master Noel is twenty years old, My Lord, and a fine, strapping young man."

That was hard to imagine. Noel had been the baby of the family, a sickly infant after their mother's death giving birth to him. Then he'd been a pampered pet to his father and two doting older brothers. He'd been a sprig of thirteen when Ted took passage to Canada, stick-thin and spotty. How could he be a man already?

"He was away at university during the scourge," Whitbread went on. "Lord Driscoll would not permit him to return home despite the physician's dire prognostications."

Which was dashed wise of Jared, not knowing if Ted could or

would ever make it back to England and the succession. He might not ever have returned. Why should he? His dreams of England had died years ago, starting in Lord Cole's estate office. He was making a new life in the New World . . . until Whitbread's letter reached him seven months after Jared's death. The passage home had taken longer than that.

Poor Lord Noel was left in a muddle, the trusted servant had written, with people dubbing him Lord Driscoll, when he knew he was no such thing. Ted was the heir, ready or willing or not.

Not.

"So he up and left?"

"He left his studies and his friends in London, rather than answer awkward questions. He stays close to home now, consulting with the steward and the solicitors. Today he's gone with the bailiff to purchase a new bull. Reluctantly, I might add. Master Noel fancied himself a regular London swell, not a farmer."

Well, Ted never fancied himself a viscount either. Or a soldier, much less a dishonoured one. He always had a head for figures so he'd set out to be a trader, a shipping magnate, a success, so he could come back to England a rich man and prove Baron Cole wrong. Too bad the old puffguts wasn't there to see.

"Learning about the estate cannot hurt him," Ted told the butler. "A bull might."

Whitbread poured another splash of cognac into both of their glasses. "To hopes he never succeeds to become the tenth Lord Driscoll, for all of our sakes."

Whitbread left to see to Ted's baggage, order his room readied and inform the cook to prepare a meal fit for a viscount.

While he was gone, Ted poured himself another glass of cognac and stared into the fire. He was home, yet he felt more lost than when he'd found himself in a log lean-to during a blizzard. He had no doubt Whitbread would have the viscount's rooms prepared for him, not his old comfortable bedchamber on the upper floor. He'd have to sleep where his father and brother had died, with their ghosts scolding him for his sins and his seven-year defection. He'd sleep next to his mother's room, the one that had stayed empty so long. Her ghost was sure to plague him to marry, to fill the nursery. Damn them all and the nightmares he'd suffer. Hadn't he suffered enough?

They should rest easy. He understood duty and obligations. He'd come home, hadn't he? Despite the bumblebroth sure to follow, despite the danger and the disappointment.

Home. This place was too quiet to be the home he remembered, with rowdy boys and a constant bustle, with boots and books and sporting dogs on the furniture, with friends and neighbours in and out all day, with dreams.

And now there was duty. And half a bottle of cognac left.

"What shall you do first, My Lord?" Whitbread asked when he returned with a tray of bread and cheese.

"After finishing this bottle? A bath and a good night's sleep. Then I'll lie low until Noel's return. He's been in charge for over a year, so he deserves to hear my plans before they are made public. I know I cannot keep my reappearance secret for long, not with the servants who saw me arrive and carried in my baggage." And not with Whitbread settling him in the viscount's suite and ordering a lavish dinner. "Please ask the staff to refrain from spreading the news in the village as long as possible."

Whitbread stiffened his spine and pursed his lips. "Driscoll Hall servants do not gossip about their employers. The secret of your survival never passed through the gates."

"Of course not. My apologies, Whitbread. I am merely used to strangers whose loyalty is as thick as one's purse is heavy."

The butler nodded. "Then once Lord Noel returns, you can take your proper place?"

"Not quite that easily. I'll speak to the solicitor before travelling to London to face the War Office. Mr Armstead still handles the family's affairs?"

"A somewhat younger Mr Armstead, the nephew of the gentleman in charge when you left. Very learned, this one, and equally as careful of the family's business. Lord Driscoll had great confidence in him. Lord Jared, that was."

"Fine. I'll ask him to call here in a few days. And I'll have to speak with the local magistrate, too. Who took over from old man Cole?"

"His son, Edwin."

"Ned? He was always as stiff-rumped as his sire. He's what? Thirty-five years old or so? I doubt he's mellowed with age. But he'll know me, so he'll have to vouch for my identity. I'd have to pay my respects at the Knolls anyway, I suppose." Which was the last thing he wanted to do, after being dead or being viscount. "Unless he's gone to London for the season?" Ted could only hope.

Whitbread sniffed. "The Coles no longer travel to the metropolis."

"No? I'd have thought that high-nosed wife of his would insist on taking her place in the ton."

Whitbread decided to let Lord Noel explain about The Incident. "Rumour has it that Lady Cole might be increasing again."

"Deuce take it, I suppose Cole has a quiverful of heirs by now."

"Some gentlemen take their responsibilities to heart."

Enough to take a shrew like Lady Cole to their beds. Ted shuddered and poured the last of the cognac into his glass. "Find me another bottle, Whitbread. Or two."

Three

Millie moved ahead. With dread.

What if Edwin tossed them out? What if there was no more money, ever? What if highwaymen stole the little money they had? What if some woman recognized Millie from her wild red hair and steered her daughters to the other side of the street? Worse, what if some man recognized her – or just noticed her wild red hair – and thought she was a lightskirt or bachelor fare?

Millie tried to think optimistically, she really did. If nothing else, once they reached Knollwood she'd get to place flowers on her mother's grave. Maybe she'd ask if anyone ever placed a marker for the neighbour's son who'd never come home. She could bring her oldest friend flowers too, and shed a few more tears. Maybe then they'd be the last tears for the young man who'd broken her heart all those years ago, first by leaving, then by dying.

Now wasn't that something to look forward to? Millie asked herself. Revisiting old graves and old dreams.

Bah! She had too much to do to turn into a maudlin miss. Next she'd get the vapours.

No, that was Aunt Mary when the hired coachman almost put their carriage in a ditch. Or when an innkeeper threatened to drown the dogs because their barking disturbed the other guests.

Millie thought about drowning them herself, and the reckless driver too. His ham-fisted driving set the coach to careening, which gave Min travel sickness. On Millie's only half-decent boots. The shouts and curses from the drivers of the imperilled carriages they passed set Finn to yipping. In her ear. And the garlic and sausage scraps the daredevil driver tossed to the dogs gave Quinn wind. In her lap.

The journey was nerve-racking. Their arrival proved only slightly less fraught.

Edwin, whom everyone but his wife called Ned, and his wife, who insisted on being addressed as Lady Cole, did not close the door to the Knolls in their faces, but neither did they welcome Millie and Aunt Mary with open arms. Aunt Mary was right that they'd be too embarrassed to send the unwanted visitors to the village inn. Millie was right that they'd be happy to send them to perdition.

Or the attic.

Lady Cole declared those were the only available rooms, forgetting that Millie knew precisely how many chambers the sprawling old house possessed. Lady Cole also decreed that the dogs could not be let loose anywhere else in the house, although her savages – her children – were permitted to run wild. The three mongrels on the top floor meant someone had to climb up and down the narrow attic stairs every few hours to let them out – on leads, of course – to relieve themselves or to eat in the kitchen. Except for that duty, Millie was to keep to her room when company came.

"And for heaven's sake, Mildred," Ned's wife declared, "put a cap over that unruly red hair so the servants don't call you a trollop."

The servants were overworked and browbeaten. They, at least, appreciated that Millie took on the dog-minding duties and offered to read to the children.

The children, all four of them, were spoiled and nasty, mean to the harried nursemaids and cruel to the dogs when they saw them. They stole Min's ball, pulled Finn's tail and chased Quinn under the furniture. When Millie tried to correct their behaviour, they went crying to their mother, who pursed her lips so tightly her teeth might get chipped. When Aunt Mary said that the dogs were complaining, Lady Cole threatened to have her sent to an asylum. Millie stopped reading to them. So what if the demons grew up ignorant and unlettered? Their mother saw nothing wrong with that, either.

Millie's young sister's welcome was no warmer. Winnie was a petulant nineteen, bored in the country, and still blaming Millie for her lack of a season, a beau, a husband. Spared the red hair that plagued Millie and Ned, Winnie was a beautiful strawberry blonde. She knew exactly how beautiful.

"To think you used to be the belle of the local assemblies and a toast of London," she said with a sneer. "You look like one of those women from the almshouse now, all skin and bones, and your skin is as rough and dark as a piece of toast." Winnie was delightfully curved, to her delight, with a perfect peaches and cream complexion that she admired in every mirror she passed. "And one would think you a ragpicker in those clothes, with those callouses! The Incident was bad enough, but you'll never pass for a lady looking like that. Why, I'd be mortified if any of my friends saw you."

Millie would be surprised if the brat *had* any friends. "I doubt I shall be here long enough to meet your acquaintances, Winnie." The Knolls was proving less comfortable than the cottage in Bristol. And less cheerful than the almshouse.

"Good. But as long as you are here, do remember that I am not a child, Mildred, so stop calling me Winnie. My name is Winifred. And no, do not look at me in that sorrowful way. You brought all of your woes down on yourself. And on the rest of us."

Aunt Mary took to her bed, surrounded by her beloved pets. They did not have much to say about the current circumstances. Neither did Millie. What was the use of sharing her dismay?

These people might share her blood, but they were not family. Even the house was no home to her, not while it was decorated to Lady Cole's garish, overcrowded taste. For this Millie had sold her diamond earbobs?

Millie counted the coins left from the journey. She swallowed her pride, her hurt, her red-headed temper, and the words she was aching to say. Instead she went to the solicitor's.

Ted's brother was so excited to have him back, you'd think Noel was released from prison, instead of from the duties of a title. He couldn't wait to go tell the neighbours, then hie off to London with Ted to settle the questions of the inheritance, the army and the funeral they'd held. Then Noel intended to resume the life of a care-free bachelor on the town: cards, clothes, horses, women and wine.

Gads, was Theodore Driscoll ever that young? No, Ted always had ambition to be something other than a rich lord's idle, indolent son. He never sought to be a London swell, only a success. He'd proved himself worthy, but it had been too late. Now he was determined to prove himself worthy of succeeding his father and brother.

The first step towards that future was the magistrate, Edwin: Lord Cole.

"No need to send ahead for an appointment like some wine merchant," Noel said. "Old Ned's always on his uppers, and under his spouse's thumb, but he doesn't mind me running tame at the Knolls. Gives him someone to talk to besides his wife and sister and those beastly children. Makes him feel important, you know, giving advice to a younger man. I never listen, naturally. He's as ignorant of the latest farming techniques as a hedgehog."

When they got to the Baron's manor house, Noel jumped off his horse, tossing the reins to Ted. A young woman was racing down the steps towards him, skirts flying, bonnet ribbons streaming behind her.

"You'll never believe what's happened," she told Noel, ignoring Ted entirely, as if he were a servant.

"Wait until you hear *my* news," Noel answered.

She grabbed his arm and dragged him around the side of the house. "Me first."

Ted watched them go. Yes, he'd been that young, once. The ache in the vicinity of his heart proved it.

The pretty female had to be little Winnie, only not so little any more, but a regular diamond. Doing mental calculations of her age, he wondered why no handsome young chap had scooped her up years ago. Most likely her father had been holding out for a duke or something.

A sullen groom arrived to take the horses, without so much as a nod to the unkempt rider. Ted shrugged and climbed the steps to the Knolls, the way he'd done for so many years. An unfamiliar butler came to the door and told him to go around back to the service entrance. Ted almost told the man to go to hell, but he gave his name instead. The fellow's jaw dropped open.

Before the butler could close his mouth, Ted said he'd announce *himself*. He knew the way. He used to know this house as well as his own.

The furnishings in the rooms he passed were different, and different from anything that should have appeared in England. Egyptian, Ted thought, with touches of chinoiserie. And Greek statues in various niches. He followed the voices he heard coming from what used to be the morning room: loud, angry voices.

"How dare you!" a female was shouting. "Keeping us in purgatory when I possess a substantial fortune!"

"You had to reach your majority to inherit your mother's portion. That's what the trust said," a man replied. Ted thought the defensive whining sounded like Ned Cole's.

"So I had to grow turnips just to eat? You could not have advanced some of the interest? Or after Papa died, laid out your own funds for the few months until my birthday? Why, if you'd bothered to inform me of my coming wealth I could have borrowed against it, rather than fret over heating the cottage in the winter."

"What? Trust a peahen like you to manage that kind of money?"

A different female shouted back. "You've already made mice-feet of your life," she shrilled. "And dragged us into the mingle-mangle to boot. There'd be a lot more gold in the Cole coffers if your father hadn't had to pay off That Man."

Ted knew it was rude to interrupt a private argument, and Zeus knew he did not want to get between warring women. The door was open, though, and one of the females, who was either very fat or very pregnant, spotted him and shrieked. 'Who let this ruffian in my house? Do something, Cole. Don't let him have the good silver. Or the children," she added as an afterthought.

Ted ignored her, the bluster coming from the other side of the room, the weeping older woman, the squabbling children, the butler puffing down the hall. The parlour could have held forty people; Ted saw only one.

She was the last person he wanted to see, and the woman he saw every night in his dreams. No, it could not be. Fate could not continue to be so cruel. This female was thin and pinched looking, like somebody's poor relation.

Then the lady angrily pulled an ugly lace cap off her head, sending hairpins and wild red curls in every direction. She threw the hat on the floor and stamped on it. "That's what I think of your opinions, and your human kindness."

There was no mistaking that hair, that temper, those flashing green eyes. His mouth went dry. His knees locked. His blood froze in his veins. But he was a man. He'd survived a rifle shot, a plunge into a raging river, capture by unfriendly natives and years in the wilderness. He could survive this too. At least until he was outside where no one could see him.

He forced his legs to move in her direction. Then he forced his spine to bend in a bow. "Lady Stourbridge. How do you do?"

She slapped him. "Is this some kind of joke, sirrah? I am not and never have been Lady Stourbridge. And who the devil are you anyway?"

Noel came flying into the room, shoving the butler aside. "He's Ted. My brother, come home to be Viscount Driscoll."

Millie fainted.

Ted caught her before she could hit her head on the cluttered furniture. He held her against him, remembering to breathe again. Not Lady Stourbridge?

Lady Cole screamed. Ned shouted, "Put my sister down!"

When hell froze over. Ted would have carried Millie right out of the house and into for ever, if the doorway was not filled with servants and children and barking dogs.

"Put her down, I say."

The older woman picked up an ugly vase and threw it at Ted. "You're dead. No ghost is going to steal my niece!"

Ted ducked, protecting the limp treasure in his arms, but the vase shattered on the floor. Now Lady Cole shrieked. Not about her sister-in-law in the embrace of a wild man in buckskins with a braid down his back, but for her ugly urn. The children chased the dogs, knocking over a table filled with a tea service. The dogs started gobbling biscuits and lapping tea while the older female begged them not to, because sweets gave them gas. Noel was laughing. Winnie was giggling. And the Baron challenged Noel to a duel for perpetrating such a hoax.

Ted smiled. How could he not smile with Millie against his heart? Millie who was not Lady Stourbridge.

"Don't be a clodpole, Cole."

Four

"Hello, Red," he said.

Millie opened her eyes. She did not want to, because she was having the most wondrous dream. She thought she'd just wake up enough to tell all of her relatives to go to the devil, then go back to—"Red?"

She'd been called Miss Cole, Mildred and Millie, even That Woman, but only one person dared to call her Red. She hated her hair and the teasing she'd suffered, so she'd learned to fight back until the teasing stopped. Ted used to say he loved the colour: a welcoming fire, a perfect sunset, a hint of passion, a rose in full glory. His rose. Now the large man who was so tenderly cradling her in his arms called her by that awful, magical name.

She raised a hand to touch the thick dark beard that covered most of the man's face. "Is it truly you, Ted?"

He lowered his lips to hers and kissed her. Gently, with the beard and moustache scratchy on her skin. But, oh, no man had ever made her feel that way, all soft and melty. "It is you, or I have died and gone to heaven." Or hell from the feelings one simple kiss aroused.

"You did not die."

"Nor you. You came home."

"Now I am home."

The others in the room were yelling. At Millie and Ted, at the dogs and the children, at each other.

"Out," Ted ordered without taking his eyes off Millie.

"That's dashed irregular," Cole protested while his wife gasped at Millie's morals, kissing in front of the children and her impressionable sister-in-law.

"If you don't wish the infants to see a lot more," the Viscount said with a growl of frustration, "I suggest you remove them on the instant. And although I'd wager young Winnie has seen more than her share of kisses, take her when you leave, too."

One of the dogs jumped on to the sofa where Ted still held Millie on his lap. "You too, old chap." Ted let Quinn sniff his hand and addressed Finn, who was snarling at him. "I won't harm her, I swear."

Aunt Mary picked Quinn off the sofa before Lady Cole could have conniptions. "Oh, I do like a man who talks to dogs. Come on, my dears. I am certain these two have much to speak of."

They did indeed.

"You first," Millie said when everyone had left and Ted shut the door behind them. She moved to a chair near the fireplace, away from his too-tempting arms.

Ted started pacing. "Lud, I wish the chaos hadn't overturned the tea cart. My mouth is dry. Where to start?"

"Where you left me, seven years ago."

"No, I'll start with your father telling me that you were too young, that my offer for your hand was laughable. I was tempted to ask you to elope with me to Scotland, but your father was right, you were too young. You hadn't seen anything of the world yet, or other men."

"I would have gone with you."

"Your father also said I was not good enough to marry his daughter and I never would be anything but a useless second son. That's when I decided to prove him wrong by making my fortune in Canada."

"I would have gone with you," she repeated.

"Into who knew what conditions after a treacherous ocean crossing? How could I subject you to such peril?"

What she'd faced without him was far worse, but Millie did not say that. "Go on."

He did, explaining that he and two other men, friends from Cambridge, founded a shipping and trading company in the British territory. The business kept growing, with more people moving to the north, more demand for the products. The company needed to expand, though, to make them all wealthy. Ted wanted to see more of the country before returning home, so he travelled along the frontier, establishing new outposts, signing new contracts.

Then war broke out, worse than the previous skirmishes between the British and the Americans. The Americans resented the English impressing their seamen to fight against the French. The British felt the colonists were trying to steal the best acreage for farming. Each had allies among the various native tribes, who had reasons of their own for defending their ancestral lands. The French were stirring up trouble, too, as usual.

Ted sympathized with the sailors and the settlers, but he was a loyal Englishman. So he volunteered to act as guide to the uncharted regions he'd been exploring. They made him a lieutenant, and soon sent him as a forward scout for a company of young, inexperienced soldiers. He was shot by men hiding in the woods, not Americans, not hostile natives. The marksmen spoke the King's English, with Yorkshire accents. Ted knew because he was just barely conscious when they dragged him off the path he'd been following.

He heard the gunfire when his green troops marched right into the ambush. Every Redcoat was killed. Then the attackers came back for Lt Driscoll, who was still alive. So they tossed his limp body into a gorge above a turbulent river. Ted did not remember much of what happened next, just the cold and the clutching for branches, rocks, dead trees. He remembered waterfalls and rapids, but not how he survived. He awoke with no idea how many days had passed, to find himself being cared for by a native tribe that spoke no Indian language he knew. Besides the gunshot, the loss of blood, fevers from exposure and the near drowning, half the bones in his body were broken or bruised. He was in too much pain, delirious most of the time, to care if he was patient or prisoner, or where they were taking him, slung between two ponies.

Months passed. He had no idea how many, but his beard grew, and his wounds healed. He learned some of the natives' tongue; they learned some English, which would help them in the white man's world. Eventually he was strong enough to leave, but more months passed at the slow pace he was forced to travel, until he found a British village that had mail service, infrequent and unreliable as it was. He sent word of his survival. Before he reached his business partners or his army outpost, though, he heard rumours that a Lieutenant Driscoll had turned traitor. That he'd led his men into an ambush.

He was ready to march into the commanding officer's

headquarters and declare his innocence. But first he collected his mail from England.

"My brother wrote that the family had received an invitation to your wedding."

"There was no wedding."

"I did not know."

"I did not know you were alive, either."

Ted could only shrug now, years later. How to describe his despair? His dreams were dead. He might as well be too. What reason did he have to return to England? Why should he prove himself to someone who did not care?

So he disappeared. He was officially dead, except to a trusted few.

"I wasn't one of those you trusted."

"You were married."

"No, but if I were, I was still your friend. I mourned for you every day."

"As I mourned my loss of your love."

She shook her head as if to say no, she'd never stopped loving him, but he stared out the window, not seeing.

He went on to explain that eventually he started to recover his ambition. After all, a man had to do something with his life. With a new name and new appearance, he conducted business away from the cities and the larger settlements. He also conducted a covert investigation into the circumstances of the ambush. He discovered that his death was no accident of war, but a planned and paid-for assassination. When that effort apparently failed, his enemies plotted his dishonour, counting on a firing squad to end his existence.

"Who would do such a dastardly thing?"

"Oh, it was easy enough to trace the orders, once I recognized one of the barbarians who tossed me off the cliff. I, ah, convinced him it was in his best interests to name his employer. He reluctantly but eventually named the commanding officer, Major Frederickson himself. Who happened to be first cousin to the only man in England who had reason to wish me dead."

"Why did you not come home and bring charges against him if you knew his name?"

"Because my enemy was highly placed. No court would convict him. I would have had to kill him myself, instead."

"The maggot deserved to die."

"Yes, but I could not shoot your husband."

Millie clutched the handkerchief from her pocket. "My husband?"

"Stourbridge wanted me out of the way so he could marry you. He needed your dowry and the other money it seems you recently inherited."

"No," she started to protest. But then she recalled the Earl's greed, his implacable determination to get his way in everything. "But we never married."

"Why? It is your turn to explain. A broken engagement is bad enough, but a cancelled wedding? That is unheard of."

Millie started picking at the threads of the handkerchief she'd so tediously hemmed. She could afford to purchase store-made ones now, she thought, irrelevantly. Ted cleared his throat.

Millie cleared hers too. She wished for tea. Or wine. "I thought you were dead. I wished I were too, but one doesn't die of a broken heart, it seems. As you said, a person has to do something with his or her life. So when Papa announced that Lord Stourbridge wished to marry me, I agreed."

She knew she could never come to love the arrogant Earl or be happy under his domineering ways, but she hoped to have children to give her existence meaning. At first the Earl was courteous and complimentary. Then he started to show his true colours, in his eagerness to begin their family long before the wedding.

Millie tried to tolerate his kisses, but he wanted more. She could sacrifice much for her unborn babes, but not yet, not until she said her vows. The Earl turned nasty at her refusal which he took, rightly so, as her reluctance to share intimacies with any man other than Theodore Driscoll.

"He . . . he tried to force me."

"Now I have to kill him twice."

"He did not succeed. I used my knee, the way you taught me before you left. He let me go, but he vowed to make me pay for my insolence after the wedding. He would take pleasure in showing me who was master."

"Three times."

The handkerchief was in shreds now, pieces littering Millie's lap. "I knew I could not go through with the marriage to that beast. Neither Papa nor Ned would listen. The contracts were signed, and they expected me to do my duty for the family. I was a silly goose, they said. I suffered bridal nerves, they said. But I knew better. So I ran away. On the day of the wedding."

Ted whistled. "You left Stourbridge at the altar?"

"St George's, with hundreds of guests. The Prince was invited. I do not know if he attended or not."

Now Ted grinned. "That's my girl!"

"No, I was no one's girl. You were dead, remember? My father disowned me and sent me off with Aunt Mary to live in poverty near Bristol. Ned did not plead my cause. I hardly blamed either of them. The Earl sued for breach of promise, of course, and won my dowry plus a huge sum for his public humiliation. He took his revenge further by seeing that every door in London was closed to my family, and by claiming I was a slut anyway, most likely carrying another man's child. We were all ruined by that evil man."

Ted left the window and stood in front of Millie's chair, brushing crumbs of handkerchief off her skirts. "Then come with me to London and we'll both have our revenge. I have written proof of Stourbridge's perfidy, and I have influential friends who will support my testimony. Come with me, Red."

"What are you asking of me?"

He knelt down and took both of her hands in his. "I cannot ask you to marry me, not until my name is cleared. But I am asking you to follow me to town. I'll leave tomorrow, open Driscoll House and fetch a special licence. By the time you arrive, I'll have Stourbridge run out of London, or run through with my sword."

"No, I cannot go. I would have followed you anywhere, to the ends of the earth, once. But I cannot marry you."

"What, because this isn't a proper proposal? I'll have my mother's rings waiting for you in town, and do it up right, I swear."

"I am not fit to be your viscountess. Haven't you listened? I am disgraced."

"Worse than a traitor and army deserter? We'll both disprove our guilt. And if people do not accept us, we can simply return to Kent and start filling the big empty house with our own family."

Millie stared at their two hands, joined, without speaking.

"Is it the money? Do you fear I cannot support you and our children? I am a wealthy man, my love, even without the Driscoll fortune. Not even your father could complain."

"I seem to have a fortune of my own suddenly. And I would have married you when you had nothing."

"But not now?" He put a finger on her chin and tipped her head up, forcing her to look at him. "You do not wish to marry me?"

"More than my hopes of heaven. But I do not trust you."

He dropped her hands. "You think I am a traitor, a coward?"

"I think you will continue to decide what is best for me, like every man has been deciding my entire life. I think you'll challenge

Stourbridge, not caring that you could lose or be hung for an illegal duel. I'd be a widow, mourning you all over again. Mostly I think we are not friends any longer. *You* do not trust *me*."

"I thought you had not waited."

"If I knew you were alive, I would have waited for ever for your return."

He dragged his hands through his shaggy hair. "Deuce take it, Red, we cannot change the past. Must we suffer for it for the rest of our lives?"

"I do not know."

"Come to London and find out. Now that you're an heiress, go buy new clothes and jewels, another three dogs for your aunt. Attend the theatre, see the opera. Enjoy yourself, my love. You deserve it, and we deserve another chance to become the friends we used to be, the lovers we should have been. No one will shun a beautiful, rich woman, I promise you, especially after we reveal what a villain Stourbridge has been. Hints of an engagement, and your aunt as chaperone, will still any gossip. As for your worrying over a gentlemanly duel, I never intended to give Stourbridge that much of a chance to shoot me in the back. He did not offer to meet me at dawn, or treat my lady with honour. The scoundrel is no gentleman." He grinned. "And I have learned how to fight dirty."

Millie still wasn't sure. She was certain of her heart, but not of her courage.

Five

"Take me instead," Winnie pleaded.

She tumbled into the room from where she'd obviously been listening with her ear against the door. "I've never had my chance in London, and they—"everyone knew she meant her brother and his wife, who were right behind her in the hallway "—will never take me because of what happened to Millie."

"You cannot go stay in a bachelor's house with no one to chaperone but a crazy old lady who speaks to dogs," Lady Cole pronounced.

At which Aunt Mary shot back: "And you should hear what they say about you, you tub of lard."

"I suppose we could all go," the Baron suggested, "since no one could find fault if my sisters are under my care. Driscoll needs my help to prove his bona fides and re-establish himself. My knowledge of the law, don't you know."

No one believed he had any such knowledge, but Winnie enthusiastically seconded Cole's offer to let her go to London. So did Noel, for reasons of his own, having to do with the little beauty.

"And if Stourbridge is routed," Cole added, "we can be comfortable again in town." Which he sorely missed, with his clubs and his convenients. "But Cole House is leased for the year."

Ted bowed to the inevitable, and the only way he could guarantee Millie going to London. "You are all invited to stay at my home, of course. I am afraid, though, that there is no provision for children at Driscoll House. The nurseries have been in holland covers for decades, and the armament collection is too dangerous." To say nothing of the priceless heirlooms.

Lady Cole loved the idea of getting back her rightful place in the beau monde, but she hated giving up control of her disappointing husband or her spoiled sister-in-law, especially to this great hairy bear of a man whose social standing had not been settled. "I refuse to travel without my children," she said.

Her husband smiled. "Good. That's settled then. I'll escort my sisters and my aunt, and you shall stay behind with the little dears."

"What? I never said—"

No one listened to her sputtering. They all waited for Millie's decision. They couldn't very well go if she didn't.

Ted knelt beside her again, his hand cupping her face. "I need you beside me, Millie Mine. Every day, every way."

A tear ran down her cheek, on to his fingers. "Heaven help me, I need you too."

Now Aunt Mary sniffled, and even Noel had to clear his throat.

"But you have to promise me, Theodore Driscoll, on your word of honour, that you will not let that man kill you. That we will run away together if your innocence is not proved. That you will never go off and leave me again."

"I promise, my love," he said, and sealed the bargain with a kiss.

Lady Cole started carping about how they'd simply cause another scandal at this rate. No one listened to her that time, either. Lord Cole called for champagne, for a toast.

They were going to London.

This trip was far different from Millie's recent one. The journey took hours, for one thing, not days. And Millie's conveyance was a fancy open curricle with a competent whip for a driver: Ted. Noel and Cole were on horseback alongside, and Aunt Mary and Winnie

– who was threatened with staying behind with Lady Cole unless she was on her best behaviour – sat in luxury in the Driscoll family coach. Mr Armstead rode with them. The solicitor joined the travellers because he knew the best barristers, if one should be needed for Lord Driscoll's affair; he also felt a debt to Miss Mildred Cole for letting her languish in Bristol so long. At first he worried about a conflict of interests, representing both families, but Mr Armstead could see for himself how the new Viscount and the former outcast were on close, even intimate terms. The distinguished, middle-aged bachelor was also relieved, and delighted, to be seated across from Miss Marisol Cole, a lovely woman of delightful nature. Her dogs were delightful too.

Ted had sent word of their arrival, so servants were lined up outside Driscoll House waiting to welcome them with every comfort a viscount's dwelling could offer. They dined at home that evening and made an early night of it after the excitement of the move. The campaign began the next day.

Ted went to the War Office. Millie went to the shops.

Ted met with the Home Secretary. Millie met with a banker Mr Armstead recommended, to transfer her monies into her own name with a separate account for Aunt Mary.

The new viscount hired six brawny men to guard his back, his home and his beloved. Millie hired two lady's maids, a dresser, a coiffeur, a seamstress, a dance instructor and a social secretary.

Ted called on his godmother, the Dowager Duchess of Southead. Millie called on her late mother's best friend, the current Duchess of Southead.

Ted visited the gentlemen's clubs, his own, his brothers', his father's. Millie visited the modiste, the corsetière, the bootmaker and the lending libraries.

Ted got his hair cut. Millie did not.

At night they all attended the theatre, the opera, even the circus at Astley's Amphitheatre. Millie was never far from the Viscount's side, while her beautiful young sister hung on Lord Noel Driscoll's arm. A maiden aunt and a well-respected lawyer provided watchful chaperonage, along with the girls' brother. They were all seen, admired and endlessly speculated about. No one approached them or sought their acquaintance, however, despite the rumours flying through town that the Prince himself was considering taking up Driscoll's cause. No one wanted to risk the powerful and prickly Stourbridge's displeasure until they saw how the cards fell.

Stourbridge was at the races in Epsom, due back in London in a week. He had to know of Ted's miraculous survival via the servants' grapevine, and of Lord Driscoll's arrival with Stourbridge's former fiancée to boot. The Earl had to be seething. Or shaking in his boots, if half the gossip were true. The ton was atwitter with the talk, aghast that one of their own could behave so reprehensibly, agog for the Earl's return and the outcome.

Millie and Ted were alone almost never. How else to restore a lost reputation? But how to reclaim a lost friendship? They stole hours at night, long after the others were abed and the servants dismissed, that's how.

Millie marvelled at how Ted was even more handsome than she remembered, now that he'd shaved. She wept over the scars the beard and moustache had hidden. The Viscount admired how Millie's figure had grown more womanly, and her glorious hair had grown longer. He spent hours combing it through his fingers, smoothing out the night plait her maid spent hours braiding. They spoke of books, Bristol and his business, of travels they hoped to take and changes they would make in the townhouse. They discussed the reforms Ted could enact when he took his seat in Parliament and which party best suited their values. Sometimes they disagreed, but they listened to each other with respect and considered the opposing views. They fell back into the old camaraderie as easily as Aunt Mary's dogs found the most comfortable sleeping nooks and the most sympathetic servants in their new residence. It was as if Ted and Millie's closeness was part of their very natures, unaffected by time or distance.

What was new was passion. Not that the pair hadn't felt attraction before or had treated each other like siblings, but they'd been young, innocent and honourable. Now they were adults, aroused by each other's scents and shapes and skin. They had grown-up desires, growing by the minute, and so many wasted years to make up for.

The household might know how Ted and Millie spent their late-night/early-morning hours and why Miss Cole's hair looked like one of the dogs had slept in it, but no one interfered. The sooner the wedding, the better for everyone. Driscoll House would have a mistress. Aunt Mary would have a comfortable home – if her hopes for Mr Armstead went unfulfilled. Winnie would have a wealthy sponsor for her season, her brother a high-placed brother-in-law, and Noel freedom to pursue his own pleasures.

Then Lord Stourbridge returned to town. Ted knew because he

had men on his payroll to keep watch at the Earl's residence and clubs.

"You cannot be thinking of calling on him at his own home, in private," Millie insisted. "Not without taking the Lord High Magistrate, the sheriff and the Horse Guards. Otherwise, he will shoot you as you walk through the door. Or have his hired thugs do it for him."

"No, I will not meet him in private. Your disgrace was made public. My supposed treachery was made public. The man succeeds by whispering. Let him hear the whispers now. Out in public, not hidden away in a fortress."

Millie had to be honest. "I do believe his humiliation was fairly public, as he waited for his bride to appear at the church. I could almost feel sorry for him, on the brink of losing everything he holds dear, except for what he did to you."

"We will never be safe if he is left alive in England."

She knew. "Be careful."

Lord Driscoll waited until the Southead Ball. The Dowager Duchess had been gracious enough to include Winifred in her granddaughter's come-out celebration. They knew Stourbridge was attending because no one declined Her Grace's invitations. Her balls were always memorable, and her approval necessary for entry to the haut monde. Stourbridge was so arrogant, so confident of his own worth that he'd count on facing down any criticism simply by appearing there. Further, common opinion held Stourbridge considering the granddaughter for his countess. He was considering her dowry and connections, at any rate. Not that either duchess would permit him within a mile of the young girl, not now.

Silence fell over the assembled guests as the elegant party from Driscoll House arrived at the ball. The Viscount's tailor, barber and valet had turned the savage colonial out to perfection, the paragon of upper-class British manhood, which meant he was dressed like every other male in the room in black and white.

Millie wore green: a green silk gown, green satin slippers, a bandeau of green velvet around her red curls and the Driscoll family emeralds. Women turned green at the sight.

Suddenly everyone wanted to know them. Millie could have danced every set, if she hadn't promised all her dances to Ted, her brother, Ted, Noel, Mr Armstead, Ted and the Duke of Southead. Winnie became equally as popular. She'd be in transports over her success, except for Noel scowling at her dance partners. Even Miss

Marisol Cole created a modest stir among the older gentlemen, she looked so handsome in the new gown Millie had shamed Ned into purchasing for her, aside from the wardrobe Millie provided.

They danced, they chatted, they strolled, and they kept looking for Stourbridge. He'd arrived, Ted's informants reported. As soon as he was refused a dance with the Duchess' debutante, he went to the card room, where Southead himself invited the Earl to play a hand in his private library. The Duke also sent word to Ted.

The Viscount left Millie with her aunt and gestured her brother and Noel to come with him. Millie waited three minutes, then followed.

So did several others who had an inkling of the coming confrontation.

Stourbridge looked up from his cards and sneered when he saw the men facing him. "Still a coward, I see, Driscoll. Too afraid to face me by yourself after those lies you've been spewing."

Ted did not rise to the Earl's bait. "No lies, Stourbridge. And these are witnesses, not reinforcements."

Stourbridge took a long, deliberate sip of his wine. Then he tossed the rest of the contents of the glass in Ted's face. "Very well, consider yourself challenged. Pick one of your lily-livered cohorts to be your second. Swords or pistols, it matters not. You'll be dead by daybreak. Permanently, I trust."

Ted had to restrain Noel from charging at the Earl. "There will be no duel. That's for gentlemen. And these others—" he waved his hand at Ned, Noel, the Duke, three men in the doorway "—will not interfere if you choose to go out to the garden with me now, man to man, no weapons but our fists. I would like nothing better than to water His Grace's roses with your blood. But you have a choice."

Stourbridge looked at Southead and raised one eyebrow. "Is this what passes for civilized behaviour in your home? Brawls and name-calling? That might occur in schoolyards and the wilderness. I expected better from your hospitality, Duke."

"He has proof," Southead said. "I am convinced you have done grievous harm to these families, and to our brave soldiers. I'd listen to his offer, were I in your shoes. Your feet are set in quicksand."

Stourbridge tried to look unconcerned, but his fingers drummed on the table. "Speak, then, savage."

Ted nodded. "Very well. You can meet me outdoors, as I said. Right now, before you can hire a gang of ruffians. You will not survive, I promise. Or you can face a trial before your peers in Parliament. The sheriff's men are waiting outside to arrest you."

"What, a peer of the realm, on the word of a deserter?"

"I have sworn and witnessed testimony from one of Frederickson's hirelings that you paid the commanding officer to have me and my troops ambushed. Frederickson confessed also, in front of several other officers. Your cousin, wasn't he? He's dead now, you know. An accident, they said, but his own men shot him."

"And I will testify that you tried to rape my sister," Cole added, which warmed Millie's heart, there in the doorway. "You will find no friends in the Lords."

The Duke concurred. "You'll be convicted and hanged as a traitor."

The drumming got louder. The sneer disappeared into a grimace. "I'll leave the country. Give back the stupid chit's dowry, if that's what you want, Cole. You can have the whore and her money, Driscoll. You've been panting after both of them since you were in leading strings."

Millie gasped, her brother turned red, but Ted forgot his best intentions and knocked Stourbridge out of his chair with a hammer-hard right punch to the mouth. Then he dragged him up by his neckcloth, which was already spattered with the Earl's blood and teeth. "Apologise to the lady."

Stourbridge mumbled something hard to interpret with his jaw broken. Ted tossed him back to the chair. "You have one other option. His Grace has offered you the use of a small room to the rear of his home. One door, no windows, no carpet. One bullet in one pistol. You can die a gentleman, even though you never lived as one."

Before Stourbridge could decide, an older man pushed through the ever-increasing crowd at the door. "No," Lord Walpole shouted. "That's not good enough! My youngest son was one of the soldiers you had murdered in Canada." He pulled a small pistol out of his inside pocket. "I came tonight to kill Driscoll. I see now I would have been a murderer then too."

"I am sorry for your loss, My Lord," Ted said, trying to calm the distraught man. "Your boy was a fine lad."

"He did not deserve to die, not that way." Tears were streaming down Walpole's cheeks. He aimed the gun at Stourbridge. "But you do, you scum."

He pulled the trigger.

The Dowager's ball was more memorable than ever.

Six

"Come to bed, my beloved."

The vows were pronounced; Millie and the Viscount were wed.

The guests had left, the families – including Mr Armstead, who was as close as a bachelor could get to parson's mousetrap without being caught – headed back to Kent for a month or so until Ted's title was made official. Then they'd all return to London for the grand ball the new couple planned to celebrate.

The servants at Driscoll House in London were dismissed for the rest of the day and night. And maybe tomorrow too, while Lord and Lady Driscoll celebrated in private.

Millie set her hairbrush aside and smiled at Ted's reflection in the mirror. She loved how his bare skin gleamed in the firelight, how he looked so at home in the massive master bed.

For his part, Ted could not take his eyes off his beautiful bride. Her red curls crackled from the brushing as they flowed down her back. She had red curls between her legs, too. He couldn't decide which he found more appealing. He smiled again. Thank heaven he did not have to choose.

"Come, Millie mine. You've been gone far too long."

"Ten minutes?"

"A lifetime, it seems."

She smiled back and returned to the bed, to his arms. They lay together, comfortable and content for the moment. Then Millie sighed. "I cannot help worrying about poor Lord Walpole. Do you think there will be an inquest and charges brought against him?"

"I do not see why there should be. At least six men saw the pistol fire by mistake while Stourbridge was examining its design."

She sighed again. "I'm glad."

"Glad the muckworm is dead? So am I. I cannot help the twinge of sympathy I have for the poor devil though. I don't know what I would have done if you kept saying no to a hurried wedding."

"I shouldn't have, not so soon . . ."

He wrapped a long curl around his fingers, and the fingers of his other hand found the short curls. "Six months? I'd have been tempted to carry you off to my lair and ravish you."

She kissed him on the lips, the chin, then breathed into his ear. "I thought that's what you just did."

"What, are you complaining about my lovemaking, wench?"

"Not if you promise to do it again soon."

He pretended to groan. "Now who is trying to kill me?"

"With love. Only with love."

With a bit of encouragement he rose to the occasion and proved his own love with tender words and passionate kisses that led to more celebrating.

"I did not know marriage could be so . . . stirring. Will it be like this for ever, do you think, Ted?"

"Now and for ever, Red, now and for ever."

Lucky Millie. Blessed Ted.

Remember

Michèle Ann Young

London – 1820

"*She* is the widow, Madame Beauchere?" Hatred pounding in his veins, Gerard Arnfield, His Grace the Duke of Hawkworth, observed the lush woman in peacock blue on the dance floor.

Charlotte. After all this time.

But not the Charlotte he remembered.

The curvaceous form looked the same. The violet eyes and glossy chestnut tresses struck achingly familiar chords. But for the rest? Pure artifice. A neckline designed to draw the male eye to the swell of creamy breasts. The full lips promised of heaven to any man who won them, but instead led to hell.

Nothing about her rang true.

Beneath the chandeliers, her skin glowed with the translucence of a pearl. A pearl he'd once claimed, only to discover he held nothing but smoke.

Something as sharp as a knife twisted in his gut. Damn her for coming back.

"You know her?" His old friend Brian Devlin stepped back, his pale, thin face rife with curiosity.

"I know her," he said without emotion.

"Biblically speaking?" Dev looked hopeful.

Gerard allowed himself a grim smile. "For a man requesting a favour, you ask too many questions, Dev."

A brief nod acknowledged the set down. "Will you do it, though? I can't think of anyone else who could draw her off. My aunt is frantic."

"Why not?" Why not pay her back in kind for her cruelty? Although, on the one hand, he should thank her for teaching a naïve youth about the ways of women, except it would be like thanking his father for beating sense into his head.

Madame Beauchere laughed up at her partner, Dev's cousin and heir to the Graves fortune. His fair, open expression beneath its thatch of carefully coiffed sandy curls reminded Gerard of a besotted calf.

Much like the expression Gerard once had plastered on his face.

Devlin sighed. His brow furrowed. "It won't be easy. She's got her claws firmly hooked."

Seeing her so beautiful, so womanly, Gerard's anger flared anew, a blazing inferno of rage – along with lust for her delectable body. Something he hadn't expected. Something he quickly controlled, but didn't fight. Yes, he still wanted her. Only this time it would be different. This time he'd make it impossible for her to leave until *he* decided she would go. This time he would get her out of his mind and his blood entirely.

He gave his friend a cool glance. "You may bank on my success."

Dev must have heard something in his voice, because his frown deepened. "Don't tell me you have fallen for the wench."

"I don't fall, Dev," he said gently. "I fell them."

The benighted ladies of the ton had called him Axe Arnfield for years, because they fell at his feet at the snap of his fingers.

And bored him nigh unto death. At least Charlotte represented a challenge.

"Well, I hope you haven't met your match," Dev grumbled under his breath.

Once she had been his match. Now, she was simply another female to conquer and leave behind.

Gerard observed her glide sensually down the set. Graceful, alluring and utterly feminine. He could see how an impressionable youth like Graves would end up bewitched.

"I'll introduce you when the set is over," Dev said.

"No need. She'll remember."

Devlin gave him a morose glance. "My aunt will pray weekly for your soul in gratitude."

He laughed softly. "Tell her not to bother. I don't have a soul." Not where Charlotte was concerned.

Charlotte couldn't shake off the sensation of being watched. No, it wasn't quite that. She had been stared at from the moment she arrived in London, mostly by jealous females. This felt more intense and not completely unpleasant.

She let her gaze wander as her feet followed the music. As a girl, she'd loved dancing, but now it was simply a means to an end. It showed off her charms and grace, and allowed her to flirt.

There. Leaning against a pillar. A tall, exquisitely tailored man with dark-blond hair, sardonic amusement in icy blue eyes. Their gazes clashed.

Heat flared in her body, the fire of desire, even as her heart twisted in pain and her stomach plummeted to her royal-blue slippers.

Gerard. The sound of his name in her head was a cry of despair.

He acknowledged the brief meeting of their eyes with a slight dip of his head. *I dare you*, those cold eyes said. Her smile suddenly felt stiff, her cheeks tight.

Her heart rattled against her ribs while her mind absorbed this latest disaster. *Nom d'un nom*. He wasn't supposed to be in town. Her spy had promised he would not return until autumn.

His gaze drifted away.

Perhaps she'd imagined the challenge. Perhaps he hadn't recognized her after five long years. Lord, she hoped so.

Dragging her gaze back to Lord Graves as he took her hand in the centre of their four, she swallowed dry fear. Serious-faced and hazel-eyed, he was the answer to all her prayers – and Father's last hope of rescue from his dank Calais prison.

She smiled and he flushed a bright pink. She wanted to ruffle his gleaming curls, pat his shoulder. He was a nice young man. The kind of man to whom she'd be a loyal and dutiful wife. That he had more than enough money to cover father's debts made him the perfect suitor. If she could bring him up to scratch.

Worry gnawed at her stomach. Gerard was here. His presence sent her mind spinning, her heart tumbling.

The cotillion concluded and Lord Graves walked her back to Miles O'Mally, her father's loyal friend and her supposed uncle. A dandy in his youth, he was still a fine figure of a man with a penchant for flashy waistcoats. Tonight ivory brocade embroidered with pink roses hugged his paunch.

With a light laugh, she fanned her face. "So energetic. I protest, I am quite parched."

"Let me fetch you a drink," Lord Graves said eagerly.

"A true knight indeed, My Lord." She gave him a glowing smile of approval. He hurried away.

A twinge of conscience twisted her insides.

Why should she feel ashamed? She was doing exactly what the nobility had done for centuries, binding two families together for the good of both. She would be good for the feckless youth. A steadying influence. Not for a moment would he have cause to suspect her lack of emotional engagement. Never would he know the sting of betrayal. Such loyalty as she promised came at a price: her father's freedom.

She leaned close to Miles, her fan hiding her lips, her voice lowered. "He returned."

The charming Irishman's florid face frowned. "Are ye sure?"

"My dance, I believe," a rich tenor murmured behind her.

O'Mally's brown eyes widened, then his brow lowered.

Dread filling her heart, her breath held fast in her chest, Charlotte turned and faced Gerard.

The Duke took her hand. He deftly turned it over, his lips brushing the pulse point at her wrist as he bowed. Her mind went blank. Fire tingled up her arm. The searing scorch of his warm lips had taken no more than the time required to blink, yet left her trembling.

"Madame Beauchere," he murmured. "Such a delight to meet you again." The modulated voice held an underlying warning.

"I—"

"The music starts." One hand in the small of her back, the other clasping her fingers, he guided her between the guests towards the dance floor. One or two heads turned to look. Her mouth dried. This was a catastrophe.

Her gaze travelled to a pair of mocking blue eyes. "This is a waltz," she said, frowning. "I don't waltz. Ever." It always felt much too personal for her taste.

"Really?" He swirled her into his arms and on to the dance floor. He was taller than she remembered. Broader. A man, no longer a boy, and more handsome than ever.

"Despicable," she muttered.

"I beg your pardon?" His drawl shimmered and danced over the skin of her shoulders as if he'd stroked her nape, yet all the while his hands remained decorously placed.

She glared up at him. "You did that on purpose. Made it impossible for me to refuse without causing a scene. So I said 'despicable'."

His eyes warmed to cerulean and one corner of his mouth kicked up a fraction. Attraction sparked, crackling in the air like unspent lightning bolts. Incendiary. Explosive. She found it hard to draw a breath.

"I suppose I should be honoured," she said. "Although we lack a formal introduction."

"We need no introduction, Charlotte," he said with dispassion. "You knew me the moment you saw me."

He remembered. Her heart leaped with joy. Expending every ounce of will power she possessed, she kept her expression coolly remote. "I wasn't sure if my memory was playing tricks, Your Grace. You've changed."

An eyebrow rose. "We both have. You even have a different name."

"As do you. My condolences on the loss of your father."

He shrugged carelessly. "My congratulations on your marriage and my commiserations on your husband's demise."

Revulsion churned in her stomach. She hated the pretence. But having killed off a non-existent husband for the freedom widowhood gave her, there was little she could do but accept his condolences. "Thank you," she said, as calmly as her trembling body would allow.

"You are all graciousness," he said.

"And anger," she replied, arching a brow. "I never waltz."

He laughed, the sound deep and dark. It tugged at something low in her stomach. Lower. A place not to be imagined in relation to this man.

"You used to waltz with me," he said. "Remember?"

She smiled at him sweetly. "Your Grace is incorrigible."

"And you, Madame Beauchere, are beautiful."

These words delivered in honeyed tones caressed her ear. A shiver ran down her spine at the promise of remembered pleasure. An offer of delights she had once mourned.

That part of her life was over. She must not let him distract her from her purpose. Father's life depended on her ability to net a husband with money. Panic tightened her throat. The Duke could easily spike her guns should he choose. He knew too much about her past. Hell. He *was* her past.

Would he expose her? He'd been fond of her once. Might she convince him to say nothing? Dash it, she'd been prepared for the chance they would meet in the small world of the ton, but she'd prayed it would be later. *After* she married.

Forcing herself to relax, she let the music and the imperceptible pressure of his guiding hands carry her where they would. In truth, she hadn't waltzed since she was a young impressionable girl, when the world seemed a much kinder place.

"For a woman who doesn't waltz, you are very accomplished," he murmured close to her ear, sparking waves of delicious heat.

With a coolly raised brow, she let him know she was not unaware of his intent to fluster. "You misunderstand, Your Grace. I do not waltz as a preference, not because I cannot." She easily accomplished the complex turn beneath his arm. When he recaptured her hands, he gazed deep into her eyes. A licking hot blue flame of naked desire, more potent than anything she'd seen in young Graves' expression, made her gasp.

This man, this duke, had no qualms about letting his intentions be known. Her heart picked up speed. Her pulse fluttered and raced. Her indrawn breaths barely filled her lungs until she felt dizzy.

Damn her for a fool. His gaze plucked another chord. A song of longing. A tune close to her heart.

A heart required too high a price. Her father's life.

For a second, she entertained the idea of asking Gerard for help. He was rich. He'd easily parted with a few hundred guineas to be rid of her once before. Her and Father.

He would surely not aid a man he'd deliberately set on the path to destruction. Given their past, allowing even a hint of her desperation to come to his ears would be a dreadful mistake.

Whirling in his arms, she pretended not to notice his blatant ardour, while her skin tingled and her blood burned its way through her veins. She lifted her chin and regarded him dispassionately. "Are you enjoying the season, Your Grace? I haven't seen you at any other ball or rout these past few weeks."

Amusement quirked his finely drawn lips. "Keeping track of me, Charlotte? I gather you only recently arrived in town yourself."

"I am honoured someone of your exalted station noticed someone as lowly as myself." She couldn't help the tinge of bitterness in her voice, remembering his cruel words delivered so coldly by his father.

"Rare beauty never escapes my lofty attention."

The wry note in his voice surprised a chuckle from her lips. At least he was honest.

He smiled, and all at once she saw a glimpse of the boy she remembered from her youth, when he'd been bookish and kind, not the cold, hard man he'd become.

But she'd been different then, too.

Plump and awkward. So innocent in her youthful adoration. Bitterness welled.

The musicians began their final flourish. She glanced around for Graves with her promised refreshment, but found herself on the other side of the dance floor and headed for the balcony doors.

"Where are you taking me?"

"The evening is warm. I thought you might like to take the air for a moment or two." He snagged two glasses of champagne from a passing footman.

She could insist he return her to her friends. She could play the haughty widow and make a scene, but the French doors were open and other couples meandered outside in the cool air on the well-lit terrace. A moment's fresh air posed no danger.

The challenge in his gaze gave her pause. Did he mean her harm? She had to know.

Young Lord Graves would wait. She rested her gloved fingertips on the fine wool of his sleeve. "You tempt me, Your Grace."

"So I hope," he said softly.

Something inside her fluttered and stirred. Excitement. Passion. He tantalized her senses. Wickedly. More than any man she'd ever met.

But then he always had.

They passed through the balcony doors and into the soft glow of torches. He guided her down a flight of stone steps, along a pathway to a grotto lit by a single lantern on a stone frieze of nymphs by water. A fountain sparkled and glittered beside a stone bench. They were alone.

"Your Grace," she protested.

"Call me Gerard," he demanded. "It will be like old times."

Remember, her heart whispered.

"A time of youthful folly," she scoffed lightly, aware of his size, his hard male form in the softly shadowed small space. She glanced around. "How did you find this place?" She laughed. "Of course, you have been here before."

He didn't deny her accusation, but handed her a glass of champagne. His fingers, long and strong and warm, closed around hers as she grasped the stem. An intimate gesture of possession she tried to ignore.

"To us," he said softly and guided the rim to her lips. He held it there for a heartbeat, then let her go.

Absurdly, she missed his touch. She forced a sultry smile. "To you, Your Grace," and tossed the liquid off, the froth of bubbles cool and tart on her tongue. "Now, if you will excuse me, I promised Lord Graves the next dance." She made to brush by him.

His arm caught her around the waist, swung her about to face him. "I will ride with you in the morning."

She gasped. "How did—"

He laughed softly. "I hoped you hadn't changed that much." His hands captured one of hers and he lifted it to his mouth. Even through her gloves the heat in his lips scalded her flesh and curled her toes. "Tomorrow, Charlotte."

The promise held a threat. If she didn't find a way to stop him, he was going to ruin everything. Heart pounding, she turned and fled.

Gerard trotted his mount back along Hyde Park's Rotten Row. She wasn't coming. The disappointment he felt surprised him, but not her absence. Cowardly wench.

He'd thought he'd forgotten her, but the scent of her fragrance – not the perfume she wore, but her own personal essence – had been as familiar in his nostrils as his own shaving soap, and far more intense.

He patted his gelding's high-arching neck. "We'll find a way to bring her to heel, old fellow." The sound of wild galloping brought him up. A grin broke out on his face as he recognized the rider. Late then, but here. And alone. Now that was a surprise.

Perhaps not such a coward, after all.

He rode to meet her. They drew up side by side.

"The dawn is all the brighter for your presence," he said, bowing over her outstretched hand encased in York tan.

She flicked her whip. "Flirt. Don't hand me false coins, Gerard."

The sound of his name in her sweet low tones aroused his lust.

She was lucky she'd fled the grotto so swiftly the previous evening or he might have convinced her to let him engage in more than mere banter. The attraction between them had sparked and flashed like a mighty storm striving for freedom.

"A race," she said and was off, strands of her chestnut hair flying in the wind, along with the ribbons of her fetching bonnet.

He kneed his mount and gave chase. The bigger horse gained ground and he soon overtook her. He slowed to let her catch up.

Laughing, she joined him. "He's a fine animal." She ran a glance over the gelding. "Will you sell him?"

"Not for any amount of money." But there was a price he'd let *her* pay.

She pouted a little and he laughed. "Walk with me while the horses cool," he said and dismounted.

He saw the suspicion in her eyes, but grasped her around the waist and lifted her clear of her mount. He held her as a groom would, calmly, impersonal. He did not want her to startle like her skittish little mare.

He gathered the reins of both blown horses in one hand and walked by her side across the sward.

"I rarely find anyone willing to proceed at more than a trot," she said, her eyes twinkling, her cheeks blooming pink from their mad dash.

She looked lovely. As tempting as hell on a cold winter's day. He bit back a curse. "I remember the way you rode the fields around Pentridge. I always expected you to break your neck."

The breeze toyed with the loose strands about her face and she held them back with one hand, her sideways glance full of amusement and perhaps even a little misty. "You were just as bad."

He put a hand to his heart, but belied the movement with an ironic twist to his lips. "Where you led, I merely followed."

She laughed as he intended she should, but amid the light tinkling sound he heard a note in a minor key. Sadness? Regret?

Hardly likely.

"How did you know I rode here in the morning?" she asked, gazing out over the Serpentine.

"Common knowledge," he said. "But where is the trusty O'Mally?"

She shrugged. "He wonders at your reason for singling me out, when it is known you display little interest in gently bred females."

"Does he now?"

She nodded. A decisive little jerk of her pretty chin.

They walked beneath the bows of an ancient spreading oak. He stopped to look down at her. "Didn't you tell him we once were friends?"

God, it had been so much more than friendship in the end. Or at least he'd thought so, until she ran off to France with another lover.

She shivered. A small little shudder that barely shook her frame. Her violet eyes darkened, like dusk over heather-clad hills, though her lips remained sweetly curved. "Yes, we were friends when we were young." She fell silent for a moment, her eyes distant. "Remember when we found the ruined castle in the woods? You were sixteen, about to go off to school?"

"We called it Camelot," he said, his heart hammering at the recollection. "Romantic nonsense."

"You rescued me from a dragon."

She'd clung to him, terrified, when they heard the noises in the bushes.

"It was a cow."

A smile teased her lips. "And we laughed until we couldn't stand up."

"I loosed your hair and kissed you because you looked like Guinevere," he said, the pain of it stabbing his heart.

They'd made love many times after that day, but that was the first time. The sweetest time of his life. A myth. Just like their castle.

She raised her gaze and there was a hard light in the depths of her eyes. "I think Miles is right. You are a man who does nothing that does not benefit himself."

A scathing condemnation from one such as her.

He stepped in front of her, the tree at her back, the horses at his heels. He tilted her chin with his free hand. He gazed into her shadowed eyes. She met his searching look without flinching.

"Then we are alike," he said. Shielded by their horses, he dipped his head to claim her mouth. Slowly, gently, he edged her hard up against the knotted bark of the great tree. He plied her lips gently. She welcomed him in. Her avid response fired his blood. He plundered her sweet depths with his tongue, swallowing her soft cries of approval. He braced to steady her soft, pliant body as she melded against his length.

She'd made him laugh and she'd made him hunger. He would have her again.

He thrust his thigh between hers and she parted her legs. He felt her heat and her desire rise to meet his own. Breathless seconds passed in a feast of the senses.

Then her hands rose to push against his chest, hard enough to let him know she meant it.

Reluctantly, he drew back and gazed down into her slumberous eyes. "I want you," he said, his voice a low growl.

Her smile hardened. "For you, the price is high."

"Name it."

"Marriage."

The word, spoken with determination and triumph, took him aback. He curled his lip in an amusement he did not feel. He shook his head and chuckled. "Charlotte. Oh, Charlotte. You are a wicked tease."

Anger flared in her gaze. Her hand lashed out, but he caught her small-boned wrist with ease. "Let me go," she said on a quick, ragged breath.

He lowered his head and kissed the back of her hand.

She tried to tug it free with a gasp of outrage. "Release me."

He smiled down at her and she stilled. His gaze searched her face. Was this what they had become? Adversaries in games of the flesh? Apparently so. He prised open her closed fist with care and pressed a kiss to her palm, then nibbled at her bare wrist above the glove.

"Don't," she whispered. "Please."

"You used to like my kisses, remember?" he said softly against her milky skin.

She closed her eyes briefly as if he'd somehow caused her pain.

He knew her too well to believe it. "I see you have a new fly in your web. He pants like a cur after a bitch in heat."

She wrenched her hand free, her colour high. "You know nothing."

She glanced over his shoulder. Her expression changed, became distant and cool. He felt the loss of her anger as he had felt the loss of her body against him.

"Stand aside, sir," she said in chilly accents. "Here comes a true friend."

He glanced back. "Ah, the so trusty O'Mally. Is he your friend? Or another of your lovers?"

She glared at him. "My escort. Sadly, he was a few minutes late or you and I would not be having this conversation."

He couldn't prevent the surge of jealousy in her trust of the elderly dandy, but he merely bowed. "Allow me to help you mount." He brought her horse around and interlocked his fingers. She stepped up, her small hands on his shoulders, a feather-light grip. He tossed her up into the saddle, helping her settle her knee around the pommel. His fingers curled around her slim ankle encased in leather as he slipped her foot into the stirrup. When he glanced up, she was looking bemused.

He returned her gaze and with effort remembered his purpose. "I will see you this evening."

She twitched her skirts into place and gathered the reins. "No."

"You and I have unfinished business." He glanced at the tree trunk where they had just recently been pressed together.

She flushed. "Our business was finished years ago."

"I find myself unconvinced," he said, raising a brow.

She flicked her horse with her reins and left at a canter.

Gerard watched her slight figure greet O'Mally.

"Tonight, Charlotte," he promised softly to himself. "And we will both be satisfied."

His body hardened at the thought. But another sensation invaded his chest. One he'd not felt for a very long time.

An ache.

Almost midnight and still no sign of Hawkworth. She should be glad. She was glad. Desperately relieved. He would have spoiled everything and the end was almost in sight. Lord Graves was a hair's breadth from an offer.

"You waltzed with Hawkworth yesterday," Graves whined.

She resisted the urge to bat him away like an annoying gnat on a summer's eve. Shocked at the disloyal thought, she smiled at him and replied in soft tones. "His Grace did not take account of my wishes."

The young man stiffened. "If he offered you some insult—"

"Not at all." She lightly touched his arm with her fan. "It was more a misunderstanding. Tonight, I have danced three dances with you, more than with any other gentleman. To dance again would not be seemly." Unless they were married. She let the unspoken words hang in the air.

He wooed her against his family's objections and she would not provide them with the ammunition of scandalous behaviour. Meeting the Duke in the park could have been a disaster. She'd thought to talk to him as a friend, beg him to leave her in peace, until he'd shown his true colours. Lust, not friendship, drove their relationship.

And her taunt about marriage had stabbed at the heart of matters between them. A duke could not marry the daughter of a debt-ridden sot, any more than the ducal heir could have. The old duke had been brutally frank. His heir would be more than pleased to set her up as his mistress, but never as a wife. Nothing had altered in the intervening years.

Gerard was no knight on a white charger arriving to save her from her dragons.

"You will let me take you to supper," Lord Graves said, his jaw jutting. "You promised."

More whining. She contained a sigh of impatience and nodded gravely. "I am looking forward to it." It would be different when they were married. He'd be less inclined to remain underfoot. "If you will excuse me, for a moment, I have a torn flounce that needs pinning." And a headache brewing.

The darling boy looked anxious. "Hurry back. I will fetch you some champagne."

Oh how she longed for respite from his constant youthful chatter and jealous eye. Feeling as if she might at any moment die of suffocation, Charlotte fled the ballroom.

It would be fine after they wed, her mind repeated like a mantra as she hurried along the hallway to the ladies' withdrawing room. She would make him a good wife. They would retire to the country. Breed lots of children she could love. And Father would be saved.

An arm shot out from a doorway, curling around her waist and dragging her into a darkened room.

Her stomach jolted. She opened her mouth to scream, but nothing came out when a warm finger pressed against her lips and a familiar voice said, "Hush."

The scent of his bay cologne swirled around her. "Your Grace?"

"Charlotte."

He spoke her name in his deep voice. He cupped her face in his hands. "Have you forgotten my name so soon, sweet?"

The endearment tore at her heart, ripped open the wounds she thought long since healed.

She jerked her head away to no avail. "Let me go."

He sighed. "I wish I could. Say my name."

"Gerard," she spat at him, desperate for release in case she committed the error of this morning. "Let me go, before someone sees us."

He released her. Her cheeks felt suddenly chill. She stared at a face shadowed from her gaze, the shadow of her girlish dreams and the shadow of her lonely nights. "Why are you doing this?"

"This?"

"Plaguing me? Following me?" *When you never followed when I most needed you,* the broken voice whispered in her head. The voice she usually ignored. She turned away, strode to peer through the gloom at a portrait above the mantel. "Why did you drag me in here?"

The striking of a tinderbox sounded behind her. Candles flared to life, the room, a library, took shape around her as he lit the scattering of candelabra and the sconce between the bow windows.

She swung around. "Why, Gerard?"

He blew out the taper and tossed it in the empty hearth. A wicked smile touched his lips. "Did I tell you how beautiful you look tonight?"

She tossed her head. "You and a hundred others."

"You've grown cruel, Charlotte. The adulation of striplings has gone to your head."

The words were spoken lightly but they lashed like a whip. "You were the same kind of stripling once," she replied, wielding her own lash.

In three strides, he came to stand before her, his body no longer that of a boy but of a powerful male. Large and full of arrogant confidence. He gripped her shoulders, his gaze searching her face, his lips thin, his eyes hard enough to break her. "That boy is gone," he said softly and his mouth descended on hers. Ravishing. Punishing. Blissfully hot. The kiss of a bold, hungry man.

How she longed to yield, to feel again the joy, to relive their passion. Her body trembled with eagerness. Pride came to her rescue. She stiffened against his onslaught, fought for command of her traitorous body and heart.

He lifted his mouth, but didn't release her. "Why?" he murmured against her lips. "Why, Charlotte?"

She shrugged free from the circle of his arms, strode with short impatient steps to the window and shifted the edge of the drape. Outside, street lamps wavered in the mist, blurring her vision. An image of her father languishing in a French debtors' prison hardened her resolve and her voice. "Why what?"

He came up behind her. "Why did you leave?"

She spun around. Incredulous. "Why would I stay?"

His jaw flickered. "And so here you are back again, married, widowed and once more plying your wiles on a green youth."

Pain like a clenched fist in her stomach almost doubled her over. "He is a fine young man."

"And wealthy."

Heat rose to her hairline. He made it sound so sordid. She paced away from him, her silk skirts catching at her legs, her heart beating a retreat. She clenched her fists against the fear. A terrible fear she could deny him nothing. "What makes you think you can once more interfere in my affairs?"

"Affairs? A good choice of words." He gave a hard laugh. "Have you forgotten what we had together?"

An ache carved a swathe through bone and muscle all the way to her soul. "We had nothing," she cried. "And you know it." She eyed the distance to the door. If she ran . . .

He cut off her retreat with one smooth step, held her upper arms. Fury blazed in his eyes along with the hotter fire of possession.

"We had this," he growled and claimed her mouth with a plundering kiss.

Even as she began to fight, he softened his mouth, wooed her with his sensual lips, planted small kisses to the corners of her mouth, the tip of her nose, her closed eyelids.

Every inch of her face garnered his attention and her heart opened like a parched rose in the desert to a gentle rain.

Yielding, she sighed and twined her arms about his neck as her body remembered the sensations of his touch. He nuzzled her throat, kissed the pulse beneath her ear, and murmured, "I missed you."

"Oh, Gerard."

More kisses rained on her face and lips, tastes and licks remembered and yearned for over long tearful nights.

One step at a time he eased her into the window embrasure. Under the spell of his delicious mouth, she startled when the window frame touched her back. He pressed into her, his thigh parting her legs, his hands cradling her face. "Remember?" he asked.

She laughed, a poor broken sound

He closed the curtain around them. Their own private world. As if they were young and innocent again. And deeply in love.

His mouth found hers. Thought slipped away as their tongues tangled and danced to the music one heart played to the other, until dizzy and breathless she broke free. "How could I forget? It was a conservatory then, though, not a library. And your father almost caught us."

He kissed her jaw, her ear, nibbled the lobe, tasted her throat when she arched back against the wooden frame to give him access.

Her insides ran hot, like melted honey, warm and golden and sweet. His scalding breath shivered across sensitive skin, his lips teased the rise of her breast.

She ran her hands through the silk of his hair, across the breadth of shoulders more manly, stronger than she remembered.

He licked the hollow between her breasts, his long clever fingers working free the tapes of her stays at the neckline of her gown. He tugged the confining fabric down and found her nipples beaded and aching.

He suckled.

She moaned at the surge of desire. She clenched her fists in his thick wavy hair and her body tightened, remembering the bliss. Yearning.

Gently his hand trailed down her hip, caressed her thigh, and inched her skirts upwards. He stroked the bare flesh above her stockings.

"Gerard," she warned half-heartedly.

"Hush, sweet," he whispered and flicked her nipple with his tongue.

She melted.

He pushed against her with his knee and the sweet pressure made her squirm. So delectable. But not nearly enough.

"Put your leg up on the seat," he said softly. "Remember how you liked it like this?"

"Gerard, we can't. We mustn't."

He chuckled, deep and low. "Say no then, love. Say it now."

Love. Her heart stilled. How many times had he called her his love? Remember? How could she ever forget? Free will seemed to flee. She could not deny him, for to do so would be to deny all the years she'd been so alone. And lonely.

Dear sweet heaven, she'd missed him.

One large warm hand raised her thigh and she rested her foot on the window seat. One hand drew her gown languorously to her waist and cupped her buttock, steadying her, the other roved ever higher.

He took her mouth as he caressed and teased her body, until she could do no more than moan her pleasure.

"You are ready, sweet," he said. "Let me in."

She gasped her assent and raked her hands through his hair, kissing his mouth as he unbuttoned his falls. He cupped both hands beneath her and easily lifted her up. She brought her legs around his waist and clung to him. A moment later, his hard flesh sought entrance to her body.

She lowered herself on to him, with a sigh.

He groaned against her neck. "My Charlotte," he said. "Mine."

Pleasure cast her on to tossing seas where tempests raged. He held her in arms of steel, driving her, deep and hard, her spine protected from the harsh wood at her back by his hand. She was transported to another realm, a place of naught but pleasure. A place where she gave as much as she took and the bright light of completion beckoned.

A place where love reigned supreme.

His ragged breaths rasped in her ear. "Now," he demanded. "Now, darling."

She ground against him, seeking to break the bonds of earth.

He thrust into her, his hips sensually twisting.

She shattered. He came with her.

Together they drifted on the warm current of hard-breathing bliss. His forehead dropped against her shoulder. "Dear God," he muttered.

Suddenly aware of her surroundings, of what they had done, thoughts rolled around in her head, while her body stretched like a luxuriating cat's. She shifted in his arms and he carefully lowered her to her feet. He fixed his clothing, then helped her with hers, tying her tapes, hiding her bosom, rosy with his kisses.

He drew open the curtain.

The library door swung back. She couldn't see the intruder as Gerard moved in front of her, protecting her from view.

"Your Grace?" Graves' voice.

Charlotte shrank into the shadows.

"My cousin said you wanted to see me? Am I interrupting some . . ."

Gerard moved, shifting as if to shield her, but somehow failing.

"Charlotte?" Graves choked out.

Her face flamed as she met his distraught gaze. All her hopes crumbled.

"Pardon my intrusion," the young lord said, all stiff and hurt.

The library door slammed shut.

Fool. Such a fool. She'd let the memory of pleasure forgone destroy her life.

Gerard turned to face her, regret in his eyes.

"He was looking for you," she whispered. "How did he know to find you here?"

"I'm sorry." He didn't sound sorry. He sounded guilty.

She frowned. "How could he possibly know?"

He shrugged.

She had to find Graves. Find some way to explain. She ran to the mirror, saw what he had seen – her hair in disarray, her face flushed. What had she done?

She turned to leave.

The door opened to admit a thin pale gentleman. "It worked," he crowed. He halted as he realized she was still there. Lord Graves' cousin, Brian Devlin, winced. "Madame Bouchere."

She looked over at Gerard, who was frowning at him. Everything tumbled horridly into place. A pain seared her heart. "You planned this. How could you, Hawkworth? You deliberately ruined my life once, you and your father. How could I not have guessed you would do it again?"

She rushed for the door.

"Charlotte," Gerard said. "Wait."

Hand on the door handle, she paused, staring at the ornate panelling. She could not bear to turn and see the triumph in his eyes. "If you ever come near me again, I'll have O'Mally run you through."

She escaped out of the door. Something hot and wet rolled down her face. Tears. She dashed them away. It was the pain in her heart she couldn't bear. The well-remembered pain of betrayal.

Damn. Bugger. He'd made her cry. He'd hurt her. The expression on her face when she saw Graves in the doorway had been like a kick to his chest by a metal-shod carthorse.

Bloody hell. He'd been so sure she didn't care tuppence for the fellow; sure he'd be able to woo her back into his life with the one thing they'd had that was perfect. Where had he gone wrong? Doubt niggled in the pit of his stomach. What had she meant about his father? He had the unusual feeling he'd made a terrible mistake.

Dev rubbed his hands together and Gerard wanted to hit him.

"That's it, then," Dev said. "I had the hell of a time convincing him not to call you out, but he finally agreed that she wasn't protesting, and therefore she must have been willing."

Gerard shot him a glare. "What do you mean, bursting in here like that! Listen to me well. Say one word about this, you or your idiot cousin, and I'll cut out your tongues and feed them to the lions at the Tower."

"What do you take me for? The lad is hurt and a little bitter, but he'll do as he's told. Now perhaps he'll find a girl of suitable station."

Red blazed behind Gerard's eyes.

"Not that she isn't . . ." Dev began. He stared down at Gerard's fist bunching his coat. "Oh hell. What is the matter with you?"

"Nothing."

His friend's eyes widened. He groaned. "Not you too. Is the wench some sort of witch?"

"Don't be stupid." Gerard strode for the door.

"Where are you going?"

Gerard thought for a moment. A wry smile pulled at his mouth. "I'm not sure," he finally said. "Heaven or hell. But first I need to find my carriage."

"Will you not tell me what happened, dear heart?" Miles O'Mally followed Charlotte from the clothes press to the trunk she was filling.

She turned and glared. "His Grace the Duke of Hawkworth happened." She dropped the armful of clothing into the trunk.

"What did he do?"

"She put her hands on her hips and sighed. "You will find out soon enough. It will be all over London tomorrow, if it isn't already."

"Young Graves didn't come up to scratch?"

"No. And he won't. He caught me in a compromising position with the Duke."

"I'll kill him," O'Mally said. "Hang him up by his thumbs. Damn! I'll make him marry you."

"I wouldn't marry him if he was the only man in London." Not that he'd ever make her an offer. He considered her nothing but a soiled dove. "Get out of my room. I'm packing." She marched back to the clothes press.

"Where are we going?"

She stopped and took a deep breath. "Damn it, Miles. I don't know." She dropped her head and covered her eyes with her hands. She choked on a lump in her throat that refused to be swallowed. She took a few deep breaths. "There's no help for it. I'll have to accept Count Vandome's offer."

"You will not." The shock in his voice made not the slightest impression on her flayed nerves. "The man is a pervert. Old enough to be your grandfather."

"I have no choice. He'll be generous. I'm ruined here and he promised to pay Papa's debts."

"Ah, damnation." The Irishman's voice was thick with tears. Miles cried easily. Unlike her. Until last night, when the tears hadn't ceased for hours. That was yesterday. Today, she was wrung out. Dry as death.

All the starch seemed to go out of the old man, he sagged on to the edge of the bed. "Don't do it, girl. I love your father like a brother, but he's not worth a life of misery. You know he will succumb again. He can't help himself. One roll of the dice and he's lost to reason. I should never have encouraged him to go to France."

"I thought if we came back to England and lived in the country. Away from temptation . . ." But there was no hope of that now.

"Your pa doesn't deserve the sacrifice. Walk away while ye can."

"I can't." Father needed her help.

A knock sounded below.

Miles cocked a brow.

"It's probably the carter for the trunks. Go away and let me pack." A deep voice drifted up from the hallway.

"Doesn't sound like a carter. Sounds more like an argument."

Her heart sank. The only person she could think it might be was her erstwhile suitor. She'd wounded him dreadfully. He no doubt wanted an explanation. She'd have to face him. She straightened her shoulders. "It must be Graves. I'll go down."

"I'll come with you. Make sure the young hothead does nothing rash."

She worked her way around the trunks piled up on the landing. Miles followed her down the stairs.

The gentleman at the bottom of the stairs was facing away from her, but he looked too big to be Graves, too broad.

"Hawkworth." Her hands clenched into fists.

He turned. "We need to talk."

"Let me at him," Miles said. "You'll talk to the point of my sword, Duke. Or better yet, speak with the mouth of my pistol."

Hawkworth would hurt him. "No, Miles. He's done quite enough damage." She stared at Gerard's hard angular face, the bleak eyes that only seemed to warm when they rested on her. Her heart quivered. No. No, she would not let him do this to her again. "Please leave, Your Grace. You are not welcome here."

He glanced up at the baggage. "You are leaving, then."

"Of course I'm leaving. You made sure I couldn't stay. I'm going back to France. Now, go away."

"Not until you hear me out. You owe me that much."

"You dog," Miles roared.

Charlotte put out an arm to hold him back. "I owe you nothing."

"Then do it for old times' sake, love."

She froze. "Don't call me that."

"Damn it, Charlotte." He grabbed her arm and dragged her down the last couple of steps and pushed her into the drawing room.

"Blackguard," Miles yelled, hurrying after them.

Gerard closed and locked the door in the Irishman's reddened face. "You will listen," Gerard said, glaring at her.

She looked down her nose at him, then sank on to the sofa. "Very well. Speak your piece."

Gerard visibly swallowed. She'd never seen him so nervous. Not since the first time they'd . . . Heat flushed up from her belly. Oh why did she have to think of that now?

Gerard stared from her squared shoulders to her clenched jaw. The look in her eyes did not bode well for his mission. Anger rolled off her in waves. While he had scripted this play to save his friend's cousin, he no longer knew the ending.

She gazed up at him. "The great Hawkworth, having once more altered the course of my life, is now here for what purpose? To gloat?" She lowered her gaze to her hands resting in her lap and bit her lip. "I would have been a good wife to Graves. I always wanted children."

His legs felt weak. "Then why not have children with me?"

Her lips parted in shock. "With you? Never."

The old anger rose to claim him. The deep bitterness of loss. "Don't tell me you loved Graves. You don't know what love is." He couldn't restrain his bitter laugh. "And neither do I."

"You don't need to tell me that," she spat. "I know."

"You must have thought a great deal of this Beauchere fellow to leave me for him."

She stared at him blankly for a moment, then glanced away. "There is no Beauchere. There never was. I could hardly come back claiming to be a maid." She shot him a look that held more than mere loathing, it held heartbreak.

He recoiled. "Are you telling me you never married?"

"How could I marry? After we . . ." She made a small hopeless gesture with one hand. "Father is ill. He needs medical attention. Relief from his debts." The stiffness in her back flowed away. She hunched her shoulders and turned her lovely face to gaze into the empty hearth. "Gerard, why are you here? You've won. Just like before."

The defeat in the slump of her shoulders jangled every nerve in his body. Her words rang bells of alarm.

A cold feeling spread in the pit of his stomach. "What do you mean, 'just like before'?"

She looked up, her eyes hopeless. "It is over with, Gerard. Let it lie." She forced a smile. The pain in her lovely eyes knifed through the wall he'd built around his heart when she left. He wanted to gather her close, kiss away the crease in her brow, promise her the world. But he didn't dare trust her. She'd lied about loving him. He was no longer a besotted youth and he wanted the truth from her lips. "What about before?"

A horrified expression crossed her face followed by a look of pained disbelief. "You must know. You sent your father to negotiate the terms of our alliance, a carte blanche as your mistress because marriage was out of the question. When he saw Father's shock and horror, he apologised for what you'd done and offered help. He agreed to pay all of my father's debts and give him enough money to take me abroad. To hide my shame. He knew about us. What we'd done. Only you could have told him."

Bile rose in his throat. "I did not. I swear it." He put out a hand.

She waved him off. "O'Mally had brought back tales of great riches to be had in the new gambling hells in France. The money was too great a temptation to my father, even though I begged him to refuse. What influence I had no longer counted. In his eyes, I was a fallen woman. And now he is ruined and near death. You knew it would happen."

The nausea in his gut turned to icy anger. Cold fury against his autocratic father. He clenched his fists. "How could you believe I'd abandon you?"

"I didn't at first. I sent you a note, begging to see you." She got up and went to the bureau and pulled a folded paper from its depths. "You seem to have forgotten your reply."

Gerard unfolded the note and read the contents. "*The choice is yours.*" His seal, cracked and flaking, clung to the bottom.

"Brief and to the point," she said in brittle tones.

"I did not write this. The only note I received from you spoke of joining a lover in France."

Her eyes widened.

He recalled his father's glee at the news of Charlotte's departure. Followed by a litany of suitable brides. But Gerard could never bring himself up to scratch. Could never quite put on the shackles of a loveless marriage.

"Don't go," he said.

"I cannot stay. I am ruined."

The pain in her voice, the humiliation, battered his conscience. He felt physically ill. She was right. He had toyed with her, his pain making him angry, when all the time she was innocent.

His was to blame. The realization stole his breath. He should have gone looking for her instead of retreating into icy pride.

"I'm so sorry," he said softly. "Is it too late? For us? Is it possible to start anew? Marry me, Charlotte?" He held his breath as if the weight of the air in his lungs could tip the scales against him.

Charlotte stared into his beloved face. He looked different today, younger, a little less sure of himself. Less like the hard-edged nobleman she'd seen these past few days and more like the youth she'd loved.

She'd let him kiss her and make love to her, because she couldn't help the way he made her feel. But his father had taken her aside five years ago. He'd explained just what Gerard owed to his family name. The duty. The honour.

Nothing had changed. She couldn't speak for the burn in her throat and the tears behind her eyes, so she gave him a watery smile and shook her head.

"Why not?" he asked, his voice thick and strange.

"A duke cannot marry the daughter of a drink-sodden gambler who can't pay his debts. A criminal. He is in prison, Gerard."

"Your name is as good as mine. Goes back further if I'm not mistaken."

"And you are seventeenth in line to the throne."

"Nineteenth, now. Believe me, it is not a consideration in my life."

Misery rose up to claim her, leaving her numb. "It still wouldn't be right. I'm a fallen woman in the eyes of society. Your duchess must have an impeccable reputation." Another thing his father had said. "It is better if I leave. Lord Graves is a kind and generous young man. I thought I would make him a good wife and, somehow, with O'Mally's help, manage to keep Father from being too much of a burden."

"And now?"

"Graves deserves more."

"And me?"

Tears blurred her vision. "You deserve more also."

He looked at her with a gentle smile. "Dearest Charlotte, are you really going to decide what is right for everyone else – for me, for your father – and sacrifice your own happiness? Think about what *you* want for a change. Because I damned well want you. I'll take your father, and Miles O'Mally to boot, as long as I can have you at my side. But only if you want me, too."

It tempted unbearably. The thought of never seeing him again, never holding him, was tearing her apart. "You still want me as your mistress?"

Anger flared in his eyes. "No, damn it. I never wanted you as a mistress. I want you as my wife. Just as we planned. Do you think I didn't know then what your father was like? My father had lectured me to death on the matter. I didn't care then and I don't care now. It's you I want. At any price."

"Oh, Gerard." Hot tears flowed down her face. "We can't."

"My love," he said. He gathered her into his arms, drew her against his chest. "My little love."

She dissolved against him, feeling wanted, beloved and terribly weak.

"I'm so sorry," he whispered against her hair. "I had no idea what my father had done. If he wasn't already in his grave, I think I'd murder him."

She gave a little sobbing laugh, joy and heartbreak warring for ascendency.

"Charlotte, marry me. Please."

She sniffed. "After what happened in the library, they'll all think I trapped you."

He handed her his handkerchief. "They won't. There are some privileges among the burdens of a dukedom. We will be married in St George's, the Prince will attend, and no one will dare say a word. Now, I want your answer. And it better be 'yes'. We have wasted too much time."

So much time. Her heart swelled with the knowledge there was only one answer she could possibly give. "Yes. Oh, yes. Gerard, I won't let Father—"

He silenced her words with a kiss. "Hush. You and I will deal with your father together. We will have the rest of our lives to solve his problems, and wealth beyond reason."

She laughed through her tears. "Oh, I couldn't."

"But you will. I want the children you promised me. A boy who looks like you and a girl who looks like me. Remember?"

"Oh, yes, darling Gerard, I remember. Yes, please, I would like that very much."

He claimed her mouth. In the heat of passion, she forgot everything but him.

Moonlight

Carolyn Jewel

One

The Ballroom at Frieth House, The Grange, North Baslemere, Surrey, England – 3 June 1815

By the time Alec McHenry Fall, who had been the third Earl of Dane for a very short time, made his way around the ballroom, Philippa was by herself. She sat on a chair backed up against the wall, her chin tipped towards the ceiling. Her eyes were closed in an attitude of relaxation rather than – Dane hoped – prayer.

Her position exposed the slender column of her throat to anyone who might be looking, which was almost no one besides him since the room was nearly empty. Her hands lay motionless on her lap with the fingers of one hand curled around an ivory fan. The other held the corner of a fringed shawl the colour of champagne.

He continued walking, not thinking about much except that Philippa was his good friend and he was glad to have had her assistance tonight. He stepped around the detritus of a hundred people jammed inside a room that comfortably held half that number. A gentleman's glove. A bit of lace. A handkerchief. Silk flowers that had surely started the evening pinned to some young lady's hair or hem.

Dane stopped in front of her chair. "Philippa."

She straightened her head and blinked at him, her shawl draped behind her bare shoulders, exposing skin as pale as any Englishwoman could wish. Her legs were crossed at the ankles and her feet were tucked under her chair. Dane was quite sure she smiled before she knew it was him. He didn't remember her eyes being quite so remarkable a shade of green. An unusual, light green. How interesting. And yes, disturbing that he should notice any such thing about her.

He grinned and reached for her hand. He'd removed his gloves for the night, but she still wore hers. "A success, my little party, don't you think?"

A concoction of lace, ribbons and silk flowers covered the top of her strawberry-blonde hair, a fashionable colour among the young ladies of society. That he was now the sort of man who knew such things as what was fashionable among the ladies remained a source of amazement to him. He'd known Philippa his entire life. Her hair had been that shade of reddish-gold long before it was stylish.

Philippa was no girl. She was a mature woman. Thirty-one, though she could easily pass for younger. Her features were more elegant than he had remembered during the time he'd been away. The shape of her face was striking. For some reason, he was just noticing this tonight. Her smile, in his opinion, came too rarely.

"My Lord." Her eyes travelled from his head to his toes, and he quirked his eyebrows at that. She meant nothing by the perusal, after all. Another smile played about her mouth. "How dare you be so perfectly put together after dancing and entertaining all night?"

Dane knew he was in splendid form. His clothes fitted with the perfection only a London tailor achieved for a man of means. He wasn't a sheep farmer any more, except by proxy when his steward forwarded the income, and he was inordinately pleased that Philippa had noticed the change. Made him feel a proper sort of aristocrat.

"I was about to ask you the very same question." He bowed, returning her smile with one of his own.

Philippa had agreed to act as his hostess for the night because he was a twenty-five-year-old bachelor, his mother was in Bath with his eldest sister, and he was alone at Frieth House for the first time since leaving four years ago. He made a mental note to send Philippa flowers the following day. Was there even a florist in North Baslemere? Gad. He might have to send to Guildford for roses. Pink or white? he wondered. Or perhaps tulips, if they could be found?

"Flatterer." She opened her fan and waved it beneath her chin. Her eyes twinkled with amusement. He liked the sound of her voice. Definite, controlled. And yet, there was a fullness to the tone that made him wish she'd keep talking. "Do go on, My Lord."

He laughed, but that he'd said such a fatuous thing embarrassed him. He'd been in London long enough that empty words came to his lips without thought. There was no good reason for him to flatter Philippa, particularly when doing so made him look a bloody damn fool.

Was it flattery if what he'd said was true?

The only other people in the room now were servants, most of them hired by Philippa on his behalf since he no longer made Frieth House his primary home. He'd come back to North Baslemere for a number of reasons. This was his birthplace, for one, and he had deep and lasting connections here despite the changes in his life. For another, Philippa was going to remarry, and he wanted to celebrate the happy event when she and her prospective groom formally announced their news.

"Not too tired to walk a little more, I hope?" He cocked his head in the direction of the terrace door and looked at her sideways. She'd taken a great deal of care with her appearance tonight. Something he hadn't noticed before, what with the excitement of a party so perfectly managed he'd had nothing to do but enjoy himself. Pink roses! "Did I remember to compliment your appearance?" This wasn't flattery, he told himself. "If I didn't, you have permission to shoot me."

"No, Alec, I don't believe you did." These days Philippa was the only person to call him by his given name. He rather liked the informality. From her. She held out her hand, and he took it as she rose. "A breath of air would be delightful."

Now that he'd spent time in London, he saw Philippa with a more experienced eye. She was not quite beautiful, but she had something that appealed. Her looks were in no way inferior, but her confidence, her utter satisfaction with herself as she was, made her interesting for more than her face and figure. During his time away, he had learned that even perfection was tedious in a woman one did not otherwise admire.

She glanced at him, mercifully unaware of his inventory of her physical attributes. Christ. London and its courtesans had made him a lech before he was thirty. What business had he noticing her that way? Before she tucked her hand in the crook of his arm, she adjusted her shawl and in the process gave him a flash of bare shoulder. He hadn't seen her in an evening gown before, and, well, this close to her and with none of his earlier distractions, he could see her skin was perfectly smooth and white from her forehead to her bosom.

They continued to the set of double doors that led to the terrace, leaving the servants to the task of cleaning up. If it were daylight they would be able to see the roses that had been his mother's pride while she lived here, before his sisters had given their mother grandchildren upon which to dote.

"I've asked a maid to make up a room for you," he said. They were outside now and crossing the terrace. He'd also never realized she was as delicate as she was, though one also had to take into account the fact that he was a bigger man now, taller and broader through the shoulders than when he'd left North Baslemere.

"It's not so late," she said. "I'll walk home."

"Nonsense." He put his hand over hers. "I won't hear of it."

Philippa tilted her head in his direction. "I'm not sure that's wise, My Lord."

"What isn't wise?"

"My staying the night."

"Why ever not? You're family." Even before the words were out, he understood, with a disconcerting thump of his heart, what she meant. He'd thought of her as an older sister for years and years. Twenty-five years, to be exact. But she wasn't his sister. Appearances were everything, and if she stayed the night, a youthful widow in the home of a London buck, there might be unpleasant speculation.

A rather explicit image popped into his head. Him covering her, thrusting into her, while she held him tight against her naked body.

Good God. Had he gone entirely mad?

"And yet, not family." She adjusted her shawl.

"If not family, then fast friends." Dane had the oddest conviction that he'd somehow stepped out of time and that now nothing was familiar to him. Not his childhood home. Not this terrace or the garden he'd grown up with. Not even Philippa, who he admired as a friend.

"Yes," she said, tightening her hand on his arm. "We are friends, aren't we? Lifelong friends." They stopped at the furthest edge of the terrace. She took a deep breath of the night air.

Dane who, by coincidence, happened to be looking down, saw the swell of her breasts against her neckline. In his out-of-place mood, he thought of sex. With Philippa. And that sent another jolt of heat through him.

Two

Jesus. He'd gone mad. Thank God she had her eyes closed because he was still looking and thinking thoughts that ought not be in his head.

She lifted her hands towards the night sky. "It is lovely out, isn't it?"

"Yes." He clasped his hands behind his back and tried to ignore his so awkward awareness of her as a woman instead of as Philippa, who, in the pages of her letters to him, had often possessed no gender at all.

The bodice of her gown was green satin with a matching bow beneath her bosom and two wide, tasselled ribbons hanging down nearly to the hem of her white muslin skirts. Her slippers matched the green. The hue complemented her hair and eyes. As for the bare skin on display, well, in London he'd learned he was a man who admired a woman's bosom. Maybe that explained his plunge into madness. Long legs were nice, of course, but to have one's eyes and hands and mouth engaged with a woman's breasts, there was his particular notion of sensual paradise.

What he could see of Philippa's breasts was very nice.

"My Lord?"

"Mm?"

She tapped his arm with her fan. "Gathering wool, Alec?"

He tore his gaze from her chest and his thoughts from the bedroom in which he had privately ensconced them while he undressed her. She was too polite to let on if she'd noticed him leering at her like some satyr from the forest deep. "I beg your pardon." He cleared his throat. "Lost in the clouds, I suppose."

"Did I see you speaking to Captain Bancroft earlier?" The crack of her fan opening startled him.

Captain Bancroft was the man she was going to marry. "Yes," he said carefully. "We did speak."

Inside, the servants were putting out the candles and lamps that had made the ballroom blaze, so their spot on the terrace was slowly receding into darkness. She glanced towards the roses. "To think I held you in my arms when you were hardly three weeks old. I was six, and so proud to be allowed to hold the baby."

Yes, he thought with immense relief. This was exactly the direction their conversation needed to take. Talk of him in nappies and his hair all curls. "Did you ever imagine I would turn out as I have?"

She faced him, her expression serious. Composed. How had he never noticed her mouth before? Such a lovely, soft mouth. "I've loved you since that day," she said. She was so sure of herself. So certain that her opinion held weight and consequence. She was right, of course. He cared very much what she thought.

He found this confidence of hers attractive. In fact, he'd sought that very quality in the lovers he'd taken. The few there had been.

Dane was certain Philippa would be confident in his arms. She would do exactly as she wished, convinced she was entitled to her pleasure, too. God save him from women who merely accepted.

Her shawl slid off her shoulders, and she brought the ends forwards so more of the material hung from the crooks of her elbows. "I loved you as if you were my own." She tipped her head towards him. Philippa, he was quite sure, had no difficulty keeping him in his proper place. "And yes, I expected all along that you would turn out well. I never doubted for a moment."

"I did."

She cocked her head. Always so serious. "I suppose we all doubt ourselves to some degree or another, don't you think?"

"Or else we're insufferable, yes." He brought her closer to his side, and she leaned in towards him. Philippa rarely smiled, and she did not now. He wondered what he could do to change that. She lifted her chin, eyebrows arched when their gazes locked. The deep awareness in her eyes was exactly as he recalled. "I've never thought you doubted yourself," he said. "Why?"

"Oh, yes," she said, and he fancied she sounded sad. "Quite often."

"But why?" he asked in a low voice. He lifted a hand to touch her cheek, but didn't. "Why so sad, Philippa?" he whispered. "What's made you so melancholy tonight?"

She kept her torso turned towards him. His heart skipped a beat. "If I ask you a question, Alec, will you answer me honestly?"

Dane considered that. While she awaited his reply, in the distance, someone's hound bayed. He'd learned a thing or two in London. "I cannot promise you that, Philippa." Her fingers remained on his arm, and he reached over and placed his palm over the top of her hand. "There are subjects about which no gentleman should ever be frank." Somehow, that seemed the wrong thing to say. "When a lady is concerned."

Her mouth thinned. "It's London that's done this to you. Isn't it?"

He froze in fear of her remonstrance against his immodest leers. Hell, he was looking even now. She knew the inappropriate direction of his thoughts. She'd always been one to divine his thoughts. "Done what?"

She looked . . . wistful. "Made you so infernally wise." She studied him. "I felt it in your letters, you know." The edge of her mouth quirked down. "Such wisdom in a man so young."

He laughed. His amusement didn't bring a smile to her mouth and it didn't dispel his odd mood, either.

She shook her head. "I'm serious, Alec." She took a step away, almost as if she were dancing with him. Her gloved hand fell slowly to her side. They hadn't danced that night. Not even once. That seemed a pity to him now. "Your opinion matters a great deal to me."

He pulled on his cuffs, but he looked at her from under his lowered eyes. "What wisdom I have is at your disposal."

"It's about Captain Bancroft."

His heart sank. If he told her the truth, she might never forgive him. "Ask me something simpler. Please."

Her mouth curved; at last a smile. For a moment he succeeded in making her back into the Philippa he'd been writing to all these years. The older woman with a life completely separate from his own. The illusion did not last long. "What would be the good of that, My Lord?"

She turned away, facing the garden and the shadowed forms of the roses. Her shawl drooped to her waist at the back. He found himself staring at the bare skin of her neck and shoulders. Another green satin bow nestled below her shoulder blades. A tendril of her hair had loosened from the curls at the back of her head and dangled just above her nape.

He stood behind her. Close enough to touch that so pale skin. Enough that he could see the curve of her breasts. "Ask me your question, then, and I'll answer as honestly and politically as I can."

Philippa bowed her head, then faced him again. Her tongue came out and tapped her lower lip just once. Dane steadied himself. They were friends. They'd practically grown up together. There had never, in all those years, been so much as a hint of sexual attraction between them. Not once.

"I think you're my only friend." Her eyes opened wide, and she was looking at him. Really *at him*, and he knew whatever she asked, he would give her the truth. "The only one whose opinion I trust." She came close enough to rest her hand on his arm. He breathed in the scent of her perfume. "Is it not peculiar that you're the only person I can think of who understands?"

"What is it you want to ask me about Captain Bancroft?"

She sighed and for a moment looked so miserable his heart broke for her. "You met him tonight. Spoke with him for a while?"

Dane nodded.

Her eyes surveyed his face. There was really no hope of him getting out of this. She'd always been able to tell when he was lying. "What was your opinion of him?"

He steeled himself against a reaction that would betray him before he had a chance to understand why she was asking. "Answer me this first, do you love him?"

She looked away, and he put a finger to her chin and brought her face back to his. His finger had a mind of its own for it slid along the edge of her jaw from the underside of her chin to the point just beneath her ear. Such soft, soft skin.

A part of him was aware that in touching her like this he'd begun a slide into intimacy that would take them well past friendship, if he let it.

"Come now." He was aware that his touch was a lover's touch and that his voice . . . Well ... He'd spoken to lovers in just such a voice, hadn't he? "Your letters mentioned him often enough. If you love him, you don't need my opinion."

"Why not?" Her mouth firmed. "Why shouldn't I ask your opinion of the man I might marry?"

Might.

"If you feel guilty for loving a man who is not your late husband, you shouldn't."

She blinked several times, and he felt like a heel for his inappropriate reaction. He pulled his clean handkerchief from his pocket and put it into her free hand while she sniffled. "I don't know. Sometimes I think . . ."

He took his hand away from her face and, somehow, his errant fingers ended up on her shoulder. On the skin bared by her gown.

The lights in the ballroom were doused now, and he and Philippa stood in shadowed night. He stroked her shoulder and ended up following the line of her collarbone. He shouldn't be touching her, and yet he was. And she wasn't moving away. Curious.

"It is difficult to be a woman alone," she said. She gazed at him. "What was your opinion of him?" Her fingers squeezed the life out of his handkerchief. "The truth. Please."

Dane sighed. The raw truth was that he hadn't liked Captain Bancroft at all. "He struck me as reserved."

Her hand tightened around his arm. "Unvarnished truth, Alec."

God, yes. If he took her to bed, she would take what she wanted from him. For the first time since the thought had come into his head, he thought perhaps he ought to.

Philippa's gaze was steady on him. "I am a grown woman and quite capable of coming to my own conclusions whatever you say about him. You won't convince me of anything I don't already suspect."

"Very well." He ought to put more space between them. He didn't. "I thought him cold and condescending and insincere in his interactions with me."

She sighed. "He is a proud man. That is a fault of his, I know. But he admires me, and I suppose I am to be flattered by that."

"He would be mad not to admire you." There. Unvarnished truth. "It's a good match, Philippa. That's what others are saying."

"And you? What do you say?"

"That a man like him will do his duty." He wanted to help her, to make her life turn out as it should, with her safe and happy and secure. She was right – a woman alone, especially a beautiful woman like Philippa, well, there were always difficulties for a woman in her situation. "He'll look after you."

She gave a tight nod. "He's an honourable man."

"Yes."

Philippa looked at the sky as if a consultation with the moon would help her through whatever she was thinking. "Shall I make you a confession?"

He took a step closer to her. "You know you may."

"I do not admire him as I ought."

He didn't answer right away and, when he found words, they weren't the ones he'd planned to say to her. "Do you love him, Philippa?"

She walked away from the house. He went after her, stopping her with a hand to her shoulder. She halted, head bowed. In a low voice, she said, "Life is often more complicated than one wishes it to be."

Dane stood behind her, scant inches between them. He put his hands on her shoulders. "Don't marry him, Philippa," he said into the dark. "Not if you don't love him. Not if he can't make you happy."

"There's a great deal to admire in him." Her voice stayed low. "He commanded a ship of the line and was twice commended for bravery, you know."

Again he trailed his index finger along the top of her shoulder. He watched the tip of his finger moving along her skin. So soft, her skin was. "More unvarnished truth for you, Philippa." He breathed in. "I didn't like him."

More lights inside the house had been extinguished. They were now standing in full darkness, with the moon bright in a cloudless sky casting shadows on to shadows. And he was touching her as a lover might.

"I've met officers who served with him." She didn't move. No shrug to dislodge his fingers. No step away. "They were sincere in their admiration of him."

He thought of Captain Bancroft, his dreary grey eyes and the disdain that oozed from him whenever he smiled. Daring you to believe the smile when the truth was in his eyes. "He's a prig."

Philippa turned around and they gazed at each other in the dark, with moonlight and the quiet falling soft around them. The light silvered her hair and deepened the shadows beneath her collarbones and between her breasts. Her mouth twitched. "I daresay he is."

He slid his finger along the side of her throat and by now there was really no denying his caress. She didn't move. He didn't stop touching her; the rest of his fingers followed. Along the side of her jaw, the top of her cheekbone. Beneath the ripeness of her lower lip.

"I ought to marry him." She turned her head away, towards the darkness, and Dane drew a finger along the neckline of her gown and, after a moment more, he leaned in and pressed his mouth to the side of her throat, breathing in the scent of verbena that clung to her skin. After one more moment, he pulled her into his arms and kissed her.

Three

Frieth House, the Rose Garden

Philippa thought she was doing quite well, managing her conversation with Alec. He had, after all, given her his honest opinion of Captain Bancroft, and that was something. She had successfully ignored the trip in her pulse when he touched her or when their eyes met. Her reaction was not proper. They were friends. Not lovers or even potential lovers. So she had suppressed all her inconvenient admiration of his person.

And then, well, things simply went wrong. How it happened, she didn't understand. But Alec, whom she had known since he was a boy, who was still, in her mind, unconscionably young, took her in his arms and kissed her.

Not on the cheek. Or the forehead.

On the mouth.

There really wasn't any misunderstanding his intent.

She'd been thinking about kissing him for some time. And, when it happened, God save her soul, her stomach took flight.

She had a single moment of clarity during which she understood the enormity of her mistake in coming out here with him. One moment when she might have put a stop to whatever madness took her over. One moment, and all her good intentions dissolved like sugar into tea.

She was caught up, swept along by the way he wrapped his arms around her as if he had every right to, as if this was something they ought to do. As if doing so was actually a good idea. Surely it wasn't. But if he thought so, who was she to object when she was so lonely without him?

He felt delicious. Warm and strong and certain of what he was doing. And she, she didn't feel quite as alone any more.

He fitted his mouth to hers and, in her last moment of sanity and good sense, she recalled that he wasn't even twenty-six and she was six years his elder, a mature woman who ought to know better.

Alec cupped the back of her head with one hand and slid the other tighter around her waist and, for the first time in her life, she had to lift her chin in order to be properly kissed. He was taller than her husband had been, and he was kissing her increasingly as if he wanted to do more than just kiss her. Something inside her wanted that. And more.

She gave up because Alec had grown into a man, and he knew, she quickly discovered, how to kiss. She had not been held like this since William died. Until this very moment, she hadn't known how terribly she'd missed the physical intimacy, the knowledge that someone found her desirable even though she was no longer young.

Not to mention the unsettling discovery that she could be aroused by another man. She'd begun to think she would never want anyone but William. In Alec's embrace, the greyness that had enveloped her since her husband's death vanished. Her body came to life with a selfish desire to be touched, caressed, and even, Lord save her soul, to be penetrated. She was mad. She must be mad. Lulled into foolishness by the moonlight.

She wanted Alec Fall inside her, this young man who had grown up and become so much more than the handsome boy he'd been.

His mouth opened over hers, and she responded in kind. His chest was solid against hers, his arms strong, and she melted against him because he felt so good, because she missed a man's embrace. He smelled of bergamot and lemon and – oh, how lovely – he wasn't tentative at all. His tongue was in her mouth, and she wasn't sure she could support her weight on her trembling knees. She wasn't sure she wanted to.

She was aroused. Sexually. Carnally. Wickedly, thoroughly aroused for the first time in months and months. All this time, she'd been afraid Captain Bancroft would do more than kiss her cheek, to the point where she'd concluded there was something wrong with her. Alec forced her to confront the lie of that. She wanted him to do more than hold her. A very great deal more.

Somehow, she found the strength to push away. "Alec." Her mouth felt bruised, her body alive. She swallowed. "My Lord."

He kept his arms around her as if he had no doubts. "Mm?"

She closed her eyes, shivering. "You are so young."

"But not too young." He kissed the top of her cheek, just below her eye. "And not too inexperienced, I hope."

"I didn't imagine you were." There was no way on earth a man could kiss like that and be a virgin. The thought of Alec in bed with a woman shocked her into stillness. But he had been. Of course he had been. Some other woman had been his first. And there had been others after that, she was certain. He seemed to have guessed what she was thinking because his beautiful mouth curved. She tried for dignity and suspected she'd failed. "You must have been very much in demand in London."

"Oh, yes," he said, a laugh in his voice. His fingers splayed over her lower back and kept her close. "All the young gentlemen are put to stud in London."

"That isn't what I meant." The whole time, she stroked his face, tracing the outline of his mouth, the slant of his cheekbones, the soft depression just beneath his eyes. She wondered about the woman who'd been his first and imagined him touching her, kissing her body, the very first time he slid into a woman. "Was she very beautiful?"

His hand on her waist slipped to the small of her back and his fingers angled down. Tonight, of all nights, she'd worn a short corset and there was, in fact, very little material between his hand and the side of her hip. "Yes. But not as beautiful as you."

Alec kissed her again and she buried one hand in his lovely, thick dark hair, while the other clutched his shoulder. Her shawl was tangled between them with one corner dangling to her feet, which she knew because she was stepping on the end. She let her neck relax until the moment his palm supported the weight of her head, and imagined how the moonlight must be silvering her face, seeping into her blood, into the marrow of her bones.

His breath felt warm on her cheek. "Philippa."

Her name was a whisper. Soft as a petal. Calling to her in a way that made her heart feel too big for her chest. No one had whispered her name like that since William. An endearment, his whisper was. So achingly sweet. She did not release him. In such moments of inaction were momentous decisions made.

He lowered his head again, and his lips slid down her throat, trailing soft kisses. Gentle kisses. Needful kisses that brought tears to her eyes. His hand on her hip moved away, but only long enough to gather up her shawl and drape the end over her shoulder. He took a step forwards, holding her, moving them, she realized, deeper into the garden.

Philippa's eyes fluttered open and her gaze locked with his. She understood the look in his eyes, the touch of his fingertips, the reason they were now standing completely out of the circle of light from the house. If one of the servants happened to look out the window, they would not be seen.

She shivered. Not because she was cold. These feelings were wrong, but, oh, since he'd been away he'd become a lovely man. Not a boy any longer. A man, fully grown. And her friend, too. They had written to each other, holding back so little of themselves. She knew so many of his secrets, and he hers. She trusted him. She knew him to be thoughtful. Principled. A gentleman.

"Don't go home tonight," he whispered. "Stay with me. Even if only for a while, Philippa." His voice slid between them, a low, enticing whisper. In the dark, in just the light from the moon, she had to strain to see him. He wrapped his fingers in the folds of her shawl and pulled her closer.

She missed the passion of her marriage and now that this so very young man had awakened such longing in her, she wanted to say yes. She wasn't sure she could do anything but assent. Seconds ticked away.

"Christ," he said, his voice low and dark. And he sounded like a man who knew what he wanted and intended to have it. "Don't say no."

She cupped his face in her hands, leaning against his torso. "Alec, how can we?"

"The usual way," he said. "The way any man and woman do."

She shook her head then realized he probably couldn't see her. Not well enough. His cheeks were smooth, but since he was so dark-haired, he'd probably shaved before he came downstairs for the ball. Once again, she didn't step away. She didn't even let go of his face.

"Good." He kissed her again, sweetly, cajoling her, keeping her close against him, and, Lord save her, she kissed him back again. Foolish. So foolish. Even while she thought that, her hand slid around to the back of his neck, and she wished desperately she wasn't wearing gloves. She pulled back, and he drew in a quick breath.

He let go of her and dug into an interior pocket of his coat. "There's a private entrance round the back. The stairs exit directly into my room. We can go there now and see where this leads us."

"No," she whispered. She pressed her palm over his hand, trapping it in his pocket. She could salvage this. Save them both the awkwardness of a moment lost to moonlight. "No. Alec," she whispered. "I can't."

"Why?"

"I never meant for that to happen. To let you kiss me like that."

He worked his hand free of his pocket and caught her hand in his. "Lie to me if you like, but don't lie to yourself."

Good heavens, he was throwing her own words back at her. Words she'd said to him years ago whenever he said something dishonest. She took a step back and shook out her skirt. She was horribly aroused. Her body tingled with anticipation and desire. "Touché, My Lord."

"I'm sorry you lost William." He caught her other hand in his and held both hands tight. Her heart gave a twist in her chest. "I am sorry. Believe that if you believe nothing else I ever say to you. If he were still alive, I'd be happy for you." He lowered his voice. "But he isn't, Philippa. Don't live as if you'd died, too."

"I thought I had." To her horror, her voice hitched.

He pulled her into his arms again. "That's the reason you think you ought to marry that prig Bancroft, isn't it? So you won't have to love anyone again." He closed the gap between them and put his mouth by her ear. "Don't deny it."

And then, the wicked, wicked man's tongue flicked out and touched the side of her neck.

"You're wrong," she said.

"Liar."

She didn't answer.

"I'm going to strip you naked," he said. "And ask you to do a hundred sinful things to me." The rawness of his voice set off a quivering need in her. He grabbed her hand and started walking and she, who could have objected, did not, even though he wasn't heading back to the terrace.

Four

A thousand times between then and now Philippa could have objected. She didn't. And the astonishing thing was that she wasn't the least bit conflicted, even though she'd let him make the decision for her. She'd done so even though, since William's death, she'd had to take control of her life and was now well used to dealing with her own affairs and making her own decisions.

She was perfectly capable of directing the course of her life.

Philippa followed him to the back of Frieth House and stayed silent when he fitted his key to the door. For now, she resisted the urge to lay her hand on Alec's back. Instead, she imagined the warmth, the play of muscle underneath his coat she would soon feel if she were to do something so bold.

Click.

Not a moment later, they were inside with the door closed behind them, away from the moonlight and enveloped in the darkness of the stairwell. He let out a breath, low and soft as silk. They stood there by the door. Alec didn't move. He didn't give her space. She didn't make any.

"It's been too long for me," she said.

"I know."

Time stretched to eternity. She might die from the anticipation of the next moments. Her stomach took flight when he leaned in. She did the same, leaned towards him. Alec took a step forwards, she took one backwards until there wasn't any farther she could go. He kissed her there, with her head and shoulders touching the wall behind her. His kiss was slow. Tender. Thorough. She melted against him. Surrendered to him.

Of course she had. She wanted this. *This*. So fiercely. The electricity in her belly, the warmth between her legs, the ache in her breasts, the way her breath caught in her throat. His mouth on hers. The taste of him. The solidness. The maleness of him.

He planted his palms above her shoulders and pressed forwards. His torso touched hers, and she put her arms around his neck. While he kissed her and while she kissed him back, she slid the fingers of both her hands up into his hair and brought him closer.

The past with Alec was exploded and had been since the moment they'd stepped out on the terrace. Now, she thought, This is Alec, this man who is holding me with such conviction. She couldn't square this impossibility with her present condition, the heat that ran just beneath her skin, her desire to touch him, her desire to have him touch her. To do those hundred wicked things to him. And a few more besides.

They broke apart, not far, and he gripped her shoulders and rested his forehead against hers, waiting, she realized, for his breathing to settle. "I can't wait. I can't wait," he said in a low voice, "until I am inside you."

His bluntness shocked her. And aroused her. She wasn't a prude, not by any means, but William had never expressed his desire for her in such frank words. She didn't know if she ought to reply in kind and so said nothing.

Alec held her hand while he led her up the stairs. At the top, she could just make out the faint outline of the doorway. Which meant there was likely someone inside. A servant. His valet most probably. He straightened his coat and ran his fingers through his hair before he glanced at her to make sure she would be out of sight when he opened the door. She stayed to one side, out of the crescent of light that appeared on the floor and ceiling of the landing.

"Burns," he said. He walked inside. His voice receded with his advance into the room. "I won't need you tonight after all."

She listened to the murmur of a male voice and then to silence.

"Goodnight, then. I'll call you in the morning. When I'm ready."

There was another silence, and then Alec appeared in the arc of light and reached through the doorway to grab her hand and bring her inside. Into his room. "Stay here." His gaze held with hers until she nodded. As if she were capable of withdrawing now. She wasn't that strong. He reached behind her and shot the bolt home on the staircase door.

He secured the other doors, too. He'd grown up in Frieth House, and this room, the master suite, had been his father's – a fact she knew because she'd practically grown up here as the Fall family's third daughter, even though she was no relation at all.

The room had changed very little from what she remembered. Alec's father had been a man of simple tastes. Spartan, even, but kind. He'd never forgotten her if he had gifts for his own children. She'd loved him as if he'd been her real father.

The desk against the far wall was oak with a fold-out leaf presently lowered to show the drawers and cubby holes that would otherwise be hidden. In front of the desk was a plain oak chair. In the corner, there was a washstand with a white and blue basin and ewer, a towel nearby. The red highboy and armoire with an uncarved door were familiar sights. A tassel hung from the key still in the armoire lock. The bed was plain: no high posts, no canopy or hangings.

Frieth House was Tudor and, like the previous Falls, Alec's father had modernized very little. The walls and ceiling were square panels of carved mahogany. The wide plank floor was covered with a carpet that had probably been in place for a hundred years.

Despite how little had changed since the last time Philippa had seen the room, there were signs everywhere of Alec's imprimatur. Books on the desk, for example, one of them still open. Alec had always been an avid reader. At the foot of the bed was a black trunk with the coronet of his earldom painted on it in gold and silver, red and blue, with an occasional splash of yellow. A decanter of brandy sat on a table, a crystal tumbler next to it.

She walked to the centre of the room just as Alec came back from locking the last door. He headed to where she stood and stopped too close to her for a man who was only a friend. Too close for safety. Not close enough for a lover.

Her stomach fluttered. Alec seemed at once ineffably familiar and a complete stranger to her. The boy she'd known her entire life, the young gentleman with whom she had exchanged frank and even intimate letters, and this handsome, unknowable man whose touch made her feel alive.

"You haven't changed your mind, have you?" he asked.

She shook her head.

"Good."

In all the time she'd known him, not once had she seen him the way she did now. As a desirable man. A man of substance and weight, of a surprising gravitas considering his age. She studied him, trying to understand what had changed. However long she looked, she didn't think she'd ever know. Her eyes saw a man now. A man she desired.

His irises were nearly black and his lashes were a thick, dark sweep across his cheeks. His father lived on in the angles of his face, the length of his nose, the distance between his eyes. The shape of his mouth was his mother. Sensitive, his lower lip slightly fuller than the upper. There was a dimple in his chin. She very much wanted to make love to him. To Alec.

"Lovely Philippa." He pushed her shawl off her shoulders, catching it at the crooks of her elbows and pulling the cashmere away to drape over the desk chair. His touch, light as it was, sent a quiver through her body. "I can hardly believe you're here." He took her right hand and worked her glove off her fingers. "That it's you," he said as he did this. He drew her glove off her arm and glanced at her before he went to work on the other one. He took the fan dangling from her wrist and set that on the trunk. When he drew off her other glove, she pulled her hand back. His gaze met hers and desire roared through her.

He dropped her gloves on top of the trunk with her fan. A smile quirked his mouth, and she was reminded of the boy he'd been. His smile had always been infectious. The man before her had no hesitations about what he was doing. "You anticipate me wonderfully well."

"I am relieved, My Lord."

He reached for her left hand. Their bare skin touched. Hand to hand. The tips of his fingers slid over hers, once, slowly, over the wedding ring she still wore. "Do you miss him?"

"Yes." She spoke over the lump in her throat.

"I miss him, too. His letters." He slipped his arms around her waist and, as he pulled her close, he made a low sound in the back of his throat. Because he was a young and healthy man. Because he desired her.

The tension in her eased. She put her hands on his chest and slid them down to the first button of his coat. Her wedding band glittered on her finger. She unfastened the button.

His eyelids closed part-way. "Mm. What wickedness is this?"

"Wickedness?" She darted a look at him before she started on the next button. "You are in your private quarters, My Lord. Surely you can be comfortable here without thinking yourself wicked."

"Perhaps you're right." He shrugged off his coat when she was done, but her hands followed the collar until the fine wool was sliding past his shoulders and down his arms until she could reach no further. He leaned away to drop his coat on the chair.

"I think, Philippa, that I am still not as comfortable as I might be. Tell me, what ought we to do about that?"

She couldn't help smiling. His waistcoat soon joined his coat. And there he stood, in his trousers, shirt and braces, and he was simply too beautiful for words.

"It strikes me," he said, still smiling that familiar smile of his, "that you must be uncomfortable, too. And here—" he gave a quick look around "—I think we may both be as comfortable as we like."

Philippa held up her hands. "I've already removed my gloves. And my shawl."

"Very bold." He ran his index fingers from the tops of her shoulders downwards, along the neckline of her gown. "But I worry that this lovely gown of yours restricts you too much to be at ease. Does it?"

"Perhaps you're right, My Lord."

"Mm," he said. He moved behind her and began unfastening the hooks and ties of her gown. Before long, he was lowering the dress and she stepped out of her best evening gown. Her corset was next. Then petticoat. When he was done, he set his hands on her shoulders and his mouth by her ear to whisper, "Is that better?"

She could only nod. She was now wearing only her shift and, of course, her dancing slippers and stockings. Alec stayed behind her and put his hands around her waist. She dissolved against his chest.

"What a slender woman you are, Philippa."

"Does that disappoint you?"

"No." His hands slid up, his fingers slanted towards the floor. His hands stopped just beneath her bosom. She held her breath, longing for him to touch her yet enjoying the building warmth. She was liquid inside, a pool of desire when she'd once thought she was no longer capable of that sort of reaction.

His fingers brushed the bottom curve of her breasts.

Philippa faced him. He was looking at her as if he wanted to eat her alive. She pushed his braces off his shoulders. Alex shrugged, and they fell to his sides. She undid his neckcloth, then the buttons on the placket of his shirt. He reached between them and pulled it over his head, turning a little to let it drop away from where they stood.

"What a splendid animal you are," she whispered. "So sleek. So well made." His body was the product of youthful vigour and lack of indolence. She touched his chest, sliding a finger over his nipple.

"More," he said on an intake of breath. He cupped the back of her neck and drew her towards him. She kissed him there, flicking her tongue over his nipple. One, then the other.

He gathered handfuls of her shift, and drew it up and over her head. She stood before Alec wearing nothing but her shoes and stockings. He stayed completely still, eyes on her body, lingering on her breasts. "So lovely."

With her eyes on his, she touched her breasts. The effect on him was gratifying. The wide-open eyes, the swift intake of breath. "Your hands," she said, "need to be here."

His attention fixed on her hands, on her fingers. He took a step forwards and his hands came between them, one then the other, pushing away hers. And then his fingers covered her and she pressed forwards and raised her face to the ceiling, eyes closed because she didn't think she could look at him and keep back the tears at the same time. She knew him so well. He would never do anything to hurt her.

"Like this?" he whispered.

"Yes."

"Tell me what you want."

Slowly, she lowered her head and, when she opened her eyes, he was looking at her with that same reverence that made her throat close up. "To feel." She covered his hands with hers. "To be alive the way I am right now. Like this."

Alec swept her up in his arms and carried her the ten steps to the bed. He spread himself over her, one hand above her shoulder, letting the weight of his hips press against her pelvis. His hair fell over his forehead and his lashes were black against his cheeks. He was looking at her body, her breasts, her stomach. He stroked his hand down her body, from her shoulders to her back and toes. "Jesus, Philippa. You're so lovely."

"The lights," she said.

He looked up. "What of them?"

"Don't you mean to turn them down?"

"No," he said. "I don't." He curled a hand around her upper thigh, pulling up so that her knee bent and his palm spread flat around the back of her leg. His other arm bore his weight and when she set her fingertips to his upper arm, she traced the shape of the muscles. "I want to see you. I want to put my mouth places that will make you scream my name, and I want to watch when you come apart in my arms."

Alec dropped his head and then his mouth was on her breast, his weight a little heavier on her now. She twined her legs around his, arching into the pressure of his mouth. Her body felt too full, the sensations too intense to bear. His fingers pulled at her garter and, after fumbling a bit, released one to slide her stocking down her leg. When he'd done that, he shifted his weight to his other arm and his mouth to her other breast. Her other garter was soon gone, her slipper and stocking tossed off the bed. She heard the sound of her shoe hitting the floor.

She moaned when he pulled away. "No," she said. "Stay."

"I want to look at you." His voice sounded thick and, when she managed to open her eyes, he was doing exactly that – kneeling between her legs, pushing her bent knees apart. "Does this make you feel alive? Tell me."

"Oh, yes," she said on a breath.

He kissed his way down her stomach, to her belly and then his mouth was between her legs and she simply hadn't expected he would be willing to do such a thing. He wrung her out. Completely and utterly.

Philippa let her body vanish into her arousal, the cresting pleasure and the damnable way he would bring her to the edge of climax and then stop.

She lost her mind.

"Alec." Her body bowed off the bed. His name was a groan, a long low note of all the pleasure that wound her body tighter and tighter. The silvery tremble of her approaching climax filled her. "Now."

She shouted, and she didn't care at all what he'd think of that. The spiral of pleasure peaked and she fell and fell and fell. When she came back to her body, he'd pulled himself over her and was grinning at her.

"Good?" His mouth twitched.

She touched his back with her fingertips, drawing them down the sides of his spine as far as she could reach. Until she touched his trousers. "You are still dressed," she said when she could trust herself to speak. "Why is that?"

"An excellent question." He pushed away to sit on the edge of the mattress. She turned on to her side, watching him. Her marriage had been a passionate one, but William had never displayed himself in this unselfconscious, uninhibited way. Her husband had come to her room at night, and never without letting her know that he would. In the dark, he slid between the covers with her, and they made love with tender quietness.

Alec's skin fitted close to his body. When he moved, his muscles flexed and bulged. He wasn't slender like William had been. She touched the top of his spine.

"Look at you," she whispered.

He turned his head towards her while he was pulling off one shoe. He smiled. "I'd rather look at you."

"What is it you do that keeps you in such health?" She moved behind him, knelt and slipped her hands around his waist.

"Boxing." He dropped his other shoe and reached for the sagging waist of his trousers. As he pushed them off along with his small clothes, his erection was free to the air and her sight.

He was naked at last. Gloriously, splendidly naked. She reached around and touched his hardness. Alec tensed. He reached to curl his palms around the backs of her arms. With a moan, he let his head fall against her shoulder. He put one heel on the mattress, letting his thigh fall open. "Philippa, yes. More of that, too."

His skin was warm, and she held him like this, stroking him, touching him until, all in one motion, he slid an arm around her and then covered her with his body.

Five

Dane was aroused beyond anything, but there was something more he was feeling, and he wasn't sure what it was, other than it had to do with Philippa. Obviously. And then, perhaps not so obviously.

"Have I told you how beautiful you are?" he said. "How perfect? Exquisite?"

He dipped his head to kiss her shoulder. At this exact moment he elected to think more about the curves of her body, the shape of her breasts, the texture of her skin, than his emotional state. He'd made love often enough without his heart being involved at all. This was different. She was Philippa, and she took his breath.

Philippa set her hands on his shoulders, her palms curving over on to his back. Her eyes were closed, her mouth parted. He shifted himself into place, and she knew exactly what it meant that he nudged aside her thighs. He knew what it meant that her hips shifted underneath him, that inviting tilt of her pelvis, the slight bend of her knees.

"Now?" he whispered. He was grateful to sound both calm and amorous when in fact he was hardly anything of the first and the second was a trite description of the emotion that made his chest tight. He hadn't ever *needed* a woman the way he needed to possess Philippa, and that frightened him.

She slid her hands along his sides to his hips. Her fingers dipped in and out of the small of his back and then around to cup his backside. Every caress of her hands made him harder yet. "Yes, Alec," she said. "Please. Now."

Her hands urged him forwards, and he slid inside her. He almost lost his mind. This moment, this moment was purely about sensation, but there was also the sound of her slow intake of breath, which shook him to his core. It enchanted him that she would make a sound like that.

He wanted – no, needed – her to find pleasure in his arms. He needed to see to her every satisfaction. He needed everything to be perfect. And then he just wanted to keep doing this, because this felt so good. She felt so good. His Philippa.

Dane groaned as the warmth of her body enveloped him. This was Philippa who was sending him crashing over the edge. She wasn't passively accepting him, something he'd worried might happen. She raised her knees so that her thighs slid up to his hips, and she rocked her pelvis into his. They were naked, both of them, and what they were doing was more than fucking. The quiver of incipient orgasm pooled at the base of his spine.

Since the moment this evening when he'd realized there was more than an intellectual spark between them, something physical that hadn't existed before, he'd been anticipating this moment. He sank down, pressing his forearms to the mattress above her shoulders. Her breasts were warm against his chest, her hips matched the rolling, rocking motion of his, her body utterly feminine, soft where he was hard, curved exactly so.

"Alec." Her voice was low and smooth, and she made him feel like he was the only man ever to satisfy her.

He wasn't so far gone that he didn't recognize the carnal element of this encounter, but he understood for the first time in his life the difference between taking a woman to bed for the physical pleasure alone and what he was doing at that moment. To be honest, he was worried about what that meant; knowing he was making love to Philippa and that she might not be making love to him.

He said, "Look at me, Philippa."

She did and he could see the faraway look in her eyes. He panicked at what that signified. She might not feel as he did. For Christ's sake, she was going to marry bloody Captain Bancroft. He fell into her eyes, into those green depths, and he knew himself and her well enough to understand he wasn't going to come away from this intact.

He thrust again and again, and she held him and matched him. He kept remembering all the times he'd seen her, talked to her, laughed with her or simply sat at her side without needing to say anything. Or sat alone in his London apartments reading or rereading one of her letters or writing one to her. Never once had he thought she was someone he could have. Not once had he thought she was the woman he was destined to love. All this time, he hadn't known. He'd never guessed.

Why hadn't he?

He pulled out and turned her over, and she understood right away what he wanted because she went to her hands and knees. God, yes.

Dane cupped her hips, and he shouted when he was inside her again, because it was even better this time than the first. They were close to the head of the bed, and he shifted them again until she had her hands on the wall above the bed frame. He was on his knees behind her, one hand holding her breast, the other around her hips with his fingers between her legs, making sure she came to climax.

Her response was, quite soon, a long, low moan. He kissed the back of her neck, moving inside her, and felt the tremor of her impending orgasm around him. He stopped.

"Alec." His name was a sob of frustration.

He held her tight, not moving. "What?" he whispered. "What do you want?"

"Finish me."

"Finish you. I'm not sure what you mean."

"You do," she said. She turned her head to him as far as she could.

"Like this?" He slid out of her almost all the way and pushed back in slowly.

"Harder."

"This?" A little harder, this time.

"More." She pushed her hips back.

"Like this, then?" Again. When he was inside her this time she came and, Jesus, he'd never felt anything like it. She called his name and what he heard was Philippa's voice. Philippa. The woman who knew him best. Who was kind and generous and thoughtful and who had always been able to make him laugh, to whom he had confessed some of his most intimate thoughts and concerns. What if she didn't feel the same?

Something inside him broke. He felt the strings of his heart vibrating with the power of what he felt for her. He wasn't the same man as when this had started.

He put her on her back again. He was trying to just fuck her but he couldn't. He was rough, but she met that without reservation. She gave him back even more until he was the one rushing to orgasm.

Moments before his crisis, with his body quivering on the edge of release, he gritted his teeth and, his heart pounding at his chest as if it would break through his ribs, it occurred to him that Philippa was not a courtesan whom he could expect to have taken precautions or who had the resources to act if there were consequences.

He stopped moving in her. When he was certain the danger had passed, he grabbed her face between his hands. Philippa pressed the back of her head into the mattress. "Alec." She wrapped her arms around him and groaned. "This is unfair of you. What are you doing to me?"

"Look at me," he said.

Her eyes flickered open and slowly focused on him.

He swept his thumbs along her temples. "Philippa." He kissed her forehead, and he couldn't help himself, he pressed further into her. Then he dropped a kiss on both her cheeks.

"What is it?" she asked. She reached to brush his hair off his forehead. "What's made you look like your heart is breaking?"

"Only you would know that."

"What is it, my darling Alec?"

Panic constricted his chest when he saw her eyes widen. He had himself in better control now. "You'll think I'm mad, but I'm not. And you know me. You know I'm not the kind of man who would put a lover at risk. I will not put you at risk of a child out of wedlock." He kissed the edge of her mouth. "Never."

Her eyes went wide. "Hush, my darling. It's all right. You can withdraw, isn't that so?"

He started moving in her again. "I could, Philippa." Very quickly, he was near the edge again, and she sucked in a hard, fast breath when he was as far inside her as he could get. "I will if that's what you want." Her eyes never left his face, which gave him hope. "You know I wouldn't ask that of you if I didn't mean every word. We're here, Philippa. Like this." He stared into her face. "You wouldn't be if you didn't love me."

He pushed up on his hands again, still inside her. Her fingers curled around his arms, and she matched him, moved with him, wrapped her legs around him. But he did not see any answer in her face, and he did not intend to take silence for consent.

"You can't marry Bancroft when we feel like this together. Not when I've made you scream my name, and I'm about to scream yours."

She put her arms around his shoulders and held him tight. Her eyes glittered with tears. But she was looking at him. "Alec."

"Say yes, Philippa." He thrust a little faster now and, when he spoke again, his words were breathless. "I'm very close. Answer me now, before we have to stop this." He felt his orgasm coming on, but he kept his eyes on her face. His heart twisted in his chest. He bent his head to kiss away a tear that escaped when she blinked.

She brought him closer yet. "Come, Alec."

"Is that yes?" He stared into her eyes, wet with tears, and didn't know the cause.

"It's madness. The moonlight made us mad."

He stilled. "Answer me, Philippa." His gaze locked with hers. "Don't make me live without you. Don't make me spend the rest of my life bereft of you."

She closed her eyes and opened them slowly, and then she smiled. "Yes."

"Jesus." He surged forwards.

Neither of them said anything more. Philippa made a tiny sound in the back of her throat as he gave in to all the physical sensations coming at him. He gave in to the emotions, too. He knew, dimly, that he was unlikely to get a child on her this time, but he still thought of how he would feel when he held his first child in his arms, by the woman he loved beyond all others.

Her sweat-slick body moved with his, her arms tightened around him and she kissed his cheek, his mouth. She let her head fall back while he drank in her face, her parted lips, until he had no choice but to give in to a climax that shook him hard and rolled him through a wave he wasn't sure he was going to survive.

He did, of course. As did Philippa.

They were married by special licence a week later by the vicar in a small ceremony in the rose garden of Frieth House. If anyone in attendance wondered why the bride and groom vanished through a blue door at the rear of the house at the end of the ceremony, no one said a word.

An Invitation To Scandal

Lorraine Heath

London – 1820

> *Your presence is requested for a private dinner at midnight at*
> *the home of Miss Arianna Vernon. A carriage will be sent at half*
> *past ten.*

Sitting in his library, which had once housed hundreds of books
and now sported only empty shelves, Nicholas Wynter, the Earl of
Harteley, squinted at the words inscribed on the invitation that had
been delivered by a dark-haired lad barely out of short pants. He
had hammered at the door until Harteley had been given no choice
except to answer in order to stop the sound from echoing through the
hollow hallways. He had few possessions left to absorb the impact of
noise. Even his own footsteps had begun to grate on his nerves and
slice into the dull ache in his head that constantly accompanied him
as he sought to finish off what remained of his father's fine spirits.

The cheeky little bugger, dressed in purple livery that looked as
though it had been newly stitched, had curled up his lip in disgust,
obviously mistaking Harteley for a maggot rather than a recently
anointed lord. Harteley's black hair had grown unfashionably long
and he'd not shaved in three days. With no servants to tend to his
needs, he saw little point in maintaining appearances while in residence. He'd discarded his jacket and unbuttoned his waistcoat.

"Give this to yer master immediately," the lad had ordered,
extending the invitation.

Harteley had merely laughed and begun closing the door. The
boy had blocked his actions by placing his foot, protected by a well-
made boot, in the doorway. It irked that this urchin appeared more
aristocratic than Harteley, that he possessed confidence and didn't
cower from his task.

"It's me mistress' business. It's important." He'd shoved the invitation and a crown into Harteley's hand. "Fer yer trouble."

That had stopped Harteley's laughter with such force that he'd nearly choked, stopped it because his fingers had closed around the coin as a drowning man might latch on to a rope tossed his way. He'd watched the lad scamper to a waiting coach and leap up to take his position at its rear, thought he'd seen a curtain at the window billow slightly before the driver had urged on the matching greys.

Now Harteley slowly savoured his whisky and wondered who the deuce was Miss Arianna Vernon. Such an unusual name. Not one he'd easily forget. But forget it he had – if he'd ever known it. He tapped the gilded invitation against his tan-clad thigh. It wasn't uncommon for women to seek his company, but never was it handled so formally.

A woman who began a dalliance with an invitation would no doubt be cold in bed. Probably the reason she sought him out. He had a reputation for melting the most solid of ice. He actually enjoyed it, took pride in his prowess. He had little enough to offer the world.

But of late, he'd grown bored. Women were too easy. Everything had become too easy – except survival and maintaining the last shreds of his dignity. It had been almost a year since he'd inherited the title and the crumbling estate that came with it. He wasn't certain how much longer he could retain the London residence. The debt collectors were knocking on his door with as much determination as had the lad with the invitation.

Through the blur of too much liquor, he again read the words. When the true state of his affairs became known – and it was becoming increasingly difficult to keep them hidden – women would no doubt scorn and avoid him. He might as well take advantage while he still had the opportunity.

The coach arrived promptly at half past ten. Harteley had bathed, shaved and donned his most flattering clothes: blue tailcoat, white shirt, white cravat, white silk waistcoat, black trousers. Oddly he felt more himself than he had in days.

The lad had once again accompanied the coach. He didn't seem surprised to discover that Harteley was the master of the house, although he did smirk.

"Have you a name?" Harteley asked, as he followed the boy to the coach where a taller and older footman opened the door.

"Jimmy," the lad responded, just before his dark eyes widened as Harteley flipped him the crown.

"For your trouble."

The lad tipped his hat. "Thanks, milord." And he scrambled on to the back of the coach.

Harteley settled on the plush bench. He recognized good crafts-manship when he saw it. Miss Vernon was exceedingly well off. The horses lurched forwards, and he had to admit it was perhaps the smoothest riding coach in which he'd ever had the pleasure to travel. He was becoming more intrigued with the mysterious Arianna Vernon. Tonight promised to be anything but dull.

He was surprised to discover that her residence was located beyond London, hidden away behind wrought iron and towering elms. The driver and horses must have known the path well, for they barely slowed as they turned off the main road. Yet no torches lit the narrow dirt trail they travelled. Even with a full moon, little was visible before the mansion came into view.

It was as grand, if not grander, than the one Harteley had inherited. Even from a distance, it was evident that it required no repairs. Here, torches flickered to reveal the magnificent estate. In the moonlight, the lawn appeared immaculately groomed.

As soon as the coach rolled to a stop, a footman was opening the door. Harteley disembarked, his curiosity piqued. This could not be the residence of an unmarried lady, even if she did refer to herself as "Miss". She was either married and in want of an affair, or her father was off tending to business and she was taking advantage. Then another thought occurred to him: perhaps she was an aging spinster, in want of a bit of fun while she was still able to enjoy it. He wasn't bothered by the possibility. In the dark, the particulars of a woman were left to a man's imagination. And he'd always possessed a grand imagination.

"If you'll come along with me, milord," the footman said.

He followed the footman up the steps and into the impressive manor. He had an eye for the finer things, and this home was filled with them: marble floors, candles flickering in crystal chandeliers, well-made furni-ture, statues, flower-filled vases, paintings created by the masters.

A butler stepped forwards and bowed slightly. "Milord, the mistress awaits you in the morning room."

The morning room. Not the bedchamber. Was it possible that she truly was interested in only sharing dinner? He suspected not. She no doubt wanted to be charmed out of her clothing. While he'd begun the adventure with a bit of scepticism, he found he was suddenly very interested in this woman of mystery.

As the butler led the way down the wide hallways, Harteley took in his surroundings. Everything was perfection, nothing was over-looked. Yet he couldn't help but feel that the elaborate surroundings were all for show, as though someone were striving to be impressive, to deflect interest away from something else. Considering what he'd inherited, he could certainly understand that desire. He'd held on to artwork as long as possible simply because it allowed him to feel civilized. As he'd been forced to sell each piece, so he'd felt as though he were whittling away at the core of who he was. He'd always known his place resided in the upper echelons. Falling from it was a painful and belittling process.

He had moments where he despised his father for his gambling habits, for his preference for selfish pleasures. But then Harteley was not so very different. It was the very reason he'd accepted the invitation. For a night of expected pleasure.

Another footman – good Lord, how many servants did she possess? – opened a door and the butler ushered Harteley inside. One wall and a portion of the ceiling were all glass. Moonlight whispered inside to shimmer along the figure standing near the far windowed corner. Her back was to him, but he was struck by the paleness of her hair, which rivalled the moon. It was caught up in a simple style that revealed the long, slender slope of her neck. He decided he would kiss her nape first and then trail his mouth along her delicate shoulders.

"Miss Vernon," the butler said, reminding Harteley he was not yet alone with her, "Lord Harteley has arrived."

She turned from her observation of the gardens, and he nearly stepped back from the unexpected beauty of her. And her youth. She was far too young for a man as jaded as he. Yet he could not deny the appeal of her innocence or the desire to regain his youth that swept through him. She reminded him of an earlier time when his life was filled with choices – and he'd chosen poorly. Why of a sudden these bothersome reminiscences when he'd astutely avoided them for years? Something about her was familiar. The high cheekbones, the delicate chin. He knew her, but from where?

"My Lord." Her voice was that of a nightingale and so enthralled him that he almost didn't notice her curtsey.

He couldn't recall ever being so mesmerized. He bowed. "Miss Vernon. Tell me, have our paths crossed before?"

"We've not been introduced."

Which was not exactly a proper answer to his question. "You remind me of someone."

"Do I? Who?"

He shook his head. "I'm not quite sure."

She released a slight laugh. "Well, when you remember, I do hope you will share." She indicated a round lace-covered table at the other end of the windows. "Please, let us not delay. Dinner awaits."

"You're very young, Miss Vernon."

She was only momentarily flummoxed by his seemingly random statement. "Two and twenty," she responded with her chin angled high. She possessed a great deal of pride. Perhaps as much as he once had.

"And I am not so young," he pointed out, rather unnecessarily.

"Two and thirty."

He fought not to reveal how it bothered him that she would know his age. It was a small thing, no secret, but he sensed she knew quite a bit more than that. Her next words confirmed it.

"Don't look so surprised, My Lord. I know a great deal about you."

"Then you must also know that I prefer women of experience."

He recognized disappointment in her expression, and it made him feel like a cad. It had been a good long while since he'd given any care to another's sentiments. Why did he care about hers?

"You are quite presumptuous, My Lord, to think my invitation included anything more than dinner."

"The hour is late, Miss Vernon. A certain amount of secrecy accompanied my arrival here. It has all the makings of a clandestine meeting."

She acquiesced with a slight nod. "I'd not expected you to object."

"Then I have correctly discerned your purpose in sending for me."

"Hardly. You see, My Lord, I am in need of a champion."

Arianna could barely suppress her disappointment. He didn't remember her. Not that she'd truly expected him to. It had been ten years. And she'd been a child. All of twelve. While he'd been a young man searching for an evening's delight. He'd spoken to her only in passing, but it was enough to win her heart.

He'd been so dashing, so joyful, so handsome. Tonight he was less so on two counts. Still handsome, he now possessed a weariness. While they sat at the table as her butler, Jones, directed the servants who were arranging their dinner, she had an uncanny urge to reach across and massage the furrows from Harteley's brow. His hair was the black of a moonless night, his eyes the blue of sapphires, rich and deep. Through the years, it had become her favourite gem because it reminded her of him.

If she lived to be a hundred, she'd never forget sitting on the stairs, waiting for her mother to finish with business so they could go to the theatre. He'd been on his way up, following a tart named Satin when he'd spotted Arianna and smiled. The wide grin, so white in the dark face that spoke of a man who possessed a preference for the outdoors, had caused her childish heart to gallop wildly in her chest.

"You're a bit young for this establishment, aren't you, poppet?" he'd asked.

She'd been so taken with him that her voice had refused to work. He'd laughed. A soft laugh, a comforting sound, as though he understood why she was so flummoxed. She amused him. Even then, she'd had little doubt that he was accustomed to attracting the attentions of the ladies, that he knew he was too handsome for his own good. He'd cast his spell over her.

"Come along, milord," Satin had urged, rubbing her silk-clad body against his.

That was all it had taken for Arianna to lose his attention. She was determined not to lose it now.

"I'm hardly the champion sort," he finally grumbled, after the servants left and Jones took his place across the room, in front of the door. She knew her butler didn't favour her plan, and that he wouldn't leave her alone with a man "the likes of Lord Harteley".

"I believe you underestimate yourself."

"I know myself very well, Miss Vernon."

She watched as he wrapped long, tapered fingers around the bowl of his wine glass. That hand possessed strength, and she knew with little enough effort, he could crush the crystal. But instead he held it with a feigned gentleness. She could see in his eyes that he was not happy with this turn of events. He'd expected something quite different from her invitation. But then she'd known he would. It was the reason she'd sent it. The reason she'd not doubted that he'd come here tonight.

She knew a great deal about Nicholas Wynter, Lord Harteley. Her mother had kept accounts on every man who had frequented her establishment. Arianna had scoured them searching for any clues regarding her father. While her endeavours had proved fruitless in that regard, she had been rewarded with bits and pieces about Lord Harteley. An overwhelming relief had taken hold when she realized that he'd never once bedded the infamous Jewel.

She watched now as Harteley savoured his wine while glancing around.

"You are obviously a lady of means," he said quietly. He pinned her with his blue gaze. "How did you acquire your wealth?"

"My mother. She is responsible for all of this. I grew up here with nannies, and governesses, and tutors."

"And what of your father?" he asked, but she detected no curiosity in his tone.

A portion of the truth would have to be revealed now, and he would come to understand the formidable task she placed before him. "I have only the foggiest notion as to who he might be."

And then only if he'd been one of her mother's numerous paramours or gentleman callers. It was quite possible he'd held a special place in her heart and she'd never noted his name in her records. It was also possible that he was someone of whom she'd been incredibly ashamed and so she'd never written out his name.

A true gentleman, Harteley didn't bring the question to his lips, but his unwavering gaze asked it just as loudly.

"They were never married," she admitted.

She saw understanding enter the depths of his blue eyes. "So by champion . . . you seek a protector. I fear you have misjudged me. I have not the means to take or provide for a mistress – not that I don't find you beautiful and utterly charming—"

"I care little how you find me, My Lord." Lie. She cared deeply. She wanted him to be infatuated, to want her as she wanted him. "It is not a protector I seek, but a husband."

"With your questionable background, you expect to entice a suitable gentleman into asking for your hand?"

She easily caught the rough edge of disbelief in his voice. She was illegitimate, born in shame, although her mother had never allowed her to feel that way. It was only as she'd grown into womanhood that she'd begun to understand her life would include the freedom to do as she wanted but never the respectability that her mother had tossed aside in order to survive. It was the very reason that she'd not asked Harteley outright to wed her. She'd fancied him since she was a child, caught glimpses of him over the years. He deserved a respectable lady. But if while in her company, he were to decide that he wanted more from her . . .

She would very likely cast aside respectability as her mother had. The heart, after all, could be far more convincing than society, and because she'd lived on the edge of society, she was more accustomed to listening to her heart. Even now it was urging her to cast aside her original plans, to take him as a lover.

The flames from the candles on the table cast a dancing mosaic of shadow and light over the rugged features of his face. He had grown into a handsomeness that was breathtaking, and yet there was a harshness to it, tempered by disappointment. She wondered if he'd known the extent of what he would inherit. So little. Mounting debt and no means to earn the coins needed to alleviate his burden.

"I intend more than that, My Lord. I intend to marry a titled gentleman."

"You reach beyond your station, Miss Vernon."

"I have coins aplenty," she stated. "I know most marriages are based on what is held in the family coffers."

"I should think you deserve better than that."

It was the first comment he'd made that gave her hope that her true reason for inviting him here might not be in vain. "And you deserve better than what your father left you."

His eyes narrowing, he leaned forwards. "How do you know of that?"

"He came to trouble by visiting the unsavoury parts of London, and I . . . well, I have some knowledge regarding those portions of town."

"A true lady would not know of such things."

"I never claimed to be a true lady. However, I wish to be, and I'm willing to do whatever is required. What of you, My Lord? What will you do to be free of debt?"

For the first time since they sat down to dinner, she could see a spark of interest in his expression. "Did you have something in mind, Miss Vernon?"

"Indeed, My Lord. I wish you to marry me."

God help him, but he wanted to laugh. Instead he excused himself from the table and wandered to the corner where she'd been gazing when he'd first entered the room. He could see a fountain and a white gazebo. He had no reason not to accept her offer. She'd spoken true. A full coffer often married an empty one.

He could restore his estate to its splendour. He could maintain his London residence. His pride would take a bit of a bludgeoning as he'd not be marrying the daughter of a peer. He'd be marrying a woman who'd arrived in the world with a shady past.

He heard her soft footsteps. He slid his gaze towards her, almost becoming lost in her eyes. He'd not been able to tell their shade until they'd sat for dinner and the flames on the table had illuminated them. They were unusual, so pale that her eyes seemed to be little beyond brightness. He couldn't explain it, but they reminded him of something.

"Must he remain while we discuss this?" he asked, indicating the stoic butler.

She glanced over her shoulder. "Jones, please leave us."

"Miss—"

"I shall be fine."

The butler grunted in obvious disapproval, before leaving the room, the door closing quietly in his wake. Harteley turned, pressed his shoulder to the window, and folded his arms across his chest. "You could have anyone. Why me?"

"I can't have anyone. The circumstance of my birth ensures it."

"Still, I am left with the impression that you're not being totally honest with me regarding this arrangement."

She nodded, glanced down, then lifted her gaze in what he was coming to recognize as her defiance against the world and its unfairness. "My mother is dying."

He heard true sorrow and bereavement in her voice, and couldn't prevent his tone from indicating the same. "My condolences."

"She's not yet dead. As I said, she's provided all this for me. My entire life, she has strived to give me what she never had. She has very little time left. I want her to know that I am to marry above my station. I believe it will bring her . . . peace."

"And you believe I can be easily bought?"

Her lips parted slightly, and not for the first time that evening he wondered what it might be like to press his against hers. He couldn't deny that she appealed to him on a primal level. Sharing a marriage bed with her would certainly be no hardship. Lord, who was he striving to convince? Bedding her would be bloody marvellous. He'd want to take her here, in this room, with the sunlight streaming in. He'd have no reason to imagine her as anything other than the beauty she was.

"Have I judged you poorly?" she asked.

"Unfortunately for you, no."

Her green eyes widened at that. "Why unfortunately?"

"I take after my father. I'm a selfish man who cares about only what benefits and satisfies me."

"I don't believe that."

Unfolding his arms, he took a step towards her. "You should, Miss Vernon. If I am to accept your offer for marriage, I believe it imperative that you understand exactly what you have bargained for." With one hand, he cradled her face and stroked his thumb at the corner of her mouth. "I would not be denied."

"I would never deny you," she said on a soft breath.

"I would expect complete obedience."

She opened her mouth, closed it, shook her head. He couldn't prevent a corner of his mouth from curling up. "That you would deny me."

"I cannot promise it, no. I fear I've been rather spoiled. I'm accustomed to having my own way."

"Would you at least try?"

"I would try, but make no promises. What else would you require?"

Her breath was coming in short little gasps; her eyes had grown languid with each stroke of his thumb.

"I believe those are all my requirements," he murmured. "What of yours? Surely you expect more from me than to simply parade me about as your husband."

"In public, I would expect you to at least pretend to love me. And we must be seen in public. As soon as possible. My mother still has visitors. Some are men of influence. She must never know that I've paid for your . . . favours. It would break her heart, and I'll not countenance that. If you cannot put on a good show for her benefit, there is no reason to go any further."

"My dear Miss Vernon, I believe I have the acting skills necessary to play Romeo." He held her gaze.

"How many men have you entertained?"

"None. I am still a virgin." He believed her.

"Pay all my debts, and we shall announce our betrothal."

"You're accepting my offer then?"

"I would be a fool not to." Before she could object or say more, he lowered his head and took possession of her mouth. It had teased him from the moment she'd first spoken. He preferred women of experience, but her innocence was an aphrodisiac. He felt within her quivering slender frame a hesitation and an eagerness. One of her arms wound around his neck, while the other formed a slight buffer between them, her hand clasping his waistcoat. She didn't object to his questing tongue, rather she welcomed it with seeming abandon. She explored as much as he did. She tasted of wine, so much so that he wondered if she'd fortified herself before his arrival. But there was nothing in her speech or actions to indicate she'd imbibed too much.

Unexpected heat scored him. He'd feared that owing her for the relief her coins would provide would haunt him, would make him unable to desire her, but his fears had been for naught. He wanted her with a desperation that surprised him. Every woman he'd ever had had been held by other men before him. There was something both sweet and enticing to realize that she would come to him pure.

He pulled back from the kiss before he was tempted to take her there and then. He owed her that much at least, to wait until their wedding night. She came with enough scandalous baggage. He had no intention of adding to it.

"Will you secure a special licence?" she asked.

"If you wish."

"I shall see that all your debtors are paid tomorrow."

He furrowed his brow. "Are you certain this is the path you wish to take, Miss Vernon?"

"I've known since the first moment I set eyes on you."

The night had gone much better than Arianna had ever dared dream. She'd prepared for bed, but she'd been unable to sleep. After that torrid kiss he'd given her, all she'd been able to do was think about Lord Harteley. She'd feared it was a childish fantasy, but now it would come true. She would marry him.

She arose early and prepared for her journey into town so she could see her solicitor and take care of all that was needed to bring this plan to fruition.

But first she needed to see her mother.

She strolled out of her room and down the hallway to the bedchamber at the end. She took a deep breath, fortifying herself, before opening the door. Morning light and a rose-scented breeze eased in through the windows. The companion who stayed with her mother through the night rose from her chair beside the bed.

"Good morning, Gladys."

"Miss Vernon."

"Please fetch us our breakfast."

"Yes, ma'am."

While Gladys' heels clicked swiftly over the polished wooden floor, Arianna approached the bed, bent over and pressed a kiss to her mother's warm brow. "How are you this morning?"

She'd learned not to ask others how her mother was doing. It brought out her mother's temper. "Talk to me, girl. I'm not dead yet," she'd lamented on more than one occasion.

"Not too bad," her mother responded now in a weary voice.

"Are you in much pain?"

"The laudanum helps."

Arianna sat on the edge of the bed and took her mother's frail hand, wondering how it could be so cold when her brow was so warm. It had once caressed her back while she wept and swiped away her tears afterwards, with a gentleness that had caused more tears to form. From the moment she'd understood what her mother was, she'd not judged her. Her mother had done all in her power to protect her. Now it was Arianna's turn to take care of her. She couldn't cure her of the cancer. Lord knew she'd consulted enough physicians and taken her to the waters. For all the money her mother had accumulated, for all that would be passed on to Arianna, she would willingly give away every ha'penny if it would ease her mother's suffering, if it would keep her with her.

But to plead for her mother to stay when she was in such pain was too cruel. So all she could do was relieve her worry.

"I've been keeping a secret from you," Arianna said quietly.

"I doubt it, dearest. Even confined to my bed, I hear of a good many things." Her mother's once bright pale-green eyes were now dull. Her once glorious mane of hair was now thin and so faint a blonde as to be almost white.

Arianna concentrated on the blue veins lining her mother's hand. "A gentleman has been calling on me. A lord. An earl. He's asked to marry me." She raised her eyes. "I said yes."

She watched as a long-lost sparkle entered her mother's eyes. "Who is he?"

"Lord Harteley."

The sparkle dimmed somewhat. "You do realize in all likelihood he is marrying you for your money."

Arianna smiled. "You do realize that in all likelihood most men would. You placed me at a disadvantage by providing me with all this wealth."

"How selfish of me."

She squeezed her mother's hand. "I shall be a countess. I shall have entry into all the homes you were denied."

"I want you to have love."

Lifting her mother's hand, she pressed a kiss to her fingertips. "It will come."

"You were always such a dreamer."

"Which is the reason you love me."

"I love you, dearest, because you are mine."

And now she would be Harteley's. Surely in time he would come to love her as well.

He'd been swept away by possibilities, by a simple solution to a complicated problem. Before last night, he'd certainly considered marrying a woman who came with a nice dowry, but the thought had rankled. Yes, it was acceptable to marry for money, but still it left a sour taste in his mouth.

Or perhaps it was simply all the whisky he'd drunk after returning to his residence last night. He was in his library now, tipping up one empty bottle after another, searching for one last drop.

"I do hope you won't imbibe to this extent once we are married."

He swung around to see Miss Vernon standing in the doorway. Even from this distance, he could see the displeasure marring her lovely features. Perhaps marriage wouldn't be such a simple solution after all. "What are you doing here?" The words were snapped and churlish.

She merely arched a finely shaped eyebrow and glided over to the window. "I went to see my solicitor. I wanted to let you know that I have made arrangements and all you need do is send him a list of your debts, and he shall see to them. I knocked but no one answered. The door was not locked and so here I am." Sighing, she glanced around at empty bookshelves and clutter that was of no value. "It's worse than I thought."

"Reconsidering your proposal?"

She gave him a soft smile. "No. I told Mother the wonderful news this morning, and she was quite delighted. And relieved. I owe you for that. Whatever the cost, it is worth it."

He wandered over to where she stood by the window and leaned against the wall. "And if the cost is your unhappiness?"

"Why would your purpose be to make me unhappy?"

"Not my purpose, but . . . ours is more a business arrangement than anything else."

"Most marriages among the aristocracy are, from what I understand."

"Don't you wish for more?"

"Of course I do. Don't you?"

He hadn't meant to reach out to touch her, but she'd left some strands of hair to frame her face and he found himself toying with them, allowing his fingers to graze the soft curve of her cheek.

"Why me? I've been sitting here ever since I returned home last night wondering why me? There are other impoverished lords who'd have jumped at your offer. Why did you choose me?"

"Because all the others turned me down."

His hand stilled, his gut clenched.

"Oh, I'm so sorry. The look on your face. No, no." She was suddenly so near that he could feel her breath against his chin when she spoke. Her hands were roaming over his face, and he imagined them roaming elsewhere, ungloved, as they'd been the night before following dinner. "I've made you feel less than you are," she said softly. "You are the only one I asked. The only one I would have asked."

"Why?"

She turned away, and in the sunlight easing through the window, he could see the blush creeping along her face. "Now it is my turn to be hurt. You don't remember me, but when I was younger, much, much younger, our paths crossed. You spoke to me and I took quite a fancy to you. I've heard tales about you over the years. I know your father didn't treat you kindly and that you were at odds. I know that he cared only for his own pleasures and nothing for the legacy he was leaving you."

"If you were a child, you viewed me through the eyes of a child. Surely, I have changed in all these years."

She faced him and flattened her hand against his chest. "Not here, deep inside. I know it seems silly, but I've always felt something special where you are concerned. I can't explain it, but perhaps it's not meant to be explained."

He glanced out at the briars and thickets. By the end of the week, he'd have gardeners to put matters to rights. He could hardly fathom how all this had come about. Who'd have thought he'd have a guardian angel?

"If we're to make an announcement in *The Times*," he said quietly, "it would do us in good stead to be seen at least once together. Would you care to take a turn about the park with me?"

Relief and joy lit her face. "I would be delighted."

Because he didn't have an open carriage, they took her coach to Hyde Park – after Harteley had made himself presentable – and disembarked to stroll among the greenery. She loved it. Had always loved it. Had loved the city, but her visits here had always been rare because her mother had sought to spare her from the mortification of her origins. She couldn't help but notice how dashing Harteley was in his fine attire. Perhaps they'd live in his residence and she could visit the park every day.

"How did your mother come by the wealth she will leave to you?" he asked.

Her arm was intertwined with his. It was the only thing that stopped her from stumbling over her own feet. She'd known he'd ask eventually.

"I'm not sure." It was a lie, of course. Not because she was ashamed of her mother or what she'd done to ensure Arianna had everything, but she knew he would find fault with it and, as a result, with her. Until they were actually married, she'd hold her secrets close. "She thought it crude to speak of money."

"But surely you have some idea."

"I never asked." That was true. She'd never had to. Her mother had always been honest with her. *It's easier to face the truth than to run from it,* she'd said. But for now, Arianna preferred to run.

"What is her name?"

"Jane Vernon." Although her working name had been Jewel. Eventually she'd become the Jewel of London.

"Did she ever marry?"

"One man breaking her heart was enough for her."

"Do you fear I will break yours?"

"It is worth the risk for her happiness."

She could feel his gaze settling on her. "You will give everything for her happiness, and then she will leave you."

"The leaving will hurt terribly, but I will find joy in knowing she goes in peace."

He released a rough laugh. "I'd not have done the same for my father."

She didn't ask after his mother. She knew that she died giving birth to him. "Your father did not sell his . . . soul to see that you never went without. My mother sacrificed everything for me."

"I thought you didn't know what she did."

"I said I didn't know how she came to have her money, but I know what she did as a mother."

"I can't imagine such devotion."

She fought not to be disappointed by his words. She still dreamed of a time when his heart would stir with feelings for her. Before she could think of any appropriate comment, a man cutting a dashing figure on a great black horse came to a stop before them.

"Harteley," he said.

"Ambrose."

While she'd never seen the fair-haired gentleman, she was familiar with his name. He was a marquess, one day to become a duke.

"Miss Arianna Vernon, allow me to introduce Lord Ambrose," Harteley said.

"My Lord."

He swept his hat from his head, his blond curls falling down to frame his elegant face. "Miss Vernon. I hope our paths will cross again. Good day." With that, he settled his hat back on his head and galloped away.

"That was rather odd," she said.

"He was trying to determine if your skirt is available for chasing."

"What conclusion do you think he drew?"

"I'm not sure, but when I see him at the club I shall ensure it is the correct one."

She squeezed his arm. "I knew I had selected the right man to be my champion."

He didn't feel like a champion. Why did she have such faith in him, and why did it suddenly seem so important that she did? The questions fluttered through his mind as he sat in the club slowly sipping a brandy.

It had been a week since the invitation. He'd taken her to the opera. He'd felt pride at having her beside him. She was beautiful and charming. Men had watched them, and he'd seen envy in so many gazes. Women had been curious. He'd seen envy there as well. As she'd promised, his debts – his father's debts – had been paid. She'd given him a hundred pounds as proof of her faith in him. She'd hired servants for his residence and had a box of books delivered to him for his library.

Their announcement had appeared in *The Times* and he'd begun the process of obtaining a special licence. He couldn't deny that he was anticipating the marriage, in particular the wedding night. He had the means now to visit various brothels but he refrained. He could argue that it was because he felt he owed her, but the truth was that no other woman interested him. No other had her smile, her belief in all things good, her loving heart. He'd never had any interest in owning a lady's heart, but he found himself unexpectedly wanting to possess hers. She had so much love to give, and to have it directed his way—

He barely looked up when Ambrose sat beside him.

"Saw your announcement in *The Times*, old chap. Can't believe you're marrying the chit. Thought she was your mistress."

Harteley levelled his gaze on him. "You thought incorrectly."

Ambrose sneered. "She'll be cuckolding you before the ink is dry on the church registry."

"Why would you think that?"

"Her mother was quick enough to spread her legs."

He felt a sickening sensation in his gut, a foreboding. Why would any woman of means need a champion? Why had he not asked himself that? "What do you know of her mother? What do you know of Jane Vernon?"

"No more than you."

"I don't know her."

Ambrose laughed and leaned forwards. "Of course you do, old boy. She's the Jewel of London."

"I need to see her now!"

Harteley didn't bother to rein in his temper or to keep his voice down, which was probably the reason the butler said, "She's abed."

"With whom?"

The old man's face hardened. "Watch your mouth, lad."

Harteley made a move to go around him, and two footmen stepped in front of him and grabbed his arms.

"You'll not stop me. Now step aside."

"You've been drinking, lad. I can smell it on you," Jones said. "Return in the morning when you're sober."

But he was beyond listening to reason. "Arianna!"

He shouted her name twice more, but she didn't appear.

"I need to see her now!" he yelled, again.

"Over my dead body," Jones said. "She's retired for the evening—"

"Hardly," she interrupted, and Harteley jerked his gaze up. She wore her nightdress and night wrapper. Her braided hair swung over her shoulder as she began her descent. "Unhand him."

With a nod from Jones, the footmen stepped aside. With deliberate slowness, Harteley straightened his clothes, his gaze never leaving her. "I know who you are," he finally said and, while he didn't shout, the words still echoed up the stairs.

She staggered to a stop. "I told you who I was."

"Your name, yes, but not who you are. Who your mother is – the Jewel of London. A whore. You expected me to marry the daughter of a whore."

All blood drained from her face. She staggered forwards and sat on the stairs. "Don't call her that."

"Why didn't you tell me?"

She shook her head, but he heard the truth in her silence. She'd known he'd not accept her offer. He'd be the laughing stock of London. The shame he'd thought his impoverished state would bring him was nothing compared with the shame that marriage to her would bring.

"What is all the frightful commotion?" a faint voice asked from the top of the stairs.

He lifted his gaze and saw her – the Jewel of London. By the time he was ready to make sport with the ladies he'd considered her too old. But even now, with death hovering, he couldn't deny her regal beauty.

And as his gaze shifted back down to Arianna, an image filled his mind of a young girl sitting on the stairs . . .

He remembered her now. Her innocence, so out of place in the bordello, as she'd waited there.

"Will you wait for me to grow up?" she'd asked as he'd headed up the stairs with some woman whose name he could no longer remember.

"Absolutely," he'd called down, laughing.

She sat there on the steps now, looking diminished and broken. There was no one to stop him from going to her.

Instead, he spun on his heel and strode away.

Arianna wept while her mother held her. This was not how it was supposed to end. She'd known that, sooner or later, he would remember her but she had hoped it would be after they'd spent time together, after he'd come to care for her, when her origins were no longer a concern. Now her mother had learned of her deception.

"It was a lovely thought, Arianna," her mother said quietly. "But you should know that I care not who you marry. I care only that you're happy."

"I thought he'd make me happy."

"Instead he's broken your heart. I could kill him for that."

How could she have misjudged him so poorly? How could she have thought he was her destiny?

The house still echoed, for he'd not replaced much of what he'd sold. But it was clean. Servants ushered about quietly to see to all the tasks that needed their attention, while he brooded in his library and downed the whisky until his mouth was numb and he no longer tasted it.

Good God, he'd almost married an infamous madam's daughter. Her mother was a trollop and she had no father to speak for her. If Arianna lived by example . . .

She would never be unfaithful. In spite of Ambrose's words, Harteley knew she would never cuckold him. She was not adept at seduction. She could have seduced him without money. She could have swayed her hips and pouted her lips. Instead she'd provided him with an honourable way to alleviate his debts.

For the love of her mother.

He bolted from his chair and strode to the window. The moonlight was less than it had been two nights before, but he could see the beginnings of the gardener's work. All would be restored. He would be restored. She'd given him back his pride. She'd given him reason to smile.

She'd asked nothing of him except that he pretend to love her. Pretend to love her smile, her laughter, her joy. He enjoyed her company more than he had any woman's in a good long while. The depth of love she gave her mother . . . he'd seen the bond as mother and daughter stood on the stairs. A woman with the determination to do what she needed to survive and provide for her daughter. A young woman with the courage to reach for a dream of happiness.

She'd been a child sitting on those stairs at the brothel. "Who is she?" he'd asked the woman leading him into a bedchamber.

"Jewel's daughter."

"What's she doing here?"

"Waitin' for 'er mother to finish up with bus'ness so she can take 'er to the theatre."

He'd known even then that she was remarkable. That hadn't changed.

He couldn't say that he loved her, but he couldn't deny that she intrigued him. Raising his arm, he pressed it to the glass and peered intently into the night. To continue on the path she'd set for them would be scandalous.

All she asked of him was that he champion her.

Such a small request for a lady who deserved so much more.

Arianna strolled through her garden. She thought it far lovelier than Hyde Park, but then her mother had always paid the gardeners well to ensure that her daughter had the finest of everything. Paid the servants with money that men had paid her.

She told herself that it was better that Harteley had learned the truth before they were married because she might not have been able to survive his turning away from her after they'd shared an intimacy. His kiss had been so very wonderful, and to contemplate losing more than that—

"There you are."

She swung around, her heart hammering painfully against her ribs. "Harteley."

He appeared so handsome, more so than ever. His clothes were the finest in which she'd ever seen him. His burgundy jacket set off his swarthy looks. His white cravat was tied to perfection.

"I've been searching for you for some time," he said quietly.

"Yes, it's easy to lose people here in the gardens. They go on forever."

"No." He stepped towards her. "I didn't mean here in the gardens. I meant . . . I've been searching for someone who makes me grateful to get up in the morning. I didn't realize it was you until I found myself unable to think of anything else."

"You called my mother a whore."

"I've already apologised to her for that. Now I must apologise to you. I have no excuse for the words. I was wondering, however, if you might find it within you to forgive me."

"Did my mother forgive you?"

"She did."

"Then I suppose I can do no less."

"Well, you could do more." He took another step nearer. "I've obtained the special licence. And I've brought a vicar."

Her eyes widened. "You want to marry me?"

"I do."

She angled her chin haughtily and lied. "Unfortunately, I no longer want to marry you. It was a foolish bargain on my part, to be willing to give you every—"

"I don't want everything. I only want you." He reached into his pocket and removed a folded parchment. "A letter from your solicitor, confirming that I have signed settlement papers that prevent me from taking any of your property or money."

"Why would you do that?"

"Because I need a champion. Someone who believes in me when I fail to believe in myself."

"You will be ostracized for marrying me. You must know that."

"At first, certainly. But you will be my countess and, in time, I think you will charm society until they no longer care about your origins."

"Why?" she asked, her voice breaking. "What changed your mind?"

"I'm not sure. I only know that I want you to be my wife, that someone who has overcome her past as you have can help me overcome mine."

"Yours is not nearly so ruinous."

"Then it should be easy enough for us to conquer it."

They were married in the gardens. Her mother was able to stand at her side and Jones stood beside Harteley. The ceremony, although brief, was almost too much for her mother. When she began to sway, Jones was the first to reach her and sweep her up into his arms.

"We'll need one more ceremony before you go, vicar," Jones said.

"We don't have a licence," her mother muttered.

"Doesn't matter. I want the words between us if nothing else," Jones said.

Her mother had merely nodded and there in the garden she married the butler.

Arianna and Harteley travelled to London for the night. His residence was far from what it would become, but that night she was only interested in sharing his bedchamber.

Wearing only her nightdress, she waited expectantly for him. Strange, considering her mother's occupation, that she was so nervous.

"Tell me what I should do," she'd urged her mother.

All her mother had given her was a smile and the soft words: "Enjoy him."

Enjoy him. How could she when she could barely draw in a breath?

The door opened. He walked in wearing only trousers and a silk dressing robe. Before she could utter a word, he took her into his arms and began to plunder her mouth. Then he gentled the kiss and she swayed into him.

Heat surged through her. She was barely aware that he'd unbuttoned her gown until it slithered along her body to land on the floor.

"My God, but you're beautiful," he whispered.

She looked up at him, held his gaze. "So are you."

He cradled her face. "How can you be so innocent?"

"Perhaps because my mother wasn't. She protected me."

He lifted her into his arms. "I shall strive to do the same."

He laid her gently on the bed. He discarded his dressing gown and began to work on the fastenings of his trousers. "Would you rather I douse the lamps?" he asked.

She shook her head. "No. I want to see you."

And she was grateful that he allowed her request. She knew the human form was beautiful, but she thought he was magnificent as he shoved down his trousers and joined her on the bed. She touched his shoulders, toyed with the light sprinkling of hair on his chest. "I've so often dreamed of this."

"I suspect I shall lie on my deathbed still wondering why you chose me," he said.

"And I shall always wonder why you came back."

He shook his head, a smile playing over his lips. "Because for once in my life, I listened to my heart."

Her heart soared, swelled to such an extent that she was surprised her chest could contain it.

Then his hands and mouth were exploring every inch of her, with tenderness and deliberation. Pleasure ebbed and flowed through her. Each caress brought her closer to the edge of something she couldn't quite fathom. Each stroke urged her to touch him as well.

She loved the texture of his body. Firm, strong muscles undulating beneath her fingers.

Then he rose above her and gazed down on her. His mouth covered hers. His body plunged into hers. His cries mingled with hers.

He rocked against her and the pressure built. Sensations she could have never imagined travelled through her. He was hers now, just as she'd always dreamed.

She was his, just as she'd always wanted.

The pleasure spiralled through her until it burst forth into a conflagration that had her calling out his name. She was aware of her name escaping through his clenched jaw as he thrust into her one last time, his body taut, his muscles quivering.

He lowered himself to her, buried his face in the curve of her shoulder. He pressed his lips to her dew-covered neck. "Arianna."

Her name was a whispered benediction.

And she knew that love wouldn't be far behind.

Author Biographies

Leah Ball
Mammoth debut author and second-prize winner in the R.W.A.
Royal Ascot's Hot & Wild Regency category, her first novel, *Secret
Possessions*, is currently on submission.

Sara Bennett
Bestselling author of historical romance for Avon, she writes passionate
Victorian- and Regency-set romances. She has just finished the second
book in her latest series, The Husband Hunters Club, and also writes
paranormals as Sara Mackenzie.
www.sara-bennett.com

Elizabeth Boyle
New York Times bestselling author of fifteen Regency-set historical
romances, including the popular Bachelor Chronicles series, she is also
the winner of the R.W.A.'s RITA award, a voracious knitter and an
occasional seamstress.
www.elizabethboyle.com

Anna Campbell
Multi-award-winning author writing passionate, emotional Regency-set
historical romance for Avon, she lives in Australia and loves to travel,
especially to the United Kingdom.
www.annacampbell.info

Robyn DeHart
Three-time *Romantic Times* Reviewers' Choice award nominee, her
Legend Hunters series is a favourite among reviewers and fans alike.
www.robyndehart.com

Amanda Grange

Bestselling author of *Mr Darcy's Diary*, she has written seventeen Regency-set novels including her popular series of Jane Austen retellings.
www.amandagrange.com

Lorraine Heath

New York Times and *USA Today* bestselling author who has penned more than twenty-five historical romances, including her popular Scoundrels of St James series. She is also a recipient of R.W.A.'s prestigious RITA award, a *Romantic Times* Career Achievement Award and several other literary accolades.
www.lorraineheath.com

Candice Hern

Award-winning author of Regency-set historical romances, her Regency World website features an illustrated glossary, a detailed timeline of Regency events and an illustrated digest of that era's notable people and places.
www.candicehern.com

Carolyn Jewel

Writer of historical and paranormal romance, who often wishes she had superpowers.
www.carolynjewel.com

Christie Kelley

Born and raised in upstate New York, she decided to write her first book after seventeen years of working in software development. She currently writes Regency-set historicals for Kensington Zebra.
www.christiekelley.com

Vanessa Kelly

Writer of sensual, Regency-set historical romances for Kensington Zebra.
www.vanessakellyauthor.com

Shirley Kennedy

Author of numerous Regency romances for both Ballantine and Signet, she's kind to animals and has never been convicted of a felony.
www.shirleykennedy.com

Anthea Lawson

The pseudonym of a husband–wife team writing spicy historical romance, their debut novel, *Passionate*, was nominated for a Best First Book RITA in 2009. Their most recent release, *All He Desires*, "deftly combines danger, desire, and a deliciously different setting into a sexy version of Victoria Holt's classic gothic romances". (*Booklist* Reviews)

www.anthealawson.com

Caroline Linden

Critically acclaimed author of sexy, suspenseful historical romance.

www.carolinelinden.com

Margo Maguire

Author of seventeen historical romances – including *The Rogue Prince*, her latest Regency-set romance from Avon Books – her adventurous and sexy novels have been translated into twenty languages.

www.margomaguire.com

Delilah Marvelle

Two-time Golden Heart finalist, a *Romantic Times* Reviewers' Choice nominee and a double finalist in the Booksellers' Best Award, she loves writing historical romances with scandalous twists.

www.delilahmarvelle.com

Barbara Metzger

Author of over three dozen Regency-set romances and historicals, plus a dozen short stories, she has won many awards, including R.W.A.'s RITA, two career achievement awards from *Romantic Times* magazine, a Madcap award for humour in historicals and, most recently, a *R.T.* award for Most Innovative Historical Romance. This year, her new book, *The Bargain Bride*, has won rave reviews from *Publisher's Weekly*, *Booklist* and *Library Journal*, as well as another *R.T.* nomination for Best Love and Laughter Romance in the historical category. She lives on Long Island with her little dog Valentino.

www.barbarametzger.com

Sharon Page

USA Today bestselling author of sensual Regency-set and historical erotic romances, she has been called "a new queen of erotic romance" by *Romantic Times* magazine. She is a two-time consecutive winner

of the National Readers' Choice award, and a winner of the *Romantic Times* Reviewers' Choice award.
www.sharonpage.com

Deborah Raleigh
New York Times and *USA Today* bestselling author of thirty-three Regency-set novels and short stories, her books have been nominated by the *Romantic Times* in the Best First Regency and in the Career Achievement in Regency Romance categories. She also writes the paranormal Guardian of Eternity series under the pseudonym Alexandra Ivy.
www.deborah-raleigh.com

Patricia Rice
New York Times bestselling author who has been nominated for the R.W.A.'s RITA awards for Regency romance, as well as for her paranormal historicals and contemporaries.
www.patriciarice.com

Julia Templeton
Writer of spicy historical, time travel, vampire and contemporary romances, featuring sexy alpha heroes and strong heroines. Aside from writing and reading, she enjoys research, haunting bookstores and libraries, travelling, riding motorcycles and spending time with family and friends. Married to her high-school sweetheart, she has two grown children and lives in Washington State.
www.juliatempleton.com

Emma Wildes
Romantic Times Reviewers' Choice nominee, winner of a Passionate Plume award and an Eppie for best erotic historical, she grew up loving books, so writing just came naturally!
www.emmawildes.com

Michèle Ann Young
Award-winning romance author of five Regency-set historicals and a variety of short stories, she is an army brat and grew up all over Britain, developing a special love for its regional history.
www.micheleannyoung.com